# PRAISE FOR THESE NATIONALLY BESTSELLING AUTHORS:

## JAYNE ANN KRENTZ

"A master of the genre..."
—*Romantic Times*

"Who writes the best romance fiction today?
No doubt it's Jayne Ann Krentz."
—*Affaire de Coeur*

## STELLA CAMERON

"Her narrative is rich, her style is distinct,
and her characters wonderfully wicked."
—*Publishers Weekly*

"If you haven't read Stella Cameron, you haven't read romance."
—Elizabeth Lowell

## HEATHER GRAHAM POZZESSERE

"An incredible storyteller!"
—*L.A. Daily News*

"Award-winning Pozzessere combines mystery with
sizzling romance."
—*Publishers Weekly*

# AUTHOR BIO

## JAYNE ANN KRENTZ

is one of today's top contemporary romance writers, with an astounding twelve million copies of her books in print. Her novels regularly appear on the *New York Times*, Waldenbooks and B. Dalton bestseller lists. First published in 1979, Jayne quickly established herself as a prolific and innovative writer. She has delved into psychic elements, intrigue, fantasy, historicals and even futuristic romances. Jayne lives in Seattle with her husband, Frank, an engineer.

## STELLA CAMERON

is the bestselling author of forty books, and possesses the unique talent of being able to switch effortlessly from historical to contemporary fiction. In a one-year period, her titles appeared more than eight times on the *USA Today* bestseller list. This British-born author was working as an editor in London when she met her husband, an officer in the American air force, at a party. He asked her to dance, and they've been together ever since. They now make their home in Seattle, and are the parents of three grown children.

## HEATHER GRAHAM POZZESSERE

describes her life as "busy, wild and full of fun." A master storyteller with over ten million copies of her books in print around the world, Heather says her first career choice was not writing but acting on the Shakespearean stage. Happily for her fans, fate intervened, and now she is a *New York Times* bestselling author. Married to her high school sweetheart, this mother of five spends her days picking up the kids from school, attending Little League games and taking care of two cats. Although Heather and her family enjoy traveling, southern Florida—where she loves the sun and water—is home.

# LEGACIES OF LOVE

## JAYNE ANN KRENTZ

## STELLA CAMERON

## HEATHER GRAHAM POZZESSERE

HARLEQUIN®

TORONTO • NEW YORK • LONDON
AMSTERDAM • PARIS • SYDNEY • HAMBURG
STOCKHOLM • ATHENS • TOKYO • MILAN • MADRID
PRAGUE • WARSAW • BUDAPEST • AUCKLAND

ISBN 0-373-83430-6

LEGACIES OF LOVE

Copyright © 1999 by Harlequin Books S.A.

The publisher acknowledges the copyright holders of the original works as follows:

LEGACY
Copyright © 1985 by Jayne Ann Krentz

NO STRANGER
Copyright © 1987 by Stella Cameron

WEDDING BELL BLUES
Copyright © 1990 by Heather Graham Pozzessere

# CONTENTS

# LEGACY

# JAYNE ANN KRENTZ

## ONE

He hadn't planned to move in on her this quickly, but Honor Mayfield was making it so easy he knew he would be a fool to waste the opening. Spinning a web was a delicate task, and one of the most important aspects of the job was selecting the beginning point. It looked as though Honor was going to provide the perfect beginning herself.

Constantine Landry sat alone in a private box fronting the Santa Anita Racetrack. One booted foot lazily braced against the partition, an expensive set of Japanese-crafted field glasses resting on the empty seat beside him, he could have been any one of a number of the more affluent racing enthusiasts who occupied the row of private boxes.

But his attention wasn't on the results of the second race that were being posted on the lighted board below. Instead, he watched with calculating eyes as a woman with golden-brown hair walked quickly along an aisle in the grandstand behind him. She had a very serious expression on her face and was obviously intent on following a flashily dressed man several yards away from her.

*Might as well make it a parade,* Landry thought as he got to his feet with an easy, coordinated movement. The first strand of the web was waiting to be strung, and unless he missed his guess it was going to be a very strong anchor thread. Honor Mayfield, it appeared, was headed for trouble. Keeping her out of it would give him exactly the kind of opening he needed.

Landry was accustomed to waiting and watching for openings. Trained hunters learned those necessary skills quickly or remained singularly unsuccessful. Landry had been very successful in his profession. He had been dealing with two-legged prey a long time. One brightly dressed, unprotected female who had no idea she was being pursued presented no real problem. What was definitely out of the ordinary was this strange restless excitement that was suddenly pervading his bloodstream.

It wasn't the cool intensity of the hunt as he might have expected. It was a deep, thrumming sense of anticipation. And it was all wrong. He knew instinctively that **it** was not the right sort of emotion for this kind of thing, but he didn't seem to be able to repress it.

The warmth of the Southern California sun beat down on Landry and his quarry with pleasant warmth. Hard to believe it was only January, he thought vaguely. He'd forgotten that on days when the smog factor was low and the California sun was living up to its promise, the towns that sprawled out from the heart of Los Angeles could still remind one of just how beautiful the countryside had once been. The San Gabriel Mountains formed a magnificent backdrop for the picturesque racetrack. If one concentrated on the scenery one could ignore the huge, modern shopping center that, in true California style, stood nearby. Southern Californians never felt entirely comfortable unless they were close to one of the many luxurious enclosed shopping malls.

Landry stalked Honor Mayfield at a discreet distance, questions without clear answers circling in his head as he moved through the crowd. He didn't understand the questions any more than he understood the unexpected sense of anticipation. He knew what he was doing, had planned the contact carefully. So why was he questioning his own motives at this late juncture? Around him people were hurrying to make their bets on the next race, crowding the aisles en route to the windows where cashiers waited patiently to accept what seemed to be an endless river of money.

It was a little difficult keeping Honor in sight without closing in on her. She was only about five feet four inches tall, easily lost amid the crowd. But the watermelon-pink of her shirt helped identify her as she slipped through the crush of bettors. One of the things Conn Landry had learned about her these past few months was that Honor had a passion for brilliantly-hued clothes.

He'd acquired a variety of such small tidbits of information about her and he still couldn't quite explain why he found each little detail so fascinating.

He increased his pace enough to close some of the distance between himself and his quarry as she, in turn, hurried after the man in the avant-garde safari suit. Landry knew whom she was following. His name was Granger and the abundance of rings he wore in addition to his clothes made him an easily recognized figure. Once again Landry wondered why Honor Mayfield was interested in him. Granger was dangerous.

But, then, so was Constantine Landry. And as far as Honor Mayfield was concerned, Landry decided objectively, she had more to fear from him than from Granger. She just didn't know it yet.

There were a lot of things she didn't know yet, and Landry made a decision. He would not tell her everything until he understood exactly why he was experiencing such a strange sense of ambivalence about what she was doing. It was the quarry who should remain uncertain and off-balance, not the hunter. He would approach her as a stranger, he told himself.

Months of hunting came to an end as Landry shortened the distance between himself and Honor.

Leaving the grandstands behind, Honor experienced a surge of nervous tension that almost broke her resolve. *Face it*, she told herself grimly, *you don't really know what the hell you're doing.* Not knowing, however, didn't solve any problems. She had no choice but to keep pushing blindly along the course she had set for herself.

The crowd thinned out as she followed Granger toward the barns. Grooms soothing high-strung Thoroughbreds and maintenance people carrying tools and equipment replaced the betting enthusiasts. Soon she would come up against the impenetrable barrier of the gates that protected the stables. Without a pass she would be unable to get past the uniformed guard. If Granger was going beyond that boundary she would be out of luck.

It was with mixed emotions that she saw him turn off to head toward the parking lot area that was reserved for people whose business was connected directly with racing. Owners, racetrack employees, trainers and similar types were entitled to use the lot toward which Granger was now moving. She knew he hadn't parked there, because she'd seen him come through the front entrance of the track grounds an hour earlier. She suddenly realized that following Granger through a crowded grandstand was one thing. Following him away from the relative safety of the crowd was quite another. Granger moved in a different world, one that existed beyond the legal fringe of racing. People in that world tended to make their own rules.

Honor took a deep, steadying breath and her fingers tightened on the strap of her turquoise-blue shoulder bag. Perhaps she should have hired a professional, she told herself. A private detective, for instance. Someone who knew the people and rules of Granger's world. How did one approach a loan shark, anyway? The idea of dashing up to him and catching hold of the sleeve of his off-white safari suit was rather intimidating. Honor was trying to formulate a list of other possible approaches when a man's hand closed around her upper arm.

"What the—? No! Let go of me!" The words came out in a frightened gasp as she spun around to confront the stranger who was laying claim to her arm. Instantly she pulled herself back under control. Panic wasn't going to get her anywhere. She was still within shouting distance of help.

"Ladies intent on tailing people like Granger should take care not to wear shirts the color of the inside of a ripe watermelon," the man said in a cool, dark, gritty voice that ruffled her already agitated nerves. "It makes you a little too visible, you see."

Honor struggled to keep the raging fear-inspired adrenaline under control. "I beg your pardon," she snapped icily, "but I have no idea what you're talking about. Kindly let go of my arm before I'm forced to scream for help."

The man gave her a curiously twisted smile that didn't have any impact on his gunmetal-gray eyes at all. "You've already got help. I'm it."

She stared up at him, conscious of feeling very vulnerable as she sensed the strength in his grip on her arm. He wasn't quite six feet in height but there was a chilling power in his lean, hard frame that made itself felt on several levels. A bodyguard, she wondered fleetingly. She'd always thought of professional bodyguards as being big and burly, men whose threat lay in their massive, rocklike bodies. But this man made her think of the elegantly lethal qualities found in a stiletto or a coiled whip. Infinitely more dangerous.

"Do you—do you work for Mr. Granger?" she heard herself ask uneasily and then realized how much information she had provided just by admitting to knowing Granger's name.

"No." The strangely bleak smile stayed in place. "I only work for myself."

Which made perfect sense, Honor realized abruptly. Men such as this one did not take orders from slick loan sharks like Granger. But that only made her present situation even more confusing.

"Then I really can't see that we have anything to discuss," she began bravely. "If you'll excuse me, I must be going. I have to take care of some business."

"So do I, lady. So do I."

The grip on her arm tightened just enough to remind her that she couldn't possibly escape it, and then Honor found herself being led back toward the barn area.

"Wait a minute! What do you think you're doing? I don't even know your name."

"Constantine Landry. Call me Conn."

"Mr. Landry, I demand that you release me. I have something I must do," Honor said with soft urgency. Granger was even now disappearing from view behind a large building. She struggled in Landry's grip and seriously considered yelling for help. There were plenty of people around. Surely this man wouldn't do anything drastic to her in front of so many witnesses.

"If you're talking about your little plan to tail Granger, I'm afraid you're going to have to think of a more pleasant way to spend the afternoon."

"You are working for that bastard!"

He slanted a wry glance down at her as he pulled her toward the guarded stable gate. "I've told you. I don't work for anyone except myself. Not anymore."

"Then why are you interfering with me now? And how do you know who Granger is?" Honor asked grittily.

"A lot of people around here know who Granger is. He's been involved in everything from loan sharking to drug dealing. Not a nice man. I can't help being curious about why a nice lady such as yourself is following him. Believe me, unless you're feeling masochistic, you don't want to go where Granger's going right now."

Honor stared up at Conn Landry's savagely carved profile. "Just where is Granger going?"

"Straight into a police trap. He's been set up. Granger believes he's about to connect with one of his drug couriers. And he is, in a sense. But the courier has been working undercover for the past six months. Today the cops pull the plug. It wasn't an easy trap to set, you know. Granger's big enough to employ others to take his risks for him. But this time he was convinced that the deal was too big to leave in the hands of employees." Landry shook his head ruefully. "Some people just can't learn to delegate when they should."

Honor dug in the high heels of her turquoise leather sandals. "How do you know all this? Who are you, Conn Landry?"

He politely allowed her to drag him to a halt, turning to confront her questioning hazel eyes. "That's simple. I'm the man who's saving your sweet tail from the rather unpleasant surprise awaiting Granger. Just how would you explain your presence to the cops when they closed in on him and found you wriggling in the net, too?''

"I don't understand any of this!''

"That's obvious. And that's why you should have the sense to stay clear. Come along, lady in the watermelon shirt. I want to introduce you to a friend of mine.''

Confused and wary, Honor again found herself being led toward the stable yard. At the guarded gate Constantine Landry flashed an owner's pass, and the next thing she knew she was inside the perimeter that protected the expensive animals. Rows of barns, horse trailers and small cottages for the grooms were scattered around the grounds. The pleasant, earthy scent of well-cared-for horses filled the air. In the grandstands all was excitement, disgust, urgency and despair, depending on the outcome of the current race. Here there was a subdued, businesslike bustle of activity.

"Mr. Landry, this is ridiculous. Please let go of my arm!''

"I told you to call me Conn. And I think this is about the safest place for you until Granger's been taken out of commission. From what I could tell you were hell-bent on following him right into trouble.''

"Why should you care?'' she snapped furiously.

His mouth kicked up briefly at the corner in that odd little smile that didn't go anywhere. "A good question.''

She waited for the answer and when it didn't come, Honor pursued her arguments for freedom. "Look, if you're a police undercover agent or something and I've gotten in your way, I'm sorry. I didn't mean to interfere in any sort of operation designed to take Granger off the streets! Believe me, no one wants him in jail more than I do!''

Landry nodded. "Mind telling me why?''

"I can't see that it's any of your business. You haven't shown me a badge or any identification.'' Immediately wary, Honor backed off from being pushed into an explanation. "I still don't have any idea of who you really are, do I?''

"The situation is mutual. You haven't introduced yourself, either.''

"I don't intend to do so. You seem to know far too much already.'' There was a certain satisfaction in being able to deny him something, at least, Honor discovered. Constantine Landry was almost frighteningly sure of himself. The rigorously austere planes and angles of his features held no trace of softness or warmth.

"I think," Landry said too quietly, "that it's time you told me who you are."

"Are you asking in an official capacity?" she demanded with a show of bravado that was only skin-deep. With a flash of intuition she sensed that introducing herself would be a small act but a crucial one. It was as though he were asking that she commit herself somehow, demanding that she acknowledge the tenuous acquaintance, insisting that she take a potentially dangerous first step. Oddly enough she could have sworn in that moment that he already knew who she was and that he was only asking to maintain an illusion. She brushed aside the uneasy thought. Of course there was no way he could know her identity.

"I'm asking. Period. No official reasons."

Honor felt the lapping waves of his will and knew that the full force of an ocean of strength lay behind them. They halted in the shade of a long barn and she looked up at him searchingly. Quite suddenly she knew that in the end he would have his answer. She had the feeling he'd gotten answers from people before; he was that kind of man. There was no point resisting the soft command in his voice.

"As I said before, I think you know too much already," she observed quietly. "But for the record, my name is Honor Mayfield."

"Yes." He took her arm again and led her into the barn. There had been satisfaction in the single word.

Just yes. Simple and certain. As if she were merely confirming something he already knew. What was going on here? she wondered.

"Mr. Landry, I've answered your question. Now tell me what your role is in all this. You owe me that much."

"Do I?" He had halted in front of a roomy stall. There was a soft rustling sound from within, and a few seconds later an inquisitive equine head emerged to investigate. "Hello, Legacy. I hope you feel like running today."

"Legacy?" Honor stepped forward, putting out a hand to touch the nose of the horse who watched her with avid interest. "This is Legacy?" For a moment Granger and all the related problems were forgotten as she stared at the beautiful bay colt.

Landry's chilled eyes studied her reaction to the horse. "I own him."

"I see." Honor couldn't think of anything to say. She was looking at a tiny piece of her past and for a moment the impact was unsettling. "I didn't realize," she went on weakly. "That you owned him, I mean. I saw his name on the program. He's running in the fifth, isn't he?"

"That's right."

Honor withdrew her hand and the sleek Thoroughbred extended his nose to follow the movement. "He's very beautiful."

"Very."

"He's favored to win today, isn't he?" She couldn't take her eyes off the animal.

"Slightly. This is only his second race and he still has a ways to go to prove himself."

Honor stepped back out of range of the questing mouth that was beginning to nip interestedly at her silk shirtsleeve. "I'm sure he'll do well."

"He comes from good stock," Landry said deliberately.

"One of Stylish Legacy's descendants," Honor didn't realize she'd whispered the words aloud until Landry responded.

"You seem to know something about the line."

She shook her head. "Not very much, really. I don't follow the details of the racing world closely. Once in a while I come to the track when I can find the time. When I was a kid I had the usual female hang-up on horses."

"But you know about Stylish Legacy?"

Honor sighed. There was no harm in admitting the truth. "My father once owned him. He and another man, that is. Is Stylish Legacy still at stud?"

"Yes. He's eighteen years old now. But still producing winners." Landry stroked the warm bay neck, and Legacy nuzzled his chest, inhaling the man's scent through the fabric of the coffee-colored shirt. The horse clearly enjoyed being the center of attention. "So your father once owned Stylish Legacy?"

"It was a long time ago. He and a partner—" Honor broke off quickly. "Look, Mr. Landry, I think this has gone far enough. Please tell me what your connection is with Granger. Is he really walking into a trap out there in the parking lot?"

"Most of us walk into a trap at some point in our lives."

"I am not in the mood for cryptic comments!"

Legacy reacted to the sharp tone of her voice, his sensitive ears flicking in irritation. Landry soothed him.

"Take it easy, boy. She's just a little nervous, that's all."

"I have a right to be nervous," Honor muttered, glancing down the row of stalls. Several curious muzzles were appearing and a half-dozen pairs of interested brown eyes were examining the scene at the far end of the long, shaded barn.

"You'd have a lot more reason to be nervous now if you were out there in the parking lot taking the fall along with Granger," Landry told her.

Honor shifted restlessly. "If what you say is true, then I suppose I should be grateful to you for stopping me."

Landry inclined his head. "Yes, you should be. Feeling grateful, Honor?"

"I'm not sure yet. Basically because I'm not sure how you're involved."

"A bystander. Nothing more. But I'd heard rumors around the track about what was being planned for Granger today. Racetracks thrive on rumors. When I saw you following the man, I decided to pull you out of the action. Somehow you just didn't look like the type to be up to your neck in loan sharking and drug dealing."

Honor shuddered, utterly repelled. "I'm not."

"But you were following him," Landry pointed out coolly.

"It's a private matter, Mr. Landry," she told him stiffly.

"Will Granger's arrest take care of this private little matter for you?"

"With any luck, yes," she answered fervently.

"Then I think, on the whole, that you really should feel grateful to me, Honor Mayfield."

Her gaze narrowed. "Are you the type to hold that sort of thing over my head?"

He looked at her, gray eyes unreadable and unyielding. "I keep track of what I owe in this life, Honor. And even closer track of what's owed to me."

For a long moment she couldn't drag her gaze free of the invisible bonds Constantine Landry was using to chain her full attention. She had never met a man like this. A part of her was genuinely apprehensive and cautious. But another part of her was deeply aware of him, and that disturbed her even more than the understandable wariness she was experiencing.

"I believe you, Mr. Landry." And she did. Completely. "You aren't a cop, are you?"

"No."

"And you do own Legacy?"

"Oh, yes," Landry told her with great sureness. "I own him."

For a moment a genuine expression of emotion flickered in the gray eyes. A mixture of pride and pleasure and enthusiasm.

Scenes from the past flashed briefly through Honor's mind. She remembered a similar expression in the eyes of her father when he had talked about Stylish Legacy. People who owned racehorses were infected with a certain kind of fever, even when they tried to pretend that the horses were purely financial investments or tax shelters. Getting involved in the racing world almost always meant getting involved on an emotional level. It wasn't just a realm of numbers and big financial transactions. It was an arena that involved the emotions. It struck Honor as strange that Constantine Landry should be interested in such a world. He looked like the kind of man who kept the emotional side of his nature under rigid control. In fact, a person could be pardoned for questioning whether or not Conn Landry would even be capable of a strong emotional response, Honor decided dryly.

"You really did just happen to hear about the police's plans for Granger and decided to rescue me when you saw me headed for the ambush?"

"Yes."

"Just because I didn't look like the type to be involved with a man like Granger?" she persisted. Her hand twisted the leather strap of her shoulder bag as she remembered the feeling she'd had that he already knew her name before he asked her to introduce herself.

"I had my reasons. That was one of them."

Honor drew a breath. "Well, then, I *am* grateful to you. To tell you the truth, I was not anxious to confront him, anyway. If the cops have him now that certainly will take a problem off my hands." For the first time since the whole mess had started, Honor permitted herself to give in to a feeling of relief. Overwhelming relief. A tentative smile lightened her eyes.

Landry saw the incipient relaxation and the hint of warmth in her and congratulated himself. The first strand of the web was in place. Honor Mayfield did not yet understand that she would have been better off taking her chances out in the parking lot along with Granger. Explaining herself to the cops probably would have been simpler and safer in the long run than explaining herself to him, Landry decided. But, then, she didn't have any choice.

*Come into my parlor, pretty fly.*

Actually, he admitted, she wasn't exactly pretty. But there was a compelling quality about her that seemed to fascinate him. The hazel eyes were expressive and serenely intelligent. Here in the shade the subtle golden highlights of her hair were hidden, but the style suited her. It was a smooth, casual curve that just touched her shoulders. A soft mouth and a slightly aggressive nose blended pleasantly enough with the wide, faintly tilted eyes, but taken independently the features would never be labeled beautiful.

Still, Landry realized, he found himself studying Honor's face, searching for whatever it was that intrigued him. Perhaps it was the hint of feminine strength in the way she carried herself. Or perhaps it was the shuttered, cautious warmth he saw in her eyes. She was not a superficial woman. Pride and intelligence and gentleness hovered just beneath the surface. Landry had spent a good many years learning to make accurate judgments of other people. His life had sometimes depended on that ability. Yes, there would be rewards in store for the man who slipped past her barriers.

The rest of her was proving unexpectedly interesting, too. A pair of pleated khaki pants that tapered to the ankles emphasized the curve of a nicely rounded derriere. The watermelon shirt was loose but didn't conceal the fact that her waist was small and so were her pert breasts.

In bed she would be sleek and responsive, Landry decided abruptly. He wasn't certain how he knew that but he was convinced of it. His whole body was convinced of it. The unexpected surge of a very ancient kind of awareness took him vaguely by surprise. It also put a piquant focus on his plans for Honor Mayfield. Once again he was forced to confront the wavering image of the goals that should have been crystal clear in his head. Determinedly he ignored the sense of ambivalence.

"Honor," he murmured, tasting her name aloud.

She looked up at him curiously. "Yes?"

"It's an interesting name."

"My father's choice," she informed him flatly.

"And do you live up to it?"

She didn't care for the direction of the conversation. "Since I'm not playing poker with you, I can't see that it matters."

"Is your father pleased with your efforts?"

"My father is dead, Mr. Landry."

Silence greeted her repressive remark. Landry didn't make the usual "I'm sorry" murmur. He merely accepted the information as if he already knew the answer. She didn't like the way he seemed to anticipate her. It made Honor nervous. She was already uneasy enough as it was today.

On the other hand, she would have been feeling distinctly more anxious right now if Conn Landry hadn't intercepted her en route to the parking lot. Her mouth relaxed into a warm smile.

"What are you thinking, Honor?"

"That I owe you one if you really did save me from getting involved in the setup meant for Granger."

"I agree."

Her smile tilted into a sardonic curve. "A more gallant approach would be to shrug and tell me your assistance was nothing, that I shouldn't feel obligated because of it."

He was silent.

"But you're not going to take the gallant approach, are you?" Quizzically she examined his hard face.

"No. Why should I? I prefer to keep the scales balanced."

He looked slightly puzzled that she should even suggest another way of operating than the one he was using. Honor knew in that moment that the words were a fundamental tenet for him, a doctrine by which he lived. He might be a harsh man in many respects, she decided, but he had his own code. Here in Southern California, where so many people ignored such archaic things as personal codes of behavior in favor of convenience and indulgence, there was something deeply intriguing about a man who lived by his own rules.

"Then you may have to write off this particular debt, Mr. Landry. I don't see how I can repay you," Honor said coolly.

"You can watch Legacy win in the fifth with me," he tossed back smoothly. "I'm using the trainer's box. I'd like you to join me. Especially since you have some connection with his sire."

Relief flared in her as she realized he wasn't going to ask too much after all. "I never actually saw Stylish Legacy run. My parents were in the process of getting a divorce during those years and there was a lot of...unpleasantness between Mom and Dad. I didn't get to spend a lot of time with my father. It was all a long time ago." Which didn't mean she hadn't been thrilled at the idea of her father's actually owning a racehorse, Honor remembered.

"You'll join me in Humphrey's box?"

"Well, if you insist," she agreed doubtfully, trying to hide her budding excitement.

"Having just saved your neck from the long arm of the law, granting me the favor is the least you can do, isn't it?" Conn said laconically.

"You have a remarkably undiplomatic way of putting things, Conn." Her words were tinged with some of the asperity she was feeling. Damn it, she did owe him some repayment for his fortuitous interference. But she didn't like the way he was using that obligation for his own purposes. Conn Landry, Honor decided, tended to be more than a little ruthless. Some of her initial excitement faded. "I can't see why you'd particularly want my company to watch Legacy run, but——"

"I do. So that settles it."

"Mr. Landry," she began fiercely, only to be interrupted by a new voice. It was a man's voice and it held a deep Southern drawl.

She turned to see a large, balding man with a paunch and an easy smile approaching. He was wearing a beige Stetson with what appeared to be a genuine snakeskin band. The rest of the outfit from the Western-cut shirt and flared trousers to the hand-tooled cowboy boots harmonized nicely with the hat. He was probably in his sixties, she estimated. The crinkles around his eyes when he smiled made her want to respond in kind.

"Have a heart, ma'am, Conn's only in town for the races. He's all alone and it seems perfectly logical to me that he might want to share Legacy's big race with a pretty little thing like you."

Landry nodded toward the newcomer. "Honor, this is Ethan Bailey. He's got a couple of horses with the same trainer I use, Toby Humphrey. Ethan, meet Honor Mayfield."

"How do you do?" she said politely, extending her hand. Her fingers were immediately crushed in a warm paw.

"Just fine, Miss Honor, just fine. It is Miss, isn't it?" He made a show of examining her ring finger. "Out here in California a man can't always be sure. You folks have a rather interesting approach to life."

"Don't let Ethan put you on," Conn advised dryly. "He may have been born in Texas, but he spends a hell of a lot of time in California."

"Only because Toby Humphrey's the best trainer around and he works here in California." Ethan Bailey sighed. "And I like to be close to my horses as much as possible."

"Just a good old ranch boy at heart," Conn said, but there was an easiness in his tone that told Honor he liked the other man. "You'd never know he made his living wheeling and dealing in West Coast real estate, would you?"

"Now, Landry, old buddy, you know damn well that my calling

is every bit as legitimate and inspirational as your own. Some objective folk might say even more so.'' Ethan Bailey grinned, reaching out to pat Legacy's neck. ''He's looking good today, aren't you, Legacy? Going to leave the rest of those clodhoppers behind in the dust.''

There was a rustle of movement from the far end of the stable and a small, wiry man who appeared to be somewhere on the far side of sixty-five came striding toward them at a brisk pace. He was accompanied by two young grooms.

''Afternoon, miss.'' The small man tipped his battered cap politely to Honor as he came to a halt in front of Legacy's stall. ''Hello, Conn, Ethan. Time to take Legacy down to the saddling ring.'' He stepped aside, and so did everyone else as one of the grooms, a young woman, moved forward to take charge of Legacy.

''Toby, I'd like you to meet a friend of Landry's,'' Ethan Bailey introduced the trainer, whose attention was divided between Legacy and the man who paid him to train the animal.

''He's in good shape, Conn,'' Humphrey pronounced. ''Real good shape.''

The horse strode out of the stall with an energy that spoke of his breeding and fitness. Honor found herself entranced by the beautifully built creature. The muscles of Legacy's strong hindquarters moved sleekly beneath a coat that had been burnished by hours of hand grooming. The center of attention now, and well aware of it, he tossed his head and pranced.

''Let's go,'' Landry said softly. He took Honor's arm and guided her after the small procession formed by the trainer, the grooms and the dancing horse.

''He's so beautiful,'' Honor breathed, no longer even thinking about getting out of her commitment to watch the horse race. She was getting caught up in the behind-the-scenes excitement and knew it.

''You've got a stake in him, you know,'' Landry pointed out, watching her changing expression. ''A family connection.''

''Maybe I'll splurge and put a couple of dollars down on him,'' Honor decided. She ignored the subtle emphasis he put on the words ''family connection.''

''We'll go place our bets after we've seen him saddled.'' They followed Legacy and his attendants to the stalls near the grandstands where the horses were saddled and the jockeys mounted.

"Who have you got on top of Legacy today?" Ethan Bailey asked conversationally as they watched the postage-stamp-size saddle put in place.

Landry hooked one booted foot over the bottom rung of the metal barricade and leaned forward on his elbows to watch the prerace activity. "Humphrey picked Milton. Says he'll have enough sense to let Legacy alone when the time comes."

Bailey nodded. "He's putting Milton on Cavalier in the eighth, too. Can't complain about the boy. Did real good by me last time he was on Cavalier."

Honor listened to the racing talk flowing around her and felt her pulse begin to quicken. At least the excitement in her system now wasn't from fear, she thought with a burst of gratitude for the taciturn man beside her. Hoping devoutly that whatever had taken place in the parking lot would result in her never having to worry about Granger again, she allowed herself to be swept up in the unique thrill of being connected, however distantly, to a real, live racehorse once again.

She was barely able to contain herself as they watched Legacy and his competitors being led out of the saddling area. Milton, the jockey, was tossed on board and then the restless animals headed toward the tunnel that opened onto the track.

"Come on, Honor. Let's get our bets down. See you around, Bailey." Landry nodded at the other man as he propelled his willing captive in the direction of the stands.

"He's going to win," Honor declared as she stood in line to place the bet. "I just know it."

"If you're sure of it, why are you only putting a couple of bucks on him?" There was a brief, teasing light in Conn's eyes.

"If you knew me better, you'd realize that's as big a risk as I ever take," she retorted.

"You were taking quite a risk this afternoon by following Granger." The hint of indulgent humor disappeared.

Some of Honor's new bubbling mood evaporated. "That was different." She was saved from explaining just why it was different because her turn came at the window. Hastily she put down her two dollars and accepted the ticket.

Two hundred on his own horse wasn't overly ostentatious, Honor decided a few minutes later as she watched Landry place his own bet at a different window. Of course, the real money for the owner would be in the winning purse and in the prestige.

Landry took her arm very firmly once more and led her into the stands.

Seated in the private box Toby Humphrey maintained for the use of his clients, Landry settled back to watch Legacy being edged into the gate. Out of the corner of his eye he could also watch the excitement on Honor's features.

She was caught up in it all now, he thought with satisfaction. She'd had no intention of getting involved with him this afternoon, yet here she was beside him, thoroughly engrossed in the coming race. He knew damn well that she was very grateful for his intervention earlier. He also knew she had been almost as wary of him as she was of Granger. But here she was, right where he wanted her.

It had all worked out very neatly. The first strand of the web was in place. There would be no escape for Honor Mayfield. He had counted on Legacy as a lure and it had worked. He'd assumed she'd have some interest in the horse because of the fact that her father had once owned the sire. Keeping her free of Granger was an added plus and she was bound to be grateful. Conn knew the starting point of the web was firmly attached. From now on he would move more and more surely into her life, taking advantage of every opportunity to get closer to this woman who was a link to the mystery of the past. He wanted her gratitude, her trust, her confidence, and he also wanted her to sense that he was the one in control.

Remaining in control was critical, Conn reminded himself. The last thing he wanted to risk was being tugged into the heart of the web right along with his victim.

# TWO

Legacy breezed in three lengths ahead of everything else in the field. Milton, the jockey, sat politely on the horse's back as though he'd just been invited along for the ride. Honor found herself on her feet and shouting along with everyone else. The excitement of horse racing was highly contagious.

"He won! He won! Conn, he did it!"

She thought she saw a brief sign of satisfaction in his expression, and then it changed to an arrogantly aloof interest in the fact. He appeared far more curious about her bubbling reaction to the win.

"Yes, he did."

"You're going to clean up on your bet and so am I. Come on, let's go. We've got to hurry. They'll be taking the photos in the winner's circle." Honor impulsively reached out to grasp his hand and hustle him out of the box.

"What's the rush?" But Conn got slowly to his feet. He sounded slightly perplexed.

"The rush is that they'll take the photo regardless of whether or not the owner is there. And you want to be in the picture, don't you? You can hang it on the wall in your bathroom or something. Didn't you get your picture taken the last time you watched him race?"

"No," he admitted. "I've only watched him race once before, and I'm not all that familiar with the track formalities. I was sitting in the stands and no one sent for me or told me how to get into the picture."

She laughed up at him, finding the trace of genuine disappointment in his voice rather endearing. "No one sends for you. You get into the picture by running. Come on, Conn, let's go!"

Swept up in the thrill of being connected to a winning racehorse, Honor was only vaguely aware of how hard she had to work to get Landry down into the winner's circle where a head-tossing, sweat-soaked Legacy was waiting to have his picture taken.

Everyone in the vicinity, it seemed, except Landry was eager to participate in the little ritual. Conn seemed almost embarrassed by the activity going on around his horse. It occurred to Honor that he wasn't accustomed to being in the limelight. A man of the shadows, she thought fleetingly and wondered vaguely what he'd done during his life. By the time Honor had pushed Conn into position near Legacy's head and the track officials had taken their customary places, a few other totally unrelated faces were already standing near the horse.

At the last moment Landry looked around and saw Honor waiting behind the barrier. Suddenly he held out his hand in a cool, commanding fashion.

"Come here, Honor. You might as well be in this shot, too."

"Oh, no, I had nothing to do with him winning," she protested. But there was more than politeness in his eyes; there was a strangely intense insistence. He wanted her to join him, she realized, and in those hectic moments Honor's instinct was to obey. Besides, how often would she have a chance to be photographed with a winning racehorse, she asked herself cheerfully. She hurried forward to take her place beside him.

It was all over in a moment. The track officials did this sort of thing after every race and had the routine down pat. Four photos of winning horses and their beaming owners had already been taken this afternoon and there were several more to go. The crowd around Legacy broke up quickly as Humphrey took charge and led the horse away toward the stables. Landry still retained his remotely satisfied look, but he didn't completely fool Honor. The deep pleasure in Legacy's win was there. Intuitively, she sensed it.

"A winner has a lot of friends," Honor observed as the strangers who had managed to push their way into the photo drifted off, laughing.

"A fact of life. Losers, on the other hand, fare a little differently," Conn Landry said dryly as he guided Honor back into the stands.

That thought sobered her. "I wonder how many friends Granger will have, now that he's been arrested. If he was arrested. What if he's out on bail within a few hours, Conn? Or what if the trap didn't close properly?"

"Since I don't know why you're worried, I can't be very reassuring, can I?"

Honor flushed and firmly changed the subject. "We'd better go collect our winnings."

He hesitated as she made to hurry toward the betting windows. "Honor?"

"What is it, Conn?"

"I think you ought to tell me what's going on."

"Why?" she asked starkly, her mood fading rapidly. The momentary excitement of being carried along with the thrill of the racing world was almost entirely gone.

"Because you owe me an explanation," he said simply.

"You said I only owed you my company while we watched Legacy win."

"That's just a part of what you owe me."

She saw the unreadable chill in his eyes and suppressed a shiver. Around them the crowd ebbed and flowed, ignoring the small confrontation as if it wasn't taking place. Honor felt alone and isolated, forced to deal with a predator on his own terms.

"Perhaps it would have been better if you hadn't interfered earlier," she said quietly.

"But I did interfere, and now it's too late."

"Too late for what, Mr. Landry?"

He smiled weakly. "You were calling me by my first name a few minutes ago."

"Just tell me what you want from me," she exploded tightly. The turquoise leather strap of her bag was damp with moisture from her palm.

"Dinner tomorrow evening?" he suggested gently.

Her eyes widened. "Dinner!"

"As Ethan told you, I'm only in town to check on Legacy's progress. I don't know anyone else except Ethan and Humphrey and a couple of other people who have horses in Humphrey's stables. Is is so strange that I'd want to have dinner with an attractive woman whose father owned Legacy's sire?"

"I don't know, Conn. Is it strange? There's something about you that confuses me and I think you know it."

"Bailey and Humphrey can vouch for me," he pointed out calmly. "If you don't trust me, ask them for a reference."

"It's not that exactly—" She broke off, floundering. "It's this other business with Granger. I still don't understand how you knew what was going on this afternoon."

"I told you. Racetrack rumors. They're rampant."

"Apparently they didn't reach Granger's ears in time!"

"Probably because most people around here would just as soon see him removed from the scene. He's lowlife."

"I'll agree with you on that point."

"I'd like to know how you got involved with his sort."

"And if I don't feel like telling you?" she challenged.

"I'd still like to take you out to dinner."

But it wasn't a simple invitation. If it had been, Honor knew she would probably have accepted without much hesitation. There was something about Conn Landry that intrigued and compelled her. But the way he was asking her out to dinner made her wary. His request contained the same sort of insistence and urgency she'd sensed when he'd demanded that she be in the photograph a few minutes ago. On the other hand, she owed him a great deal, probably more than she knew, for his interference earlier in the afternoon. And then there was the fact that Ethan Bailey and Toby Humphrey seemed to like him, for whatever that was worth.

He must have seen the flickering uncertainty in her eyes, because Conn gave her his strangely sardonic smile and pushed her lightly in the direction of the pay windows. "Give me your address and I'll pick you up at seven."

"I don't think—"

"Where's your ticket?" he asked as they reached the window.

"Here." Her fingers moved nervously in her purse, searching for her winning two-dollar ticket. A small plastic envelope fell to the floor during the awkward shuffling. Honor stifled a small sigh as Conn reached down to pick up the business card case and read:

Mayfield Interiors

Designs for Commercial and Residential Space

After noting the title of her business, Landry calmly pocketed one of the cards and then handed the case back to her. "I'll give you a call tomorrow when I find out Granger's status."

Honor shook her head once in silent acceptance of fate. Conn now knew her business address and her phone number. It would be a simple matter for him to get in touch any time he wished. Her last hope of retaining some anonymity and therefore some protection from him evaporated. The disconcerting part of it all was that she wasn't sure but she was glad the matter had been taken out of her hands.

Half an hour later, after watching a proud Legacy being given his cool-down walk by a groom, Honor finally made her escape from the Santa Anita racetrack. The afternoon had proved a total surprise, she decided as she drove back to Pasadena. On the one hand she had been saved from that tricky business with Granger. But the other side of the coin had revealed a situation that, in its own way, was fraught with just as much risk.

So many questions surrounded Constantine Landry. How would he know Granger's status by tomorrow? Was he really in town just to watch his horse run? What had that vague crack of Ethan Bailey's meant? The one about real estate being a bit more legitimate than Landry's occupation. Perhaps she should have done as Conn had dryly suggested and asked Bailey and the trainer for a reference. No, that would have made her feel ridiculous. Obviously they would say reassuring things about him, or Landry would never have made the suggestion in the first place. Besides, Landry was a good client of Humphrey's. It was unlikely the trainer would have said anything negative, anyway. And as for Bailey, well, the older man had seemed to like Landry.

And then there was the little matter of Landry having saved her from having to deal with Granger.

That alone put her deeply into his debt, Honor decided. There was no way around the issue. When it came to paying her debts, Honor made a point of living up to her name. The family's reputation had been tarnished enough fifteen years ago to last more than a generation. Yes, she would meet Conn Landry for dinner if that's what he thought she owed him.

The phone was ringing as Honor turned the key in the lock of her apartment door. She didn't rush to answer it because she was almost certain she knew who was on the other end. She was right.

"Hello, Adena."

"You're back!" her younger sister exclaimed in frantic tones. Adena rarely spoke in mild or neutral tones. Everything was exaggerated, dramatic, excited or outrageous. Adena fit very well into the Southern California life-style. "What happened? Did you see Granger? Talk to him? Oh, Honor, I've been so scared."

"Yes and no, respectively." Honor tossed her blue bag down on the kitchen counter, aware of the irritation behind the act. She was very fond of Adena but lately the bonds of sisterly affection and family loyalty had been pushed a bit far.

"Yes and no! What on earth does that mean? Did you work something out with the man or not?"

"Calm down, Adena. Things didn't go exactly as planned. But

it may all be for the best. You'll be glad to know that Granger is currently in police custody."

There was a stunned silence on the other end. "The police have him?" Adena finally asked in confusion. "But how? When? I don't understand."

"Apparently a trap had been planned for him today," Honor explained steadily and then gave her sister the few details she had.

"But a man like that will be out on bail in a few hours," Adena cried.

Honor said nothing. She was well aware of that possibility.

"And who is this Landry person?"

"Beats me. Owns a beautiful horse, though. A colt sired by Stylish Legacy."

"Stylish Legacy?" There was a questioning note in Adena's voice. "Wasn't that the horse Dad used to own?"

"That's right." Adena had been only eight years old when Nicholas Mayfield had been killed. She remembered the horse only because of some of the mementos that had been left behind. Honor, at thirteen, had been fascinated with the idea of having a horse in the family, even though she had never gotten to watch him run. Stylish Legacy had only been in a handful of races before the two men who owned him had both died in a bloody scandal that had traumatized Honor more than anyone else in the family. Adena had been too young to understand fully what had happened, and Mrs. Mayfield, who had been in the midst of messy divorce proceedings, had been almost relieved to have everything ended.

"Well, I don't see what this has to do with anything. Where does Landry fit into all this?" Adena asked anxiously.

"He kept me out of the trap that had been set for Granger. And when he found out I had some distant connection to his horse, he, uh, invited me to watch the race." "Invited" was something of a euphemism for the command Landry had issued, but Honor didn't feel up to explaining her own wariness of the man.

"And he's going to tell you what happens to Granger?"

"He said he'd find out tomorrow."

"Honor, this is getting messier and messier. Why couldn't you just have paid off Granger and put an end to it all?"

Honor closed her eyes, momentarily seeking patience. "Because by the time I was about to catch up with him, the police were waiting."

"So this Constantine Landry says. What if he was wrong? Or playing some weird game? This doesn't solve anything! I'm in the same mess I was in before. What are we going to do now?"

"Adena, I don't know. I have no way of knowing what was happening out there this afternoon," Honor said flatly. "You'll have to forgive me if I'm not handling this in the proper manner, but I haven't had a whole lot of experience dealing with sharks such as Granger!"

"Meaning I have?"

"You're the one who owes him five thousand dollars, not I!" Adena broke into tears and, as usual, Honor felt guilty.

"Forget it, Adena," she soothed wearily. "I'll take care of everything. I'm seeing Landry tomorrow and he'll tell me whether or not we still have to worry about Granger."

"Are you sure you can trust this Landry person?" Adena demanded through sobs.

"No." The initial response had been immediate. But then Honor thought about the man with the gunmetal-gray eyes. "Well, maybe," she temporized.

"What kind of an answer is that?"

"The truth is, I just don't know yet. But there's something about him, Adena. I think he might be quite ruthless on occasion but I also have a feeling that he's, well, concerned with keeping the books balanced."

"What books?"

"Never mind. I'll call you tomorrow after I find out more. Goodbye, Adena." Honor put down the phone before her sister could get in another question.

Then she moved deliberately across the living room with its red, black and yellow furnishings on a white carpet and into the red-and-black-tiled kitchen. It had been a rough day in several ways, and she deserved some compensation. Pouring herself a glass of cool Napa Valley Riesling, Honor went back into the living room. She sank down into a black-webbed rocking chair and propped her feet on the red hassock. Silently she toasted the palm tree outside her window.

"Here's to you, Constantine Landry, whoever you are. I'm not sure yet whether I should be thanking you or running as fast as I can in the opposite direction. But one thing's for sure. You aren't going to make my life dull."

By the time Conn showed up at her door the following evening, Honor had decided that running really wasn't necessary. In fact, she told herself as she took in the sight of him standing on her doorstep, she was beginning to look forward to the evening.

He wore an immaculately cut gray linen jacket that had a subtle slub weave. Charcoal trousers that ended above hand-sewn calf-skin shoes emphasized the coiled strength of his body. The crisply striped shirt and silk tie completed the quiet look of expensive power.

The only factor that bothered Honor was that she couldn't identify the type of power that emanated from Conn Landry. It wasn't, for example, the muted ritualized power associated with the corporate world. Nor was it the flashy, tacky, heavy-handed power of the Southern California film crowd. It crossed her mind briefly that what she was seeing was the cool arrogance of a professional gangster, but she dismissed the idea at once. Instead, the strength in Landry seemed to be uniquely his own. And she had the sense to know it was, therefore, more dangerous in some ways than the more easily recognized sources of power. It was always simpler to deal with a factor that could be labeled and understood.

But for some reason, although she was warily respectful of the potential danger in him, Honor didn't fear Conn. That knowledge gave her the poise to smile warmly at him.

Landry saw the confidence in her and told himself he was amused. Yet a part of him knew a sense of reluctant admiration. The lady had guts. Having just recently finished with a rather blunt heart-to-heart chat with Granger, he now knew just how much nerve she must have buried beneath that bright, stylish exterior.

She was wearing a yellow-gold chemise that was sashed low on the hips with a crisp, wide band of black. The effect was both rakish and self-confident without being outrageous. The black sandals and the ebony bracelet on her small wrist completed the outfit. Her hair swung in a sleek curtain around her shoulders and as he stood there on the threshold, Landry had an almost overpowering urge to run his fingers through the golden-brown stuff. He wanted to touch her with the familiar intimacy of a lover. She'd look good a little mussed from his touch, he decided.

Once again he realized he should be questioning his own reactions. It was reasonably safe to admit he found himself responding physically to Honor. Conn decided that he understood that part and could deal with it. But it definitely was not on the program to uncover this vein of whimsically indulgent tenderness.

"The desk clerk at my hotel recommended a little restaurant downtown," Landry said as he walked her toward the silver-gray Porsche that waited at the curb. He told her the name. "Know it?"

Honor nodded. "It's an excellent choice." She allowed him to slip her into the front seat and then had to wait impatiently while he circled the front of the car and slid in beside her. "Well?" she invited cheerfully. "When are you going to tell me all the details?"

His promised phone call that afternoon had been brief, disappointingly so, Honor had discovered after she'd replaced the receiver. Landry had only asked for her home address and then said quite calmly that Granger was no longer a problem. He'd refused to tell her more at that point.

"I'll give you the full story over dinner," Landry promised now as he pulled away from the curb. The quiet, tree-lined streets near the California Institute of Technology campus were relatively empty at this hour, and he made his way through them with an ease that told Honor he didn't need directions.

She wondered briefly how he happened to be so familiar with the Pasadena streets, and then promptly forgot the matter as her mind went back to Granger.

"He really is out of the way, though?"

"He won't bother you or your sister again."

Her head snapped around. "How did you know about my sister's involvement in all this?"

"I'll tell you that over dinner, too." He threw her a sidelong glance. "Relax, Honor. I've taken care of everything."

Some of her breezy confidence faded. "*You've* taken care of everything? I thought it was the police who had handled Granger."

"Whether or not they do doesn't affect you anymore."

"Do you know, Conn Landry, you have a remarkable talent for the cryptic comment?"

"Since my talents are rather limited, I try to perfect the few I have."

"I get the feeling your sense of humor may not be numbered among your few perfected abilities."

"Probably not," he admitted without any show of concern.

"Pity," she said dryly, trying to sound just as cryptic as Conn.

Driving ability was, apparently, one of his limited number of talents, Honor observed as he parked the Porsche with neat precision in front of the casually elegant little restaurant. When Conn opened her car door and took her arm to escort her across the sidewalk she decided that he had another talent: He had the ability to make her feel safe.

It was an odd sensation on her part, she reflected as she was seated. Honor had never been aware of needing or desiring a man's protection. Whatever protection a man offered his women had disappeared when she was thirteen, and she hadn't depended on any since then.

Containing her curiosity until after she'd obediently ordered her meal of broccoli salad and scallops, Honor waited for an opportune opening. When the Sonoma County Chardonnay arrived at the table after much deliberation between the wine steward and Conn, she decided she had waited long enough. Smiling expectantly, she sipped the beautiful white wine and repeated her question.

"Tell me what they did to Granger."

Landry shrugged, reaching for his own glass. "He's out on bail. Eventually he might wind up in jail on a more or less permanent basis, but probably not this time."

Honor's expectant smile disappeared. "You said everything was all right now, that Granger has been dealt with and was no longer a problem. I was afraid of this," she went on morosely. "As long as he's running around loose, I'm going to have to find him."

"You're not going anywhere near that scum. I told you the situation is under control." There was cool command in Conn's gaze again.

"I haven't got much choice," Honor shot back.

"You're right. You don't have much choice. You're going to do as I say in the matter."

"You don't have any conception of what's going on!"

"No?" Broodingly he studied her set face. "I know your sister owed him five thousand dollars because of that loan he gave her to pay off her gambling debts. And I know she didn't have the money. Apparently she went to you for it."

"How do you know all this?" Honor demanded fiercely.

"Some of it I learned from Granger and some of it I figured out for myself," Conn explained easily.

"You've actually talked to Granger today?" She was stunned by the news. "You saw him?"

"He headed for the racetrack as soon as they released him. He's a real racing addict. But, then, you must know that, or you wouldn't have been there yourself yesterday looking for him."

"Adena told me she thought that was the most likely place to find him," Honor admitted slowly. "But I don't understand why you approached him."

"Don't you?"

"Well, no. None of this is any of your business."

"It is now."

"Conn, this is ridiculous. You can't just choose to involve yourself in my personal life!"

He watched her intently for a long moment and then reached across the small table to draw a thumb along the back of her wrist. His hand, Honor realized uneasily, was as strong-looking as the rest of him. Large, square, powerful. At first glance a woman wouldn't guess that those blunt fingers could be so amazingly sensitive. Yet the small pattern he traced on her wrist sent a tremor of awareness through her.

"I've already involved myself in your affairs, Honor. I paid Granger off and told him not to go near your sister again."

Honor's gaze reflected her shock. "You paid him off! You gave him five thousand dollars?"

"That's what your sister owed."

"Yes, but—"

"Honor, it's all over," Conn told her with a surprising twist of gentleness in his voice. "You don't have to deal with Granger. I've already handled him for you."

Confused and alarmed at the implications of having this man take charge of such a personal and dangerous matter, Honor found herself fumbling for words of anger and protest. "You have no right! You should have consulted me. Now I owe you the five thousand dollars. That's assuming you're telling me the truth in the first place. Maybe this is all some sort of scam to take me for another five thousand. How do I know that you're any less dangerous than Granger?"

"You don't."

"Damn you and your cryptic comments!" She tossed her napkin on the table and prepared to get to her feet. The large, square hand that had only moments ago been tantalizing the back of her wrist suddenly closed around it like a manacle.

"Sit down, Honor," Conn ordered quietly.

"Why should I?" she hissed in response.

His mouth lifted in the now familiar faint smile. "Because you owe me five thousand dollars?" he suggested smoothly.

Honor went very still. She couldn't have gotten out of her chair now even if the room were on fire. Her eyes met Conn's unreadable gaze. "My checkbook is at home. Take me back to the apartment and I'll give you your money. The same money I was going to give Granger. I get the feeling it doesn't much matter which of the two of you I pay. You seem to have a lot in common, you and Granger."

For a split second she was certain she'd gone much too far. The fingers shackling her wrist were now tight bands of steel and the cold of Conn's eyes could only have its source in the farthest reaches of the universe. In that taut instant of time Honor's instinctive wariness of the man made the transition to genuine fear.

And then, quite suddenly, she was free. Landry released her hand and sat back in his chair, reaching for his wineglass. He took a long swallow before he spoke. When he looked at her again, the frightening ice of his eyes had disappeared, leaving only his usual, remote expression. The wry tone of his words dissipated most of the remaining tendrils of alarm that curled through Honor's body. He inclined his head once, very formally.

"Congratulations, lady, you nearly managed to push me over the edge with that last crack. Not many people have the power to do that to me."

She swallowed awkwardly. "My guess is not many people care to make the attempt."

"Did I frighten you?"

"I don't know how to take you, Conn," she said honestly. "Yes, you frightened me for a moment. After all, I don't know much about you, do I? And now I owe you five thousand dollars."

"Wouldn't you rather owe it to me than to Granger?"

"I don't know yet. At least I have a fair idea of where Granger fits into the grand scheme of life. He's a loan shark. Once I'd paid him off he would have been out of the way. You're not so easy to classify."

"I'll take that as a compliment. A minute ago you were pointing out how much I had in common with Granger. Apparently my status isn't really that low in your eyes."

"Why did you do it?" she asked starkly.

He didn't pretend to misunderstand. "Because I didn't want

you going near that man," he declared with absolute conviction. "You don't know anything about dealing with people like him. How did your sister get involved?"

Honor sighed, relaxing a little now that Conn seemed under control. "For a while this fall she was dating a man who, among other things, gambled heavily. I guess he made it all look so easy and so much fun. He took her to Vegas and to the races and encouraged her to try her luck. At Santa Anita he introduced her to Granger. I gather he often used Granger as a banker. Granger made the money so readily available that my sister couldn't resist. She wanted to keep up with the high-rolling crowd she was moving with and eventually got run over, instead. She luckily came to her senses and dropped the boyfriend."

"But by that time she was already into Granger for the five thousand?"

"Actually, she only borrowed three thousand," Honor said bluntly. "But the government doesn't regulate interest rates in Granger's world."

"Two thousand dollars in interest on a three-thousand-dollar loan. Yes, Granger is a step ahead of most banks. Well, if it's any consolation, he won't be approaching your sister again, even if she shows up at the track."

Honor considered that. "Because you told him to stay clear?" "That's right."

"Why is Granger so willing to take orders from you?"

"Maybe I make him nervous the same way I make you nervous," Conn offered laconically as the broccoli salads arrived.

Honor ignored her food. Leaning forward intently she said, "Conn, I will repay you tonight. I have the money."

"It's not necessary."

Honor shook her head violently. "It is most definitely necessary. I will give you the money tonight."

He watched her expressive face for a moment as if trying to make up his mind about something. Then he nodded. "All right. If it will make you feel more comfortable."

"It will!"

He smiled faintly. "Yes, I can see that it will. And I do want you to feel comfortable around me, Honor."

"Do you?" she asked skeptically.

"It's a priority of mine," he assured her calmly.

Honor had to admit that by the conclusion of the meal, Conn had achieved at least a portion of his goal. Her sense of caution around him was still very much alive, but the compelling attraction he held for her was stronger than ever. There had been no argument over the matter of her giving him the money, so he obviously didn't intend to hold it over her head in any way. His main objective, apparently, had been to protect her from having to face Granger.

Strangely enough his protectiveness left her feeling in some ways more deeply in his debt than she would have felt if she'd simply owed Conn five thousand dollars. It was an odd bit of irony, she reflected as she gave him the key to open her front door.

"Would you like some brandy while I write out the check?" she offered politely as she stepped inside the apartment.

"Thank you, I'd appreciate that," he murmured, prowling through her strikingly decorated living room. "Just tell me where it is. I'll get it."

"In that red lacquered cabinet by the window."

He nodded and paced across the white carpet. He was taking in every detail, Honor thought fleetingly as she went quickly down the hall to her bedroom to get her checkbook. How much could that man read from the design details of her living room? Probably far too much.

It was as she stepped into her Japanese-inspired bedroom that Honor experienced her first sense of something being subtly wrong. For an instant she stood poised in the doorway, frowning as she looked into every corner of the room.

A moment later she shook her head in self-annoyance. Everything was in order. The red-and-black gilt-trimmed drawers of her dressing table were closed, just as they should have been, and her bed was dramatically neat, with its embroidered quilt in place. The room was a visual interpretation of subtle, sophisticated serenity. The only jarring note was the television set, and it was discreetly concealed behind a folding screen.

Honor nibbled on her lower lip for a few seconds, trying to shake off the feeling that there was a new element in the room. Then, half-disgusted with herself, she strode over to the closet and yanked open the shoji-screen doors. Inside, her brilliantly colored clothing hung in place above the array of equally bright shoes. Everything was as it should be.

"You're turning into a nervous little old spinster, my girl," she told herself bitingly. Determinedly she bent over the dresser and scrawled out the five-thousand-dollar check. After signing it she straightened, aware that the eerie trickle of uneasiness was still thrumming in her veins.

The only place in the room she hadn't checked was under the bed. Surely she wouldn't give in to the impulse, she chided herself.

"Oh, nuts!" She went to her knees on the white carpet and peered beneath the bed. Conn's blandly interested voice from the doorway sent a jolt through her.

"Well, I'll be damned. I've heard tales of single ladies who reach the point where they start looking under the bed before they go to sleep at night, but I didn't imagine you were one of them."

"I was right earlier this evening when I decided your sense of humor was not among your limited selection of talents, Mr. Landry." Awkward with embarrassment, Honor got to her feet and turned to pick up the check that lay on the dressing table. Aware that her cheeks were stained with a strong shade of pink, she spent an extra moment studying the check so that she wouldn't have to meet his mocking gaze.

But when Honor swung around with a flippant remark ready on her lips she suddenly found herself in Conn's arms. He had crossed the white carpet without making a sound, coming up behind her as stealthily as any predator.

"Conn?"

"There's no need to go looking under your bed, Honor. I'm right here."

Standing very still in his arms, Honor watched with fascination as he lowered his mouth to hers. He was there, all right, filling up every inch of her beautifully designed bedroom with his own brand of strength and presence. All thoughts of a vague wrongness in the atmosphere went out of her head as he took her lips. Conn Landry felt very, very right.

It was not the sort of kiss she normally expected and received the first time she kissed a new date. Landry's mouth did not move on hers with the tentative, questioning approach a man generally used in the beginning.

Instead he took her mouth as though he had been anticipating the action for a long while. The hunger in him was blunt and dangerously near the surface. What should have bothered her was that her body seemed to respond with the same feeling of being suddenly on the verge of discovery and release. It was an exciting, exhilarating sensation.

Her arms came up to wind slowly around his neck as he coaxed apart her lips. She shuddered a little as his tongue swept behind the barrier of her teeth. His response was to tighten his hands on her waist. Conn pulled her into his heat with irresistible pressure, gently forcing her into total awareness of the tautness of his thighs. And all the while he explored her mouth, drinking hungrily from the intimate, moist depths.

Honor's lashes closed slumberously and her body was invaded with a sweet lethargy that was shot through with red threads of anticipation.

"Honor, honey, you taste so good," Conn murmured in a husky growl as he reluctantly freed her mouth. He sampled the hidden skin behind the curve of her hair, his teeth nibbling with exquisite gentleness. "Spicy, sweet and sexy. I knew you'd taste this way."

Reflexively her nails kneaded his shoulders, the coral tips sinking deeply into the gray fabric of his jacket. He groaned and raised his hands slowly along her rib cage until his thumbs rested just beneath the curve of her unconfined breasts.

"Oh, Conn."

"We're going to be good in bed together, you and I," he interrupted with soft satisfaction. He grazed the pad of his thumb across the crest of one breast and felt it flower to life beneath the yellow-gold silk.

His absolute certainty got through the sensual haze that seemed to be clouding her senses. "No," she whispered. "Not bed. Not yet." And, if she had an ounce of genuine intelligence, she added silently, not ever. She should know better than to play with fire at her age.

"I won't rush you," he vowed soothingly as he continued to glide the flat of his thumb across her silk-sheathed nipple.

Questioningly she lifted her head to meet his intent gaze and found herself staring into gray, bottomless seas that swirled with masculine desire. The depths of his hunger startled her even as it called to her.

"I think," she began carefully, "that you'll do things exactly as you want to do them, regardless of whether or not it means rushing me."

"Don't be afraid of me, Honor," he rasped against her ear. "There's no need."

"What's that supposed to mean?" she asked urgently, a strange panic sizzling through her.

"Nothing. Just relax. I want you, but I can wait." He used his strong hands on the nape of her neck, gentling her tense body until she did as he asked and relaxed against him. "I can wait," he repeated half under his breath.

There was something about the way he touched her, the way his hardness felt against her softness that was undermining all her defenses, Honor realized vaguely. The attraction between them was so unexpectedly strong, so out of the ordinary, that she wasn't fully prepared to handle it. Time was the key. She sensed that much.

Apparently Landry did, too. Slowly he eased himself away from her, mouth crooked just a bit at the edge. "I'll give you a little time, Honor." He brushed his mouth lightly across her parted lips. "But I think I'd better get myself out of your bedroom or I won't be able to keep my promise."

Without a word she followed him out into the living room, the check clutched in her hand. He finished his brandy while standing by the window gazing out into the darkness. They spoke little during those few minutes but the atmosphere was heavy with unsatisfied male desire. When at last he turned to leave, Honor thrust the check at him. Conn took it without glancing at it, stuffing it into his jacket pocket.

"Feel better now that you've paid the debt?" he asked softly.

"Yes." But she didn't feel she had paid the debt, Honor decided as she said good-night to him at the door. He had protected her from having to deal with Granger. She didn't have any way to repay that part of the obligation and the knowledge caused a faint tingle of unease.

It wasn't until she had turned out all the lights in the living room and walked slowly back down the hall to the bedroom that the sensation of wrongness returned. Once again she found herself standing in the doorway, trying to understand what it was that bothered her.

This time she finally focused on the cause. The large, folding screen with delicate Japanese artwork wasn't standing in quite the same place it had been earlier this evening when she had left the house. It didn't quite hide the television behind it.

The designer instincts in her had always insisted on using the screen to hide the brash, high-tech look of the portable TV. The twentieth-century technology had seemed to clash with the elegant serenity of the room.

Curious, Honor walked over to where the screen stood and

examined the flattened areas of carpet where the legs of the screen had once pressed it down. She knew she hadn't moved that screen in two weeks. It had been that long since she'd used the television.

It was such a small thing, she told herself nervously. But designers were trained to notice small details in a room. It was often the little things that made the difference between a room with dynamic, personal impact and a simple showplace that had no warmth. The little things could also destroy the image. People in her profession soon learned to recognize odd little details that could produce great effects or ruin beautifully planned projects.

Someone had been in her bedroom that night.

# THREE

"She's a nice young lady, Conn," Ethan Bailey said. He was focusing a set of field glasses, watching a fast filly go through her morning workout on the track.

"Your horse or Honor Mayfield?" Landry leaned against the railing, his eyes following Bailey's expensive filly.

"Both, I reckon. But to tell you the truth it was that sweet little Honor I had in mind."

"You trying to tell me something, Ethan?" The odd little smile flickered at the edges of Landry's mouth.

Still gazing through the glasses, Bailey shrugged. "None of my business, of course, but, well, she doesn't seem quite your type, son."

"I agree. It's none of your business and she's probably not my type." But Conn kept his tone easy, not wanting to offend his friend. "On the other hand, I've never been really sure exactly what my type is. And Honor is turning out to be…interesting."

Ethan's brow held a trace of a disapproving frown. "You planning on playing games with Miss Honor?"

"You're certainly concerned about her."

"Like I said, I like her. Back where I come from a man's not supposed to play games with a lady like her."

"She can handle them." Conn relented. "Look, Ethan, don't worry about her. And don't worry about me, either. I know what I'm doing."

"You always seem to be in control of things, I'll grant you that." Ethan grinned abruptly. "Forget I tried to give you the dose of fatherly advice. A man my age sometimes takes a few liberties he's got no right to take. Besides, if you scratch deep enough, you'd probably find out my motivations weren't exactly pure as the new driven snow."

"Meaning you're jealous?"

"You bet," Ethan acknowledged fervently. "The reason a man my age starts offering fatherly advice is precisely because he's a mite envious of a man your age. It's our way of getting even with you young folks. Spiteful. Downright spiteful.''

Landry's eyes lightened with fleeting humor. ''That showgirl I saw hanging on your arm last month in Vegas didn't seem interested in finding anyone younger than you!''

Ethan sighed grandly and shook his head. ''Sad to say, I'm afraid my main attraction for that little gal was my bank account. Unfortunately I doubt that Miss Honor would be similarly impressed.''

''You don't think so?'' Landry asked thoughtfully.

''Well,'' Ethan drawled lightly, ''I suppose it might be worth a try.''

Landry was startled by the sudden, unexpected tension that flashed through him as he pictured Ethan Bailey or anyone else trying to impress Honor Mayfield. He must be crazy, he told himself. Ethan was only teasing him. Deliberately he summoned up a determined casualness. ''Hands off, Ethan, old buddy, I saw her first.''

''And when do you plan on seeing her next?''

Landry glanced around at the quiet grounds. ''This morning. I invited her to come watch the workouts.'' His eyes narrowed faintly as he glanced at his watch. ''She said she'd try to make it.''

''Maybe something came up,'' Ethan said. ''The lady's got a business to run, didn't you say? Some kind of decorating work?''

''Interior designs for offices. Homes, too, I think,'' Conn answered absently, beginning to wonder if Honor might be going to stand him up after all. He'd called her yesterday, the morning after their dinner date, and issued the invitation to join him at the track today. The lure was an attractive one, he'd told himself. He had a hunch she'd enjoy watching the horses working out. She had seemed initially hesitant and then in a little rush of enthusiasm, she'd said she'd try to make it.

He'd been certain she'd show. Everything seemed to be falling into place quite neatly. When he'd accepted the check the other night they'd both known it didn't erase the debt between them. He'd seen the gratitude in her eyes. It had been coupled with caution, but it had been genuine.

She'd been frightened of Granger and he'd assumed the task of dealing with the man on her behalf. In addition, he'd kept her from getting mixed up with the police trap that had been set in the parking lot. A real knight in shining armor, Landry told himself sardonically. Then he wondered why the image bothered him.

There were a lot of things bothering him that shouldn't have been making him uneasy. He didn't understand it. Everything had seemed so simple and straightforward when he'd originally decided to track her down. The decision had been based on an intuitive, gut-level feeling that there were questions to be asked and that the only one left who might have some answers was Honor Mayfield. It wasn't that he thought she would really know what had happened all those years ago, but she was a Mayfield. Through her he might be able to satisfy the uncertainties, the *wrongness*, the sense of injustice that had haunted him so long. But she would run if she found out who he was. In fact, she would probably be wise to run. So he had to ensnare her firmly before he revealed himself.

And now that he'd kissed her, Landry knew the first strands of the web were securely locked in place. The response from her had been unmistakable. His body still remembered it, along with the seething frustration of knowing that the time was not yet right to push her into bed.

Yes, she'd show up this morning, he told himself, aware of a sense of satisfaction. The bonds of gratitude and sexual attraction were in place. The combination was a strong one—with any luck at all, an irresistible one.

"Here she is." Ethan Bailey interrupted Conn's thoughts to wave cheerfully at Honor, who was walking toward them with a foam cup of coffee in her hand. "Over here, Miss Honor."

Conn turned his head to look at her, aware of a certain possessive pleasure. She looked good this morning, her hair brushed back behind one ear and held with a clip. An indigo-blue chambray shirt was belted over a pair of snug-fitting jeans. Something about the way she moved as she walked toward him sent a flare of anticipation through him. Conn got to his feet.

Honor saw the hunter looking out at her from Conn Landry's eyes as she came up to the railing. It sent a tiny jolt through her, even as she acknowledged the sense of pleasure she felt in his presence. Perhaps she had been right early this morning when she'd told herself it might be better to forgo the invitation. Every time she was with Conn she risked deepening an involvement that she sensed was dangerous. Yet here she was, unable to stay away.

"I was beginning to think you might not make it," Conn said

quietly after the greetings had been exchanged. His gaze moved over her, seeming to take in every detail.

"I wasn't sure myself." She smiled politely and sipped her coffee, refusing to elaborate. "Is that one of your horses, Ethan?"

"Yes, ma'am," Bailey declared proudly as he set a stopwatch to time the filly. "Paid a handsome sum for that little lady. Expect great things from her."

"Ethan expects great things from all his horses," Conn remarked.

"I want more than tax shelters, I want a winner," Ethan said firmly. "All the tax sheltering in the world ain't as satisfying as one good win."

"How long have you owned racehorses?" Honor asked curiously.

"Oh, years. More than I care to count. Gets in a man's blood."

"Is it in your blood, Conn?" she asked, looking directly at him.

"I don't know yet. Legacy is the first horse I've owned," he told her flatly. The gray eyes were very cool as he returned her questioning glance. "A lot of things besides racing can get in a man's blood."

Honor felt a prickle of alarm. "Such as?" she challenged with false lightness.

"A woman."

"Or hot coffee," Ethan Bailey inserted suddenly, as if sensing the new tension in the air. "That cup of java sure looks good, Honor."

"I got it at a concession stand. They've opened one to serve people who are attending the workout session this morning. If I'd known you didn't have any I would have picked up an extra couple of cups." She felt oddly grateful to the older man for having dispelled the momentary uneasiness caused by Conn's words.

"What say we get ourselves some, Conn?" Ethan suggested promptly.

Landry got to his feet. "I'll get the coffee." He turned and paced toward the concession stand.

Honor watched him, conscious of the smooth coordination of his stride. He was wearing jeans today and an open-throated khaki shirt that suited the hunter she had seen in his eyes a few moments earlier. Honor shifted restlessly and took another sip of her coffee. For the hundredth time since he had left her the night before last, she told herself she would be wise to ease out of the relationship that was developing between herself and Conn Landry. And for the hundredth time she decided she'd wait just a little longer before making a firm decision in the matter.

"He's an interesting man, Honor." Ethan spoke quite gently as he picked up the field glasses and focused them on his filly.

"Have you known him long, Ethan?" She wasn't quite sure how to ask all the questions she wanted answered about Conn.

"Just since he bought Legacy. He's new to the racing world."

It seemed to Honor that Ethan was about to say more and then changed his mind. She felt an overpowering urge to push a little further. "Do you know what, uh, kind of business he's in?"

Ethan lifted one shoulder indifferently. "Well, I believe he's made a few substantial investments."

"In what?"

Ethan lowered the field glasses and gave her a vaguely troubled look. "Business investments. You know, a bit of this and a bit of that."

"Where are these investments?" she tried to ask casually, deeply aware of the older man's hesitation.

Ethan cleared his throat. "I think he mentioned Tahoe at one point." Then his face brightened. "Lots of lovely land up around Lake Tahoe."

"Lots of lovely gambling casinos, too," Honor noted dryly. "Is Conn involved in gambling, Ethan?"

"Don't you think you should be asking Landry these questions, Honor?" the older man asked with obvious unease. It was clear he was feeling awkward.

She felt a wave of embarrassment. "You're probably right. Sorry. It's just that he's a difficult man to get to know. Doesn't talk about himself much."

"There's usually a good reason why a man doesn't want to talk about himself," Ethan said very soberly. "Sometimes it's best to respect that privacy."

Honor considered her next comment but went ahead and made it anyway. "He did me a big favor yesterday, Ethan."

"Handling Granger for you? Yeah, he said something about that. Everyone knows Granger's bad news." There was a meaningful pause. "But a lady probably ought to be careful about taking favors from Conn Landry."

She went still, aware of more than just a subtle hint of warning in Ethan Bailey's words. Impulsively she put out a hand and touched his arm. "Ethan, please. Is there something I should know about Conn?"

Bailey exhaled deeply. "Honor, I like Conn Landry. I like him a lot. But the plain truth is, I'm not sure he's the sort of man a woman such as yourself should be getting mixed up with, if you take my meaning."

"I'm not sure that I do," she said quietly.

"Oh, hell, listen to me," Ethan growled with what sounded like forced humor, "I've been sounding like someone's Dutch uncle all morning. I surely didn't mean to go and make you nervous. You're a big girl. Last thing you need is advice from an old goat like me."

Honor smiled warmly at him, knowing he wanted to be off the hook. "You're hardly an old goat, Ethan Bailey."

He slanted her a quick glance. "Are you kidding? I'm old enough to be your father. Or Landry's father, come to that."

"Don't you know that owning horses makes you fascinating to most females?" She chuckled as she spotted Conn on his way back with the coffee. "Women love horses."

"Is that a fact?"

"Is what a fact?" Landry asked as he handed Ethan a cup.

"Honor, here, was just telling me that women love horses, and that men like me who own them are *fascinating*." He seemed vastly pleased with the word.

"Let's not forget I own one, too," Conn said blandly, his gaze raking Honor's features. "Does that mean I'm in the fascinating category?"

Honor was saved from having to answer because at that moment Bailey's beautiful filly came thundering past. Immediately all attention went to the horse. Morning workouts were, after all, a serious business.

An hour later, when Honor finally decided she ought to be getting back to work, Conn walked her to her red Fiat. It was the first time they'd been alone that morning. As they halted beside the car, he turned her to face him, his strong hands settling on her waist.

"Did you miss me the other night after I left?"

It was difficult to lie to a man with eyes the color of gunmetal, Honor discovered. She compromised. "Actually, I had other things on my mind," she informed him flippantly.

"Another man?"

She didn't like the way he said that. "Not quite. A little matter of a folding screen that wasn't where it should have been."

He frowned. "What are you talking about?"

Honor sighed. "Remember when you came into my bedroom and found me checking under the bed?"

"I remember."

"Well, I was doing that because I had a funny feeling that something wasn't quite right. I know it sounds ridiculous, but a designer develops an unconscious eye for the details of a room. And I know my own place so well that when the least little item isn't in the right location, I'm aware of it."

"A screen wasn't in the right place?"

"I use it to hide my television set," she explained, feeling vaguely silly. "It had been moved a few inches. Figuring out why and when kept me busy for a while."

He tilted his head to one side, studying her. "And what kind of answers did you come up with?"

"The most logical one is that my younger sister visited the apartment while we were out that evening. She has a set of keys, and she's been known to make raids on my wardrobe."

"Had she visited your place?" Conn persisted.

Honor shook her head, remembering the phone call she had made the next morning to Adena. "She said she hadn't, but to tell you the truth she was so busy singing your praises for having handled Granger that I'm not sure she was paying much attention to my question! You've got a real fan in Adena."

He ignored that last comment. "So what about the screen?"

"Well, another possibility is that the apartment manager let herself in for some reason or another. Unfortunately she went out of town yesterday morning and won't be back until tomorrow. I won't be able to ask her until then. And then there's the last possible reason."

"Which is?"

Honor smiled humorously. "That my so-called trained designer eye isn't quite as good as I assumed. All in all, the whole incident doesn't amount to much."

"Nothing was missing?"

"Nothing."

"Then it wasn't a robbery attempt."

"Fortunately I was saved that bit of melodrama," Honor said feelingly. "One of my friends got hit six months ago. The thieves cleaned out everything except the carpet. Don't look so concerned, Conn. Obviously there's some perfectly logical explanation for the screen having been shifted a few inches. I've stopped worrying about it."

"But it kept you from thinking about me that night," he murmured, rubbing the edge of his thumb along the line of her jaw.

No, it hadn't kept her from thinking about him but Honor decided it was best to let his assumption stand. Instinct warned her that it would be risky to let Conn know just how much he filled her mind. What was it Ethan had said? *I'm not sure he's the sort of man a woman such as yourself should be getting mixed up with.* She wasn't at all sure, either.

"Will six o'clock be okay for dinner tonight?" Conn asked softly, his thumb caressing her chin now.

Almost violently aware of the small, intimate touch, Honor reminded herself of her own uncertainties regarding this man. The way he asked told her he had no doubts at all but that she'd be free for him tonight. His confidence scared her.

"I'm sorry, Conn, but I have a business engagement tonight."

The gray eyes chilled. "A date?"

"You could call it that." She owed him no explanations, she assured herself.

His thumb stopped its gentle stroking and she felt his fingers as he lightly touched her throat. "Cancel it, Honor."

She swallowed, a frisson of fear flickering through her. "I can't do that. I have a business to run, Conn. Don't you know anything about the pressures of business?"

"I know about business pressures. I also know something about nervous fillies. Relax, Honor. Cancel your other engagement and come to dinner with me." His voice was rough and persuasive, a lover's voice.

Honor reacted to it, hovered on the brink of surrender and then retreated barely in time. "No, no, I can't do that, Conn. I'm sorry but I really do have to be going. Thank you for inviting me to the workouts this morning. I enjoyed them. How much longer will you be in town?" She made the question casual, subtly emphasizing the short-term nature of their association.

He watched her slide quickly into the front seat of the Fiat, closing the door as if it were a locked gate behind which she would be safe.

"It all depends."

Honor frowned up at him, eyes narrowed against the sun. "Depends on what?" she asked as she turned the key in the ignition.

"On some business matters I'm handling."

"I thought you were only here to see Legacy run."

"I'm taking the opportunity of tying up a few loose ends," he said coolly.

She hated it when he was so damn cryptic. "Well, I certainly wouldn't want to keep you from attending to business." Honor put the car in gear and drove off without glancing back.

She had been undecided about whether to attend the private party being held to celebrate the opening of a new restaurant that evening. The interior had been designed by a friend, however, and Honor knew Susan Mallory would appreciate having her show up. A finished project gave a designer the same sense of pleasure and satisfaction as a finished painting gave an artist. By the very nature of the business, neither could retain possession of the creations. There was only a limited period of time for the creator to enjoy it and show it off.

Honor didn't try to kid herself as she dressed for the event. She had made the decision to attend based almost entirely on an instinctive desire to put some distance between herself and Conn Landry.

Ethan Bailey's awkward but well-meant warnings had only served to crystallize her own uncertainties concerning Conn. He was getting too close, too fast.

Honor checked the sweep of the magenta-colored blouson dress she had chosen to wear and then brushed her hair back into a neat twist at the nape of her neck. It was difficult to get excited about the evening ahead. All she could think of was how much anticipation she would be feeling now if she were waiting for Conn Landry to collect her.

The festivities were in full swing by the time Honor arrived. She drifted through the crowd of fellow designers, reporters, friends of the proud new owner and local restaurateurs, idly searching for Susan. En route she helped herself to the unlimited quantities of exotic cheeses that had been set out. When the crush of people maneuvered her close to the bar, she ended up with a plastic cup of a low-budget Italian wine that helped wash down the cheese. She wondered what Conn was doing at that moment.

"Honor! You made it! I'm so glad. Tell me, what do you think?" Susan Mallory, attired in the latest of oddly layered Japanese fashions, pushed through the crowd toward her. In one hand she held a plastic glass of wine and with the other she waved at the art deco interiors she had designed.

Honor smiled at her attractive dark-haired friend. "It's wonderful, Susan. Absolutely wonderful. It's just too bad that it's not customary to put up a little plaque saying who designed the space."

"I know." Susan sighed theatrically. "No one ever thinks to credit the designer." She brightened. "But I have gotten some good referrals out of it."

"Good. How are the wedding plans going?" Honor helped herself to a chunk of imported Camembert.

"Perfectly," Susan enthused. "As a matter of fact I was going to call you next week and ask if the beach cottage was going to be available."

"Second week in June?" Honor tried to reconstruct the rental schedule in her head. "I think so. The agent said he'd booked it for the month of August, but part of June was still free. What made you decide to honeymoon in Ventura? Isn't that a bit ordinary? I thought you were going to Hawaii or Puerto Vallarta?"

"Everyone goes to Hawaii," Susan informed her blithely. "And those who don't, go to Puerto Vallarta. Richard and I discussed the matter the other night, and when I told him that you owned a charming, secluded place right on the beach just up the coast, we decided to ask if it was available. Going to use the house yourself this year?"

"I rarely use it," Honor said quietly, thinking of the beach cottage that had been her only inheritance from her father, other than a small trust fund that had helped see her through college. "Once in a while during the winter when it's not being rented out I spend a weekend there, but that's about it."

"I don't see why you don't use it more often. I love the marvelous country retreat look you achieved with all that lovely rustic furniture and those horse-racing photos scattered on the walls. I had a great time there last summer."

Honor thought of the pictures of Stylish Legacy that had belonged to her father and that she had left in place at the cottage, along with a variety of other racing mementos and paraphernalia. It was difficult to explain that she had always found visits to the cottage vaguely depressing. Memories of that traumatic year when she was thirteen seemed to be waiting for her there. It was easier to give a more rational explanation for her failure to use the beach house.

"I'd lose the rental tax advantages if I spent too much time there," she said easily.

"Oh, of course," Susan said. Being a Californian, she understood the implications of tax-advantaged investments immediately. People in California worried a lot about such investments. "Does your sister use it?"

"Rarely. My mother used to go there occasionally before she remarried and moved back east. Basically I'm just hanging on to the place for the appreciation and for tax purposes. And if it's free that second week in June, you're welcome to use it."

"Great, I'll tell Richard. Come along, I want to introduce you to my client."

"The gentleman in the mauve suit?"

"That's him."

By ten o'clock Honor decided she'd had enough cheese to supply her calcium needs for a month. She was tired of the party and tired of the endless cocktail chatter. It was time to leave. It was with a feeling of relief that she headed out into the parking lot to find her Fiat.

She didn't notice the headlights in her rearview mirror until she was only a few blocks from her apartment. Honor didn't know when it occurred to her that the same pair of headlights seemed to have been behind her for quite some distance, but when the thought finally did strike home she felt her palms grow damp on the steering wheel.

It was not unheard-of for a lone woman driver to find herself being followed, forced off the road and assaulted. Honor had read that one technique for dealing with the situation was to drive to the nearest police station. On no account were you supposed to lead the trailing car to your home.

But she was only a block away from the apartment house now and she couldn't be absolutely certain she was being followed.

The headlights edged in closer behind her as she turned onto her quiet street. If she was being followed the vehicle could probably close in so quickly that it would slip through the automatic gate of the apartment garage when she opened it to let herself inside. Honor could easily find herself trapped inside the locked garage with whoever was driving the other car.

Then, again, it could be her imagination at work. The same vivid imagination that had insisted on believing someone had moved the screen in her room the other night.

Honor considered her options and decided to drive on past her apartment. She would circle the block and see if the other car followed. If it did, then she would lose no time racing back out onto a more crowded thoroughfare and heading toward the nearest police station.

The other vehicle was suddenly very close behind her, its headlights on high beam so that she could see nothing in the mirror except a blinding glare. She was about to accelerate past the apartment complex when her own lights picked out the silver-gray Porsche parked at the curb. There was a dark figure in the driver's seat.

Quite suddenly Conn Landry's presence seemed the most reassuring sight she'd seen in a long time. Without pausing to think, Honor pulled in to the curb behind him, aware that the car behind her was slowing, too.

Switching off the ignition, she was out of the Fiat and running toward the Porsche before the tailing vehicle could edge in to the curb.

She saw the door of the Porsche swing open and then Landry was in front of her. In that moment his quiet power offered precisely the comfort and safety she wanted. Honor threw herself into his arms.

"Honor? What the hell—?"

The angry roar of a pickup truck motor cut off his startled demands. A second later the black truck accelerated past and disappeared around the corner.

Honor glanced up briefly to get a quick look at the vehicle but she made no effort to pull free of the iron-hard embrace in which she was wrapped.

"I think...I think that truck was following me," she managed as relief surged through her. "It had been behind me for blocks. I've heard of weirdos who do that, you know, follow a woman home and then attack her. I was going to drive on past when I saw your car. Oh, Conn, I've never been so glad to see anyone before in my life! What on earth are you doing here, anyway?"

"Guess," he growled succinctly. When she looked up at him with puzzled eyes, he sighed and loosened his grip on her long enough to close his car door. "I was waiting for you, naturally. Why else would I be sitting out here in front of your apartment building at this hour of the night?"

Honor's racing pulse slowed to a more normal level as the full implications of his presence hit her. "I'll assume that last crack is a rhetorical question." She pulled free of his encircling arm, smoothing her dress. "Don't get me wrong, Conn, I really was glad to see you, but I think it would be interesting to know exactly what you thought you were going to accomplish sitting out here in the first place."

"Let's go inside and I'll explain it all in great detail," he murmured, taking her arm. "But first of all tell me about that truck."

"I honestly don't know any more than I just told you. A California crazy who gets his kicks following single women, I suppose. I should report him to the cops."

"Report what? That truck didn't even have a license plate on it."

"Well, he's gone now, thank heavens."

Conn propelled her lightly through the gate and up one flight of stairs to her apartment. It was as he took her key to open her front door that Honor realized she still didn't know what he was doing here.

"Conn, about this business of you waiting for me," she began with what she hoped was a suitably imperious air, "I'd like to know just what you thought you were going to accomplish."

He slanted her an unreadable glance as he stepped around her and headed for the red lacquered cabinet that contained the brandy.

"Priority number one was to see who would be bringing you home." He poured a shot of brandy into a glass. Then he raised the glass in a faint salute. "Priority number two was to make sure you didn't take him upstairs."

Honor heard the quiet arrogance in his words and swallowed uneasily. "As you can see, I'm really not into truck drivers." She decided to go on the offensive. "Did it occur to you that I might object to your making yourself right at home with my brandy?"

He stalked toward her with cool, masculine grace. "It seems to me that offering me a drink is the least you could do under the circumstances."

"What circumstances?" she flared.

"I've been around when you needed me lately, haven't I?"

She licked her lower lip. "No one asked you to be around, Conn."

"But you've been grateful, nevertheless, haven't you?" He took a large swallow of the brandy and regarded her with his gunmetal eyes. "How was your *business* engagement, Honor? Have a good time?"

"Reasonably so," she said, mustering her composure. "Until that truck picked me up on the way home."

He nodded, taking another sip of brandy. Conn was wearing the jeans and the khaki shirt he'd had on earlier that day, Honor realized vaguely. The dark clothing combined with his somber, dangerous mood made him a formidable force in her living room.

"I think it's time for a little honesty from you, Honor Mayfield," he told her considering.

"What, exactly, do you want me to be honest about?"

"The reason you wouldn't have dinner with me tonight will do for a start."

"I told you, I had a business engagement."

"A very convenient one."

"Are you accusing me of something, Conn?"

"Yes. Avoiding me. And I'd like to know why."

Honor tried to move around him and found he was somehow blocking her path. She lifted her chin with cool hauteur. "Because there's too much I don't know about you. You frighten me a little, Conn, and I think you realize it."

The gray eyes flickered. "Yes."

"Then why put me through the third degree about this evening?" she challenged tightly. "Unless you really want to scare me for some reason."

She had the oddest feeling that he was forced to stop and think about the answer to that question. There was a tension in the room that wasn't doing much to dry her already damp palms. This evening was turning into a full-scale disaster.

"You have a point, Honor," Conn said finally. "I don't have any right to dictate how you spend your nights, do I?"

"No," she got out in a thin whisper.

"The problem is that I'd like that right," he continued.

"Conn, please..."

"I'd like you to know that I'll be there when things turn nasty the way they did with Granger and the way they did tonight when that truck followed you. I'd like you to trust me, Honor. I want you to know you don't have to get nervous and make up excuses for not seeing me."

His words poured over her in a rough, sensual cascade that caught at Honor's senses. But they weren't simply smooth lover's lies. There was an underlying urgency in them that forced her to accept their sincerity. In that moment she wasn't even sure Conn himself realized the intensity with which he was speaking.

Honor watched him as he moved toward her, aware of the swirl of male hunger in his gaze. She remembered the reassuring feeling of his arms going around her earlier out on the street and realized she wanted to know that sensation again.

"Conn, there's so much we don't know about each other," she tried with a touch of desperation.

He set down the brandy glass and touched the base of her throat with a remarkably sensitive fingertip. The desire in his eyes was an endless gray sea.

"I agree. There is much we don't know about each other. But I think tonight would be a good time to discover some basic truths."

Whatever her answer would have been, it was swallowed up in the depths of his kiss.

## FOUR

It came as a shock to Conn to discover that he didn't want her to be afraid of him, that, instead, he wanted her to trust him. It was a further surprise to find out just how protective he now felt toward her. The image of himself wearing a suit of polished armor should have made him laugh but it didn't. He was beginning to experience a possessiveness that should have made him uneasy.

When he'd found himself sitting in the car out in front of her apartment, waiting to see who would bring her home, Conn had finally acknowledged that he had a problem, one he hadn't counted on having to handle.

He'd planned on being the one who spun the web; he hadn't anticipated the danger of getting tangled up in the delicate, sticky strands himself. He would never remain objective enough to sort out the truth if he lost control of himself and the situation.

Now, tonight, it seemed very important that he regain control over events and in the process satisfy this dangerous desire that was threatening to undermine his original goals.

Yes, Conn told himself as he felt the trembling response on Honor's lips, that's what he was doing tonight. He was simply regaining control.

Her mouth was soft and warm. He wanted to crush it beneath his own, just as he wanted to crush her body into the embroidered quilt on her bed. The uncertainty in her was turning rapidly into passion. He was holding a woman who wanted him, even if she wasn't sure she ought to want him. Sensing her desire, his own soared.

"It's all right, sweetheart," he breathed as he freed her mouth to taste the warm sweetness of her throat. "Just let go. Just let it happen. I'll be right there with you and I'll take care of everything."

"Conn," she whispered shakily, "I wanted time. I'm not sure of anything right now."

He wrapped his fingers lightly around the nape of her neck and used his thumbs to lift her chin so that she had to meet his eyes.

Her gaze was half-drugged with a combination of desire and wariness.

"I'm the man who's there when you need him, remember?" he reminded her softly. "And you need me tonight. We need each other. I don't make a habit of sitting in front of a woman's apartment waiting to see who will bring her home. I was there for nearly two hours, trying to imagine how I would handle the other guy."

"What...what would you have done if I'd been with someone else?"

He groaned and pulled her fiercely against him. "Don't ask. Finding out you'd been followed by some punk in a pickup truck was even more of a shock, though. I don't like your living alone. It's dangerous."

"Yes, I know." She made the comment into his dark shirt, and Conn knew she meant it to cover him as well as stray hoodlums in black trucks.

"Don't be afraid of me, Honor."

He didn't know how to counter her caution with words, but Conn did know that he needed to touch her more intimately. The scent of her was tantalizing, beckoning, full of womanly promise. "I couldn't resist you tonight even if I wanted to try. And the last thing I want to do is try," he grated. He slid his palms down her back to the rounded curve of her hips. She murmured something into his shirt as he pulled her lower body against his own. Conn knew from the way she tensed and then softened that she was now fully aware of his arousal.

"Conn, we should talk..." Her voice trailed off beneath his mouth.

"In the morning," he promised when he released her lips. "We'll talk in the morning. We'll settle everything in the morning."

"Will we?" Her eyes were questioning, luminous pools in which a man could get lost.

"Please trust me tonight, Honor." Was that him pleading for a woman's trust, Conn wondered vaguely. Tomorrow when he was more rational he would probably be shocked at the husky words. But tonight he longed only for an affirmative response.

"Can I trust you, Conn Landry?"

He moved abruptly, lifting her up into his arms.

"Yes, you can trust me!" The vow was ground out with a force that amazed him. She seemed to accept the rough promise.

Her arms wound around his neck and surrender flickered through her body, making her even warmer and gentler than he had imagined.

Conn left the lights off in her bedroom as he carried her through the door. The pale glow from the hall provided all the illumination he needed. Standing her carefully on her feet he fumbled for the fastenings of her bright-magenta dress. When she leaned against him, her head nestled on his shoulder, he wondered what the hell had happened to his normally coordinated hands. His fingers never trembled like this.

It seemed to take forever before the silky garment obligingly gave way and fell into a frothy heap around her feet.

"Honor," he murmured wonderingly, drawing his hands lightly around her shoulders and down to the curve of her breasts. He touched the lacy edge of her bra, sliding one finger underneath to find the peaking tip of her nipple. "Honor, I want you so much."

She said his name into his shoulder, her nails sinking into the fabric of his shirt. "You make it impossible for me to even think tonight. Why is it like this with you, Conn?"

With a small, impatient gesture he unsnapped the front hook of her bra. His palms slipped over her breasts. "I don't know," he heard himself say with unexpected honesty. "I could ask you the same question. Why do I feel like this with you? I never meant—"

"Never meant what?" She raised her head to look up at him through her lashes.

"Never mind. Don't think about anything other than tonight, sweetheart. Heaven knows you're all I can think about at the moment." He framed her face with his hands and kissed her drugingly, glorying in the vibrant response he received. "Take off my shirt. Let me feel your hands on my body," he ordered thickly.

She obeyed willingly, her fingers shaking faintly as she struggled with the buttons of his shirt. But in a moment she had it off and then she tugged awkwardly with the buckle of his leather belt.

Trying not to hurry, but knowing he could barely contain his need, Conn finished undressing her. He slid his hands down the length of her, dragging off the satiny underpants and the gossamer panty hose. When she pushed at his snug-fitting jeans, he stepped back and tugged at them himself.

A moment later his jockey shorts fell to his feet and he heard

Honor's sharp intake of breath as she saw the evidence of his rising desire.

"I told you I wanted you, sweetheart. Did you doubt me?" he said in a husky voice, aware that he needed some sign of her acceptance of him as a lover. Why it mattered he couldn't have said. He only knew that he wanted her to affirm her desire for him. He wanted her to need him as much as he needed her. "Are you still afraid of me?"

She shook her head, stepping close so that she could feel his excitement pressing hungrily against the smooth skin of her stomach. She cupped him gently with her hands and Conn thought he would lose all control.

"I want you, Conn." There was a mesmerizing sincerity in her throaty voice. "I don't completely understand all of my feelings tonight, but I know I want you."

"Honor, I'll make it good for you, I swear it."

Her mouth curved gently in an age-old smile of feminine promise and provocation. "What if I'm the one who doesn't make it good for you?"

"Little cat," he murmured, determined to kiss the sensual teasing out of her. "You couldn't be anything but perfect for me." He lowered his head and parted her lips with his mouth, forcing his tongue deep inside. Then he shaped her buttocks in his hands, letting his fingers graze tantalizingly over her flesh. When he heard her gasp of anticipation he stroked around to the front of her body and touched her intimately between her thighs.

Honor moaned, and his own pulse beat heavily as he felt the dampening heat of her. When she seemed to lose her balance and collapse lightly against him, Conn knew a primitive sense of masculine satisfaction. Leaning down he yanked back the quilt on her bed and then he lifted Honor and settled her gently into the depths of the bedclothes.

She fell back sensuously, her hair fanning out on the pillow, hazel eyes gleaming up at him through her lashes. "Have you hypnotized me, Conn Landry? It's either that or I must be slightly out of my head tonight."

He felt the fire in his veins as he stood staring down at her. If he'd experienced a feeling of possessiveness earlier it was nothing compared to this inferno leaping through him now.

"I'm glad you're feeling disoriented," he muttered as he came down beside her in a heavy rush. "This is just the way I want you, warm and welcoming and all mine. I don't want you to be able to think straight. Not tonight.''

He buried his mouth against the base of her throat, stroking his palm down her stomach to the treasures below. She whispered his name in aching desire and he felt the readiness in her. When she arched her hips against him in silent demand he told himself he'd make her wait a little longer. He wanted her so hot and passionate that she would not be able to imagine living the rest of the night without having him inside her. It was, after all, exactly the way he himself was feeling.

''Tell me about it, Honor, honey. Tell me how much you want me.'' He made the demands in a husky tone in between stringing kisses across her breasts.

''So much, Conn, I want you so very much. I've never felt like this.'' She lifted her hips again, grasping his shoulders to urge him to her.

He pushed one knee between her legs and felt her open immediately for him. The invitation jerked a rough cry of passion from him and he knew he couldn't wait any longer. Conn settled himself between her thighs, aware of her fiery need teasing him.

''Take me inside, sweetheart. I have to be inside you or I'll go crazy!'' He moved his hand down to touch the folds of exquisitely sensitive feminine flesh, assuring himself once again that she was ready. She murmured in passionate response.

''Please, Conn. Please, now!''

He couldn't hold back any longer. Catching her shoulders, he thrust deeply, embedding himself in her pulsating, clinging warmth. He felt the shudder go through her as her body adjusted to the masculine invasion. Instantly he stopped.

''Honor?''

She didn't open her eyes but her legs moved slowly to wrap his lean hips. He felt her nails in his back and the small pain sent another ripple of excitement through him.

''Love me, Conn. Please make love to me.''

''Honor, I couldn't do anything else!'' He began to move within her, feeling her body growing increasingly tense around him.

''Conn, Conn!''

He sensed the uncertainty in the breathless way she called his name and dimly realized she wasn't quite sure of what was happening to her body.

"Let go, sweetheart," he rasped against her breast. "Just let go. I'll catch you."

She cried out as the heightening tension suddenly unleashed itself in one shattering conclusion. Conn lifted his head to cover her mouth, drinking the passionate sounds she made far back in her throat, and then he felt his body arching heavily as it sought its own release.

For long, timeless seconds he rode the storm with the woman in his arms, holding on to her more tightly than he'd ever held on to anything or anyone in his life.

Honor came slowly out of the hazy world into which she had drifted. She was aware of Conn's heavy frame sprawled along hers, felt the weight of his thigh chaining her leg. She was still wrapped securely in his arms, and the knowledge filled her with deep pleasure. Languidly she toyed with the silver-shot blackness of his hair, studying the dark lashes that were the only hint of softness in his face. Then he opened his eyes.

Like a cat, he was fully alert instantly, no hint of sleepiness or sensual lethargy in his gaze. But there was a strong element of satisfaction there, Honor realized—sure, arrogant, masculine satisfaction. She found it somewhat amusing until he spoke.

"No more nights like tonight," he said bluntly.

"No? You didn't enjoy tonight?" she teased lightly, knowing he couldn't possibly be referring to what had just happened between them.

Conn shook his head once, impatiently, and then lifted himself off her body with obvious reluctance. "I meant no more nights where I sit in front of your apartment and wait to see who's bringing you home." He cradled her possessively in the crook of his arm. The musky scent of him filled her nostrils as she burrowed willingly against his shoulder.

"How many more nights will there be to worry about, Conn? Soon you'll be going back to Tahoe and you won't be terribly interested in how I spend my evenings."

The wave of unhappiness that washed over her as she listened to her own words occupied her for several seconds. Then she noticed in astonishment that Conn had gone dangerously still.

"Who told you about Tahoe?" he asked, his voice low and harsh.

Honor stirred uneasily. "Ethan said something about your having business interests there." She turned her head to meet his eyes.

"That's all I have there. I don't make my home in Tahoe," he said in clipped tones. "I just own some real estate there."

"I see." Honor wasn't certain what to say next. Clearly he didn't want to talk about Tahoe or where he actually did live. And she didn't want to spoil the magic intimacy of the moment. There would be time enough in the morning for discovering all the facts that mattered. "It's all right, Conn. I didn't mean to pry. And you don't owe me any promises or commitments. I understand that."

The information didn't seem to please him. "The hell I don't," he growled, twisting to pin her gently back against the pillow. "Honor, you and I are bound together now. Don't you understand that? You just gave yourself to me."

"Do you realize what you're saying, Conn?" she asked carefully, afraid to let herself hope for too much from him.

"I know exactly what I'm saying," he told her evenly. "I couldn't walk away from what we've started. And I won't let you walk, either."

She smiled tremulously. "Do I look as though I'm trying to get away?"

"You tried to avoid me this evening," he pointed out gruffly. He sounded as if the fact had hurt him in some fashion.

Her fingers moved in delicate patterns on his broad shoulders. Unintimidated by the harsh lines of his face, she looked up at him with the soft eyes of a woman who knows she's falling in love.

"That was earlier. This is now," she explained as if it were obvious.

"You're not frightened of me any longer?"

"I don't think I was ever really scared, just wary," she said dismissingly.

"And you're not still wary?" he pressed.

"Should I be?" she countered lightly, not understanding why he was so insistent.

"No," he rasped, lowering his mouth once more to hers. "There's no need any longer."

A part of her wanted to ask what that meant, but he was already restoking the fires it seemed only he could ignite. Honor felt the throbbing intensity in him and had no wish to resist.

The commitment between them was new and untried, fragile and unexplored, but it had been established. Conn was right. Neither of them could walk away from it now.

Hours later Honor came slowly awake, aware that the man beside her was not asleep. She snuggled against his side.

"Conn? Is something wrong? Can't you sleep?"

"I'm just doing some thinking, honey."

"What about?"

"About that pickup truck that followed you home tonight. Among other things." The last three words were tacked on in an almost inaudible tone.

"What about the truck?" she pressed, yawning.

"I don't like the fact that somebody tried to get at you tonight."

She frowned slightly in the darkness. "You don't suppose there's a chance Granger sent someone after me?"

Conn shook his head once. "No, he'd have no reason to go after you. It would be your sister he'd try to terrorize and she——", He broke off as Honor suddenly sat bolt upright.

"My sister! Conn, what if he's going to do something to Adena?"

Conn reached up to pull her down. "Relax. As I was about to say, she's paid her debt. Granger wouldn't go after her now."

"You sound awfully sure of that."

"I am sure."

For some reason Honor believed him. The quiet strength in his words spoke volumes. She relaxed. "Then the incident tonight was just another crazy Southern California event."

"Unless you add it to that business of your screen being moved the other night," he said thoughtfully.

Honor was silent for a moment. "I'm sure that was just a mistake on my part."

"Positive?"

Lying there in the darkness with Conn's easy, masculine strength to cling to, it was easy to be positive. Honor nibbled invitingly at his lower lip.

"Positive."

Honor awoke early the next morning with the feeling that her whole life had changed overnight. When she turned her head to gaze down on Conn's magnificently sprawled form, she knew the intuition was right. Even if he walked out on her today her life would never be quite the same because she would never be able to put him completely out of her head.

His body was lean and tan against the tangled white sheets. The intriguing darkness of his hair on the pillow made Honor want to reach out and run her fingers through it as she had last night.

Weren't harsh-faced men supposed to appear more relaxed and even gentler in sleep, she wondered idly as she studied the grim planes and angles of his face. If that was true, Conn didn't fit the mold. His strength and determination were too much a part of him to disappear temporarily while he slept. In the fresh light of a sunny morning he still looked like the kind of man only a fool would want for an enemy, the kind of man a woman would not risk pushing too far.

The realization sent a wave of restlessness through her that drove Honor out of bed. Barefoot, she padded into the black-and-white-tiled bath. The full-length mirror threw her nude image back at her, revealing a mussed halo of golden-brown hair and eyes that reflected a deep, feminine wonder.

Conn had made love to her last night in the most satisfying way possible. He had not played sophisticated games, trying to dazzle her with technique and style. Instead he had lost himself in her, at the same time possessing her completely.

Admittedly her experience was limited, but Honor instinctively knew that the kind of passion she had experienced last night could not be a common thing.

Stepping into the shower, she let her pleasantly sore body soak beneath the hot spray. Every time she moved today she was going to be reminded of Conn's elemental style of lovemaking, she thought wryly.

She heard the bathroom door open and close. A moment later Conn appeared on the other side of the glass shower door, smiling lazily. One thing had changed about him, Honor realized suddenly. The smile was a full-fledged one this morning, not that strange, grim twist of his mouth with which she had become so familiar. That knowledge pleased her deeply.

He opened the shower and stepped inside, reaching for her. "Mmm," he murmured through a long, luxurious kiss, "you taste good in the morning."

"Considering the amount of goat cheese I sampled last night, that's saying something." She grinned, winding her arms around his neck.

"I consider it a part of the earthy side of your nature." He slicked his hands down her wet body to her hips, squeezing gently.

"I'm a Southern Californian. I'm not supposed to have an

earthy side to my nature. I'm supposed to be all gloss and cutting-edge glitter," she complained.

"Then you're a failure as a Southern Californian. But I knew that the moment I met you."

She tilted her head. "You did?"

To her surprise he gave her a sober, intent look. "The last thing you are is superficial, Honor. Even if your apartment does resemble a picture in a design magazine. I knew when I realized why you were going to confront Granger that you had guts. And your enthusiasm for Legacy's big win the other day was genuine, even though you only had two dollars on him. Last night you gave yourself completely to me. No games. I could list a lot of other reasons why I know you aren't the kind who flits along on the surface of life."

"But?" she prompted, a little shaken by his blunt observations and determined to lighten the atmosphere a little.

"But all my glowing compliments would probably go to your head and spoil the basic sweetness of your nature." He chuckled, slapping her affectionately on the rear and turning to pick up the soap.

"Beast. I was just getting to like the compliments. I'd rather hear them than listen to you yelling at me for daring to have another engagement last night."

"I didn't yell at you." He stuck his head under the full force of the water, eyes closed. "I simply explained a few facts of life."

She went still as she listened to the possessiveness in his voice.

"Conn?"

"Hmm?"

"It works both ways, you know."

He pulled his head out from under the shower and opened his eyes. He looked down at her searchingly. "Both ways?"

"I won't be involved in a one-sided relationship," she said with quiet insistence. "I have to know that you'll live by the same rules you're imposing on me."

"You think I won't?" There was soft challenge in the words.

Honor studied him for a moment longer, thinking over what she knew of this man. It wasn't all that much in some respects. Yet a part of her longed to trust him implicitly. "I think you will." She finally smiled tremulously. Hadn't she sensed from the start that he was a man who lived by a code? He kept the scales balanced.

Conn moved, wrapping her close against his warm, wet chest.

"Does that mean you trust me, finally?"

Her fingers splayed through the damp, curling hair that covered him in a sexy pelt. "Yes."

"Thank you, Honor. I'm glad," he said simply.

*So am I,* she thought, *because I'm in love with you.*

An hour later Honor was slicing papaya and sprinkling it with lime while Conn made coffee. The doorbell chimed just as she was putting the fresh fruit on the table. Wiping her hands on a red kitchen towel, Honor went to answer it.

"Adena!" she exclaimed. "What are you doing here?"

"Just dropped by on my way to work to see if I could borrow that great chunky leather belt you bought the other day. Hey, is that an extra slice of papaya? Great, I didn't have time for breakfast this morning."

With her usual impulsive approach to everything, Adena whipped around the edge of the door and came to a halt, staring at Conn. Conn stared back, politely examining the flashy little gamine in front of him.

Adena's bright blond hair was cut in an eye-catching wedge that framed her outrageously made-up hazel eyes. While Honor's tastes in clothing were stylish, her sister's were definitely trendy. A less charitable observer might have termed them outrageous. This morning Adena was wearing knee-high cavalry boots, tight-fitting red pants and a huge, boxy, loosely woven cropped top. She carried it off with her usual enthusiastic panache.

"Good grief," Adena said in obvious astonishment, "who are you? Honor *never* has men stay for breakfast."

"I insisted, I'm afraid. You're Adena?"

"That's right." Adena swung around with a grin. "Where did you dig him up, Honor? He's much more interesting than those designer types you usually hang out with. Good grief! This one's not even wearing mauve!"

"This is Constantine Landry," Honor said very firmly. She could feel the faint flush on her cheeks as her inquisitive sister began to pry for information. "I believe I mentioned him," she continued sardonically.

"Landry! The guy who handled Granger for me. Of course," Adena almost pounced on a somewhat startled Conn. "You're an absolute jewel, you know." She kissed him noisily before he realized what was happening and then she released him to leap for the coffeepot. "Can't tell you how much I appreciate your help.

Took a terrible load off my mind. Granger gives me the creeps. And if I was worried, that's nothing to what poor Honor felt!'' Adena shivered theatrically as she helped herself to coffee.

''Then I trust you will stay away from him and others like him in the future. I don't expect to have to handle that kind of situation again, and if I find out you've tried to coerce Honor into doing it for you, I will be very displeased,'' Conn said flatly as he picked up the coffeepot and set it down on the table.

Honor heard the cold, lecturing tone and saw that Adena had heard it, too. Her volatile sister was not accustomed to having men lecture her.

''Hey, what's with the big brother attitude?'' Adena demanded, plunking herself down at the table. ''It's too early in the morning for that sort of thing. Any more papaya, Honor?''

''There's another one in the refrigerator, if you want to cut it.''

''Too much work. I'll share yours.'' Adena leaned forward to scoop out a sizable chunk of the deliciously colored fruit.

Stifling a sigh of resignation, Honor quickly began to eat the rest of the papaya, knowing that if she didn't she would lose most of it to Adena.

''I'm not your brother, big or otherwise,'' Conn pointed out grimly. ''My only interest is in your sister. I will therefore hold you responsible for anything you do that gets her into a difficult situation. Do I make myself clear?''

''Conn, there's no need to come down on her like a ton of bricks,'' Honor said a bit stiffly as she saw the uncomprehending expression on Adena's face. ''It was all a mistake and Adena knows it. She won't be getting into that kind of trouble again, will you, Adena?''

''Golly, I feel as if I'm sitting in the middle of a scene from 'Father Knows Best.' Doesn't it strike either of you that it's too nice a morning for lectures?'' Adena complained.

''What kind of a morning was it the day you first started borrowing from Granger?'' Conn calmly ate his papaya, oblivious of Honor's frowning glance.

''I get the point,'' Adena said disgustedly, shooting to her feet with lively grace. ''If you'll excuse me I think I'll be on my way. Something about the atmosphere around here is depressing. How about the belt, Honor? Okay if I take it?''

''Help yourself,'' Honor agreed, as she nearly always did. ''Oh, and Adena...?''

''What?'' Adena was halfway down the hall.

"Are you sure you weren't in here the other evening?"

"Positive. I went with Gary to see that new slasher movie I told you about." She disappeared into the bedroom and reappeared a moment later carrying the prized belt. "My goodness, you two certainly did something energetic on that bed. Well, see you guys later." She was gone before either Conn or Honor could respond.

For a moment after the whirlwind left, silence hung over the table. Then Conn said very thoughtfully, "I can see that she's been something of a handful for you. Your mother...?"

"My mother remarried a few years ago and moved to the East Coast. Adena wanted to stay out here with me. There are times when I'm afraid I may not have handled her all that well, but she's basically a good person."

"Perhaps," Conn suggested carefully, "she needed a firmer hand while she was growing up."

"She was only eight when Dad was killed." Honor tried to put a lot of finality into the sentence.

"How old were you?"

"Thirteen. Conn, I don't really like to talk about the past," she explained quietly.

He stared at her for a moment. "You can't pretend it doesn't exist."

"Because I want to know everything about you."

Honor closed her eyes. "Believe me, you don't want to know about that aspect of my life."

"Yes, I do," he countered in a soft but steely voice. "And I won't stop asking until I get all the answers."

She slammed her cup down into the saucer, growing annoyed with his insistence. "All right, I'll tell you. I'm the daughter of a man who was killed, along with his partner, while running an illegal shipment of guns into the Middle East. Does that answer your question? It was tacky, embarrassing and traumatic. The papers had a field day with it. They called my father a traitor and

"I don't pretend it doesn't exist," she said coolly. "I just prefer not to discuss it. The circumstances surrounding my father's death were, well, traumatic for all of us. It nearly devastated me. Thirteen-year-olds tend to take things very seriously, I'm afraid."

"What happened, Honor?"

She looked at him over the rim of her coffee cup. "Why **do** you want to know?"

a criminal. The general implication was that in the end he got what he deserved.''

''Along with his partner,'' Conn said slowly.

''If you want my opinion,'' Honor said bitterly, ''I've always thought that the real criminal probably was his partner. I'll bet my father caught him with the shipment and his good buddy pulled a gun. In the end they both died. My father was apparently armed, too.'' Honor swallowed some of her childhood anger. ''They were supposed to be respectable oil executives.'' She sighed.

Conn's eyes narrowed and the fingers around the handle of his coffee cup tightened as he regarded her tense face. ''You've always assumed that your father's partner was the guilty one?''

''No one will ever know. The authorities said they were both in on the gunrunning.'' Honor shook her head, striving to return to normal. ''And I guess it no longer really matters, does it? It was all a long time ago.''

''Some people aren't satisfied until they've tied up all the loose ends,'' Conn Landry said so softly that Honor wasn't certain she'd heard him.

Her head came up quickly as she scanned his face with her growing knowledge of him. ''You're one of those people, aren't you?'' she hazarded. ''The kind who ties up loose ends. You like things balanced.''

''Yes.''

Honor absorbed the loaded sound of the single affirmative word. It had all the impact of a poised knife. Constantine Landry was being honest, straightforward and utterly truthful, she decided. He wasn't telling her anything she hadn't already guessed, but by reinforcing the knowledge he reinforced the sensation she had of danger hovering like an aura around him.

Memories of the night tangled in her mind with the trickle of unease Conn seemed to generate in her. Adena had been right in saying this man was unlike the other men in Honor's world. Honor reflected for a moment on the wisdom of terminating the relationship and knew in her heart of hearts that she would not be able to do it. Not yet. Conn had claimed there was a bond between them now and a part of Honor recognized it. There was a hunger in her to follow the dangerous path that might lead past Conn Landry's emotional barriers. For a few minutes last night she had been allowed through the gates. She wanted more opportunities to discover the man behind the seemingly impervious walls of cool control.

Honor made a decision in the warm light of a new day. She would take the risks inherent in becoming involved with Constantine Landry. She had no real choice.

# FIVE

It couldn't be love, Honor told herself at least fifteen times several days later on a Friday as she worked on some space-planning arrangements in her office. She'd only known the man for approximately two weeks, and if she were truthful with herself she actually knew very little about him.

But Conn was making a habit of staying for breakfast, and she realized she wanted him at her table tomorrow morning, too.

Idly she pushed around the little cutouts that represented various sizes and shapes of office furniture, but it was hard to keep her mind on the floor plan in front of her. All she could think about was the fragile new relationship she had begun with Constantine Landry.

It shouldn't be love, not so soon and not when there were so many unanswered questions, but she was very much afraid that it was. She'd never felt so vulnerable before in her life. Only love left a woman of twenty-eight feeling so precariously poised on the brink. Why was she fighting it, she wondered.

But she knew the answer. Conn Landry didn't fit any mental image or preconceptions she'd had about the man to whom she would one day give herself so completely. His background was still exceedingly vague, for example. He'd alluded briefly to various investments and mentioned that he'd spent a great deal of time overseas until two years ago. Something to do with being a go-between for corporations. Whatever that meant. And he'd told her he lived in the San Francisco area.

Honor sighed and reached for another cutout of a table that could be used for large meetings. It was oval and would be far more interesting in the office space she was designing than the square one she'd been trying. She could see it now in rich gray slate on a black steel pedestal. It would give an impression of solid reliability to the clients of the securities brokerage house for which she was doing the design.

When you got right down to it, Honor told herself, what she knew about Conn revolved around impressions of him as a man rather than knowledge of the realities of his life. As a man he appealed to her senses on every level. She knew it was far more than a physical attraction. It had been from the first, even when she'd been so wary of him.

Some of her initial caution still existed, she had to admit, but she had shoved it far to the back of her thoughts. Instead, she now focused on ways of gently penetrating the emotionally controlled exterior that surrounded Conn. So far her only real success in that area seemed to take place in bed. Honor grimaced ruefully. She didn't like the idea that the only way she could really reach him was with sex.

Honor glanced up from her desk as the front door opened. Ethan Bailey smiled genially as he stepped inside the sleekly furnished room. He glanced around with interest.

"This is right nice," he observed, touching the finely-grained beige leather of a chrome-and-leather chair. "Is that real marble?" He indicated her desk top.

"Absolutely." She smiled, motioning him to one of the chrome-and-leather chairs. "Nothing like a sheet of black marble to impress potential clients. What can I do for you, Ethan? Don't tell me you need some design work!"

He chuckled, lounging back comfortably in the chair. His hand-tooled boots were revealed as he extended his legs and steepled his fingers. "To tell you the truth, I hadn't thought much about it until now." He glanced around at some of the photos on the walls. "Looks to me like you know your business. I like that one there."

Honor followed the direction of his glance. "Ah, my one shot at the Southwestern look. I can see why that would appeal to you." She smiled at him. "What on earth made you decide to stop by and see me, Ethan? I would think you'd be out at Santa Anita."

"Already watched the morning workouts," he said easily. "Conn was there, too."

She nodded composedly. "Yes, he said he wanted to discuss Legacy's future with Toby Humphrey."

"Well," Ethan said as if he weren't quite certain how to continue. "He did. He also talked a bit about Legacy's past."

Honor's gaze was quizzical. "Is something wrong, Ethan?" she finally asked gently.

The older man shifted uncomfortably. "To tell you the truth, I don't rightly know. But I've been around a long time, Miss Mayfield. Maybe too long. A man can get cynical in his sunset years.''

''You're hardly in your sunset years. I don't think you'll be the type to ever hit them,'' Honor grinned.

He returned her smile but there was a measure of seriousness in his normally cheerful eyes. ''Honor, I wonder if I could speak quite frankly.''

''Of course.''

''What I'm going to say is probably none of my business. But I feel obliged to say it, anyway. You're such a nice young lady. And seeing you off and on with Conn at the track I've come to think of you as a friend.''

A trickle of warning went down Honor's spine. ''What's wrong, Ethan? Why are you here?''

He sighed, glancing up at the photo of the Southwestern-style office. ''Your last name is Mayfield.''

She blinked in astonishment. ''Well, yes.''

''Conn said this morning that your father had once owned Legacy's sire, an animal called Stylish Legacy.''

''That's right.''

Ethan closed his eyes briefly and when he opened them his gaze was very level. ''Your father's full name would have been Nick Mayfield?''

The warning sensation was stronger now. ''Did you know him, Ethan?''

The older man shook his head. ''I've been in racing a long time, Honor. It's kind of a small world. When I heard your last name was Mayfield, I just brushed the whole thing off as a coincidence. After all, it's been a long time...''

''It's been fifteen years since my father died, if that's what you're trying to say.''

Ethan cleared his throat. ''Not exactly. That is, I remember the newspapers really played it up big.''

''Yes.'' The residual anger of a helpless thirteen-year-old girl still simmered. ''Everyone seems rather interested in ancient history these days. Did you know my father?''

''Not well. But I was certainly aware of the horse he owned. Stylish Legacy was the most promising colt on the West Coast fifteen years ago. Since he was sold to that syndicate he's lived up to that promise. Legacy cost Conn a fair-size fortune.''

''Ethan, I still don't understand what you're trying to say.''

''I'm making a mess of this,'' he grumbled. ''Honor, this is real tough on me. Lord knows I don't want to get involved in anything personal between you and Conn, but I don't want to see you hurt, either. Conn, well, he can take care of himself, but you're just a little thing and you don't know what's going on behind the scenes. I didn't know myself, or rather, I didn't want to admit I knew until this morning when Conn mentioned that your father was the Mayfield that had owned Stylish Legacy."

"Please get to the point, Ethan," Honor said tensely. "It's obvious you're trying to tell me something."

He inhaled deeply. "Honor, you probably know your dad had a partner."

"I'm aware of it."

"The man the newspapers said was with him in that nasty business in the Middle East," Ethan went on doggedly. "Do you remember that man's name?"

"Vaguely. I think it began with an S. Stone or Stanton or something. Why?" Honor realized she was tapping the tip of a pencil against her floor plans and leaving small small black marks. Annoyed, she forced her hand to remain still.

"His name was Stoner. Richard Stoner," Ethan said flatly.

"So? I'm afraid I don't understand where all this is leading."

"All right. I don't know how else to give this to you except straight. Landry is Conn's middle name. He's used it for years because he was working overseas for a lot of fancy corporations that might have been nervous about dealing with Richard Stoner's son."

The pencil in Honor's hand snapped in two. Blindly she stared down at the broken halves. Slowly she raised her head to meet Ethan's unhappy expression. "Conn Landry is the son of my father's partner?" she whispered uncomprehendingly. "But why didn't he tell me?"

Ethan leaned forward anxiously. "Honor, you were only a kid when your father and Stoner killed each other during that quarrel. Conn was twenty-three, just out of college and starting his first job with the oil company for which his dad and your father had worked. Leastways, that's what I recall. The scandal hit him pretty hard, I gather. It's not something he talks about, but I heard rumors around the track when the story hit the papers. Racing people talk. Too much sometimes."

"Racetrack rumors," Honor echoed huskily.

"They said—" Ethan halted abruptly, as if searching for the right words and then tried again. "They said Conn was convinced your father had betrayed his. People said he swore vengeance on your family fifteen years ago.''

''Vengeance!'' A man who liked to tie up loose ends. A man who kept the books balanced. The words went through her head in staccato fashion.

''It's the kind of thing an angry, hurt twenty-three-year-old man would say,'' Ethan pointed out gently.

''The kind of thing a twenty-three-year-old Conn Landry would say, I suppose,'' Honor said bleakly.

Ethan was silent for a moment before continuing.

''Fifteen years have gone by. I expect most everyone's forgotten now. I hadn't thought of the story in ages. When Landry bought Legacy and his horse and mine wound up in Humphrey's training stables, somebody remembered that Richard Stoner had had a son who used the name Landry. I kept my questions to myself. Didn't seem like any of my business, after all. Not until you showed up in the picture.''

''I see.'' Honor's eyes narrowed. ''And then you started wondering?''

He nodded forlornly. ''It was the coincidence of the whole thing that worried me. It didn't seem strange that Conn might have returned to the States after several years and decided to buy a colt sired by the stallion his father had once owned. But when he picked you up at Santa Anita the other day, I started remembering all those stories about how he'd vowed to make your family pay for what your father did to his.''

''My father didn't do anything to Richard Stoner! Certainly he didn't betray him,'' Honor hissed, the old anger welling higher within her. ''I always thought there was a damn good chance that Stoner was the one who was smuggling weapons and that my father had the bad luck to discover him doing it.''

Ethan held up his hands in a placating gesture. ''Please, Honor. I don't know anything more about that end of things than anyone else who was reading the papers at the time. From what little I knew of your father personally, I have to say he always seemed a decent man. He never spent much time around the track, so I really didn't get too well acquainted, but I was under the impression that folks respected him.''

''Really?'' There was a scathing tone in her voice as Honor remembered the humiliation that her mother had been forced to endure as so-called friends turned their backs on her after the scandal hit the papers. The fact that her mother had been filing for divorce hadn't lessened the humiliation Mrs. Mayfield had to handle. And nothing could have mitigated the pain Honor had gone through.

"I knew I shouldn't have come here today," Ethan growled in embarrassment. "But I just couldn't stand by and not tell you who Landry really was. You have to make your own decision about the man, but I thought you ought to know that his interest in you might be based on something besides...besides..."

"I think you're trying to tell me that he might have some motivation other than love at first sight," Honor observed coolly.

Ethan stared at her for a moment. "I tried to tell you that the other day. Men like Conn Landry don't know much about love, Honor. But that was just an old man trying to pass along a little advice to a young woman who was in danger of getting swept off her feet. I knew then that you weren't his usual kind of date. But I also figured you were old enough to make your own judgments. This morning, though, when Landry mentioned your father as having been the Mayfield who owned Stylish Legacy, I got rather worried."

"Why would Conn bring up the subject?"

Ethan shrugged. "I don't know. He doesn't realize I know who he is. I suppose he didn't think I'd make any connection. Or maybe he wouldn't care if I did."

"You've never told him you're aware he's Richard Stoner's son?" she asked in amazement.

Ethan's mouth firmed. "You have to understand how it is in the racing world, Honor," he said gently. "For the most part a man's past is his own business. As long as he's honorable in his dealings, sees to it that his horses are well cared for, tips his jockeys properly when they win, no one really questions his past. At least they wouldn't do so to his face. People around the track might gossip about it, but that's as far as it goes. A fellow owner wouldn't dream of confronting another owner and demanding explanations. Our only association is through racing. I don't generally pry into matters that don't concern me."

Poor Ethan, Honor thought distractedly. He was very upset at having taken on the responsibility of warning her. She could see he was already regretting his involvement.

Her own mood was precarious, she realized. In all honesty, Honor wasn't sure how she felt as she absorbed the implications of the news of Landry's identity.

But it explained so many things, she thought grimly. Looking back over the past several days she began to see the pattern of his actions, and it was almost frightening. He had kept her from getting involved in the trap meant for Granger. Then he'd handled the business of Adena's debts to the man so that Honor wouldn't have to deal with him. It was after that that Honor had begun to experience the odd sensation of being in Conn Landry's debt. Conn had done nothing to ease that sensation.

Then there had been that incident the other night when his presence had scared off the punk in the pickup truck. Following that, Conn had made fiercely passionate love to her, placing bonds on her that chained her senses.

Honor was appalled, seeing herself as a small female animal that had been neatly driven into a strange sort of trap. What was Conn Landry Stoner planning on doing next, she wondered in frozen pain. What was the point of the trap?

"I suppose I ought to thank you for telling me all this," she managed distantly.

"Not hardly!" Ethan exploded in self-disgust. "If I were you I'd kick me out of this office. I probably had no business coming to see you about all this. But I swear, Honor, I just didn't know quite what to do. If you'd been anyone else except the daughter of the man Conn blamed for betraying his father, I wouldn't have opened my mouth any more than I did the other morning when you started asking questions about his, uh, investments. I figured I'd overstepped myself then. Now I've really put a foot in it, haven't I?"

"I know you meant well, Ethan."

"Meant well! Hell, Landry's a friend of mine. I felt torn apart, not knowing which way my duty lay. Heaven knows what he'll say when he finds out I'm the one who told you who he really is," Ethan sighed.

"He couldn't have expected to keep it a secret forever," she pointed out.

"That's true," Ethan agreed. "But what if I've got this all botched up? What if it's all perfectly innocent? A genuine coincidence? He meets you by accident at Santa Anita, takes to you and decides to keep his identity quiet because he knows you might be nervous about seeing him if you know who he really is."

"Do you believe that, Ethan?" she asked soberly.

"I might. If it weren't for one thing," Ethan admitted slowly. She frowned. "What's that?"

"That business about Granger being about to walk into a police trap the other day?"

"What about it?"

"Well, I got to thinking about it. I hadn't heard any rumors about that ambush. So I checked with some folks I know. Granger wasn't arrested that day, Honor. Best anyone can figure out, he didn't walk into a police setup. He wasn't set free on bail, either. Just been running around loose as usual."

Two hours after Ethan Bailey had left her office, Honor finally accepted the fact that she wasn't going to get any productive work done that day. She locked her door and walked out onto the busy thoroughfare that fronted the building in which her office was located. It was another of the days for which Southern California was famous: temperatures in the mid-seventies and reasonably clear of smog. A good day to go to the beach, she thought. The water would still be uncomfortably cold for anyone except surfers, but it would be pleasant to take off her shoes and walk in the sand.

This wasn't the first time since Ethan had left that she had thought of the beach and of the cottage her father had bequeathed to her. She rarely used the house, as she had told her friend the other evening at the party. But quite suddenly she had begun to see it as a place to which she could escape. Honor had a strong need to lick some very raw wounds and she wanted to do so in private.

How did one confront the Conn Landrys of this world and demand explanations, she asked herself as she sat down at a table in an outdoor café. The menu wouldn't come into focus long enough for her to concentrate on the special of the day, so she ordered her usual avocado-and-sprouts sandwich. When it arrived she barely tasted it.

Her fingers trembled as she sat beneath the huge umbrella that shaded her table and tried to picture Conn's face. Such a harshly carved face, with eyes that reminded her of the color of a lethal weapon.

Dangerous. She had known from the beginning that he was dangerous. He had told her he was a man who kept the score even. But she'd had no way of knowing then that he had a score to settle with her family.

Honor didn't finish the sandwich. She paid for it and walked to the parking lot where her Fiat waited. Slowly she drove home, her mind in a turmoil. By the time Ethan Bailey had left she was feeling sorry for the older man. It was obvious he had been in a terrible quandary about whether to come to her with his information. Now he was no doubt consumed with guilt for having warned her about a man he considered a friend.

Looking back, Honor was sickened by the easy way she had allowed Conn Landry to get close to her. What a fool she had been to fall in love with a man who was driven by some twisted notion of revenge.

Assuming, of course, that revenge really did lie behind his actions, Honor reminded herself without a great deal of hope. She knew the odds were against it all being some horrendous coincidence, and there was that business of Conn's having lied about Granger. But what if there was some viable explanation for everything, she asked herself over and over again as she parked her car in front of her apartment.

The only thing she could do was confront Conn and ask him. She had to know the truth and she had to hear it from him. Nothing else was going to kill the love that had begun to grow within her.

It was impossible to concentrate on anything that afternoon as she waited for Conn. He had said that morning that he would be at her door at six this evening. As the day dragged on Honor realized how much she was beginning to cling to the hope that he would have explanations for everything.

It was ridiculous to allow herself that hope. She was setting herself up for a fall. But there was no real alternative. Nothing would convince her completely that she had been manipulated for some bizarre reason of revenge until she heard the damning words from Conn himself. The catch, of course, was that in all probability he would simply lie to her.

"Surely I'll know if he's lying. We've become so close in the past few days," she said half under her breath as she paced the white carpet. Another illusion. What made her think she would know if he was telling her the truth, she thought. After all, if everything had been a lie until now and she had believed it, there was no reason things would be any different tonight.

Close. That was another illusion. The only true closeness they had achieved had been in bed, and for all she knew, that feeling had been entirely one-sided. There was no reason to believe their mutual passion had been more than a good toss in the hay from his point of view.

Pausing by the window, Honor stared sightlessly out at the palm tree and wondered what kind of revenge Conn Landry Stoner would go after from a woman. She wasn't wealthy. She wasn't married, so there was no relationship for him to spoil with insinuations or threats. She had inherited nothing from the partnership formed by their respective fathers, so there was nothing of value to demand from her, at least nothing she knew of except that beach cottage up the coast. As far as Honor knew, it had belonged only to her father. It had never been a part of the partnership. Stylish Legacy, the most valuable remainder of that business arrangement, had long since been sold and the profits evenly split between Nick Mayfield's widow and whoever had inherited Richard Stoner's estate.

But there was no denying that some way, somehow, Conn would want to even the score. She had to accept the fact that he seemed to have chosen her as the one who would pay for that betrayal fifteen years in the past.

The old resentment washed through her. As a young girl who had loved her father, she would never have been willing to believe that he had betrayed his friend. The evidence of that bloody night was fated to be forever vague and uncertain. The killings had taken place in a far-off land, and those who had been in charge of the investigation had been more concerned with dealing with the embarrassment the incident had caused a huge oil corporation than with getting at the truth. The main goal of the company for which Richard Stoner and Nick Mayfield worked had been to hush up the whole mess. Both men had been working for the company until just prior to the discovery of the gunrunning. Stoner and Mayfield had formed their own firm, but still had ties and contacts in the larger corporation they had just left. The huge conglomerate had its image to consider.

By rights, Honor told herself violently, she had as much reason to want revenge as Constantine Landry Stoner. She ought to be thinking of a way to turn the tables.

But all she could think of this afternoon was how she had fallen in love with a man who apparently wanted only vengeance.

Honor was in a pair of old jeans and an emerald-green dolman-sleeved top when she went to answer the door at six o'clock. She had pulled her hair back into a strict knot at the nape of her neck. It must have been obvious immediately that she was not dressed for an evening out. Conn took one look at her unsmiling face and stepped inside.

"I take it we're staying in this evening?" he said coolly as he shrugged out of his impeccably tailored dark linen jacket.

"I think we need to talk, Conn." Honor was remotely pleased that her voice was calm. She watched him toss the jacket over a chair and marveled at his easy familiarity with her apartment. He hadn't hesitated to move right in on her private space, she realized.

He slanted her an assessing glance and sank easily into a chair. "Something wrong, Honor?"

She drew in a deep breath and walked back to the window to stare into the darkness. "That's what I want to ask you, Conn."

"You're the one who's being cryptic now."

She heard the hard-edged caution in him and wondered at it. He knew enough about her to realize that matters were serious, she thought bleakly.

"You never bothered to mention that your last name was Stoner," she said quietly.

There was a second of dead silence behind her. Honor was almost afraid to move.

"Stoner never has been my last name."

Startled, the wild hope leaping up within her in spite of her efforts to quell it, Honor spun around. "You're not Richard Stoner's son?"

"I'm his son."

Hope died. "I see."

"In all the ways that count, Richard Stoner was my father. I was twelve years old when my mother married him. My biological father was killed when I was a baby, but she never wanted me to deny his existence. Stoner agreed with her, so there was never a formal adoption. But I grew up thinking Richard Stoner was the kind of man I wanted to become."

Honor stared at the granite-hard expression on the face of the man she loved and knew there was no more reason to hope. Some perverse element in her nature insisted on spelling it all out, however, and she found herself asking the next question.

"You knew who I was before you met me?"

He leaned his head back in the chair, watching her through narrowed eyes. "You've been busy today."

"Just answer the question," she pleaded.

"I knew. I've known for several months."

She closed her eyes briefly and turned back to the window, her hands clasped tightly in front of her. "Other than making me feel like a fool, what did you plan to accomplish, Conn?'' she asked steadily.

He came up out of the chair without making a sound. Honor didn't know he was so close until he spoke from only inches behind her. ''The flat truth is that I didn't really know what I wanted from you in the beginning. I only knew there was something to be settled between my family and yours.''

''You wanted revenge. You believe my father betrayed yours,'' she whispered starkly.

''The official investigation of what happened that night concluded there had been a quarrel between partners, that Nick Mayfield had planned to kill my father and finalize the sale of the guns himself. Something went wrong. Richard Stoner had managed to get off a couple of shots before he died and neither man came out of it alive. Personally, I think my father discovered yours was using his cover as a respected executive to smuggle those arms shipments and confronted him.''

''And in the ensuing fight, they killed each other,'' Honor finished distantly.

''Something like that.''

''Either way, you're convinced my father was guilty of betraying yours.''

''I've had no reason to think otherwise for fifteen years,'' Conn said levelly. ''I knew Richard Stoner well. He wouldn't have been involved in anything like gunrunning.''

''My God,'' she breathed. ''Fifteen years. Fifteen years of plotting your revenge. It must have eaten away your soul.''

She sensed a slight movement, and then his fingers touched her shoulder. Honor froze.

''It wasn't like that, Honor. If it had been, I would have done something drastic long ago. Are you willing to listen to me tonight?''

''I don't have much choice.''

''No,'' he agreed grimly, ''you don't. You're the one who brought up the subject.''

She wished he would take his hand off her shoulder. His touch made her want to turn around, bury her face against his chest and cry out all the anger and pain. ''How long would it have been before you bothered to bring up the real reason you've been sleeping in my bed, Conn?''

His fingers tightened dangerously, and she sensed the tension in him. ''Listen to me, Honor, and listen well. This isn't going to be easy to explain. I've had a hard time comprehending it myself."

"It seems quite simple to me."

"That's because you don't know what the hell it's all about! I haven't been hidden away in some dark hole plotting vengeance for the past fifteen years, for heaven's sake. I've been working overseas just as I explained to you. It was a good job, a high-paying position. I was busy and I was always on the move. What's more, I was very good at what I did."

"You never got around to explaining just what a go-between does, Comm," she pointed out dryly.

He bit off an exclamation of impatience. "I was a sort of troubleshooter. I got sent in when a company was having problems on a foreign job site."

"What sort of problems?" she pressed dismally. "Don't tell me you handled labor disputes."

"No," he said, gritting his teeth, "my specialty was security problems. Honor, my former job hasn't got anything to do with this. I only mentioned it because I was trying to show you that I haven't been exactly brooding for the past fifteen years."

"But you haven't exactly forgotten the night our fathers shot each other, either, have you?" she flung back.

"Neither have you."

She inclined her head once in aloof acknowledgment of that truth. "No, neither have I."

He applied pressure to her shoulder, turning her easily under his strong hand. She found herself forced to face the full intensity of those gunmetal eyes. The implacable hardness in him was almost overpowering.

"Honor, I'm a man who believes in tying up loose ends. I've told you that."

"Yes."

"When I decided to resign from my job and return to the States two years ago, a part of me started thinking about the unfinished business between my family and yours. I remembered my father's interest in horse racing, too, and something made me decide to find out what had happened to Stylish Legacy. Discovering what had happened to the horse seemed like a place to begin the search for the truth about what had happened between our fathers that night. The next thing I knew I was buying one of the colts. It seemed the right thing to do. Perhaps I absorbed some of Richard Stoner's fascination with Thoroughbreds. Or maybe I find the horse a link to the past. Buying Legacy was a mistake in some ways, though."

"Because every time you looked at him you thought of his sire and of our fathers' partnership," Honor guessed unhappily.

"Honor, I have a thing about betrayal. Perhaps it all stems from the way my stepfather died. I don't know. Perhaps I've seen too much of it in my line of work. Whatever the reason, once I'd bought Legacy, my need to settle the past became more and more important. I told myself I would at least find out what had happened to Nick Mayfield's kids. It wasn't hard to track you down. Once I had located you, I decided to keep going. Something kept pushing me."

"A need for revenge." She met his eyes with a level gaze of her own, refusing to flinch from the grimness in him.

"All right," Conn replied, "maybe that's what it was. Call it what you want. But I think it was something else. I had this feeling, you see, that if I found out what Nick Mayfield's eldest daughter was really like I might learn something about what Mayfield himself was like. I might be able to decide once and for all if he was the kind of man who would have killed his partner in cold blood. I'd be able to put the past to rest. And once I'd bought Legacy, I couldn't seem to stop the search for the truth. One thing led to another. For the past three months I've known where you lived, where you worked, whom you dated and that you occasionally went to the track."

"You had me followed!" She was appalled.

"Only for a week. Long enough to find out the critical details. Then I took over the job myself. It's the sort of thing I've been trained to do." His mouth tightened.

"You must hate me very much, Conn Landry," she whispered.

"No, damn it, I don't hate you! That's what I'm trying to explain," he snapped furiously. "After I bought Legacy I had to keep going. Don't you understand? One thing led to another. After I had discovered the whereabouts of Mayfield's elder daughter I had to find out what she was like."

"Why?" she cried. "Because of some criminal theory out of the Middle Ages that states the tendency toward betrayal runs in a family?"

"Maybe I just wanted to see if she'd turned out like her father. I don't know exactly why I had to track you down and meet you. You were another link, like Legacy. I only knew that it was important."

"Because there was unfinished business to settle," she finished savagely. "Why the trap, Conn?"

"What trap?" But she saw the wariness shimmer in his gaze.

"Come on, there's no need to pretend. From the first moment I met you, you've been boxing me into some kind of cage. There was that incident with Granger, for example."

There was rough-edged steel in his response. "You want the truth? I'll tell you. In the beginning I wanted to make certain that when I made contact, I would be the one in control. The best way to manage that, I decided, would be by spinning a web around you. I wanted you in my debt at first and later—," He stopped suddenly.

Honor already knew what he'd been going to say.

"And later you decided that seducing me would add to your sense of control. You're a very thorough man, Conn."

"It's the reason I was successful in my job while I worked overseas. And it's the reason I've been successful in my investments during the past two years. Being thorough is part of the way I do things, Honor."

"I still don't understand what you want from me," she said stonily, all hope dead within her now. "You seduced me. Believe me, that's about all I have to give. There's a little money, I suppose—,"

"I don't want your money, damn it!"

"My father left me a beach cottage up the coast," Honor went on doggedly, her gaze never wavering. "It's worth something. You've met Adena. You must realize there's not much to be had from her. She's still just a kid in a lot of ways. I imagine you could successfully seduce her, too, if you put your mind to it, but that seems a bit tacky, doesn't it?"

"Will you shut up? You're not even trying to understand!"

"What exactly am I failing to comprehend?"

He released her, removing his hand so quickly she wondered if he'd been afraid of losing control and actually hurting her. It was so hard to imagine Conn losing control in any situation. Stepping around her he reached inside the red lacquered liquor cabinet and found a bottle of Scotch. Honor watched as he splashed some of the amber liquor into a glass. He swirled the liquid once and then took a swallow.

"It's hard to explain what I've been feeling for the past couple of months, let alone the past few days. I only know that my feelings toward you were, well, ambivalent. You were the elder daughter of the man who had betrayed my father. Something in me has always wanted to put to rest what happened between our parents fifteen years ago. There was nothing I could do at the time. I was a twenty-three-year-old kid, and none of the honchos in the corporation would give me any real help in finding out exactly what had happened that night. I had to piece it all together for myself between what I knew of Richard Stoner and what the newspapers told me. It's never felt right, never felt finished." He ran his fingers restlessly through his hair.

"Did seducing me somehow put an end to it for you?" Honor asked coldly.

Conn looked at her. "Seducing you changed everything."

She caught her breath. "Is this the part where you tell me you've fallen madly in love? That since meeting me you've given up all notion of revenge? That the past doesn't matter any longer?"

The gunmetal-gray eyes were colder than the landscape of the moon. "Look, Honor, I'm trying to be completely honest with you."

"That's a change."

"You little——" He took a step forward and halted abruptly, visibly restraining himself. The poised-to-spring tension in him now was very evident. "Honor, I don't know much about love. It's an undefined, vague concept that usually doesn't sustain itself for long from what I've seen. And I won't tell you that I've completely forgotten what happened between Richard Stoner and Nick Mayfield fifteen years ago. But something very basic has changed in this equation and that's the way I feel toward you. My feelings about you are no longer in the least ambivalent. I want you. And I have some first-hand evidence that you want me. I'm prepared to start over on that basis."

"Start over?" She couldn't believe what she was hearing. "Are you out of your mind?"

His face was a set mask. "I've been asking myself that question for the past few days. No, I'm not out of my mind. At least I don't think so," he added wryly. "There are bonds between us, Honor, and I suspect you realize that as much as I do. There are ties, factors that link us. Factors that brought us together and that we can't shake off very easily. Whatever the initial cause and effect was, the result exists. You and I are together now."

"I would never have guessed you were a believer in fate!" she stormed.

He shrugged. "Maybe I've spent too much of my life in parts of the world where people believe in things such as fate and destiny."

"Well, I'm from Southern California," Honor flung back fiercely, "and here we shape our own future. I was a fool to get involved with you, Conn Landry, but I can assure you I'm not going to stay involved. Please get out of my apartment. Now!"

He set down the half-finished glass of Scotch. "You know it isn't going to end this simply."

"Get out."

"I'll be back. We'll talk this over when you've calmed down. There is too much between us." His mouth lifted in the faint cynical smile. "Murder and betrayal fifteen years ago between our fathers, passion and *obligation* between you and me. Don't forget that last bit, honey. You owe me. We're all tangled up together in this now."

He turned and walked out the door before Honor could find an answer.

## SIX

He would give her twenty-four hours, Conn decided. Hell, who was he kidding? He needed the time just as much as she did. Conn piloted the Porsche to his hotel, parked the car in the lot and stalked inside to the English-pub-style bar. It wasn't until he ordered the Scotch that he realized just how much of his tightly controlled sense of frustration and anger must be visible. The bartender acted as though he were serving a shark who had casually wandered into the comfortable lounge. From across the room Conn recognized a couple of men who had horses at Santa Anita. They were staying at the same hotel, but neither of them made any move to invite Conn to join them. His dark mood must have been evident even from this distance.

Landry downed a long swallow of the Scotch after it was placed gingerly in front of him and then sat glowering at his reflection in the back-bar mirror. A grim-faced man with eyes that were sheets of frozen metal stared back.

Twenty-four hours. That should be long enough, he thought. She was shaken and upset right now, but twenty-four hours hence she would have calmed down enough to listen to reason. With any luck he would have calmed down a little himself.

He hadn't expected it to happen this way, hadn't thought she would learn the truth on her own. He'd intended to give her the facts carefully so that she wouldn't be alarmed. He would have told her eventually, when he judged the time was right and when he'd sorted it all out in his own mind.

That was the most complicated part, he realized. Sorting it all out in his own head was taking some work. Faced with having to put his strange initial ambivalence toward Honor into words, he'd fumbled badly and he knew it. He hadn't done a good job at all of soothing her fears or of explaining something he barely understood himself. If only he'd had some time to prepare.

But his feelings toward Honor had been crystallizing slowly and in fragments. He hadn't yet put them together into a complete whole that would be comprehended. It was as if he'd started fitting together the various glittering shards of a broken mirror. Some things were clear already, Conn realized. He knew beyond a shadow of a doubt that he wanted her. He'd accepted his need to protect her. And he no longer struggled to ignore the strange possessiveness he felt.

But other images in the mirror were still jagged and out of focus. He wasn't sure of Honor's feelings, for example, other than a certainty that he could make her respond magnificently in bed. When he'd told her that seducing her had changed everything, he hadn't been lying. It had. What she might not have realized was that matters hadn't been fundamentally changed just for him. They had altered just as completely for her.

At least, Conn admitted in a flash of clearheaded honesty, he wanted very badly to think they had changed for her. The possibility that the lovemaking hadn't been as intense and meaningful for Honor as it had been for him created a sick dread in the pit of his stomach. He drank some more Scotch to mask it.

There were other fragments of certainty, he assured himself. He sensed a basic integrity in her that he hadn't expected to find in Nick Mayfield's daughter. When she was with him he had a feeling of rightness that he couldn't explain. He liked the expressiveness of her hazel eyes and he liked the way she had run to him the other night when the guy in the pickup truck had frightened her. He'd liked the feeling of playing hero and protector, Conn decided. He appreciated the courage it had taken for her to try to deal with Granger on behalf of her sister. So many things about her seemed to draw him.

For those reasons and a thousand more he had told himself that he needed time while he reevaluated the situation. But something had happened today to steal that factor from him. How the hell had she found out that he was Richard Stoner's son? For the record, he'd have to clear that up the next time he saw her. Racetrack gossip, probably.

His mouth thinning dangerously, Conn ordered another Scotch and considered the lonely dinner that lay ahead. Maybe he'd just stay here until it was time to go upstairs and face an even lonelier bed. Plenty of nutrition in good Scotch.

Several blocks away from the hotel, Honor locked the door of her apartment and picked up the red leather suitcase at her feet. She'd left a message for Adena on her sister's answering machine. Adena could handle anything that came up that affected the apartment. Honor carried the bag down to the garage and stuffed it into the Fiat's trunk. Then she slipped into the driver's seat and shoved the key into the ignition. It was going to be a long drive, but she would have plenty of time to think en route.

She was so wrapped up in her churning thoughts that she didn't notice the black pickup behind her until she was on the on-ramp of the freeway. When a casual glance in her rearview mirror picked it up, Honor's stomach twisted into a sudden knot of fear.

*You can't be sure it's the same truck,* she told herself. But she couldn't see any license plate, and Conn had mentioned the other night that the black pickup that had followed her home hadn't had plates. It was dark now, however, and she couldn't be certain of the image in her rearview mirror.

The tension in her doubled as she considered the possibility that she'd been singled out by a genuine lunatic. Perhaps some crazy had decided to follow her around terrorizing her. She could try driving to a police station to see what happened, Honor thought as her knuckles went white on the wheel.

Just as she was deciding which off-ramp might take her to a station, however, the truck dropped back several car lengths. Two other vehicles filled the space between herself and the pickup, and Honor began to relax. Perhaps it had been just a coincidence or her imagination. The potential perils of freeway driving claimed her attention for the next several miles as the lanes became crowded. The freeways around Los Angeles were packed at this hour on Friday evenings. She lost sight of the pickup completely and told herself it had been nothing to worry about. There were a heck of a lot of pickups on the roads these days.

The temporary nervousness quelled, Honor's mind went back to the festering emotions that had driven her into leaving town. The pain of discovering that Conn Landry had lied to her wasn't diminishing. If anything, it was far stronger now that she'd had his deception confirmed from his own lips. There was no denying that she'd been secretly hoping there would be some logical explanation for everything.

And, of course, there had been a logical explanation, she thought bitterly. What Ethan Bailey had told her was the truth. Explanations couldn't get much more logical than that.

She'd fallen in love with Richard Stoner's son. She had been so very stupid. Landry had manipulated her from the moment they had met. No, he'd begun setting her up long before that. He'd admitted he'd been stalking her for months.

She was being pursued by a dangerous man, all right, but not the one in the pickup truck. Her nemesis drove a Porsche and harbored a taste for revenge that was more than old-fashioned; it was primitive. Her only choice was to escape the vicinity while she tried to deal with the traumatic turn of events.

Honor fled up Highway 101 as if she were being chased by demons.

Conn had good reason to remember his decision to drink his dinner the previous evening when the phone in his hotel room rang shrilly at seven-thirty the next morning. The simple act of trying to answer it kick-started a throbbing headache that had apparently been waiting in the wings.

"Hell," he groaned as he fumbled for the receiver. "I didn't leave a wake-up call," he grumbled before the person on the other end could greet him.

"Conn? Is that you, Landry?"

Conn sprawled back against the headboard, one hand on his throbbing temple. His stomach was definitely unsteady, he realized. "Who is this? Ethan? What the hell are you doing calling me in the middle of the night?"

"Sorry to wake you. I'm at Santa Anita. Came to watch the morning workouts." There was a pause.

"I plan to skip them this morning," Conn muttered, closing his eyes and inhaling carefully. "I've got some other things on my mind." He thought he could handle the stomach. It was his head that would be the death of him.

"Yeah. Listen, Conn, I'm not calling about that. There's something else. Something strange. I think you ought to get out here."

"Give me one good reason."

"It has to do with Legacy," Ethan said levelly.

Conn opened his eyes and immediately regretted the violent exercise. "Legacy? What's wrong with him? Is he okay?"

"Well, yes, but—"

"Where's Humphrey?" Conn sat up in bed, ignoring his head with a fierce act of willpower. "If there's anything wrong, get Humphrey to look at the horse. I'll be out there as soon as I can."

"Legacy's all right, Conn. But this has something to do with him, and frankly, I'd rather not talk about it. This is a public phone."

Through the pain in his temples, Conn heard the man's concern.

"Okay, okay. I'll be right out. You're sure the horse is all right, though?"

"He's fine, Conn," Ethan said wearily.

Landry slammed down the receiver and swung his feet to the carpeted floor. It took guts just to get out of bed, but he made it to the bathroom. Unzipping the shaving kit, he found a bottle of aspirin and gulped down a few tablets. Then he turned on the shower and stood under the spray for several minutes brooding about how long it had been since he'd gotten drunk because of a woman. He couldn't even remember if he'd ever deliberately set out to get stoned because of a female. A first for Honor.

He'd have to tell her just what she'd done to him. He'd put it on the list of grievances he planned to present to her when the twenty-four hours were up.

His head had settled down a bit by the time he located the Porsche in the hotel parking lot and started out to Santa Anita, but Conn was still moving with a bit of care as he walked through the track parking lot toward the barns.

Ethan Bailey met him just outside the guard gate. One glance at the older man's face and Conn knew there was a truly major headache waiting. Bailey's normally laid-back, easygoing manner was nonexistent this morning.

"You'd better tell me the worst and get it over with," Conn said, sighing.

"Let's go out to my car," Ethan suggested gently. He didn't wait to see if Conn would follow, but started toward the parking lot.

"What the hell are you being so mysterious about this morning? I'm really not up to this sort of thing today. If something terrible has happened to Legacy, just tell me." Conn paced beside his friend, his unsettled temper bubbling just below the surface. He felt angry at the whole world this morning. The past, the present, Honor Mayfield, Scotch, the whole world. And now Bailey was playing games.

No, that was unfair. Bailey was very concerned. He wasn't playing games. In fact, in the couple of years he'd known the man he'd never seen Ethan Bailey this upset.

"You look worse than you did the time that real estate deal in Orange County went sour," Conn grumbled.

"That was business. This is personal," Ethan told him in a troubled tone. He paused beside his big white Mercedes and turned to look at Landry. "Maybe too personal. Maybe I handled this all wrong.'' He wrenched open the door and reached inside to pull out a bundle wrapped in burlap. ''You can tell me where to get off if I screwed this up, Conn. But I wanted you to see this before I did anything too dramatic.''

''What is it?'' Frowning, Conn glanced down at the harmless-looking bundle.

''I found these inside Legacy's stall this morning. I went past it while he was out having his morning gallop and I just happened to glance inside.'' Slowly Ethan unwound the burlap and revealed two green apples. Conn stared at the fruit in mild surprise. ''A couple of apples. So? One of the grooms probably brought them in for him.''

Ethan shook his head. ''You know how strict Humphrey is about the horses' diet. None of his grooms would dare bring in anything special for Legacy or any of the others. Humphrey's got all his animals on scientifically formulated feed. Conn, someone brought these in for Legacy and put them in his feed while he was out getting his morning workout. Look at this.'' Ethan turned over one of the apples, revealing that it had been cored.

The carefully honed instincts of several years spent in the security business finally emerged. Conn reached for one of the apples and examined the hole in the base of it. Without a word he moved his hand to the pocket of his blue denim work shirt and removed a small star-shaped metal object.

Ethan's brows came together in a thick shaggy line. ''What the heck's that widget?''

''Something I picked up a few years back,'' Conn explained absently as he used one of the sharp points of the star to neatly slice the apple in two. ''Kind of a good-luck piece, I guess you could say.''

''Didn't know you were the superstitious sort,'' Ethan observed.

Conn cleaned the star on his jeans and dropped it back into his pocket, his attention completely on separating the two halves of the apple. ''A man picks up some odd habits when he works in some of the places I've worked. Well, what do you know?'' he concluded in a whisper as the large capsule hidden in the apple was revealed.

Ethan stared at the powder-filled capsule. ''I was afraid there wasn't going to be any real good explanation for those apples being in Legacy's stall.''

Landry lifted chilled eyes to meet the other man's dismal stare.

"I wonder if Granger decided he didn't like being told to lay off Adena Mayfield."

Ethan looked back at him steadily. "Conn, Granger's from the bottom of the barrel, but he's sort of old-fashioned."

"Spell it out, Ethan."

"From all accounts he's what the women's movement would call a genuine, dyed-in-the-wool male chauvinist pig. He doesn't hire females."

Conn went very still. "What the devil are you talking about, Bailey?"

Ethan made a visible effort to steel himself to deliver the rest of his news. "When I found those apples this morning, I casually asked the guard if there'd been a lot of strangers coming into the stable area. He said no."

"Granger could have bribed someone who works here," Conn interrupted irritably.

"That was my next thought." Ethan heaved a sigh and glanced at the wall of mountains in the distance. "But the guard went on to say there had been one person through the gate on a visitor's pass. A woman. A lady with light-brown hair who wore a pair of yellow pants and a blue windbreaker. She didn't stay long."

Conn didn't move for a timeless instant, images of Honor's bright-brown hair and vivid wardrobe flashing into his aching head. Honor, who saw herself as a woman who had been used, the victim of a man who had tracked her down out of revenge. Honor, the daughter of a man who had once betrayed and killed his best friend.

Like father, like daughter? "No," he whispered under his breath.

"You all right, Conn?" Ethan squinted at him worriedly.

"I'll live." Maybe. He suddenly wasn't sure. There was a strange, painful tightness in him, a nausea that had nothing to do with his hangover.

"Do we go to the track authorities with these apples?"

Conn forced himself to deal with one thing at a time, although his mind was racing in a hundred meaningless directions. "No."

"Damn it, why couldn't he think straight?

"I don't know," Ethan said uneasily, "maybe we ought to get the contents of that capsule analyzed before you make any decisions. After all, we don't know for sure just what's in there."

"How many reasons can you think of for stuffing a capsule inside an apple and feeding it to a hundred-thousand-dollar race horse?'' Conn asked sardonically as he rewrapped the apples. He was amazed at how much effort the small task required until he looked down at his hands and realized they were shaking.

''I can't rightly think of any good reasons. Unless Toby Humphrey was trying to trick Legacy into taking some medication?'' he added hopefully.

''I had a long talk with Toby yesterday about Legacy's health and future. The horse isn't on any medication.'' Conn spoke flatly, without any emotion. ''Whatever's in this capsule was meant to poison Legacy.''

''The authorities—''

''No!'' The denial was much too harsh, too loud. He brought himself under control with savage willpower. If he wasn't very careful his voice would soon be shaking as badly as his fingers. ''I'll handle this on my own.'' Conn held the wrapped apples in one hand and looked at his friend. ''You knew I'd want to deal with this myself, didn't you? That's why you called me first instead of the track authorities.''

Ethan nodded gloomily. ''When the guard said something about a woman, well, I...'' He didn't finish the sentence.

''You knew who the description fit.''

''Conn, this is just about the most goddamned miserable mess I've ever seen. What did you do to that little lady to make her want to do something like this?''

Conn glanced down at the bundle in his hand. ''Made her mad, I guess.'' He turned and started toward his Porsche. ''But that's nothing compared to what she just did to me.''

That was the truth, he added silently, as he flung himself into the Porsche and tossed the burlap bundle onto the floor of the car. He probably shouldn't even be behind the wheel of a car right now. If he had any sense he would go somewhere and calm down before confronting Honor.

Then, again, if he had any intelligence he wouldn't be in this situation. Everything he'd learned about human nature during all those years working security for multinationals around the world seemed to have evaporated around Honor Mayfield. What the hell had happened to his normal, realistic approach to people, he wondered.

He ought to have expected something like this, Conn thought in disgust, glancing at the incriminating bundle. She was the daughter of a man who had betrayed and killed his best friend. Did that sort of inclination run in the blood? There were places in the world where people believed it did. Even if the instinct wasn't hereditary, there were other factors he should have taken into account last night, such as the fact that he hardly qualified as her best friend.

Honor had been infuriated yesterday when she'd learned the truth. He knew she was capable of passion. It stood to reason that such a fundamental capacity would affect other areas of her life in addition to her responses in bed.

Reason. He couldn't seem to reason clearly at all this morning and not just because of the effects of his hangover. It took Conn almost the entire distance of the drive from Santa Anita Racetrack to Honor's apartment house to acknowledge that his own passions were running dangerously close to being out of control. Between the throbbing ache in his head and the twisting pain in his gut he was incapable of calming himself.

It was the pain he didn't fully understand. It should have been the cold, hard tension of fury. Instead it was something else, something he wouldn't have guessed himself capable of feeling anymore. He *hurt*, not just physically but on a primitive emotional level that hadn't been touched since the day they'd told him Richard Stoner had been murdered.

As he slammed the Porsche to a halt at the curb in front of the apartment complex the simmering caldron of his emotions threatened to explode. He was actually having to fight for self-control, and the knowledge only served to increase the level of explosive tension. He'd never had this kind of problem. He was always the one in command of himself and any given situation. Such talents had been a necessary skill in his job and he had come by those abilities naturally. For years he'd taken his chilled, controlled, efficiently ruthless approach to life for granted. The fact that this particular woman had pushed him beyond those boundaries was almost stunning in its impact.

Conn took the stairs to the second floor, loping up them two at a time, and came to a halt in front of Honor's front door. There he drew a couple of deep breaths in a useless bid to pick up the leash on his anger. Then he pounded brutally on the door.

It took several minutes of pounding and the frowning inquiries of a couple of Honor's neighbors to convince Conn that his quarry had fled.

"Look, mister," a man damp with sweat he'd worked up jogging said, "I just came up through the garage. Her car isn't down there. Take my word for it. She's gone for the weekend." Wiping the perspiration off his forehead, the jogger dug out the key to his own apartment.

"Do you know where?"

The knife blade buried in Conn's tone brought the man's head up just as he unlocked the door. "Sorry," he said crisply. "I don't." Rather hurriedly he stepped inside and slammed the door behind him. Conn heard the bolt being shot home.

Terrifying Honor's neighbors wasn't going to achieve much. Time to track down Adena. He had the younger woman's address in that pile of information he'd garnered during the past few months. Driving back to the hotel and digging through the data took time and chewed at his insides, but it was the only approach. He was about to walk out of the room with the piece of paper in his hand when he remembered the aspirin. He could use a few more. His head was not improving at all. At least his stomach was staying under control. Pausing to gulp a couple more tablets, Conn wasted no more time. Ten minutes later he was pounding on Adena Mayfield's door. This time he got an answer.

"Good heavens, what do you want? It's only eight-thirty and it's Saturday. If you're here to give me another lecture about Granger, kindly skip it. I have an excellent memory." Adena glared at her visitor, clutching at the red-and-purple kimono-style bathrobe she'd apparently slung on to answer the door. Her stylish haircut had not yet been blow-dried into its proper wedge shape and her blond hair was in a tangle. Without her normal-outrageous makeup she looked much younger, Conn realized.

"I'm looking for your sister," he spat out.

"Honor?" Adena blinked vaguely. "How should I know where she is? You're the one who's been spending so much time with her lately. You've probably got a better idea of her whereabouts than I do."

"She's not at her apartment." It was taking a savage effort to keep his voice even remotely level.

"Don't blame me if you've managed to misplace her," Adena grumbled. "Hey, what is this?" she added in a gasp as Conn suddenly pushed open the door and stalked into the entry hall. "Look, she's not here, if that's what you're thinking." Something about his mood finally hit her still-sleepy brain. "What's wrong, Conn? Is Honor okay?"

"I have to find her."

"Why?" There was a sudden, wary concern in her voice. Conn heard the change in her tone and forced himself to contain his fury. If he alarmed Adena too much it would be tough to get information out of her. "We argued last night. She's apparently left town. I'm trying to locate her."

"Ah," Adena said, her face clearing. "You want to do a little groveling, is that it?"

Conn stared at her. "I hadn't thought of it quite that way."

"Well, don't worry. Honor is a very forgiving, tolerant soul. Heaven knows she's put up with a lot from me during the past few years. Let me see if she left any messages for me on the machine. She usually tells me when she's leaving town." Stifling a yawn, Adena padded into the kitchen and switched on the tele-phone-answering machine.

Conn listened to two calls from young men begging Adena to go to the same punk rock concert and a call from a young woman wanting to know if Adena cared to go to the mall to check out the latest fashion scene before Honor's tense voice was heard. Unconsciously Conn's hand clenched so tightly the knuckles went white.

"Adena? This is Honor. I'm going out of town for a couple of days. Thought I'd get some use out of Dad's cottage before the season starts. I'll call you when I decide to return. Please don't tell..." There was a pause before Honor's voice continued. "I'd appreciate it if you wouldn't let anyone know where I am. I need some time alone."

"Uh-oh." Adena grinned wryly as she switched off the ma-chine. "Looks like I should have vetted that call before letting you listen, hmm? Then again, I expect Honor's ready to hear your abject and humble apologies. Are you going to the cottage?"

"I'll need directions."

"Sure." Quickly Adena rattled them off and then she eyed her visitor keenly. "What did you and Honor fight about?"

"It's a private matter," Conn said stiffly, heading for the door.

"Oh. Well, as I said, I'm sure Honor will take you back," Adena assured him cheerfully. "I've never seen her this way about a man before. Of course, I've never seen her with a man like you, either. You're not her standard fare."

Conn halted halfway through the door. "Because I don't own a pair of designer loafers and wear mauve ties?"

"Somehow," Adena said dryly, "I think there's more to it than that. Goodbye, Conn. Don't forget to practice your groveling tech-nique while you're driving. I think it needs work."

Conn left before he gave in to the impulse to explain to Adena that groveling wasn't exactly what he planned to do when he finally tracked down Honor.

He made one more stop at the hotel to pick up his shaving kit and a couple of other items and then climbed back into the Porsche. An hour out on the freeway he still couldn't detect any change in his unstable mood. Maybe he should have had something to eat. Taking all that aspirin on an empty stomach probably wasn't such a bright idea. On the other hand, the thought of eating didn't do much for his seething temper, either. He only had to glance at the burlap bundle on the floor of the car to rekindle the simmering pain and its accompanying rage.

Betrayal shouldn't hurt this much, he decided. It was, after all, just another fact of life. Why was it that a woman's act of betrayal could slice a man to the bone? The image was apt. He felt as though he were, indeed, bleeding.

When she arrived at the cottage late the previous evening, Honor had experienced the sense of unease and distant, unhappy resentment that she always felt when she opened the door of the beachfront house. The feelings had lessened with time. They weren't nearly as strong as they had once been, but they had remained forceful enough through the years to keep her visits to a minimum.

Saturday morning she rose after a restless night's sleep and prepared a breakfast of dry cereal and coffee. As she ate she glanced around the walls, absently noting the framed photos of Stylish Legacy in various winner's circles. Honor rarely studied the pictures closely. It hurt to see the face of her father smiling back at the world as if the future looked good to him.

There were other mementos of her father's interest in racing scattered about the room. A bridle hung on the wall beside a small racing saddle that had been left over after the sale of Stylish Legacy. In one corner stood an old wood-and-iron chest containing various racing memorabilia. One of Stylish Legacy's blankets was folded on top. Locked in a drawer in the bedroom were copies of the *Daily Racing Form* from fifteen years ago, containing glowing accounts of the promising colt. There were also some copies of the horse's pedigree and other papers that had once held meaning to her father. Honor kept those locked away, too.

Perhaps she'd made a mistake coming here after all, Honor thought. The cottage depressed her. But she had been running the way a wounded animal runs, and this was where she instinctively headed. It was either this or check into some anonymous motel. Somehow that alternative seemed even more depressing. Maybe a walk on the beach this morning would lighten her mood.

Honor changed into a pair of jeans and some tennis shoes and pulled a heavy peach-colored velour top out of the suitcase. It was turning chilly. By the evening the coastal fog would no doubt be rolling in and blanketing this stretch of beach. The promising warmth in Pasadena did not extend this far north today.

The empty sandy beach didn't prove as therapeutic as she had hoped. It stretched for a distance of a couple of hundred yards before terminating in a rocky outcropping. At the foot of the rocks the water foamed dangerously, driven by a current that made swimming unsafe. It helped to walk, and the crisp wind from the sea was invigorating, but nothing eased Honor's pain. She found herself going over and over the sequence of events surrounding her relationship with Conn Landry, looking for the point at which she should have seen what he was doing to her. It appalled her to realize that she had been so incredibly vulnerable.

It was even more appalling trying to deal with the turbulent mix of emotions that shook her to the center of her being. She had fallen in love with the man. *In love!* Remembering all her initial wariness of Conn, Honor wondered how she could have been so stupid.

Giving up on the walking therapy after forty minutes or so, Honor turned reluctantly back toward the house. It really was turning cold, and the fog would be arriving earlier than she had originally anticipated. She could feel it in the air.

Her father's cottage stood isolated and alone on the bluff over-looking the beach. There were a couple of other cottages nearby but they were both empty at this time of year. The region had remained underdeveloped because it was just a little too far from Santa Barbara to become chic. Someday, Honor had told herself, when development caught up with this area of the coast, her in-heritance would be a gold mine. She had used that rationalization whenever logic had dictated that she sell the cottage.

The truth was that a part of her never wanted to sell. Although the place depressed her and made her strangely uneasy, she couldn't bring herself to get rid of it. It was as if too many ques-tions remained unanswered about the past, questions that should have been settled fifteen years ago. Honor had been unable to settle the questions or let go of the things in the cottage that raised those questions in the first place.

She was pondering the vagaries of her own nature when she heard the roar of the Porsche engine as the sleek black-and-silver vehicle pulled into the cottage driveway. Honor halted abruptly, all her swirling emotions threatening to consume her.

Conn Landry had come after her.

In stunned silence she watched as he thrust open the car door and strode to the cottage. She was several feet away, standing in the shadow of the house, but she could see the implacable expression on his harsh face. Honor let him raise his hand to pound on the door before she stepped around the corner, her head high, hands shoved into the pockets of her velour top. The breeze caught her hair, whipping it around her shoulders.

"Hello, Conn. Still looking for your revenge? I should think you'd have had your fill by now. Even if you haven't, it's all you're going to get."

He spun around to face her, his lithe, strong body dangerously balanced. The cold gray eyes raked her with a simmering emotion she couldn't name. It couldn't possibly be pain, she thought.

"Lady, you could teach me a few things about revenge," he retorted softly. "You surprised me, do you know that? I would never have guessed you'd try to get at me through the horse. God only knows why, but I would have staked my life on the belief that you weren't the type."

Honor felt a jolt of fear. "What are you talking about?"

"Your little scheme to poison Legacy."

"Are you out of your mind?" she gasped out.

He inclined his head once, in brutal mockery. "That possibility exists. I've been asking myself the same question for the past couple of hours. I must have been crazy to think you were a different breed from your father."

"Don't bring my father into this!" she flared furiously.

"Why not? It all started with him. But it's going to end here, Honor Mayfield. I swear, it's going to end here between you and me."

"Don't touch me," she breathed, truly frightened now. At the same time her own fury wouldn't allow her to turn and run, as all her instincts dictated.

"I've got to," he told her roughly as he came toward her. "I have to find a way to get you out of my system. You've pushed me over some edge I haven't come close to since the night they told me Richard Stoner had been killed. That was the last time I felt this wild, Honor. But fifteen years ago there was no one who could be made to pay for what had happened. This time it's different. This time I've got my hands on you."

## SEVEN

Honor turned and ran, not because she had some misconception that she might actually be faster than Conn or that he wouldn't come after her. She ran because one glimpse of the rage in his normally remote gray eyes convinced her she was dealing one hundred percent with the avenging, predatory side of his nature. And when you were the potential victim in a situation like that, you ran.

She fled around the corner of the house, heading for the beach simply because there was nowhere else to go. She knew he was right behind her even though the sound of his movement was inaudible above the slap of the surf and the rising rush of the sea breeze. Honor also knew that fleeing was hopeless. She had yearned to get past the barriers of Conn's self-control but she had never dreamed of doing it this way.

He didn't call out to her or order her to stop. Conn simply bore down on her with the silent intensity of a large hunting cat intent on bringing a gazelle to the ground. Running across the sand was like running through snow. It dragged at her feet, making Honor think of those odd nightmares in which the sleeper found herself being pursued but was unable to escape. She sucked in the cold air, her heart pounding from exertion and fear, and as she reached the water's edge Honor felt Conn's hand on her waist.

"No!" she shrieked, spinning around to strike at him in desperation. "Let me go, damn you!"

"Did you think you could run from me? There's no place on this planet you could hide." He pulled her against the hard length of his body, trying to control her struggles.

But as far as Honor was concerned at that moment, she was fighting for her life. She lashed at him with her nails, kicked at him with her feet, twisted relentlessly in his grasp and tried to use her teeth on his arm.

"You little——" Conn's words were muffled as Honor's constant struggling threw both victim and pursuer off balance. They landed in a sprawl on the cold, wet packed sand. "I'll teach you to betray me," Conn rasped, throwing his thigh heavily across her legs to still their thrashing movement.

"I didn't betray you!" The words were torn from her as she pushed uselessly at his descending weight. "I don't know what you're talking about, but you can't do this to me. You have no right to hurt me!"

"I haven't even begun to hurt you. After the way you've hurt me——"

He broke off abruptly, but not before Honor had heard the startling rawness in his voice. She wondered at it, trying to make that evidence of pain mesh with the rage she was certain was governing his actions. Breathlessly she pushed at him.

He pinned her relentlessly to the damp sand, using his weight to crush her beneath him until her struggles finally stilled. For a long moment Conn stared down into her blazing eyes. He held her wrists above her head as he lay on top of her.

"You bastard." The anger and fear were still warring within her. There was no time to analyze the flash of emotional agony she thought she'd detected in his gaze. She had her own pain to deal with. Honor felt Conn's strength overwhelming her, leaving her physically helpless.

"You've got a hell of a nerve calling me names."

Her head moved on the sand. "I never even knew you, did I? I never had a chance. You lied to me about yourself from the beginning."

His face was a harsh composition of hard lines and flaring eyes. As she stared up at him Honor was vaguely aware of the twin red marks that coursed down the side of his cheek. She was vaguely shocked at the wound she had inflicted. He would carry the sign of her struggle for a few days, she knew. Yet other than holding her helpless, Conn hadn't physically hurt her.

"I wasn't the one who lied," he gasped. "You lied to me every time I took you to bed. All that softness and warmth, it was all an illusion, wasn't it? I had begun to think you were different."

"Different from what?" she flung back, stricken that he could believe she had somehow faked her reaction in bed.

"Different from other women. And different from your father!"

"Leave my father out of this!"

"I can't. What he did is at the middle of this whole damn thing. I should have realized that. Should have known that his daughter wasn't likely to be any different. She's just as capable of betrayal."

"I haven't betrayed you!"

"Then why hide? Tell me why you ran, Honor."

"I'm not hiding. I just wanted to get out of the vicinity of the man who had been using me for his own warped notions of revenge. Is that so strange? Damn you, Conn Landry, who gave you the right to inflict your warped sense of justice on me? And who says I have to let you do it?"

"I wasn't inflicting any punishment on you," he exploded. "I haven't done a thing except take you to bed, come in handy when you were being followed by a punk in a pickup, and rescue your sister from the mess she was in with Granger, remember? I never hurt you! I never wanted to hurt you!"

"You tracked me down just so you could 'tie up loose ends,'" she hissed. "You wanted to settle old scores. You admitted it! Taking me to bed was part of your twisted idea of getting even. And now you have the nerve to accuse me of betraying you!"

"You tried to poison Legacy!"

She gasped in amazement and then her eyes slitted in fury. "Never. I would never hurt your horse. Or any other horse, for that matter!"

"It was the only way you could get back at me after I told you I hadn't simply been swept off my feet by you, wasn't it? After you found out that I had other reasons for meeting you than because I'd fallen in love at first sight or some such idiocy, your feminine ego was enraged, wasn't it?"

"I was upset that you didn't feel the same way toward me as I felt toward you! Yes, I was angry. I had a right!"

"You were the one who wanted to punish someone, Honor. You wanted to get back at me and you chose Legacy as the means to do it."

"That's not true," she cried, appalled. "Do you really believe I would do such a thing? Is that how little trust you have in me, Landry? I admit we haven't spent a lot of time together and I'll also admit that you told me lies for most of that time, but everything I said or did was real. I meant everything. *Everything!*"

"Then why did you try to feed those apples to Legacy this morning?" he almost shouted.

Honor stilled as she heard the agonized plea for an explanation in his words. If she was feeling torn apart, Conn was also in shreds. "I've been here at the cottage since late last night. I haven't gone near Legacy.'' The cold from the sand seemed to be seeping into her. She was chilled emotionally and physically. The only warmth in the world right now was the heat from Conn's hard frame.

"You were seen at the stables this morning. A bright pair of yellow pants and light-brown hair. The only visitor through at that hour. It had to be you.''

"If you believe that, then why don't you go ahead and finish whatever it is you're going to do to me? What are you planning to do, Conn? Strangle me? Beat me? Call the cops? Make up your mind. I'm getting cold out here on the sand.''

"Damn you!''

For an instant she thought he really was going to strangle her. The frustrated fury in his eyes was terrifying. But before Honor's instinctive scream could leave her lips her mouth was crushed ruthlessly beneath his.

It was not a kiss of either passion or gentleness. There was nothing but naked despair and masculine outrage involved. Conn tore through her mouth, annihilating resistance as he went until she stopped fighting altogether and went passive beneath him. There were no other options for her, Honor thought. It was the despair she sensed in him that made it impossible for her to struggle. Some fundamental part of her wanted to offer comfort and warmth, even though she was putting herself at risk.

It seemed forever before some of the emotion began to drain out of the marauding assault. When Conn finally raised his head, Honor risked lifting her lashes just far enough to examine his features. Her mouth felt bruised and her body felt as if it were trapped under a granite boulder but she knew that Conn wasn't going to strangle her. That realization went deep, and she could not have said just why she was so certain. But the relief she felt was in her eyes.

"Don't get the impression that it's all over, Honor,'' Conn snarled softly. "It's hardly begun.'' He rolled off her, uncoiling to his feet and reaching down to pull her roughly up beside him. Without a word he started back toward the cottage, his hand locked around her wrist.

Honor stumbled along behind him, confused and still frightened. She pushed her sandy hair out of her face as the wind caught it. "What now, Conn? How are you going to take your revenge?'' she challenged.

"I haven't decided." He slanted her a cold sidelong glance. "Believe me, when I do, you'll be the first to know."

"You think I'm going to be dumb enough to hang around and wait for your bizarre brain to come up with something suitably satisfying for you?"

"You're going to hang around, all right. You're not going anywhere, Honor. Not until I've had my fill of you. I'm going to work you out of my system and then I'm going to get as far away from you as possible."

She heard the ruthless promise in his words and shivered violently. The cold within her worked deeper into her body. "Not a chance, Conn. I'm no masochist."

"You don't have any choice. You owe me, lady. More than you can ever repay. Somehow I'm going to collect. I swear it. I won't let you rip me to pieces and then walk away!"

He shoved open the door of the unlocked cottage, tugging Honor in behind him. Then he kicked the door shut and released his victim. His gray eyes raked her. "Go take a hot shower and change your clothes. You're a mess."

Honor didn't argue. She fled to the single bedroom and locked herself inside. On the other side of the door she took several deep breaths, fighting to get herself back under control. So many emotions roiled within her—anger, shock, pain and a sense of loss. Unsteadily she began to undress. Conn was right. She needed that hot shower and dry clothing. She had never felt so cold in her life.

When she emerged from the shower sometime later and tugged on a fresh pair of jeans and a bulky knit sweater, Honor felt more in command of herself. She stood in front of the mirror blow-drying her hair and wondered why she didn't look as bruised and battered as she felt. Only her eyes reflected the pain she had suffered. But even as she stared at her reflection Honor saw the courage return to her gaze.

The man she had been stupid enough to love was dangerous, but he was back in control of himself. She finished pulling a brush through her hair, clipping the soft tendrils at the nape of her neck. Then she turned and walked out of the bedroom with a determination to hold her own with the man who waited for her.

Conn was in the kitchen, running water into the coffeepot. For a moment Honor stood in the doorway watching him in taut silence. He didn't look up, but she knew he was aware of her presence. The set of his face was as grim as ever and there was a tension in him that communicated itself across the room.

"By all means, feel free to make yourself at home," Honor muttered.

He ignored the small piece of sarcasm, concentrating on the task of getting the coffee going as if it took all his attention. "Sit down, Honor. We have to talk."

"About what? Your mind is apparently made up, and I don't recall your asking for any input from me." She sank wearily into one of the white wicker chairs at the table. "I've been tried and convicted, haven't I?"

"The evidence is pretty conclusive. And then there's motive." He threw himself into a chair across from her, regarding her with a deep, brooding expression. "We both know you think you had a motive, don't we?"

Her hand curved into a fist. "I had a motive, all right. I was the one who felt betrayed. But I'll tell you this, Landry. If I had set out to get even I wouldn't have used poor Legacy to achieve my ends. I'd have gone after you directly. I wouldn't have involved an innocent animal." She shook her head in despairing wonder. "You must think I'm as low and filthy as...as that loan shark, Granger."

Conn shifted restlessly. "No, I think you were furious. A woman scorned. Isn't that how you saw yourself? They say a woman who feels that way is capable of just about anything. True?"

"It doesn't matter." She stared at him. "It just doesn't matter." Conn was about to say something else and then thought better of it, apparently. He got to his feet and stalked across the kitchen to pour the coffee. With his back to her he stood for a moment staring out the window, watching the sea. Slowly he sipped the piping-hot black brew.

"Maybe it does matter," he finally growled. "You're a passionate woman. In a moment of rage and hurt you might have lost your head and—"

"I didn't do anything to your horse, so don't bother searching for excuses for me to use. I can't imagine why you'd want to find reasons, anyway."

"Believe me, I'm asking myself the same question. I'm going to get you out of my system and then I'm going to leave." Honor felt the renewed tension but she didn't move. "Why should you need to get me out of your system? How could you possibly let a woman you think so little of get so close?"

"I was a fool." He didn't turn around.

"Well, that makes two of us, doesn't it?"

"Yes."

Honor blinked back the tears, refusing to give in to them. "At least we aren't trying to shoot each other the way our fathers did when things went wrong in their business relationship. Although I wasn't altogether certain just what you had planned out there on the beach. I suppose it's lucky for me you don't pack a gun, isn't it?"

He swung around with controlled violence. "This isn't a joke."

"Do I look as though I'm joking? Conn, this is the end of it and you know it. Unless you're going to physically hurt me, you might as well leave. You hate me, and the sooner I'm out of your sight, the better," she whispered.

He slammed down the coffee cup. "I'm not leaving. Not yet. I told you yesterday that I want you and I'm going to have you. On my terms."

"I thought I made it clear that I'm not a masochist. I won't play victim for you, Conn, not anymore." She got slowly to her feet, one hand on the edge of the table for support. Her gaze was unwavering.

"And I thought I'd made it clear you don't have any choice."

He started forward with a cool, measured stride.

Honor stepped back. He wasn't enraged this time, but she knew she was in just as much danger. She edged backward until she was in the main room of the cottage, standing beside an end table that held a lamp. "I won't let you do this to me, Conn."

"From what I remember about the way you respond in my arms, you want me as much as I want you!"

"Damn you! I went to bed with you because I fell in love with you!" For an instant she regretted letting the truth emerge, but a moment later her pride surfaced. What did it matter if he knew she had gone so far as to fall in love? He already despised her.

Conn halted, his eyes blazing. "Love? You expect me to believe that? After what you've done?"

"Believe what you like," she replied steadily. "It's the truth, I only went to bed with you because I cared. Because I was in love."

"Prove it," he taunted coolly.

Her eyes narrowed. "What are you talking about? There's no

way I can prove a thing like that. How should I prove my love? Go out and throw myself off a cliff into the ocean? I doubt that you'd believe me even if I did. I don't think you know how to trust anyone, Conn Landry. That's probably why you're so hot to settle old scores and collect all outstanding debts. Life is safer that way, isn't it? You don't have to worry about taking a risk.''

"Skip the psychoanalysis. If you loved me a couple of days ago, you must still love me now, right? By all accounts true love isn't an emotion that dies easily.''

"How would you know?'' she flung back tightly. "You don't even believe in it?''

He came another step forward. "So why don't you try to convince me?'' Conn taunted.

"How?'' She eyed him with renewed wariness, uncertain of his mood now.

"Tonight when we go to bed you can give yourself to me without any arguments or recriminations. Just the way you did last week. Let me have all that warmth and sweet passion as if they were for real! Maybe you can convince me that it was unrequited love that made you try to poison Legacy!''

"Prove my love for you by going to bed with you? Conn, you're supposed to stop using that line the day you graduate from high school!''

"I take it you're not still in love?'' he mocked cruelly. "A somewhat short-lived emotion, wasn't it?''

"It didn't die a natural death. You murdered it.''

"Then it wasn't a very sturdy emotion, either, was it?''

"Stop goading me,'' Honor hissed. She reached out and scooped up the small brass table lamp. Her hands were trembling. Conn glared at her. "Put that down, Honor.''

"Not until you get away from me.''

"You really think you'd use that on my skull?''

"Anyone who would deliberately try to poison a horse would be capable of cracking a man like you over the head,'' she warned half-hysterically.

For some reason that halted him in his tracks. He stood staring at her in stunned amazement. "Are you saying you did put those apples in Legacy's feed?''

"I don't know anything about any apples. But I do know I'm not going to let you touch me as long as you hate and distrust me so much,'' Honor vowed. Her grip on the lamp base tightened. The passionate fury that sparked between them seemed to flicker and then, very slowly, it began to fade. Conn didn't move for a long moment and then he asked softly, "Is my trust so important?"

"It's the most I could have hoped for from you, isn't it? You don't know the meaning of love." Honor heard the raw truth in her own words as she slowly lowered the lamp.

Conn hesitated. Then quite coolly he stepped forward and removed the lamp from her unresisting fingers. "You'd come to me without any guarantees of love?"

"I haven't had any guarantees for the past week, have I?" She stood very straight, hazel eyes brilliant. "But I was under the illusion that there was at least some mutual trust and respect between us."

"And that's enough for you?" he pressed deliberately.

"I was fool enough to think so," she admitted, knowing deep down that she had been banking on the wealth of her own love for him to fill in the gaps.

"If I said I believed you, was willing to accept the possibility that it wasn't you who put the apples in Legacy's feed, would you let the situation between us go back to the way it was before...before yesterday?"

Honor caught her breath at the implications of what he was saying. He was going to back her into a corner from which there would be no escape except into his arms. It took her a moment to comprehend why he was doing it. Then the truth hit her in a cold shower of realization.

"That's the only way you'll feel safe with me, isn't it? The only way you'll be able to handle an affair with me now. I'm to tell you that I love you and give myself to you without any reservations. In turn you'll tell me you believe I might not have been the one to poison your horse."

"It sounds like a fair split to me." He shrugged carelessly. "Both of us take a risk."

"What risk are you taking?" she demanded tightly.

"That I might wake up one morning to find you've tried to crush my skull with a handy object such as that lamp," he said dryly.

"And in turn I get to love a man who doesn't know how to love me and who might still be using me to satisfy his need for revenge. That's a hell of a bargain, Landry. You must have been playing in some rough leagues for the past few years to learn that kind of wheeling and dealing," she told him scathingly.

He ignored that. "As I said, we both take a few risks. Does this famous love of yours give you enough guts to make the deal?"

He was walking on ice he couldn't measure, Honor realized sadly. Conn Landry was terrified of having it crack beneath him and finding himself in water that was way over his head. He wanted her, perhaps so much so that he was even willing to believe she might not have tried to poison his horse. But he was afraid to risk loving her.

The other side of the coin showed her wanting him. But she wasn't nearly so adept at bargaining with emotions. The only way she could give herself to him was if she simultaneously took the risk of loving him.

"A few minutes ago there wasn't any doubt at all in your mind but that I was the one who had tried to poison Legacy. Why are you willing to consider other possibilities now, Conn?"

He looked at her, silent for a long moment. Then he said softly, "You're wrong, you know. During the past few years I have learned how to take a few risks. I don't like them. I do my best to minimize them whenever I can, and I prefer to plan matters so that there are as few chances as possible. But that doesn't mean I don't know how to take them. What about you, Honor? Can you take them?"

Honor drew a long breath and then she sank wearily into the chair beside the end table. She clasped her hands in her lap, not looking at him. "I might. For the right man. But you're not that man, are you, Conn? The right man for me would never have believed me capable of trying to avenge myself by poisoning a horse. The right man for me wouldn't have threatened violence. The right man would have trusted me when the chips were down."

She sensed his restless movement, but he didn't try to touch her.

"The chips are down," he bit out huskily. "And I'm willing to...to consider your side of the story. I could almost believe that even if you did it, you might have thought you had a reason."

The awkward, uncertain way he said it infuriated Honor. Her head snapped toward him. "Oh, golly gee, thanks. You don't know how terrific that makes me feel. Your generosity of spirit overwhelms me, Landry."

He glowered at her, shoving a hand through his tousled hair. "You don't know what I've been through last night and this morning. I woke up with a hangover that would have constituted a reasonable excuse for turning myself in to a hospital emergency room. Then I get a phone call telling me to come down to the track, where I'm shown some very convincing evidence that the woman I've been sleeping with has tried to take some revenge by poisoning my horse. I haven't had a thing to eat since yesterday and I can't think of anything except the fact that the woman I'd decided was different from her father has probably made a fool of me. She tells me she loves me in one breath and then turns around and deliberately taunts me when I give a little ground and admit I'm willing to look at her side of the matter. Is it any wonder I'm not feeling extremely charitable?"

"What about me? I've been through the wringer myself. I discover that the man I've fallen in love with has only been playing some kind of strange game with me. I come to the beach for a little peace and quiet and find out he's followed me, intending to punish me for a crime I didn't commit. He succeeds in terrifying me and then announces he's willing to make a deal. I'm going to be allowed to go to bed with him a few more times so that he can work me out of his system. In exchange, he's willing to concede I might not have tried to injure his horse. No guarantees, no nonsense about falling in love, no promises for tomorrow. Heck of a deal you're offering, Landry."

He moved then, reaching down to haul her abruptly to her feet. "Believe me," he muttered, his face very close to hers, his eyes ablaze with a strange light, "it's better than the deals I usually offer." Conn's arms locked around her as he brought his mouth down on hers.

But this time the kiss was different. Honor sensed the change at once and knew that this time she didn't have to fight back. She relaxed faintly, letting his frustrated, demanding need wash over her in waves.

She shouldn't have had even a vestige of concern for his emotional state. It was her own she ought to have been worrying about. But she was a woman in love, and in spite of what she had told him earlier, nothing could alter that. Her palms stroked slowly down his back in a gentling fashion.

"Honor," Conn growled softly. "Honor, don't fight me. I want you the way you've been since our first night together. Warm and sweet and welcoming."

She wondered vaguely if he'd even realized what he'd just said and decided that he probably didn't. Not entirely. Regardless of what had happened between them, she was coming to understand this complicated man. He needed love whether he knew it or not. And a part of him was trying to reach out and take it even though another aspect of his nature was warning him that she was capable of betrayal. The conflict within him was almost palpable.

Slowly she pulled free of his embrace and he let her go reluctantly.

"Honor?"

"You said you hadn't eaten since yesterday," she murmured, starting back toward the kitchen without meeting his eyes. "It's almost lunchtime."

He hesitated and then followed her. "Are you going to feed me?" Conn asked with deliberate mockery.

"I'm going to feed myself. I can make an extra sandwich for you, if you'd like." Honor opened the refrigerator door.

"Yes," he said so quietly she wasn't sure she heard him. "I'd like." He sat down at the kitchen table, watching her intently as she went about the business of slicing bread for sandwiches. He didn't say a word as she finished slathering the chutney-and-cream-cheese mixture on the bread and set a plate down in front of him. When she sat down on the other side of the table, Conn finally spoke again. "You were right about one thing."

"What's that?"

"At least we're not at each other's throats the way our fathers ended up all those years ago." He picked up a sandwich half and took a large, healthy bite.

"Could have fooled me," Honor said bluntly. "I could have sworn you were at my throat."

Conn's gaze narrowed as he munched his sandwich. "You don't know me all that well, Honor. If I'd really gone for your throat..." He let the sentence die, turning back to his food with a vengeance as though he didn't want to finish his words.

Honor swallowed and stared at him for a long moment. "Yes, I know. If you'd really gone for my throat you'd have torn it out by now. What's been holding you back, Conn?" For the first time she allowed herself to think about the full ramifications of his behavior. Intuitively she knew she was right. If Conn Landry had been intent on tearing her apart, he'd have done it by now. Men like Landry didn't compromise.

Yet Conn was willing to compromise with her.

He looked at her, considering. "Beats me," he finally said, shrugging.

Honor sighed. "I like a man who knows his own mind."

"I'll admit that right now I'm not entirely sure of myself or of you. I don't like the feeling, but I'm stuck with it."

"You prefer everything cut-and-dried, don't you?"

"I prefer everything clear and comprehensible," he drawled. "There are a lot of things going on between us that aren't either clear or comprehensible. They make me——" he hesitated and then concluded "—uneasy."

"Did you really have a hangover this morning?" Honor asked suddenly.

His glance was mildly savage. "I went to bed very drunk last night."

"Because of what had happened between us?" she pressed.

"I was annoyed. Irritated. Disgusted. Impatient. I decided to medicate my emotions with an old-fashioned remedy. What the hell's so amusing about that?"

Honor's faint flicker of humor disappeared at once. Indeed, she wasn't even sure from where it had sprung. "Nothing. I guess it's just, well, *interesting* to think of you deliberately getting drunk because of a quarrel with a woman. Somehow it doesn't sound like something you'd do."

"You're such an expert on what I'm likely to do in any given situation?" he challenged roughly.

"I'm learning fast," she shot back. "Do you want another sandwich?"

He chewed for a moment before answering, his gaze reflective. Then he nodded briskly. "Yes, please. I think I'm going to live."

"Poor Landry," Honor said with surprisingly gentle mockery. "You really have had a hard day, haven't you?" She got to her feet and went over to the counter to construct another cream-cheese-and-chutney sandwich. Then she poured some more coffee.

Carrying both over to the table, Honor sat down again and silently asked herself the question she couldn't decide how to ask aloud. *What now?*

"This cabin belonged to your father?" Conn asked after a moment, glancing around at the rustic interior.

Honor had the distinct impression he was searching for a topic that, while it might not be completely neutral, because nothing was neutral between them right now, was at least less emotional.

"Yes." Compelled to further his efforts at nonlethal communication, Honor sought for something else to add. "He used to bring Adena and me and Mother here whenever possible. I don't use it much anymore. Generally I keep it rented out, but this time of year it's often empty.''

''That's Stylish Legacy?'' Conn nodded toward one of the winner's circle photos. A framed clipping cut out of a fifteen-year-old issue of the *Daily Racing Form* hung beside it.

''Yes.'' Again Honor struggled for neutral words. ''All the photos are of Stylish Legacy.''

Conn finished his sandwich and picked up his coffee cup. Then he got to his feet and wandered over to the nearest photograph. The picture showed the stallion, head high, jockey still perched on his back, posing for the camera with the usual assortment of people crowded around. Nearly twenty people had squeezed into the photo, most of whom were total strangers who had dashed in front of the photographer just for fun.

Richard Stoner and Nick Mayfield stood nearest the groom, who held Stylish Legacy's head. Conn studied the fifteen-year-old photo of his father and his father's best friend for a silent moment and then he turned away.

''You've kept all your father's records and mementos of Stylish Legacy?'' he asked, wandering out into the living room to glance at some more of the pictures.

''I couldn't bring myself to throw them away, but I didn't want them in my apartment, either. Too many memories,'' Honor confessed.

''Too many unanswered questions, you mean.'' Conn fingered the small racing saddle.

''Perhaps.''

''They look very pleased with themselves, don't they?'' Conn stopped again in front of another winner's circle photo.

''Dad and Richard Stoner? Yes, they do,'' Honor agreed, getting up to go stand in the kitchen doorway. She watched Conn as he studied the picture. ''Proud and excited by the win.''

''They trusted each other at that point.''

''Yes.'' She waited, uncertain what to say next. ''They were partners and they owned a winner.''

''Apparently that wasn't enough to hold the partnership together.'' Conn swung around, pinning her with his eyes. ''I wonder what it takes.''

''To hold a partnership together?''

''To hold two people together. A man and a woman, for instance,'' he said deliberately.

"I don't know," Honor retorted carefully. "I suppose it depends on the particular man and woman involved."

"There would have to be trust," Conn suggested too quietly.

"At a minimum." She decided to ask the question she hadn't dared ask earlier. "What now, Conn?"

He set down his coffee cup and looked at her. "A walk on the beach?"

"I've already been for a walk on the beach."

"I could use the fresh air."

It was an overture, Honor realized. Tentative, cautious, uncertain, but an overture nonetheless. "All right."

## EIGHT

Honor lay alone in bed that night and wondered for the hundredth time what was going through Conn Landry's head. He was out there in the living room, supposedly sleeping on the couch. He'd accepted the arrangement without a murmur of protest, as if he couldn't have cared less where he slept. She had been very calm, very deliberate, about fetching pillows and a quilt from the closet and setting them out on the sofa. He'd simply watched her, sitting by the fire, his head back against the cushion of the chair.

She'd been deeply aware of his intent stare all evening, aware of dark, unspoken questions hovering in his mind, aware of the tightly restrained desire in him. All of Honor's feminine instincts warned her that the smoldering caldron of emotions tormenting Conn tonight constituted real danger for her. But a part of her was resonating in response to the mixture of sensations emanating from him.

Honor turned on her side, twisting restlessly amid the sheets and blankets. She hadn't slept at all since going to bed an hour and a half earlier. Dinner had been a quiet affair. Neither Conn nor Honor seemed able to make casual conversation under the tense circumstances. Honor had considered various ways of telling Conn that he couldn't stay the night, but all the phrases of rejection had died on her lips.

It wasn't just that she was afraid he wouldn't leave; it was that, deep down, she didn't want him to leave. A tentative truce had been established out there on the beach that afternoon. She wanted time to pursue it, time to rebuild some basis for trust.

She was a fool to want to reestablish something that had never really existed in the first place, Honor told herself again and again as she lay listening to the insistent pulse of the sea. There was nothing to be salvaged between herself and Conn. He had been using her from the beginning to work out a warped notion of revenge, and now that someone had menaced his extremely valuable racehorse he would probably never trust Honor, even if she could somehow prove her innocence.

And how could she prove her innocence? Someone had apparently seen a visitor at the barns who looked like her. Given the shaky situation between herself and Conn, that was more than enough to damn her in his eyes. Furthermore, he was convinced she'd had a motive.

He'd arrived at the cottage in a fury, full of threats and retaliation. But somehow none of those promises of menace had really materialized. There had been moments of genuine danger; Honor was well aware of them, but Conn hadn't actually carried any of them to the ultimate conclusion. He hadn't hurt her, and tonight he was sleeping on her sofa, not forcing his way into her bed.

Honor tried to think logically, to analyze Conn Landry's actions since his arrival at the cottage. There was no doubt in her mind that he was coiled like a whip, poised to strike. But this evening he seemed uncertain of his target, even though she had been within range all day. She wondered what was holding him back.

Perhaps the part of him that seemed to need her was stronger than the side of him that couldn't trust her. The need in him would involve much more than physical desire, Honor realized. A man like Conn Landry would not be at the mercy of his hormones. He was too self-contained, too controlled. If he was in a turmoil because of a woman it was because he wanted or needed something from her more than physical satisfaction. By the same token, Honor decided, it would be difficult for him to accept that he needed more from a relationship. It would force him to acknowledge a certain vulnerability and that would be hard on Landry.

It was all very confusing, deeply troubling, and it was definitely making it impossible to sleep. Honor moved uneasily, adjusting the covers with a futile gesture. She wished she wasn't so pulsatingly aware of Constantine Landry's presence in the next room. It was as though his own turbulent emotions were reaching out to tangle with hers. Lying there alone she couldn't be certain how much of the tightly-wound sensation she was feeling was due to her own jumbled thoughts or to her awareness of his. The sensation of commingling was strange, adding to her restlessness.

Surmounting all the questions, anger, doubts and fears, however, was a gradually strengthening desire to ease the pain she had seen in his eyes. The tension that had been flowing back and forth between herself and Conn all evening had taken its toll on him as well as on her. She wanted to ease the fierce intensity she sensed in him and in so doing, ease the uncertainty within herself. But she would be a total idiot to go out into the other room and make any such efforts. There was enough of the predator in Landry to make such a move dangerous in the extreme. True, he had himself under control now, but if she wandered out there dressed in her nightgown, her hair tumbling around her shoulders, her feet bare, he was liable to read an open invitation in her actions. And who could blame him?

Still, she wasn't going to get to sleep tonight at this rate, and the turbulent state of her emotions demanded some positive action. The knowledge that Conn was experiencing his own heightened tension was enough to push Honor into doing something decisive, even if it was reckless.

With a surge of determination she pushed aside the covers and reached for her robe. When she stepped off the small rug beside the bed, her toes curled in response to the cold hardwood floor. But Honor ignored the chilly sensation and walked to her bedroom door. She opened it slowly, softly, and found the living room illuminated only with the faintly smoldering ruins of the fire.

Standing there in the doorway, her fingers clutching the lapels of the robe, Honor swept the shadows with her gaze. She was seeking the man whose unsettled state seemed to have been tangling with her own. When her eyes found his lean form still sprawled in the overstuffed chair in front of the hearth, some of her initial determination faltered. She stood very still in the doorway, not certain what to say now that the moment was upon her.

"Conn?"

"Go back to bed, Honor." The words were spoken in a flat, inflexible tone of warning. Conn didn't move.

Honor took a step forward, the robe flaring gently around her ankles. "I want to talk to you," she said.

"I don't think that's such a good idea right now." He kept his brooding gaze on the fire.

Honor took another step and then a third. She kept going until she was standing beside his chair. "I can't sleep, and it doesn't look as though you've been doing much sleeping, either. We need to talk, Conn."

"About what?" he asked roughly. The pale flicker of the remnants of the fire highlighted the harsh lines of his face as he continued to gaze down into the embers. "We've had trouble talking all evening, in case you haven't noticed. Why should we try it again now? I think it would be much more intelligent on your part if you went back into that bedroom and closed the door."

Honor caught her breath and sank down onto her knees beside the chair so that she could meet his eyes. Her movement finally forced him to look at her, and when he did, she saw the turmoil of frustration and pain and hunger in his gaze.

"Maybe you're right," she said softly. "Maybe now isn't the time to talk."

"Get out of here, Honor. Believe me, it would be best if you went back to your room. I'm not—" He broke off, searching for words and then continued evenly, "I'm not sure of myself right now. I'm not sure that I'm in complete control."

He sounded vaguely dazed by the admission and the words released much of the restraint Honor had tried to put on her own emotions. She reached out and touched his fingers as they lay curling tightly into the arm of the chair. "It's all right, Conn. I'm not in complete control, either. But, then, I never am around you." She risked a tentative smile.

He stared at her. "Woman, do you know what you're doing?"

"Yes. No. Not completely. I only know I can't go back into that bedroom alone. There is too much going on between us. Too much that is unsettled."

The hand she had been lightly touching moved, shifting abruptly to catch her questing fingers in a grip of iron. "Unsettled questions are dangerous, Honor. Don't you know that?"

"I'm learning."

He drew in a deep breath and she could see the decision in his burning eyes. "Why are you so willing to take risks tonight?" he demanded softly.

"I don't seem to have any choice."

Conn gave her a strange look. "You may be right." For a moment longer he simply gripped her hand, not moving as he continued to search her face. "No more choice than I've got in the matter. We're trapped in this web together, you and I. It's been like that from the beginning. I should have realized how it would be. But how could I have guessed?"

"Conn? I don't understand—"

But he didn't allow her to finish the question. Instead, he uncoiled to his feet, retaining his hold on her and drawing her up to stand in front of him. Honor felt the fine trembling in his touch as he pulled her slowly, inevitably, against the length of his body. The heat in him seemed to reach out, engulfing her, and she responded with a soft cry. Her arms went around his waist and she let her head sink down on his shoulder.

"Neither of us can find the words right now," he grated hoarsely. "There's no point trying. You've come to me when you could have stayed safely in your room."

"Yes."

"Then there's nothing else to talk about." He lifted her face with the edge of his palm. For a few intense, vital seconds he stared down into her soft eyes and then he muttered something incomprehensible. Whatever it was got swallowed up in the kiss that followed.

Honor gave herself over to the drugging emotion of the embrace. It seemed to her now that only the flaring passion that ignited so quickly between them could bridge the chasm that stretched between herself and Conn. A part of her would pay any price to cross that abyss tonight. Even if the bridge was made of rainbows and fire and would disintegrate before morning, she would build it because the need to reach him was so overwhelming.

Conn's mouth was a furnace of damp heat that communicated his passion without any restraint. His hands slid down her back to her hips, moving possessively on her. The fierce urgency in him sought to overtake her and bring her to the ground. The predatory quality in Conn that Honor had sensed from the beginning was fully alive tonight, but she understood it because there was an echo of it in herself. Her own need to communicate, even though the communication was on the sensual level, approached the violent in its intensity.

"Honor, I have to have you now. I couldn't stop even if I wanted to try. Woman, you don't know how it is with me tonight, what I feel like inside. I'm burning." Conn's mouth moved heavily on hers, staking a claim before moving to the curve of her shoulder.

Honor gasped as she felt the light touch of his teeth on her bare skin. Then her robe was being loosened, pulled free of her body and discarded at her feet. She shivered as his hands shaped the curves of her breasts, the heat of his palms sinking into her through the soft nightgown. And then the interior of the cottage spun around her as Conn abruptly swept her up into his arms.

She closed her eyes and drew her fingers lightly along the nape of his neck as he carried her into the bedroom. The strength in him made her feel secure, even though a small voice whispered that perhaps she should fear it.

Conn settled her into the depths of the tousled bed and stood for a moment looking down at her. His eyes never left hers as he unbuttoned his shirt and unfastened his belt. When at last he stood naked, his maleness an aggressive force dominating the room, Honor moved. She put out a hand to draw him down to her.

"Honor, honey. Oh, *Honor!*"

He came to her, stripping off her nightgown in a swift, impatient movement that left the material crumpled in a heap at the foot of the bed. Then Conn moved across her body with the power of a wave breaking on a reef. Honor felt herself responding vibrantly, her body achingly alive and aware. The emotional tension that had been tightening within her all day was transmuted into a physical tension. It sang through her nerve endings and throbbed deep in her lower body.

She traced the outline of Conn's hard, muscled frame with soft fingers that held a woman's demands. He groaned in response to her touch, pushing himself into her palm when she drew her hand down his thighs.

"Conn," she whispered as the driving power in him throbbed under her touch.

"I want you, Honor. I can't stop wanting you," he rasped. His lips roved from one nipple to the other, exciting and challenging. When Honor lifted her hips instinctively, moving against him with unconscious need, he traced a sensuous path down her body to the apex of her legs. "Open for me, sweetheart. Let me feel the passion in you."

She writhed beneath him, obeying the command. His husky words of encouragement and demand were dark and heavy in her ears. Then she felt his fingers working exotic magic amid the secrets of her body and she cried out again.

"You want me," he growled, pushing his strong legs between her soft thighs. "Say it. Say you want me!"

"Yes, darling. I want you. With everything that's in me. I've never needed anyone the way I need you."

Her words seemed to thrust him over the edge. Conn muttered her name between clenched teeth, and then he was forging into her warmth, claiming her fire for his own with relentless force.

"Hold me," he ordered with an aching harshness. "Hold me, Honor. Wrap yourself around me and don't let go!"

Honor had the fleeting but vivid impression that Conn wasn't even aware of his own rough command but she reacted to it with everything that was in her. With all her strength she clung to him, riding the whirlwind. The final burst of unraveling excitement sent shivers through her that generated a powerful reaction in Conn. His fingers sank into the skin of her shoulders and he arched heavily into her softness. There was a thick muffled, wholly male cry of release and satisfaction from far back in his throat and then he was collapsing damply along her body.

For a long while Honor lay quietly beneath Conn's muscled weight, recovering her energy and her senses. She was beginning to think he might have gone to sleep when he finally stirred and opened his eyes to look down at her flushed face.

"I wonder," Conn murmured at last, "if you have any idea of what you've done."

"They say that in reality it doesn't work," she whispered soberly.

"What doesn't work?"

"Going to bed with a man in order to achieve some sense of communication. The conventional wisdom has it that in the end all you get is a few moments of illusion. In the morning everything's the same."

His lashes lowered until she couldn't read the expression in the gray eyes. "Is that what you were doing? Trying to communicate?"

"I suppose. I couldn't stand the distance between us any longer. I guess a part of me thought that if we...if I..."

"A part of you thought that if you seduced me the distance between us would disappear?" He toyed with a tendril of her hair as it lay along her bare shoulder. "You took a big risk."

"Did I?"

He paused a few beats as if thinking it over. "Yes. I could lose you now. Let you think that you were achieving your mystical, nonverbal communication for a few days."

"While you worked me out of your system?" she dared.

"Umm. And when I've had enough I could simply walk out the door." He twisted the tendril of hair between his fingers and tugged slightly, his mouth tightening.

"Yes," she agreed. "You could do that."

"There's just one problem," Conn continued thoughtfully.

"What's that?"

"I don't think I could ever get enough of you to work you out of my system. I'd be deluding myself if I decided to try that route.''

Honor closed her eyes briefly, aware of the precarious balance between them. "I was deluding myself when I decided to try going to bed with you in order to communicate more effectively.''

He went still. "Were you?''

"I went to bed with you because I love you,'' she admitted softly. "I suppose communication is a part of love, but the truth is that I would have walked out into that living room tonight even if I knew that I'd never see you again afterward.''

"Honor,'' he breathed, lowering his head to brush his mouth against hers, "I'm glad.''

"You probably are,'' she agreed wistfully. "The way it stands now, I get to take all the risks, don't I?''

"Loving me is a risk?'' He frowned.

"A big one. I never dreamed I'd fall in love with a man who couldn't give me his trust. But, then, I never thought I'd be foolish enough to fall in love with a man I couldn't trust, either.''

Conn's frown metamorphosed into cold anger, but he didn't move. "You're saying you love me but you don't trust me? I don't believe you, Honor. I've never given you any reason not to trust me.''

"You didn't tell me you were Richard Stoner's son,'' she reminded him.

"That's different,'' he flared, visibly offended by her interpretation of his silence on that score. "I never lied to you about it. I simply decided not to mention it until...until I got to know you better.''

"Until you'd decided how you'd take your revenge?''

He shook his head once with savage impatience. "No. I knew it would introduce a problem into our relationship and I didn't want to do that. Not when everything between us was so new and fragile. I wanted to move cautiously until I knew you understood how things were between us.''

She stared up at him. "And how are things between us?'' Honor whispered.

Conn's head lifted with faint masculine challenge. "I want you and you love me. That pretty well sums it all up, don't you think?''

"I think I'm getting the short end of the deal,'' she tossed back. "Other than that—''

"No," Conn interrupted grittily. "You're not getting the short end of the deal. You're getting everything I have to give."

Dumbfounded, Honor looked up at him. "All you have to give? I don't understand."

His hands framed her face, holding her still. "I want you," he said evenly, "more than I've ever wanted any woman in my life. It goes beyond wanting in a physical sense. I could handle that if it only involved a desire to take you to bed. But it's more than that. I need you in some way I can't explain. And because I have to have you in order to stay sane I'm prepared to take a risk. More of a risk than I have ever taken with another human being. I've been thinking about it all afternoon. It's what was going through my head out there in front of the fire. It's been eating at me since I got here this morning. I have to trust you. I don't seem to have any choice. Tell me again that you didn't try to poison Legacy."

"I didn't try to hurt Legacy in any way," she answered in a low but very steady voice.

He sighed and she felt something in him relax. "I've met a lot of people who can lie while they smile and look you straight in the eye. Enough of them to know you're probably not one of them. It's taken me a few hours to work it out because everything hit me like a ton of bricks this morning."

"And you instinctively expected the worst from me because I'm Nick Mayfield's daughter, right?" she asked with resigned bitterness.

"I'm accustomed to expecting the worst from people in general," he admitted calmly. "Life is safer and simpler that way. That philosophy has been responsible for keeping me alive on occasion."

"I can imagine." But she knew he missed the note of irony. Conn was too busy finishing what he had to say.

"But there's a softness in you that wouldn't mesh very well with a woman who would try to get revenge on a man by poisoning a horse. You give yourself too completely when you give yourself to me. You don't hold back. Even tonight when you thought you were only seducing me in order to reestablish communication you weren't careful or cautious. There is no restraint in you when you take me in your arms. You wrap yourself around me and make it very clear that you want me and need me. You're *vulnerable* to me, aren't you?"

"Not by choice."

A cool, laconic smile flickered briefly at the edge of his mouth. "No, not by choice. In spite of yourself. You know you should be wary of me. You're smart enough to realize I could be dangerous. From the very beginning you've tried to be careful around me, put some distance between us. But it didn't work, did it?"

"No."

He nodded in deep satisfaction. "When you opened the door and walked out into the living room tonight, I knew for certain."

Honor moved her head uneasily on the pillow. His palms slid down to her throat. "Knew what for certain?"

"That you couldn't stand the space between us. The knowledge that what we had together was teetering on the brink was eating at you, wasn't it? You couldn't bear to let it all fall apart. When you came out into that room to find me, I realized you couldn't let me go any more than I could allow you to walk away from me."

"You make it sound as though we're trapped together."

"We are. Caught up in a web from which neither of us can escape. We need each other. You label your emotion love and I call mine wanting, but it amounts to the same thing."

Desperately Honor tried to think it all through. "You believe I didn't try to get at you through Legacy?"

"I believe you didn't try to poison the colt," Conn stated quietly.

The breath Honor had been holding escaped in a long sigh. "Thank you, Conn."

His thumb moved slowly along the base of her throat. "It's your turn. Do you believe I didn't deliberately seduce you in order to get revenge for what happened between our parents?"

"I think," Honor said very honestly, "that you would use some other method if you were really out to punish me for what you think happened fifteen years ago. As I said earlier, if you ever went for my throat, you'd be quick and brutal about it. You wouldn't make love to me the way you do."

The smile reappeared fleetingly. "And just how do I make love to you?"

"Completely. Overwhelmingly. I can't believe that you're playing bedroom games with me. There's too much of...of *you* in the way you make love." It was the truth, Honor realized. There was a quality of blatant, fundamental honesty in the way Conn staked his claim of passion and possession. No games, no fancy techniques such as another man might employ to achieve a woman's surrender. Just rock-solid desire that carried its own kind of reassurance and established its own integrity. She, too, had had a chance to do some thinking this afternoon and evening, Honor decided with sudden insight.

"I think we both needed the breathing space we got this afternoon," Conn said, his eyes intent.

"Did you mean what you said a minute ago? That your idea of wanting and my notion of love amount to the same thing?" She wasn't certain why she risked the question. There was too much riding on it, too much hope. It was reckless to ask questions like that, but she needed to know exactly how he felt about her. If he chose to label his love for her "wanting" and "needing," she could live with that. So long as underneath she knew that what he really felt was equivalent to what she felt.

The gray eyes softened indulgently. "Why do women always want to dress it up by calling it love?"

"It's not a matter of dressing it up. Love is what it is. Why not call it by its proper name?" It was Honor's turn to be indulgent. "I think you're the one who's searching for labels. Do you love me, Conn? Are you playing it safe again by hiding behind more acceptable macho words like *want* and *need?*"

His eyes narrowed faintly. "I'm not trying to play it safe. I'm trying to be honest with you. I want nothing but honesty between us from here on in, Honor. We have to establish that if we're to have a basis for a future."

"I agree," she whispered tremulously. "We need honesty. But if we're to have a future, we also need love. I thought—that is, I was beginning to think—that maybe you were falling in love with me and that you just weren't sure of the words yet. But that's not the case, is it?"

"I know the words don't mean much. Do you want me to say them even though I don't believe in them?" he challenged roughly.

"No." She shook her head quickly. "No, I don't want you to lie to me. Not ever."

"I won't, honey," he soothed, stroking her cheek with infinite care. "You can believe anything I tell you."

"What about the things you don't tell me?"

He shrugged, his sleek shoulders moving easily in the shadows. "The things I don't tell you aren't important for you to know. They don't impact us."

She swallowed, a little stunned. "You're so incredibly arrogant at times. And the most arrogant thing of all is that I don't think you even realize it. You just take your own assurance for granted. Will you take me for granted, I wonder?''

He moved his head in a gesture of absolute denial. ''Never. I'll take care of you, Honor. I'll protect you. I'll take you to bed as often as possible and I'll always tell you the truth. But I swear I'll never take you for granted. How could I? I've been around long enough to realize that some things are unique in the universe.''

''But you don't love me,'' she concluded sadly.

Anger flashed quickly across his face. ''What I feel for you hasn't got anything to do with something as rosy and soft and ephemeral as love. It's a hell of a lot more certain and more real. I'm making a commitment to you, lady. And I'm asking for a commitment in return. Something we can both count on, something solid and sure. If I'm going to get tangled up in this web with you, I'm going to pull all the strands as tight as possible.''

''Because you always tie up loose ends,'' she finished for him.

''Always.'' He relaxed again. ''Why do you keep pushing, sweetheart? You know it's settled now, don't you?''

''I think it is. For you.''

''It works both ways. Whatever chance you had of freeing yourself from the trap in which we're caught disappeared when you came out into the living room to find me tonight.'' He lowered his head to seal the words against her mouth. ''I don't want to talk anymore for a while, Honor.'' His palm slid meaningfully down her arm until his fingers twined with hers. Then he raised her hand to a level with her ear and turned it so that he could kiss the vulnerable inside of her wrist.

Honor hesitated for a moment, trying to hold back long enough to force him to continue the dialogue that had just been established. Then she gave up the effort. What was the point? She'd accomplished so much. She would make herself be content with what she had achieved tonight. After all, she had known from the beginning that Conn Landry did not understand love. She could hardly expect the revelation to hit him on top of everything else that had happened today. At the moment she would be grateful that the relationship between herself and the man she loved had not fallen over the brink on which it had been so precariously balanced. Together she and Conn had rescued it.

Love would come eventually, Honor reassured herself as she surrendered to the insistence of Conn's touch. For him the trust was the hard part and she hoped that tonight his belief in her integrity had been established. There was time to work on building the rest.

Honor awoke a long time later, vaguely aware that she was lying alone in bed. It took a moment to reorient herself, and when she did, she sat up with a sudden, panicked jerk.

"Conn?"

"I'm in the kitchen. Be back in a minute. I just wanted a glass of water."

"Oh." In relief Honor glanced at the clock beside the bed. It was two-thirty in the morning. Now that she was awake, she felt a little thirsty herself. Sleepily she pushed aside the quilt and padded barefoot into the kitchen. Conn was standing near the sink, drinking his glass of water while he studied yet another shot of Stylish Legacy.

"Hey, it's cold out here," he murmured as Honor reached into the cupboard to get a glass for herself. "You should have put on your robe."

"You're a fine one to talk," she grumbled, eyeing his attire, which consisted solely of a pair of white briefs. "You've got on a lot less than I have." She yawned as she filled the glass.

"I was planning on using you to warm myself up as soon as I got back into bed," Conn informed her absently as he bent a little closer to Stylish Legacy's photo. "You know, I think Legacy inherited his sire's basic conformation, especially the strong hindquarters."

Honor gave him a small, amused smile. "You've got it bad, Conn."

"What?" He turned his head to glance at her in surprise.

"Racing. I can see it's really getting a hold on you. My father was that way about it. He tried to keep Stylish Legacy just a business deal, a tax shelter. But the truth was that he was hooked on the whole racing scene."

Conn watched her drink her water. "So was my father. Just look at the two of them in this photo. You'd think they'd won the Kentucky Derby instead of just another stakes race."

Automatically Honor's gaze followed his. She rarely looked at the photos closely. Whenever she saw the pictures of her father and his partner, the old, unsettled sensation swept over her. As a result she had gotten into the habit of never really studying the photos.

But for some reason Conn's deep interest in the pictures of

Stylish Legacy intrigued her. For the first time in years she found herself looking at the jumble of people around the winning horse. Conn was right. Regardless of what had happened between them later, at the time this picture was taken Richard Stoner and Nick Mayfield were two very happy, very satisfied racehorse owners.

"They do look quite pleased with themselves," she acknowledged softly.

"So does everyone else in the photo. How do all those strangers always manage to crowd into the picture?"

"I expect it's kind of a game. Like getting yourself on TV when a television film crew shows up." Honor realized that she wasn't feeling the usual uncomfortable sadness she remembered experiencing in the past whenever she'd looked at these pictures. Out of curiosity she moved across the kitchen to glance at another. Her trained eye began to pick out details, automatically recording the color of the riding silks the jockey wore, the fifteen-year-old suit her father had on and the cowboy hat on the head of the man standing directly behind Richard Stoner.

Honor blinked and leaned closer.

"What is it?" Conn asked, moving across to stand beside her.

"I think this guy in the hat behind your stepfather is also in that other photo."

"The trainer, probably."

"No, I don't think so. There's something familiar about that hat, Conn." Thoughtfully Honor went back to stare at the other picture. "Same hat. I can't really see his face, but I'd swear there was something about him...." Honor moved to yet another picture, and in this one the face beneath the brim of the cowboy hat was much clearer. "Conn! It's Ethan Bailey. A lot slimmer than he is now and fifteen years younger, but I'd swear it's Ethan."

Conn leaned over her shoulder to stare at the man in the hat. "You're right. But Ethan barely knew either of our fathers. Why would he show up in three winner's circle photos with Dad and Mayfield?"

"At three different tracks, too. He's hardly the type to run down into the circle to get into the picture just for kicks. That sort of activity is for kids and pranksters."

Conn straightened, shaking his head. "We'll have to ask him about it sometime." He reached for Honor's hand. "Come on, honey, let's go back to bed. My feet are getting cold. Along with a few other parts of my anatomy."

"You expect me to warm all of those parts?"

"It would be a nice, considerate gesture."

*A wifely gesture,* Honor thought wistfully. But she kept the comment to herself.

"You know," Conn observed lazily as he snuggled Honor down into the covers a moment later, "I feel as though I'm finally able to think normally again. I spent most of the day feeling bruised, battered, hung over and furious. Now at last everything's begun to settle down."

"That must be a relief," Honor murmured, running her fingers through his hair. "I have a hunch you're not used to being shaken up and confused, are you?"

"No," he growled. "I'm not." He curled Honor closer into his body, luxuriating in the warmth of her.

"Well, if it's any consolation, neither am I," she told him gently.

It was then that Conn's new clearheadedness reminded him of the question he had intended to ask Honor. He paused, his mouth hovering just over hers.

"How did you find out I was Richard Stoner's son?"

Honor was quiet for a moment and then she said calmly, "Ethan Bailey told me."

Landry swore very softly and sat up in bed. "Why is it that every time I turn around lately, Ethan Bailey seems to be nearby?"

# NINE

"Didn't you realize that Ethan Bailey knew who you were?" Honor asked. She lay propped up on the pillows, watching Conn as he swung his feet over the edge of the bed and turned on the lamp.

"The subject never came up with Ethan."

"You've said yourself that racetrack rumors are prevalent. And Ethan's been around racetracks for years. Other than using your own name instead of Stoner, did you ever make any effort to hide your connection with Stylish Legacy and his original owners?"

"No." The answer was clipped, impatient, as if Conn's mind was busy tracing a pattern and didn't want to be bothered with side issues. Conn stared unseeingly at the wall for several tense minutes, his face set in familiar, harsh lines.

Uneasily Honor leaned forward to touch his shoulder. "Conn?"

"Ethan was the one who found the apples in Legacy's feed this morning. The one who told me you'd been seen around the barns very early today."

"Oh." She didn't quite know what to say in response. Her hand dropped from his shoulder.

Conn twisted around to meet her eyes, his gaze cold and intent. "When did he tell you who I was?"

"Yesterday. He came downtown to my office and said he felt obliged to warn me that you might not be telling me the whole truth about yourself," Honor said in a low voice. Conn's mouth became even grimmer. "It wasn't the first time he'd tried to warn me about you."

Conn caught her chin on the edge of his hand and held her still. The gunmetal-gray of his eyes was almost lethal in the soft light. "What else did he tell you about me?"

Honor licked her suddenly dry lower lip. From out of nowhere the fear of Constantine Landry resurfaced. A knot of tension began tightening in her stomach as she felt the power in his hand. He wasn't hurting her, merely anchoring her in place for the moment, but the leashed savagery in his eyes was more than enough to trigger elemental alarms all over again. Forcibly she fought down the doubts and uncertainties. Conn's violence was not aimed at her.

"He implied at one point that you might be mixed up in gambling up at Tahoe. I wondered if that was why you knew how to bring pressure to bear on Granger," she admitted unsteadily.

"That bastard," Conn said far too calmly. He didn't release her.

Honor wasn't certain if he was referring to Ethan Bailey or Granger. Taking a grip on her nerves she continued more firmly.

"He told me that I wasn't your usual type."

"As if he'd know."

"Yes. Well, then yesterday he said he'd realized who both of us were and he wanted to warn me that you'd once sworn revenge on my family. He implied you were playing some kind of cat-and-mouse game with me." With a touch of anger Honor wrenched herself free of Conn's grasp and drew her knees up under the sheet. She balanced an elbow on each knee, folded her arms and rested her chin on them. "Which you were, in a way."

Conn exhaled slowly. "Which I was, in a way," he agreed coolly.

He made no immediate move to touch her, but Honor could feel the implacable intensity of his eyes. "For the record," she asked softly, "just how do you make a living that allows you to buy expensive racehorses and gives you the free time to hang around Pasadena looking up old family acquaintances?"

There was a measure of silence before Conn retorted, "Does it matter?"

She slid him a sidelong glance and then returned to her contemplation of the foot of the bed. *Did it matter?* She could practically feel the challenge in him. He was deliberately pushing her, she thought, and wondered why. There were two possible causes: arrogance and insecurity.

The idea of Conn Landry feeling insecure and needing reassurance was laughable. But even Landry's arrogance had its limits. She took another risk.

"Do you mean, does it matter in terms of how it affects our relationship? No, it doesn't. But I guess I'd like to know whether or not I'm going to be expected to entertain business acquaintances like Mr. Granger on a frequent basis."

"Relax, Honor," he murmured, his voice softening with a combination of amusement and satisfaction, "I don't make a living by investing in Granger's kind of business. The investments I've made are mostly in real estate. I was paid far too much for the kind of work I did overseas, and since I had no one to spend it on and was too busy to use it myself, I just kept funneling it into stateside property. By the time I came back to the States, there was a nice nest egg waiting for me."

The way he said it was just a little too smooth, Honor decided, not without a trace of amusement. She lifted her chin off her arms and looked at him. "How is it you were able to deal so effectively with Granger? Or was he just intimidated by your, uh, forceful personality?"

Honor could have sworn that a red stain appeared momentarily along Conn's cheekbones. She found it almost endearing.

"I occasionally do some consulting work," Landry admitted with great care. "You get to know people that way. Make certain contacts."

"Consulting work for whom?" She pressed more out of curiosity now than uneasiness.

"Businesses," he said very easily. "It was my field of expertise, you know. People hired me to analyze security procedures and come up with ways to minimize risks overseas. The same needs exist here in the States."

"Go on," she encouraged, intrigued now.

"Well," Conn continued cautiously, "one of my first jobs when I got back to the States was to analyze the security arrangements around a certain, er, businessman who deals heavily with some of the rougher elements of society."

"You did consulting work for a gangster." Honor nodded in sudden comprehension.

Conn's expression turned distant and forbidding. "He was a friend of mine. Someone I met a long time ago. He and I had a lot in common at one time but he chose to take a slightly different route to success. When I got back to the States he got in touch. Said I was the only man he could trust to set up a security system for him. I owed him, Honor. He saved my life once when we worked together briefly several years ago. I always pay my debts. At any rate I used my connection with my former, uh, client, when I confronted Granger. Clout, you might say."

"It's all right, Conn. I trust you," Honor said with a smile. "No more questions about how you managed to intimidate Granger."

He frowned. "Are you sure?"

"I'm sure."

"That still leaves us with the current problem," he remarked, clearly relieved to be able to put the other aside.

"Ethan Bailey."

Conn nodded, saying nothing.

"Ethan did more than tell me you were looking for revenge," Honor offered offhandedly. "He also told me you lied about Granger."

"Lied about Granger! What did he say?" Conn demanded.

"That Granger had never been picked up that day at the track. That he hadn't walked into any trap."

"The implication being, of course, that I hadn't saved you from getting mixed up in the mess. That the whole story had been a fabrication designed to establish a link between you and me. A link I could use." Conn sounded coldly bitter.

"You've implied more than once that I was under some sort of obligation to you," she reminded him gently.

"Damn right," he shot back. "You were. But it was a legitimate obligation. I didn't fake it."

Honor shook her head, another flash of amusement lighting her eyes. "So arrogant."

Conn's mouth curved wryly. "I must seem that way to you at times."

"So Granger really did walk into a trap set by the authorities that day?" she queried.

"Oh, yes. And he was released on bail shortly thereafter."

"What would you have done if I hadn't conveniently needed rescuing?" Honor asked, accepting his version of the truth.

"Found another way to approach you. When I realized you were following Granger, I decided to wait and see what was happening. It raised a lot of questions. Brought up the possibility that you were in trouble."

"So you decided to take advantage of the situation."

Conn shrugged. "That's the way I am, Honor. I take advantage of my opportunities. I wanted a solid approach to take with you, and that business with Granger gave it to me. I would have been a fool to let it slide."

"I can see why you've been financially successful," she said dryly. "The predator in him would never be far below the surface. "I suggest we get back to Ethan Bailey," Conn said harshly. "It seems very clear that he's the reason we're both here instead of having dinner in Pasadena. He warned you off of me."

"Perhaps out of genuine concern," Honor pointed out.

Conn brushed that aside. "He did more than warn you, he lied to you about Granger. Implied I had lied to you."

Honor heard the emphasis on his last words. "That really bothers you, doesn't it? That he made it sound as though you'd been less than truthful with me."

"I told you earlier tonight that I've never lied to you," he said grittily.

Honor nodded quickly, aware of the simmering fury in him. "All right. We've got a situation in which Ethan Bailey keeps cropping up, apparently with the goal of making each of us distrust the other."

"He sure as hell implied that it had to be you who tried to give the poison to Legacy," Conn said. "But why? It makes no sense."

"I know. No sense at all. Why should Ethan care about you and me getting together?"

"There's another name that keeps recurring, too—Granger." Conn became thoughtful for a long moment. "It seems to me we've found ourselves talking about him almost as often as we've talked about Bailey."

Honor put her chin back down on her arms. "Remember the evening that guy in the pickup truck hassled me?"

"Yes." He looked at her sharply.

"Well, I could have sworn a similar sort of pickup followed me when I left Pasadena yesterday evening."

Conn was suddenly tense. He leaned forward and caught her shoulder, pulling her around to face him. "You're sure?"

"No. No, I'm not sure," she said honestly. "Traffic was heavy and I could have been mistaken. There are a million pickups on the road these days. You know that. I didn't notice it after a while. Just for a time there, after I got on the freeway, I got nervous. Then it disappeared. It was probably just my imagination."

"Right now I'm not willing to write anything off to imagination," Conn said bluntly. "This is getting screwy."

"We've got so little to go on. Ethan in those photos with Dad and your stepfather. The guy in the pickup truck. Granger."

"The guy in the pickup truck could be associated with Granger," Conn said slowly. "But I don't know why. Granger and I did business together. When it was concluded I thought each side was reasonably satisfied with the results."

"Maybe he didn't like the way you got involved in the affair," Honor suggested. "After all, it was between him and Adena."

Conn shook his head. "I guess he might have decided to teach me a lesson." He sounded as though he thought it was highly unlikely.

"If he did would he have been capable of hurting Legacy in order to punish you?"

Conn gave her a pitying glance. "Granger has been successfully collecting money from his loan shark operations for years. Believe me, he's resorted to more exotic techniques than poisoning a horse."

"So I'm a little naive," she mumbled. "I just can't see someone deliberately poisoning a beautiful animal like Legacy."

"You're right. You're a little naive." There was affection in his tone as Conn threaded his fingers through her tangled hair. "You know, we're forgetting something here," she went on musingly. "Legacy never was actually poisoned. You said Ethan showed you the evidence?"

"That's right. Claimed he got it out of Legacy's stall."

"And then he told you I'd been seen around the barns."

"Yes." The affection disappeared from Conn's voice. Honor shook her head. "You must have hated me for a while."

He hesitated. "I felt betrayed," he finally acknowledged.

"Like father, like daughter?"

He winced. "I'll admit the thought went through my head. But you must have felt the same way after Ethan told you his tales."

"I did. Betrayed."

There was another moment of silence before Conn said softly, "Ironic, isn't it?"

"Because of the betrayal that occurred between your father and mine? Maybe it was inevitable once you and I made contact."

"No, it was not inevitable," Conn muttered tightly. "The sense of betrayal you and I experienced was deliberately fostered by a third party."

"Ethan Bailey. But he had the material with which to work, didn't he? And he was right, in a way," Honor added.

"Right about what?"

"I'm probably not your usual type," she explained lightly.

"Am I yours?" he retorted.

"Well, no, you're not. Adena was right about that fact, I'm afraid."

"Lady, are you teasing me?" Conn moved abruptly, pushing

her back against the pillows and pinning her there. He searched her face, daring her to admit it.

"Maybe. A little."

Conn groaned and then gave her a quick, hard kiss before sitting upright again. "If it matters, I don't think I have a usual type. There haven't been a lot of women in my life, Honor." He looked down at his hands.

"I'm not surprised," she said calmly.

He slid her a startled glance. "Why do you say that? Am I that poor a catch?"

"You wouldn't make a poor catch, just an extremely difficult one to land," she drawled thoughtfully. "A woman would need a very carefully built net."

His eyes narrowed. "It's academic now, isn't it? You and I wound up in the net together. We're both caught."

*No,* Honor thought, *not quite. I don't have you, not completely. But you do have me. A little unfair, but that's the way the world works, I guess.* Aloud she said, "As you say, it's academic. Especially tonight."

"Especially tonight. Tonight we've got to think a little more about Ethan Bailey."

"And Granger," she added.

Conn suddenly surged to his feet, reaching out for his jeans and pulling them on quickly. "Maybe I can get a few answers about Granger at least."

"Right now?" Honor asked. "In the middle of the night?"

"Some of the people who would know about Granger tend to work the night shift," Conn informed her, buttoning his shirt. "In my line of work I tend to make just as many contacts on the right side of the fence as I do on the wrong side."

"What are you going to do?" Honor slid out of bed and tugged on her robe.

"Make a few phone calls." He started out into the living room with a purposeful stride. "Good thing you keep a phone here."

"Have to. The people I rent to usually can't afford to be without access to a telephone, even when they're on vacation. They're always wheeling and dealing or pretending that they are. Part of the L.A. image." Honor followed him, stepping into her slippers en route. She reached the bedroom doorway just as Conn reached for the phone.

She saw the sudden hardening of his expression even before he started to dial.

"Damn," he muttered, tossing the receiver back into its cradle.

"What's wrong?"

"Phone's out of order." He stood staring at her, gaze unreadable.

"Are you sure? There hasn't been a storm or anything recently."

"No, there hasn't, has there? Get dressed, Honor."

"Dressed! But it's three o'clock in the morning."

"I'm aware of that. It's three o'clock in the morning, the phone's out of order, and we're miles from town. Add to that a short list of rather pithy questions that remain unanswered and the fact that I'm finally starting to think clearly again—and you've got a very messy situation. I want us both out of here. Now. Go get dressed and don't waste any time on the job." He started toward her.

"All right, all right, I'm going," she said quickly. Honor spun around and headed back into the bedroom, spurred on by the cool command in his words. "Are you always like this when you're working?"

He was busy stuffing a few of her things into her suitcase. "Like what?"

"Overbearing and intimidating. You sound like you've had a lot of experience giving orders." She yanked on the jeans and a vividly striped cotton sweater.

"Maybe. Frankly, I've never thought about it." He snapped the case shut. "Ready?"

"No."

"Too bad. Let's get going." He took her arm and towed her toward the door.

"Do you think it's possible you're overreacting to a dead telephone?" Honor inquired dryly.

"Possible. Even probable."

"But that's not going to slow us down, is it?"

"Not a bit." He opened the front door, slamming it behind them and fishing the Porsche keys out of his pocket in one movement. "Get into the car, Honor."

She was beginning to absorb some of his strange sense of urgency, Honor realized, as she hurried around the front of the Porsche and opened the passenger door. He was inside, twisting the key in the ignition even as she dropped into the seat beside him. The normally responsive engine came alive briefly, shuddered and died.

Conn swore and tried again. This time there was even less reaction. He didn't bother to try a third time. Instead he drummed his fingers lightly on the steering wheel and stared out into the darkness.

"We," he announced mildly, "have very big trouble."

"We could try my car," she volunteered tentatively, sensing his deadly serious concern.

"We could, but I have a strange hunch it wouldn't do any good." He shoved open the car door. "Come on, Honor, let's go."

"Where are we going this time? And what do you mean about my car being dead, too?" Anxiously she leaped out of the Porsche, wresting her own keys out of her purse.

Conn glanced around, sweeping the night-dark scene around the cottage. He seemed to make a decision. "Okay, let me have the keys. We'll give it a try."

When her car didn't start on the first attempt, Conn didn't bother with a second. He was out of the seat, grabbing Honor's wrist and yanking her along behind him before the car door had swung shut.

"You think someone sabotaged the cars?" she gasped in amazement, stumbling a little as he pulled her back toward the cottage.

It wasn't Conn who answered her. Another voice responded to the question. "If he does think that, he'd be right," drawled the man who had last been seen driving a black pickup truck. He stepped around the corner of the cottage, allowing the weak moonlight to illuminate the gun he held.

Honor was so startled that she stumbled heavily against Conn. He automatically reached out to steady her but somehow managed to pull her even more thoroughly off balance. In the next instant they both tumbled to the ground with Honor landing in an undignified sprawl across Conn's body.

"Golly, lady. You got a problem or something?" demanded the man with the gun. "Get up. Both of you. Mr. Granger don't want no delays."

"Granger!" The astonishment as well as the anger in Conn's tone was real. Slowly he got to his feet, using his left hand to steady Honor. She was trembling, he realized, but there was little he could do at the moment to reassure her. "Granger sent you?"

"I guess you must have made Mr. Granger mad, moving in on

his turf and all." The young punk motioned with the nose of the Saturday night special. "Let's go. Don't got all night."

Conn kept his hold on Honor's arm, pulling her with him as he slowly obeyed the gunman's orders.

"Conn?" Honor spoke his name softly, questioningly, but she followed the urging of his grip as they set out toward the beach.

"Do as he says, honey. He's wired," Conn said in a low voice. The sound of the surf covered his last words but they were dangerously true. The guy with the gun was probably only eighteen or nineteen, street-tough, but riding some kind of high. Perhaps it was just the tense excitement of holding a gun on two people or the rush of power that undoubtedly was coursing through him. Perhaps he'd indulged in a few chemicals to work up his nerve for the task. Whatever it was, the man was lethally high-strung and therefore very unpredictable. Conn had seen the syndrome before. The only way to deal with it at this point was to keep him talking. Conn needed an opening.

"I thought Granger and I had a deal," Conn said, projecting his voice over the increasing noise of the surf. "I was under the impression Mr. Granger stuck by his deals." The gunman was herding his captives out onto the beach where there was virtually no cover behind which a desperate man could dodge. The sand became a further barrier to quick movement, dragging at Conn's shoes and causing Honor to stumble occasionally.

"Mr. Granger don't like the way you conduct business, slick. He said to tell you that you won't be getting in his way again after tonight. It's me that's got a deal with Granger," the punk added with pride.

Conn seized on the hint of arrogance. "Granger trusts you to take care of us?"

Beside him Honor gasped as her foot collided with a stray piece of driftwood. Other than that she hadn't said a word, Conn realized grimly. She was scared to death, but she wasn't panicking. He felt a possessive admiration for her self-control. The last thing he needed right now was a hysterical woman. The next few minutes were going to be extremely precarious.

"Granger's sent word that he's giving me my chance to prove I can handle jobs for him," the gunman explained. "And you can bet I ain't gonna let him down. Getting in with Granger's a quick way to the big time and I ain't gonna do nothing to blow my chances."

Honor spoke for the first time, glancing over her shoulder to search the man's face in the watery moonlight. It was cold and there was a stiff breeze snapping the air from off the waves. She shivered again under Conn's hand. "You're the man in the black pickup truck who followed me home the other night, aren't you?"

"You got it, lady."

"And you also followed her out of Pasadena?" Conn put in coolly.

"Had to see where you were heading. We knew that wherever the broad went, you'd be sure to follow."

Conn thought about that for a few seconds. "Is that right?"

"You should of stayed in your own league, Landry. Shouldn't have tried to mess around with Granger. He's big-time."

"I didn't realize he was extending his scope of activities to include this kind of thing," Conn admitted dryly. "But I guess it's safe enough for him. After all, you're the one taking all the chances."

The gunman's eyes narrowed in the moonlight. Conn saw the hot, tense anger in the man's face and the uneasy way he lifted the weapon. "I ain't taking no chances, Landry. I told you, Granger's big. He's got this all planned out. All I got to do is carry out instructions and everything's going to be just fine. No sweat."

"The only reason Granger got to be big-time is because he pays people like you to take the risks for him," Conn pointed out calmly.

"Shut up, unless you want it here and now," the punk rasped.

"I take it here and now isn't the way Granger wants it done?" Conn retorted. He felt the fury in himself and wondered at it. It wasn't just that he knew he'd been stupid for having allowed this situation to occur. It went beyond that, centering around his self-disgust at having failed to properly protect Honor. She was his woman, he thought tautly. It was his responsibility to protect her. Yet he'd allowed the reckless passion and the conflicting feelings of betrayal and inexplicable trust to swamp his normally cold-blooded, clear thinking to the point where he'd put Honor in jeopardy. It was traumatic to realize just how deeply involved he was with Honor Mayfield.

"Granger was real particular about how he'd like this done, but if you get tricky, I'm supposed to go ahead and finish things any way I can."

"Where are we going?" Honor asked softly.

"What's that?" the punk demanded suspiciously.

"I asked where we're going," she repeated obediently.

"Down to the far end of the beach. The water's supposed to be dangerous down by the point. Couple of bodies might not resurface for days, if ever."

"I see," Honor muttered.

Conn felt her drawing in deep, even breaths, trying to control her fear. The knowledge that she was so frightened enraged him further. Savagely he clamped a lid on his emotional reaction. It wouldn't help matters if he allowed his own control to disintegrate. He was unaware of how roughly he had begun to grip Honor's arm until she looked up at him questioningly. He relaxed his hold but he didn't release her. It was cold out here, he thought vaguely. The water would be unbearable.

"You seem to know a lot about the ocean currents around here," Conn managed to observe as they reached the water's edge and turned toward the rocky point at the far end of the beach. There wasn't much more time. The point was only about fifty yards away, looming dark and forbidding in the shadows. Around its base white water foamed evilly.

"I got all the instructions," the gunman informed him sullenly.

"Were you the one who moved the screen in my bedroom?" Honor asked tightly.

"I don't know what the hell you're talking about, lady. I ain't never been in your bedroom."

Conn slanted a quick, curious glance down at Honor but she was concentrating on her footing. It seemed to him that she was having more than the normal amount of trouble walking in the sand. After all, yesterday morning she'd been running on the beach without this degree of awkwardness. Her present lack of coordination suited him perfectly, however. So perfectly that he wondered whether she was stumbling on purpose. There was no doubt that the gunman wasn't paying much attention to her troubles as long as she stayed on her feet and kept moving. But he must be accustomed to her awkward progress by now. If she were to suddenly stumble to her knees, he probably wouldn't panic and pull the trigger.

Tentatively, uncertain how to get the message across to Honor, Conn tugged at her arm. Was it his imagination or did she actually incline her head slightly? His right hand tightened around the object he had palmed back at the cottage when he'd tugged Honor off balance the first time. He was only going to get one chance, so it would have to count and count heavily. Beside him he felt Honor's new level of tension as she seemed to pull herself physically together.

She was going to do it, Conn realized. She knew what he wanted. He felt another overwhelming rush of pride in her perception. Honor Mayfield was quite a woman to have beside you in a crisis, he decided.

"Let's move it, you two. Hurry up, lady. What's the matter with you? Can't you walk straight?"

"I'm a little scared," Honor retorted flatly.

"Tough. That's your problem, ain't it?" The gunman sounded pleased with the power he was wielding. "If it makes you feel any better, Granger wants this to look real romantic."

"Romantic!" Honor repeated, sounding horrified.

"Yeah. You know. A lovers' quarrel. What the cops like to call a *domestic*."

"My heavens," Honor breathed. And then she stumbled to her knees.

Conn released her at once, making no attempt to break her fall. Instead he swung around in a smooth rush, hurling the metal star-shaped object that had been nestled in his palm.

"Damn you—" the gunman began to yell at Honor, outraged at her clumsiness. But he never finished the sentence.

The razor-sharp blades that formed the points on the star sliced into his shoulder, cutting through the denim shirt he wore as though the material were delicate silk.

The punk screamed in fear and rage. His arm jerked spasmodically and the gun went flying. It landed on the wet sand at the water's edge and an instant later was lost below a breaking wave.

Conn didn't waste any time looking for the weapon. He was on top of the other man in an instant, his body uncoiling with controlled violence.

"Conn!" Honor shot to her feet, her eyes going from the sight of the two men locked together on the beach to the gun that appeared briefly, half covered with wet sand. She started to reach for it but stopped when Conn's gritted words halted her. Even as he spoke another wave covered the weapon.

"Forget the gun. It's useless now. And our pal here isn't going anywhere."

Honor swung back to see Conn releasing his captive. The man on the sand was whimpering softly, clutching at his bleeding shoulder. Conn was wiping the star-shaped weapon against his jeans. Honor realized it was blood that was leaving the damp streaks on the denim fabric. Then he dropped the lethal object into his shirt pocket. There was a respectful casualness about the way he handled the object that spoke volumes.

"On your feet," Conn nudged his victim with the toe of his shoe. "I'm afraid that your fast-track route up Granger's corporate ladder just met with a delay. Probably a permanent one. Young, ambitious executive types like you don't usually get second chances from people like Granger."

The man glowered in mute rage but stumbled to his feet. He didn't let go of the bleeding wound in his shoulder. "I got to have a doctor," he muttered.

"I don't think they make house calls anymore," Conn said easily. "And since both our cars are out of commission..."

"My truck," the man gasped, shambling ahead as Conn pushed him forward. "I got my truck parked down the road a ways."

"Good. We can use it to drive you into town and turn you over to the cops."

"Granger will take care of me," the punk declared. His own uncertainty about that fact was quite clear in his voice. "The guy who hired me said Granger always takes care of his people."

"Which brings us to an interesting question," Conn murmured, glancing back at Honor who was moving beside him without her former clumsiness. "Just who did hire you? Not Granger himself, apparently."

"I ain't talking," the man informed him haughtily.

Conn didn't bother to persuade him to make the effort. He turned his attention to Honor.

"Are you all right, honey?" he asked as they neared the cottage.

"I'm okay." But she couldn't disguise the stark, too-flat tone of her voice. Nor could she understand why she was still trembling. Reaction, she decided. It must be reaction.

"You handled yourself well back there," Conn went on, his voice husky with approval and pride.

"Gee, thanks. Maybe I've missed my calling somewhere along the line." The flippancy didn't feel any more natural than the tremor in her limbs, but Conn seemed to understand.

"It's all right, Honor," he soothed as he waited for her to open the door of the cottage. "You'll be fine in a little while."

He stayed back for a moment, watching the wounded man carefully as he followed Honor through the door.

It was Honor, therefore, who first realized there was another visitor to the cottage that night. She stopped short at the sight of a familiar face studying a photo of Stylish Legacy.

"Ethan!" she whispered.

Ethan Bailey glanced up and then swung around to cover the trio in the doorway with the gun in his hand.

"So things didn't go quite perfectly, I see," he noted in pained resignation.

"They rarely do," Conn said, sighing.

## TEN

"It wasn't my fault, Mr. Bailey! I swear it wasn't. You got to explain that to Mr. Granger. I did exactly like I was told. I put the cars out of commission. I took the two assignments out to the point where the water's rough. I did my part exactly right. But you never told me about that knife thing he carries. He cut me bad. Real bad. I got to have a doctor."

"Knife thing?" Ethan favored Conn with a mildly questioning eyebrow. "Oh, yes, that fancy letter opener you said was a souvenir. Let's have it, Landry." He didn't point the gun at Conn but at Honor instead.

Honor stood very still, alert to the fact that without the element of surprise Conn would not be able to use his weapon before Ethan could shoot her. Wordlessly Conn removed the star blade from his pocket and dropped it down on the floor.

"Much better," Ethan approved. Then he turned his attention to the wounded man. "You'd better go find yourself a doctor. Although it's going to be tricky explaining that wound to an emergency room medic, isn't it?" He shook his head. "I should have realized you wouldn't be able to handle this by yourself."

"But you said Mr. Granger had everything planned out, right to the last detail. You said nothing could go wrong," the man whined.

"Well, son, I was wrong. It happens occasionally. The older you get, the more you realize that." Ethan waved the gun encouragingly. "On your way."

"I don't know if I can drive like this. I'm bleeding pretty bad."

"Try," Bailey suggested coolly. "Try real hard. Mr. Granger doesn't like screwups. If I were you, I think I'd get out of his vicinity. Find some new territory, Tony. I think it would be healthier for you if you did."

The man called Tony stared at Ethan's mildly implacable face and then he turned and walked out of the cottage without another word. The door closed behind him.

Honor stood staring at Ethan Bailey as a strange silence descended on the small room. She felt the renewed tension humming through her, mingling with the reaction from the first incident out on the beach. All of her nerves felt as though someone had seared them with a flame. Over and above her own shaky, unnatural sensation of fear and anger, Honor could have sworn she felt Conn's fierce reaction. But he seemed under control, as always. The knowledge steadied her on the one hand and raised grim questions about his past on the other. Conn's self-control was unnerving. What had he done to learn it?

"I take it," Conn said finally, "that poor Tony is under a slight misconception?"

"About the identity of his real employer?" Ethan nodded blandly. "I'm afraid so. Seemed simpler to have the boy think he was working for Granger. Kid was so anxious to make it big in a hurry. I couldn't resist taking advantage of all that drive and ambition. There he was, hanging around the fringes of Granger's crowd whenever Granger appeared at the track. I heard through the rumor mill that the boy was looking for work, Granger's kind of work. I decided that since I needed some temporary help, I might as well use him. He seemed happy enough with the job until a few minutes ago."

"I don't understand," Honor said in a whisper. "Isn't Granger involved at all?"

It was Conn who answered. "No. He was just a very convenient red herring, wasn't he, Ethan?"

"Yup. Would have been even more convenient if old Tony hadn't made a mess of things. But I learned a long time ago that a man has to be flexible, has to take advantage of his opportunities and be prepared with a backup plan when things go wrong. Didn't get where I am today without practicing what I preach."

"You want us dead," Honor said in a remote tone that didn't sound at all like herself, not even to her own ears.

"It would have been mighty convenient if you two had played your parts out correctly," Ethan explained. He stood easily, the gun in his hand held at a relaxed but alert level.

"You mean if I'd really believed she was the one who tried to poison Legacy?" Conn put in casually. He moved slightly, taking a few steps away from Honor.

"Stay where you are, boy. That's far enough." Ethan's gun hand tightened fractionally. Conn stopped.

Honor hastily interrupted, trying to divert Ethan's attention to herself. "You wanted Conn and me to distrust each other, didn't you? You wanted us to quarrel."

"It set the scene nicely. Everyone at the track saw Conn leave this morning and knew he was in a rage. Couple of owners had even seen him drinking purty heavy the night before. They knew the two of you had ties that went back a long, long way."

Conn's eyes slitted. "They know it because you made certain they found out, right?"

Ethan shrugged. "You know what racetrack gossip's like, son. Especially when it concerns a stallion like Stylish Legacy and the men who owned him. Bound to be some talk when one owner's son shows up with a colt sired by the famous horse. When you started dating Honor, here, why folks were just downright fascinated. Leastways, they became fascinated after I reminded them of the old story."

"Do you mind explaining just why you're going to all this trouble, Ethan?" Conn asked coolly.

"I'm afraid it's a long tale. And I'm not sure we have time to go into it tonight. I looked up the tides before I set this whole plan in motion. The high tide will be peaking right soon. I want you and the little lady here following it out to sea."

"Assisted by a couple of bullet holes?" Conn tossed back.

"Something like that. Might as well head back down to the point. Looks like I'll have to take care of the little job I hired Tony to do. Hard to find good help these days."

Honor felt Conn tense. He would make a suicidal effort, she knew. He would do anything he could to protect her. That knowledge was as sure and solid in her mind and heart as the knowledge of his passion. She had to act first or risk having him throw himself straight into Ethan's gun.

"You can take care of us, but it's going to be tough to stop the gossip that will be hitting the track when this is all over," Honor told Ethan with sudden conviction.

Ethan frowned. "You don't have to worry about the gossip. You won't be around."

"I'm not talking about what people will say of Conn and me. It's what they'll be speculating about you that should interest you. My sister, Adena, knows everything I know. I called her this afternoon and left the information on her telephone-answering machine."

Conn shot her a startled glance, fully aware that she hadn't used the telephone. His attention went back to Ethan almost immediately.

"Now just what the devil are you talking about, little lady?" Ethan demanded impatiently.

"I'm talking about the fact that Adena won't keep her mouth shut. When I don't return from this little jaunt she's liable to go straight to the police."

"With what?" Ethan snapped, more of his patience disintegrating. On the opposite side of the room, Conn stood balanced and poised. Ethan was focusing entirely on Honor.

Honor drew a deep breath and played her one and only card. "With the information that there was another owner of Stylish Legacy fifteen years ago. A silent partner named Ethan Bailey."

The effect on Bailey was electric. The easy, good-old-boy image disappeared in a flash, leaving the face of a raw, embittered and infuriated man.

"You're lying, bitch," he breathed tightly. "You don't know what the hell you're talking about!"

"Don't I? It's all there," Honor said, gesturing calmly toward the wood-and-iron locker that sat in the corner, draped with the folded horse blanket. "All the proof anyone could ever need."

"What proof?" Bailey hissed, his gaze momentarily riveted on the locker. But he seemed to sense that Conn was waiting for an opening. Ethan kept the nose of the gun firmly pointed at Honor. It would still be a simple matter for him to pull the trigger before Conn was halfway across the room. "What proof?"

Honor sucked in her breath and tried to think logically. She had to make this sound good. She badly wished the fear-inspired adrenaline racing through her system would calm down. As it was she could see the tips of her fingers trembling as she bent down toward the locker. Awkwardly she patted the black-and-white blanket lying on top.

"Dad was a businessman. First, last and always. As excited as he used to get about Stylish Legacy's wins, he always claimed the horse was really nothing more than an elaborate tax shelter. Nothing more than a business matter. And because it was a business matter, he kept very good records."

"I don't believe you," Bailey snarled. "If you knew anything you would have put it all together a long time ago."

Honor shook her head. "I didn't put it together all these years because I never wanted to go through all the records and souvenirs my father had left to me. It was too painful. Every time I looked at this trunk I was forced to remember what had happened to Dad. On the other hand, I couldn't bear to throw it all away, either. So I told myself I was putting the various mementos to good design use by decorating the cottage with them.'' She gestured at the photos and racing paraphernalia on the walls. ''Creates just the right ambience, don't you think? Casual but chic, rustic but elegant. It's made the cottage very popular, you know. I rarely have any trouble keeping it rented.'' Her voice broke a little on the last word and Honor quickly stopped talking while she regained her control.

''If you haven't investigated the contents of that trunk in all these years, why would you have done it on this visit to the cabin?'' Ethan challenged.

''If I hadn't met you at the track, I would never have recognized the third man who always seemed to show up in Stylish Legacy's winning photos,'' Honor told him simply. ''I've rarely studied the pictures, anyway, but after Conn arrived yesterday and became so interested in Legacy's sire, I started looking at the photos a little more closely. And when I look at things closely, Ethan, I tend to see things. I've been trained to see details,'' she added with a wry touch of apology. ''It's something designers get very good at, I'm afraid. The smallest details make all the difference in a well-designed room.''

''You little bitch,'' Ethan breathed.

Honor plowed on determinedly. Ethan was still holding the gun with far too much concentration. She turned back to the trunk. ''Once I realized you were in so many of those winner's circle shots and once I saw the expression on your face—''

''The expression on my face!''

Honor inclined her head ruefully. ''It's always the same, the expression on the face of the owners and trainers. That look of satisfaction and victory and excitement. It's really unique. Look around, Ethan. That expression is on my father's face in all the photos. It's on Richard Stoner's face, too. I saw it on Conn's face the other afternoon when Legacy won. And it's on your face in all the photographs of Stylish Legacy in the winner's circles. No matter how hard people try to keep it on a business level, racing seems to get into the blood. It's always more than a business.''

''That proves nothing! Absolutely nothing!''

''True, but it was enough to make me curious. I opened the trunk, Ethan. I started looking through some of Dad's records and papers. As I said, he was a businessman. In his own fashion, he paid as much attention to detail as I do. It's all here, Ethan," she concluded, hoping she wouldn't have to fake it any further. It was very difficult being creative on your feet when someone was holding a gun on you. Out of the corner of her eye she saw Conn advance on catlike feet, making no sound as he approached Ethan. The older man's attention was still zeroed in on Honor.

"You're lying," Ethan muttered, his eyes moving uneasily now from Honor to the trunk. "There's nothing in that trunk."

"Want to see the records?" Honor taunted, her hand hovering just above the horse blanket.

"You're damn right, I want to see them! Show me your fancy proof, little lady," Bailey growled furiously.

Honor bent down and lifted the heavy wool horse blanket.

"Bailey!" Conn snapped loudly.

Instinctively Ethan swiveled around at the clipped command. He panicked as he realized that Conn was much too close to him. But Honor already had the blanket in motion, whipping it toward Bailey.

"Damn you!" Bailey shouted, pulling the trigger reflexively. But the blanket was floating over him, settling around his head and shoulders, and the shot went wild.

In the same instant Conn was on him, propelling the older man to the floor and wrenching the gun free. It was all over in a moment. Conn was far younger and stronger than Bailey and the struggle was fated to end in only one way. Ethan lay still, sagging with the knowledge that he had lost. Slowly Conn rose to one knee and picked up the weapon. He stared down at the fallen man and then he flicked a quick, assessing glance at Honor.

"Are you all right, honey?"

"Peachy keen," Honor mumbled, sinking down onto the top of the trunk. "Just peachy keen. Except for my knees. They don't seem to be functioning properly." She took several deep breaths, willing herself to calm down. "I don't think I can take too much more of this tonight, though, Conn. A little seems to go a long way."

He was on his feet now, squeezing her shoulder tightly. "I know what you mean. Why do you think I gave up those cushy security jobs overseas in favor of a little consulting work and real estate investment? This sort of thing gets to you after a while. I've never been so scared in my life as I was this evening. Twice someone held a gun on you and I was terrified I wasn't going to be able to protect you."

She glanced up at his ravaged features and her love for him shone softly in her eyes. "That's funny. I never had any doubts at all. I just don't tolerate the tension well."

Conn looked at her, his gaze unreadable. "No doubts?"

"I knew you'd do whatever you thought had to be done," she said quietly. It was the truth. Conn would have given his life for her tonight and she was fully aware of that. She had been equally determined that he wouldn't make the sacrifice.

"Thank you, Honor," he said softly.

"For what?"

He shrugged. "For having faith in me."

Honor touched his hand but she couldn't find any words. Her eyes met his in a silent communication that was shattered by Ethan Bailey's groan. She turned to look at the man as he sat up slowly. There was something different about Ethan now. He looked like a broken man. Or one who has come to the end of a long road. It was Conn who spoke first.

"I think," he said, "that it's time we had some answers." He sat down on the trunk beside Honor, the gun held almost casually in his right hand. There was a grimness to him that was frightening. "Were you really a silent partner in Stylish Legacy?" he asked, staring at Ethan.

"Ask her, she seems to know all about it," Bailey muttered, massaging the back of his head.

"It was an educated guess," Honor confessed. "I've never looked inside the trunk. I made a stab in the dark, based on your appearance in all those photographs. No one can resist getting into the photo when the horse wins, least of all the owners."

"You might as well tell us everything," Conn suggested, watching Bailey with a brooding expression. "Now that the connection has been made, it shouldn't be too difficult to dig into the past and find out the whole truth. It just hinged on knowing there was an association between you and our parents. I have a hunch that association involved more than a racehorse. There was something more, wasn't there, Ethan? Something you had to cover up, even if it meant killing the son and daughter of Stylish Legacy's original owners."

Bailey glowered at him and then went limp. "If you really start digging you'll probably find it," he admitted. "For fifteen years I've been afraid of what would happen if someone went looking for answers. I thought I was safe because no one seemed inclined to probe too deeply. The most dangerous time was right after the *incident*."

"Incident?" Honor demanded. "You mean after Stoner and my father died?"

Bailey nodded. "I thought that if I got through that part okay, I'd be home free. I had to let you sell Stylish Legacy, of course. I didn't dare come forth with a claim on the horse. That would have been too risky, because I'd taken such pains to make sure no one knew I was involved financially."

Conn thought about that for a moment. "You didn't want anyone to know you had a financial interest in the horse," he finally repeated carefully. "Because if someone knew that he might suspect that you were involved with our parents in other ways?"

Honor shot him a swift, questioning glance. What was Conn after?

Bailey nodded with a dismal air. "Couldn't take any chances. It hurt to lose Stylish Legacy. Best colt on the West Coast in those days. Could have made a fortune off of him. I didn't even dare to buy one of his offspring. I didn't want to risk it. But I kept track of how the runners he sired were doing. Couldn't help myself. When I learned one of his colts was picked up by Richard Stoner's son, I had a feeling . . ." His voice trailed off sadly.

"A premonition that something was going to go wrong?" Honor suggested.

Bailey nodded. "It seemed dangerous. As if fate had stepped in and forced me to get involved with everything I'd closed the door on fifteen years ago. I thought I'd just make contact with you, Landry. Easiest way to do that was transfer a couple of my horses over to Humphrey's stable. It was simple to introduce myself to you as a fellow owner using the same trainer. I could keep tabs on you that way. Make sure you never got too curious. Or at least have some warning if you did."

"And then I got in touch with Nick Mayfield's daughter," Conn murmured. "You must have really gotten nervous then."

"It all seemed to be getting too dangerous, too close. Fate."

Honor frowned. "You tried to plant a few seeds of doubt at first, hoping I'd back away from any relationship with Conn, didn't you?"

"If you'd backed away from him everything might have gone back to being safe," Ethan sighed. "But you didn't. I could see the two of you getting more and more involved with each other. I knew that once you knew who he was, you'd probably get angry,'' Bailey explained. ''And I thought that if Landry realized you had betrayed him by trying to poison Legacy, he'd be furious.''

''So you set up the situation and then you hired good old Tony to pull the trigger, right?'' Conn growled. ''Okay, I can figure that much out for myself. But why don't you save us all some time and explain why you didn't want your association with my stepfather and Mayfield to come to light? Seems to me, there could only be one reason for that.''

Honor held her breath as her mind leaped to the same intuitive explanation. ''You killed them?'' she whispered tightly, staring at Ethan. ''You killed my father and Stoner?''

A forbidding silence settled on the room and then Bailey nodded once. ''Had to, don't you see? They found out I'd been running guns, using their connections and facilities in the Middle East. The night they got wise, I had to act. There wasn't time to think,'' he went on, his eyes becoming remote as he looked back fifteen years. ''It all happened so quickly. I didn't know they'd been suspicious. I thought they believed I was just curious about the operations. After all, they'd let me put a lot of money into their business.''

''Once again as a silent partner?'' Conn asked with ice in his voice.

''Had to insist on that. I didn't want anyone connecting me with the guns if they were ever discovered. I'd been small-time until then. Don't get me wrong, I'd made money selling weapons to anyone who'd buy them and I'd made a fair amount of money, but I wanted to expand. I needed a safe cover for really big shipments. There was so much more money to be made in that line. Somewhere in the world there's always someone wanting to go to war, you know. Big wars, little wars, guerrilla wars, revolutionary wars. Bandits with political motivations and just plain outlaws. A never-ending market. A businessman's dream. But you got to take precautions.''

''You needed a legitimate cover and you needed reliable transportation facilities.'' Conn nodded with a degree of understanding that rather shocked Honor. ''You needed an established business that had contacts in places like the Middle East.''

''I met your father and Mayfield when they first got interested in buying a racehorse together. I used to own a couple of horses back then, although none of them were in Stylish Legacy's league. But I've always been involved with the track. And I kept up with track rumors. I knew your fathers were international businessmen and I made friends with them. I'm the one who put them on to Stylish Legacy. I'd planned to buy him myself, but when I suggested we all go in as partners, they were happy enough to agree."

"One kind of partnership led to another, I suppose?" Conn said.

"That was right about the time when Mayfield and Stoner were thinking of leaving the big corporation they'd been working for. They planned to set up their own business. I offered to pour some money into it. Any new business needs capital, and they agreed to let me invest. Things worked real well for a while after they'd established their new business operation. I greased a few palms, used a few contacts, and the first thing I knew, I had shipments of rifles riding right alongside the steel piping and oil field equipment your fathers were shipping overseas. No one looked too closely at the other end because Mayfield and Stoner were trusted. They knew folks. The right folks."

"And if anyone had looked too closely, you'd have been in the clear because you were just a silent partner," Conn finished. "No one knew you were involved."

"I made sure my name was left off all the paperwork. Just a private gentlemen's agreement."

"Then one night Stoner and Mayfield became suspicious." Conn's thumb moved with a hint of restlessness on the grip of the gun.

"They set up a trap," Ethan snarled with a trace of returning belligerence. "One of the men I'd bribed talked, and they found out when I had another shipment due to arrive overseas. They knew I had to be there in order to conclude the deal. They got there ahead of me. What they didn't realize was that the man who'd sold them information also sold me information. He was playing both sides of the fence, and I got lucky."

"You were able to set up your own trap," Honor hazarded bleakly. "You made it look as though my father and Richard Stoner had been smuggling the guns and had quarreled over a shipment. You killed them both."

"After that I got nervous," Bailey admitted. "I figured my luck was running out. Decided to get out of the gunrunning business altogether. After all, I'd made a pile. Time to invest it in more legitimate things. Investments people wouldn't be inclined to question."

Conn and Honor looked at him for a long time. Bailey seemed unaware of any of their emotions. He was lost in his own world, examining where it had all gone wrong.

"You bastard," Conn finally said but there was no heat in the words. Only a weary acceptance that the past could not be changed.

"I knew," Honor said softly. "I knew there was something wrong with the notion that Stoner and Mayfield had betrayed each other. It never felt right."

Conn nodded. "I know. Too many loose ends. Too many unanswered questions. That's one of the reasons I came looking for you, Honor. I can't deny it. And I don't regret it, because otherwise we would never have met."

"The questions needed to be answered," she agreed quietly.

He looked at her. "That was pretty slick, the way you pulled the basic connection out of thin air. If you hadn't realized that Bailey's association with Stylish Legacy was a solid one, the rest of it wouldn't have fallen into place so neatly. You're fast on your feet, lady. You've got guts."

Honor smiled shakily. "Coming from you, I'll assume that's a compliment."

Conn blinked in surprise. "Of course it is."

"You moved fairly rapidly yourself when the occasion warranted," she returned dryly.

He lifted one shoulder in a gesture of dismissal. "I spent a lot of years learning to do it. It was just part of the job."

"Some job!" Honor broke off thoughtfully, glancing back at Ethan. "What do we do now?"

"We've got all the evidence we need to get Bailey here out of our lives," Conn began slowly. "But I'm not sure we'll ever be able to pin the past on him. Unless there really are some incriminating records in this old trunk."

"I doubt it," Honor said. "I did glance briefly through the stuff when I moved it here to the cottage. I don't recall anything that might be useful in connecting Bailey with what happened fifteen years ago. But who knows? I didn't realize the significance of Ethan being in all those photographs until yesterday. Maybe there is something buried in this trunk." She paused. "It was all a long time ago, wasn't it? It's over now."

Conn glanced at her. "We know the answers. There aren't any more loose ends." He sounded strangely satisfied.

Honor understood the feeling. There was a deep sadness underlying the sensation, but also a sense of peace. No more loose ends.

Well, maybe one. Honor remembered the question that still hovered at the back of her mind. She turned to Ethan. "Was it you who moved the screen in my bedroom?"

He came out of his gloomy reverie long enough to appear vaguely startled. "How did you know I searched your room? I hardly touched a thing!"

Honor's mouth twisted wryly. "One thing slightly off is all it takes, I'm afraid. I'm beginning to think my eye for detail is going to be the bane of my existence."

Bailey slipped back into his memories. "I just wanted to see if you had any stuff on Stylish Legacy lying around. I needed to know how much you knew about the horse and who had owned it. Didn't realize you had all the answers here at the beach house."

It was midmorning by the time Ethan Bailey had been taken into custody and the necessary paperwork completed. The authorities notified the hospital emergency rooms in the area to be on the alert for a man of Tony's description seeking care for an odd knife wound.

Honor and Conn returned to Pasadena late that afternoon.

They talked quietly over dinner at Honor's apartment, both of them coming to grips with the results of the traumatic events. Gradually they both began to relax and accept what had happened. There was a feeling of companionship, of being bonded together, Honor thought at one point. She and Conn now shared a past and the secrets that had been buried there. It deepened the sense of commitment she felt about the future, but something was missing. Something wasn't right about the way they were preparing to face that future.

It wasn't until later that evening that Honor realized that soon she would have to deal with the problem that had precipitated the entire matter: her relationship with Constantine Landry. If she didn't confront it directly it would haunt her, leaving an element of uncertainty deep in her mind. And it was a cinch that Conn himself would never of his own accord resolve the gray area because he simply didn't admit it existed. But by the time the thought flitted through her mind, Honor was slipping rapidly into sleep. Her body curled deep into the comforting warmth of Conn's as they lay together in her bed.

Tomorrow, Honor promised herself just before she closed her

eyes. Tomorrow she would find a way to make Conn understand that what he felt for her was love. He needed to acknowledge that fact for both their sakes. He had to know that what they shared was something that went beyond an amalgam of want and need and desire.

Unless he took that final step, Honor realized, Conn would never be able to give himself as completely to her as she was willing to give herself to him. There would always be a part of him that was remote and untouchable.

Was it selfish, she wondered, this need she had to make him understand that he was vulnerable to her? Possibly. No, *probably.* Perhaps it wasn't right to expect him to lower his guard as far as she had lowered hers. He had been alone a long time in a harsh world, and the barriers he had built around himself made sense on many levels. She had seen the fierceness in him at the beach house, had come to know the relentless, utterly determined side of his nature. The predatory part of him had helped save their lives; she could hardly quarrel with its existence.

But the hunter in him made it difficult for Conn to admit to love. He could commit himself; she didn't doubt that. He could also give passion and protection. In turn he demanded a great deal. Loyalty, respect, commitment, passion—all of those and more he wanted from Honor. She had given him more. She had given him her love. But so far he hadn't shown any willingness to take the dangerous step himself. He wasn't able yet to admit that he was vulnerable and that what he felt for her was love.

Until Conn could do that there would always be loose ends in their relationship.

## ELEVEN

Honor awoke with the conviction that there were still matters remaining to be settled between herself and Conn, but she hadn't even begun to formulate a plan for resolving the uncertainties when he unwittingly pushed her into a corner.

Honor opened her eyes to find Conn sitting up against the headboard, the sheet carelessly bunched at his waist. He wasn't wearing anything that she could see but he'd obviously arisen earlier because he had a mug of coffee in his hand.

"You're certainly bright-eyed and chipper this morning," she complained, stretching languidly. "Isn't it a little early to be looking so alert? After all we've been through during the past couple of days, I think we deserve some extra sleep."

"I've been thinking," he told her very seriously. He didn't respond to her light greeting.

A small warning bell went off somewhere, but Honor couldn't imagine why. "Oh?" She eyed the coffee with increasing interest.

"We can fly to Vegas this afternoon, spend the night in one of the big hotels and be back here in time to see Legacy run tomorrow afternoon."

Honor tried to assimilate all that. "I suppose we could. Any reason why we should? And did you make me a cup of coffee while you were at it?"

Conn frowned and reached around to lift another mug off the end table. "Here. And the reason we should go to Vegas is because it would be the quickest and easiest way to get married."

"Married!" Honor nearly spilled the hot coffee on the sheets as she accepted the mug and struggled to a sitting position. As it was, a few drops struck the bodice of the black-and-white-striped nightgown. She dabbed at them furiously while she tried to think. "Married?"

Conn reached out to hold the mug while she finished attending to the small drops. "I suppose we could go ahead and apply for a license here in California, but there's a waiting period, and I'd just as soon take care of things as quickly and neatly as possible."

Honor finally ceased her efforts at cleaning the nightgown and went still. She seemed to be having a problem focusing on the main issue. Her mind was skittering around in circles, looking for an escape. In that moment Honor didn't bother to question why she wanted to escape.

"Are you quite certain you want marriage, Conn?" she asked slowly.

His expression grew even more implacable. "It's the only logical conclusion. We could simply live together but somehow that doesn't seem *formal* enough for what we have. You belong to me now. We belong together. There's a commitment between us. Obligations, duties, responsibilities. All those things go with marriage, not a casual affair. And I think you know it." He took a sip of his coffee and added blandly, "After all, aren't you the one who keeps saying you love me?"

Honor paled beneath the well-aimed thrust. The man was, indeed, a hunter. He knew exactly where to strike. Frantically she rallied her forces.

"Yes, I'm the one," Honor agreed bleakly. "I'll take my coffee back now."

He handed it to her, faint wariness flickering in his eyes. "Honor? What's the matter?"

She took a long swallow of hot coffee. "Nothing, Conn. But I need time. We both need time." Her mind seized on the only escape it could find. "There's so much to work out, so many plans to make. Where are we going to live, for example? I have a business established here in Pasadena. I can't just pick it up and move it elsewhere. And I imagine you have your business headquarters well established up in the San Francisco area."

"My business is movable," he interrupted flatly. "I can shift my operations to Pasadena without too much difficulty."

Honor blinked uneasily, sensing he had deliberately acted to forestall her protest before she could even get it properly outlined. She rushed to find another excuse. "There's Adena to consider."

"Believe me, from what I've seen of Adena, she wouldn't care at all if you got married. I think she approves of me."

"Well, it wasn't exactly her approval I was worrying about. I just thought it might be nice if she were invited to the wedding!" Honor flared.

"You can invite her if you wish. I don't mind picking up an extra airline ticket for her," Conn said.

"The police may have more questions for us to answer during the next few days," Honor fretted.

"They know where to find us."

"I have clients to see," Honor went on doggedly. "I really shouldn't take any more time off just now."

"We can plan a honeymoon for some other time. You won't be away from Pasadena except overnight. Not unless you want to take some time off again to go away for a few days."

"My mother—"

"We'll notify her," Conn said promptly. "Later, when we take the honeymoon we can visit her, if you like."

Honor groped for other excuses and found she had exhausted the lot. Except for the truth. "It's just too soon, Conn. I need time."

He drained his coffee and set down the mug with an air of finality. "You're stalling."

"Well, maybe I am!" she blurted, feeling cornered.

"Why should you want to stall?" he challenged softly. "You love me, remember? I can make you come alive with passion. I've saved your neck. We share a bond that goes back fifteen years. We're committed to each other. Are you going to deny it?"

"No, I'm not denying it but I'll be darned if I'll let you push me into marriage when you don't know how you feel toward me!"

He stared at her in astonishment. "What the devil do you think you're saying? I know how I feel toward you. You're mine. I'll take care of you, protect you, make love to you. What more to do you want from me?"

"Love! I want you to understand that what you feel for me is love!" She could no longer control her tongue. Her emotions overwhelmed her, causing her to say things she was very much afraid she would regret later. Already she could see the anger beginning to burn in Conn's eyes. It frightened her, but she couldn't stop.

He reached out and caught her wrist, removing the coffee mug from her fingers and dragging her across his chest. Beneath dark lashes he gazed grimly down at her. "I asked you once if you wanted me to lie to you. You said no. Have you changed your mind?"

"No, of course not," she gasped.

"Then are you trying to blackmail me into saying the words you want to hear? Are you setting a trap of your own, Honor?

Trying to push me into a corner by saying I can't have you unless I do things your way?''

"Typical of you to decide that I'm trying to trap you. You're the one who's so skilled at weaving webs, remember? I fell into all the nets you strung, all down the line, but it stops here. You want everything from me but you're not willing to give everything of yourself. I want a man who is as vulnerable to me as I am to him. I don't want a one-sided relationship, Conn."

"Vulnerable?" he grated. "I doubt you even know the meaning of the word. Vulnerable people don't survive long in this world unless they've got someone else to take care of them."

"I'll take care of you," she promised rashly. "I won't betray you or hurt you. I love you."

"You seem to enjoy your power over me," she flung back furiously.

"You meant that you wouldn't be playing word games with me."

"You don't understand," she cried.

"You're trying to force me into conforming to your mental image of a husband and a lover. You want to know you have power over me. That's what you really mean by *vulnerable*, isn't it? You want to know I'm weak when it comes to you.''

"So you're trying to even the score?''

"Maybe I don't happen to like unbalanced accounts, either! You're not the only one with a monopoly on keeping the score even." By now she was no longer making any attempt to keep her words rational and calm. Honor's emotions had taken over completely as she sensed herself being pushed into yet another of Constantine Landry's intricate webs.

"You don't have any choice in this case," he told her savagely.

"**You** belong to me."

"**It** works both ways."

"All right, so I belong to you. That's grounds for marriage, lady."

"It's grounds for an affair," she retorted. "Not marriage."

"You're going to split hairs over a four-letter word?" he demanded.

"Love is more than a four-letter word. If that's all it was, you wouldn't have so much trouble dealing with it!''

"I'm beginning to realize exactly what it does mean," he said grittily. "In your mind, at least. It means vulnerability and weakness and a knowledge of your own power over me. Admit it, Honor. That's what you're looking for.''

She stared up at him helplessly. ''If that's what you think it means, then there's not much point in continuing this discussion, is there?''

His jaw tightened as he sensed her weary withdrawal from the argument. ''Oh, no, you don't, Honor. You're not backing out of this that easily. You're going to marry me. I'll make you a good husband. There will always be honesty between us. Honesty and commitment. And passion. Nothing else matters.''

She fought for composure. ''You mean it wouldn't bother you at all if I stopped loving you? As long as I continued to supply my share of the honesty and commitment? Oh, and the passion, naturally.''

He looked slightly startled. The expression was immediately replaced with a taut frown. ''What you call your love for me is really your sense of being vulnerable to me. And you can't change that, honey. By marrying me you'll be admitting that you trust me with that kind of power. I won't abuse that trust.''

''You're the one who's playing word games.'' Freeing her wrist, Honor slipped away from him. He let her go, watching through narrowed eyes as she tugged a robe out of the closet and tied the sash. When she dared meet his gaze again she realized that all the soft, gentle comfort she had known from him during the night had vanished. The predatory challenge was radiating from Conn in a way that effectively destroyed her last hopes.

''You're throwing a tantrum because you can't find a way to reassure yourself that you have as much control over me as I do over you. That's all this is about, isn't it?'' he asked icily.

''From the beginning you seem to have been manipulating me,'' she said, sighing. ''You've woven so many webs around me that I haven't always been able to think straight. I suppose that's why you now assume I'm trying to reverse the process. I'm not, Conn, but I've got to draw the line somewhere.''

''So you can keep the books balanced?''

''You taught me the importance of that.'' She turned and walked into the bathroom, not trusting herself to stay in the same room with him any longer. Mingled despair and anger were causing her to be almost as unsteady as fear had the previous night. Honor decided she was sick and tired of being at the mercy of such strong emotions. They took too much out of a person, send ing her to euphoric highs one moment and despairing lows the next.

As she switched on the shower, she lectured herself on control. The kind of self-control Conn seemed able to exert much of the time was suddenly an enviable attribute. She'd work on it, Honor vowed as she stepped under the spray. She'd work very hard to develop it. No more would she allow herself to be swept up in her responses to Conn. Never again would she allow him to manipulate her or weave nets around her. She was a strong-minded woman, or at least she always had been. You didn't make a success out of yourself in Southern California without a fair degree of fortitude and determination. She could handle Conn Landry on her terms. She would force him to acknowledge his true feelings, force him to become really emotionally committed to her. She didn't want a man whose sense of commitment seemed to stem almost entirely from the harsher sides of his masculine nature. Possessiveness, sexual satisfaction, a feeling of protectiveness were strong factors, important factors. But they fell short of love.

Honor was still telling herself that fifteen minutes later when she stepped out of the bathroom and discovered Conn had left the apartment.

Twenty minutes after he'd stormed out of Honor's apartment, Conn walked into the barn where Humphrey stabled the Thoroughbreds in his care. Two grooms with whom he was on friendly terms took one look at the expression on his face and discreetly disappeared. A goat that had free run of the stables because it had a calming effect on the high-strung horses showed the intelligence goats are noted for and ambled off out of range.

Conn found Legacy's stall and came to a halt. The colt turned inquiringly and didn't seem particularly put off by the dark tension in the man. He shuffled to the door and thrust his nose into Conn's hand.

"Sorry, fella. Absolutely nothing special for you today. You have to run tomorrow. Can't take any risks," Conn murmured, stroking the sleek neck. The horse's ears pricked at the approach of another man.

"Hello, Landry," the trainer said easily as he came to stand in front of Legacy's stall. "Come to check up on your horse?" Humphrey peered perceptively at his client. "He's looking very good. Very good indeed. No reason he shouldn't do as well for you tomorrow as he did in his last race. I've scheduled Eddie

Campbell to ride him. Told him to hold him back a bit at the start and then just let him have his head.''

Conn nodded, only half listening to the familiar trainer patter. If Legacy lost tomorrow there would be an equally reassuring patter listing all the reasons why: The track was muddy, the horse was too nervous, the jockey didn't handle him right on the course and so on. It was all part of the horse-racing scene. Just like the rumor mill. Conn wondered if any rumors about Ethan Bailey had filtered into the network yet. Apparently not, because Humphrey didn't mention them. The trainer came to the end of his analysis of the horse and then arched an eyebrow inquiringly at his client.

''Did you have a question?''

''No,'' Conn shook his head, unable to come up with any form of idle conversation. What he really wanted right now was to be alone. He probably shouldn't have come to the track. But the thought of going back to his hotel room was depressing. ''Just wanted to take another look at Legacy. Do you think he has the potential of his sire?''

''Stylish Legacy? I believe he does.'' Humphrey nodded toward the colt. ''Legacy got the best of Stylish Legacy's genes, if you ask me. Good shoulders, strong hindquarters. Smart. Fast. Likes to run. Can't ask for more from a horse.''

How much could you ask of a woman, Conn wondered silently. How much could a woman ask of a man? Legacy was a friendly animal, willing to give his all on the racetrack. He'd respond with everything that was in him when called upon. But that didn't mean he was emotionally involved with human beings.

*Damn it,* Conn thought violently, *I'm going crazy. How dumb can you get, Landry? You can't draw parallels between animals and humans. Not when it comes to relationships.*

''Well, I'll be around if you need me,'' Humphrey announced with a nod of farewell. ''Want to use the box today?''

''No thanks. I'm not going to watch the races.''

Humphrey nodded again and departed, leaving Conn alone with his horse. Absently he continued to stroke Legacy's nose.

Honor wouldn't be able to maintain the distance she had put between them this morning, Conn told himself. He had been saying the words in various formats since he'd left the apartment. In her own words, she was vulnerable to him. She wanted him, needed him. Hell, she loved him! And she knew he was committed to her. She *knew* it! She had to know it in the depths of her soul. He'd never felt like this about any other woman. The impact she had made on him had thrown his whole life off balance.

He knew his impact on her had been equally strong. He was sure of it in his bones. She couldn't hide the completeness with which she surrendered in his arms. Yet she had balked at taking the final step of marriage. Conn racked his brain trying to understand why. He had accused her of wanting power over him, but now he wasn't so certain. Another infinitely more devastating possibility flashed through his thoughts.

What if she was nervous about formalizing their relationship for the simple reason that she still didn't trust him?

Conn's hand stopped moving on Legacy's nose as the knowledge exploded within him. Of course she trusted him. She had to trust him. She'd said she'd trusted him, damn it!

But something was holding her back from making the final commitment. She claimed she wanted love, and Conn had told her that she was using the word to mean power. But perhaps he had been wrong. Perhaps what the word really meant was trust.

Legacy nuzzled Conn's shoulder in a puzzled fashion, seeking more attention. When Conn didn't oblige, but simply stood staring unseeingly into the stall, the colt moved philosophically back to his feed.

It was intolerable to think that she might not trust him after all they had been through, Conn thought, dazed. Absolutely intolerable. The realization that she might lack faith in him was shattering in its intensity. Didn't she understand that he would do virtually anything for her? Protect her with his life?

Conn turned away from the stall and walked as if in a dream to the far end of the long barn. There he found a bench. No one was around. Slowly he sank down onto the hard wood surface and tried to understand what was happening to him.

He trusted her, he thought. Completely. At least he assumed he did. But perhaps he hadn't actually trusted her to know her own mind. She'd said she was in love with him. And he hadn't really trusted her to know what she meant.

She must think him incredibly arrogant. And he was, Conn realized. Unbelievably arrogant. How could she trust him totally if she knew deep in her heart that he didn't even trust her to know her own mind? When you gave something, you wanted something equally valuable in return. He hadn't given her what she needed.

Instinct guided Honor as she drove out of the underground garage and headed toward the freeway. Conn would head for the track. She knew it intuitively. It was where she would go if she were he. He wasn't the type to sit and sulk in his hotel room.

What a fool she had been this morning. She'd risked so much for so little. Conn was right. She'd been playing word games, searching for reassurance when all along she'd known intellectually that he was giving her everything he had to give a woman. She would find him and tell him that it was enough, more than enough. She loved him and what he felt for her had to be very close to that emotion. What did it matter if he couldn't or wouldn't verbalize it?

If only she'd kept her head this morning and not allowed emotions to rule her tongue. Bitterly Honor castigated herself for the way she'd handled Conn's proposal of marriage.

Except that it hadn't actually been a proposal, she reminded herself with a rueful sigh. Perhaps if he'd actually asked her properly instead of arrogantly assuming she would want to marry him as quickly as possible she wouldn't have lost her temper and her head.

Life with Conn was not going to be entirely uncomplicated. The man was made of iron, and he surrounded himself with almost invincible emotional barriers.

But they weren't totally invincible and that was what she had to keep in mind. It would take work getting him to trust her to the point where he could lower them, perhaps years of work. Honor told herself she was more than willing to make the effort to gain his complete, unqualified trust. She had no choice because she loved him.

She parked the car in the lot and made her way to the barns, flashing the visitor's badge Conn had provided for her. Then Honor turned toward Legacy's stable. Blinking a little as she walked from brilliant sunlight into cool shade, she glanced around and saw the horse looking out of his stall. There was no sign of Conn. Slowly she walked toward Legacy, wondering if she'd been wrong in her guess as to where Conn had gone.

"Hello, Legacy," she murmured soothingly. "Have you seen him?"

The horse went into his attention-getting routine, nuzzling her shoulder. Honor obliged for a few moments, her gaze searching the shaded interior of the long barn. It took a while before she realized Conn was watching her from a bench at the far end of the building.

He didn't move as she turned to look at him, but his eyes absorbed the sight of her standing there in the jeans and bright-coral sweater in which she had hastily dressed. Honor had been so certain of what she wanted to say when she left the apartment, but now she couldn't seem to get the words straight in her head. Slowly she lowered her hand from Legacy's muzzle. Then she started toward Conn.

He stood up as she approached, the lean, tough quality of his body outlined beneath snug jeans and a white long-sleeved shirt. He let her come to him, not moving as she walked forward. There was a moment when Honor feared she had made the wrong decision, taken too big a risk. It seemed to her in those few seconds that the predatory side of him was the ruling side and that she stood no chance of suppressing it. Then she was close enough to read his eyes and at that point nothing could have kept her from going into his arms. She ran the last few steps, coming into his waiting embrace with a small rush. His arms tightened around her with reassuring urgency.

"I'm sorry, Conn," she whispered breathlessly. "I never meant to push you this morning. Of course I'll marry you, if you'll still have me. We belong to each other. I don't know why I doubted it. I know you'll give me everything you can of yourself. I realize you wouldn't talk of commitment unless you meant it. What more could I ask for?"

His hands moved roughly on her back. "How about a little trust?" His voice was hoarse with barely controlled emotion.

She lifted her head from his shoulder, her eyes widening in shock. "You trust me, don't you?"

"I thought I did, Honor," he groaned, pulling her head back down against his shirt. His fingers tangled in her hair. "I sure as hell trusted you more than I've trusted anyone else for longer than I care to remember. But in the final analysis, I guess I didn't trust you completely."

Panic surged through her. "But why? What have I done to make you think I'd betray you? I thought everything was resolved between us. I love you, Conn."

"That's the part I wasn't willing to believe. I didn't give you credit for knowing your own mind because you were talking about an emotion I've never really believed existed. I stormed out of the apartment this morning thinking that you were simply trying to push me into saying the words you wanted to hear, that you wanted to hear them because they would give you some assurance of your own power over me.''

"No—," she began desperately but he silenced her gently with his hand.

"Even though I was furious, I had to admit that you had the right to know that I wasn't going to dominate the relationship completely. It must seem to you that I've been running things between us from the beginning. I tracked you down, engineered our first meeting, kept tightening the strands of the web until there was nowhere for you to turn except into my arms. I thought that by demanding some wild declaration of love from me, you were really just trying to reassert yourself in the relationship.''

"I was, but not because I wanted to control you,'' she explained in despair.

"I realize that,'' he admitted thickly, lacing his fingers at the nape of her neck and bending his forehead down until it touched hers. "Now I realize it. I didn't trust you enough to give your feelings and emotions full credit. I kept trying to assume that what I felt had to be what you felt. You were either mislabeling or dramatizing or looking for a wedge. I didn't trust you to simply have fallen in love with me.''

Honor heard the aching unhappiness in him and her arms went around his waist. "And now?'' she whispered tremulously, her eyes bright with unshed tears.

"I trust you, sweetheart. Really trust you.'' He caught her chin under his thumbs and lifted her mouth for a quick, hard kiss that conveyed the full scope of his feelings. When he freed her mouth he went on huskily. "I want everything you can give me, including this thing you call love. I'm not altogether sure just what you mean by it but I want it.''

"It's yours, Conn. It will always be yours.''

He shook his head once. "I'll give you everything I can in return, honey.''

"I know.''

"I'm not sure yet just what that includes. Will that hurt you? I can't bear to hurt you.''

"No,'' she denied. "You won't hurt me if you give yourself as completely as possible. And I know you will. With you, there is no other way.''

He exhaled slowly, as if a great weight had been lifted from him. Then Conn folded her close, holding her in silence for a long moment before he spoke again.

"Vegas?"

She nodded her head against his chest. "Yes."

"I'll get the tickets this afternoon. Do you want Adena to go with us?"

"It's not necessary. She'll understand. I was just using her as an excuse this morning."

"You were looking for a way out," he growled.

"I guess I wasn't able to trust you completely at that point, either."

"And now?"

"Now I do," she told him simply.

"I thought we'd settled all that at the beach cottage." He sighed, easing her against his side so that he could start them back down the length of the barn.

"We talked about trust and we promised it to each other, but we didn't think about all that it meant. We assumed it was only a matter of telling the truth about facts. We didn't realize it also meant trusting each other's emotions and feelings," Honor said with a small smile. "But I expect we can make a few excuses for ourselves. After all, everything has been happening so quickly. It's no wonder we were still feeling our way with each other this morning."

Conn nodded wryly. "I was sitting there on that bench a little while ago, trying to think of how to approach you. I've finally realized just how arrogant I must seem to you."

"Terribly arrogant at times," she agreed cheerfully.

He winced. "I'm going to try very hard to control that part of me."

"Uh-huh."

He slid her a sidelong glance. "You sound skeptical."

"You don't seem worried about it any longer," he noted with interest. His gunmetal eyes softened, and Honor could have sworn there was both relief and amusement in his gaze.

"Oh, I believe you'll try," she told him with a tiny grin.

"But not that I'll succeed?"

"I think it's a very basic part of you. And I think it's been well tempered over the years."

"I imagine I'll be obliged to point out the error of your ways occasionally to you in the future. Part of my wifely duties,"

"You can yell at me until doomsday as long as you marry me," he assured her emphatically. Then he brought them to a short stop in front of Legacy's stall. The colt thrust his head out again and eyed the two humans curiously.

"You're going to win tomorrow, aren't you?" Honor asked the animal.

"He'll run his heart out," Conn said quietly. "He'll give it all he's got out there on the course."

Honor glanced at Conn as she patted the horse. His face had reset into harsh, all too familiar lines. "Legacy's a fine horse," she observed tentatively.

"But he'll run because he was born and trained to do exactly that. And there's an instinct in him that makes him want to lead the pack. That makes him a winner. But he doesn't run and win to please me or Humphrey or the guy on his back. He doesn't do it for any of us. He does it because that's just the way he is."

Honor hesitated, trying to read between the lines. "Are you trying to tell me something, Conn?"

Conn swung his gaze from the colt to Honor's face. "Legacy's not emotionally involved with humans except on a very superficial level. He enjoys our company but he could get along fine without any of us as long as he had access to food and other horses."

Honor felt as though she were missing something important, but she couldn't put her finger on it. "Well, he is an animal, after all."

"Just an animal," Conn repeated in a low voice.

"And he operates on his own kind of logic. I understand." She smiled. "Still, if he does win tomorrow I'd like to think he's doing it as a wedding present for us."

Conn relaxed and took her arm again. "Speaking of a wedding, I have to go get one arranged. Why don't you go on back to the apartment? I'll meet you there as soon as I've made the reservations."

"All right."

But Honor still had the feeling she had missed a crucial piece of communication from Conn. He walked her out to the parking lot in silence. She nodded in the direction of her car and he turned to guide her toward it. She was struggling to find a way to ask him if there wasn't something more he wanted to say on the subject of Legacy when two men dressed in a style that was strongly reminiscent of Granger walked out from between a row of parked cars.

"Damn." Conn stopped abruptly, yanking Honor to a halt beside him. "Why is it that just when I think everything's finally settled with all the loose ends tied up, something like this happens?''

It was clearly a rhetorical question and neither of the two men seemed inclined to respond to it directly. Large diamond rings flashed in the sunlight as one of the men made an apologetic gesture.

''We're here on behalf of Mr. Granger,'' the first man began.

''I was afraid of that,'' Conn groaned.

Honor felt the tension in him, but it wasn't the coiled, lethal kind of tension she had sensed when they had faced first Tony and then Ethan Bailey. This time Conn seemed wary but not unduly alarmed. Honor wished she could be that much at ease around two men who had openly stated they worked for a loan shark, but it was impossible. Living in Southern California might give one a certain amount of panache, but there were limits.

''Mr. Granger would like you to know that he's really sorry about the inconvenience you've recently experienced at the hands of a certain person named Tony,'' the second man said very civilly. ''Mr. Granger don't do hits. And he don't like people saying they're on his payroll when they ain't. He told us to keep an eye out for the aforementioned person here at the track. Just in case. We been watching most carefully. Me, I said old Tony would be heading for the border, but Joe here figured he might just try to sneak back. Looks as if I lose another one to Joe.''

The man called Joe grunted but said nothing.

''Mr. Landry?'' the first man said with an air of grave politeness. ''Mr. Granger says to tell you he's really sorry about all this. He'll take responsibility for cleaning up the mess. Says you and him had a deal and he don't want you to think he reneged.''

Conn kept his fingers wrapped around Honor's arm. ''Tell Mr. Granger I appreciate his integrity. Tough to find businessmen with integrity these days.''

''Mr. Granger looks after his reputation,'' Joe remarked with a certain air of pride. He obviously appreciated the fact that he worked for a man with a good business reputation.

''I'm aware that Mr. Granger's word can be relied upon,'' Conn said coolly.

''Good.'' The other man nodded. ''He'll be pleased to hear that. Well, no sense holding you folks any longer. Just wanted you to know Mr. Granger has taken care of things.''

''Do I assume, then, that you've picked up Tony?'' Conn asked quietly.

"Got him trying to sneak into the barns," Joe said with obvious satisfaction. "Mr. Granger was real pleased. Picked him up an hour ago."

"You picked him up?" Honor broke in, startled. "You've got Tony?"

"Yes, ma'am. No need for further worry."

"But what are you going to do with him?" she gasped, ignoring Conn's suddenly tightening grip.

"Why, ma'am, we intend to make certain Tony don't go around misrepresenting himself in the future," she was told very gently.

"If...if I might suggest," Honor began carefully.

"Honor, shut up," Conn hissed under his breath.

She licked her lips as the first man and Joe turned polite, inquiring gazes on her. "Just...just a thought," she managed weakly.

"What's that, ma'am?"

Behind her Conn groaned and his fingers dug into her arm. She knew he was ready to yank her back against him and shut her mouth completely if she said anything dangerous.

"The police are already looking for Tony. They want him in connection with a certain, uh, incident over on the coast. You say your Mr. Granger doesn't do, er, hits?"

"We can handle Tony," Joe explained as though she weren't very bright.

"Honor, these gentlemen know what they're doing," Conn began firmly.

"I was only going to suggest that they turn him over to the cops. Then Mr. Granger wouldn't have to worry about him and neither would we. It would certainly keep things cleaner for your boss," she added helpfully to the one called Joe. "He wouldn't have to get his hands dirty protecting his reputation. He could let the police do it for him. Don't you think he'd appreciate that?"

To everyone's apparent astonishment, Joe seemed to find the suggestion mildly interesting. "I'll pass your notion along to the boss," he finally said with a nod. "He might like it. Might at that. Appeal to his sense of humor. Come on, Carl. Let's go see Mr. Granger."

The two men disappeared down the row of parked cars.

Honor was left shivering in Conn's grasp. She turned stricken eyes up to meet his wry expression. "Do you think they'll kill him?" she asked uneasily.

"Honor, you're a babe in the woods." He sighed. "Too naïve for your own good."

"I am not naïve! I'm from Southern California. No one is naïve out here!" she exploded.

"It's all right, honey," he soothed. "I'll take care of you."

"Well, if your lack of naïveté is due to the fact that you've been dealing with people like Granger and Joe and Carl and Bailey and Tony all your life, then you're the one who needs protection. I'm the one who's going to have to take care of you. I'll keep you from getting mixed up with bad company."

He glanced down at her in surprise as he opened the door of her car for her. "I never thought of it like that. You may have a point."

He bent down to kiss her possessively and then slammed the door shut.

# TWELVE

Legacy won by a full three lengths the following afternoon. No sooner had the results flashed on the board than Conn was dragging his new bride at a dead run toward the winner's circle. Adena, who had attended the races with Conn and Honor, grinned delightedly as she hastened along beside her sister.

Laughing with excitement, Honor allowed herself to be swept up in Conn's wake, her new gold band sparkling in the sunlight. Breathlessly she stood beside Legacy's proud owner as the photograph was taken. The usual assortment of gawkers, pranksters and miscellaneous folk crowded into the shot but no one minded. Least of all the colt who tossed his head with spirited arrogance.

"Are you quite sure he isn't emotionally involved in all this?" Honor murmured to Conn as she watched the groom and trainer lead the horse back toward the barns.

Conn's mouth curved briefly. "I'll admit that at the moment it's tough to tell just what that horse is thinking."

"He gave you both a great wedding gift," Adena observed. "When are you leaving for the beach house?"

"Just as soon as I can get Honor back to the parking lot and into the car," Conn vowed determinedly.

"Don't you just love a forceful man?" Adena cooed mockingly to her sister.

"Just this particular forceful man," Honor replied so softly that no one heard her.

"How long are you going to be gone?" Adena went on interestedly.

"Just a couple of days." Conn was striding briskly through the crowd, towing the two women behind him. "Honor has to get back to work. She's finishing some projects and can't afford to be away too long."

"That was great news about the police locating that awful Tony person, wasn't it?" Adena commented. "Imagine finding him locked inside a tack room. Makes you wonder how he got inside in the first place, doesn't it?"

"It certainly does," Conn said with great feeling. "Racing gear is expensive, though. They have to keep it locked up. I suppose Tony went into one of those rooms and someone came along behind him and shut and locked the door, not realizing he was inside."

"Sure." Honor grinned. "And then a casually patrolling guard just happened to check the tack room and find him. Recognized him instantly and turned him over to the cops. Very neat."

Conn slanted her a look. "Very." He paused. "You're looking a trifle smug, darling."

"Am I?" Honor feigned surprise.

"Listen," Adena broke in, waving energetically at a young man dressed in leather and silk, "I see someone I know. He'll give me a ride home. Have a good time at the beach and I'll see you when you get back. We'll throw a real bash. 'Bye!"

Conn swung an assessing glance at the young man in the exotic clothes. "You know him?"

"Oh, yes. That's Jason. He's very sweet, really. Works in the men's department of a local high-style boutique. Adena's dated him on and off for ages. Quite safe, Conn. You don't have to play big brother."

He shrugged and turned back to the task of getting her out to the waiting Porsche. "I only do it for your sake," he explained almost apologetically.

"What? Play big brother?" Honor smiled. "I know. You're trying to assume the responsibility so that I won't have to watch out for her. But I've been keeping tabs on Adena for years. And she's really getting to be quite grown-up. Soon she won't need anyone watching over her."

"As long as you worry about her, I'll worry about her, I suppose." Conn reached the Porsche and opened the passenger door.

"I know." But she wound up saying the words to herself because he'd already closed the door. He would worry about Adena because he was in love with Honor and what affected Honor, affected Conn. It was an intricate, tightly woven web, one neither of them could escape. And one day, Honor promised herself, Conn would know that the kind of emotional involvement he was feeling was called love.

Conn slid into the driver's seat and thrust the key into the ignition. There was a strange mixture of satisfaction and hunger in his expression. The combination had been there since last evening when he'd slipped the ring on Honor's finger and repeated his vows. She still shivered when she remembered the passionate, possessive way he had made love to her later in the elegant hotel room.

The drive back up the coast to the beach cottage was a pleasant one. The sun was shining but the clouds were gathering far out at sea. There would be a storm later, Honor knew. The thought of a pleasant fire in the fireplace and a glass of warm brandy made her smile. By the time she and Conn unlocked the front door of the cottage she was feeling surprisingly content with life.

The first thing she noticed as she walked back into the cottage was that she no longer experienced that vague air of depression she had always sensed in the past. The beach house felt right, now. No lingering questions or disquieting memories. It felt good.

Conn took her for a long walk on the beach before they sat down to a home-cooked meal of paella and wine. Honor teased her new mate about his ability in the kitchen and he assured her she had gotten a real bargain of a husband.

It wasn't until they were sitting together on the sofa in front of the fire, sipping brandy, that Honor's gaze fell on the old iron-and-wood trunk. She stared at it thoughtfully for a long moment. "What are you thinking, honey?" Conn asked softly.

"I was just wondering what, exactly, might be hidden in that old trunk. I never really did go through Dad's stuff properly. It was just too painful a process. Maybe it's time I took a look."

Conn watched her for a moment or two and then without a word he got to his feet and went across the room to unlatch the iron lock. The top groaned as he pushed it open. Honor stood up and went across the room to join him, looking down into the trunk.

"Just more photos and form books and copies of the racing trade journals," she observed. Kneeling, she began to lift out some of the yellowed papers. Conn dropped down onto one knee beside her.

They spent nearly two hours going through the contents of the trunk. Much of the time was taken up by Conn who paused to read everything he found on Stylish Legacy.

"Humphrey says Legacy might do just as well as his sire in another year or so," he told Honor proudly. "Then we'll retire him to stud."

"Legacy will probably enjoy that." Honor grinned, reaching for yet another folded copy of the *Daily Racing Form*. "Being a male, he probably does a lot of thinking and fantasizing about that sort of thing.''

"There you go again," Conn complained. He stopped as a small, leather-bound book fell from the folded newspaper. "What's that?"

"Looks like a diary or a notebook," Honor said, turning the volume over and over in her hands. She opened it cautiously and stared at the bold scrawl on the pages inside. "My father's. I'm sure of it. It looks like some sort of financial record.''

"Here, let me see." Conn reached over to take the book from her hand. "You're right. It's a running account of a debt. Want to take a guess who was being systematically paid every three months?''

"Ethan Bailey?" Honor leaned over his shoulder to peer down at the page in front of him.

Conn nodded. "There had to be some record. You just don't borrow a huge sum of money from a man like Ethan Bailey and not keep track of the payback. It's all here. A good accountant could probably trace the whole history of the transaction, given this book.''

"And prove that Bailey was involved with Dad and Stoner," Honor concluded. "I don't know how far that would get us, though. It's been so long.''

Conn kept turning the pages, working his way toward the back of the volume. The precise account of the debt continued to be recorded, but now there were remarks at the bottom of the page. Conn paused so that he and Honor could read them.

"Dick says he's getting uneasy feelings about Bailey. Says there's something about the man he just doesn't trust,''' Conn read.

"Dick was your stepfather?" Honor asked curiously. "Short for Richard?''

"Right. Listen to this." Conn picked another passage and read it aloud.

I have to agree with Dick. This business with Bailey needs to be checked out. I'm going to start leaving more complete notations in this account book. It will serve as a record in the event that what Dick and I fear is taking place is actually happening. If we're wrong, Ethan will never need to know we distrusted him. If we're right, the new firm of Stoner &

Mayfield is in big trouble. A scandal of this size will be difficult to smash.

From there on, the details of suspected weapons smuggling were given along with the name of the man who was selling information. There was a brief description of the trap that had been set and then there were no further entires in the leather volume.

Honor sighed a long time later as Conn closed the book and set it back inside the trunk. "It's all there."

"Do you want to make it public? I still don't think we could make it stick. It's an old tale and it happened in a foreign country a long time ago."

"I wonder what story Bailey is giving the police?"

Conn shook his head. "I doubt he'll open up that weapons-smuggling scandal. He's too smart to raise more questions about his past than necessary."

"But what if he does, Conn? He could drag our fathers' names through the mud again."

"This time around we'll have the book." He indicated the leather volume.

"That might not stop him," Honor fretted. "Bailey might decide he's got nothing to lose. We never really thought about that aspect of it. If he talks, really talks, it will open the whole mess up again."

"I think we could both survive another round of scandal, don't you?" Conn asked softly.

She smiled gently. "I think we could survive just about anything together."

He reached out to close the trunk. "This is such old news now that very few people would be interested, anyway. Except, naturally, for the folks who hang around racetracks. It would probably just focus a lot of attention on Legacy. Make a mystery horse out of him or something. Might be just the touch of magic he needs to make his name in racing circles. Great horses always have stories and myths told about them."

Honor couldn't help it; she broke out laughing. "You're one very determined owner, Conn Landry. You've got the fever."

He straightened and reached down to pull her into his arms, his gunmetal eyes suddenly intent. "Not nearly as bad as the fever I've got for you, Honor Mayfield Landry. And I think I've finally got a word to describe it. It's been burning in my mind ever since I made you my wife."

She went still in his arms. "Has it, Conn?"

"I love you, Honor." The words came from him in a thick, husky voice that shook her to the core. "I don't know why it took me so long to realize it. But I know. I'm sure now. So very sure."

"I'm glad, Conn," she whispered, touching the side of his face with gentle fingertips. "I love you so much."

"I'm sorry it took me all this time to get the words straight. I was worrying about other things, like trust and honesty. I didn't stop to realize until tonight that I wouldn't have been so concerned about those other things if I wasn't already in love with you. It's all so simple once you look at it from the right direction. Heaven only knows why I was so blind."

"As you said, you had other things on your mind." She smiled invitingly. "But I was sure that you weren't a racehorse."

"What?" He looked blank.

"That's what you meant earlier, wasn't it? When you talked about the reasons Legacy runs and wins? You told me he wasn't emotionally involved with humans. He gives them his best when they ask it of him, but he does it because that's just the way he is. But you're involved with me, Conn. You don't protect me and care for me and occasionally yell at me just because I ask it of you. I never did actually ask it of you, as I recall," she added thoughtfully. "I knew you did all that because you were involved on some deeper level than even you realized. At least, that's what I kept telling myself."

"Completely involved. I've never been so involved with another human being before in my life! I know it sounds ridiculous but I knew I didn't want it any other way with you. I didn't want to be separated from you in some manner. I didn't want to be like Legacy. I'm a human being, not some Thoroughbred who doesn't really need people." He seized her abruptly, lifting her high into his arms with a fierce joy. "I knew I needed you, honey, but I thought most of that need was tied in with the way I wanted you physically. But it's so much more. I never understood. I just never understood."

His surging wonder was contagious. Honor's own happiness was shining in her eyes as Conn carried her into the bedroom.

The storm that had been building out at sea broke just as Conn came down onto the bed alongside Honor. He gathered her into his arms, all the words that had once been so alien to his tongue tumbling forth in a glorious litany of love.

"Hold me," he breathed as he flowed over her body and let himself sink into her welcoming warmth. "Hold me, Honor. I love you so much."

Honor held him, giving herself up to the passion that was binding them together as Conn proved beyond a doubt that he was, indeed, emotionally involved with her.

Conn Landry knew how to love.

# NO STRANGER
# STELLA CAMERON

## Chapter One

"What love life?" Nick laughed. He leaned against the window frame and twined the telephone cord through his fingers.

"Don't fence with me, Nick Dorset. Who are you seeing? We all refuse to believe you've turned into a saint. I'm your sister, remember? I know you."

Some things never changed. "Sure you know me, Janet. Boy, do you know me." He enjoyed the calls from his sister in Omaha. The banter was always so comfortably predictable. Janet, two years older than himself and ecstatic over marriage and motherhood, felt it her duty to nag him into similar bliss.

"Are you listening to me?" Janet demanded his attention.

"Sure, sis, I always listen to you. And I know everyone in the family thinks it's time I settled down and had ten kids. Unfortunately, no one's offered to fill the bill."

"You mean you never give anyone the chance to offer, or accept, either." Janet's high silvery voice sputtered along the line. Nick was twenty-nine, she persisted. He'd had his flings. He was established. If he had to settle in a dreary, wet place like Seattle, at least he could have the comfort of a wife to share his home and to come back to from all those awful planes he piloted. Didn't he ever think of giving up flying? They'd all thought he would be tired of playing airplanes by the time he got out of the air force.

"Mmm. Nope. Not yet, Janet. I enjoy commercial flying even more than the service. Faraway places with strange-sounding names and all that. The only thing I'd like better would be my own planes—my own business. But that'll come in time." Absently he twisted the rod to open the vertical slats of the wood blinds. Instantly the gray light of an October afternoon made fuzzy lines on the opposite wall. He'd lived on Seattle's east side for six months, and the area's moody grandeur never bored him.

"By the way," he added. "Seattle isn't dreary, kiddo. Wet, but never dreary. I'll have to get you out here sometime."

"Don't change the subject, Nick. You left a trail of disappointed hearts behind you here. There *has* to be a woman in your life. You just aren't talking.''

He sobered. This sister, physically so like him, also had an uncanny habit of picking up emotional vibes he'd hardly acknowledged. ''Rein in that imagination, Janet.'' The muscles in his broad back had tightened unconsciously and he shrugged, trying to relax. ''How's wonder kid and Crete?'' *What kind of name is Crete?* He smiled despite himself. Janet's husband might have an unlikely name, but he was a decent sort, and Nick thoroughly enjoyed him.

''Great.'' Her voice became warmer. ''Oh, Nick, it's so good to have someone to share everything with. And Penny's gorgeous. Her ballet teacher says...''

Nick tuned out. He'd have several minutes in neutral before he was forced to add anything to the exchange. Two-year-old Penny was a subject on which Janet could expound indefinitely and without prompting. He let the words pour over him. He could see Janet, tall and well built, her tawny eyes flashing animation while she repeatedly pushed back her wavy brown hair. He realized one of his hands was buried in his hair right now and shook his head slightly. As teenagers, they'd often been mistaken for twins.

A vehicle door slammed outside. He edged around the bay window to sit on the arm of a dining chair. From there he had a clear view of the corner outside his condominium building. His unit, on the third floor, overlooked three converging streets.

''I know you'd love to watch her,'' Janet was saying.

''You bet I would,'' he agreed, narrowing his eyes to see who was loading a chest of drawers into a U-Haul truck parked directly in front of the Lake Vista condos. ''You'll have to let me sit in on a lesson next time I get home. But isn't she a little young for ballet?''

''The best dancers start at two. Her teacher told me that Nureyev and Gallina...''

Russian ballet dancers, or any ballet dancers, weren't high on Nick's list of fascinating topics. The scene he was witnessing held far more interest.

Surely that was John Winston from next door. The guy was in some hurry. With the help of a man whom Nick didn't recognize, Winston bundled pieces of furniture carelessly into the truck.

A silence in his right ear snapped his concentration. ''What'd you say, Janet? There's a lot of noise on this line.'' John Winston and his buddy were shoving a rolled carpet in now. Every few seconds, John glanced over his shoulder.

"Say it again, Janet. I can't hear you." His own lack of attention wasn't helping.

Winston had stopped, holding an end table at waist height. Rubber squealed, and an old brown Pinto slowed to a halt a few feet from him. A tall woman got out, and Nick took a deep breath. The familiar jolt hit somewhere deep inside him. Abby...John Winston's *wife* Abby, he reminded himself. Her brother, Michael Harris, flew for the same airline as Nick. Michael had given him the lead on this condominium.

Nick rolled onto the balls of his feet to peer down on John and Abby Winston. John had gone into action again, shoving the table into the other man's hands, grabbing a cardboard carton. When Abby grasped his shoulder, he shrugged free and turned his face from her. She just stood there then, both hands shoved deep into the pockets of that baggy black coat she always wore. There was an ethereal quality about her, an intriguing air of deep preoccupation. She was an artist of some kind, store display design, Michael had said—whatever that meant.

Janet was asking if they should hang up.

"Right," Nick managed. Her voice was really fading in and out. He didn't feel like talking anymore. "Okay, I'll call you in a few days, and maybe we'll get a better connection. Give my love to Mom and Dad and everyone. Hug Penny for me. I should get a couple of days layover back there sometime next month...No, I don't think it'll be Thanksgiving, but as long as we see each other... Yes. Love you, too. Bye."

He reached to hook the receiver into its wall cradle. This could turn into a long day if he didn't come up with something to occupy himself. If it weren't for the fog, he'd be on his way to Honolulu, but Seatac International was socked in.

An ember spat from the fireplace. Nick hurried to retrieve it from the hearth and piled another log on the flames. He sat on his haunches, thinking, as he so often did, about John and Abby Winston. They'd proved to be disconcerting neighbors. It struck Nick that he hadn't seen John for weeks. The guy must have been on a trip. A merchant seaman, a big, handsome man, he always had a hearty greeting when they passed. He had that gift for meaningless banality that made Nick vaguely uncomfortable. Particularly when he was often forced, only minutes later, to listen to John's raised and angry voice through an adjoining wall. No audible reply ever came, and in contrast to her husband, Abby Winston had little to say in the hall or the parking lot. Invariably she muttered something indistinct before dropping her shadowy gaze. But she was beautiful. Very, very beautiful.

Nick returned to his vantage point at the window. Something odd was in progress with these people. John's job took him away regularly, sometimes for long periods, but with a U-Haul truck? No sea trip would require transporting dressers and rugs—and a grandfather clock? And why the rush? They must be moving out. The sinking feeling in his stomach was easily identifiable: disappointment. And he couldn't pretend it would be John he'd miss. He frowned. Maybe some of what Janet had said was right, and he was jealously guarding his bachelor status. Burying himself in an adolescent infatuation with a married woman who scarcely knew he was alive was a pretty safe way to stay unattached.

John threw a paper cylinder into the truck cab and hurried back into the building. Nick heard his running footsteps on the stairs and the thud of the door across the hall. The man who'd been helping load nodded to Abby and climbed into the passenger seat of the truck.

Minutes passed. Abby stood, the toes of her boots overlapping the curb, rocking slowly back and forth. The breeze that swirled the fog into shifting wisps flattened her short black curls to one side of her head. She was thin, too thin. The coat also flapped dispiritedly, first wrapping her slender back tightly, then billowing wide. Nick imagined her eyes, huge and gray, thickly lashed; the fine, upsweeping brows. Oh, Abby Winston was very beautiful all right, and very out of reach.

Footsteps sounded on the stairs again, going down this time, leaping, two, three steps at once. John Winston wanted to be gone. The woman at the curb didn't turn as her husband passed her, a kit bag over his shoulder, a large suitcase in his other hand. He hesitated a few inches from her, shrugged, threw his baggage into the truck, and latched the back handles.

Then she moved. Nerves leaped all over Nick's body. Her hands hovered close to John Winston's sleeve for seconds before she touched him, and he turned. No expression on those masculine but almost too pretty features and in the eyes that Nick knew were blue. Fair curls blew this way and that from beneath a watchman's cap while the man stood like a carving, waiting. For what?

Abby drew frantically closer, gripped both of John's arms, and in profile Nick saw her lips move. The man only shook his head and broke contact.

Instinctively Nick opened the window a few inches, knowing at the same time he was too far away to hear anything that was said.

John raised his hand and Nick did hear something. "Goodbye," John Winston's shout came. "Good luck." And now he was smiling broadly, backing away, running around to climb into the driver's seat and gunning the engine to life.

Abby's hand was also raised. The truck swung in an arc and headed west, toward the freeway. Her pale fingers remained uplifted, gradually splaying, before she dropped her arm.

At last she turned, and Nick found he couldn't breathe. She hunched, looking closely at something he couldn't make out. Her feet scuffing, she came close to the building until he had to crane to keep her in sight. Immediately below his window, she stopped, and he saw what held her interest. With the thumb and index finger of her right hand, she turned her wedding ring in slow circles. Her bowed head hid her face.

The breeze increased to a whining wind, rattling the windows. Unlikely hailstones fell in smattering handfuls against the panes. Fog and wind and hail—only in Seattle, Nick acknowledged wryly. She'd lifted her head now. She must be cold, and the hail would hurt her face.

Good, she was coming in. He stood. It wouldn't do for her to realize he'd been watching. *Oh, my God.* He leaned his forehead on the cold glass. Those haunting gray eyes were flat, and she continued to turn the ring, around and around.

In his mind, he saw again the closed gaze John Winston had given his wife. The nonchalant wave, the empty words, "Goodbye. Good luck." The running, wanting to be gone.

Abby had clutched her collar tight to her neck. Nick saw the pinched set of her normally soft, full mouth. She'd just said goodbye to her husband. And, without any proof more tangible than his own gut feeling, Nick knew it was a last parting.

John Winston wouldn't come back.

# Chapter Two

"You're uptight as hell. Are you going to make this easy on both of us and tell me what's wrong?" Marie Prince spoke with her usual harsh bluntness.

Abby wasn't in the mood for a woman-to-woman confidence session. She ignored her friend and looked around the living room. This place needed attention. Immediately. Michael was supposed to drop in on his way from the airport. If she didn't figure out a way to camouflage the gaps in the decor left by John's departure, her brother would ask questions she wasn't ready to answer. She pulled a potted areca palm beside the couch to fill a space vacated by an end table and assessed the effect. Now an empty spot glared where the grandfather clock had stood with the palm beside it.

"I'm not going to go away, Abby, so you might as well break radio silence."

"What?" Good Lord, she was losing it. For a few seconds she'd almost forgotten Marie was there, draped over the one remaining armchair. "Sorry, Marie. Guess I was thinking about something."

"That'll do for a start." Marie flipped her long honey-colored hair behind her shoulder and arranged her body more comfortably. "Why are you pacing like a caged cat? And rearranging furniture? Not typical, my friend, not at all like our dreamy girl."

"I'm not—" Why was she shouting? She never shouted. "I'm not a dreamy girl, Marie. I'm twenty-seven. Too old to be any kind of girl. And I'm not uptight. Michael's coming for lunch, and I was deciding what I could fix him, that's all. Don't you have to get back to work?" Sometimes Abby wondered why she and Marie had remained friends for so many years. They were completely different. Maybe that was the attraction. Marie was direct, always let you know exactly where you stood. Abby couldn't overcome her reticence and knew she never would.

"I've got time yet." Marie watched her narrowly, calculating. "John's been gone again for two weeks?"

Abby sank wearily onto the couch. "I don't remember telling you that."

"You don't seem to remember much these days."

She let the wise remark pass. "Yes, John's been gone again for two weeks." Two weeks since she'd had to accept that he meant to finish what he'd started.

"What did he say when you told him about your job? That must have rattled him. You were always so into display design."

Every inch of Abby's skin turned clammy. "I don't know what you're talking about." There was no way Marie could know about that.

"I tried to reach you at the store. They said you left on the fifteenth of October. I called and called you here. No answer. That's why I came over. Where have you been keeping yourself? The jerk who fired you wouldn't give me any more information."

Unfamiliar anger started a slow burn in Abby. "Connie Reese isn't a jerk. I hope you didn't give her a bad time. She couldn't tell you where I've been because she wouldn't know. And I wasn't fired. I quit after falling off a ladder. Under the circumstances, I thought I should find a job where I could keep both feet on the ground for a while."

Marie crossed her legs and leaned back. "You were probably right." Her green eyes flickered over Abby. "How are you feeling now?"

"Great." She didn't want to discuss all this. She wished Marie would leave. "Do you still like working for the secretarial agency?"

"Sure. It's a living." Her long pink nails danced, typist style, back and forth on her jean-clad knee. "And I like variety. At least I know I'll be with a new set of faces every few days."

Abby tapped her fingertips together. Whatever happened, her family mustn't get wind of the mess she was in, not yet. Yet she needed someone, a sympathetic ear.

"Abby, you didn't say what John thought about the job change. I expect he understood, didn't he? When is he coming home?"

Questions, questions. Marie had been in the condo fifteen minutes, and already Abby felt battered, exhausted by the incessant questions. "John doesn't know I quit. He walked—he left before I could tell him. I'm not sure when he'll be back. This could be another long trip." She'd better keep her own counsel, after all. Less danger of complications. Fortunately she hadn't revealed where she'd found work. "Marie, I'd love to talk with you all morning, but I'd better get on. I want to whip up some lunch for Michael.''

Marie pouted theatrically. ''Michael, Michael, Michael. Always *has* been Michael first with you. Why can't I stay for lunch, too? That brother of yours was a crummy kid, but he sure grew into some hunk, and—'' She caught Abby's eye and held up a hand. ''All right, all right, I get the message. I'm leaving.''

Abby was instantly contrite. ''I'm sorry. It's just that you and Michael rubbed each other the wrong way from the day you called him an undersized runt. Doing that to a fourteen-year-old boy in front of his first girlfriend was a good way to make an enemy for a long time.''

''He asked for it.'' Marie laughed. ''He said I was fat in front of half the football team. My pride has never recovered.''

Abby couldn't help grinning. ''I think you two could have been great friends if you didn't hate each other so much. You have such a wonderful gift in common—elephant memories.'' She looked away, remembering how uncomplicated childhood had been. ''Don't go just yet, Marie. Michael won't be here for an hour or so.''

''*Is* there something you're not telling me?'' Marie asked tentatively. ''Are you in some sort of trouble?''

The temptation to unload the accumulated bitterness soured Abby's mouth. She rubbed her face with both hands.

''Hey, hey. Don't get upset, please. You know what a chicken I am about a crisis.''

True, Abby thought and looked up, a bright smile fixed in place.

Marie came to sit beside her. ''What's happened?'' She looped an arm awkwardly around Abby's shoulders.

''A lot,'' Abby said and remembered what she really liked about this sultry woman, had liked since they were grade-school kids together. Marie, so determinedly tough, hid her own pile of disappointments behind a brittle wit, but only to protect a kind heart that had gotten her into trouble too many times. A pretty face and sexy figure had brought her very little real happiness.

''Okay, friend. You don't want to talk about it, and I'm pushing you. Sorry. I never was Miss Tact.'' Marie smiled crookedly.

''But I do care about you.''

Abby took a long, shaky breath. ''Give me a little time. I've got some things to sort out in my head, alone. There's so much

I haven't faced and still don't understand, I—I just need some time, that's all."

"It isn't John, is it?"

Buzzing filled Abby's head, and little disjointed sounds. "John?" There wasn't enough air in the chilly room.

"Oh, Abby. It is John. You started to say he walked out just now, then stopped yourself. But that's what you meant, isn't it? He's left for good this time. Damn, I should have known. And now of all times."

"No, no, no." Abby shook her head. The blurring at the edges of her vision frightened her. Just like the day she'd fallen from the ladder in the store. "I'm not going over this now."

"You two never were right for each other." Marie shook her gently. "Look at me. This is awful, but it's not the end of the world. I went through a divorce and lived to tell the tale. And I didn't know anything was wrong with my marriage until I was told I wasn't wanted anymore. At least you had warning. John's been giving signals for ages. I was surprised—" She closed her mouth firmly and rested her head against Abby's. "I'm sorry."

Everything Marie had said was true. She and John had been on a direct path to disaster from the day they married. Now it was hard and painful to remember the first blush of their love and that careless certainty that they'd go on as they were, carefree, forever. How soon the freshness had died, been killed by John's increasing indifference and infidelity. Her head throbbed.

"What happened, Abby? Did he— Has he been— Oh, hell."

Abby met her friend's gaze steadily. "You're right: John has left me. Actually he left me before the last trip. He only came back to get his things." Surprisingly it didn't hurt so much to tell the truth. "We're getting a divorce. He filed back in September, and it will probably all be over before the end of November. I knew it was coming, but I kept hoping we'd pull things together. I wouldn't face that it was useless. People in my family don't divorce."

"Damn it, Abby. I always felt you two were really different types, and—and it had come to this in the end." She inhaled sharply. "I know how you feel about marriage, about not giving up. But you don't love him anymore, do you? Not really?"

"Don't!" Abby implored. She got up and crossed to the fireplace. Charred remnants of wood gave off a faint, acrid odor. "No." Resolutely she faced Marie. "It's true. I don't love him. I haven't for a long time, a year or more. He destroyed what we had—'' She paused, pressing a finger and thumb into the corners of her eyes. ''I'm trying not to lay it all on him. It takes two, isn't that what they say?''

Marie nodded mutely.

Abby spread her hands wearily. ''Not by what I said. More because I never said anything, I think. He's only worked when he felt like it. His mother's been so good to him, sending money, thinking she was encouraging him to make something of himself. But it didn't work that way. Knowing he could always get money if he needed it seemed to make him believe he shouldn't have to settle down. But, Marie, he's thirty-two years old. *Thirty-two.* He knew he wasn't being fair. And feeling guilty made him angry, and it just kept getting worse. This past year has been awful. I was never sure he was really at sea when he said he was. I know there was— I'm sure he met— I think—'' She stopped. Some things didn't have to be said, should never be said.

The green eyes watched intently. ''You think what? Don't hold anything back now. It'll help to get it all out.''

''Please—'' Abby willed steadiness into her voice. ''My parents are my main concern right now. If they knew how things stand with me, they'd, well, first they'd be so hurt about the divorce. They'll have to know, but it doesn't have to be now, not while I'm trying to get on my feet. I've got to make myself financially secure. John and I split what we had, but it wasn't much to begin with, and with all the expenses there will be, I need a chance to build up some savings. If Mom and Dad found out, they'd try to help, and they can't afford it. So, Marie—''

Quickly Marie broke in, ''Don't say it. You don't have to. I wouldn't **tell** a word of this to anyone unless you said you wanted me to. But I want a promise from you in exchange.''

Abby raised a questioning brow.

''You'll talk to me regularly. I want to know exactly how you are all the time. You're going to need a friend, and I want to be that for you. Promise?''

''Oh, Marie.'' They met halfway across the room and hugged. As always, Abby felt gangly beside her diminutive friend. ''Yes. Of course. Thank you for everything.'' She sniffed and laughed. ''I feel better already. Now if I can just keep snoopy Michael from catching on, I'll be doing fine.''

''He won't.'' Marie wrinkled her nose. ''Men don't pick up on

''I guess I made him feel guilty, and he couldn't handle that.''

''Guilty? How do you mean?''

other people's vibes the way women do. No sweat. Just don't say anything. John's on a trip, so what else is new?"

*No sweat.* When Marie left, Abby surveyed the room again. Marie had never yet failed to say what was on her mind. She hadn't mentioned how bare the place was, so she couldn't have noticed half the furniture was missing. Michael, always rushing, fitting from subject to subject, was even less likely to realize anything was different.

She checked her watch. Michael wasn't due in at Seatac airport for another hour. Postflight formalities and driving here would take forty-five minutes more. Time for her to make a run to the store. The cupboard was definitely bare. She needed to watch what she spent for a while, but a few groceries would be a good investment, both to divert Michael's suspicion and to provide a couple of the balanced meals she'd neglected for too long.

THE FAMILIAR navy blue uniform and peaked cap caught her eye the instant she swung the decrepit Pinto back into her parking slot. Darn. Michael had beaten her to it, and she'd wanted to set the stage before he arrived.

She switched off the ignition, waited for the predictable rattling sound in the engine to stop and rolled down the window. "Hi, Mike," she yelled, grinning broadly. "Be right with you." It was so good to see him. He'd bent down to fold his flight bag in half. Then he straightened, and her smile faded. The uniform was the same, but it was her neighbor, Nick Dorset, and not Michael who approached her car.

Abby rubbed her chilled hands together. A panicky fluttering assailed her nerves. The man had thought she was calling to him. He must think she was a nut.

"Hi, Abby." He stooped, bringing his face close. "How's it going?"

"Fine, thanks." She fiddled with her keys and reached for her bag on the passenger seat. "Sorry I shouted like that. I thought you were Michael." In all the months Nick had lived next door, she'd never initiated a conversation. But that didn't mean she hadn't noticed him.

"I was going to stop by and see you."

"Oh?" She looked directly into his eyes, puzzled. Coming to see her? Her skin heated. There was no reason for Nick Dorset to stop and see her. He was merely being nice, trying to ease the awkwardness she must be giving off in signal waves.

"Yep. Michael asked me to talk to you." He had unusual eyes, deep-set, a kind of gold-brown. Dimples formed lines beside his full mouth. She'd never seen him so closely before.

He smiled, evidently not noticing she was tongue-tied. "He's hung up in Chicago. Iced-up wings or something. I said I'd stand in for him, keep him out of trouble with you."

"Oh," Abby said again and blushed. She must sound like an airhead, but she couldn't seem to think of anything else to say. Nor could she look away. His mouth was wide, and his teeth were strong. Abby glanced at the deep cleft in his chin, the vertical shadows his smile made beneath high cheekbones, the straight nose. A big, unnervingly handsome man, only made more appealing in the perfectly cut airline uniform. She made much of shoving her keys away. Even if she were in a position to think of another man taking an interest in her, Nick Dorset would be the last to consider Abby Winston as anything but his married neighbor, the sister of one of his colleagues.

"Mike said he hopes to get out by this afternoon. That means it'll be late this evening before he gets in. He said to tell you not to worry, and he'll call when he's at his apartment."

Abby rallied. "Thanks." She put her hand on the doorhandle, but Nick opened it first and stood back for her to climb out. "Thanks," she repeated and cringed. This was ridiculous. "I would have worried. He's not always too good about letting someone know when he's held over. We should all be used to him by now, but I guess we can't help being human." There, she sounded together now, in control. She'd also just said more to Nick than she'd ever said since he'd moved in. Somehow she'd almost been afraid to look at him too carefully before. There was an air about him, a force field that moved with him. Even with the few words they'd occasionally exchanged in passing, she'd felt a stirring of interest she couldn't afford to feel.

She opened the hatchback, expecting him to leave. He came beside her. "Let me help you with those." One long hand, tanned from Hawaiian stopovers, closed around the top of a grocery bag.

"No," Abby said too vehemently. She swallowed uncomfortably. "I mean, you have your own things to haul in. I can manage a couple of grocery bags." She laughed, and the sound was unnaturally high. "I need the exercise. Thanks for letting me know about Michael."

"You're welcome." He took a step backward, keeping his eyes on hers until Abby buried her head in the hatch. She was lonely, that's all, and reacting to the long absence of a strong man's presence in her life. John had ceased to be there for her months ago.

She juggled the two sacks and slammed the trunk shut. The bags weren't heavy, just unwieldy, and they ground the handle of her purse into her wrist.

"That much exercise no one needs." Nick's voice stopped her as she shoved through the outer doors to the building. He'd pushed his cap to the back of his head. Thick curly brown hair stuck out in all directions. "Give me those." He slung the strap of his flight bag over his shoulder and took the bags into one arm. With his free hand, he guided Abby upstairs.

She mustn't puff. The three flights were no steeper than they'd ever been, they just seemed that way each time she climbed them.

At her door she hesitated. He made no move to give up the groceries, he simply stood there, smiling amiably, waiting. Abby took a deep breath and fumbled for her door key. "You must need to get on. Set those down, please. I'm a hopeless loser of keys. This may take time." She scrabbled along the torn bottom lining of her purse.

He only broadened his smile and leaned against the wall.

"Really," she said. "Don't bother—"

"It's no bother," he cut in. His was a **gravelly** voice with a warmth no woman would miss. "Take your time."

Her fingers closed around the elusive keys, and she unlocked the door. "There. Finally. I—" She couldn't dismiss him like a delivery boy. He was Michael's friend. "Would you like to come in? I'm dying for a cup of coffee myself. And I bought stuff for Michael's lunch. It shouldn't go to waste." Of course, he'd refuse. She was vaguely horrified she'd included lunch in the invitation. Coffee would have been enough for conventional politeness.

"Sounds wonderful. I like cooking, but I'm always lazy when I've been out on a trip."

Abby led him inside, her heart thudding uncomfortably. She had to be crazy. What must he think of her? A woman who rarely spoke, let alone issued lunch invitations, and now she was allowing him to carry her groceries and come into her home as if they were old friends. He wouldn't know John was away. She shut out the start of the thought that John was gone permanently—not simply away. But Nick didn't know anything about them or her, and he'd think she was just being pleasant to someone Michael knew.

A thought did strike her fully, with a blowlike force. She must guard against any slip with this man, as closely as she'd intended to do with Michael. If Nick Dorset discerned anything amiss, he was likely to mention it to Michael, and the damage done would be just as great.

Nick cataloged every move Abby made. She was as edgy as a cat. He could almost see her nerves, tight as fiddle strings, a hair away from springing wildly from her control. And, oh, was that control ever tenuous.

For two weeks he'd watched and waited for some sign of exactly what was happening next door. Nothing. Running into Michael Harris in Chicago today had been the answer to a dream, an excuse to actually talk to Abby.

He carried the brown bags to the kitchen. The living room was Spartan, each piece of furniture tasteful, but widely spaced as if a lot was missing. But he knew it was. Muscles knotted along his jaw. He could not allow himself to give away that he knew something was wrong. She must be the one to tell him if she wanted to. And she wasn't likely to open up with a man she scarcely knew.

"Here?" He smiled over his shoulder at her, then set his burden on the kitchen table when she nodded. "Ah," he sighed, deliberately cheerful, dropped his bag and took off his cap. It bothered him that they were strangers. He wanted to know Abby. He wanted to know her very well.

She wore the baggy black coat and made no attempt to remove it. "Sit down." She waved toward the living room. "I'll make that coffee and rustle up something to eat." The attempt at lightness didn't quite come off.

"Let me help."

"Well. Oh, I guess." She smiled, the soft mouth parting in a way that made his eyes follow the motion. "You can make the coffee. It'll have to be instant, I'm afraid. The mugs are in the cupboard over the sink."

How many women could manage to look exotic in a worn old coat? She did. Its starkness intensified the beautiful fragile bones in her face, the big, almond-shaped eyes beneath her sweeping brows. *Had John Winston left for good?* Nick felt instantly guilty. He was actually hoping John had cut out permanently and left the field wide open for him. *Good God.*

"Did you find the mugs?"

He started. "Yes. Right where you said they were." All two

of them, not counting a chipped one set off to one side. He filled the kettle and put it on to boil, found a jar of coffee and scooped a spoonful into each mug. Glancing sideways, he confirmed what he thought he'd already seen—she still wore the wedding ring. It slipped loosely around her knuckle. He frowned. She was thin, thinner than she used to be. And the air in her condo was arctic, which must be why she kept on her coat. She probably didn't even realize she hadn't taken it off.

"Do you like tomato soup?" Abby lifted a small can from the bag, then a package of sprouts.

"Love it." His thought tightened. Her face was drawn now, anxious while she thought he wasn't studying her. An insane longing to take her in his arms shocked him. *Whoa, buddy. Watch it.*

"Here," he said, reaching to take the sprouts, "you start the soup, and I'll finish unpacking these things for you."

Her eyes turned up to his, luminous yet strangely empty. Beaten. That creep had left her, and she was struggling to hold her life together. And there was very little money around here. Nick straightened his shoulders. Abby was a tall woman, but beside her he felt huge and very masculine. Protectiveness was a foreign sensation, but she made him want to take care of her.

She hadn't moved. "You must have better things to do than unpack my groceries," she said in a small voice. "I feel like a nuisance."

Nick laughed with a heartiness he didn't feel. "A nuisance? Don't kid yourself. I was lonely and wondering what I would do with myself this afternoon. I almost invited myself to lunch. I'm the one who should feel like a pest."

Abby laughed too, softening the pale line around her mouth.

"Right. You are a pest. But I'm glad you're here." She reddened and turned away to open the can.

Once she must have been spontaneous like that all the time—the way Michael was. Somehow the natural sense of humor had been ground out of her, and Nick had a good idea by whom. He reached into a sack. He'd never been easily put off from anything he really wanted. And he really wanted Abby Winston. With some patience, he might just find a way to get her. A flash of amusement rose in his mind. Ten kids might not be what either of them would ever want, but she'd certainly fill the bill very nicely as that "someone to come home to." Janet had mentioned so often.

Boy, did he have a way of getting ahead of himself. Way ahead.

Pots and bowls clattered as Abby prepared soup. Nick lined up her purchases on the table. Four loose carrots in a plastic bag. An apple. A small package of ground meat and a single, thin piece of whitefish. Cheddar cheese and a loaf of unappetizing-looking store-brand bread. Food intended for one and not much of it. She had bought two large cartons of milk.

Nick held back the million things he wanted to say. Another person's pride was sacrosanct. Abby was clearly trying to keep up appearances. She must have a chance to become comfortable with him before he tried to gain her confidence.

"Oh, good grief." She shoved the pot to the back of the stove.

"I forgot the sandwiches. Cheese and sprouts okay?"

"Perfect," he said evenly. He knew perfectly well cheese and sprouts were all she had, but he'd have said yes to turnip and liver sandwiches if that's what it took to stay with her as long as possible.

He finished making coffee and carried it to the living room. He'd been inside the Winstons' condo once, when Michael first brought him over to see the one he'd actually bought himself. Nick was almost certain there'd been a glass-topped dining table in the bay window. Now the area was empty except for a pile of brightly colored cushions heaped in one corner.

Uncertain where to set down the mugs, he stood in the middle of the room. Damn, he didn't want to embarrass her. He sat on the couch. There wasn't even a coffee table anymore. What had happened here? Why would Winston feel it necessary to strip the place like this?

"Here we are." Abby carried a tray. She took what was clearly an instinctive step toward the window and stopped. For a second she seemed disoriented, and Nick almost went to her. "Uh, here we are," she echoed faintly.

Nick breathed hard. "Let's sit on the couch. We'll be comfortable." One end table remained. He put the mugs by his feet and reached to take the tray. She handed it over and watched him slide it onto the end table.

"Good idea." Her lips came together, and the eyes became vast. She stood, pressing her palms together, swaying slightly as if uncertain what to do next.

What could he say, should he say? *Has your husband left you? I know he has and that you're having a hard time; please let me help you. I'm crazy about you; I have been from the first time I saw you.* Instead he patted the couch beside him and said, "Come on. The coffee and soup are getting cold."

She crossed her arms tightly. "Are you cold? I'm not." Her chin came up, and a spark of defiance lighted her eyes. "But I can turn up the heat if you like. If you...if you think the coffee and—" She looked down at her coat, and a hint of pink swept over her pale cheeks. Then she laughed.

Of course, the heat was turned down to conserve money, and that's why she kept on her coat. Nick experienced the closest thing to panic he remembered since his first solo flight. He was out of his depth. And far from helping Abby Winston, he was making her acutely miserable.

She almost rushed to the thermostat, rotated it sharply, much higher than it ever needed to go. In the next instant she unbuttoned her coat, fumbling until it was off and she could hang it in the closet by the door.

"There." She faced him in a loose dress of some gauzy blue stuff assembled in horizontal panels. When she crossed to stand in front of him once more, the fabric floated about her slightly. It was too light for the time of year.

"There," Nick agreed in a voice that didn't sound like his own and handed up her coffee.

She took a sip. The feverish color remained in her cheeks. "Not so bad for good old instant brew, huh?"

Nick said nothing. He clutched his own mug so tightly he could feel every groove in the pottery. Desperately, his heart jamming his throat, he tried to concentrate on her face. Not that it mattered where he looked. He'd finally discovered what any fool would have seen a long time ago.

Abby Winston was pregnant.

Chapter Three

*Pregnant.* Nick slammed his front door behind him and tossed his flight bag down the length of the hall. What a bloody fool. And what a bloody fool he'd almost *made* of himself. A few more minutes of ignorance, and he'd probably have been concocting some way for them to get together again. Inviting her to go somewhere, even. Thank God for small mercies. At least they'd been spared even more embarrassment.

*Hell, hell, hell.* He skimmed his cap after the bag and dragged off his jacket. She would have expected him to know she was pregnant. Whether or not he'd actually seen the obvious shouldn't have been a factor. Why hadn't Mike mentioned the baby? Nick started for the bedroom, loosening his tie as he went. Mike hadn't mentioned the baby because he was Mike. The guy only sat still when he was driving a bird. That was probably also the one activity capable of keeping his mind on a single course for more than ten seconds.

Nick slumped on the edge of the bed. He had embarrassed her. In those few seconds after he'd glanced at her stomach, while he'd riveted his eyes on hers, he'd given the whole show away. She knew he hadn't been aware of her condition and that he was shocked. He'd gulped the coffee and the soup, forced every bite of sandwich down his throat, prattling on all the time about absolutely nothing. And Abby had pushed the spoon around her own bowl, not eating, and hadn't touched the sandwich.

Pregnant women were supposed to eat properly, weren't they? Janet had been a fanatic... *Oh, damn it.* It was none of his business. Nick stripped quickly, trying not to think, and pulled on running pants. If all else failed, there was always exercise. He'd run this mess out of his brain.

Warm-up first. Stretch. He dropped to the rug and gripped his ankles, pressed his knees to the floor with his elbows. One, two, three. Press and release. He closed his eyes, concentrated on breathing, in, out, fill from the bottom, in out. Shoot. That son of a bitch Winston had left her alone and pregnant. He'd taken his pick of what they'd owned and gone away. Did Michael know?

Push-ups. They were the thing to fill the mind. He rolled on his stomach and stretched out. Jeez, he must be getting old, his calves felt like warped shoe leather. What had happened to the college track star of a few years ago? Up, hold, down. Ten of these were going to feel like a hundred and ten today. He'd never make his usual fifty.

How would she keep on working and care for a child? *Concentrate, Dorset.* Twelve, thirteen. He was moving more smoothly, breathing better. If Mike knew, she wouldn't look so alone and desperate. He'd never allow her to go short of money or live in a bunch of cold rooms and not have enough to eat or— The Harrises were a close family. They had to know. If they didn't it was because Abby didn't want them to, and it wasn't his place to interfere.

He flopped onto his back, clasped his neck in both hands and did a series of rapid sit-ups. Now he'd go to the track at the junior high school across the street and run until he was too tired to do anything but sleep. He grabbed a shirt and sweat jacket and left the building at a trot.

The track was a godsend. It had been one of the factors that helped him make up his mind on the condo. Gravel scrunched beneath his feet, flew up in damp little clumps behind him. The air felt good, cold, whipping his skin, riffling through his hair.

*None of his business.* The words kept time with his thudding feet. Abby Winston was none of his business. She wasn't the only lovely woman in the world. And plenty of them were neither married nor expecting a baby. Who needed someone else's grief? Janet had been right: it was past time for him to spread out, meet people, women. Next week he was due to visit Omaha. Maybe he'd look up some of those disappointed hearts his sister never failed to mention. Yeah, maybe he'd just do that.

"ABBY, HONEY, eat one of these turnovers. Your dad made them specially because he knows how you love them."

Abby smiled at her mother and took a pastry from the proffered plate. She wasn't hungry, but she wouldn't disappoint her silent father. "Thanks, Mom." She smiled at Wilma Harris. "And you, Dad." George Harris watched and waited, unsmiling, until she took a bite. "Mmm. Dad, like I always said, no one bakes an apple turnover like you do."

The pale face rumpled into a thousand wrinkles that seemed permanently flour-lined. George had been a baker since he was sixteen, and his skin had long ago taken on a powdery quality as if the residue in the air where he worked followed him everywhere. Even his thinning hair was dull white.

By comparison, Wilma was florid, an energetic, rotund woman never seen without a splash of magenta lipstick and highly rouged cheeks. Her hair, steel gray now, was still brushed up at the neck and sides into the crinkled puff she'd worn as long as Michael and Abby could remember.

"Don't I get a magic confection?" Michael stopped pacing the tiny room and hovered at Abby's elbow. "We know who's the favorite around here. I don't get special tidbits baked for me."

Abby grinned up at him and punched his ribs playfully. "Sure, Mike. No one does anything for you, including all those poor girls you keep on strings in every city you fly to."

He sat on the rug by her feet and hung his dark head. "Not true, not true. I'm maligned. Any one of them is free to go whenever they like."

Wilma laughed delightedly as she invariably did over Michael's inflated reputation as a lady-killer. Even their father grunted, shaking his thin shoulders convulsively.

"About time you settled down, son." George's voice, always a surprise since he spoke so rarely, crackled deep, yet oddly papery. "Like your sister. Your mother and I are getting into this grandkid bit. You should see the stuff she's piling up for the baby." He smiled fondly at Abby. "That little man's not going to want for anything, I can tell you."

Abby kept the corners of her mouth turned up. "Little man, Dad? If it's a little lady, doesn't she get anything?"

"Oh, George, listen to you." Wilma laughed comfortably. "In a while I'll show you the christening gown I've started, Abby. Two yards long. All lawn and Austrian lace." A happy blush rose in her cheeks. "Cost a bit, I can tell you. But nothing's too good for that baby—our first grandchild. And it doesn't matter whether it's a boy or girl. Either can wear a gown like that. I was thinking maybe all your children could use it. Like a sort of heirloom. And Michael's, too."

All your children. Today, while they were all together, Abby had hoped to find the courage to explain what had happened with John. The baby was due in less than two months now. She couldn't pretend much longer.

"Mrs. Winston wrote to me," her mother continued. "What a lovely lady. She thinks the world of you and John. And she's so happy about the baby. She'd like to come out when it's born, but the trip from New York would probably be too much for her, and she's sensible enough to admit it. That heart of hers..." Wilma clucked sadly.

A deep breath drained Abby. She felt herself sink and shrivel. What would the news of John's defection do to her mother-in-law's heart? The sensation of being closely watched prickled over her skin, and she met Michael's piercing blue stare. He raised his brows, and she felt he could see inside her head. Quickly she looked away.

"Wilma, tell Abby the rest of what Mrs. Winston said." Her father had leaned forward in his reclining chair. "About after the baby and all."

Abby studiously avoided Michael's unwavering stare but knew he hadn't taken his eyes off her. He'd guessed something. Unwittingly, by what she'd said, or not said, she'd given herself away. He might not have figured out exactly what was wrong, but he was suspicious. Nick could have alerted him. Nick had definitely guessed she had a problem—in addition to the pregnancy that had so patently surprised him. Hot blood rushed to her face at the memory. How could he not have known that? He'd looked so shocked when he realized. And he'd almost fallen over himself making a hasty retreat. She'd seen him twice in the week since that disastrous lunch. Each time he'd nodded briefly and headed for the running track, looking too spectacular in shiny clinging blue pants and muscle-hugging shirt. Damn. She wanted to go home. Instead, she said, "What did Mrs. Winston say, Mom?"

Wilma finished pouring fresh coffee all around. She sat again, slid on the pair of half glasses that hung from a chain around her neck and fished an envelope from her apron pocket. "This only came this morning. I'll read you the bit George is talking about. Mrs. Winston's as proud of you as we are. Your art and everything and the way you've settled John down. I'd have thought she was more old-fashioned than me, but she even says she's glad you've kept up with your work, and she hopes you'll go back to it when the baby's old enough."

The expensive paper rattled as she looked for a specific page. "Here it is. She says: 'I've been thinking so much about them, John, Abby and the baby. I know I can't make the journey, but

I've only got one son, and I'm not going to give up the pleasure of holding his baby. As soon as Abby's up to it, I'm going to pay for them all to come to New York and stay for a few weeks. We'd probably better wait for the weather to be a bit warmer before the baby travels, but then I'm going to have them come. I think looking forward to that is all that keeps me going these days.''

Wilma folded the letter slowly and pushed it back into her pocket. ''Poor soul,'' she muttered. ''She doesn't have the pleasure of seeing the pair of you the way we do.''

Abby coughed and put a hand over her mouth.

''What is it?'' Michael said, instantly on his feet. ''Are you all right?''

She nodded, coughing more loudly as tears filled her eyes. Pointing to her throat, she muttered, ''Just a tickle. Excuse me,'' and rushed from the room.

In the tiny rose-papered bathroom off a narrow hall, she locked the door and sat on the toilet cover. The too-familiar pounding had started in her temples once more. She reached to run water over her fingertips and touched her lips, her brow and jawline. Nausea hadn't been a problem since the first few weeks of her pregnancy, but now she was sure she would throw up. The apply turnover sat, a leaden lump, in the pit of her stomach.

''Abby! You okay?'' It was Michael, calling through the door as he had so often when they were kids and she'd run away from his teasing to find a place to hide. ''Abby, please say something. You aren't fooling me.''

''Coffee went down the wrong way,'' she managed. ''Thought I was going to choke to death. Go tell Mom and Dad I'm okay so they don't worry.''

''They aren't worried. Open the door, sis,'' Michael whispered.

''I want to talk to you.''

Oh, God. Nick Dorset had let the cat out of the bag. Slowly she reached to shoot back the bolt, and Michael came in, closing the door behind him.

''Okay. We don't have long, so come clean. Is it money? I know John's at sea again, and the checks don't always get through on time. Is it that?''

She stared at him. ''No, no, not really.'' He didn't know anything. Relief slackened her muscles.

''Oh, Abby.'' He dropped to his knees and hugged her, smoothing damp curls back from her face. ''This isn't a good time to be alone, is it? You want John with you. How could I have been so dumb? No experience, I guess. Forgive me for being an insensitive jerk?''

She nodded against his shoulder. ''If you were, I would.''

He leaned away, a sage expression on his boyishly good-looking features. ''Pregnant ladies get blue for almost no reason. I know I read that in a magazine once. Must have forgotten, that's all. I'll come over more often. We can go to the movies. Yep, that's what we'll do, go to the movies.''

Hopeless. She was steadily drowning in her own cowardice. But how did you tell all these happy people, all these people who thought your world was rosy, that you were getting a divorce and the whole damned sky was about to fall around your ears?

''Thanks, Mike. You're sweet. You always were.''

He grinned, instantly cheerful again. ''That's what all the girls say. Come on. Let's get back.''

Abby laughed and let him lead her to the living room. Their parents stood side by side near the black metal fireplace, the top of George Harris's head barely reaching his wife's eyebrows.

He cleared his throat loudly. ''Abby, your mother and I have been talking things over, and we want...'' He paused, and Wilma elbowed him gently. ''We wondered if you and John would like it if the baby was christened in New York. After all, John is Mrs. Winston's only child, and she couldn't make it to the wedding, either—''

''We'd come too, of course,'' Abby's mother broke in. Excitement heightened the color along her cheekbones. ''Your dad and I've got a bit put by, and we always talked about taking a trip one day.'' She lowered her lashes. ''Kind of like the honeymoon we never had. Anyway, that way John's mom would get to be at the christening, and we wouldn't miss it, either, and we'd have a trip. It'd be a real adventure,'' she ended in a rush.

Abby felt marooned, isolated and gradually slipping farther and farther from safe ground. While she smiled and heard her voice saying the right things, laughing, an intangible bubble walled her off. Michael wrapped his parents in a bear hug and talked of being the only one who could fly them to the East Coast. After all, he'd have to go, too. He'd also arrange for them to pay a fraction of the normal fare; dammit, he'd pay it himself. It was all a wonderful, wonderful idea.

An hour later Abby set out on the twenty-mile trip back from her parents' house in the north end of Seattle to the east side and the hateful job she must keep as long as possible. She despised herself for not telling her folks the truth about John and getting it over with.

When she crossed the Evergreen Point Bridge over Lake Washington, a setting wintry sun cast cool orange chips over the choppy waters. Abby glanced from the road, to the dense evergreen forest, to Mount Rainier, a giant gold-lit snow cone to the south and began to smile. She loved this place and loved her baby and her family, and she'd make her life come right. She didn't need a man to help her.

By TEN, ABBY was counting off the minutes until the notice on the Laundromat wall could be flipped over to the side that read, No Attendant on Duty. In Case of Complaint Call: with her own telephone number added in black wax pencil.

*Her art.* Abby eyed the drunk snoring in a green plastic chair by the door. His ragged laundry had long since fallen to the bottom of the dryer, but she shied away from waking him. Her art seemed very distant. What would her parents say if they knew their daughter, their pride and joy, was managing a twenty-four-hour Laundromat? And Michael? What would he think, and Mrs. Winston? She felt sick again and sat with a thump at the end of the central row of chairs.

No one knew about this except Marie, and no one else would, if she could help it. Marie had badgered the truth out of her, and somehow being able to talk to someone made the discomfort easier to bear. The day would come when Abby could go back to her own profession, Marie insisted; this was temporary, and jobs were hard to come by when you were pregnant.

Abby pushed herself to her feet. Every move was becoming more difficult. She transferred two loads of wash to a dryer and inserted coins. The noise helped late at night, made her feel less alone. ''Manager'' was a laugh. She was the only employee. The man who'd given her the job came by every few days to empty the coin boxes. He said little, never looked directly at her but handed over her paycheck regularly every other Friday. The paycheck, Abby reminded herself when she was dejected, was all that mattered.

She wished someone else would come in. The drunk showed up regularly, always late, always reeling, and although she figured he only wanted a warm place to sleep, he frightened her. Her car had been acting up lately, and she worried it wouldn't start one night. The thought made her claustrophobic.

Some people left their laundry for her to do. They usually tipped. So did the customers who had her tend their dry cleaning in the large do-it-yourself machine at the rear of the store. Abby began folding a pile of towels and squelched her dislike for the work by telling herself for the hundredth time that in her condition she was lucky to have found something. Thanks to this job, her savings were still untouched.

"Good Lord!"

Abby froze. She'd know that voice anywhere. Still folding a towel, she turned slowly and looked into Nick Dorset's surprised amber eyes. She put the towel into a laundry basket and smoothed her dress. "Hi, Nick. Off your beaten track, aren't you?" *Oh, please, please, don't let him tell Michael.*

"You too." He dropped a bulging pillowcase and tugged off his gloves. "Never struck me I might not be the only one with washer trouble. Yours is out too, huh?" He met her eyes directly, and she saw him swallow. She made him uncomfortable, and she hated that. But he hadn't cottoned to the reason for her being there. If she could just keep up the pretense...

"You're lucky." Her brain seemed to be scrambled. "Uh, lucky. You can get your stuff right in. All the washers were full when I got here, or I'd be long gone."

"Right." He nodded, unzipping the black leather jacket. "Yeah, I'm lucky. I'll just get this load going. I didn't realize this was the closest Laundromat to our place." While he spoke, he shoved clothes into a machine, then shut the lid.

Several miles from Lake Vista; Abby hadn't realized it was the closest, either. The possibility of someone she knew coming in had never crossed her mind. Nick was looking around vaguely.

"If you didn't bring soap, you can get it from the dispenser," Abby said before she could stop herself. She mustn't risk any kind of conversation with this man for more reasons than one. He stirred feelings in her she shouldn't have, feelings that would horrify him if he as much as suspected them. And he represented a threat to her hope of finding an acceptable way out of her predicament.

He bought a box of detergent and started his machine. Abby finished folding and cast about for something else to do without giving herself away. She glanced at the wall clock. Fifteen more minutes, and she'd find an unobtrusive way to flip the sign. Then she'd breathe more freely, certain no one would ask for assistance and give her secret away.

"Abby, could we talk?" Nick had sat and pulled a book from his pocket, but it lay unopened in his lap. "About the day we had lunch?"

She lifted her chin with a sense of having to clear an air passage to her lungs. He was going to say he'd guessed everything about her and John.

"Please?" His smile made those long shadows beneath his cheekbones. "I feel bad about it."

She sank down beside him, clenching her hands together. "I'm the one who should feel bad. The food wasn't very appetizing, and I was lousy company." The dryer behind them stopped, and she glanced quickly over her shoulder. What would he think when she didn't take the clothes she'd folded with her? Nervously she added, "I was a bit down that day, I'm afraid."

"Because your husband's gone again so soon?"

Her scalp prickled. "He, er—" Overreacting would be death. The comment had no hidden meaning. "Yes."

"When will he—"

She leaped up. "Oops. Dryer's stopped. Don't want wrinkles."

"Abby." He walked beside her. "Is there something you'd like to share with me, something that wouldn't hurt so much if you had someone to talk to?"

Her pulse thundered. She'd been right to fear this man's intuition. "No," she replied with a forced laugh. "Of course not. Whatever makes you think that?" Her eyes went to the clock. Eleven. Instead of locking the customer's laundry in the supply room, she'd take it with her and make sure she was back before the woman came for it in the morning. That way Nick couldn't guess she worked here.

He didn't move away. "Let me help." Without making a fuss, she couldn't stop him from taking the other end of the sheet she held. He snapped the fabric efficiently, folding and passing in a manner that spelled practice. "Like old times," he chuckled. "This was always one of my jobs at home." With the last fold he approached her to take the sheet and covered her hands with his.

Abby parted her lips. Why couldn't she get enough air anymore? His fingers were warm and hard, strong. She closed her eyes and let him take the sheet from her. He must think she was strange. He was probably laughing at her behind those deep, deep eyes.

"I guess you're on your way now," he said quietly, and when she glanced up, she saw no hint of laughter. "It's icy out there now, Abby, and foggy. Be careful. You shouldn't be driving in conditions like these."

*And in a condition like mine,* she thought self-derisively. "Thanks," she murmured. "I'll be fine." The truth was she was terrified of slippery roads and the long deserted stretches where she feared her increasingly temperamental car would break down. She said, "No one needs to worry about me."

John Winston no longer mattered to her. She was glad they'd soon be divorced. But although she wanted her baby, she resented the way John had effectively spoiled her for another romantic involvement. How could she expect Nick, or any man, to show a woman alone with a child anything but decent concern? She piled one of the store's baskets high and gathered her coat and purse.

A rumbling grunt snapped Abby's attention to the man by the door. He snuffled and rubbed his bleary eyes. She dropped her coat and redistributed the load in the basket.

She kept her head down. Nick picked up her coat and leaned close beside her against the washer. "I'll carry that load out for you. It's too heavy."

Shuffling footsteps approached, but she didn't turn around. "I can manage." The old coot might be half pickled, but he could decide to notice any change in routine.

"You got a problem, missy?"

Abby gripped the rim of the basket in both hands. "No," she said too sharply and glanced sideways at the man. He swayed slightly. "Everything's fine, thank you."

He hiccuped and rubbed the back of one hand over his mouth. "Mister." His eyes didn't quite focus, but he aimed a glare at Nick. "If you don't want trouble, you better not mess with the help around here."

## Chapter Four

For seconds, Nick's face was blank.

Abby waited, her fists clenched on top of a washer. The too-familiar numbing sensation edged into her head.

"You got anything to say, mister? Or you ready to move on?" The drunk took a stumbling pace forward and clutched Nick's arm.

Nick carefully unwound the grimy fingers from his sleeve. He made no attempt to answer the man. Instead, he looked at Abby, and she read the expression in his eyes all too clearly: smoldering anger. "Abby," he said quietly, "do you work in this place?"

"Yes," she said. What else could she say? "But it's only temporary until..." Why had Nick, of all people, shown up and found her out?

He shook his head. "You don't belong here at all. Come on, you're leaving."

"The lady don't need your help." The man swayed. His stale breath constricted Abby's throat. "You want a fight, boy, you got it." He bared nicotine-stained teeth while he made a wavering jab at Nick's chest. The blow glanced off. Nick grasped the thin wrist as it passed and shoved the man into a chair.

"Sit still and shut up, buddy." He glared menacingly at the slumped form. "Better yet, go find somewhere else to make a nuisance of yourself."

She was going to die right here and now. "Please, Nick. He's okay. Everything's fine. I can't—I mean—I work here, okay? And I need the job." The game was up, all over. Nick would tell Michael, and then her parents would know. She made an effort to rally. "I can handle things. Really. I'm used to it."

"Is that supposed to make me feel better?"

He wasn't *supposed* to care one way or the other. Abby walked past Nick and stared unseeingly out the windows. Nick Dorset was a decent man with decent instincts. He must be wondering why John would allow her to do a job like this now. Warm hands on her shoulders startled her. She glanced up into

Nick's face. A wonderful face, lean, unforgettable. This was madness.

"Sit down, Abby—please. You look bushed." He steered her to a chair. "My stuff will be finished in a few minutes, and I'll drive you home."

Abby watched him silently. She'd have to think fast. He didn't know about John's desertion, but now he did know where she was working, and the set of his jaw showed his disapproval. He'd tell Michael for sure. The worst possible way for any part of her secret to come out would be secondhand. Her family would never forgive her if someone else told them the news. Somehow she had to appeal to Nick, to make him understand she needed the money she made here and persuade him not to say anything to Michael.

When the washer stopped, Nick piled his laundry, still wet, back into the pillowcase and met her eyes. "Is that yours?" He inclined his head to the basket of linen he'd helped her fold.

"No," she said quietly and felt heat rush up her neck. "If you'd like to leave your things, I'll dry them and drop them off later." By then she'd have come up with a plausible explanation.

"There's nothing wrong with my dryer. You're coming with me now."

Abby bit the inside of her lip. "I'm not finished. And I have my own car. But thank you." She might like a strong man around, but not here, and not now.

"I'll wait." He slung his load over one shoulder and leaned tensely against the doorjamb.

"I said I've got my car," Abby said faintly. She didn't have the energy to keep up a battle of wits. "There are things I have to do."

"Do them." This was the flip side of Nick Dorset: totally intractable. "The heap you call a car will be okay in the parking lot overnight. From the noise the thing makes, I'm surprised it starts at all. You shouldn't be driving it."

A rumbling snore sounded. Her "protector" was once more drowsing and snuffling.

Abby picked up the book Nick had forgotten and said as she handed it to him, "I do have to drive myself. How would I get back tomorrow otherwise?" She was so tired.

"Something tells me you won't be coming back tomorrow. Michael doesn't know about this, does he?"

"Oh, please..." The right words, she must find the right thing to say. "Look, Nick," she stated resolutely, "I'm going to ask you a favor, but I need a little time to explain. Could you wait before you say anything to Michael?"

He studied her until she glanced away. "All right. I don't know what's going on with you, but something is. Maybe it's none of my business, but…" His sharply expelled breath was audible. He sat beside her. "Michael's my friend, and he feels about you the way I feel about my sister. If he'd found Janet working in—in a dump, I'd slug him for not clueing me in. But I won't say anything if that's the way you want it. Only, Abby, I'm not leaving you here tonight. You need the car tomorrow? Fine. I'll bring you back, and it'll already be here."

Abby started to protest, then changed her mind. "Whatever you say." He held all the cards. A few more weeks at this job were all she asked. They wouldn't make her rich, but they'd help.

Nick said, "Good," and leaned back in the chair. He smiled at Abby when she got up and willed all emotion from his eyes at her slight awkwardness. He'd like to get his hands on that son of a bitch Winston. Thank God the damned washer had chosen tonight to go on the fritz. He glanced at the creep snoring through flapping lips at the opposite end of the line of seats. No way would he leave her here with that.

Within minutes, she'd locked several baskets of laundry in the storage room, flipped over a sign on the wall and pulled on her coat.

They didn't speak until Nick had closed Abby into his car and climbed behind the wheel. She leaned against the door. Her uplifted profile, her neck, showed pale against the darkness outside. He started the engine. "You leave the place unlocked at night?"

"The shop itself, yes. Anything portable is shut in the back room. A watchman checks the front from time to time."

"Is anyone really likely to wash clothes at one or two in the morning?"

He felt her look at him. "I guess, or they wouldn't keep it open."

Now what? Would she volunteer information, or should he ask direct questions? He waited, and the silence only lengthened.

Fog swirled in shifting tunnels before the headlights of his BMW. He'd tried to put her out of his mind. How he'd tried. In the past two weeks he'd worked up to seven miles a day on the track whenever he was in town, and Abby Winston ran every step of the way with him.

"I feel ridiculous," she said suddenly.

"Why?" He knew the answer. She was proud, and he'd made her feel as though she were a burden.

Abby rested her elbow on the window rim. "The lady-in-distress role is foreign to me. I'm a manager, Nick, a survivor. And I was fine back there—", she turned sharply toward him "—honestly I was. I know how it looked. But who's going to bother a— I'm fine there."

*Who would bother a pregnant woman?* she'd almost said. He pursed his lips. Her self-esteem was zero. She might be pregnant, she was also extremely, hauntingly lovely, more so to him because she was pregnant. He closed his eyes for an instant. There was definitely something wrong with his psyche.

He parked near the entrance to the condo, reached behind the seat for his laundry and leapt out to open the door. "We could both use something hot. Have soup or hot chocolate with me."

"You've done enough already." She held the railing beside the steps tightly, moving without her usual light step. "Let me make you something."

Still trying to save face, he thought. He was glad darkness hid the evil expression he knew he couldn't control well enough. "I bought this new drink mix I'm dying to try," he lied, praying he could keep her out of the kitchen while he found the old can of chocolate he knew he'd put somewhere in a cupboard. "This is just the night for it. Humor me."

She glanced back into his face, and for the first time in weeks he saw that marvelous, impish smile. "Okay," she said. "Lead on." He knew she was twenty-seven. When she smiled like that, she could have passed for seventeen, except for the fine lines of fatigue around her eyes and mouth.

A swift glance around Nick's condo unsettled Abby, made her feel like an intruder into his comfortable world. He wasn't a tidy man. As she stood awkwardly in the entrance to his living room, he toured the area, sweeping discarded clothes from couches and chairs, shoving newspapers and magazines into piles on tables, pausing for an instant to grab two pairs of shoes from a corner.

He grinned as he passed her, arms laden. "Sit. I'll do my famous hide-all trick, then make us that drink." He paused in the hall, looking back, laughing. "Sometimes I have nightmares my mother will show up and open the wrong closet. In my mind I see her lying on the rubble that falls out, calling me 'Nicholas Stuart.' That always meant big trouble.''

Abby laughed, too, and walked farther into the room. The layout of the condo closely resembled her own. Nick's kitchen, open to the living and dining room, had a common wall with her kitchen. At the far end of the hall he would also have a master bedroom with its own bathroom. She could see the second bathroom door and the small bedroom beside it. In her own place, that would become her baby's nursery.

Nick breezed back and went straight into the kitchen. ''Sit down, sit down,'' he called. ''Oh, wait. Let's have a fire.''

She'd already noted he did everything quickly. On his knees before the fireplace, he crumpled newspapers between the andirons and heaped logs rapidly on top. His shoulders moved powerfully beneath a dark turtleneck sweater. ''There. Let there be flames.'' He set fire to the paper and rested on his heels an instant before checking over his shoulder. ''Let me have your coat, Abby.''

''I'm not—'' Yes, she *was* warm enough for once. And she couldn't go on trying to hide her stomach from him. He already knew how pregnant she was. She shrugged out of her threadbare coat, annoyed at her own self-consciousness.

''Great.'' Nick took it and laid it over a chair, his housekeeping efforts evidently already forgotten. ''Now, sit.'' He pointed imperiously to a smoky-blue couch. ''I'll be a jiffy in the kitchen.''

She crossed her arms and sank into the plump corduroy cushions. The blues and magentas were strong and appealing. Clearly he'd spared no expense on the decor.

''This is lovely, Nick,'' she said.

He stuck his head around a partition. ''What did you say?'' His hair stood on end in front, and he was in the act of pushing it more awry.

''This.'' She made herself look away. ''Your home is lovely.''

He had that rare and irresistible mixture of masculine magic and total lack of self-awareness.

''Thanks. Coming from you, I'm flattered. Michael says you're very artistic.'' He went back to clattering with things she couldn't see.

Abby pushed herself upright. Her back ached. That was a new development she'd have to mention to the doctor. Wasn't it too early for backaches? She shook her head impatiently. Everything was fine.

"Let me help you." The kitchen was small, with counters lining two sides and a third Formica-topped space forming a central island.

Nick's muffled voice came from the recesses of a narrow corner pantry. "No need." He stood on tiptoe, reaching to the back of the top shelf.

Abby craned to see what he was doing. Two mugs were already arranged on a teak tray, and hissing milk climbed steadily up the sides of a pan on the stove. "There's a need!" She snatched the pan from the heat and held it over the sink.

"What's the matter?" He stepped back, holding a rusty tin in one hand.

"Well, one more second, Nicholas Stuart, and..." She laughed and it felt good. "Cleaning baked milk from stoves is pretty low on my list of fun activities."

"Mine, too. Thanks." Nick laughed, too, and took the pan from her. Then he caught her staring at the tin he held. "Ah, I can manage now," he said, the laugh fading to a sheepish grin. "Your new drink mix?"

"Oh, what the hell. I was always a lousy liar." With a flourish, he inserted a spoon beneath the lid and pried it off. "There wasn't a new mix. I just didn't want to come in here alone, and I needed an excuse to lure you. Forgive me?"

When he looked like that, what woman could *not* forgive him? "I forgive you," she said softly, meeting his fine eyes. "And I love plain old chocolate of any kind." She started to turn away. "And I also didn't feel like going into an empty apartment any sooner than I had to." She'd said too much, but it didn't seem to matter.

They sat side by side, drinking silently, watching the fire, for several minutes before Nick spoke. "How do you feel?"

Tension shot back into her body. "Great," she said. "There's nothing like a fire and a hot drink to bring you back to life." Let him leave it at that.

"Mmm." He looked into his mug. "That wasn't exactly what I was asking."

Abby didn't answer. She couldn't answer.

"When—when—I'm not very practiced at this, Abby. When will the baby be born?"

A shaky feeling started in her arms and legs. "About the beginning of January, I think." As if the baby knew its mother was anxious, what felt like a tiny foot jabbed at Abby's side. She shifted involuntarily.

Nick watched her closely. "So, there's only a couple of months to go. You're seven months pregnant?"

"As far as I know." She'd never had this kind of conversation with a man other than her doctor. Even Michael was—well, he was Michael, and he glossed over any subject he considered outside his range.

"Is everything going smoothly? Does the doctor think you're as well as you should be?"

The baby kicked again, and this time Abby saw Nick's eyes catch the movement. She blushed violently. "I'm fine."

"What does that feel like?" He nodded at her abdomen. "You must feel very close to the baby when it's inside you."

The man was disarmingly natural. Abby took a deep breath. "At first I felt like a cage full of fluttering birds. Now I think an elephant house might be more appropriate."

He didn't smile or move his gaze. Tentatively, he placed a hand on her belly and waited. The baby performed on cue, and Nick looked up, smiling broadly. "That's something," he said. "Marvelous." He smoothed her dress, pressing harder.

Abby blinked, her eyes stinging. John had never shown any interest in his child's development. He'd certainly never wanted to feel movement. From the instant he'd discovered she was pregnant, he hadn't touched Abby at all. She closed her eyes. For a crazy instant she was tempted to lean against Nick's chest, to ask him to hold her.

"Oh, good Lord. I'm sorry, Abby." Nick withdrew his hand as if it burned. Color stained his high cheekbones. "I'm sorry if I embarrassed you, Abby. I didn't think."

She cleared her throat. "It's okay. Nick, can we talk about my job?" *Keep on track,* she ordered herself.

He stood and set down his mug before putting more wood on the fire. "I thought Michael said you designed those display things in stores." His back was toward her.

"I did. I—" She swallowed. "I had a fall from a ladder and—"

Nick stood forcefully. "When? When did you fall? Did you see the doctor?"

His concern shouldn't make her feel so good, so warm. "It wasn't serious. I just decided to do something else until after the baby's born."

"You intend to go back to work then?"

She didn't meet his eyes. "I'll have to." She set aside her mug.

"Nick, things will get better. But for a little while I'm not—"

This was impossible. She'd never cried poor mouth to anyone, and she wouldn't now.

"You need money," Nick supplied bluntly. "I understand. We've all been there. But do you need it so badly you have to work in a Laundromat? I shouldn't have thought John would go for that. Or doesn't he know?"

This had to be over quickly. "He's at sea. He doesn't know I quit my job." At least she hadn't lied.

"I see. But Michael, and your folks——"

She cut him off quickly. "No! No, Nick. I can't go into it, but they're the real reason I'm asking, no, begging you not to mention any of this. I promise you I can work it out on my own. If I find I can't, I will go to Michael, and I know he'll help me."

Nick returned to the couch and sat sideways, facing her. "Do you know what you're asking?"

"Yes," she said evenly. "I'm asking you to pretend you know no more about me now than you did before you walked into that Laundromat tonight."

Abby thought she saw a glint of anger darken Nick's eyes. She was imagining things. "Can you do that, Nick?" she pressed. "Forget you saw me there?"

"Let's just say I'll forget it around Michael. Is that a deal?"

She hesitated. "A deal, I guess." He'd stick to it; she knew he would.

Nick made up his mind. He would ask now and her reaction would give him the confirmation he needed. "Abby." He waited until she looked at him. Her eyes were huge, the gray softer and more veiled than ever, if possible. "John is...he's at sea."

"So you said. I wondered when he was coming back."

She stood and picked up her coat, bowing her head while she slid an arm into one sleeve. Silently cursing himself, Nick got up and stood behind her to help.

Her lips parted. Damn, he shouldn't have done that. She was going through enough already. But he had his answer.

"John?" The last traces of color drained from her cheeks. Nick made fists to stop himself touching her. "John is due back? He's been gone a lot recently."

"This could be another long trip." Her voice was level but

reedy. She gave a high little laugh. "I've learned to expect John when—when I see him."

"Sure." Nick wished he could haul back everything he'd said in the past two minutes. Abby headed for the door. "What time do you have to be at work tomorrow?" he asked.

"Oh, I don't know." She dug in her pockets, and he heard keys rattle. "I have to check my schedule."

He let her out and smelled the faint scent of some sort of wild flower as she passed him. "Will you call me when you're ready to leave? My number's on the tenant list. I'm on layover for ten days, so I can take you anywhere you need to go." He was sticking his heart firmly on his sleeve, and he'd sworn not to do that.

"Thank you," Abby said, without meeting his gaze.

He made sure she got into her condo and returned slowly to his own. Standing at his favorite place by the window, he stared into the street. Streetlights cast an eerie glitter on frost-covered shrubs.

The cold was in Nick's soul. He was no longer safely fantasizing about another man's off-limits wife. He was falling hard and hopelessly for a pregnant woman who still loved the husband who'd deserted her.

## Chapter Five

Abby moved quietly around the condo. She'd finish getting ready and catch a bus to work before Nick had any idea she'd gone. Today she had the early shift, and he'd have no way of knowing that. When she failed to call, he was likely to contact her and discover she'd already been to the Laundromat and returned home. Soon he'd get over his natural protective urge and forget her. She was still worried he might make a chance remark to Michael, but all she could do was pray he wouldn't.

With exaggerated caution, she tiptoed to the door, with a brown sack containing a thermos of coffee and a cheese sandwich scrunched beneath one arm. She would find a way to thank Nick for his kindness of last night, but not now. The bus stop was a block away, out of sight of their building. All she had to do was get there.

Grimacing, she eased off the deadbolt, turned the handle and slipped onto the landing. With equal care, she slid the locks into place and turned toward the stairs.

"Morning. Thought I heard you up and about. Early shift?"

*Nick*. He sat sideways on the top step, his feet crossed at the ankles, his back braced against the wall.

"You couldn't have heard...I mean...I didn't make any noise." She bent her head and smothered a laugh. "What are you doing, Nick? Sentry duty?"

"Am I so awful you have to sneak away?"

"You know better than that. I just hate being a nuisance, that's all." She was glad to see him, even thrilled, and the feeling disquieted her. Abby sobered. "How long have you been out here? It's only eight o'clock. You were waiting for me, weren't you?"

"Yup. I figured you might try something like this. I was going to camp here all day if necessary."

Abby approached him, unsure what to say next. Nick swung his legs aside and offered her a hand. After a second's hesitation she gripped his fingers and sank awkwardly beside him on the step.

"What's in the bag?"

"Coffee and a sandwich. Want some coffee?" She only had one cup, but she could wash it out at the store.

"Thanks. Not now. I'll have some in the car." He smoothed a curl from the corner of her eye, and she flinched. "Abby, what's wrong—really wrong? You aren't doing so well, are you?"

She met his gaze defiantly. "I'm doing just fine, Nick. Terrific. Why shouldn't I be? Pregnancy's no big deal—happens every day."

"You're too alone with it."

Abby fashioned a brilliant smile. "Every woman's alone with pregnancy. No one else can do it for you."

"You know what I mean."

"**Do** I?" She set down the sack. Nick Dorset was a bright, bright man, and too perceptive. And she was beginning to like him too much.

"When are you going to give in and admit you aren't making it?"

Abby drove a hand into her hair. "I *am* making it, Nick. What makes you think I'm not? And why would you care?" She didn't want him to answer that. "For some reason you feel responsible for me—don't ask me why, unless it's because my brother's your friend. I'm perfectly in control, and if I weren't, it wouldn't be your problem. I had to take a little interim job, that's all. Why the big deal?"

He put an arm around her shoulder and shook her gently. "That's what I keep asking you." His strength acted to weaken her. She wanted to put her head on his shoulder.

"You're the one who's keeping secrets from her family," he continued. "If I wasn't pretty sure you were having a rough time, it would be one thing, but I am sure, and I'm going to have to play stand-in until you've got someone else around to help. I want to be here for you, because—for—for Michael's sake." His brown eyes reflected specks of light from the window over the stairs. He touched her chin lightly. "Would you be offended if I offered to lend you some money?"

"No! I don't need anything." Abby stood, immediately became dizzy and grabbed the banister.

Nick didn't notice. "Only till John gets back?" He picked up the bag and held his left hand toward her.

Abby looked straight ahead. "Thanks, but I've got enough

money. I have to leave. All I need to ruin my day is to miss the bus.''

''Okay, forget I mentioned a loan. Come on. The guy what brings you, takes you back. That's something else my mother taught me.'' He grasped her unresisting hand and tucked it through his arm.

''Your mother sounds like a nice lady. You and your family are close, aren't you?''

''She is and we are, thank God.'' He turned a sharp gaze on her. ''But you think a lot of yours, too. I know that from Michael and from your overprotective instincts toward them.''

She nodded. Confiding in him might feel good; it could also be very dangerous. Abby walked downstairs beside Nick. At five foot ten, she looked up to few men. Her eyes only reached his chin. She looked at him now, at his clear-cut profile, the sensitiveness of his slightly parted lips, his strong teeth. If only— She flexed the muscles of her jaw. If only Nick were part of her life? She was truly an idiotic dreamer. And a very pregnant, not-quite-divorced dreamer. What else did that kind of thinking make her?

Further argument about accepting a lift was pointless. Nick ushered her firmly to his car, and within fifteen minutes they sat outside the Laundromat. A fragile sun failed to stroke away the frost on the parking lot. Abby made ready to get out.

''Wait.'' Nick reached across and took her hand. ''When do you get off work?''

She rested her head back and closed her eyes. He was like the proverbial dog with a bone. ''I'm not sure. Look.'' She turned toward him. ''Don't worry about me, okay? You've already gone far beyond the call of duty. I give you full marks for chivalry, recommend you for white knighthood, even.''

He didn't laugh. ''You sound flip.''

''I'm not.'' She became uncomfortably warm. She had sounded flip and rude and ungrateful. ''Thank you for everything, Nick. But forget me and get on with your life, huh? I'm not your concern.''

He looked at her mouth while she spoke. She brought her lips together, but several seconds passed before his eyes returned to hers. She saw him swallow. The instinctive sensation inside her, long buried but not forgotten, spread fast and powerfully. Not now, maybe never again, should she allow this reaction, and never with a man she had no right to.

''Have dinner with me,'' Nick said quietly.

Abby received the invitation like an unexpected blow. She couldn't form a reply.

"Will you, Abby?"

"I've got to get into the store."

"Abby?"

What did he want from her? He couldn't be attracted to a woman seven months pregnant whom he thought happily married. Even without the pregnancy, he wasn't the kind of man to interfere in the marriage of a friend's sister.

"Can't you answer me?"

She started. "I...yes, yes, I guess so. Yes, I'll have dinner with you." *Fool. Poor, lonely fool.*

"What time shall I pick you up?"

Panic gripped her. "I don't know. Maybe we should do this another time. I'm not sure when I'll get off."

"I'll just stay and wait for you, then."

"Wait?" she croaked disbelievingly. "I've got a full day's work to do."

"How long is a full day's work?"

He had her. "Eight hours," she muttered. "Please don't stay or come back. I must drive my car home today."

He seemed to consider for a while. "Okay. But give me your keys for a minute. I'll bring them in to you."

Abby dithered, then found the keys in her purse. Nick took them and came to help her from the car. He smiled, bouncing the keys in his palm. "See you in a jiffy."

She still didn't move.

"Get in out of the cold." He waved, and she took a few steps backward. "Go on," he insisted. "I won't make off with your chariot, honest."

"Yes. Right." Abby clutched her brown paper bag to her chest and turned away. She didn't look back until she was inside the empty store. The place was cold, great misty moons swelling on each windowpane. She rubbed a hole and peered out.

At first she didn't see him. Then the noise of an engine grinding pulled her attention to the windshield of the Pinto. Beyond it's white-coated surface, she saw his silhouette. He was checking out her car. The heavy warmth trembled into her again.

Nick slid out of the car and lifted the hood. He got a rag from the trunk of his BMW and bent over her engine. Checking oil and water—all those things she'd sworn to learn about as soon as she felt stronger. Day by day she became more aware of the need to become totally self-sufficient. But at this moment she loved watching Nick's lean body bend and stretch, his muscular jean-clad legs stiffen against the side of the car. Abby's sigh drained her lungs. The feelings she was developing for Nick Dorset were pointless and could be disastrous if they made her careless in what she said to him.

The hood slammed. Nick came toward the shop, wiping his hands. His straight back, the slight swing of his wide shoulders, accentuated the loose-limbed confidence of his walk.

"Whew." He expelled a cloudy breath as he came in. "It's almost as cold in here as it is out there. Here." He handed over the keys. "Believe it or not, everything seems fine. How's seven for picking you up?"

Abby spread her hands. "I really don't think I should, Nick. And you must have better things to do. You've very kind, but—"

He waited patiently, not attempting to interrupt. When she stopped, her lips parted and he took a single step and kissed her cheek. "Seven?" he asked, his fingers lightly circling her neck.

Abby nodded, keeping her hands at her sides with difficulty.

"And, lady, you can trust me—with anything. I'm not a fool. I can figure a few things out for myself, and they're safe with me. Okay?"

She nodded again.

"See you." Fleetingly he smoothed her hair and left.

Abby stood motionless, watching him stride to his silver car and swing his long legs inside. He rolled down the window and waved, his grin broad, before driving away.

*What? Abby wondered. What things have you figured out, Nick?*

HE HAD TO TALK to someone, and Janet was the obvious victim. Nick ran upstairs and let himself into his condo. He calculated the time difference between Seattle and Omaha. Janet probably would be getting Penny's lunch.

Jeez, he wished it was a respectable time of day for a drink. What was happening to him?

Janet's phone rang seven times. Nick started to hang up. Damn. Maybe she was driving Penny somewhere, or meeting Crete at that little café in the basement of the building where he worked.

"Hello."

The receiver glanced off the cradle as he pulled it back. "Janet? Is that you?"

She laughed. "Yes, Nick. I'm me." "Smartie. You always were a smart mouth. I thought you weren't there."

"I'm here."

Nick shook his head and smiled. "Good. Now we both know where we are. How's Crete?"

"Wonderful."

"Penny?"

"Wonderful."

"Mom and Dad?"

"Nick..."

"Are they okay?" He sounded mentally incompetent.

A sigh gusted along the line. "Mom and Dad are wonderful, too. What's the deal, Nick?"

He pulled out a dining chair and slumped into it. "Just felt like talking to you." That much was true. He crossed his legs on top of the table and grimaced at the marks the heels of his boots made on the glass.

"I feel like talking to you, too, brother. But why do I get this feeling you're about to drop a bombshell?"

"Because you don't have enough to occupy that fertile imagination of yours." Nick scrunched down, rested his neck on the chair's back and stared at the ceiling. "I'm on a long layover. I get bored, that's all."

"Thanks a lot. So bored you're reduced to calling me."

He ignored the remark. "Janet, have you ever had the feeling there was something different about me?"

Janet didn't answer.

"Are you still there?"

"What do you mean, *different*?"

He rolled his eyes. "*Unusual.* Not the same as most guys."

Janet giggled.

Nick shifted to rest his elbows on the table. "Listen, you. Be serious. This is serious to me. I wonder about myself sometimes. I mean, I've gotten fairly serious with one or two women. There was Lisa; I almost thought she was it for a while. But I could never quite... I don't know. Maybe I'm...different."

A muffled choking sound suggested Janet was working at control. "Nick, is there something you haven't told me?"

He groaned. "Like what? I don't mean I'm into whips and chains, if that's what you mean. Or that I've got a thing for some male flight attendant. Although——'' he paused for effect ''——there was this one who——''

''Stop!'' Janet snuffled the way she always had when she laughed hard. ''If there's one guy I'm not worried about in that area, it's you. Remember, you were the kid who ran the longest kiss contest behind the girls' locker rooms, and won. And if I'm right, you were only twelve at the time. So quite being squirrelly and spit out your problem.''

''I can't.''

The line pinged and popped while Janet digested his announcement. Then she said, ''You're in love. I knew it. The last time we talked, you sounded funny, and I knew you'd fallen for someone. Who is she?''

Nick scrubbed a hand over his face. He was in a big mess. How did he explain that to his sister? ''You're running ahead,'' he said at last. ''Way ahead. I don't know what I feel for sure yet.''

''But you feel something for *someone*, correct?''

''Yep.''

''So, follow your heart and see where it leads you.''

''Straight into hell,'' he muttered.

''What?'' Janet's voice rose. ''What did you say about hell?''

''I'm in a bind, Janet. I don't think she really knows I'm alive.''

She gave a short derisive laugh. ''That would be a new twist. Who is this gorgeous paragon?''

''I can't say.''

''That's ridiculous.''

''I can't. Not yet.'' He stood and walked slowly around the table. ''Maybe never.''

A hard breath sounded. ''You're driving me nuts. What do you want me to say? First you ask a bunch of questions about your mental health—at least I think that's what you were asking. Then you tell me you've fallen for someone. And now you can't tell me who she is. Tell me how to react, and I'll do it.''

''Janet.'' He squeezed his eyes shut. A pain started in his temples. ''This isn't your average situation. I'm not sure how to…I'm not sure… Dammit, I don't know what's the best thing to do next, and after that, and after that. She's kind of off-limits in a way.''

''Oh, God, Nick. Don't tell me.'' Janet gave her famous tuneless whistle. ''She's married.''

''On the head, kid. She's married to a one-hundred-percent creep who doesn't—''

"Understand her?" Janet broke in. "Nick, every man or woman who wants out of a relationship is misunderstood."

He paced, placing heel and toe deliberately. "You didn't let me finish. He doesn't want her anymore, only I'm not supposed to know that. He's left her, and I'm not supposed to know that, either. She's protecting the bastard, sorry, protecting him. She's not telling anyone he's taken off, not even her folks. I think I'm the only one who knows, and she doesn't know I do."

"Whoa! How do you know? Did you turn clairvoyant?"

"I just know, okay?"

Loud music blasted his eardrum. He jerked the phone away. Janet covered the receiver, then came back, sounding breathless. "Sorry, Nick. Penny gets bored when I'm on the phone. She does things to make sure I know she's still around. Kids are a challenge sometimes."

His throat tightened. "You're lucky. Kids are neat."

The following silence went on and on.

"Janet, I know this woman's on her own. She's my neighbor, and I saw her husband move out. I can see it all in her eyes, too, do you understand?"

"Yes," Janet said slowly. "Does she have children?"

"Uh, no. Why do you ask?"

"No reason, no reason. Just a feeling. You don't normally extol the virtues of parenthood."

Nick felt bone tired. "I didn't know I had."

"Forget it. Maybe I'm reading too much into everything you say. Tell me more about this woman, Nick."

He dropped to the floor and sat cross-legged, an elbow on each knee. He wished Janet were here, flesh and blood, looking right at him. "She's gentle, Jan, very quiet and soft, the kind of woman a man—this man—dreams about meeting. And she's got guts. I've been kind of trying to draw her out, and she covers up. She's more worried about hurting her parents and brother than what happens to her."

"You are in love!"

"Come on, Jan, help me, don't clown around."

He heard her tap her fingernail against the mouthpiece. "I'm coming to visit. Mom will help Crete with Penny. She's wanted me to get out there and see what you're up to. She thinks you'll open up to me better than you would to her."

"You're overreacting. No one needs to come. I just wanted

advice. You asked questions and I answered. Now you're rushing out here. And why are you and Mom talking about me?''

''She's always talking about you, Nick. You should know that. 'When's that boy going to settle down?' You've heard the line. But you asked why I think you need help, so I'll tell you. You never said a word about what your friend looks like, that's why. She's gentle, quiet, soft. This is the guy who used to measure female brains in inches, thirty-six and above.''

Nick couldn't help laughing. ''That was in my youth. Abby's tall, five-ten or so, and thin—too thin. Short black curls, big gray eyes. Janet, she's the loveliest woman I've ever seen.''

''Abby? Nice name. And she's married to someone else.''

He sighed. ''And she's married to someone else—at the moment.''

''You intend to change that.''

''Maybe. Hell, that's the problem. I don't know what I intend to do. But I do know I can't get her out of my mind.''

Janet cleared her throat. ''You've tried?''

''I've been running seven miles a day.''

''You tried.''

''Yeah, and it didn't work. Well, Janet, you must have things to do. Give my love to everyone.''

''Nick.''

''Yes?''

''Would you have room to put me up if I came for a day or two in a couple of weeks?''

He drove his teeth into his bottom lip and calculated. Abby would be seven and a half months pregnant then. *Oh, God.* ''Of course I've have room. I'd love to see you. It's been a long time since just the two of us were together.''

''I'll let you know the date. Hang in there. If Abby feels anything for you, she'll tell you the truth about her husband.''

''You're right.''

''I am, Nick. She has to be the one to mention it, remember that.''

''I'll remember. Bye, Janet.''

He heard the way she slid the phone into its receiver. She was thinking. Nick checked his watch. Nine hours before he could pick up Abby. He'd be thinking, too.

An open fire made up for almost anything lacking in the home decorating department, Abby decided. She'd stopped at a supermarket and bought two bundles of logs. This was the first fire she'd ever lit, and she was pleased it had caught and drawn so well. All those years of watching her father and Michael at work must have taught her something.

She stood back to look at the room again. Moving the couch and chair closer to the fireplace had produced a more intimate look. A hideous gap glared behind the grouping, but with luck she could keep Nick's mind focused on eating, and he wouldn't notice the emptiness in the room.

John had taken the turntable, but she still had her cassette deck and speakers. For the first time in weeks, she slipped in a favorite jazz tape and jogged in time to its beat into the kitchen.

Nick had better like Japanese food, particularly sushi. She'd tried to reconstruct comments Michael had made about Nick and she was certain she remembered something about eating sushi in Honolulu. She'd even splurged on a bottle of good sake. Nick might argue that they should go out as he'd suggested, but she'd soon convince him this was better, and after all he'd done, she owed him a meal at home and a chance to relax.

The house and her efforts in the kitchen were as appealing as they were going to get; now she'd better see what she could do with herself.

JAZZ. NICK SMILED and fingered the knot in his tie. Abby was playing jazz again after God knew how long. He used to hear her doing that late some afternoons when she got home from work. That was in the days when she occasionally smiled her shy smile on the stairs and wasn't quite so thin.

She was looking forward to a night out on the town. His hand shook slightly, and he studied his fingers with disbelief. Old Dorset, Mr. Cool, shaking like a high school senior going to his prom. He hoped she'd like the restaurant where he'd made reservations. Canlis was one of the best places in Seattle. Its location, overlooking Lake Washington, was spectacular. He wanted to give Abby wonderful things. And wonderful food, things to make her feel good and be healthy, seemed a good place to start. He'd bought flowers, too, long-stemmed pink roses. Later he'd find a way to give her the rest of what she should have. He'd find a way to be with her...all the time....

Nick tried to ignore his other thoughts and reached for his suit jacket. How long was it after a woman gave birth before she could—*Hell.*

ABBY TRIED NOT to watch the clock in her bedroom. She already knew she had less than ten minutes left, and nothing she'd tried on made her look less like a melon. She avoided the mirror. Looking at herself wouldn't change a thing.

The dress she chose was one she wore in summer when she wasn't pregnant, another of her favorite cotton peasant dresses. She liked its blue-gray color because it did nice things for her eyes. The loose shape floated free from her shoulders and at least her legs looked good in it. Too bad it was intended for seventy degrees rather than thirty.

That was it, the best she could do. If Nick Dorset had wanted a glamorous companion tonight, he wouldn't have chosen her. Abby considered lipstick and discarded the idea since it only heightened her pallor, then returned to the kitchen. Where they would eat was still the big question.

NICK STOOD IN FRONT of Abby's door and shifted the roses from one hand to the other. He could think of a lot of guys who would laugh at this exhibition. He ran a hand over his hair and felt it spring awry again. To button the jacket or not to button the jacket? He did it up, undid it and grinned, shaking his head, before jabbing the bell.

The door opened at once. "Hi. Come in." Abby fiddled with a satin tie at the neck of her dress. Color swept into her cheeks. Nick's thighs tautened. She was fantastic.

"Here." He shoved the roses at her, and she almost dropped them.

They laughed.

"Roses?" She smelled them deeply before looking up at him, clutching the crackly package to her breasts. "I love roses. Thank you. I can't remember the last time... Thank you, Nick."

He shrugged. "They aren't anything." From the corner of his eye he noticed the fire. The room was warmer, less Spartan somehow. "Are you ready?"

She opened her mouth and closed it again before pulling him inside and reaching to push the door shut. "Do you like Japanese food?"

Nick looked more closely at the room. It had been prepared for guests, or a guest. His heart made an unaccustomed rotation. "I love Japanese food. Why?"

"Because I thought...I mean... Well, Nick, you've been such a dear to me it's time I did something for you, and I make a pretty mean sushi. No one would employ me in a sushi bar, mind you, but I'm pretty good just the same." Her hands grasped the rose stems tightly. Nick wanted to warn her about the thorns but kept quiet.

She rushed on, "I made some stops on the way home and got all the stuff. They pounded the octopus for me. Do you like octopus?"

"Love it." He didn't want to be paid back for a couple of car rides. He wanted to take her somewhere special.

"You'd enjoy eating here, then? I got sake. I couldn't find that green mustard, but they had some hot stuff. And I found ginger slivers." Her eyes were huge and anxious.

Nick swallowed a sigh. Being with her, anywhere, was all he wanted. But he hated the thought of her spending money she couldn't afford and working some more after a day at that dump of a Laundromat.

"I messed up, didn't I?" she whispered. Her gaze swept over him. "You're dressed to go out. I expect you'd rather do that."

"No." Nick smiled, snapping to life. What Abby needed most was cheerful company and a chance to do whatever pleased her. "I'd much rather eat here." He took the flowers and wrapped an arm impulsively around her shoulders, pulling her close. "I'll cancel our restaurant reservations. But you have to let me help." Her face was inches from his, her mouth a whisper away.

Abby felt his breath on her forehead. He felt so good, smelled so good, clean. She slid an arm around his waist and squeezed quickly before letting him go. He continued to hold her, gazing down at her body.

She rested a palm on his chest. "What is it?"

He started, looking at her face again. "I never held a pregnant lady before, that's all."

"I guess it seems strange," she said, trying not to stiffen.

"Different, that's all." He spread his fingers on her back, stroked lightly. "I was thinking how special it is to watch a life grow, to feel it."

Hesitantly Abby smoothed his lapel. She didn't want to move. "You're a special man, Nick."

"I doubt it, but thanks." He smiled into her eyes. His mouth was irresistible, wide, naturally upturned at the corners. Abby caught the glimmer of his teeth. How would his mouth feel, taste? "What are you thinking, Abby?"

Her attention shot to his eyes. The expression there was intense. Did he sense how attracted she was to him, share some of the sensations that tempted her to reach up and kiss him?

She was dreaming, and she hadn't answered his question. Abby took a deep breath. "I was thinking we should get my roses in water and do something about dinner."

He laughed softly, tilting back his head. "You're right." He released her. "Come one. Let's create our masterpiece."

Abby followed him slowly into the kitchen, where he set about proving he knew a lot more about preparing sushi than she did. While she arranged the roses in a vase and found chopsticks, he mixed and chopped, wrapped concoctions in kelp and arranged them on platters. Soon one counter was laden.

"I'll heat the sake in the microwave," Abby said, decanting the colorless liquid into a glass jug. She assembled small pottery cups on a tray with a pot of green tea.

Nick stood back, surveying their handywork. "All ready," he announced and glanced toward the living room.

He had to notice the absence of tables. Abby swept up plates and chopsticks and napkins. "I thought we'd eat buffet style. Take what you like and come back for more." She avoided his eyes. "I have to do something about getting a dining table one of these days."

"I like buffet style and knees," Nick assured her. He leaned close, pushed back a curl from her temple and waited until she met his gaze. "Everything looks terrific in here. You light a good fire."

Abby started to relax. "My dad and Michael are the experts. This is the first one I've made myself, but I remembered watching them and did the same."

"I can't wait any longer for this food," Nick said, piling sushi on a plate. He poured a glass of sake and looked inquiringly at

Abby, who shook her head. "Of course. Tea for pregnant people, I guess." He held a steaming cup and his glass in one hand. "Load up, and we'll sit on the couch."

Was he really as enthusiastic as he sounded? She could choose to believe so, and she would. "Sounds great," she said and put several pieces of sushi on her own plate, and mustard and soyu.

In the living room Nick put his food and the drinks on an end table and shrugged out of his jacket. He draped it over the chair and waited until Abby was seated on the couch before sinking easily down beside her and balancing the plate on his knee. "Oh, I love this stuff," he commented, sinking his teeth into a piece of tender salmon. "Mike and I have this favorite place in Honolulu, but I guess he told you that."

"Mmm," Abby managed around a mouthful of yellow tuna.

"Do you like Hawaii?"

"Love it. The climate's great—in small doses. I prefer the seasons we have here."

"You come from…"

"Omaha, Nebraska. Nice. Home. But too cold in winter, and I just happen to think Seattle's the only place on earth I want to spend the rest of my life."

Abby's stomach tightened. Being relieved this was where he wanted to be would do her no good, but she was relieved just the same. "I love it here, too. I've never lived anywhere else. I was born in the north end of Seattle, in the house where my parents still live. Michael was born there, too. We went to the same schools, knew the same people—although Michael's two years older than me, and back then he never missed a chance to rub it in." She held her bottom lip in her teeth, smiling, remembering.

"That makes you twenty-seven."

Abby inclined her head, watching him get up and put more sushi on his plate. "It's not supposed to be polite to ask a woman's age." She sipped her tea and regarded him archly over the rim of her cup as he sat again.

"I didn't," he retorted and brushed a knuckle along her jaw. "But Michael's twenty-nine, the same as I am. I'm not Einstein, but I can figure it out from there. And by the way—" he took her in thoroughly from head to toe "—twenty-seven looks fantastic on you."

"Hah!" Abby pursed her mouth in mock skepticism. "I bet you tell every female you meet the same thing,"

"Wrong," he retorted. "Only the fantastic ones."

She chuckled. "You know a lot about me from Michael. All I know about you is that you come from Omaha. Spill."

He finished his sake, set his plate on the rug and spread an arm along the back of the couch behind her. "I'm a very complicated man, so this may take time."

"We've got time." She elbowed his ribs, and he caught her hand and held it.

He let out a bored sigh. "Nick Dorset, 29, six-two, one-eighty. One narrow escape but never married. Father an architect, mother a grade-school teacher. One sister, Janet, 31, degree in early childhood education but busy being married and raising one two-year-old daughter—Penny-the-prodigy." He sighed and frowned. "What else?"

"Achievements? Hobbies?"

"Boy, maybe I should go see if I can find my pedigree. You really want to know the little stuff?"

"I've got a feeling it's not so little."

"Where were you when I needed a fan club?" He rested his head back and looked at the ceiling. "Lettered in track in high school. Got an athletic scholarship to the University of Nebraska. Didn't make the Olympics. Did make it through the school of engineering. Air force—pilot. Fell in love for the first time, and can't get planes out of my blood. Got out of the service and went straight to commercial flying. Now I'm dreaming of owning my own business. I'd like to operate a float plane service between the San Juan Islands. How am I doing?"

"Great. You sound marvelous. And you'll do it with the float planes, Nick. I know you will."

He'd turned his face toward her. The room's subdued lighting deepened the shadows beneath his cheekbones and made his eyes unfathomable. Abby cleared her throat. He still held her hand, and she concentrated on the warmth of his strong fingers on hers.

"There isn't anything very earth-shattering to know about me. I was an art major and went into store design, which I'm crazy about. Obviously, I didn't escape attachment. I'm looking forward to the baby: it's what I always wanted, although maybe not..." She blinked rapidly. "Maybe I could have timed my first pregnancy better."

"What do you mean?"

She'd slipped, said something she hadn't intended to say. "Nothing, really, except it would have been nice to be better established and settled."

"You can't always get things exactly right."

He was so direct. "No," Abby agreed. "You can't." She searched for a way to change the subject and grabbed for the first inspiration. "Running. You like to run, don't you? I've seen you heading for the track."

"Running keeps me sane sometimes. I—" He stopped abruptly and turned away. "Shall I turn the tape over?"

"Yes, please." His reaction puzzled her. "I'm going to start jogging."

Nick faced her, instantly frowning. "Not now, you're not."

She stared at him, irritated. "No, not now. Of course not now." He seemed to think she was some kind of invalid. "I meant after the baby's born. Having a baby doesn't mean a woman has to languish on a couch for the rest of her life, you know."

He smiled faintly. "I know that. My sister says she's never been fitter than she is since she had Penny. You should see that little kid go. I was just afraid you'd decided to handle exercise the same way you're handling the rest of your life."

Abby made fists at her sides and had to grab for her sliding plate. "How am I handling the rest of my life?"

He gathered their dishes and carried them wordlessly into the kitchen.

One step behind him, Abby tapped his back. "How am I handling the rest of my life, Nick?"

"As if you're invincible. Superwoman. Abby can do anything, and she doesn't need anyone, right?" He turned the faucet sharply to run water into the sink.

"I don't need someone to wash dishes, if that's what you mean." Immediately she hated the words. "Forget I said that. It was snippy. But leave that, please; I'll do them later."

He did as she asked, wiping his hands on a dish towel. "Can we sit and talk for a while? Or am I being kicked out?"

She *had* offended him. "Stay, Nick. I'm sorry if I'm not very good company. It's just that...I seem to fly off the handle easily these days. I would like you to stay." But not to ask questions, she thought.

Nick put in another tape and added wood to the fire. He sat on the couch and kept his eyes on Abby's face while she joined him.

"Any trouble at the Laundromat today?"

"No. I wasn't even busy."

"How many days a week do you work?"

"Six."

He loosened his tie and undid the top button of his shirt. "Seems like a lot when you're pregnant."

"It won't hurt me."

"I hope you're right, Abby." He slid a hand behind her neck and swayed her toward him until her shoulder rested on his chest. "If I'm pushing in where I don't belong, forgive me. But I care what happens to you. You're one of the world's special people."

She closed her eyes, grateful he couldn't see her face. "Thank you. But I'm fine, really. I can manage." He felt so strong, so very masculine.

Nick ruffled her hair and removed his hand. "And John will be back, and everything will be fine again."

The joy died. "Yes," she said. How would she cope? "Would you like some coffee?"

"Sounds great," Nick replied, and watched her slide forward and stand before going to the kitchen. Every second made him want her more...want her and the baby. He passed a hand over his face. The woman was still in love with her husband. She must be, or she'd admit the guy had dropped out for good.

"You take it black, don't you?" Abby called from the kitchen.

"Please." He noticed two books on the floor beside the couch and picked up the top one. *Becoming Parents.* The front cover showed a pregnant woman in a leotard lying on her side. Behind her a man reclined, also on his side, a hand on her belly, his face resting against her hair. Nick swallowed and began turning the pages.

Dishes clattered in the kitchen, and he closed the book quickly, but Abby didn't appear. She was running water over the dirty dishes in the sink, and he heard the dishwasher open. He should help.

Quietly he flipped through the book again, stopping at a section with the heading, "Guidelines for the Labor Companion." Brief instructions followed for dealing with various stages of labor. "If she loses control, be firm, keep talking, help her resume proper breathing. Massage her back or abdomen if this is helpful." Nick ran a finger down the page, picking out sections on irritability, nausea or vomiting, the urge to push or bear down, what to do when the mother wanted to give up. "Encourage. She may say she can't do it, that she's losing control or can't go on." Sweat broke out on Nick's forehead. All this stuff was foreign, the way women coped with natural childbirth—women and their husbands. Who would Abby have?

A small sound broke his concentration. Abby hovered in front of him, a tray of coffee cups in her hands. She stared at the book in his lap.

"Let me take that." Nick reached for the tray and put it on the end table. "Sit down and tell me about all this." She didn't need to be made to feel awkward. He took a deep breath through his nose. "You're going to use this method of natural childbirth?"

Abby sat down and took the cup he offered. "Yes. It's best for the baby, and I want to know everything that's happening."

Nick swallowed some of his own coffee and made himself turn another page in the book. "Sharing a baby's birth is a unique privilege," he read. The sensation in the pit of his stomach was like nothing he'd felt before. He'd like to share the birth of Abby's baby. His skin turned cold. Now he knew he was becoming unhinged.

"Are you taking classes or something?"

"I've had one. I go to Seattle for them."

He knew what he was going to ask, and that he shouldn't. "Isn't John supposed to go with you?"

She averted her face. "His work makes it tough to plan like other people do."

Nick pressed on, hating himself, yet unable to stop. "So who will coach you? That's what it's called, right? Coaching?"

Her hands shook. She gripped the cup tightly, her fingers curled. "I have a friend, Marie Prince, she.... Well, she'll help if I ask her. If she's got time." Her chin came up. "And if that doesn't come off, I won't be the first woman to make it through without a coach. I'll learn the techniques well, and I'll do just fine."

How had she missed those books when she was cleaning up? Abby thought. She didn't want to discuss this, not with Nick. She didn't want to dwell on how alone she was likely to be when the time came. When she'd asked Marie to stand by, she'd admitted simply that she'd probably pass out and be useless. The class leader had volunteered help, if she was available, but that was iffy. Abby made herself smile at Nick and relax against the couch. How like him to immediately assume every father would make sure he was present for his child's birth. Nick would have been. The subject was something she'd never even broached to John. Nick was watching her thoughtfully. "My brother-in-law was with Janet when Penny was born. Afterward he carried on as if he'd given birth himself. He said it was the greatest thing that ever happened to him." He grinned and set down his cup. "Seems to me great experiences should be shared."

"You mean I'll be selfish if I go it alone?" She forced a laugh.

"If the horror stories are true, I might be prepared to spread a little of the greatness around. I have nightmares that I'll yell something stupid and make an ass of myself." Warmth flew up her neck. No one had ever made her tongue as loose as Nick did. Single men didn't want to hear all this.

"Do you suppose—," he began, then pressed his lips shut. He colored slightly. "I wondered if I could come to some of the classes with you."

Goose bumps shot out on Abby's arms. "Come? To childbirth education classes? Nick, you'd hate it."

"No, I wouldn't." He took her cup and put it beside his, held both her hands in his. "I'd be really interested. And then, if you needed me, I could...I could be with you for the delivery." He blushed furiously now. "I mean, I could take you to the hospital and cheer from the sidelines or something."

She doubted she'd heard correctly. He chafed her hands almost painfully, and she concentrated on watching his fingers move.

"Would you let me do that, Abby?"

"I don't know," she said slowly. Why would a man want to be present for the birth of another man's child? She'd curl up from embarrassment with Nick there.

"Will you think about it? Let me come to the classes, anyway. While—just while John's away. He'd probably be glad to know you had someone with you. And I know Michael would."

John, Michael. Abby's mind clouded. John didn't give a damn, and if Michael found out he'd fire questions with both barrels.

"Don't talk to Michael about the baby or the classes. He's not comfortable with the whole thing."

Nick felt an unaccustomed trembling in his limbs. He could hardly believe he was pressing for this. "Stop worrying about what I may say to Michael. I've got the message you want him kept out of your business." She hadn't asked him not to tell John, he noted with more satisfaction than he was proud of. And she hadn't totally refused to let him be part of what was happening to her.

She was quiet now. Far from relaxing her, he'd managed to heighten her anxiety. Tentatively he stroked the side of her face until she looked directly at him.

"Just like you say, Abby, everything's going to be okay," he said, pushing his fingers into her hair. He mustn't go too fast or risk confusing her.

Abby nodded and covered his hand. She blinked rapidly, and his throat tightened. The lady was determined not to cry, not to give herself away. He started to pull her head toward him and met no resistance. Leaning back, he settled her face against his shoulder and rested his chin on top of her head.

"You're a kind man, Nick, the best. I'm going to look forward to seeing you with a wife and children of your own."

Nick stared ahead and through the window at a dark, moonless sky. Oh, he was sterling, honesty itself. How fast would she run if she knew what he really wanted?

"Rest, Abby. Close your eyes. You look beat."

Her body untensed slightly. He felt the baby kick against his hip and suppressed a smile. Maybe he was going to pull this off, although a psychiatrist might enjoy figuring out why he wanted to.

Abby's breathing had become regular. Nick was surprised. She wouldn't be comfortable with the idea of falling asleep in his arms.

Despite himself, he drowsed.

The sharp click of a key in the lock snapped him wide awake. John Winston! Nick glanced down at Abby's bent head. She must be exhausted to hear nothing. His thoughts were scrambled. He heard the door sweep open. If he tried to put distance between himself and Abby, she'd be disoriented, then frightened. God, they couldn't do anything but face the music and find a way to explain the truth—nothing was happening here.

Careful not to awaken Abby, Nick craned to look over his shoulder, with a pleasant smile arranged on his lips.

The door slammed, and a man coughed. Heels clicked down the hall. "Hey, sis. Where are you?" Michael Harris said and halted in the entrance to the living room.

## Chapter Seven

Nick quelled the urge to laugh hysterically. Michael Harris, of all people. And Nick was alone, at night, with Michael's married pregnant sister and holding her while she slept. *Think quickly*, he commanded himself.

"What the hell—," Michael began.

Nick cut him off, "Shhh." He pressed a finger to his lips and raised his brows. "She's sleeping."

Michael, still in uniform, slowly removed his cap and walked to stand in front of the couch. He shoved back his overcoat and splayed his hands on narrow hips. "What's going on here, Nick?"

"Shhh," Nick whispered again, making exaggerated pointing motions at Abby, who began to stir. "She'll be uncomfortable enough when she realizes she did this."

Michael sucked in his cheeks and took in the room through narrowed eyes. "This place looks different."

Abby started and lifted her head. "Nick?" She flattened her palms against his chest, looking at his face, bemused. He saw her sense Michael's silent figure an instant before she pulled quickly away and turned to her brother.

She'd fallen asleep, Abby thought frantically, actually fallen asleep in Nick Dorset's arms. She put a distance of a few inches between them and braced her weight on both hands. "Hi, Mike," she said lamely. He looked like an enraged parent, tight-lipped, stiff-backed. Good Lord, what was he thinking? Sure, it must appear weird for her to be with Nick like this, but she was hardly a candidate for some clandestine affair.

"Michael dropped in," Nick said, and Abby glanced at him, horrified. He sounded…*guilty*.

"If I'd known you might be busy, Abby, I'd have called first. You did give me a key to use—remember?—whenever John's away. Which seems to be most of the time, lately."

"Of course I remember." She wished Nick would say something intelligent. He was giving off awkwardness in signal waves. "I didn't think you were coming today," she said to Michael.

He took his cap from beneath his arm. "I guess not."

"Mike, listen," Nick stood, "whatever you're thinking, you're wrong. Abby and I are friends, we—"

"I'm not thinking anything," Michael interrupted. "Why would I?" His slitted glare, first at Nick, then Abby, suggested he was most certainly thinking something. She began to feel sick.

"It's good to see you, Michael," Abby said and heard her tone hint otherwise.

Michael didn't reply.

"It really is," she persisted.

"I don't understand this," Michael said. "It's wild. I didn't even realize you two knew each other, and I walk in on a cozy little domestic scene while my brother-in-law's away. Or is it domestic? How long have you two been 'friends'?"

"Michael, don't," Abby's skin crawled.

Nick gripped her shoulder. "Abby doesn't need any extra grief now, Mike. She's got enough. She needs to be calm," he finished uncertainly.

"Thanks for the instruction." Michael threw his cap on the armchair. "I didn't realize you were such an authority on what pregnant women need—apart from a broad shoulder to lie on." Abby had never heard him sound this way.

Nick dropped his arm from her shoulders. "Don't say things you'll regret, Mike. Abby and I are friends who decided to share a meal. She fell asleep while we were talking. Big deal. Let it go."

Michael looked anything but convinced.

Abby's heart did ugly things. "Nick," she said, keeping her voice level, "I apologize for zonking out on you like that. Some hostess. And I apologize for putting you through this scene, but Michael and I are very close, and we look out for each other when we can. He's doing his protective routine." She gave Michael a smile she hoped wasn't too fixed. "You always could be a pain when you felt righteous about something. In case you've forgotten, Nick played messenger for you the time you got held over in Chicago. Remember that?"

"Yeah," Michael said, while his expression flashed with the rest of his reaction. So what?

Abby sighed. "Well," she pressed on. "Well, that's when Nick found out John's away, and he's, well—" She glanced at Nick who smiled thinly. He'd probably never speak to her again after this. "Nick's been very kind and helped me with—with a couple of things I needed done. So I persuaded him to let me make him dinner tonight.''

"I see." The skeptical light remained in Michael's eyes. "And then—because John's away—you helped each other out with a little TLC?"

"For God's sake, Michael," Abby snapped. "I'm hardly a femme fatale. I'm more than seven months pregnant.''

He looked first at her, then at Nick, and sat down suddenly on top of his cap. He pulled it from beneath him and hung it loosely between his knees. "I'm sorry." He ran a hand through his mussed black curls and met Abby's eyes. "I'm really sorry, Abby. I was caught off guard, that's all. You can imagine how it looked when I walked in here."

"Sure, I can," she said dully. This was her fault. She'd caused a rift between Michael and Nick. And because of her, Nick had been put on the defensive. "I'm sorry I caused this—for all our sakes."

Nick stopped her from turning away. "We're all sorry," he said with a laugh. "Forget it. I'm going to get out of here and leave you and Michael to talk."

"No." Michael leapt up. "Stay, please. I only stopped to see how you are, Abby." He grimaced. "You were a whole lot better before I arrived. Forgive a protective old brother?" He leaned to kiss her cheek.

Abby wrapped her arms tightly around his neck and shook her head before kissing him soundly. "Of course I forgive you. Only idiots don't like being cared about. Nick's the one you may have to convince not to punch you out."

"I'll let you off this time, Mike," Nick said. Both men laughed, but tension still arched between them.

"Why don't we all have coffee?" Abby suggested. "Or you two could finish the sake." She smiled at Michael. "You told me once that you and Nick enjoyed sushi, so that's what we had tonight, and I got sake to go with it."

"Nothing for me, thanks," Michael responded. "I think I'll get home and crash." He buttoned his coat, scanning the room quickly. His gaze came to rest on the empty dining area, and he opened his mouth before catching Abby's eye and bringing his lips together again.

She wanted him to leave and hated herself for the thought. He was telegraphing silent questions, and she wouldn't be able to put him off much longer. "Will you be in town for a few days?" Abby said.

"Until Friday. How about lunch tomorrow? I could come to the store and pick you up, if you like."

"No, no." She avoided looking at Nick. "I mean, yes I can get off, but let's not meet downtown. Does Hiram's at the locks sound good? I'm in the mood for seafood."

"I could still pick you up."

"I'll meet you there—say, at one? There's no point in you fighting the jam."

Michael showed signs of arguing. Abby put an arm through his and urged him toward the door. "Would you mind calling the restaurant for a reservation? Sometimes they get busy on nice days."

"Nice days?" Michael raised one dark brow. "We'll be lucky if it doesn't snow."

"Do it anyway, Mike," Nick said, and she caught his knowing grin at Michael. "You never know. There could be a crowd to watch sea gulls ice-skating or something."

"Oh, right." Michael slid on his cap and tipped it over his eyes. "Hiram's at one."

"I'll be there," she said faintly and listened until the front door clicked shut.

She couldn't look at Nick. She'd never be able to look at him again without blushing.

"Pretty bad, huh?" He turned her toward him. "But I guess I can't blame him for the outraged act."

Abby bit her lip hard. "I'm so sorry, Nick. I don't know what made me fall asleep like that. I've never been one of those people who nap for no reason."

"You've never been pregnant before, have you? I should think that's a pretty good reason, particularly when you keep insisting on overdoing everything."

"I've never been pregnant before, no. Maybe I am doing too much. I don't know what to say about Michael, about the way he behaved."

"Forget it. We must have made quite a picture. Poor guy had a right to overreact. But, Abby—" Nick breathed into his fist, watching her thoughtfully "—I do think you'd better consider confiding in Michael. He's suspicious."

She moistened her lips. "How could he be? I mean, of what?" Nick shrugged. "I'm not sure. I just have a feeling he's looking for something. Anyway, think about it before you see him tomorrow. I'm sure if you appealed to him he'd agree to keep quiet around your parents. After all, it won't be long before John gets back—will it?"

Abby felt blood drain from her face. She was in a mess, and the situation could only get worse. "I'm not sure," she said evasively. "It could be awhile. But I'll think about what you say." She wanted to be alone now, to think. In two days she'd be signing final divorce papers. John was almost completely out of her life.

"Should we get those dishes finished?" Nick asked, beginning to unbutton a cuff.

She stopped him. "I'm going to leave them, tonight. I'll get up early, and they won't take any time. You must be ready for bed. I know I am. Thanks for the roses, Nick, and the lovely evening. And again, forgive my nutty brother."

"I've already forgotten the whole thing." He picked up his jacket and slung it over one shoulder. "I'm only next door if you need me, Abby."

"Thank you."

"You would call me, wouldn't you?"

"Of course." She wasn't sure she would, but she liked him more than ever for offering.

"Good night, then."

"Night, Nick."

He walked slowly down the hall. Abby followed, her hands clasped in front of her. She stretched around Nick to open the door and bowed her head as he passed.

On the threshold, he paused and turned back. "Thanks for a great dinner."

"You're welcome."

"This is the best time I've had in years, Abby."

She searched his face and found no trace of humor. "Well, thanks again, but I find that hard to believe."

"Believe it. Can we do it again? Next time I cook?"

What could she say?

"Abby? Will you spend another evening with me...soon?"

"We'll see. Good night, Nick."

Nick jammed his free hand into his pocket, stepping backward and feeling like a man moving through deep water. One pace in the other direction, and he could have kissed her. He kept smiling until she closed the door.

Drained, he leaned against the wall and rested his head back. He hadn't heard the last from Michael Harris about this evening. Michael could become a big problem unless he could be won over. Nick found his key and went into his condo. Michael would come around in time; he'd have to.

In the bedroom Nick looked at his bed, deciding what to do next. He was exhausted, but sleep was likely to be an elusive commodity. The answer to the problem came easily. He shucked his clothes and put on running gear.

ABBY PUSHED AWAY her plate. "That was wonderful, Michael. Sinfully good."

"You need to eat more."

Not again. "I eat plenty. I don't want to be a blimp after this baby's born."

Michael made a grumping sound. "Not much danger of that. How about dessert?"

"No, thanks. I couldn't. Don't let me stop you, though."

The waitress refilled their coffee cups, and Michael waited until the woman left. "About last night, Abby."

Here it comes, she thought, and concentrated on the boats gathering in the locks outside. "It's interesting, isn't it?" she said.

After a short silence Michael said, "What?"

"The locks," Abby replied. "The way the boats gather in this huge pen to go from salt water to fresh, forcing their way upriver like salmon."

"They're going into a lake," Michael remarked shortly. "Lake Washington isn't a river. And the boats don't have to force anything, they wait for the lock water to pump them up between Puget Sound and Salmon Bay, and off they go—upstream, no sweat."

Abby glowered at him. "Thanks for the lecture. You know what I meant."

"You meant to avoid the issue, and it's not going to work. What's going on with you?"

"Nothing, dammit." She pushed back her chair, collided with the diner behind, and cringed. In a lowered voice, she added, "There's nothing going on with me that I can't handle," and immediately regretted the last few words.

Michael leaned across the table. "And what does that mean, nothing you can't handle? If everything's peachy, why is there anything to handle at all?"

Abby let out an exasperated breath. "You're putting words in my mouth. Why are you so determined to find problems?"

"I'm not. But I'm not a fool, either. Abby, I really feel rotten about last night. I'll have to apologize to Nick. But something's going on. I knew it the last time I saw you at the folks'. Will you let me in on the big mystery?"

The temptation to confide in him almost broke her. Abby drank some water, trying to stay calm. "I've had some difficult weeks, that's all. That isn't unusual, I'm sure." If she told him even that she was short of money there'd be no turning back, and he'd dig out the rest of her sordid little story before she was ready.

"Okay, you aren't going to come clean without a fight, so I'll just have to push you, Abby." He covered her hand on top of the table. "Last night was the first time I've been in your condo in weeks. There are things missing, Abby. The dining set? The clock? I didn't take inventory, but there was a lot gone, and I don't understand it."

Her heart had started a heavy thudding. So much for her theory that Michael wasn't observant. "I'm making some changes." Changes came in many forms, she thought, divorce was just one of them.

"Changes?" Michael repeated. "Waiting until John's away and getting rid of half your furniture? What's he going to say about that?"

Abby stuffed her hands in her lap and made fists. She didn't want to hate John, but at this moment her feeling for him came close to that. "We did it before he left. He knows."

Michael regarded her for a long time. He rested back in his chair, never taking his eyes from her face. "Abby, you have to have some idea when John's due home. You always did before."

She started pulling on her coat. "I don't know this time. He has to take trips when he can get them." Getting out of here was all that mattered to her for the moment.

"Funny he's making back-to-back trips suddenly. I never got the impression John was that dedicated. At least not as long as good old Mom kept coming through with the bucks." He paused, clearly stricken by what he'd said. "Forgive me. I—I should never have said that."

"It's okay," Abby said. What Michael implied was absolutely true: John was an overindulged only child who needed to grow up. Not that his development was her problem anymore. She stood, reaching for her purse. "Lunch was great, but I've got to run. I'll call you, Michael, okay?"

"I don't leave until tomorrow." He paid the bill and hurriedly trailed her outside. "Could we get together tonight, go see Mom and Dad maybe?"

She faced him, smiling, praying her eyes wouldn't give her away. "I can't tonight, Michael. You see them and give them my love. I talked to Mom this morning. Remind them I'll be over for dinner on Sunday. Have a good trip, huh?" She pecked his cheek, holding back tears. "See you when you get back."

"Take care, Abby."

She turned and half ran to her car. Behind the wheel, she set her face in a grim mask. All the books said babies sensed if their mothers were unhappy, even before birth. She would *make* herself be happy. She'd concentrate on this little person of hers and nothing else.

AT LEAST THE DRUNK hadn't shown up tonight. Abby had already locked the storage room and put on her coat when the big hand on the wall clock clicked to the half hour. Ten-thirty. She flipped over the sign, made one last tour of the shop and walked out to the Pinto.

Isolated flakes of snow fell, and a thick film of ice covered the little car's windows. Snow in November, particularly before Thanksgiving, usually boded a hard winter in the Northwest. Abby searched for an ice-scraper and remembered breaking the one she'd had last winter. She took a credit card from her wallet and went to work, shaking her hands every few minutes to keep her circulation moving. Tomorrow night she'd put newspaper over the windshield to avoid this.

The engine didn't want to turn over, but on the fourth try it caught sluggishly and she set off, peering over the wheel at slick streets. The defroster wasn't enthusiastic about its task, either.

The bad weather made hermits of all sensible people. By the time Abby turned onto Coal Creek Parkway and headed west, not another vehicle was in sight. Widely spaced streetlights served only to highlight a thickening snowfall. Dense evergreens crowded the sides of the road, and Abby drove slower and slower, knowing, without having to see, that a skid could land her in a deep brush-choked ditch.

She stopped for a red light, and the engine died. Pumping the gas while she turned the ignition key, Abby noted a service station on one corner. Lights illuminated the pumps, but no attendant was in sight. She turned the key again and closed her eyes with relief when the car jolted forward.

Another six miles, and she'd be safely home. When the car quit again, Abby figured she still had five miles to go. This time repeated efforts produced only flat clicks that let her know the battery was dead.

Abby got out and lifted the hood. She waited fifteen minutes, flapping her arms and stamping her feet. One car sped by. Both she and the Pinto were probably next to invisible, Abby decided and started walking back to the intersection.

By the time she reached the service station, her feet felt nonexistent, and every muscle in her body ached. The place was closed, but at least there was a telephone booth. She tried Marie's number and hung up after fifteen rings.

Abby walked out of the booth and stared up, narrowing her eyes against the snow. Cold air seared her throat. Nick would come, but did she want to ask him? The answer troubled her deeply. More than anything else at this moment, she longed to see Nick's tall figure walking toward her. She had no right to want him.

Abby searched the phone book and found Nick's number. She inserted a coin in the slot and began punching buttons, pausing between each digit. She almost hung up when she heard his voice.

"Hello," he said, and then, when she didn't answer, added, "Who is this?"

"Nick," she replied quietly, "it's Abby."

He hesitated. "Abby, you sound funny. What's wrong?"

She gritted her teeth, screwing up her courage. "My car's broken down on Coal Creek Parkway. I'm near Sunset Highway, at a gas station. It's closed. Everything is because of the snow. I've tried to get hold of—"

"I'll be right there. Stay put."

"Nick, just a minute. I'll walk back to the car. It's on the right side of the road heading—"

"You'll stay where you are. Close the door of the phone booth and try to keep warm." He hung up.

The telephone booth had no door, but Abby huddled inside the glass sides, her arms tightly crossed. She shouldn't have called Nick. She was being unfair, preying on his goodness.

Within minutes she heard a powerful engine. A car swept to a partial stop at the intersection, then the silvery gray BMW roared into the station forecourt, screeching to a halt inches from where Abby stood. Nick got out and ran around. Abby was surprised to see him in his airline uniform, gold stripes glittering around his jacket cuffs. He wore no overcoat or hat, and speckles of snow clung to his hair by the time he caught her hand and pulled her into the car.

"Get in," he ordered. His features were strained. The muscles in Abby's jaw trembled. She wished he would hold her.

When he sat beside her, with the car still running, he turned up the heater and then stared through the snow-caked windshield, his arms crossed. "I've been watching for you," he said. "I needed to see you."

She drew up her shoulders. Something was happening between them—had happened—and it shouldn't have. "This is a pain, Nick. I guess you were right about my rotten old Pinto."

"That's not the point."

"What...what is the point?" Could she dare to hope they were held together by something more than his concern for a friend? Nick slid his hands around the steering wheel. "It's about time you guessed the point, but you won't face up to the truth."

If he'd touched her, run his hands over her, he couldn't have produced a more electric reaction. She mustn't read too much into his words. "I'm not sure what you mean."

"Aren't you?" He reached behind his seat for a blanket before speaking. "I can't get further into it now. But we will. And in the meantime, this has got to stop," he said tightly. "This crazy job you insist on doing must go. I got called in. Another hour, and I'd have been gone. It's too dangerous for you to be driving around at night in a car that's only fit for the scrap heap."

"You're overreacting," Abby retorted and immediately turned her face away. "I shouldn't have called you. Why didn't you say you had to leave, Nick?"

He draped the blanket over her. "I'm just glad I hadn't left yet. Like I said, I'd been waiting for you to get back." His hands lingered at her sides, and his face was close. Abby could see the light from the dash reflected in his eyes, feel his soft breath, almost believe his lips had pressed hers. "I always seem to be waiting for you, Abby. Even when I don't realize it." He passed a palm slowly over her cheek, ran his fingers into her hair, and he did kiss her fleetingly on the temple before he turned back to grasp the steering wheel.

Abby looked at him. His face was inscrutable in the muted

green light. "Why were you waiting for me?" The ache in her thighs, the swelling heat from her breasts, was an almost forgotten sensation. It felt right and she wanted it.

He continued to stare ahead. "I—I needed to ask a favor."

"Ask. What is it?"

"Nothing. I'll tell you when I get you home."

She must concentrate, she thought. "Nick," she said barely audibly. "I think a dead battery's all that's wrong with my car. Could we jump it, do you think? I've got cables in the back."

His mouth turned down. "I don't want you driving that thing." He turned eyes that glinted toward her. "I realize I don't have the right to ask anything of you, but I'm going to, anyway. Please, Abby, give up this job. If money's the big problem, let me lend you what you need until you're on your feet. No one need ever know, not John, not Michael and your folks. If it would make you feel better, you can write out some sort of note and pay me back when you can."

Miserably, she shook her head. "I can't—"

He rested two fingers on her mouth. "You can. All I have to worry about is me, and I can afford to help you."

Getting Nick involved had been a terrible mistake. Abby gently removed his hand. "Thanks, Nick. But it's not as bad as you think. I really can manage very well. Just drive me home. I'll get a new battery and put it into the car tomorrow and get it checked over. Now, let's go, or you're going to be late."

Unthinking, she pressed her fingers into the hard muscle of his thigh. She heard breath escape Nick's lungs and started to withdraw her hand. He covered her hand quickly, holding it in a vise. His leg was rock hard, and his fingers twined through hers, pulling hers fractionally higher. He was aroused, unbearably aroused. *Oh, God.* She bowed her head and willed her clamoring responses to stop.

"Nick, this is no good. I don't understand it, but I know it's no good."

"Abby," he blurted out. "If only...oh hell, not now. This isn't the right time to get into anything that means so much. But, Abby, I wish you'd give up working at—"

"No," she interrupted, "stop worrying. She laughed and withdrew her hand while a cold place formed around her heart. Her body pulsed. "You're a frustrated mother hen, and I love you for it." The breath lodged in her throat. What a dumb thing to say. She prayed he hadn't noticed.

Nick was quiet for seconds, his head bowed, then he silently let in the clutch and drove back to Lake Vista.

Outside her door, Abby stopped and faced him. "Thanks a million, Nick. You saved my life. I'll try not to bother you again." She put a hand against the wall behind her for support. "Have a good trip."

"I'll be back on Monday." His smile didn't reach his eyes.

"Can you stay out of trouble till then?"

He felt responsible for her, Abby thought and looked away quickly. "Just concentrate on taking care of yourself, Nick."

"Wait," he said. "I almost forgot. Get your door unlocked while I fetch something."

Abby watched him go into his condo. By the time she'd switched on the light in her own hall, he was back, with a large cardboard box in his arms.

"This is why I was waiting for you to get back." His smile was almost a boyish, caught-in-a-half-truth smile. "One of the reasons, anyway. I didn't want to leave it on the step because it's heavy." He carted his burden past her into the kitchen and set it on a counter.

"What is it?" Abby asked, but he held her arm and walked her back to the doorway. "Leftovers," he said. "I'm famous for going out of town with partly used stuff in the refrigerator and then coming home to a bunch of ruined food. Do me a favor and use it up for me. Throw out anything you don't want. The meat's been frozen once, so I didn't want to freeze it again, and it was too much for dinner. I always overestimate." He was hurrying now.

"Anything else I can do?" Abby asked to his back. He strode inside his condo and emerged with a flight bag, his raincoat and cap. He settled the cap on his head and dug in his pants' pocket.

"I've got one plant still trying to live." He worked a key off his ring. "The one by the living room window. Don't ask me what it is." His golden eyes met hers, then lowered fractionally to her mouth. "If you think of it, would you water the thing?" There wasn't enough air. "Yes," she said softly. "Can I do anything else?"

He hesitated. "You could... Abby, don't take any chances, please." The key clinked against her ring as he dropped it into her palm.

"Have a safe trip, Nick."

He took a step toward the stairs, then turned back and shot his free arm around her shoulders. Tipping his head sideways to keep his cap visor cleared, he kissed her mouth briefly. "For luck," he said and pulled away an inch to study her. "Luck for both of us." He kissed her again, harder, his lips parting hers, his tongue passing her teeth to reach far into her mouth.

Abby moaned deep in her throat and clung to him, weak as she never remembered being weak. Nick pulled back, his eyes somber and penetrating. "We'll have luck, Abby. We'll see to that." He left in a rustle of waterproof fabric.

Abby stood still, listening until the downstairs door banged, closing out the sound of his running footsteps.

"Go away," Abby mumbled and pulled the quilt over her head. The intercom rang again, more insistently this time. Someone was leaning on the button.

She rolled onto her back. Monday, her one day off, and some clown had to bug her first thing in the morning. *Monday!* Nick was due back today, and she had his key. Abby scrambled from bed and tottered down the hall to the intercom speaker. "Hello," she said, cleared her throat and repeated, "hello."

"Finally," a woman's voice said. "Let me in, will you? It's freezing out here."

Marie Prince. Abby looked heavenward and released the latch on the outer door. Just what she needed, Marie's pseudo-bored don't-give-a-damn act on the very day Abby was due to sign away the marriage she'd thought was forever.

She opened her front door, left it standing wide and scuffed back to the bedroom. There would be no more sleeping now.

Seconds later she heard the door slam. Abby tossed aside her nightgown and pulled on her underwear. She took a sleeveless dress from the closet and rummaged in a drawer for a turtleneck to wear underneath.

"You're all belly," Marie entered the room and flopped on the end of Abby's bed. She laughed. "And boobs. The rest of you is as thin as ever, thinner maybe."

Abby kept her mouth firmly closed and struggled into the sweater.

"Why don't you buy some proper maternity clothes? They've got some cute stuff."

"Why bother?" Abby said from inside her dress. "Seven weeks, and this will all be over. And—" she wiggled her head clear "—as you just got through pointing out, I haven't gained much weight, so my regular things will fit as soon as I get back in shape."

Marie, propped on her elbows, swung her feet while she assessed Abby minutely. "You're a good-looking woman, beautiful in a way. The sooner you start making a new life, the better."

Abby found a pair of panty hose without runs and sat to put them on. "You're talking about finding another man, aren't you, Marie?"

"Mmm. What else is there?"

Not for the first time, Abby felt deeply sorry for Marie. She really wasn't whole without a man in tow. "Marie," she said patiently. "A woman with a newborn baby is hardly every man's idea of desirable. And, believe it or not, there are even women— me, for one—who don't spend every minute dreaming of Mr. Wonderful. I'm a bit soured on romance these days." Perversely, Nick's face, his tawny eyes smiling, passed through her mind. And his touch. They'd passed to a new level, and there'd be no going back. She slipped on flat shoes and began making her bed around Marie.

"You said you'd keep in touch," Marie said, standing and helping with the covers. "I haven't heard a word from you in ages."

Abby glanced up, contrite. "I'm sorry. Things have really been a bit crazy. Today…" She faltered, deciding how much to say. Then Marie's eyes settled on hers, and the old understanding was there. Abby warmed to this little woman all over again. "It's been almost three months since John filed for divorce. Everything's ready. This afternoon I sign the papers, Marie. It only took ninety days and a date in court, and that was that—over. I knew what was coming, and I'm glad in a way, but I still feel a bit upset about it." She made much of smoothing the pillow shams.

In an instant, Marie was at her side, standing on tiptoe to hug her. "I thought it must be about that time. Call it second sight. Something made me decide to come over here today. I'll come with you to the lawyer's office, if you like. It's rough to do those things on your own."

Abby smiled. She pushed Marie's long hair behind her shoulder. "You've got a good heart, Marie. Too good for your own comfort sometimes. Thanks for the offer, but I'd rather do this alone. The lawyer said John's signing *in absentia*, which I suppose means he won't be there, so at least I don't have to face him. He's probably sunning himself on some beach in the West Indies." She sounded bitchy, and she detested that. "How about some coffee?"

"I thought you'd never ask," Marie said, leading the way to

the kitchen. Abby noticed she didn't push her offer of company at the lawyer's office. Poor Marie, she tried so hard, but she wasn't heroine material.

Abby started coffee while Marie toured the living room, picking up magazines, dropping them, always on the move. "Where did the roses come from?" she called.

Abby stopped, holding the filter suspended over the percolator. "My neighbor gave them to me," she said.

"The guy who works for the same airline as Michael?"

"That's the one." Let it drop, Abby thought uncomfortably.

"The one who looks like a male model?"

Abby closed her eyes and suppressed a smile. "Nick's a good-looking man. He's also very nice."

"He didn't find these beside the road. These are strictly hot-house variety."

Trust Marie to pick up on every little thing. "You don't take anything in your coffee, do you, Marie?"

"No. Let's talk some more about this neighbor of yours."

"There's nothing to discuss." Abby carried two mugs into the living room and handed one to Marie. "Sit down somewhere."

Marie remained standing over the vase of roses. They'd been buds when Nick brought them, now they were wide open and fragrant. "He just rang your doorbell one day and said 'I brought you these. Not for any reason, just because I'm nice.' Right, Abby?"

"Don't be silly." She was remembering the box of "leftovers" he'd dropped off. The meat he'd "overestimated." Everything was fresh and untouched, and carefully selected for her, she knew. To back up his meat story, he'd thought to take off the original wrapper and use fresh plastic. She wondered how he intended to explain the chicken he'd included, and the box of chocolates.

Marie had sat on the edge of the armchair. Abby became aware of being studied closely. "Are you going to say any more about this man, or do I have to dig it out of you?"

"There isn't any more to say. You have a vivid imagination. I made him dinner one night, that's all, and he brought flowers. No big deal."

"No big deal!" Marie came half out of the chair. "Of course it's a big deal. Here you are having a relationship with a perfectly marvelous male, and you don't even bother to keep me posted."

Why had she told Marie anything? Abby wondered. She could have said she bought the flowers herself, if she weren't so honest.

"Have you been out anywhere?"

Abby shook her head. "Stop dreaming, Marie. For my sake, turn off the fairy-tale syndrome. Look at me, will you? Really look. What man in his right mind would want to take me anywhere? Nick is just a good neighbor. He's the kind of man who likes to do nice things for people. Can we leave it at that?"

Marie gave a short laugh. "Good neighbor Nick, sure, if that's the way you want it. But I'm not fooled, and neither are you. Pregnant or not pregnant, the guy's got a thing for you. I've heard some men get turned on by pregnant—",

"Marie," Abby broke in threateningly. "End of subject, understand?"

Marie buried her nose in her mug. She slid back in the chair and crossed her ankles.

They drank in silence, and Abby got up to refill their coffee. Another hour, and she'd have to leave for the lawyer's office. She checked her watch and remembered Nick. She should have made sure what time he was due in just in case he didn't have a spare key.

"Abby, have you thought about what you'll do after the baby comes?"

Abby set down her mug. "I've thought about it." And she didn't want to talk about those thoughts to anyone.

"I've been thinking about it, too, a lot." Marie glanced at Abby, faint pink spreading over her milky skin. "You're still keeping everything to yourself, I suppose? Not telling your family?"

"Yes," Abby said. "I have to. I told you I wanted to make it through on my own as much as possible."

"Bringing up a child alone can't be so easy."

Deep inside Abby, something twisted tightly. "A lot of people do it. I won't be a pioneer."

"A lot of people do it, and a lot of little kids suffer because they do."

Abby stared at Marie. "Are you saying my baby's going to suffer because—"

"Because it won't have a father around? I guess that's what I'm saying. Who'll look after it? Are you going to stay home?"

"You know I can't do that." Cold slipped over her skin.

"Your mother, then? I suppose she could baby-sit."

"No!" A panicky feeling gripped Abby. "My mother's too old

for that, now. She didn't have Michael and me until late. I couldn't let her try to bring up another child."

Marie got up and knelt on the floor beside the tape deck, reading cassette titles. "But someone does have to bring up a kid, right? Is it right to let some stranger do that while you run a taxi service, picking up and dropping off, and always too tired to enjoy any of it?"

"I don't know what you're getting at, Marie. I'll just have to do the best I can with what I've got. At least my baby will be loved. A lot of single mothers, and fathers, manage very well."

"So you already said. I just wondered if you'd considered the alternatives, that's all."

Abby massaged her temples as if she could stop the ache there.

"There aren't any alternatives." She wanted to add that she needed encouragement, not more doubts to worry about.

"Yes, there are." Marie scooted around to face her. "One, anyway. Children do best with two parents. A real home. Abby, there are dozens of couples who'd give their eyeteeth for this baby you're expecting. There's someone out there—a couple—who would take it and give it everything you can't: security, the best food and clothes, an education when the time comes—"

"Stop it." Abby's jaws hurt from gritting her teeth. "This is my baby, *mine*. And no one else can give it the kind of love I can give. I can't believe you would say this to me. You're supposed to be my friend."

"I am." Marie scooted across the rug to sit at Abby's feet. She held her knees. "I'm sorry if I always come on too fast and too strong. But I am thinking of you."

Abby's mind retreated. What Marie suggested was unnatural; it was madness. "Don't talk about it again."

"Are you really worried about how you'd feel if you gave up the baby, or is it your family's reaction you're thinking about?"

"I don't want to discuss this."

"Then there's John's mother, I suppose. I wonder if John's told her about the divorce."

"Marie, I can't take any more of this. These are things I have to face, and I can't, not yet. I don't think Mrs. Winston knows about the divorce. In fact, I'm sure she's still waiting to see her grandchild for the first time." Abby choked and covered her mouth. "I didn't want to do this to any of these people. And I didn't want it to happen to the baby or me. I'm no martyr, Marie:

I do care what happens to me, and in the end I'll come out okay. Will you leave it at that?''

Marie crossed her ankles and stood effortlessly. "For now, Abby. But someone has to make sure you do keep looking out for yourself. I've got to get to some office in Bellevue, so I'd better go.''

"Yes," Abby said faintly. "Thanks for stopping by."

"I'll be back," Marie commented, winding a blue angora scarf around her slim neck. "I won't push. But I know you'll think about what I've said.''

MICHAEL OPENED THE DOOR to his apartment before Nick had time to ring the bell. "Hi, there, Mike," he said, a prickling sensation climbing his spine. "Do you see through doors these days?''

The other man wasn't smiling. "You got my message. Good. Shut the door behind you. I'm having Scotch. Is that okay for you?''

Nick followed him into the living room with its vaulted ceiling and glass wall overlooking Lake Washington. The apartment complex was ten miles from the condos but still in Seattle's east side suburbs. "Scotch is great. Ice, no water." He pretended not to notice Michael's grim mood and went directly to the window. "You've got a hell of a view here, Mike. I never could figure out why they called my place Lake Vista. When the leaves come off the trees, we could probably see a corner of the lake if we climbed on the roof, but that's about it.''

"We?''

Nick glanced quickly at Michael, who shoved a glass into his hand. "Just a figure of speech. What's up?" Something was eating Michael Harris. His blue eyes had that opaque quality they sometimes took on when he was trying to control his anger. Nick's stomach contracted. The guy was angry about something.

"I wanted to talk.''

"No kidding." Nick felt the unfamiliar stirrings of anger himself. "The message I got when I landed made it sound like I was slated to be the star witness at an inquisition." He fished a crumpled sheet of paper from his pocket and read aloud. "'I need to ask you a few things. I'll be at my place as long as it takes.''

Michael gulped his drink. "That says it.''

"You could have started with a 'Dear Nick,' or even 'Hey, you.' What's eating you, Mike?''

"My sister," Michael announced without preamble.

Nick took a slow sip of his own Scotch, leveling his gaze on Michael over the rim of the glass. He clinked the ice cubes together. "Are you still trying to make something out of the night you found us at Abby's place? I thought we'd covered that."

"Not well enough. I need answers, Nick, facts. And I can't get at Abby. She's closed herself off from me—something that's never happened before—and I'm worried to death, dammit."

The going could get rocky, Nick recognized. He'd have to tread carefully. "Aren't you making too much out of things? Her condition could account for her changed attitude toward you. She's kind of drawing in with her baby, maybe gathering strength. She'll come out of it."

"There you go again," Michael said tightly. "Spouting like a professor of obstetrics, or female psychology or something. And when did you get so all fired close to Abby? You're very comfortable interpreting her moods, aren't you?"

"This won't get us anywhere, Mike. Why not spit out exactly what's on your mind, so we can face it."

"Okay." Michael slammed down his glass on the teak dining table. "Okay, if that's how you want it."

"I don't want it at all," Nick retorted, exasperated. "You do. I'm just an unwilling participant."

"Are you saying you aren't involved with my sister at all?" Nick's scalp tightened. He passed a hand over his face. "We aren't...haven't been romantically involved, if that's what you mean."

"Nick, my folks are asking questions. Where's John? they want to know. Why doesn't Abby talk about him? She had dinner with them on Sunday—yesterday. I got back late last night, and my mother was on the phone almost before I got through the door here. Evidently Abby hardly said two words all evening, and when my mother tried to talk about the baby's christening—there's been talk of going to John's mother's home in New York for that—Abby clammed up. Mom said she thought Abby was going to cry. I tried to get her at work this afternoon and couldn't." Michael stepped close to Nick. "She's left the store. She doesn't work there anymore. Hasn't for over a month. If the folks knew that, they'd have said so. Something's going on with her that she's not talking about. I'm afraid to push her in case she moves even farther away. But you do know, don't you, Nick?"

Nick repressed an urge to flinch.

"I may be out of line," Michael continued, "but a man doesn't take an interest in a woman who's carrying another man's child. He doesn't find ways to be with her and spend time snuggling up to her—"

Nick's fist connected with Michael's jaw almost before he knew he'd moved. "Oh, God," he muttered and grabbed to stop Michael from tripping backward over a chair.

Michael wrenched away, touching his fingertips to the corner of his mouth where a thin trickle of blood showed.

"Mike," Nick began, reaching for Michael's shoulder.

"Forget it, I didn't realize defending a maiden's honor was big with you."

When Nick swung again, Michael dodged and caught his wrist. He gripped Nick's tie, backing him up a step before he held his ground. "I ought to kill you," Michael muttered hoarsely. "Do you think I'm mad? You messed around with Abby, and John took off. That's what happened, isn't it? You've ruined her life, and when you get sick of your little games, you'll take off, too, you son of a bitch."

Something snapped in Nick. He straight-armed Michael, smacking the heels of his hands repeatedly into his chest, pushing him away, step by step, until his calves met the edge of a couch and he sat with a thump.

Nick stood over him. "Shut your filthy mouth, Michael. Shut it. What Abby told you about our friendship is true. I wouldn't be living by her in the first place if you hadn't told me the condo was for sale. Abby and I were only nodding acquaintances for months. We didn't meet properly until a few weeks ago when you asked me to let her know you weren't getting in on time from Chicago.

"When I found out she'd left her old job, I asked her to tell you, but she was afraid of worrying you. The same as she's afraid of worrying your folks with her problems."

Michael found a handkerchief and wiped the blood from the corner of his mouth. His hand shook. "What's happened between Abby and John? Not that I like the bastard." He colored and looked away.

Nick sat beside him. "Mike, we're being asinine. Neither of us has the right to tell Abby what to do with her life. She hasn't told me what's happened between her and John Winston." That much at least was true. "And it's not my business, any more than it's yours. She has said she wants to get on her feet—on her own—and prove she can cope without help.''

"She's not in a condition to cope alone. Is she working somewhere else? I've got to know what's happening.''

"If you interfere, she'll close you out. I'm an outsider, and I can see things more clearly than you. If you love her as much as you say you do, don't push, and don't tip her hand about the job or your suspicions about John to your parents. Let her tell you everything when she's ready.''

Michael rallied. "Why would she confide in you if you hardly know each other?''

"Probably because we've been messing around, don't you think?'' Nick was irritated. "I moved in next door about the same time as she must have become pregnant, but, being the swift mover I am, I'm the father of her child. How do I know for sure why she's confiding in me? Maybe she needed someone non-threatening who wouldn't tell her what to do, and I was the only available candidate.''

"Oh, hell.'' Michael buried his head in his hands. "I'm sorry, Nick. What else can I say? I love Abby. She's always been so gentle, and I hate feeling helpless. I can't stand by and do nothing.''

"Mike,'' Nick said and fetched their glasses, "drink this and listen for once.''

Michael looked up questioningly at him.

"Abby's a big girl, and she's letting all the people in her life know she wants to go it alone now. Stay out of her business until she invites you in.''

Michael drained the liquor. "Do you think John's left her? Be honest with me, Nick.''

He considered how much to say. "I think it's possible.''

"So do I.'' Michael leaned back and closed his eyes. "And maybe it's for the best. I'll do what you ask, if you'll do something for me.'' He lifted his lids to gaze unblinkingly at Nick.

"Name it.''

"After what I've said, this is going to sound off-the-wall, but I do trust you, Nick. Keep an eye on Abby. Let me know if you think she's in real trouble, or if she seems ready to open up. And in the meantime, look after her for me.''

Nick bowed his head over his glass. "Sure, Mike, I'll do that for you.''

## Chapter Nine

Nick drove too fast, Abby decided. But now that she thought of it, so did Michael. Flyers had to have quick reflexes, and they were probably naturally attracted to speed and challenge. She winced as Nick cut between two cars in the fast lane. They were crossing the floating bridge between Mercer Island and Seattle itself. A steady drizzle fell, and lights on tall standards cast wavery reflections across the west surface of the span. Blackened rims of crusty slush were all that remained of the previous week's snowfall.

Abby glanced at Nick. She'd been repeatedly glancing at him ever since they'd left the east side shortly before seven. "Are you sure you want to go through with this?" she asked, willing him to say he'd rather not go with her to a childbirth education class, after all. "If you've changed your mind, I don't have to go tonight." So far, she'd attended only one class, read the course books and halfheartedly practiced the conditioning exercises they outlined. If Nick hadn't pressured her, she probably wouldn't be going now. "I could make up this class later."

Nick kept his eyes on the road as they entered a tunnel. "You don't have a whole lot of time left to squeeze these classes in, my girl. And, no, I don't want to change my mind. You did put those pillows and books in the car?"

"In the back seat," she confirmed, her heart sinking lower. Since he'd returned from his last trip, all of her efforts to dissuade Nick from taking her to this class had failed. On Monday, he'd shown up on her doorstep and persuaded her to share pizza. The following evening he'd "made too much" Chinese food and "needed her help." Last night she'd worked, but when she got home, Nick sat on the top step outside her condo, waiting, with his irresistible smile and a request for her to watch a movie with him, because he "**hated** watching movies alone." And each time they'd been together, he'd found a way to raise the subject of childbirth preparation. Finally he'd lulled her into revealing the class schedule and accepting his offer to take her tonight. Abby pulled her shirt farther down over the one pair of maternity jeans she owned. The prospect of his being there while she went through the ungainly exercises mortified her.

"You're supposed to go to eight sessions?" Nick asked, startling her. He took the exit to Rainier Avenue. He didn't wait for her response. "You waited too long to finish the course. You'd better figure out a way to graduate early." He laughed as he changed down gears.

Abby laced her fingers tightly together. She couldn't echo his laughter. When the time came for her to deliver her baby, she'd be alone, anyway—wouldn't she? Going to the classes without a partner had seemed pointless. Nick was...Nick was a special person, but even if he offered, could she suffer the embarrassment of having him present during her labor? She couldn't. She flexed her hands and wound her fingers together again. Whatever she learned would be useful. Everyone said proper breathing alone could make all the difference in coping with contractions.

"You're quiet," Nick said. "What are you thinking about?"

"Not much."

He smiled at her. "Can't you tell me? No? Okay, I'll tell you what I'd probably be thinking." Ahead a light turned amber, and he braked. "I'd be thinking I had six weeks before the most scary event in my life. I take that back—at the risk of quoting clichés—I wouldn't go through this at all. I'll never understand where women get the guts."

Now Abby laughed. He was wonderful to be with, natural and warm. "I'm not afraid, Nick. It's a thrill to look forward to meeting someone who's been invisibly with you for months. I know this person of mine. He likes music—jazz, of course. He's happy when I'm happy, and when I'm miserable, he gets real quiet, just like I do." She stopped and stared unseeingly at shop windows.

At the firm pressure of Nick's hand on hers, Abby looked down at his long fingers. His palm was wide, and the thumb that he ran briefly up and down hers was strong. The light changed to green, and he shifted gears again.

"You keep calling the baby *him*. You really think she's going to be a boy?"

"No," Abby said, aware he was trying to keep her mind occupied. "I think *he's* going to be a boy."

"Uh-uh," Nick said. "Wrong. This baby's a girl. I've seen her hip action, and no boy could manage that." They arrived at a square red-brick building, and Nick parked beside the curb. "This is the place, and we're two minutes late."

Abby watched him get out and pull her pillows and the books from the car. She joined him on the sidewalk. "Hip action? What's with the hip action?"

"Come on." He put an arm loosely around her shoulders and started for the glass double doors. "Just believe me. That kid sashays in there. Definitely feminine."

Abby smiled, concentrating on what he said with a small part of her brain. She walked automatically, then nodded when he checked a board for the room location. Distantly, she heard him continue to joke. Their footsteps echoed along a deserted corridor that smelled of wax. They turned a corner, and he said "This is us" while he looked at a number over a door.

The room felt crammed and airless. Abby registered other couples, smiling, sitting on pillows on the floor, then started at the sound of her own name.

"Abby, that's you," Nick had bowed close to her ear. "Yes," he said loudly and continued to look at her, frowning. "This is Abby Winston."

A petite middle-aged woman smiled and indicated a vacant area. Abby walked there with Nick, let him take her coat and held the hand he offered tightly while she sat on a pillow he dropped. He sat beside her, holding the other pillow on his lap. "Nick," she heard him say and glanced at the blond woman again. She must have asked his name. He'd only given his first one. Abby took a deep breath through her mouth. This was the instructor, and she'd think Nick was Abby's husband. Stinging heat rushed to her face.

"Six weeks," Nick was saying. "We're taking the crash course."

The ripple of laughter that circled the room brought Abby's mind into focus. She was sitting like a zombie, allowing Nick to pinch-hit in a situation he wasn't qualified to deal with or responsible for. Movement all around her followed the instructor's request to get comfortable. Some women remained seated, others curled up on their side. Each man faced his partner.

"Abby and Nick." The instructor bent over Abby. "I'm Louise. Ask questions whenever you need to. You won't have a problem catching up with the rest of the class if you put in some extra time between sessions."

Abby avoided Nick's eyes. "Yes," she said firmly. "What should I do now?"

"Lie down," Louise said, "or sit. Most women are more comfortable lying. We're going to get into partner awareness of tension. Have you spent any time with the course books?"

"We both have," Nick put in, taking Abby's hands. "It looks as if the side position with the pillow under the knee would work best to begin with."

Louise patted Abby's shoulder and grinned. "They say some men get the same physical sensations as their wives during pregnancy. Nick's obviously worked out how that heavy tummy feels. Use the side position for a start."

The woman went to the next couple, but Abby didn't move. She closed her eyes.

Nick made circles with his thumbs on the backs of her hands. "Lie down," he whispered. "Everything's okay. Open your eyes and look at me. Concentrate on my face and forget where you are and all the other stuff that's bothering you."

Abby opened her eyes but couldn't seem to move. "I can't do this, Nick," she said. "We shouldn't be here, you shouldn't be here." But she couldn't look away from his eyes. They smiled, touched her soul.

He put the second pillow on the floor and laid a palm on her cheek. "We're both exactly where we should be. Unwind, sweetheart. Lie down. This is going to help you."

Under his hand her skin turned to fire. The rest of the room, the people, went away. Mesmerized, she let him guide her down. He lifted her upper leg and positioned the pillow she'd been sitting on between her knees.

Nick sat cross-legged and leaned close. "You did read the books, didn't you?"

Abby passed a hand over her brow. "Yes. But how do you know all this stuff?"

"I got my own copies. Remember, I said I was interested and I wanted to come?"

"You got your own copies?" She couldn't believe he would go out and buy books he didn't need and read them. "Why did you do that?"

He touched her face again, and this time he kept his hand across her cheek, his fingers ruffling the hair at her temple. "I did it because I care what happens to you, Abby. I want to be here, with you. Now concentrate. What are we going to do next?"

She only felt his hand. His voice lulled her. She looked directly into his eyes. He meant what he said. Nick really wanted to be here for her.

"Abby, are you listening? What comes next?"

"I don't remember."

"Yes, you do. Tense and relax. Tense and relax. Let me see how you look when you tense—scratch that." He laughed softly. "Show me relaxed. I know tense; I can see it right now. We've got to learn what it takes to touch-relax you. The gate theory makes sense to me—cutting down the perception of pain by blocking its path with a gate of skin stimulation. But I have to be able to tell which areas you tighten up and what kind of touch works to reverse the process."

Abby grimaced. "The directions are coming back to me now. Are you sure you want to go on with this, Nick? I won't mind—"

"Relax," he ordered. "I'm going to lift your left arm. I'll move it around. You let it go limp and heavy."

He supported the arm, bending and flexing her elbow, rotating the shoulder, flapping her hand back and forth. "Okay, Abby. Now go limp."

"I *am* limp." She wasn't limp; she was tight, and trembling inside and responding to him in the last way she should be responding now.

"Abby, you are *not* limp. I could stake a tree with this arm. Are you ticklish?"

She narrowed her eyes. "Why?"

"Because of something I read in that book. You know the piece I mean?"

"If you tickle me, Nick Dorset, I'll never forgive you." She pulled her bottom lip between her teeth, and Nick watched, somber for an instant, before bowing to press his mouth to her ear. He kissed it gently, and the little hollow behind the point of her jaw. Abby's spine felt formless. Instinctively she turned her cheek to brush his. The slight roughness of his beard area electrified her.

His fingers tightened on her arm, and he hesitated before lifting his face away a fraction. "You are ticklish," he breathed. "And I want to feel the weight of this arm now, or I'll find your sensitive spot and do my worst. The relief when I stop will make you relax."

"Sadist." She closed her eyes and tried to do as he asked. Her muscles softened slightly, and warmth crept steadily into her cold hands and feet.

Nick set down her arm and supported her bent knee. With his other hand he massaged her thigh. For an instant Abby tautened. She looked at his face, his freshly anxious eyes. He smiled. "Let go again, Abby. But keep your eyes open this time. We'll have to figure out a method of keeping you focused—a piece of music, or something visual to concentrate on. The book says you aren't supposed to drift too much, or you won't be ready for each contraction."

"I...Nick, why are you doing this?" As soon as she asked, she knew what she longed to hear.

Nick stroked her calf with long, sweeping motions. "Because I want to."

She grappled with his words. They were simple, beautiful to her...too simple. Her mind darted back to the night he'd rescued her in the snow. Then he'd let her know how aware he was of her as a woman. But he'd never mentioned that encounter again. She returned her attention to his face. "Thank you for helping me, Nick. I wish I could do something for you."

"You are." He rested both hands lightly on her side. "This feels tight. Think about the muscle over your rib cage and imagine the tension flowing from there, through my hands and into me."

"What am I doing for you?" she persisted, every nerve in her body fluttering.

Nick regarded her solemnly. "You're giving me the pleasure of getting to know a beautiful woman and appreciating that she's also very bright and talented. No woman ever affected me the way you do, Abby."

He spoke as if he meant what he said, as if he cared. Abby opened her mouth, and Nick immediately pressed a thumb against her lips.

"And now," he said, unsmiling, "could you please give me some encouragement here by cooperating? I want to lead you through the relaxation series in the book and make sure the instructor thinks we're doing it right so we can practice at home. It's also past time to start getting the breathing patterns and contraction timing down."

She tried. Each gentle order he gave, Abby attempted to follow, constantly pulling her mind back from the stray trails it followed. "Take another long sigh and concentrate on your shoulders," he said. She shrugged them loose. He'd spoken of their practicing at home, as if he were her husband. "While I rub the back of your neck, see warmth coming in there and the stiffness going into my fingers.'' She felt his fingers. She remembered how they'd looked holding hers in the car. Whatever was happening to her with Nick, she'd lost the will to fight it, didn't want to anymore.

''Do you feel more peaceful?''

''What?'' Abby lifted her head. ''Oh, yes, yes I do. Thank you.'' She didn't feel peaceful. Even the skin on her face and scalp responded to him with an intensity she'd never known, she realized with surprise.

''You two are good at this.'' Louise, making her constant tour of the room, paused and knelt beside Nick. She placed his hand on Abby's belly. ''She'll be getting more Braxton-Hicks contractions from now on. You'll be able to feel them too, a kind of pulling up.''

Nick frowned, passing his hand higher, then lower. ''Are they the start of labor?''

Louise smiled. ''No, just the uterus's way of getting ready for the real thing. They increase uterine circulation and help the cervix thin and soften. You'll both know the difference when true labor begins.''

At nine, Abby and Nick collected their belongings and headed back to the car. Once more Nick put an arm around Abby, this time holding her more firmly to his side. She glanced up into his face, and he smiled at her.

''Feel less threatened?''

''About the classes? Yes, I guess.''

''Good. But I really meant do you feel better about having me with you. It embarrassed you at first.''

''No——''

''Yes, Abby, it did. And that's understandable. But you won't feel so badly next week, will you?''

''I...no. Not if you want to come. But I do feel guilty. It isn't your job.''

''It's someone's job, and I don't see anyone else around.''

''So your conscience makes you feel you have to fill in. I could cope on my own, Nick. I'm a very capable woman.''

He opened the car door and helped her in. He rested an elbow on the door and stared down into her face. ''I already know how capable you are. But you *do* need a partner for these classes. And wanting to be that partner has nothing to do with my conscience. When are you going to figure that out?''

Before she could reply, he slammed the door and stood in front of the hood, waiting for a break in the traffic before he got behind the wheel.

Abby kept the pillows on her lap, clutching them. Okay, he was one of the world's gentle, responsible people, and he wanted to help her for a time. So be it. She'd leave the subject alone. She could certainly use someone to rely on. She trusted Nick. If there was one person she'd like to have with her now, he was it. Her mouth dried out. What if he were around only for a while? Just long enough for her to—love him? Yes, she was afraid she'd fall in love with Nick, and then lose him.

He started the engine but didn't immediately pull away. "Are you tired?"

She turned questioningly toward him. "No. Why?"

"Did you eat dinner before we left?"

"No—yes, yes I did." Good Lord, if he found out she hadn't, he'd be plying her with food again.

Nick met her eyes briefly before he maneuvered from the parking lot to cross two lanes of traffic. "You're a lousy liar. You haven't eaten. Neither have I. Let's go out on the town."

Abby held the pillows closer. He couldn't mean that in the traditional sense, but she should be the one to make sure he at least had a meal after all he'd done this evening. "My treat this time," she said lightly. "What kind of food do you feel like?"

"When I invite a lady out, I pay. And I choose the place, too—no arguments entertained. It's my masterful side sneaking out, the one I keep hidden most of the time."

"A closet chauvinist," Abby said and gave a short laugh while she visualized how she looked in her baggy blue flannel shirt worn with jeans and tennis shoes. Her coat was the favorite black wool, voluminous and comfortable, but rapidly taking on the greenish tinge of age. Nick also wore jeans, she remembered. A good sign. He wasn't likely to pick a restaurant where they'd both feel out of place.

Nick took a left turn from Denny Way onto Fifth Avenue and headed for the gulches between the towering glass and concrete buildings of Seattle's business district.

"Do you like the kind of music George Winston plays?" He leaned forward over the wheel, checking in each direction, and took a sharp right onto Pike Street. "I know I usually hear nothing but strains of Dixieland coming from your place."

Apprehension sickened Abby. She wanted to go home but couldn't hurt him. "I like George Winston very much," she said.

"His stuff is different, melodic, not typical modern jazz. Why do you ask?"

"Because he's playing at a place off Pioneer Square. We could eat and catch his second set. Would you like that?"

Why now? Abby thought. Why did a man who liked the things she liked and seemed on her wavelength in almost everything have to come along when there seemed no way their relationship could go anywhere?

"Abby? Will you let me take you there? The fare's strictly American-bar: beer and nachos. If you want something else, we can go to another restaurant first."

"No," she said hurriedly. "I enjoy that kind of thing." She'd agreed to go. Abby ran her eyes glumly over a group of bums slouching beneath the pergola in Pioneer Square. With luck, the dress where they were going was strictly Army and Navy store, and she'd fit right in.

The dim interior of the club they entered was a blessed equalizer for all patrons. Nick found a corner table, and Abby took a chair facing the stage. A backup group played soft synthesized music, and a few couples danced slow and close on a minute floor. Conversation hummed loudly enough to dull the music, and blue cigarette smoke hung beneath the thin beams of spotlights directed at the ceiling.

Abby ordered orange juice and tonic water and laughed when Nick said "Make that two" as if he drank the concoction all the time.

"You don't have to be on the wagon just because I am," she said when the waitress had left.

"I have to get in shape for the big event, too." Nick pushed a candle to one side of the table and leaned closer. "Do you think all this smoke could be bad for the baby? I didn't think about it."

A helpless urge to cry almost undid Abby. She glanced away, feeling the tears well up. "You're wonderful. I hadn't even thought of that. But I don't think one trip into a smoky room will do any harm."

He stretched his hands, palms up, across the table.

Abby stared at them and slowly put her two clenched fists on top. Something was happening between them, and it wasn't born of Nick's sense of decency. Pregnant or not, the tingling in her thighs was purely sexual, and the glimmer in his eyes was anything but that of a concerned friend.

Nick bent his elbows, closing her hands inside his and lifting them. He kissed each of her knuckles slowly, as if lost in thought before he said, "I'm afraid to say what I want to."

Her body ached. Simply looking at him, the sensation of his fingers, his lips on her skin, aroused Abby as she'd never been aroused. "You can say anything to me." Her voice was husky, hardly more than a whisper that he strained to hear. She cleared her throat. "What is it, Nick?" Wanting him to be completely open, afraid what that could mean, Abby smiled and felt her insides draw together. Every silent message he sent told her he was falling in love with her. If he said as much, what would she say, what could she say now?

He was quiet for a long time, then a deep breath lifted his broad shoulders. "It's not such a big deal, really. I shouldn't have made it sound so dramatic." He smiled and pressed her hands before releasing them. "My sister, Janet, is coming in a couple of days. She's one of those people who clean corners with a toothbrush and cook gourmet meals three times a day. I wondered if you'd mind using a critical eye on my condo before she gets here and helping me figure out some good places to take her."

Abby's stomach felt as if a large hand had squeezed it. Disappointment sent goose bumps crawling over her skin. She rallied, tapping her fingernails on the checkered tablecloth. "I'd like to do that, Nick. Give me a few hours to think about it. She might like to see this area of town. When I think of Seattle, I always think of Pioneer Square and the waterfront. And Snoqualmie Pass. I bet she'd fall in love with the mountains. There's a pretty good snow pack already, and there could even be skiers. If we have a clear day, you could take her up one of the lifts."

"Great idea," Nick said, but his eyes held an intense light. Sad? Why would he be sad? "Would you meet her, Abby? Come over to my place and visit? She'll only be here three days."

Abby crushed a desperate longing to hear Nick say she mattered more to him than his sister, than anyone. She wanted too much. His friendship should be enough. "I'd be pleased to," she replied mechanically, wondering what his sister was likely to make of Nick's interest in her.

George Winston played his set. His music, poignant modern interpretations of beautiful old pieces, brought joy and longing. Nick's hands, covering hers once more, gripped tighter.

"You loved that, didn't you?" he asked when it was over.

Abby turned her head away.

"Didn't you?" Nick pulled her wrists toward him. "Look at me."

She kept her face averted. "His music twists my heart, if that isn't trite." He mustn't know that listening to beautiful music with him was almost more magic than she could bear.

"You twist my heart," Nick said softly. "I don't want this night to end, Abby. I...oh, Abby, I wish I could take you home and know I'd never have to let you go."

Blood throbbed in every part of her body. Some emotion he hadn't analyzed must be carrying him along. He couldn't know what he was saying.

"You'd soon get sick of that, Nick. I'm a bit much to hold these days. But it's a nice idea. And her heart said, *I wish I could hold you forever.*

He released her hands. "One day you'll understand. When you stop believing whatever mind tapes you've been taught to play. You're beautiful, my...you're beautiful."

She could hardly breathe. "We'd better hit the road. Some of us need more beauty sleep than others—not that it helps a whole lot."

Nick sighed, then smiled brightly and presented his profile. "I resent that. Many women have said this is an irresistible face. And the body, well..."

"You know perfectly well I meant *I* needed beauty sleep." Abby smiled wryly. "We both know how gorgeous you are. I'm sure you're as bad as Michael. He leaves trails of broken hearts wherever he goes. At least, he does if you believe what he says."

Nick held her hand as they wove a path to the door. On the sidewalk they both stood beneath a streetlight, fastening their coats against an arctic wind that slapped discarded newspapers against buildings.

"Abby," Nick said and cupped her jaw, "I'd like to kiss you again, and not for luck this time."

Her throat closed. She stared up at him.

"Do you understand?"

She shook her head, afraid he'd somehow see the uprush of emotion she felt.

"What is it—loyalty to John? Is it so wrong to kiss someone who cares about you? I think you want to."

Abby rested her weight against him. His fingers splayed wide in the small of her back, then slid up between her shoulder blades. She lifted her head, and he lowered his mouth slowly over hers, opened her lips languorously and slipped his tongue inside. A quiet place formed inside her, but only for a moment before the clamoring came, and she returned the kiss with an ardor that rocked them both. Nick pressed his mouth hard from side to side and drove his fingers into her hair. He brought his teeth together on her lower lip, and she moaned. Abruptly Nick raised his head and guided her face beneath his jaw. She felt the rapid beat of the pulse in his neck.

Seconds later she roused herself, hugged his broad body quickly and pulled away. She trusted him, knew he'd be there for her if she needed him, but she couldn't allow the sexuality between them to escalate, not until she knew what the future held.

"You are so lovely, Abby. I thank God I know you," Nick said, shielding her from the wind with his body.

"The light's changing," she said shakily.

"A lot of things are changing," he responded.

"Let's cross."

Holding each other close, they hurried to the other side of the street where the BMW was parked. Nick helped Abby get settled and climbed in beside her.

He locked the driver's door and faced her, hooking his knee over the console. "About what you said back there, just before we left the bar—" he pulled her chin up "—about me and other women. I've been pretty much a loner the past few years, Abby. I'm not into breaking hearts. And what I hate most is to watch the heart of someone who means a lot to me being mangled and not being able to do much about it."

His face mesmerized her; the serious glint in his eyes, the hint of white where his teeth showed between slightly parted lips. He knew something was very wrong in her life and was obliquely asking her to let him help.

Abby fixed her attention on the signal. "You're a good man, Nick. Maybe too good. We should get home."

"YOU'RE QUIET, JANET."

"So are you. You haven't said a word in ten minutes."

Nick spread his fingers on his thighs. "I didn't realize. Sorry."

"You're nervous."

He laughed and stood. "You noticed. Observant girl."

"I'm known for my sensitivity."

"Oh, Janet, it's good to have you here, even for a little while." Nick faced her, looking down into her upturned face. Scrubbed.

Janet always looked scrubbed and healthy…and dearly familiar. "Did you sleep well? Is the bed okay for you?"

"It's great. But you didn't have to give up your room for me. I could have slept in the spare one, or on the couch."

"No way. Nothing's too good for my sister. How's everyone back home?"

Janet crossed her arms. "We did that number last night, remember? Everyone's just terrific. Nick, for God's sake, settle down. You're as nervous as a cat. I already know your Abby is married…I'm not shocked. Worried about how things are going to work out, but not shocked. So stop chewing your fingernails."

Hell, Nick thought, Janet *didn't* know Abby was pregnant, but she soon would. "She's not *my* Abby, unfortunately. And I never chew my fingernails." He should tell the whole story, just spit it out.

"I was speaking metaphorically."

"Look, Janet—" he had to tread carefully "—don't say anything. I mean, be careful what you say to Abby. We understand each other, you and I. Our brand of humor and so on, but—"

"What do you think I'm likely to say to the woman? I won't make cracks about penalties for bigamy or anything. Quite panicking."

Skirting an issue was always hazardous, Nick thought. What if Janet drew the same conclusions Michael Harris had at first? He turned his back and leaned against a wall. "She doesn't know how I feel about her," he said in a rush. "Not for sure."

Rustling behind him was all he heard.

"Janet, do you understand what I'm saying?"

"I understand," she said softly. "You idiot, Nick. You never did know how to let your feelings out."

He pressed his temple to the cool plaster. "I guess I didn't."

"And you haven't let her know she means a lot to you?"

"No. Not really. And, Janet—" he swung around "—she mustn't find out yet. You said I had to wait for her to come clean about her marriage, and she hasn't. She's too vulnerable now. If she thought she'd hurt me, if she couldn't…feel something special for me, she might insist she did, anyway. I don't want that."

The doorbell rang, paralyzing him. Abby. He shouldn't have suggested she come. It was a rotten idea with things the way they were.

"Nick," Janet whispered. "Trust me."

He nodded.

"Well?" The door bell rang again. Nick couldn't concentrate. "Well what?"

"Let her in, Nick." Janet stood and faced the door.

"Right, right." His brain felt like mush. He rushed to the door and swept it wide, grabbing Abby's elbow and hauling her inside. "Abby, this is my sister, Janet. Janet Ross. Janet—Abby Winston."

When he sought Janet's eyes, she looked not at him but at Abby. He saw a swift downward glance, and then Janet was striding forward, smiling, to shake Abby's hand.

"So you're Abby," Janet said loudly. "Nick's been telling me all about you."

Nick's blood drained to his feet. Great going, Janet, he thought. *Great going, Nick. It's your fault.* "Come on in, Abby," he said and shook his head slightly at Janet. "We're plotting Janet's itinerary. She thinks Seattle's dreary, so I've got to reprogram her opinion."

Abby looked into eyes the same tawny brown as Nick's, with the same warm, humorous quality. Brother and sister strongly resembled each other. The woman was also tall, a feminine version of Nick with her curly brown hair grown to shoulder length. She was going to like Janet Ross, Abby decided, even though there'd been a flash of surprise not quickly enough hidden when the woman realized Abby was pregnant. Evidently Nick hadn't told his sister quite everything about her.

"Hello, Janet. I'd have known you even without Nick being here." Her hands felt too big, and there was nowhere to put them. She soldiered on. "Are you sure you two aren't twins?"

"I'm the baby," Nick said and immediately reddened.

"He's fourteen months younger, and I never stop hearing about it." Janet laughed, looking at him hard before she indicated a coffeepot and cups on the dining table. "How about some coffee, Abby?"

Abby longed to touch Nick, to tell him to loosen up. Clearly her pregnancy was an embarrassment to him. She didn't want to be here.

Janet had started pouring coffee. "I'm sorry, Janet," Abby said, her smile wavering. "I can't stay. But thanks for the offer." She felt Nick looking at her but kept her attention on Janet, who set down the pot. "Are you sure? Nick said you'd be able to spend the day with us."

Abby retreated, taking slow steps backward. "My work sched-

ule changed. I'd really like to come, but you know how it is."
He'd be glad of her sudden change of mind—they both would.

"I don't think I do know how it is," Nick said quietly.

A shiver climbed up Abby's spine. His mouth had settled into a hard line. She wiped her right palm on her skirt. "Just one of those things." Her tone wasn't light enough. "I'm sorry if I've upset your plans."

He eyed her squarely. "Are you? Thanks. Maybe you should have thought about my plans before."

Abby swallowed, aware that Janet stood motionless by the table. What must the woman be thinking? "I never intended to complicate your life." She turned her face away. Every word they spoke sounded damning.

"Isn't it time you quit that dump you insist on working in? You know it worries me. Doesn't that count for something?"

"Nick," Janet broke in, "isn't this a conversation you'd rather have without me?"

Nick didn't appear to hear. He'd come so close to Abby that she had to lift her head to meet his eyes. His face was pale now, even his lips. "Michael knows something's wrong with you. After that…after he was here with us, he took a few more potshots at me, and he's figured out…" He stopped, with one hand raised, as anguish slowly darkened his eyes. He looked over his shoulder at Janet, then back to Abby. "Oh, my God. I'm sorry." He pulled her into his arms. "Forgive me. Please forgive me. I don't have any right to speak to you like that."

Abby's body became rigid. "It's okay." She touched his sides, but he didn't release her. What did Michael know? That she was working in the Laundromat? Had he told their parents? "Let me go, Nick," she whispered. Nick, she thought, had presented Janet with a picture she'd find as hard to decipher as Michael had the night he'd found her with Nick. Because of her, this visit would probably be strained, ruined. "Please, Nick." She closed her eyes. He smelled clean, fresh from the shower. His hair was still damp.

"Do you really have to go to work?" He lessened his grip, then slowly moved away until he held her at arm's length. His eyes pleaded with her.

"Nick," Janet interrupted. "If Abby has to work, she has to work." She gave Abby a painful smile. "Pray your baby's a girl. Boys never stop wanting their own way from the day they're born."

Abby returned the smile gratefully. "I think you're right, but I also have a feeling this is a boy. Nick insists otherwise, something to do with the baby's hip action, whatever he means by—'' She stopped. Sweat broke out on her back and the palms of her hands. Every word she spoke twisted the situation more. She must get away.

"We've got a girl,'' Janet said, coming to stand beside Nick. "Penny. I expect Nick's told you how I go on about her all the time.'' She grimned broadly, and the atmosphere softened. "I won't bore you with pictures now because I know you're in a hurry. But I'd like to show her off. Could we get together before I go back? I've got tomorrow, if I can get rid of Nick for an hour. There's nothing I like better than a chance to share war stories about early childhood survival—for the parent.''

Abby wanted to hug the woman. "I'd like that. Yes, let's do it. Lunch at my place.''

Nick wasn't listening. "It's slick out there again, Abby,'' he said. "Drive carefully, please.''

*Shut up,* Abby wanted to say, *before you make your sister draw totally wrong conclusions.* "I'll be fine.'' She turned back to Janet. "Your brother is a frustrated father. He thinks he has to look out— He worries about me,'' she finished lamely.

"He's always been a bit like that,'' Janet agreed.

"Did you get a new battery?'' Nick continued as if no one else had spoken.

"Yes,'' Abby said, exasperated, and opened the front door. "My car runs like a Rolls-Royce these days.''

As she entered the hall, she called to Janet, "See you tomorrow, Janet. Come whenever you like. Thanks for being so understanding about today.'' And to Nick, she added, "Make sure Janet sees the good stuff around town. The Seattle Center. Take her on a ferry across Elliott Bay. And, Nick, is there something I should get in touch with Michael about quickly?''

He shook his head sheepishly. "No. I was lashing out, I guess. He is worried about you because he found out you aren't at the store anymore. But I put him off. There's nothing to worry about.''

Nick's next action left her weak. Janet had returned to his condo, leaving them alone. He moved swiftly, held her face in both hands and kissed her mouth possessively. She responded instinctively until they drew away, breathless.

"We're going to talk, Abby. If you insist on keeping up that job, make sure you're free on Monday morning. I'm taking you out—somewhere away from here—and we're going to get a few things straight."

"I don't know—"

"Monday, Abby. Promise me."

She pushed open her unlocked door, a million confused thoughts tumbling through her mind.

"Abby Winston, will you answer me?"

"Yes, Nick," she said quietly. "I'll see you on Monday morning."

She closed the door behind her, shutting him out, and dropped to sit on the floor. Pressure was going to come from all sides and blow apart her carefully made plans; she could feel it. Her head throbbed. What she needed was sleep, but for Janet and Nick's benefit, she'd have to go out, even though she wasn't really working.

Her back ached. Tightening in her belly made her wince, and she leaned back on her arms. The Braxton-Hicks contractions the childbirth education instructor mentioned had been coming more frequently in the past twenty-four hours. She lay flat on the carpet, and her uterus pulled in sharply. The baby rolled. Abby closed her eyes and tried to relax. A few more weeks, and her baby would be here.

A tear squeezed from her closed eyes and seeped, hot, across her temples. *Her baby.* She laughed and cried at the same time.

NICK HALF LISTENED to the Seattle Space Needle elevator guide spout facts. "The Needle is five hundred feet high. It was built as part of the 1960 World Fair Grounds and left as a permanent structure for the city residents and our visitors to enjoy." The girl spoke fast with little inflection. Nick studied his shoes and wondered what Janet was thinking. She'd said little after Abby had left the condo or during the half hour drive into town. What was Abby doing now? He passed a hand over his hair.

"From the observation deck you may enjoy a 360-degree view of the city and the surrounding scenery," the guide droned on.

They shot steadily up the graceful structure toward its space saucer crown. Nick met Janet's eyes, and she returned his regard steadily, her thoughts unreadable.

At the top, they started a slow circle of the deck and Nick pointed out landmarks as they went. He dropped a coin into a telescope and made Janet look at the Olympic Mountains and

Elliott Bay with its jumble of commercial and pleasure craft and the smattering of container ships and grain vessels.

When they'd walked the perimeter of the circular structure twice, Janet planted herself in a deserted area and confronted Nick. "Are you going to tell me?"

He swallowed. He'd known the questions would come, more questions, and that they might be stickier than the others. "What do you want to know, Janet?"

She brushed back her shiny curls. Janet only seemed to get lovelier, Nick thought abstractedly. "Well, brother," she said, "if you're going to be difficult, I guess I'll have to help you out. You love Abby. I'd have to be blind or mentally incompetent not to gather that."

He looked past her toward Puget Sound. "I do love her."

"You were pretty rough on her at your condo."

"I know. But I wanted her to come."

Janet turned to rest her elbows on the window ledge. "Didn't it strike you she might be embarrassed?"

He shoved his hands into his pockets. "To be with us?"

"Stop hedging. You omitted one little thing when you told me about her. That was dumb, Nick. Was I likely *not* to notice she's pregnant?"

For an instant he didn't know what to say. He cleared his throat. "I wasn't sure how to explain."

Without looking at him, Janet reached out a hand and waited for Nick to hold it. She urged him beside her at the window. "Is it your baby?"

Nick exhaled, bowing his head. "No, dammit. I wish it were, but it's not. Do you believe that?"

"I believe it. You've really let yourself in for something, haven't you?" She looked up at him. "Are you sure her husband is out of the picture?"

"I'm sure he's left her. Her brother is, too, although Abby doesn't know that yet. The only thing I'm not sure about is whether she still cares for John Winston."

"But you want her...to marry her."

He sighed. "It's all I want. And I want that baby, too. I know it sounds crazy, Janet, but I feel as if the kid were mine. Am I mad?"

"No." She patted his shoulder. "Just a very unusual man. And from what I've seen of Abby, she's just as unusual. And, Nick, I think she loves you, too."

His stomach dropped. "How could you know that?"

"I saw it in her eyes. In the way she looked at you."

"What am I going to do, Janet?" Helplessness shaded the new hope she'd given him.

"Keep on loving her until she's ready to admit she loves you, too."

# Chapter Ten

"Hold my hand," Nick said. "This probably isn't such a hot idea."

Abby took another step and slipped.

Nick cursed under his breath, shooting an arm around her waist. "I told you to hold on to me, Abby. Those boots of yours weren't made for packed snow. I don't know why you suggested coming to—"

"I didn't."

"—a ski area in your condition." He stood still, waiting for her to look at him. "You did suggest it. You said—"

"No, I didn't. I did suggest Snoqualmie Pass would be a nice place for you to bring Janet while she was visiting," she interrupted evenly. "I agreed to talk to you today, that's all. Coming here was your idea. So can we have this discussion you insisted on and be civil to each other and maybe enjoy the scenery now that we're here?"

Nick turned her toward him. "I've been rotten this morning, haven't I?"

"Absolutely rotten, Nick Dorset. Horrible."

He touched her cheek hesitantly and tucked a stray curl inside her woolly cap. "What should I do about it?"

She caught his hand and held it in both of hers. "Tell me what's eating you, Nicholas Stuart."

"Oh, oh, Nicholas Stuart—that bad, huh?"

"That bad." She studied his face, his hair whipping this way and that, the way his tan intensified against the snowy backdrop below a glaring blue sky. He should be dressed in brilliant gear like the few skiers who passed, skis and poles over their shoulders, on their way to the lifts. She imagined him rocketing downhill, sleek, powerful...laughing...white teeth...crinkling eyes...

"What is it, Abby?"

She inhaled sharply, focusing on his eyes. "I was just thinking. I guess I was miles away."

"Thinking about what?"

She shook her head, laughing. "Sometimes a vivid imagination is a curse. I could see you skiing, and you looked——" She released his hand. "You looked marvelous. Do you ski?"

"Yes, you?" His regard didn't waver.

"Yes. Michael and I both learned when we were little, and we kept it up. Our folks couldn't afford it, really, but they always managed to give us the things they were sure we had to have."

"They sound like special people. I'd like to meet them one day."

Abby turned clammy inside her old parka. "I'm sure they'd like that, too," she mumbled.

Nick tucked her hand firmly through his elbow. They picked their way toward an alpine-style lodge, its roof sharply sloped and edged with painted flowers.

"I'd like to ski with you," Nick said. "Can we do that next winter, do you think?"

Abby watched their breaths make white clouds and tried to decide how to answer. "That would be nice." Her tone had the right noncommittal note. There was no denying what she felt for Nick, and he'd given enough signals that he could see himself as more than simply her champion while she was alone. But he didn't know she would always be alone. When he did find out, he could decide to run. Heading off deep involvement now could save them both.

"It's bound to be pretty quiet in the main lodge," Nick said. "Not too many people come up on a weekday this early in the season. We could hole up in there and talk. At least it'll be warm, and we'll have a good view of the slopes."

"I don't want to do that." Abby pulled him to a halt. "We can ride the chair to the top of the Thunderbird run and sit in the little lodge up there. They always have a fire, and you can see forever."

"No," Nick said, turning incredulous eyes on her. "You're not riding a ski lift in your——"

"Condition! Why not? They stop the chair for nonskiers to get on and off. I'll be fine and I want to go."

"You sound like a spoiled kid," he said grimly. "I want to go.' You aren't warmly enough dressed, and I don't want you falling."

She pulled her hat firmly over her ears. "Are you coming with me, Nick, or am I going alone?"

He grumbled under his breath, the word "women" sounding clearly from time to time while he guided her with exaggerated care to the lift station. When the operator had stopped the rotating cables, Abby slid quickly into a chair and fastened the safety bar under her belly. The fit was snug, but she made no comment. When Nick was beside her, the machinery ground again, and they swept slowly upward, swinging gently, the distance beneath their feet and the slopes widening.

"Isn't this something?" Abby shouted, lifting her face to the stinging wind. The sun turned the snowpack to an undulating carpet of glitter. Isolated skiers sped downhill, knees flexing to absorb each turn, poles flashing as they nicked the snow's surface. Abby laughed. "I can hardly wait to be down there again."

"You will be," Nick called back. "I've seen some fairly small kids up here, too. The baby should be able to start before too long."

Abby tipped back her head, laughing delightedly. "He's not even born, and you've got him on skis. You're wonderful."

"Am I?"

She glanced at him and quickly away again. "The old male ego never quits, does it? Sure, you're wonderful, Nick." The top station was in sight. She unhooked the seat bar. "We're almost there."

A strong arm immediately pressed across her stomach. "Stay put. Don't move a muscle until they stop the chair."

Heat crept beneath the cold skin on Abby's cheeks. "I didn't intend to jump off in midair." How could he be so aware of her pregnancy yet so unconscious of her swollen shape. He always touched her naturally with no sign of the distaste John had shown from the beginning.

Slipping and sliding, leaning on each other, they made their way from the chair dismount and up an incline to the circular lodge. Warmth rushed to meet them as they opened the door, as did the smell of burning cedar from a central fireplace.

At ten in the morning most skiers had already started their day on the slopes. Apart from Abby and Nick, only two other men and a counter hand were in the lodge. Abby chose a table with a clear view across the Cascade Mountains and peeled off her parka and cap. She stuffed the cap and her mittens into a sleeve and laid the coat over an empty chair. Nick shed his outer clothes and went to the counter. He returned with two mugs of hot chocolate, pulled the chair from the opposite side of the table and sat beside her.

"Janet said you two had a nice lunch on Saturday," he said.

"A 'good talk,' she said. Whatever that means."

Abby blew holes in the cream on top of her chocolate. "It means what she said: that we got along well. We found a lot in common. I really like her. It's too bad she couldn't stay longer." She glanced at Nick. "From her pictures, Penny's a doll. She looks a lot like you and Janet."

Nick gave her a sidelong look. "I've been called a lot of things, but never a doll."

She elbowed him, grinning. "You know I didn't mean that. Although, according to Janet, you are certainly God's gift to the world."

"What's that supposed to mean?" The mountains seemed to hold his attention now.

"Only that your sister thinks you're wonderful. I know all about what a good student you were, the star you were on the college track team and your sparkling service record—crack flyer and so on. And, more important, you're a nice guy."

"According to Janet."

Abby met his eyes and didn't hesitate. "According to Janet and me. You're the nicest man I've ever met." She hadn't meant to add that.

But Nick's face showed only the faintest flicker as he wrapped his hands around his cup. "Thanks," he said. "Every man needs a fan club."

The tiredness she'd come to dread edged into her muscles, her bones. Nick made no attempt to start a serious discussion. A sudden brittle silence yawned between them, and Abby sensed that whatever was said to break it could change things for good.

"Do you trust me, Abby?"

"Yes."

"You came right back with that. Are you sure?"

"I'm very sure. But why did you ask?"

Nick rested an elbow on the table and supported his chin. "Because I'd like us to be...I'd like to feel we were very good friends, the best."

His tone, the rigid attitude of his body, puzzled her. "I don't think I've ever had a better friend than you, Nick."

"But you aren't comfortable enough to be honest with me about everything."

She didn't like the direction he was taking. "I am honest with you."

"I don't think so. Or perhaps 'honest' isn't the right word. 'Open' might be better. I don't think you're open with me about the important things in your life. Maybe I don't have the right to expect you to be, but—"

"You have the right. I gave you the right by making you a part of my life. It's me who doesn't have the right to ask so much of you."

He turned to look at her. "You can ask anything. Could you tell me what's really going on with you right now?"

She covered her mouth, expelling a slow breath.

"Try, Abby. Start anywhere." He rubbed her shoulders and rested his hand on the back of her neck.

"I don't know where to start," she replied, so low that he brought his face closer. She added, "I don't know what I should say and what I shouldn't say."

Gently he brushed a kiss across her temple. "It's okay. Just be quiet if you want to. I didn't mean to push you."

Instinctively Abby leaned toward him. The force of her need for him terrified her. "Thanks for understanding." She'd made what could only be a terrible mistake. She'd fallen in love with Nick Dorset.

It was there in her eyes, Nick thought exultantly. The shy surprise of early love. He was winning. If he could keep himself from rushing in and frightening her off, she'd come to him whole, without John Winston's ghost.

She gazed at him for a long time, her lips barely parted, before she straightened deliberately. "I have been doing a lot of heavy thinking lately," she said. "Do you remember seeing a woman coming to my place? Small, with blond hair?"

"Not really."

"Marie Prince. I've known her since grade school. She comes over quite often. You must have seen her."

She was anxious. Nick scooped her hand from her lap and squeezed it. "Maybe I have. I just don't recall," he said.

"Anyway, Marie said something a couple of weeks ago that made me think. Sooner or later you have to face up to things, don't you?" The great gray eyes pleaded for a response, a specific reaction he couldn't give without knowing what Abby was thinking.

"Marie was talking about what children need," she went on.

She tugged at the neck of her green sweater. "Not just material things, although everything seems to come from that in the end."

A coldness climbed Nick's spine. Abby was close to some sort of panic. "Kids need love most of all, Abby," he said as calmly as he could. "Like the rest of us. It doesn't sound as if your friend told you anything you didn't already know."

"No, no, Nick. That's not it. I mean, that's not what I'm trying to say."

"Okay," he responded carefully, "go on. But take it easy, Abby. You're uptight suddenly."

"Do you think it's a terrible thing for a mother to give up her baby?"

Nick realized his mouth was open and brought his lips together. Abby snatched her hand from his and began pulling on her cap and gloves.

"Abby," he whispered urgently. The lodge was fuller now. "What are you saying?"

"Nothing." She dragged on her parka.

Nick stood and reached for his own jacket.

"You don't have to come," Abby insisted. "Stay and enjoy the scenery. You have to leave tomorrow. You should enjoy your last day off."

His brain felt numb around the edges. "Where are you going?"

"Home. I'm tired."

"Home?" A blast of icy air hit his face as she opened the door and walked onto the broad deck surrounding the lodge. "How can you go home if I don't? You came with me." He caught her arm and swung her around. "Why are you running away from me? And what...Abby, why did you ask about mothers giving up their babies?"

Wind snatched at the curls not covered by her cap. He saw the start of tears in her eyes.

"I don't want to talk about it." She hurried across the deck, her boots slithering on glassy ice. "I shouldn't have said anything."

Nausea hit Nick with weakening force. He closed his eyes for an instant. "Stand still, Abby. Now." The deadly apprehension he felt flattened his voice.

"Let me go, Nick. Just let me go. Stop feeling responsible for me."

He grasped her elbow and pulled her under the eaves of the building. "Don't tell me what I can or can't feel," he said. She was crying now, her head bowed. He held her against the wall, and she clutched the front of her jacket. "Abby, look at me. Finish what you started to tell me."

"I need a tissue." She sniffed and raised her brimming eyes to his. When she blinked, tears made their way down her cheeks. Nick searched his pockets, finding nothing but his keys and wallet. Abby wiped her face with the backs of her fingers and sniffed again.

He remembered the kerchief he wore around his neck, took it off and handed it to Abby. "Blow your nose with this. Then start talking." Whoever coined the phrase "slowly dying inside" must have felt what he was feeling now. Watching her cry tore him apart, but he couldn't comfort her without softening too much to be able to keep pressing for answers.

"Marie called me last night." The blue scarf, held to her lips, moved with her breath. "She asked if I'd thought any more about what we talked about before."

"About what babies need, what children need?"

"Yes. Marie mentioned how many people can't have children and want them desperately. She...she was saying how hard it is to work and look after a baby. And how expensive things like day care are."

Heaviness pressed into Nick's chest. Her tears flowed again, and the scarf muffled her voice. He folded his arms, gripping the fabric of his parka at his sides.

Abby made a choking noise and blew her nose again. "When you spend all your time getting a child ready to go to a day-care place and then picking him up and working in between, you've got to be too tired to enjoy him. A child knows when you don't have what it takes to be a real parent, when everything he does—the things children *should* do—makes you mad. That isn't fair, Nick. I don't want my baby to be unhappy."

Anger began to eat at Nick. "And this Marie what's-her-name says you're going to be the kind of mother who makes her child's life a misery?"

"No! Well...she just wanted me to think about the future, and whether or not I'd be doing a better thing if...if...oh, Nick." Her shoulders came up, and she seemed to shrink.

"If?" He was being merciless, but backing away now could only harm them both. "If what?"

She lifted her head and wiped her eyes once more. "I don't know why I'm blubbering about this. I'm just trying to decide if it would be kinder to give the baby up for adoption.'' Struggle contorted her features. ''Some couple could give him everything a child needs. A nice home and clothes and toys and good schools. I—''

''Don't!'' His head was exploding. ''Don't say any more. Dammit, don't say it again.'' He put a hand on each side of her face and rested his forehead on hers. ''I can't believe you let this…this *friend* make you even consider this. Abby, you told me how you know your little person. You said he liked your kind of music and was happy when you're happy. You said you were excited and just looking forward to meeting him. And you meant it, Abby, you really meant it. God, how can you think of giving him up? How many children has Marie Prince had?''

''None.''

''So what makes her someone you'd listen to? *Nice* clothes, *nice* toys? What about love, Abby, what about the most important gift you can give any human being?''

''Adoptive parents love their children. I have to be sensible, realistic.''

''You have to live with yourself. If you don't keep this baby, you'll be destroyed. And your family, what about your family?'' He squeezed his eyes shut, willing her to mention John. She had to know he ought to be asking how John would react to the idea of losing his child to strangers. Her face, when he touched it, was icy. He tipped up her chin, smoothing her cheeks. ''What is it you're not telling me?''

''Nick.'' Her voice came faintly, high and thin. ''Hold me, please.''

He hesitated, vaguely conscious that he was also close to tears. ''Sweetheart…Abby, I—'' *I love you,* he thought vehemently. But he mustn't say it. She wasn't ready to deal with another possible commitment. ''It's okay, love. It's all right.'' And he did hold her, wrap her tightly in his arms, rock her gently until the choking noises faded.

''It's not, Nick. There's only me to decide what to do and to cope.''

The air seemed abruptly thinner. He stopped breathing altogether. ''Why do you feel that?''

Her sigh fanned his neck. Her nose was a cold spot against his chin. ''I'm divorced. John and I are divorced now. He filed in September, and it's all over.''

Nick gritted his teeth against a whoop. She'd finally told him what he'd longed to hear, and it was more, far more than he'd dared hope for. John Winston wasn't her husband anymore.

"John never wanted a baby. Things hadn't been very smooth for us for a long time, and the pregnancy was the end for him." She looked up at him. "John isn't all bad, Nick. I don't want you to think I'm blaming him for all that's happened. But he's out of my life now, and it's going to take a while for me to get completely stable again—financially, I mean. I can do it. I'm good at what I do, but I had to quit until the baby's born because I couldn't work on ladders or climb around like I have to."

"I understand," Nick heard himself say. At this moment he felt he understood the world's most obscure mysteries, that he could take on any challenge. *Abby, marry me*, his heart told her, *be my wife and let the baby be mine, as well as yours*. He had to hold back. The timing must be perfect, and she must have a chance to recover from the hurt and disappointment of one failed relationship before he could expect her to risk trying marriage again.

A rolling movement against his belly surprised him. He stepped away, still holding Abby's shoulders, and glanced down.

"Oh, dear." She gave a jerky laugh. "Another country heard from. The baby's been listening to all this discussion, and he's probably...cold." Her lips came together in a straight line, and she turned her head away. "I can't give him up, Nick. I'm too selfish."

"You're not selfish, my love. You're just a mother with a normal mother's instincts. Let's get down to the car and back home. We both need to warm up." He chuckled. "I guess I should say we all need to warm up, although I think you do a pretty good job of keeping the little tyke snug."

*My love*. Abby nestled into the arm Nick put around her. He'd called her his love, and sweetheart. His behavior all morning had been that of a man in love.

"When we get back," he was saying, "you should rest. You've had quite a workout for a lady as pregnant as you are. Have you seen your doctor lately?"

"Last Friday. He said I'm in great shape," Abby responded. Nick sounded like a concerned...husband. Her need was creating the illusions her starved soul yearned to be true.

Driving back to Bellevue, Nick kept up a stream of chatter and laughter. He touched her hands frequently, lifted the backs of his fingers to rub her cheek or jaw, reassured her constantly that everything would be fine, that *they'd* work out her problems.

The BMW wound downward between snow-laden banks and evergreen forests, droopy branches sagging beneath the white coats they'd wear until spring. Abby tried to use the relaxation methods from her childbirth books, concentrating on first one tight muscle, then another, clenching harder before deliberately letting go. Her efforts failed. What kind of a woman fell in love with a man while she was carrying someone else's child—when she'd been separated only months and divorced a few days? Was she depraved, without moral standards?

"Speak to me, Abby. Let me know you're still here."

She breathed in sharply and glanced at Nick. "I'm here. A bit tired, that's all. Thanks for taking me into the mountains. It's so lovely. Clean and new."

"That's the way your life's going to be, Abby," he said softly. "With the baby. You'll see, it'll all come straight."

"I hope so." Unthinking, she laid a hand on his thigh, then drew in a sharp breath at the instant jolt in the hard muscles and tried to withdraw it.

Nick stopped her. "I like your hand where it is." He pressed it closer. "Don't hold back from me any longer, Abby."

"I—," She turned hot and cold by turns. "I don't want to. But we both have a lot of thinking to do."

Nick fell silent. He was digesting what she'd said. Surely he couldn't fool himself into thinking their future—if they had a future together—wouldn't be tough. Abby pulled her hand from beneath his and played with the zipper on her parka. They still had so much to figure out about each other. Or maybe they had nothing, nothing at all, and this little dream she'd slowly allowed to form would drift away like their breath on the cold mountain air. Abby closed out the idea. Whatever happened, this man had made a place in her heart that would always be his.

"I'll be out and back in a day on this trip," Nick said.

Abby turned sideways. "I see." He behaved as if he owed her an accounting of his schedule.

"I leave again Thanksgiving Day, but I'll be in town for the class on Wednesday night."

"I'm glad you made me carry on with the course," she said.

He kept his attention on the winding roads. "We'll both be glad I did when you deliver."

Shyness paralyzed her tongue. His being there while she gave birth would be more humiliation than she could take.

Abby clenched her fists. "Nick, you're a dear, but you probably won't even be in town when the baby's born. The chances are he'll decide to arrive while you're on the beach in Waikiki."

He laughed easily. "I'll arrange my schedule to let me be around when your due date gets close, and I can keep switching if it takes a bit longer than expected. The book says first babies are often late."

"No, Nick," she insisted, keeping the desperation she felt out of her voice. "Don't make any special arrangements on my account. I'm going to use a birthing room and midwife for delivery. Midwives are great at helping out these days. The daughter of one of my mother's friends had a baby last year, and her husband couldn't cope, so the midwife took over. It went perfectly."

The sudden pull of the brakes jolted her forward. Nick slowed rapidly and drove into a turnout. He switched off the engine and swung his long body to face her, drawing up one knee. "Let's get a few things straight, Abby."

She concentrated on a point outside the window and said nothing.

"Okay, clam up if you like, but listen, anyway. Some things shouldn't be done alone. You didn't get pregnant alone, and you shouldn't have to deliver the baby alone."

She felt her face turn scarlet and bowed her head.

"Sorry if that's blunt, but it's true. John's out of the picture. No one else has shown up to hold your hand through this, and you haven't even told your family what's happening. That leaves me, and I'm going to be as hurt as hell if you shut me out."

"I'm not shutting you out," she said. Her cheeks were throbbing now. He *couldn't* be there, he simply *couldn't*.

"So you'll tell me when the baby comes?"

"I'll tell you." God forgive her she was telling Nick what he wanted to hear. And she hadn't exactly lied. She'd tell him—afterward.

She heard leather squeak as Nick moved, felt him bend over her. "You're all very organized and logical, Abby." He stroked her hair, pushing it back from her ear. Softly he kissed the side of her neck, the hollow beneath her cheekbone. "But I'm going to have to make sure one person isn't left out of the calculations."

"Who?" she whispered.

A finger and thumb, strong but gentle, tipped up her chin. "You, Abby. I'm going to make sure you come out of this happy."

"I——"

His firm lips covered hers, cutting off what she'd been about to say. What was she going to say? Nick's mouth moved slowly, opened slowly. His teeth were smooth against her tongue. Carefully he slid his arms around her shoulders. For a second he pulled back, looked down into her eyes, glanced at her mouth and gradually, so gradually, lowered his lips to hers once more.

MARIE HELD OPEN the door to Jake's and shivered, hopping from foot to foot until Abby passed her and they were both inside the warm bar.

"Boy, Bellevue's come a long way from the dead burg it used to be," Marie said, pulling off her gloves and eyeing the customer-crammed sea of dark marble tables. "Remember when this town was just a place for extra Seattleites to sleep? Over there," she announced triumphantly. "In the corner. Quick, before someone gets it." She took off, arriving at the empty table neck and neck with a man built like Mr. Universe. Marie put a hand on the biceps bulging under his left sleeve, smiled coyly and slipped into a seat. Abby saw her friend's shake of the head and knew Marie was turning down an offer of company.

Abby waited for the man to leave before she joined Marie. "How could you do that poor little guy out of a place to sit, *and* your delightful company?" she asked through her teeth.

Marie's eyes became widely innocent. She flapped a hand. "Sometimes you just have to make sacrifices. Beneath those muscles I could feel a tender heart, and you know my record for breaking hearts. I decided to spare him."

Abby laughed and unbuttoned her coat. She and Marie had spent the afternoon trudging around the Bellevue Square shopping mall while Marie bought clothes and Abby attempted to keep her mind off her aching feet. Marie lived in Seattle but insisted that the fifteen-mile drive to the east side was a small sacrifice to get at "all those yummy shops." Abby could make it from the condo, south of Bellevue, to the downtown area in ten minutes. Today she'd rather have spent her spare time on the couch.

"How many kinds of rum are you going to try, Abby?" Marie asked when a waitress arrived. "I'll have a sampler of beers, please—ah, Ballard Bitter, Anchor Steam and Watney's."

"Perrier for me, please," Abby said, and to Marie, when the waitress had walked away, she added, "Do they really have the world's largest selection of rums, do you suppose?"

Marie shrugged. "Who knows? But it sounds good and makes a great gimmick." She slid into the corner of her bench and stretched out her legs. "Let's get back to you and your Nick."

"He's not my Nick," Abby responded testily. Her straight chair did nothing for her throbbing back. The pain had been there all day and no position seemed to relieve the discomfort. But at least she could breathe more easily this afternoon, and for some reason she'd begun to feel she had a waist again. "I don't want to discuss Nick."

"But you have fallen for the guy. You said so."

"I say too much to you. And I didn't say I'd fallen for him."

"You said you felt something different for him, and that he was different from any other man you've known. That sounds like more than casual interest."

Abby's Perrier and Marie's three miniglasses of beer arrived. Abby took a swallow and arched her back. Her belly tightened almost painfully, and she shifted, taking a deep breath.

"Are you okay?" Marie swung her feet to the floor and leaned across the table. "You look a bit green."

"I'm in pain," Abby said grimly. "It's called sick-of-being-pregnant pain. Everything aches."

Marie looked startled. "Pain? It's too soon, isn't it? Do you have to go to the hospital or something?"

"Good Lord, no." Abby shook her head wearily. "I've got three or four more long weeks of this to go, so loosen up and drink your beer."

"If you say so," Marie muttered skeptically. "Nick went to the class with you again on Wednesday, you said. He must really be something."

"He is," Abby said and snapped her mouth shut. Marie was fishing, and catching too much. "Did you spend yesterday with your folks?"

"Yesterday? Oh, Thanksgiving, yes," Marie rolled her eyes. "Always go home to good old Mom and Pop for turkey day. How about you?"

"I did, too." Abby instantly relived the previous day's joyless celebration, her parents' puzzled faces, Michael's failed attempts to get her alone.

"Did Nick go with you?"

"Mmm? Oh, no, of course not, Marie. What are you saying?"

"You still didn't let on about the divorce—to John's mother, either?"

The baby made a sluggish revolution in Abby's belly and settled in a position that put pressure on her bladder. "Drop the subject, please, Marie. It's nice of you to be interested, but you can help me most by leaving that part of my life alone."

"Sorry." Marie buried her nose in a glass.

"I don't mean to be snippy," Abby apologized. "I'm not sure of my own feelings or anything anymore. You must see how it would feel to be pregnant by one man and in love—"

"With another?" Marie's brilliant green eyes stared unflinchingly into Abby's face.

"I…yes, dammit. And he feels something for me, too. He's wonderful. For the first time I feel—loved, I guess, is the only word. He loves me, but I don't think it's the same kind of love I have for him. He wants to be there for me." Abby ran a finger down the outside of her cold glass. "I won't need him so much soon, and then he'll go on his way. He's got too much to offer to get tied down by a woman with a child. Nick will marry someone gorgeous and have kids of his own."

"You're gorgeous."

Abby looked away. "This isn't his baby."

"That doesn't seem to be putting him off. Abby, the guy's got to be crazy about you, or he wouldn't be around now. He's got a case on you despite the baby, and he's waiting until the two of you can get together—really together."

"Marie, don't." Abby blushed. Whoever had suggested that pregnant women couldn't be turned on sexually was either male or had never been pregnant.

"You want him, too, Abby. Admit it."

"No…yes, yes I do. But I can't see how he could feel that way about me like this." She splayed a hand on her belly.

"Abby." Marie lowered her voice. "Like you said, you won't be pregnant much longer. Don't give up a chance at a fresh start. Sure, you're probably right that a baby could put a man off. Do something about it. I'm not a hard old bag, just dead cold sensible when it comes to looking at what's out there for each of us. If I was in your place and a Nick came riding out of the dust to carry me off, I wouldn't think twice about going."

Abby swallowed more Perrier and carefully set down the glass.

"And if he is just hanging by a thread waiting for me to come to him—do I allow him to take on the dead weight of a woman with an infant? I don't think so, Marie. He's been one terrific friend, and I couldn't do that to him."

"You're not getting my message, Abby. I know how mad you get every time I suggest this, but you keep leading into the obvious. Come to Nick fresh. You can be the one to have his children—if that's what you're aching to do—later."

"Give up my baby. That's what you're telling me to do again, isn't it?" Abby stood and buttoned her coat. "I'm going home." Marie moved swiftly, cutting off Abby's exit. "Think about it, will you? Everyone would be better off. You, Nick and the baby."

"Excuse me, Marie."

"I'm coming with you."

"It would be better if you didn't. Give me time to get over what you've just made me feel."

"What have I made you feel, Abby—uncertain? That would be a start."

"I've never been more certain in my life. Whatever happens between Nick and me, this baby will be part of it because he's part of me. I'll see you later, Marie."

Abby's heart thudded. She held her back straight and walked the length of the bar, past a counter banked with crushed ice and studded with fresh fish, then the restaurant beyond. Her hand was on the plate-glass door to the street when the heavy rolling sensation hit her belly once more. Three times in the past two hours she'd had to empty her bladder, but she'd never make it home if she didn't stop again.

The ladies' room was to her left. In the bathroom, she locked the door and and hung her purse on a hook. Uneasiness made her hands shake.

Minutes later she slowly took down her purse. She hadn't really had a bloody show, but there was some pinkness.

At the sink, she ran cold water and splashed her face. What had the book said about membranes breaking? It could happen early, she knew, but that didn't mean the baby was ready to be born.

A sharp line of pain burned down one groin and into her thigh. She'd done too much walking today. For once she'd be sensible and ask the Laundromat owner to find a replacement for her tomorrow. A day in bed, and she'd be fine again.

## Chapter Eleven

Abby pulled up her knees and waited for the pain to pass. This one hadn't been bad, not as bad as some of the others. Breathing deeply through her mouth, she checked the bedside clock. Almost an hour since the last contraction. All afternoon there had been regular twenty-minute intervals between each wave of discomfort.

Thirty-seven weeks, or thirty-eight, she wondered? The sweat on her body turned cold as the pain dulled. No, thirty-six weeks. She was thirty-six weeks pregnant. Healthy babies were often born a month early. But this was probably only something the book had called false labor. Were false labor pains longer or shorter than true ones? She couldn't remember. Her longest contraction had lasted less than a minute, thank God.

Sweat burned the corner of her eye. She was tired. If this was the real thing, she didn't have the energy to go through with it, anyway.

After returning from Bellevue the previous afternoon, she'd gone to bed and slept until the first pain had awakened her at two in the morning. The day had passed, long and gray. After the early morning pangs there had been lengthy periods of physical relief. But she'd struggled with bursts of panic. And thirst; she'd drunk glass after glass of water and trudged back and forth from the bathroom too many times to remember.

Abby pushed the covers down and shoved awkwardly to sit on the edge of the bed. She needed to urinate again, and walk. The temptation to lie on her side had been overwhelming, and she'd given in, but the position did nothing to lessen either the pains when they came or her anxiety.

Another surge of agitation welled up in her, like the others, and indecision. Earlier she'd lifted the phone several times to contact the doctor, then changed her mind. She turned her head to see the clock again. Four. Her doctor's office hours were over. Too late to call for advice now—except to the hospital.

The patch of sky visible between the bedroom drapes was already dark again. Another night would start, endless and empty, except for the pains and this frantic tightening in her muscles.

She ought to eat something, Abby thought, or at least get another glass of water. In the bathroom, she drank more water and washed her face. Without knowing why, she combed her hair and put on some lipstick. She began to feel more human and sat on the toilet seat gathering energy to go into the kitchen for food.

Nick had returned in the early hours of the morning. His familiar step had sounded on the stairs, hesitated outside her door and continued into his condo. He must think she'd gone to work today. Her car was in an end slot. He wouldn't have seen it when he'd left to go running. Abby always knew when Nick went running by the softer thud of his shoes. He'd be expecting her to return from the Laundromat soon. The wretched tears welled up again. She wanted to see him. She was frightened.

Abby folded her arms on the side of the sink and rested her forehead. On the other side of the wall, Nick was doing...what? Lying on the floor, as she'd seen him do often now, and listening to music? Reading one of his ever-increasing pile of magazines about aircraft and flying? If she asked, he'd come to keep her company. She smiled against her arms. He'd want to practice breathing, or making her relax. No, she couldn't ask him to come, not when she might be in labor. If she was, he'd insist on coming with her to the hospital, and that was out of the question.

*Don't underestimate the power of water.* Somewhere in the book she'd read how a warm bath could relieve backache.

While the water ran into the tub, Abby collected clean clothes. She wanted to be dressed, in case.... This was labor, she admitted to herself. Early, but real, and she would have to organize her thoughts enough to get ready.

The bath felt wonderful. Even the pain that came, pulling her instinctively to a sitting position, seemed easier to take with the warm water lapping over her skin.

Abby climbed out reluctantly, fresh determination shooting a sense of urgency into her. She walked about the condo, gathering the supplies she'd need for the hospital. At one side of her small suitcase she packed a little pile of clothing for the baby. Her contractions became regular again and more frequent, still more localized in her back than her belly. There was time, but she should call the hospital.

Before she could dial the number, the urge to use the bathroom came once more, and a stronger pain, much stronger. Abby concentrated on her hands, flexed the fingers, while she took a deep breath and then let it out slowly. She felt sick. Think, she ordered her straying brain, think. Her next breath, through her nose, was hard to hold, but she kept the air in her lungs, drawing it down to her stomach, then letting it escape through her mouth.

This spasm left her drained. The trip to the bathroom was punctuated by two stops for contractions. "It hurts," she said aloud, then covered her mouth. If she allowed herself to go to pieces, she'd be lost, and maybe the baby would suffer.

When the next contraction had peaked, she returned from the bathroom to the bedroom and called the hospital. The midwife's calm voice reassured Abby. She answered "Five minutes apart. About a minute and a half" to the woman's question about the frequency and length of the pains. "I don't know," she said when she was asked if her membranes had ruptured. The instructions were short: "You should come in now, Mrs. Winston. We'll be expecting you."

Abby hung up and snapped the suitcase shut. She walked slowly to the living room, taking her coat from the closet as she passed. Her car keys were on the kitchen counter.

In the dining area she hesitated, looking at the wall phone. What if the pains were so bad that she'd have an accident while she was driving? She arched her back, clamping her hands on her hips. She *could* do it. She *would* do it.

"Oh, no," she groaned and leaned against the wall. A contraction hit, a blow that pierced her back and bore downward. Her fingers, instinctively splayed over her stomach, felt the bulge strain outward, then sink slowly back. "Fool, fool," she muttered. No, she *couldn't* do it, not all of it, not completely alone. She mustn't drive.

Her breathing came in bursts now. She was out of control. Gasping, she wrenched the phone from its cradle and dialed Nick's number.

"Where have you been?" he almost shouted when he heard her voice. "I've been watching for your car for hours. I've got my coat on. I was going to the Laundromat. How did you get in without me seeing you?"

*Shut up*, Abby thought, closing her eyes.

"Abby? Abby?"

*I need you.* Organize the breathing. That was what she should do. The book said...damn the book.

"Abby! For God's sake, answer me."

"Nick," she whispered. "Could you drive me to the hospital? It's all I need...the drive..."

"Oh, hell. You're in labor. Get to the door. Unlock the door."

His phone crashed down.

The pounding on her door seemed to come before she'd taken a step. She worked her way along the walls, hanging on. She heard her name. Nick was shouting her name and hammering on the door. She had to stop. For an instant she was afraid she would vomit, but the nausea passed, and she shuffled on.

The chain on the door had never felt heavy before, or stiff. It came loose, clanked down, and the deadbolt clicked in slow motion. Abby swung back against the wall, sinking into darkness with yet another contraction. She couldn't do this anymore.

"Good God, Abby. How long have you been like this?"

She didn't answer. Nick put his arms under hers and eased her to the floor. He knelt beside her and held her chin, tilting it up.

"Look at me and stop panicking," he said loudly. "Keep your eyes open. Use my face as a focal point."

"Yes," she said and began to cry. Useless, she thought, she was useless, and she couldn't go through with this. "I can't do it," she told him. "I don't want to."

"I know," Nick said. Beneath his tan he'd paled. "But we'll make it, my love. Did you pack a bag?" When she nodded, he stroked her hair back. "Where is it?"

"In the bedroom."

He was back in seconds and kneeling again. "How close together are the contractions?"

"I don't know. Close. All the time." She opened her mouth and closed her eyes.

"How long have you been on your own?"

She grimaced. "Since yesterday. I thought I was just tired."

"I should have called to see if you were home, dammit. I didn't think." Nick kissed her closed lids and carefully pulled her up.

She laid her face against his neck, pushed her fingers into his vibrant hair. His familiar scent and the feel of his skin on her cheek calmed her. She loved him. Abby lifted her lids and looked into his face, deep into his dear, beautiful eyes. "I love you, Nick. I'm sorry. I love you so much, my darling. I shouldn't say it, but I do." She must be delirious, but if she didn't tell him now, she might never have the guts. He could forget her afterward and go on, but he was with her when she needed him most, and she wanted him to hear the words.

His lips on hers brought her eyes wide open. His own eyes were closed while he kissed her lightly, sweetly. "You're my life, Abby," he said when he lifted his head. "I love you, my sweet lady. I have since I first saw you. Everything's going to be okay."

He half carried her downstairs, pausing when she couldn't make it through a contraction without stopping to breathe over the wave of pain.

"No," she complained weakly when he fastened the seat belt loosely under her belly, but he held her hands until she stopped trying to push it away, and she felt a warm sleepiness for several seconds before the next contraction.

Nick joked, held her hand, shook her gently each time she began to sink away from consciousness. "Concentrate," he said again and again. "Count the streetlights. Out loud. Let me hear how many."

Abby counted. And Nick counted each time another contraction swept in. She did as he instructed, organizing her breathing, changing the pattern sometimes if he told her to, making it somehow. They'd make it, just like he'd said. On the bridge between Mercer Island and Seattle, her legs began to shake uncontrollably.

"Nick," she said, bracing her hands on the dashboard.

"Everything's great," he said. "Start contraction. Breathe, one——"

"Nick," she interrupted urgently. "The pain's changing. I feel strange. I'm going to throw up."

"No, you're not. What do you feel, shaky?"

She nodded.

"Transition," he commented. "You're really moving, kid. Good girl. You may be so good at this you'll want to do it every year."

She couldn't smile. "How much farther?"

He steered the car up a steep hill between tall old buildings. "We're there. I'm going to get a wheelchair." He drove to the hospital entrance, flipped off the ignition and ran around to open her door. He put his face close to hers. "Do as I say. Take several shallow breaths."

"I can't."

"Do it. Count in your head. Then blow. Do it!"

She used the tops of her lungs, keeping her eyes on Nick's face. In her mind she thought *one, two, three*, and then she blew.

"Good," Nick said. "Do it again while I get a wheelchair."

He ran through the doors, and for an instant the panic rushed back into Abby. She clutched her coat. Her body trembled. Then Nick was back, easing her forward into the chair. He slammed the car door and pushed her into the brightly lit foyer.

"I have to sign papers," Abby said through gritted teeth. "They told me that."

"Later," Nick replied, punching an elevator button. "Which floor for obstetrics?" he called to a passing nurse.

"Three." She smiled broadly and patted Abby's hand.

She'd be looked after here. The tension drained out of her once more. Another contraction broke the moment of relief, and Abby breathed deliberately.

When the elevator doors opened on the third floor, a woman in surgical greens turned from a desk to face them. She looked critically at Abby and took the wheelchair from Nick.

Questions came fast but calmly. Abby answered as best she could, with Nick filling in what he knew. No one challenged his presence. Twice he was called "Mr. Winston," and both times he answered unflinchingly.

The birthing room, all pastels, mauve and pink and blue-gray, was warm without a sign of the equipment Abby had expected.

"Help your wife put this on," the midwife instructed Nick, handing him a gown before she drew a curtain across the open door and left.

Abby took the gown from Nick. She was too tired, too desperate, to blush. "Thanks for everything," she said. "I'll always be grateful, Nick."

He didn't move.

"Stop worrying," she said and paused, gripped by another pain.

"Keep your eyes open," Nick said. He held her shoulders, massaging. "Give it to me, sweetheart, give up the pain. Come on, one, two, three, four—blow. Let's get you into that fashion piece and finish this thing. I'm ready to meet your little person."

She shook her head. "You can't go through this, Nick. I can't—" She had to bear down. She stared at him, stricken, and he smiled, stroking her cheeks, then her belly with broad motions. "The baby's going to be born," she said faintly. "I can feel it. I want to push."

Nick frowned. "Don't push until they examine you. Hold your breath. The cervix has to be fully dilated, or you'll tear."

Abby managed a smile. "Dr. Dorset. Oh, Nick, you really read that damned book. Thank God you did. I think I refused to concentrate on the words for some——'' The pushing sensation came again.

"Up," Nick commanded, taking her weight with one arm around her waist. He unbuttoned her coat, tossed it over a chair, then leaned her against him to unzip her dress.

She should feel horribly embarrassed, but she didn't. She let him undress her to her slip.

"Okay, love. I'll hold the gown. You get out of the rest of your things."

He made a screen with the shapeless striped garment and they managed to maneuver her into it. Nick sat her on a chair and gathered her clothes into a heap before calling the midwife.

Abby found she didn't want to lie down. She sat on the jointed birthing bed with her knees drawn up. Nick stood at her shoulder, holding her against his chest.

"Your cervix is dilated to eight centimeters, Abby," the midwife pronounced. "Doing a beautiful job. But we need two more centimeters before you do any more real pushing. We could use warm compresses on the perineum to help soften things up and avoid tearing. Would that be okay?"

Abby agreed, and the wet, warm cloths were applied between her legs.

"The baby's early," she said, holding the hand Nick offered. "Is it all right?"

The midwife, Rosa, as indicated by her name tag, rubbed Abby's legs. "Everything seems perfectly fine, Abby," she commented, moving the compress to check the cervix once more. "According to your records, you're coming up to thirty-seven weeks, which isn't unusually early. When did your membranes break?"

Abby pulled her thoughts together. "I'm not sure, but it could have been in the middle of yesterday afternoon. I'd been shopping. There wasn't much fluid."

The pressure began again, and Abby dug her fingernails into Nick's hand.

"Okay," he said, "okay. You're doing beautifully. We're almost there, right, nurse?" He pressed the heel of one hand into the base of Abby's spine, freed his other hand and began a rhythmic massage of her belly.

Rosa studied her watch. "Almost there," she agreed. "It'll be soon, Abby. It's ten o'clock now, so your membranes ruptured about thirty hours ago. Next time, dear, remember to call when it happens.''

Abby felt disoriented. Another desperate desire to push came, and she held her breath until it passed. ''I wasn't sure it had happened.'' She sighed, then yawned, and the tension seeped away slightly.

''Mr. Winston.'' The midwife looked at Nick. ''It might be a good idea if your wife bore down gently each time the urge passes. Do you have a preference for position?''

Abby raised her chin, and Nick kissed her mouth before looking back at the smiling midwife. ''Maybe we could move back to a chair? She doesn't seem to like lying down.''

The midwife agreed and left them alone again as soon as Abby was settled on the edge of a chair.

''We don't have long to go, Abby.'' Nick knelt between her knees. He surrounded her with his arms, and she pressed her face to his neck, clinging to his shoulders. ''Lean forward, sweetheart. Put your weight on me. Tell me the minute you feel something different...so I can yell for help.'' He chuckled. ''I'm still working on that medical degree. I'm only up to almost-delivery in my studies.''

A distant question made fleeting contact in Abby's head. How could Nick be so calm? Then she let him take her weight.

Another contraction came, then several minutes' respite. Leaning on Nick felt so good. Two more pains, almost without interval, swept in, rose and ebbed, and Abby breathed as Nick instructed. He stroked back her damp hair, and she turned her lips to find his palm.

''Did you discuss anaesthetic with them?'' he asked. ''I guess you'd have to have it pretty quickly if you were going to.''

The response was hard to form. ''I don't want it,'' she managed. ''I'm going to make it through, and it'll be better for the baby.''

''Brave kid,'' Nick said against her hair, and she felt him smile. ''But it's okay if you feel you need it. The book——''

''Says so,'' she finished for him, trying to laugh, but ending with a sharp intake of air. ''This is it, Nick. It's burning hot there. I can feel the baby's head.''

''Nurse!''

His shout startled her. A second later, two nurses swished through the curtain, and Nick was already lifting her onto the birthing bed.

"I don't want to lie down," she said, desperately holding his shirt. "I want—," She couldn't say anymore.

Nick moved behind her, supporting her whole weight. "You don't have to, darling. Squat," he ordered, then said to the midwives, "That's okay, isn't it?"

"Whatever works," Rosa said. She held one of Abby's thighs while her companion supported the other. "The baby's crowning. Burning now, Abby?"

"Yes," Abby groaned. "Yes."

"Now," Rosa said, all business, "grunt and push, then let go and let the baby do some of the work."

Abby tightened her gut. The pain meant something, was achieving something. She laughed and choked and lost her focus. The contraction overwhelmed her, and she cried out.

"Concentrate, Abby," Nick said into her ear. "Force back against me, and think about your breathing."

Abby panted, waited for Rosa's command and pushed again. A popping sensation made her gasp. She glanced into a hanging mirror and saw the baby's head emerge. Excitement threatened to scramble her efforts again.

"The head!" Nick's voice came to her in an unnatural yell. "I can see it. God!"

The second midwife squeezed Abby's thigh. "A small push, Mrs. Winston, and we'll have the shoulder," and within seconds she said, "and now the other shoulder."

Abby squeezed her insides tightly, and the tension flowed away. The baby was born.

Abby sobbed and turned her face up to Nick. "We did it."

"Yes. Oh, yes." His face was drenched. Sweat and tears. His hair clung to his temples. The effort must have drained him, too.

Abby slumped. "Is he all right?" she said, gasping, sliding more heavily into Nick's arms. "Is he?"

"Looks good, so far," Rosa said, working rapidly over the baby. She wiped the tiny face Abby could hardly see, and the body. "A boy, Abby. But it sounds as if you already knew that. And no tearing from you. Excellent."

The tiny body moved, arms and legs flexed and jerked, and the baby cried.

Emotion expanded Abby's lungs, filled her throat, and then was let go in another wash of tears. "I want to hold him." She laughed through the tears, looking up at Nick.

"That's something," he said in a voice she'd never heard him use before. His lashes clung together. "That's really something." Fresh tears welled along his lids, let go, and he ignored them. He stroked Abby's hair absently and helped settle her back on the pillows.

"Now, Mr. Winston, I expect you'd like to cut the cord." Rosa had clamped the umbilical cord in two places and held surgical scissors toward Nick.

"Yes," he murmured, taking the instrument without hesitation. He snipped through the now-limp cord in the spot Rosa indicated, and Abby saw his throat move. He let the midwife take the scissors from him before he passed the back of a shaky hand over his eyes.

Abby swallowed her sobs, watching Nick, watching his face show the same emotions she felt. She loved this man so much, couldn't imagine having or wanting another here in his place. This child, in this moment, belonged to both of them.

"Here." Rosa lifted the baby and placed him in Nick's hands. "Why don't you introduce your son to his mother?"

The nurses busied themselves with Abby. She felt more pressure and knew the placenta was being expelled, but she only saw Nick and her son.

Nick stared at the little boy for several seconds. With one hand, he unbuttoned his own shirt and pulled it loose before lifting the baby to face level. His heart thumped painfully, and the blood in his veins; his body yearned toward this tiny creature an instant ago unborn, in this fragment of time thrust into the world—and, through Abby, become a part of himself. He cradled the infant against his naked chest, closed his eyes at the blind snuggling and reaching of the wobbly face and minuscule fingers. Blood and mucus streaked his skin. He held the baby closer, kissed his forehead, his downy cheek, bent over him, murmuring, not knowing what sounds he made, yet sure they were right.

Abby made a sound, and he looked into her bright eyes, returned their gentle smile. He leaned close. "You made a perfect child, Abby. Hold him."

The miniature body squirmed against Abby's breast, and she couldn't stem her sobs. "He's beautiful." Her throat burned. This little one was so soft, so helpless. Fierce protectiveness tightened her grip, and she smiled at Nick through her tears. His face blurred. "He's going to have a good life; you'll see."

His reply shocked her. "John Winston's a bastard," he said, his voice harsh and strangled. "I hate his guts, but I love the son of a bitch for giving me this day."

# Chapter Twelve

"Wake up, buddy."

Nick stirred, opened his eyes a fraction and yawned.

"Nick, wake up."

Consciousness hit him in shock waves. "What? Abby, what's the matter?"

A hand, clamped over his mouth, silenced him, and he looked up into Michael Harris's serious blue eyes. "Keep it down," Michael whispered urgently. "She's asleep. Come into the hall where we can talk."

Nick scrambled from the couch, shoving at his disheveled hair, rubbing the stubble on his jaw. Early daylight from a gap in the blinds made a pale stripe on one wall. He went to Abby and pulled the sheet higher over her shoulders. Her face was smooth and untroubled, faintly shiny, her heavy lashes flickering occasionally. She sighed and threw a hand over her head in a childlike way. Thank God, Nick thought, at last her hard times were over.

"Come on. Before she wakes up," Michael insisted, gripping Nick's elbow to propel him through the door.

"When did you get here, Mike?"

In the dimmed light of the hospital corridor, Michael faced him. He was in uniform, and his tie was pulled loose. "I got in at five this morning and decided to risk calling Abby. I had the damnedest feeling I ought to, and when she didn't answer, I called here. Nick, is she okay? And the baby? He's early."

"They're both fine," Nick said. He was still groggy. "Did you see Justin? He looks like Abby."

Michael's expression cleared, and he smiled. "I haven't seen him yet. Justin, huh? I'll be damned. It's hard to think of him as here and real."

"Come on," Nick said. "I'll get the nursery nurse to bring him to the window where you can see."

Michael followed him down the hall. "Can't I hold him? Amend that. I've never held a baby, so I'll need time to get used to the idea, but I'd like to see him up close."

"Only mother and father get to hold the baby for the first couple of days," Nick said and immediately clamped his mouth shut. He scrubbed at his face. "Michael, they may call me 'Mr. Winston.' I brought Abby in last night, and they thought I was her husband. There wasn't time to set them straight. Don't say anything about who I really am, okay? Abby needs someone around, and..." Nick's stomach tightened. "It's the way we want it, do you understand, Mike? The baby may be John Winston's son because he fathered him, but last night—and today—I've got more right to call him mine."

"I see." Michael stared into Nick's eyes. "It is definitely over between John and Abby, isn't it?"

"Yes."

"And you two are in love."

"Yes. But we didn't say more than four words to each other until John was out of the picture. I want that absolutely clear, Michael."

Michael hesitated, pulling the knot of his tie farther awry. A low cry came from one of the birthing rooms, and he flinched. "I believe that, Nick. Thanks for being here for Abby. Were you with her when the baby...?"

"Was I there when Justin was born?" The tentative light in Michael's eyes made Nick laugh. "Yes, I was. And boy, that was something, Mike. She was great. I couldn't handle that number, but she sailed through."

"It wasn't too hard on her?"

"Hard enough. I can't imagine it's ever too easy." He grinned. "In fact, there were a couple of times when she said she'd changed her mind, but I persuaded her to go through with it, anyway. Let's have a look at Justin."

Outside the nursery, Nick tapped on the glass, and a nurse in a rocking chair, holding a baby, glanced up and smiled. She got up and rolled a plastic infant bed in front of Michael and Nick.

"What do you think?" Nick asked, turning his head sideways to peer at Justin. "Good-looking guy, huh?"

Michael didn't answer.

Nick elbowed him. "How about all that hair?"

"Jeez," Michael said under his breath. "Five pounds, ten ounces. How does anything that small make it?"

"He's not so small," Nick said. "They've got one baby under four pounds. The one in the incubator at the back. Justin's about three and a half weeks early. The midwife said he probably wouldn't have been more than seven pounds if Abby had made it to term. And he's healthy as he is."

"He looks like a little gnome," Michael said, grinning. "All wrinkled. Like a prune."

Instantly indignant, Nick looked critically at Justin. "That's a hell of a thing to say, Mike. He's a good-looking kid." He pushed his fists into his pockets. "Abby's been to hell and back in the past few months. Trying to do everything alone. She's going to need help, and I don't just mean financial help."

Michael rested his elbow on the windowsill and continued to study the baby. "You don't think John will come through with support once he sees the boy? How could he resist someone this cute?"

"I thought you said Justin was a gnome." Nick spread an arm across Michael's shoulders. "I don't want John Winston's support. Abby won't, either. They're divorced and he's out of the picture."

"Divorced?"

Nick's arm slid off when Michael straightened. "They've been divorced several weeks. I don't think she's heard anything directly from him since he left."

"Do you want to marry Abby?" Michael asked quietly.

"Don't jump the gun," Nick replied. "We need time to know what we want for sure. But I do love her, Mike. Do you know how that feels?"

Michael's blue eyes fixed reflectively on a point above Nick's head. "I don't know. I guess not."

"It's weird," Nick said. "I know I never loved a woman before. It's like...nothing can get in the way of it, nothing else is as important as it used to be."

"Sounds dangerous to me. But you've got good taste, I'll give you that," Michael said. "Maybe if I met someone like my sister, I'd risk my reputation and get involved. I've got to call my folks. And I'll have to tell them the truth about Abby and John...and you." He set off purposefully toward Abby's room.

Nick caught up and stopped him. "Let Abby explain to her folks in her own way, when she's ready."

"It's time they knew. You see that, Nick—"

Nick interrupted quickly. "Of course. But Abby wants her mother and father to have a chance to enjoy Justin first. I know how they feel about divorce. Abby told me. She hopes once they're involved with the baby, they'll accept the other more easily. And I'd like it if they didn't view me as an undesirable intruder."

"When do you intend to spring it on them?"

"I don't intend to tell them at all," Nick said patiently. "You aren't listening to me. This is Abby's show. If you want to do something for her, then play it her way and let her know you're behind her whatever she decides. And Mike——," he took a deep breath and passed a hand over his eyes "——Abby and I haven't gotten past the stage of admitting we feel something for each other. She's got...we've got a way to go to know what we want in the future. So don't say too much about this conversation, okay?"

"Okay." Michael's smile spread slowly. He grasped Nick in a bear hug. "For what it's worth, I'm rooting for you if you're right for Abby. Can I see her now, please?"

Nick knew his own grin was sheepish. "I know I come on a bit strong sometimes. I've got a lot at stake here. We all do. Go see her. And if you say Justin's anything but wonderful, I'll flatten you—later."

Chuckling, Michael led the way back to Abby's room, passing a midwife in the doorway.

"Good morning, Mr. Winston," she said to Nick. "Dr. Morris would like to have a few words with you when he gets here."

Cold shot up Nick's back. "Who's Dr. Morris?"

"Consulting pediatrician on call," she replied. "Don't worry. Everything's going to be all right. Justin needs some intravenous antibiotics, that's all. He'll also need some pretty close monitoring for a couple of weeks, but then he'll be ready to go home."

Nick looked from the nurse to Michael, who frowned. "Antibiotics for what?" Nick asked. "What's wrong with him?"

"Dr. Morris will explain in more detail. But Abby's membranes ruptured a day and a half before she delivered. That invites infection. We automatically suction gastric fluids on any baby in those circumstances, and Justin has a Group B strep. Not uncommon. The bath Abby took yesterday afternoon probably didn't help."

"You mean Abby and Justin are sick?" Nick shook his head, confused. "They're going to be here for two weeks?"

The midwife twisted the stethoscope hanging from her neck. "Mrs. Winston is asymptomatic. No symptoms. She'll be transferred to a lying-in room shortly and go home in a day or two. The baby must finish the course of antibiotics the same as an adult. In this case the medication is administered intravenously and can only be done under medical supervision. There's nothing to worry about. You can spend as much time as you like with him. Please try to make sure Mrs. Winston understands all this, too. She's bound to be apprehensive, and she'll need your reassurance.'' A buzzer sounded. ''Can you do that?'' she asked, waiting for Nick's affirmative nod before leaving at a trot.

''Damn it all,'' Nick groaned. ''What else? I might have known things were going too well.''

''Save it,'' Michael said sharply. ''You heard what the woman said. No big deal. Now, let's make sure Abby doesn't get uptight.''

Abby strained to hear the masculine voices outside the curtain. One was Nick. Relief warmed her, and she deliberately unclenched her fists. Waking to find him gone had filled her with desperation. The other man spoke again, and the curtain was pushed a few inches aside.

''Michael!'' she exclaimed, delighted. ''Get in here, Nick called you.'' She saw his uniform. ''You came straight from the airport? You must be exhausted.''

He smiled, still poised half inside and half outside the curtain. ''Not as exhausted as you, I bet.''

Abby swallowed. Every few minutes she wanted to cry with happiness. ''Will you come in here, Michael Harris?''

''You look great.'' He edged just inside, and Nick had to steer him farther into the room.

''I feel great.'' She looked at Nick, at the dark shadow of his beard, his dear, smiling eyes. ''Thanks to Nick,'' she added. Michael might as well know how she felt.

''I didn't do anything,'' Nick said, crossing to slump on the edge of the couch.

''Sis—'' Michael approached the bed, and she patted the edge. He sat gingerly. ''Nick and I had a talk. I know about John and the divorce.''

''This isn't the time, Mike,'' Nick said firmly. ''Abby, I took Mike to see Justin. He's a handsome kid, isn't he, Mike?''

''Fantastic,'' Michael said, reaching for Abby's hand. ''Exactly what I would expect from you. You're going to have to give me lessons in holding babies, though. He's such a little guy.''

''Not too little,'' she replied and turned her face to Nick. ''Did the nurse tell you about the infection?''

Nick shifted to the very edge of his seat and propped his elbows. "Yes. Abby, you were in labor on your own for a long time, weren't you?"

"It wasn't bad at first. I wasn't even sure it was the real thing."

"I was next door, and I didn't know. You should have called."

Michael cleared his throat. "Abby, I've got to get Mom and Dad here. They'll never forgive either of us if we keep them in the dark much longer."

She sighed. "I want to see them, too. But, Michael, I'm not ready to tell them the truth about John and me, okay? I've got John's mother to think of, too. He obviously hasn't told her, or she'd have contacted us."

Michael stood slowly and buttoned his coat. "Whatever you think is best. I'll pick up Mom and Dad now and tell them there wasn't time to alert them when you were brought in. And I'll explain how Nick came to your aid." He glanced at Nick and gave a wry grin. "I am grateful for that, Florence. And I honestly believe you two might make a great item." He worked his cap on and tilted it over his eyes before pushing up the knot in his tie. "It'll probably be about an hour before I get back. Anything else I can do for you?"

"Yes, please." She rummaged in her purse on the bedside table and produced a scrap of paper. "Give Marie Prince a call for me. She'll want to know about the baby."

Michael grimaced. "Do I have to?"

"Michael," Abby said admonishingly, "Marie's okay. Just give her a call and tell her not to come to the hospital. I'll see her when I get home." She ignored the grumbling noise Nick made. "I know you two never hit it off, but she's had a rough time ever since she was a kid. You never saw her rotten home life. Underneath the tough act she's soft, and she's always been a friend to me—as best as she knows how."

"Okay, okay," Michael muttered as he slipped past the curtain. "I'll call her."

Nick immediately took the place Michael had vacated on her bed. He placed a hand each side of her and leaned close. "I've probably got morning breath, but could I please kiss you?"

She smoothed his hair, watching his eyes, and kissed him slowly. "You must want to go home, Nick. You've been so wonderful."

"You mean I do have morning breath, and you're telling me to go home and clean my teeth."

Abby laughed and immediately winced at the pulling in her

womb. "There's an extra toothbrush in the drawer—especially for fathers. You almost qualify, and I don't want you to leave—ever." Heat burst into her cheeks. "Nick, what I said at my place before we left. You know, about love?"

He sat back and held her hands. "I remember."

"Well—" she bowed her head "—I don't want you to think you owe me anything, or that I'm going to be a nuisance." She couldn't go on.

"You could never be a nuisance to me, unless—" Nick put a finger beneath her chin and tilted up her head. "Did you mean what you said?"

All the air had gone out of the room. "Yes," she whispered.

"So much it hurts. I do love you, Nick. But—"

"Shhh. I love you, too, Abby. Sometimes it feels as if I've loved you forever. I don't want to remember the time before."

Tears again, Abby thought, and felt them slide down her cheeks. "I don't know how you could have fallen in love with me, the way I've been."

"You don't know much. I couldn't not fall in love with you. You were one sexy pregnant lady, and now, well..." They laughed. "Do you understand all this stuff about Justin?"

Abby sobered instantly. "It's my fault, Nick. I should have realized the membranes had ruptured. Then I took a bath, which was totally stupid. But the nurse said he's absolutely normal and very strong, and the medication will set him right."

"It's going to be tough driving back and forth for two weeks. You probably should find a place to stay close by."

Impossible, Abby thought. She couldn't afford a second apartment, even for two weeks. "As long as I can spend a couple of hours a day with him, it'll be okay," she said.

"But how will you make it here from the east side every three hours for feedings?"

Abby pulled her hands away. "I'll give him a bottle when I am here. Otherwise a nurse will do it. They'll hold him—"

"Bottle?" Nick interrupted. "I don't understand."

"I'm not nursing Justin," Abby said evenly. "That's why I had the shot after delivery."

Nick screwed up his eyes. "I don't remember any shot."

"I had a shot," she explained patiently. "Some stuff called Trace to suppress lactation."

"Isn't mother's milk best, particularly for a baby who's premature?"

"Yes. But not essential. And this is a decision I had to make because——" She hesitated as a nurse entered the room.

"Good morning, I'm Linda Acres. I'll be with you until this afternoon." The woman's broad smile took in Nick and Abby. She settled her rimless glasses more securely on her snub nose. "Justin's already getting his medication. We'd like to move you to another room, Mrs. Winston. But we wondered if you and Mr. Winston would like to stop by the nursery and give Justin his bottle. He can be held quite easily even with the drip, and I'm sure you'd enjoy it."

Abby looked at Nick, met his eyes and saw a softening there. "We'd like that, wouldn't we?" she asked him.

"I'll get a wheelchair," Linda Acres turned away.

"No." Abby swung her legs over the edge of the bed. "The sooner I'm on my feet, the better. I can make it."

Nick helped her into her bathrobe, and they walked, their arms around each other, to the nursery.

Justin had been moved to a separate room, and a long tube ran from one tiny leg to a drip bag suspended from a hook. Abby gripped Nick's arm convulsively, but he shook her gently and smiled.

"Your boy's waiting for you," the nursery nurse said brightly as they pushed open the door and went inside. "Dr. Morris was already here and left. He had an emergency, but he'll talk to you later. He said to tell you he's very comfortable with Justin's condition."

The nurse lifted the baby from his bed. "You can use the rocking chair, or a straight one, whichever you find more comfortable."

Abby sat in the rocking chair and took Justin in her arms. She looked up at Nick, smiling. "He's so soft, Nick, and lovely to hold."

Nick pulled another chair close and sat. He gently stroked the baby's head. "Feed him, Mom. He's starving."

"Yes, sir!" Abby accepted a bottle from the nurse and offered it to Justin.

"Look at that!" Nick said loudly and colored. "Look," he repeated softly. "He knows to go after it." Justin's mouth was already securely fastened on the nipple. Nick put an arm around

Abby's shoulders and stared into the scrunched-up face. "I love you," he whispered. "Both of you."

Abby kissed the corner of his mouth quickly, then caught the nurse's eye. The other woman smiled before going to check her charges in the main nursery.

Nick was quiet for a long time. With the deftness of an expert, he tucked the receiving blanket securely around Justin's squirming arms and legs. When a minute hand worked free, Nick stroked it and spread the fingers, examining them.

Twenty minutes later, the bottle empty, Abby cuddled her son and felt the same protective urge she'd experienced when he was born. Her boy would be safe and free and have what he needed. He'd always be loved.

"We'd better get you to whatever room they want you in," Nick said. "If Michael gets back with your folks while we're here, there could be more explaining to do than you're ready for."

The new room was smaller than the first, but still bright and comfortable. Nick helped Abby get settled and was about to go home to change when Abby's mother burst into the room without knocking.

"Sweetheart, where is he?" Wilma Harris squeaked, rushing to bend over Abby and plant a kiss on each cheek. Her face was even more florid than usual, and her hair sagged slightly from its upswept puffs. "Justin," Michael said. She stood and crossed her hands, her chest rising and falling visibly. "Now where did you get a name like that? George Michael would have been perfect. You young people have such funny ideas about names." She gave no sign of having noticed Nick.

"Now, Wilma. Justin's a fine name." George Harris emerged from behind his wife and approached Abby uncertainly. He stopped beside her, an old tweed cap clasped in both hands. "How's my girl?" His pale eyes were suspiciously filmed.

"I'm fine, Dad." Abby said and rubbed the fingers that turned his hat around and around. "You've got a neat little grandson. You'll have to teach him to make those prize-winning apple turnovers of yours." She truly loved this quiet man who'd always stayed in the background of her life, an anchor when needed, but never intrusive.

"Mike says the little one's got a bug of some kind, and he'll have to stay in the hospital," George commented. "Does John know about it?"

Abby shook her head.

Her father rocked on his heels. "He'll be back soon. Don't you worry, girl. And if you need help—money or anything—your mother and I will take care of things."

Abby opened her mouth to breathe.

"Don't you worry about a thing," Wilma echoed. "I want you to come home with us until John gets back."

"No," Abby began, instantly desperate, then she repeated "No" with more control. "It's important for me to settle in my own place again. Everything's set there." It wasn't, but she wouldn't think of that now. Maybe the baby taking longer to come home was a blessing. She'd have time to get his equipment together.

"Well, if you say so." Wilma settled her head into her neck but kept a smile on her lips. "But I still think—"

"Abby knows what's best," George interrupted. He looked at Nick, not for the first time. Michael stood silently in the background. He must have forgotten to mention Nick to their parents, Abby decided.

Finally Wilma noticed Nick. She took him in from head to foot, finishing with a long stare at his unshaven face. "Are you a doctor?" she asked skeptically.

Michael came to life. "This is Nick Dorset, Mother," he said, moving to the center of the group. "I should have explained. Nick is Abby's neighbor, and he was kind enough to drive her to the hospital last night."

Abby watched her parents' expressions anxiously. Her father smiled politely and extended a hand for Nick to shake. Her mother's ample bosom swelled, and she crossed her hands over her stomach. "I don't remember you mentioning Mr. Dorset, Abby."

This was not going well, Abby decided.

"Nick, Mom," Michael interjected, "my friend Nick who bought the condominium next to Abby's. Remember, I mentioned it to you at the time. He's a flyer, too."

Reservation slowly faded from Wilma's eyes. "That's right, of course I remember. Thank you for helping Abby—Nick. I'm sure John would thank you if he was here." She looked more closely at Nick. "Did you wait here all night?"

Nick glanced at Abby before saying, "Yes. You kind of get swept along in these things. Once I was here, I stayed to find out if she had a boy or a girl. You know how it is, Mrs. Harris." He grinned conspiratorially.

Abby saw her mother's answering smile and silently blessed Nick's resourcefulness. "Michael, take Mom and Dad to see Justin. I'm a bit tired, or I'd go."

"You didn't lie."

"I didn't tell the truth, and neither did you."

"I—I'm sorry I've involved you in all this."

He jammed his hands deeper into his pockets. "I want to be involved. But I'll be glad when everything's in the open."

Abby played with the sheet. "It soon will be. Once I'm on my feet, I'll explain. I want to get Justin settled in day care and find a job in my own field, so I can prove I'm coping. Then I'll tell Mom and Dad."

"I don't think you can put them off that long. And you don't have to rush back to work. A baby needs his mother around for a little while at least."

"I want to get on with my life. I've got to start over. And, Nick, being in charge of my future is going to feel so good." She did feel exhilarated. "I've made the right decisions."

He studied the toes of his shoes, then her face. "Let's talk about this later. Sleep now, sweetheart. You'd better rest while you can."

AT THE FIRST SOUND of footsteps on the stairs, Nick's mind went blank. Should he stay where he was, or go out and meet them? Without giving his own question deeper thought, he hurried into the hall. He looked over the banister. Michael had paused between flights with Abby holding his arm tightly.

"Stay there!" Nick yelled. "Wait!" He leapt downward, two, three steps at a time, until he was beside them.

"Hi, Nick," Abby said, clearly out of breath. "I planned to run up, but I guess that'll take another hour or so."

They laughed, and he touched her face.

Michael coughed. "Why don't you take Abby's other arm, Nick. She may be skinny, but I wouldn't mind a little help."

Instead of her arm, Nick held Abby's waist. Then, without meeting Michael's eyes, he swept her into his arms and carried her the rest of the way. At her door, he waited for Michael to let them in and took her to the couch.

Nick as he went.

"Thank you," Abby said simply.

Nick stared out the window. "I don't like lying."

Michael ushered his parents out, winking broadly at Abby and

Abby scanned the room, her lips parting slightly. "What happened in here?"

Nick arranged a pillow behind her back. "You should take off your coat."

She slowly undid her buttons and let Nick pull the coat from beneath her. He spread the bright quilt he'd bought over her legs.

"Where did all this stuff come from?" Abby asked. "Nick, did you do this? How...." She chewed her fingernail. "You only had two days, and you spent most of the time at the hospital."

"Excuse me, folks," Michael broke in, giving a theatrical wave. "I hate to interrupt, but if you'll excuse me, I'll start bringing up the botanical display in my car."

"Thanks, Michael," Abby began, but he'd already ducked out.

"Can I make you some tea?" Nick asked, afraid to meet her eyes. He'd probably done all the wrong things in here.

"No, thanks," she replied. "Nick, I can't accept furniture from you. Or plants and pictures. I'm so embarrassed."

"You don't like them."

Her fingers closed on his wrist. "I love them," she said urgently, glancing from his face to the door, watching for Michael's return. "But I don't have any right to them. You've showered me with flowers until even my father has started making comments, and now this—all this. Filling up the empty spaces here must have cost a fortune."

"I saw John moving out, you know, Abby. I saw him taking your things."

Her fingers trembled on his wrist. "He took half of what we had. That was fair."

"It stunk," he hissed. "You're not living in a half-empty condo any longer, do you understand?"

She sank back, and he heard Michael whistle as he came in carrying several floral arrangements, as Abby's suitcase slipped steadily from under his arm. "Hey, Nick. Most of this lot is your fault. Give a man a hand, would you?"

Nick escaped gratefully to the cool parking lot and took his time gathering more plants and flowers. He had to handle Abby just right. She'd already let him know she wouldn't be manipulated by another man.

He passed Michael on the stairs. "She's all yours, Nick. I'm due at the airport." Michael checked his watch. "The folks are planning to come over at six. By my figuring that gives you about three hours to work with."

Nick watched Michael's back for an instant. "What's that supposed to mean?" he said.

Michael resumed his whistling then called over his shoulder, "Whatever you want it to mean" before he slammed the outer door behind him.

When Nick tapped Abby's door, it swung open under his hand.

"May I come in?" he asked tentatively.

He jumped when Abby stuck her head around the corner. "Yes. And quit the tiptoe bit. This isn't a hospital. It's a kept woman's quarters."

Nick recoiled. He *had* done everything wrong, and what he'd say in the next few minutes could make or break his future.

"Lie down, Abby," he said with more assurance than he felt.

"It's too soon for you to be walking around."

"I'm not sick," she retorted. "I've had all the nursing I need. In the bush, women have their children and carry straight on with whatever they were doing."

"This isn't the bush." His temper was rising. "And for the record, when a friend lends you a few things to make your life easier until you can get your own stuff, you aren't a kept woman."

"Would you like tea?" Abby said as if he hadn't spoken.

He opened and closed his mouth. "Yes," he said through his teeth. "And you're going to stop being pigheaded and at least sit down."

Abby lifted a hand, lowered it abruptly and sat on the closest chair—a rattan chair with brilliant tie-on cushions—one of the two he'd bought.

Nick pulled the matching chair close and took one of Abby's hands between both of his. "All morning I've felt like a kid waiting for Santa Claus. If you'd taken more than another minute to get here, I'd have been in the street hopping up and down."

"I'd like to see that. I was waiting to see you, too, Nick. I...will you hold me?"

"It'll be a pleasure," he whispered, going to his knees beside her. He pulled her into his arms, at first carefully, then with a shaky force he couldn't quell. He could smell her perfume, light, faintly rose. "I'm never going to be able to stay away from you."

"Nick," Abby said quietly and played with the hair behind his ear. "I'm frightened."

He tilted his head against her hand. "Frightened of what, darling? There's nothing to be frightened about."

She swallowed. "I can't believe you'll keep on wanting me."

"You think I could stop wanting you? Oh, Abby, I never will. Could we get married, do you think?" He'd promised himself he'd wait, dammit.

"Married?" Abby became still, her eyes wide. "Nick, do you know what you're saying?"

He held her face firmly, looked into her eyes and planted a kiss hard on her lips. He drew back. "I want you to be my wife. I want to help you bring up Justin. And I know exactly what I'm saying. Will you?"

"Get married," she whispered. "I don't know how to answer. I'm not sure what's right yet, for either of us. But I do love you."

"You don't have to answer now." He attempted a laugh that died too quickly. "I'll give you as long as you need—about two seconds."

She touched his chest, ran her fingers along his tensing muscles. "It's going to take longer, Nick."

He watched her eyes, her mouth, and waited.

"Can you see that?"

"I'll try to," Nick said.

At last she locked her wrists behind his neck and kissed him; a hundred tiny kisses rained over his eyes, his jaw, his neck. Firmly he stilled her face and pressed his lips to hers, ran his tongue lightly along her lower lip.

Abby reached between them and unbuttoned his shirt. She stopped, arching her neck to see his face. Her eyes shone dark and anxious before she slipped her hands beneath the shirt and bent her neck to put her mouth to his collarbone.

Nick's arousal unnerved him. She wasn't ready for more than gentle closeness. He eased her lips back to his before enfolding her against him and holding very still.

"We've got lots of time," he said and closed his eyes. "As much as it takes."

## Chapter Thirteen

Streams of headlights, laser stripes through the restaurant's rain-spattered windows, wound along the Alaskan Way Viaduct. Elliott Bay lay beyond, polished obsidian in the faint glow from shore.

Abby pressed her shoulder to the glass and peered down from the sumptuous, understated Penthouse Lounge on the cars speeding by below.

"You aren't eating." Nick's hand closed over hers on the table, but she continued to look outside. "Abby," he persisted, "is anything wrong?"

"No, Nick. Everything's right. I'm a bit afraid, that's all. You know, that old 'this is too good, so something's bound to go wrong' feeling?"

"It's not going to go wrong. Eat, sweetheart."

Abby smiled, kept her eyes down and managed some more of the delicious chateaubriand and béarnaise sauce. She felt Nick's still watchfulness. He was waiting, and they both knew why.

"You look lovely, Abby," he said softly. "The lady in gray. Your dress is the same color as your eyes."

The steak caught in her throat, and she coughed, reaching for her water glass. "Thank you," she said when she could speak. "It's an old dress. I haven't worn it for years." At least her red face could be passed off on the coughing fit. Compliments were something she'd never handled easily.

"I don't think many women could look as terrific as you do so soon after giving birth."

This time she took a deep swallow of red wine. Her skin was hot and cold by turns. "You aren't eating, Nick."

"I've finished." He laughed and leaned across the table. "You're shy because I said you look good. Look at me." He tilted up her chin. "When we walked in here, every man in the room gave you the once-over. I didn't know whether to preen or punch them out."

"Oh, Nick. You exaggerate. And there's nothing like a straight dress to hide a not-very-flat tummy. No man would be too thrilled by that, or stretch marks.'' She shook her head, hardly believing what she'd said.

Nick held his glass in front of his mouth while his eyes passed slowly over her. ''I'd be thrilled by every inch of you.''

''Nick, don't.''

''Don't what? Be honest? You know how I feel about you.''

Abby met his earnest eyes unwaveringly. Her body sent its own signals, and they only grew stronger. ''This is tough on me, too.'' Once she gave in to her desires, there'd be no turning back, and if it proved to be a mistake, she'd hurt them both.

Nick scooted his chair around to her side. ''It's been ten days since you came home from the hospital. I've asked you the same question every day, and every day you make some excuse not to answer.''

''We haven't had any normal time together, Nick. How can you know for sure what you want?''

His thigh touched hers. He stroked the soft fabric of her dress over her legs, then rested his hand on her knee. ''What's normal? For months we've spent time together. This is our fourth date since Justin was born, and we've been together every other day or evening I've been in town. Abby, we've been closer than most men and women could hope to be before deciding they want to spend a lifetime together. What else is it going to take?''

Abby turned his hand over and touched her fingertips lightly to his. ''Are you sure marriage is right for us?''

''I'm sure.'' He laced their fingers together and brought her hand to his lips. Gently he nipped the end of her forefinger. ''Justin will be released in two days. You're pretty much ready for him at home. We could get married, and all you'll have to do is move next door.''

She met his eyes, dark now; looked at his mouth, the white collar against his tanned neck. In the dark suit he wore, he resembled...Abby smiled, remembering Marie's comment: a male model.

''Let's dance,'' he said abruptly and slid an arm around her waist to guide her onto the floor.

When they faced each other, Abby stood still, gazing up at him. She tried to take a breath. Only part of her lungs expanded. ''I'm not sure I remember how to dance,'' she said.

''It's like riding a horse, or swimming,'' Nick replied, taking her in his arms, moving smoothly to the music of a combo playing soft and easy. "It comes back to you."

He didn't allow any space between them. His hands, spread wide on her back, held her body tightly against his. The muscles in his chest moved against her breasts. His hips pressed into her belly, his thighs transmitted rhythm to hers—and longing.

Abby kissed the underside of his jaw and rested her cheek on his shoulder. The pulse in his throat beat hard. "I keep expecting to wake up," she said, "and find I've dreamed you. I'll go next door and ring the bell, and a stranger will stare out at me."

"I wish you'd try it, love. I'll be there all right, I promise you." His hand moved to the back of her neck, over her ear, rubbing lightly. "It'll be you and me—and Justin. Come, Abby, come."

He was whittling away her resistance steadily. Abby looked up at him.

Nick kept up the swaying motion but stopped moving around the floor. He framed her face, kissed the spot between her brows, her nose, each corner of her mouth. A slight thrust of his hips caused her eyes to fly wide open. His arousal sent a burning ache between her legs.

Abby tightened her own grip. Concentration took more will-power than he'd ever know. "Have you really thought what you'd be taking on if you married me? Not just a wife, but a baby who'd need a lot of my time?"

"My time, too." He grinned broadly and whirled her around. "I'm looking forward to it. I'm pretty good at the bottle and diaper bit. In fact, the nurse this afternoon said I performed like a pro."

Abby grimaced, tracing his shirt pocket. "I saw the way she looked at you. She'd have said what a good job you did if you'd diapered Justin's head by mistake."

"She would not," Nick retorted. "And it's not my fault if the only woman who doesn't find me devastating is the one I've fallen in love with. How about the way I gave him that sponge bath? Not bad, huh?"

"Not bad," Abby replied with difficulty. He did love her. And she loved him. Could she risk agreeing to marry him?

"You okay, sweetheart?" Nick bowed his head to meet her eyes. "You look faraway and sad."

"I was just thinking I'd like to be alone with you. Really alone. Somewhere we could talk."

He regarded her seriously. "Me, too. Let's get out of here."

He held her hand and hurried her back to their table.

"There's nowhere to go, Nick. We can't walk. It's raining.''

"Trust me." He signaled the waiter and dropped a charge card on the bill.

They followed the man to the reception desk, and Nick signed the voucher before retrieving Abby's coat. "This thing has character," he said as he held up her black relic. "But I think my Christmas present to you is going to be something spectacular, maybe gray mohair.''

Christmas. He was leaping ahead as if their future was a smooth trail. "I don't accept expensive gifts from men," she said and immediately turned her eyes to the ceiling, waiting for his comeback.

He was on cue. "I'm not *men* as you put it. Am I?"

"No, of course not.''

In the elevator, which was deeply carpeted and surrounded them with soft music, she felt Nick's irritation. "I didn't mean to say the wrong thing. Sometimes I have a real flair for stupid comments. This coat is a rag. I'm surprised you put up with being seen with me in it.''

He grunted. "I won't anymore. Tomorrow we'll shop for the mohair.''

"Nick Dorset, you take advantage. I said I was sorry I was rude, not that I'd let you buy me a coat.''

"Well, you will, anyway. And we have something else to buy, don't we? Something to seal a promise, I hope.''

After the warmth of the fern-studded lobby, the night air was an icy breath-stealing blast. Abby didn't answer Nick's question.

The BMW was parked under the viaduct, but Nick, with Abby's hand firmly clamped between his body and elbow, headed directly for the waterfront.

"Where are we going?" Abby asked, shivering. "The car's back there.''

"Have you ever taken the ferry anywhere?''

She tried to halt, but he kept walking, causing her to trot. "I have when I wanted to go somewhere.''

"Want to go somewhere now?''

"It's after ten, Nick. Where would we go at this time of night?''

"Who knows?" They crossed railroad tracks to the water. Nick led the way into the brightly lit ferry terminal. At a ticket booth, he bent to see the clerk inside. "Where's that boat out there going?"

"Bremerton." The bald head didn't lift.

"Two, please," Nick said. "Round-trip."

The man took Nick's money, slapped down two tickets and some change and turned a page in the book he was reading.

"Nick, you're a nut," Abby said, stepping beside him while he walked, stuffing his wallet in a back pocket. "Bremerton? That's almost an hour's ride. And we're just going to go up there and turn around and come back?"

He glanced up, grinning broadly. "Unless you'd like to find a place to spend the night there."

She poked his side, and he doubled up, laughing. "Seriously," she insisted, "we'll be on the water for two hours at least. We won't be back till midnight."

"Hmm. Watch your step." They clattered down the metal gangway. "Two hours should be enough to get an answer out of you. If it's not, I'll just keep taking you back and forth until you do answer me."

Abby groaned, climbing ahead of him up a narrow stairway to the enclosed passenger lounges. The vessel was almost empty. Within minutes the aft doors where vehicles drove aboard clanked shut, and squealing winches hauled in the mooring lines. The huge ferryboat chugged from the terminal, rolling gently through the dark waters of Elliott Bay and Puget Sound.

Nick and Abby settled on a bench overlooking an aft deck. Rain slashed diagonally across the windows, and although the lounge was warm, Abby moved closer to Nick.

He hugged her. "Isn't this great?"

"I'm being kidnapped," she responded without conviction.

"Funny." Nick craned to get a clearer view of her. "You don't appear to be tied up or gagged. I thought kidnappers always restrained their victims."

"Unless they use sophisticated methods like brainwashing."

"Have I brainwashed you?"

She played with a button on her coat. "I think so."

"Did I do a good job?"

"I'm afraid you did." Abby pulled away and stood. "If we went just outside those doors, we wouldn't get too wet. There's an overhang from the upper deck, I think."

When she reached the doors, Nick blocked her path. "It's got to be freezing out there, Abby. Are you sure you want to go out?"

She dodged around him and pushed into the rain-laced wind. Nick followed. He undid his raincoat and wrapped her inside it. They leaned against the deckhousing, watching a luminous spume V out from the vessel and the red and green tinge of its running lights on the water. The scent of tar and oil hung heavy in the sodden air.

Abby turned inside Nick's coat, pushed her hands under his jacket and molded their bodies together. In the darkness, unspeaking, with the sound of the wind and the rotating radar scanner the only distractions, they kissed. The meetings of their mouths were wild, desperate attempts to assuage a deeper hunger.

Tentatively Nick unbuttoned Abby's coat. He touched her breasts carefully, bringing his thumbs to rest at their soft sides. She spread her palms over his flat belly, pressed down until she met hard resistance. The sound Nick made, deep, breaking, was lost on the wind before he held both of her wrists and put her arms around his neck. He kissed her again and again, forcing her mouth wide open, driving his tongue far into her mouth. His lips and face nudged, tipping her head back, until he could follow the soft skin of her neck down to the buttons closing her dress. Down, down, his lips and tongue moved, probing between the tops of her breasts until she moaned and urged his mouth back to hers. They must take this slower, much slower.

"I love you, love you," Nick said against her ear. "God, how I love you."

"You said all I'd have to do was move next door," Abby whispered breathlessly. "There'd be two of us, Nick."

He leaned away, his eyes glinting in the night. "Yes. So you've reminded me before. Then there'd be three. You, Justin and me. What do you say, Abby?"

"Yes. I say yes. If you're sure, Nick, so am I. Thank you, I'd like to marry you very much."

He laughed. "How about getting the baby home and giving me a day or two to let my family know what's happening? They probably deserve a few hours to take everything in, don't you think?"

"Michael already expects it. He'll stand up for me. I'm sure he will. Janet will have warned my folks."

Now Abby laughed. "How about getting the baby home and giving me a day or two to let my family know what's happening? They probably deserve a few hours to take everything in, don't you think?"

"Michael already expects it. He'll stand up for me. I'm sure he will. Janet will have warned my folks."

''That's fine. But my mom and dad don't expect it. I suggest we plan on about four weeks from now, mid-January, for more reasons than one.'' She was grateful he couldn't see her blush.

Nick blew gently on her ear. ''I do believe you're a very sexy woman, Abby soon-to-be-Dorset. I'd be happy to marry you tomorrow and just hold you for the next month. But—'' he held up a hand to stop her protest ''—we'll do it your way.''

''Thanks,'' she said. ''I also need to line up some job interviews. I had enough money to pay for the delivery, but I'll have a big bill still owing for Justin. And I owe Michael money now. I want to get to work as soon as I can.''

Nick had turned his head away. He said nothing.

Abby's heart thudded. He mustn't think she expected him to take on debts she'd already incurred. ''I will be able to deal with it all, Nick. You don't have to worry.''

''I'm not worried,'' he responded, his voice muffled. He cleared his throat. ''How about dropping by to see Justin on our way home? We could tell him our news.''

''Oh, yes.'' She hugged him. ''You always know what I want, Nick. I want to see him.''

Nick pulled her coat together and fastened it. ''I want to see him, too.''

The rest of the trip to Bremerton and back seemed interminable. Nick bought hot cider and cinnamon rolls from the cafeteria, and they retreated to their quiet corner to watch the waves.

Finally the ferry docked in Seattle once more, and Nick hurried Abby to the car. The heater quickly warmed her cold nose and icy hands. When the hospital loomed ahead, she felt the odd jiggle of excitement in the pit of her stomach the thought of Justin always brought.

''Have you noticed how he watches your face when you feed him?'' Abby asked while Nick swung the car into the parking garage.

''He follows movement, too,'' he said. ''He's going to be a bright kid.''

Abby laughed. ''You sound like a proud father.'' She bowed her head and clasped her hands together.

''I feel like one,'' Nick said evenly. ''And, after all, I'm going to get to share him.''

The awkwardness evaporated. ''I'm so lucky to have you, Nick.''

He pulled on the emergency brake and leaned to kiss her cheek. "We're lucky to have each other. Now, let's go and see our boy."

"You don't think they'll mind us turning up so late?" Abby whispered when they left the elevator on the third floor of the hospital. "It's so quiet in here."

"We were told to come anytime, weren't we?"

She nodded as they turned the corner. Muted light from the nursery windows washed the opposite wall.

A man was standing there, his face framed by his hands and pressed to the glass.

"Oh, no," Abby whispered. Water seemed to replace the blood in her veins. She gripped Nick's forearm.

Nick glanced down into Abby's face and back to the man. For the first time he knew what feeling *murderous* meant.

John Winston sensed their presence and straightened.

## Chapter Fourteen

He approached them slowly while Nick's brain formed and rejected a dozen comments.

"Abby," John said when he stood in front of her. "How are you, baby?"

Nick's hands instantly curled into fists, but he held himself rigid. Abby's fingers dug into his arm.

"What are you doing here, John?" She began to shake.

John Winston ran a hand through his blond curls, looked at his feet, then beseechingly at Abby. "I couldn't stay away any longer. I wanted to see him—and you."

"Why? You didn't care before." Abby's voice sounded high.

"You don't belong here."

"I got in from a trip this afternoon and tried to call you," John said. "When there was no answer, I called Michael. He told me the baby had been born." The man's blue eyes filled with tears, and Nick hated him for it. "I knew if I came here and waited long enough, you'd show."

"We should see Justin and get you home, Abby," Nick broke in, taking her past Winston. "It's late."

"I like the name Justin. Justin Winston is nice."

Abby stopped and turned back. "What else did Michael tell you, apart from Justin being born?"

"That you wouldn't want to see me. That I didn't have any right to come here. But I do, Abby. Justin's my son, too."

He had to keep hold of himself, Nick thought. He worked the muscles in his jaw and tried vainly to put his thoughts into neutral. *Don't hit the bastard, not here*, he ordered himself. And, his brain registered, Abby must deal with this in her own way. She wouldn't accept anything else.

"You didn't want him, John," she said clearly. "You didn't want him or me. I didn't ask for a divorce, you did, and it's final. We're strangers now. Please leave."

For the first time, John looked directly at Nick. "I understand you've been kind to Abby—Nick, is it? Thanks for that, buddy.

She obviously trusts you. Maybe you can talk her into letting me see my boy just once—holding him just one time.'' A tear slid down his cheek.

Nick glanced away. ''Abby makes her own decisions,'' he said, praying she'd tell the son of a bitch to get lost.

Her voice cracked when she said, ''Cut the dramatics, John. They make me sick. Why don't you just get lost?''

''Please, Abby.'' Winston took a step toward her. ''I made a mistake. I've been a bastard to you. I'm sorry.''

Abby held her purse in front of her like a shield. ''It's too late for 'sorry.'''

''I deserve this. But I hoped you'd understand a man needing to see his son.'' John covered his face.

When Abby touched the man's arm, Nick swallowed his rising nausea and rage. This creep, this manipulator who'd entertained himself by shouting at a lovely, gentle woman, by walking away away when she needed him most, was working on her too-tender heart again.

Winston put a hand over Abby's on his arm, joining her to him. ''If I can be with him—and you—for a few minutes, I'll go away. I promise.''

Abby looked at Nick and back to John. ''Okay, a few minutes, but that's it,'' she said, dull distress in her eyes. ''I'll do the talking to the staff. You're a friend, nothing more—understand?''

''Yes, of course.'' John Winston smiled a grateful little-boy smile that deliberately included Nick. With his blue, blue eyes he said *I'm wayward, and I know it, but I can be good if I'm given a chance.*

And Nick detested him.

Abby pushed open the nursery door. A nurse worked busily with a baby in an incubator. She glanced over her shoulder and raised her brows when she saw Abby and Nick had someone with them.

''This is a close friend,'' Abby said in a low voice. ''He's just passing through town, and he wondered if he could see Justin.''

The nurse hesitated, withdrawing her hands from the incubator sleeves. ''Well,'' she said and smiled at Abby and Nick, ''I suppose it's all right. Gown up, though, please. You know the routine.''

After the woman left, Nick donned a gown and Abby did the same before handing one to John. He took off his heavy pea coat, and Nick was struck afresh by the man's massive build inside a dark blue turtleneck and jeans. A vital man. The kind women went for. Nick turned away and went to see Justin.

The child slept, his tiny fists curled beneath his chin. "Hi, fella," Nick whispered, touching a whitened knuckle. "How's it going?"

"Oh, Abby, he's a beaut."

John Winston stood on the other side of the baby's bed, staring at his son with an amazement that Nick doubted could be feigned, and it wouldn't have to be. Justin *was* beautiful.

"He was born a bit early," Abby said. "Then he got an infection, so he had to stay here for a couple of weeks."

"He's going to be all right?" John gripped the edge of the crib, glancing at the antibiotic drip.

"Justin's due to go home in two days," Nick interjected. The raw sensation closing his throat was foreign. Then he identified it: jealousy of this interloper, possessiveness toward Abby and Justin. He wanted John Winston gone.

Abby smoothed Justin's cheek, and the child's eyelids parted, closed, then opened fully. He stretched, and Abby bent over him, making the soft noises she always made when she was with him. She lifted him and rubbed her chin on his brow.

John went to her side, and Nick saw their eyes meet. Either he was dying or very very sick. He couldn't stand this. Abby smiled and placed Justin gently in John's arms. He held the bundle stiffly at first, slightly away from his body. Justin whimpered, and John looked startled before he smiled and relaxed, pushing a large forefinger into one miniature fist.

"He's perfect," John moved close to Abby where they could look together at their child.

Abby straightened the receiving blanket, her features soft. "He's strong, John. They say he'll do very well."

When John put an arm around her shoulders, Abby didn't seem to notice or mind. The couple stood, rocking gently, their baby between them.

Numb, Nick reached back to untie the neck of his gown. "Winston, do you have a car with you?" he asked. The pain in his throat was suffocating now.

The other man didn't look up. "Yes. It's in the garage."

"Could you give Abby a ride home?" Nick felt Abby's stare, the stiffening of her body. "I forgot I'm supposed to check in with the airline tonight." The excuse sounded pitiful in his own ear.

"Sure I can," John said quickly. "Be glad to."

*I'll bet you will.* Nick turned to Abby. "Hope you don't mind being abandoned. But I'm sure John will take good care of you. We'll touch base soon."

"Nick…," she began, then nodded mutely, her eyes, shaded in the dim nursery, showing nothing—or everything. Nick didn't know anything anymore except he had to get out of here.

In the corridor he tossed his gown into a hamper and braced his arms against the wall, bowing his head and waiting for desperation to pass. Abby and John had appeared so natural together, holding their baby. He, Nick, was the interloper. On legs that seemed boneless, he passed the nursery without looking sideways.

Abby watched Nick go, every nerve within her jumping. Tears sprang to her eyes. His attempt at nonchalance before he walked out hadn't fooled her. Through no fault of hers he felt hurt, betrayed. Nick felt she had betrayed him simply by allowing John to hold Justin. And the excuse about having to call the airport office hadn't fooled her. He'd wanted to escape. Damn him. Damn him for doubting her. Panic clamored in her brain. She pulled her bottom lip between her teeth and bit hard.

"I must get home," she said abruptly. What counted was getting to Nick and making him see he'd overreacted to a situation she'd been unable to control.

John continued to hold Justin. He studied the baby closely. "He's got the shape of your face, but I think he'll be blond like me." He stroked the dark fuzz. "This comes out, doesn't it? I'm sure he'll end up blond."

Abby shifted restlessly. "It's hard to know yet. John, they don't like long visits." Not strictly true, but a necessary excuse to follow Nick as soon as possible.

"Okay. I hate putting him down, though." John replaced Justin in the plastic bed.

"Come on," Abby insisted, backing through the swinging doors and tearing off her gown at the same time. In the entry, she shifted from one foot to the other until John joined her and followed her example, disposing of the green gown and swinging his coat over one shoulder.

The clock in the hospital foyer showed 2:00 a.m. as they passed. Abby couldn't repress a shudder when the deepened cold of early morning drove into her. John put on his coat and pulled her against his side, shielding her while they crossed to the garage. The drawing together in Abby's belly was easily identifiable—

revulsion. John's nearness alone was enough to sicken her now. The realization shocked Abby, and she shrugged away.

He drove a brown pickup she'd never seen before. In the cab he made much of making sure she was comfortable. Abby cringed at his touch. She calculated how long ago Nick had left. Too long. While John drove, he tried to make conversation. She hardly heard what he said. Nick mustn't, couldn't think she wanted to be with John.

"Why are we stopping?" Abby asked and moved closer to the door.

Several blocks from her condo, John steered onto the shoulder of the road and turned off his engine.

John let seconds click by before he answered, "We have to talk. You know that, Abby."

"I don't," she said, tears of frustration springing into her eyes.

"Take me home, please."

"These past few months have taught me a lot."

She didn't want to know anything about what his life had been.

"Just drive," she said.

"You never used to be so hard." He tried to hold her hand, but she crossed her arms. "We all make mistakes, baby. Even you, maybe. Would it be such a bad idea to give us another chance?"

A scream sounded deep in her head. But she hadn't really screamed, had she? "We were wrong for each other from the start," she said carefully.

"You never used to say that. Baby—"

"Don't call me baby. I'm not your baby. Will you take me home, or do I have to get out and walk?"

"Hell! I'm asking for a fresh start. What do I have to do, crawl?"

Abby bent over, rocking, the tears breaking loose.

"Justin's my child, too, remember that," John said harshly. "A father has rights these days. Rights just as strong as a mother's."

"You left me. You can't come back and...and..." She couldn't go on.

Keys jangled, and the engine turned over again. Abby felt the pickup swing back onto the road and kept her face bowed.

When the motion stopped once more, she peered up fearfully. Relief almost choked her. She was home.

John stopped her from opening the door. "I came on too strong, too fast back there," he said. "Tonight was more than I could handle. I didn't know it would be. Can you accept that?"

"Yes." She'd accept anything if he'd just let her go. She must get to Nick.

"Can I at least talk to you some more?"

"Not now, John. I've had it for tonight."

"Tomorrow, then?"

Strategy was what counted at this moment. "We'll see. Good night, John."

He removed his hand slowly. "I'll call you tomorrow."

Abby pushed open the door.

"Wait," John said urgently. "I brought this for you. I was going to get flowers, but it was too late."

She hardly looked at the envelope he pushed into her hands. Had John ever given her a card before? She didn't remember.

Leaving the pickup door swinging open, she ran through the parking lot and around to the back of the building. By the time she stood in the hall between her own door and Nick's, her breath came in gasps. She stood, her fingers an inch from his doorbell, willing her heart to slow.

She rang, waited, rang again. No footsteps sounded inside his condo. Abby pressed the button again, then knocked. Nothing.

Trembling, she let herself into her own rooms and dialed his number on the phone. He didn't answer. Tears started afresh, and she wiped at them disgustedly. She cried so easily these days. Nick wasn't the kind of man to ignore his doorbell or his phone.

An idea formed slowly, and with it, terror. What if he'd been hurt and never got home? She ran back downstairs to check for his car. The BMW wasn't in the lot.

Abby returned to her condo, trying to think. The first thing to do was call the police, or should she check the hospitals?

She had a key to his place. Nick had given her a key.

He'd understand if she went in—just to check.

Minutes later she closed her own door behind her and went directly to the bedroom. Without removing her coat, she fell facedown onto the bed. She should be glad. Nick had returned home safely, his discarded suit proved that. But he'd left again, and God knew where he'd gone.

In one hand she still held John's card. She sat up and tore open the envelope. Her tears were bitter now. If Nick had truly loved and trusted her, he wouldn't have rushed away at the sight of John.

She pulled a folded sheet from the envelope. Money, bills in larger denominations than she'd seen often, slid into her lap.

"Abby," John's note read, "I never did know when I had it good. Leaving you was the biggest mistake of my life. Michael told me some of what you've been through since I went away. I can't take it all back, but I can say thank-you for the baby and ask you to try and forgive me." He signed, "Love, John."

"You never knew what love was," Abby muttered. She picked up the money and stuffed it back into the envelope with the note.

"YOU LOVE THE GUY." Marie chewed her fingernail and paced while she talked. "You're obviously crazy about him, or you wouldn't have said you'd get married."

Abby stretched full length on the couch and closed her eyes. "Yes, I love Nick." Why did Marie always show up at the least convenient times?

"So fight for him. Tell him he's all you want in the world. Don't let John spoil this chance for you."

"As I've already told you, Nick isn't here for me to tell him anything," Abby said patiently. Her head ached. Three or four hours of shallow sleep had done nothing for her health or the state of her mind. And Marie's hour-long interrogation since her uninvited appearance at nine had only increased the tension.

Marie picked up her purse and rummaged until she found a cigarette and some matches. "Where is he?"

"Like I told you when you arrived, I don't know. When did you start smoking again?"

"I never really gave it up. Nick saw you with John and took off?" She drew deeply on a cigarette, shaking out the match's flame. "He must have thought there was still something between you two. Is there?"

"There's nothing between John and me, dammit, Marie. You know that. But John's going to make it tough. I feel it in my bones. For some sick reason, he's going to try and stake a claim to Justin."

Marie whirled toward her, one elbow braced on the other forearm. "Why would John want Justin?"

Abby turned her face to the back of the couch. "How do I know? He never liked kids. Maybe he just wants what he can't have."

"And while he tries to get it, you'll let him ruin what you and Nick have?"

"I don't need this, Marie. I didn't sleep last night, or this morning. I'm scared of what John intends to do. And I miss Nick."

"He'll be back, and when he is, make sure he knows that nothing and no one matters to you as much as he does."

"What if he won't believe me?" Abby said miserably. "What if John keeps showing up on some pretext…saying he intends to see Justin? He could even try to get custody. Some of the things he said last night made it sound like he was thinking about it."

"Give him the baby."

"What!" Abby leapt to her feet. "What are you saying, Marie? After all that stuff about adoption I thought you'd know better than to make any more suggestions about giving up Justin."

Marie recoiled and sat with a thud on the edge of a chair. "Calm down and think." She ripped the tip of one nail completely off and glared at it. "How long do you think John would want to play house with a baby? If you gave him a few weeks at it, say until you and Nick are married, Justin would be back on your doorstep so fast your head would spin."

Abby couldn't believe what Marie had suggested. "My baby isn't a weapon," she said. "He isn't a thing to be used. Let John fight; he won't get him. And if Nick doesn't trust me enough to know I don't want John back, our marriage would be a mistake. One rotten marriage is enough, thank you."

"As long as you're free, John is likely to keep coming around."

"How do you know?" Abby was exasperated.

"I don't. But you're the one who said he's the type who wants what he thinks he can't have."

"'Thinks'? I— Darn, there goes the intercom. That had better not be John."

Marie got up, stubbed out her cigarette and grabbed her purse. "Don't let him in if it is."

Abby went to the speaker and heard Michael's voice before she could say anything. Relieved, she buzzed him into the building. Michael was exactly what she needed today.

She turned to Marie. "Michael's—"

"I know, I know. I'm going." Marie pulled on her coat. She'd grasped the front doorknob when Michael knocked.

Abby reached around her to let him in and suppressed a smile at her brother's strained expression on sighting Marie.

"Hi, Mike," Marie said brightly, edging past him. "I guess

today is Abby's day for visits from beautiful people.'' She smiled winningly into his cool indigo eyes and trotted out of sight.

''You might try to be nice to Marie,'' Abby told Michael reprovingly. ''She's really okay.''

''I'm not interested in Marie,'' Michael cut in, marching past Abby. ''What the hell happened between you and Nick?''

She turned instantly cold. ''You've talked to him.''

''Greg Schulz, another pilot, told me Nick took off from Seattle early this morning and that he's going to use Omaha as his home base for a while.''

Abby closed her eyes. ''Oh, Michael. What am I going to do?''

''Damned if I know. But you could start by giving me a hint of why he went, and why John Winston turned up at the folks' this morning all sweetness and light and crowing about seeing Justin for the first time last night. Abby, for God's sake!''

She felt his arms around her before she knew she'd begun to faint. Michael helped her to the couch and sat beside her.

''Stay here,'' he said. ''I'll get you some water. Or should I call a doctor?''

''Just water, please.'' John had been to her parents'. He intended to get back into her life. She wouldn't let him, but it didn't matter. Nick had gone.

A cold glass shoved into her hands made her glance up into Michael's troubled eyes. ''Tell me what happened,'' he said. ''Take it slowly and quit worrying. Whatever's happened, we'll work it out.''

Yet again Abby stumbled through the events of the previous night and early morning. Each time she paused, Michael steered the glass to her mouth and rubbed her nape. When she'd finished her story, he sagged back beside her, expelling a long, low whistle.

''So Nick has limped off to lick his wounds. Idiot,'' he said finally. ''If this is what love does to a guy, keep it away from me.''

''Are the folks going to show up here, too?'' Abby asked weakly. ''I don't think I can face them today.''

''No. From what they said, John made it sound as if the two of you needed a lot of time alone, so they intend to give it to you. I wouldn't be surprised if he'd try to see you.''

She sighed. ''He said he would, and I didn't have the smarts to put him off properly. Michael, all I want is Nick—and Justin. If John fights for custody of Justin and gets it, and I've lost Nick, too, I don't know...I just don't know. Tell me what to do, Michael.''

''You won't lose either of them.'' He turned toward her. ''Use your head, Abby, John wouldn't have a hope of getting his hands on Justin. And if he makes a nuisance of himself, I'll deal with him myself. Let's concentrate on Nick. You said you got along well with his sister.''

''Janet, yes,'' Abby agreed.

''Call her.''

''Call...oh, no, no, I couldn't.''

''You can and you will—now.'' He went into the kitchen and returned with a telephone directory. ''What's her last name? And her husband's first name? I'll call the operator.''

''Crete Ross,'' Abby said faintly. ''I don't think this is a good idea. Nick might not like it.''

''You aren't going to call Nick. He can't tell you who you should talk to.''

In what seemed to Abby like far too short a time, she heard Janet's voice on the phone and floundered into a series of confused remarks. She asked about Penny and about Janet's husband, the weather in Omaha, where they all intended to spend Christmas.

''Nick's at my parents','' Janet broke in quietly. ''He got there this morning with some story about flying out of here for a while so he can spend Christmas with the family. What's wrong?''

Abby's heartbeat pounded in her throat. ''He asked me to marry him.''

After a brief silence, Janet said, ''I'm glad. So why is he here?''

Once again, Abby explained John's unexpected appearance and Nick's reaction. When she'd finished, Janet launched into a short tirade about the immaturity of the male that brought a smile even to Abby's lips. By the time she hung up, she was almost sorry for Nick. If Janet delivered the lecture she'd said she intended for her brother, he'd come away minus most of his skin.

''She's on my side—Nick's and my side,'' Abby said distractedly.

''I gathered,'' Michael said. ''She'll get through to him.''

''If he'll listen.''

ABBY TURNED JUSTIN on his tummy, patted his bottom and leaned to kiss the dark fuzz behind his ear. She closed her eyes, breathing in the clean scent of baby powder. Notes tinkled from the slowly twirling mobiles attached to his crib. When she was sure he was asleep, she tiptoed into the kitchen, leaving his nursery door ajar. Christmas night. Justin had been home a week, and she couldn't imagine the condo without him anymore.

In the kitchen she rinsed his bottle and poured a glass of wine. She went to sit at the dining table Nick had bought while she'd been still in the hospital. As soon as she could find a job and get Justin settled in day care she'd start paying Nick back what she owed.

She left the lights off and nestled her chin on her crossed arms atop the glistening rosewood surface of the table. Outside, a dusting of snow sparkled on shrubs and outlined naked tree limbs. A Christmas Day had never been so lonely, or, at the same time, so special.

Tomorrow she was to visit her parents. Today, her mother had told her on the phone, should be Abby and John's first Christmas alone with their son. And Abby hadn't had the guts to set Wilma straight. So there had been no one but her tiny boy and the special magic he brought. No word from Nick. Michael hadn't called. And for the first time this week John hadn't turned up on the doorstep. For that, at least, she was grateful.

He'd refused to take back the money he'd given her. More had arrived by mail. He'd come at different times, bringing gifts for Justin, flowers and perfume for her, and champagne he'd insisted on sharing to celebrate their son's birth.

Abby opened the shades and rubbed at the condensation forming on the window. She didn't want to celebrate anything with John Winston.

What was Nick doing tonight? Laughing by the fire with his family? Evidently Janet hadn't managed to sway him. Abby compressed her lips. Nick wasn't any happier than she was. Suggesting, even out of anger and desperation, that he might be was immature. But he didn't trust her and wasn't about to be hurt any more badly.

A lone set of tires crackled in the street. She peered down, feeling the same rush of hope she'd felt a dozen times this week. The vehicle that drew up to park half on the curb wasn't a silver BMW, but John's brown pickup. She drew back from the window, her first thought that she'd pretend not to be at home. But that wouldn't work. He'd know she was there.

When the buzzer sounded, Abby released the main door latch

without talking into the speaker. Then she opened her front door and returned to sit by the window. She closed the shades.

"Merry Christmas, baby." John came in, bringing cool air with him. He stood, framed in the entrance to the living room, with a grocery sack in one arm, a pile of brightly wrapped packages in the other.

"Hi, John."

"Is that the best you can give a man bringing Christmas cheer?" He swayed slightly.

Abby held the edge of the table with both hands. He was drunk.

"Shh, please. Justin's just gone to sleep."

"Shhh," John echoed, rising to his toes and walking with exaggerated care into the room. "Shhh, Justin's sleeping. Good, 'cause that means his mommie and me can be all alone."

"I was just going to bed," Abby said and pursed her lips at the instant flash in his bloodshot eyes. "I think you should go, John. No, I want you to go."

He made it to the couch and flopped down, still holding his packages. "No, no, no." He shook his head repeatedly. "This is celebration time. We're going to celebrate."

Abby was afraid to move, afraid that he would reach for her. "Don't make this harder, John. You're drunk. Please get out of here."

"Nope." He stood and came toward her. From the bag he produced a bottle of bourbon, already open, and two bottles of pink champagne. The wrapped parcels slid to the floor, and he retrieved them clumsily, piling them on the table beside the liquor before he took off his coat.

Abby watched, horrified, while he worked his sweater over his head, unbuttoned his shirt and pulled the tails free of his jeans. He planted his hands on his hips, flexing the muscles in his chest beneath a heavy covering of blond hair.

"Just getting comfortable." His words slurred together. "I was surprised you hadn't told your mom and dad about the divorce. Why didn't you?"

"I'm not talking to you while you're like this." He'd struck another chord. Why hadn't he mentioned the divorce himself?

"How come you felt so confident you could walk into my family's home when you must have expected them to know about the divorce?"

His eyes slid away. "I was ready to tell them what I've told you: I'm sorry about the divorce, and I don't want it anymore.

Then I realized they didn't know, so I let it go. You don't want to stay apart, either, do you, Abby? You never wanted it, or you would have told them. We can get married again, and they never have to know we've been separated."

"Stop it," Abby said, getting to her feet. "It's over with us, John. If you think about it—soberly—you'll know you want it over, too."

"Oh, baby, you don't mean that." He clamped a hand on her shoulder, pulled her toward him. "We were always good together."

Even her mouth trembled. Her lips wouldn't stay together. If she shouted, no one would hear but Justin. "Either you go away and stay away," she said, drawing up to her full height, "or I'll call the police. Then I'll make sure you never get within a mile of my son again."

He stared into her eyes, his pupils widely dilated, then concentrated on her mouth. Slowly he drew her closer until she could smell the bourbon on his breath. She turned her head away, but he easily turned it back with a finger and thumb.

The instant before his lips would have met hers, Abby slapped him. With splayed fingers she hit the side of his face, baring her teeth as she did so and wrenching away.

John touched the reddening marks on his cheek and stepped back. "You bitch," he mumbled. "You make me go away tonight...you try to keep me from seeing Justin, and I'll find a way to get him. And that doesn't have to be through the courts."

Abby sat again, holding her head in her hands. Would he kidnap her baby if she didn't play his game? For some warped reason he wanted to get back in her life. She wouldn't take him. She couldn't take him. And she couldn't lose her baby.

John's hand on the back of her head brought a cry to her lips. She started to hit it out, but he held her wrist until she went limp. He slackened his grip, turning the vise into a stroking action. And his hand on her head became the caress of a parent for a child.

"I'm sorry, Abby," he said quietly. "I was out of line, as usual. You're right: I'm drunk. It took me all day to get up the guts to come here and ask you to marry me again. And it took booze. I'm an ass. Forgive me?"

She couldn't form any words.

"Look," he said, backing away. "We can't talk now while I'm like this. But I can't drive any more either, baby. Let me sleep this off on the couch for a while, and I'll get out of your hair until we can talk rationally. Will you do that?''

If she refused, he might start shouting again, or try.... He could force himself on her. As long as he was here, she wouldn't dare sleep, but she'd have to agree to his staying.

''You'll sleep it off, then leave?''

''I promise.'' He stripped his shirt all the way off and worked out of the soft Western boots he'd always favored. The socks followed. ''Can I just look in on Justin?''

He didn't wait for her approval before going into the hall.

Abby stood in the middle of the room. She could call Michael for help. As she formed the idea, John reappeared, and at the same moment, her doorbell rang.

She hurried forward, only to be stopped by John's powerful arm across her breasts. He slipped his hand around her waist, holding her slightly behind him.

The doorbell rang again.

''Who would come at this time of night?'' John asked. ''You could be alone here. Never answer the door when you're alone.''

''I won't. I won't.''

He gave her a hard look and opened the door.

Nick had his back to the door while he stooped to pick up several packages. ''Abby, I've been trying to get out of Omaha for two days.'' He rose, turning slowly, balancing his load, leaving his flight bag in a heap while he looked up. ''Abby....''

# Chapter Fifteen

"Little late for social calls, isn't it, buddy?" Abby heard John's drawl but looked, stupefied, at Nick. He seemed to see only John.

"What can we do for you?" John moved farther in front of Abby, filling the doorway with his half-naked body.

"I came to see Abby," Nick said in a menacing voice. He met her eyes over John's shoulder. "We have things to discuss."

"Anything you have to say to Abby, you can say to me," John said, stepping back, sweeping wide his arm. "Come join our celebration. We always have a holiday drink for a neighbor, right, Abby?"

She shook her head. John was drunk, and Nick looked as if the packages he held were all that kept him from swinging his fists. They mustn't fight. She had to find a sane way out of this.

"John needed a place to spend the night, Nick," she said lamely. "You and I can talk in the morning."

Nick's mouth set in a hard line. "Good night, Abby." He managed to haul the flight bag over his shoulder without dropping the packages. With a last long stare at her, he turned away.

John shut the door an instant before Abby heard Nick's latch click sharply. He had come back. He'd said he'd been trying to get to her for two days. And now he thought he'd made a fool of himself, that she'd made a fool of him. What else could he think after seeing John dressed as he was, and hearing her admit she was allowing him to spend the night?

With her arms crossed, she dragged her leaden body into the living room. John followed, evidently finally at a loss for words. She glared at him and set about gathering his clothes.

"Put these on, John. And get out."

He spread his hands. "But you said I could stay."

"I've changed my mind."

"Because loverboy came back?" he sneered. "You want me out so you two can get together. I saw the way he looked at you at the hospital that night. And he was going to walk in here tonight like it was home, wasn't he? He must be used to coming home to you, Abby. Well, it isn't going to work anymore because I'm home now."

Abby shoved his shirt into his arms and waited, holding his sweater and socks in front of her. "Get dressed. And don't say another word about Nick."

"I'm not going anywhere."

"You are, unless you want me to scream. Nick's sober, John. This might be one fight you wouldn't win."

"Don't make me go." He crumpled to the arm of the couch, his shirt balled in one fist. "I'll go in the morning, like I said."

"If you ever want to see Justin again, you'll go now. *Now*, John, or I'll get a court restraining order to keep you away from us altogether."

He passed a jerky hand over his face. "I'll go. But I'll be back." The shirt went on, inside out, and she handed over his sweater. "You're going to be sorry, Abby. I need Justin, and I'm not going to give up."

"You're threatening me." Abby heard her voice waver. "What can you do to me? You were the one who left, not me."

"I can do plenty." He pulled on the sweater without tucking in his shirt and struggled into his socks and boots. "Keep a close eye on Justin, baby. Make sure you're always watching him."

Abby retreated to the nearest wall for support. He was talking about taking Justin, kidnapping him if she wouldn't play some warped game. "Get out," she whispered.

He stood and dragged on his coat, stumbled and held the back of the couch to steady himself before drawing himself upright. His skin had taken on a gray tinge. "I'll be back," he said, walking a ragged line to the door. "You'll see me again, real soon."

The bang of wood on wood reverberated in Abby's head. She covered her ears. She needed help.

As soon as John's pickup pulled away from the curb, she checked Justin and went to Nick's door. He answered her soft tap, still dressed in his white shirt and navy uniform pants, his tie hanging from beneath his collar. His brown eyes were expressionless.

"John's gone."

Nick braced his arms each side of the doorway. "You didn't have to chase him off on my account." He bowed his head.

"You said we had things to discuss."

He sighed deeply. "I guess I was wrong."

Abby touched his hand hesitantly. "I'm glad to see you, Nick. I've missed you."

When he raised his head, his eyes glistened. He turned his face away. "I missed you too, dammit. I wanted to get things straightened out between us. Janet told me you'd called."

"Come to my place and talk." Abby glanced over her shoulder. "Justin's asleep, but I don't like to leave him."

"Is he okay?"

"Yes," Abby said, smiling. "He's wonderful, Nick. Such a little sweetheart."

"I know."

"Will you come with me?"

He sighed again. "No, Abby. Not tonight."

Blood rushed to her cheeks. "Why?"

"You have to know why? John Winston was in your condo, getting ready to spend the night. I'm not saying there's any grand passion between you two. I don't know what's between you. But *you* don't know what you want for sure yet."

"I do know. I want you." She was begging and didn't care. Nick stuffed his hands into his pockets, and she felt him struggle not to reach for her.

"Please, Nick. Give me a chance to explain what's been going on."

He hesitated, and for a moment she thought he'd give in. Then he straightened and met her gaze. "I'm not ready, Abby. And if you're honest with yourself, you'll admit you aren't, either. You have to decide what you want for sure. And I'm not convinced you're prepared to cut the ties with John. If you had been, you'd have told your family you were divorced instead of deceiving them."

"I didn't—"

"You did. And wasn't it because you hoped, deep down, that you and John would get back together? I wouldn't blame you. He was your husband. You must have felt something for the guy."

The thudding in Abby's chest hammered against her eardrums. Weakness clawed at her limbs once more. "I don't want John," she whispered. "I want you."

"Go back to Justin." Nick stroked her arm and let his hand fall away. Longing shone in his eyes. "I've got feelings, too, sweetheart. If you have any doubts, it can't work for us. If you come to me, it has to be whole. Give us time to think. A week.

A couple of weeks. As long as it takes. Let's stay out of each other's way, and if we're meant to be together, we'll know.''

Abby jammed her fist against her mouth, backing away. One more word, and she'd be in tears yet again. She heard Nick's door close before she'd shot home her own dead bolt.

"THEY TOOK IT even worse than I expected," Abby said. Justin in her arms, she stood beside Michael in the driveway outside her parents' house.

"Giving them the silent treatment for two weeks didn't help anything," Michael commented. "They've been expecting to see you since the day after Christmas. I'm amazed Dad managed to stop Mom from calling you."

"I should have called them," Abby said miserably.

Night had closed in, and she shivered while Michael helped her settle Justin in his car seat.

"It's late, sis," Michael said. He tucked a blanket securely around the baby and closed the door. "You'd better get home. And try to unwind, okay? You've got us all behind you—Nick, too, when he comes to his senses."

"I hope so," Abby said, crossing her arms tightly. "Mom called Nick a stranger. She didn't seem to understand at all."

"Give her time." Michael held Abby's door open and leaned on the window rim when she was inside the car. "You know what you have to do, don't you?"

Her head ached. She could hardly think. "Tell me, Michael. I need someone to tell me what to do, step by step."

"First you tell John to get lost." He straightened, balling his hands in his parka pockets and surveying a star-encrusted sky. "Don't worry about anything he might do. I can take care of John Winston. Only I won't have to with Nick around."

"Nick isn't around. I haven't seen him since Christmas night. I think he deliberately stays out of my way."

"He will be around, because when you've told John off for good, you'll go to Nick and threaten him with breach of promise proceedings if he doesn't marry you pronto."

Despite herself, Abby laughed. "Sure, Mike, sure." She sobered. "But you're right, brother of mine. That's what I have to do. That's what I will do."

She started the car, gave the belt around Justin's seat a last tug and drove off, waving to Michael. In the rearview mirror she saw his tall figure in the driveway. He was still there as she turned the corner.

In her purse was a scrap of paper, the corner of an envelope, showing John's address. She'd torn it off and kept it without ever intending to write to him or go near his home.

With one hand on the wheel, she unzipped the purse and scrabbled in a side pocket until she found what she wanted. Keeping an eye on the road, she glanced back and forth at the address.

Instead of heading east and home, she turned toward Elliott Bay and found her way to an area of old houses perched on the side of a hill. Lower Queen Anne was a district inhabited by many singles and young married couples. Abby had little trouble locating the street and house she needed.

She parked against the steep curb and lifted the still sleeping Justin carefully from his seat. The clock in the car showed nine-thirty. Late, but what she had to do wouldn't wait.

A doorplate beside the leaded glass door showed three names, one of them John's. From his number, three, Abby decided he must have an apartment on the top floor of the three-story building.

No light showed from inside. Abby tried the handle and was surprised when it turned easily. Inside, the smell of cooked cabbage and something fried—fried a long time ago—assaulted her nose.

A door on her left showed an inked-on number one. Narrow stairs rose from the right side of the hall. Abby bowed her head over Justin, praying for enough strength to deal with John, and started up. She passed the second floor, each footstep sounding thunderous on the bare linoleum. Sweat broke out along her spine.

On the third floor, a short hall led to a door with a brass number three screwed to it.

For one moment, with her knuckles poised to knock, Abby thought she would lose her nerve and flee. Instead she rapped firmly.

Seconds passed. John didn't come to the door, but she heard movement inside. Narrowing her eyes and holding Justin more tightly, Abby knocked again.

Justin stirred and whimpered. She jiggled him. He needed a bottle. "John," she said aloud, "I'm not leaving until I see you." He wouldn't hear, but the sound of her own voice was reassuring.

This time she thudded on a door panel with the side of her fist and kept on banging until a shout came from inside.

"All right, all right. Hold it down, will ya?"

Abby kept thumping.

The lock clicked, and a slender wedge of raw yellow light outlined the small woman who stood before Abby. The long honey-blond hair was caught in trembling fingers as the woman pushed it back. The lush body inside a flimsy turquoise nightie didn't need any help from backlighting, but every curve was accentuated.

Only a strong, strong man would turn Marie Prince away on a cold night—or any night.

## Chapter Sixteen

"Stop it! Hold still!"

Abby had reached the second flight of stairs when John caught her. He trapped her against the wall, covering her with his body until Justin struggled and cried.

She pushed at his chest with one forearm, trying to keep his weight from the baby. "Get away," she gasped. "Let us go. Get away! You're hurting Justin."

"God, oh, God," John muttered, pulling back, but placing himself below Abby. "I can't let you leave like this. We're going to talk. You'll understand everything if you just listen for once."

Abby closed her eyes and slid to sit on a step, her body curled over Justin. "I already understand, John. There's nothing else to be said." She looked up and met his eyes steadily in the ghastly half-light seeping down from his apartment. "Nothing, except goodbye and don't ever come near us again."

He jammed his fingers into his mussed curls. A T-shirt ended an inch above the jeans he hadn't had time to snap. "Up, Abby," he ordered. She heard each rasping breath he took. "You came to see me, and you're going to."

In one motion, he stooped and swept her to her feet, and holding her with one arm, propelled her upward. Abby's mind cleared as they went, and the fear slipped away. The next minutes, or however long it took, would be tough, but she'd get through, and then John would be out of her life. Why wasn't she terrified? Abby didn't know why, but she was sure she and Justin would be safe.

John gripped her shoulders as they entered his apartment, clutching as if she were an animal trying to escape. She saw the dingy room that was his home: an unmade bed beneath the window, wallpaper that had once been sprigged with pink roses that were brown splotches now, pieces of furniture they'd once chosen and shared. A striped plastic curtain, pulled back and sagging free of several hooks, served as an enclosure for an ancient stove on legs and a free-standing sink. In one corner a door stood open to reveal a cramped bathroom.

"I'm sorry, Abby."

She jumped and glanced around. Marie, a long down coat wrapped over her nightgown, cowered behind John. Her lovely face, perfect even without makeup, shone unnaturally. Her green eyes seemed glued open and unblinking.

Abby shook her head. "You poor fool. He used me and used me. Did you think he wouldn't use you, too?"

Marie looked away. "I was alone. And John was alone. We both needed someone. I didn't go after him, Abby, honestly."

"Keep your mouth shut," John snapped and wrenched Marie from behind him, shoving her into a chair. "This is between Abby and me."

Fury burst inside Abby. "You're a bastard, John, a bullying bastard. I'll never know why you wanted me in the first place. I'm a bit bigger than most of the people you like to push around. "You conned Marie, didn't you? You played on her loneliness, then put her to work keeping tabs on me. But you're right about one thing—I don't understand why."

"Listen," John began.

Abby waved for him to be quiet. "How long have you and John been together?" she asked Marie. "Why would you do this to me—all the visits, the suggestions I give Justin up for adoption or give him to John—why?"

Marie spoke through her splayed fingers. "I don't live here, Abby. We just...we just...I loved him," she finished, and the tears started, sliding noiselessly from her still wide-open eyes. "We were together before you two ever met, remember? Then he didn't want me anymore. But it was all right, Abby; I never blamed you. I got over him until he came to me after he left you. He told me what I already knew: that you two weren't making it, that your marriage was ending. I never meant this to happen, but it did. If I could change it, I would."

"Did you ever go to sea?" Abby asked John. "Or have you been here all this time, knowing how tough things have been with me and doing nothing?"

He made as if to touch her, then dropped his arm. "I went out on a couple of short trips."

"But you knew I'd had to leave my job and I was short of money?"

"I couldn't do a damn thing about it." Sweat gleamed on his

unshaven face. "Look at this place. I'm not exactly rolling in green stuff. And with my mother...." He paused, bunching muscles in his jaw.

"What about your mother, John? She kept writing to my folks as if nothing was wrong, but her letters to us stopped. What did you tell her?"

He scowled. "I told her we'd moved and gave her this address. She thought I was doing okay, being a 'good boy.' And she kept on and on about 'when the baby's born' and how she could hardly wait to fly us all back there so she could see him."

Justin whimpered again, and Abby rocked him. "And that's what all this is about. Of course. If your mother finds out you left me—threw away your child—she may just cut off the little hand-outs you rely on. Why didn't I figure that out before?" She gave a hollow laugh. "I was going to ask where you got the money you've been throwing around for the past couple of weeks, but I don't have to. It's the money we were supposed to use for the trip to New York, isn't it?"

John didn't answer.

"You should have thought farther ahead," Abby continued. "You should have known your mother would never understand how you could give up a child—her grandchild. Now you think if you can patch everything up between us she never has to find out. Too late. As of today, my folks know. Your mother will have to know, too. I don't want to hurt her, and if I can manage it, she'll see Justin, but there's no way to save her from this."

"Don't tell her," John said urgently. "If you do, I'll never see another penny from her. She'll change her will."

Abby approached Marie. "What was your angle on wanting me to give up Justin? If you knew John was going to need the baby to keep milking his mother for money, why would you push for that? The adoption, I mean."

Marie hunched over, driving the heels of her hands into her eyes. "The baby was the tie between you. I was afraid he would bring you back together. I never knew about John hoping to get money from his mother. All I wanted was to see you remarried and happy and make sure there'd never be a reason for you and John to see each other. I dreamed everything would come right, and we'd all be happy."

She dropped her hands between her knees and laughed. "I am a fool, and I'm no damned good. But we all know that, don't we? Only I do care about you, Abby. You'll laugh at that one, and I don't blame you, but it's true. All my life I've loved people who didn't give a...didn't love me. Why I believed it, I don't know, but this time I actually thought a man wanted me for myself, and I grabbed for the love with both hands. But I never wanted to lose your friendship. We know what the winner takes—what does that leave the loser?''

''You never did get over John, did you? I didn't realize how much he meant to you all those years ago.'' A shaft of pity pierced Abby. ''I can't talk rationally about this now, Marie, but give it some time. I'm not a saint, but I understand loneliness.''

At a slight sound from John's throat, she turned to him. ''Marie wasn't taking anything I wanted anymore, John. She was wrong. Lord, she was wrong, but she deserves better than you.''

John didn't meet her eyes. He pulled Marie to her feet. ''It's time you went home,'' he said, and his voice shook. ''Abby and I have things to talk about.''

''Wrong,'' Abby retorted. ''You and I have nothing to talk about, ever. I'm going home.''

''You're not going anywhere,'' John said, keeping his body between Abby and the door.

A steady trembling started in her belly and legs. ''Back off, John. You've lost. Marie, get your things together, we're leaving.''

''Not you, Abby,'' John said. ''You and Justin stay with me, please.''

There was no threat here. This big, usually confident man, was deflating before her eyes. ''Forget it,'' Abby said, watching Marie gather her possessions and cram them into an overnight case. She pushed her bare feet into knee-high boots and zipped them.

John made no further attempt to make Abby stay. Her last impression of him was the defeated slope of his shoulders as he dropped to sit on the edge of the bed.

Within seconds, she stood on the sidewalk with Marie. ''Where's your car?''

''Over there,'' Marie nodded across the street. ''I don't know what to say, Abby.''

''Nothing now. Give us time. And, Marie—'' Abby gripped the other woman's hand briefly ''—try thinking of yourself as worth something, will you? Stop believing you don't have anything to offer another human being.''

Without a word, Marie hurried away, switching her case from one hand to the other, her boots scuffing.

"So long," Abby said, almost to herself, while she thought, *Goodbye, Marie.*

## Chapter Seventeen

What if he didn't come? What if he did and he was furious to find her here? Abby walked back and forth in the living room. Nick would come. He would. He'd left his lights on, so he couldn't have intended to be out long. And if he didn't want to see her, she'd leave. Simple. She shuddered. There was nothing simple about any of this.

She'd come straight from John's and used her key to get into Nick's condo. Justin, propped in his car seat on the rug, sucked his fist loudly. Abby didn't want to be feeding him if Nick…when Nick got home. She moistened her dry lips. It was late. Where could he be this late?

She was standing in the hall when she heard a key rattle the lock. "Nick," she whispered, and silent dread swelled in her head, and longing. She must be calm and rational, and—

Nick came in, his head down, and slammed the door behind him.

Abby's heart began a slow drumroll. "Hi, Nick. We came."

He dropped his key and grabbed her in one steely arm. "Where have you been?" His grip was so tight she could hardly breathe. He repeatedly smoothed back her hair while he searched her face. "Are you all right? Were you at John's? I've been out of my mind with worry."

Abby couldn't move. "How? Michael talked to you. He called you."

"I went to Michael's to talk. He told me you were upset. Then I came back here to wait for you. When you didn't show, I started out to find John, only I forgot I don't know where he lives. I was going to call Mike to find out." He half dragged her into the living room and pushed her onto the couch. "Are you all right? Did you go to John's?"

She nodded. "It wasn't easy, but it is over, Nick. Completely finished."

He gave her a long look before he turned away to crouch over

Justin. He lifted the baby and held him close. "Your boy needs some attention."

Nick wore the bright blue running pants she'd tried so often not to notice, and a baggy gray sweatshirt. Sitting behind him now, Abby made no attempt not to study his broad back, the way his shirt hung in folds at his slim waist and rode across solidly muscled hips. Every sinuous line in the long, strong legs showed through the clinging fabric of the pants.

He glanced around an instant before she could raise her eyes.

"You look great," he said, his voice barely audible.

Abby's cheeks heated. He knew she'd been assessing him. "So do you, Nick. I've missed you."

Nick regarded her steadily.

Why, when she needed to say something profound, did the air have to rush from her lungs and logical thought flee?

He sat on the arm of the couch and ruffled her short curls.

"Whenever you feel like it, Abby—if you feel like it—we'll talk." His tawny eyes, when they met hers, held his heart, and Abby felt a tightening low inside that was almost a blow.

"Is there anything to talk about, Nick?" she asked uncertainly.

"You said all we'd have to do was move in next door, and we came. If you still want us."

"I still want you." Nick slid down beside her. "You know I'll never stop wanting you."

He brought his face close to hers, and she shut her eyes, waiting for the pressure of his lips. "Do you know I can see those gray eyes of yours whenever I try to sleep?" His mouth brushed hers. "And feel your hair? I've reached out my hand expecting to find you beside me." The next kiss was harder, and Nick's tongue met Abby's.

Justin wiggled between them and wailed. "Ahh," Nick sighed, and she felt his breath. "You did warn me about this moment. He needs changing and a bottle."

Before she could react, Nick strode to lay Justin on the rug. Deftly he found a waterproof sheet in the bag and slid it under the kicking legs. "Is there a bottle in here somewhere?"

Abby shed her coat and went to the kitchen to warm a bottle of formula. By the time she returned to the living room, Nick was crooning to Justin, holding him high and punctuating his hum with kisses to a face crumpled with fury. While she watched from across the room, he fed the baby, stopping the greedy sucking at intervals, coping as expertly as she ever could.

"I think you actually enjoy him," she said when the bottle was empty. "I wish..." She mustn't say it.

"You wish?"

"Nothing."

"You were going to tell me something you wish, Abby. We've been through too much together for you not to be able to tell me anything that comes into your head."

She turned her back. "I almost said I wished Justin was your son."

"He almost is, sweetheart, in a way. Didn't you tell me just now that you'd come to me, like you said you would? Didn't that mean we're going to be married?"

Her skin was cold, then fiery. "If you're still sure we should. You don't owe me anything, Nick. Just because we talked about—"

"Shhh. Can we put Justin down on a regular bed in my spare room? Would he roll off?"

"Not if we make bolsters out of towels or something."

"Look at me, Abby."

Slowly she turned to him.

"Will you stay with me tonight? Sleep with me? I only—No, I don't only want to hold you: you know what I want. But if you're not ready, I'll settle for just having you with me."

Words formed but came slowly. "I'll...I'll stay with you." She should tell him so much. "Nick, I've dreamed about you, too. And imagined you with me, beside me. I was afraid I'd lost you."

"You couldn't. I'm one of those pests who won't stay gone."

They settled Justin in a makeshift bed, surrounded him with fat rolls of towels, and within moments he fell into an exhausted sleep.

Nick held Abby's hand and started for the living room. She pulled him to a halt, tried a smile that didn't quite work, and walked backward, leading him to his bedroom.

When they stood at the foot of his bed, Nick asked, "Do you want to get some of your things?", and his voice broke.

"I don't need anything," Abby managed. "I came to you whole, the way you said I had to."

His gaze swept slowly over her, and she blushed.

"Oh, just a minute." Nick squeezed her hand before reaching to open a closet. "Remember the coat I said I wanted to buy you? I did buy it while I was in Omaha. I hope you like the thing. It can be changed if you don't." He was rushing now, filling the awkward moments for her. "I was going to give it to you when I got back, but—"

Abby caught both of his wrists. "Nick, you don't have to worry about me. This is where I want to be, with you, totally with you."

He looked at her, desire straining every feature tight. "God, I'm afraid to let go, Abby. I'm only a man, and I've wanted you for so long."

She ran her fingers into his hair, reached up, pressing close and kissing him with all the pent-up passion she'd suppressed for too long. Their mouths met again and again and with force. Tongues sought, breath became one breath, and it was Abby who grasped Nick's hips, clamping his hard body to hers.

He arched back, his eyes closed. "We've got to be careful, Abby. It's soon for you, maybe too soon."

She wanted to argue. Instead, she broke away and walked to the far side of the bed. Her eyes riveted on Nick's, she took off her sweater. Self-consciousness thickened her fingers as she unbuttoned the silvery silk blouse she wore.

"Is this too soon?" Nick asked. "We don't have to push." She heard him swallow. "Maybe I belong on the couch for a few nights."

Abby shook her head and undid the impossibly tiny buttons at her cuffs. When the blouse lay on a chair, she stood very still, aware of the rise and fall of her breasts. Reaching back, she undid her lace bra and let it fall.

"God, Abby," Nick said, "you're lovely. I knew you would be."

He pulled the sweatshirt over his head, and Abby felt the last vestige of air sucked from her lungs. His body showed the lean conditioning of an athlete. Broad shoulders, well-muscled chest, a dark shadow of hair fanning wide before it narrowed to a diminishing V at his waist.

Abby felt her breasts swell and flush. She unzipped her skirt, kicking aside her shoes, and slid off the rest of her clothes. Instinctively she covered her stomach, certain it must still carry the signs of pregnancy.

"Don't," Nick whispered. "Don't hide any part of you from me. You are so beautiful." He leaned on the bed to untie his shoes before stripping away the running pants.

Abby laid trembling fingers against her lips and waited until he stood inches from her. His back was straight, his stance unconscious and comfortable with the honest display of his desperate need for her. He kept his arms at his sides while she looked at him. She wanted to tell him it was he who was beautiful, he who was perfect. But speech was impossible.

"Sit by me," he said, throwing back the quilt and covers and sinking down. He smoothed the sheet beside him and offered his hand.

Abby lifted her hand, held it out until Nick threaded their fingers together. When she sat, she was half facing him, their hands still joined, her thigh pressed to his.

Nick tipped up his jaw, the tendons in his neck flexing, and she kissed him there, kissed the dip above his collarbone and followed unyielding muscle to touch her tongue to an instantly erect nipple.

"You must be tired, Abby," he said hoarsely. His chest rose and fell, and he turned her hand over his heart. Rapid thudding met her sensitive fingers. "Are you?"

Abby shook her head, smiling. "I've never been more wide-awake."

She pulled her knees onto the bed and moved behind him. "You're tense, my darling. You don't have to be. I'm not made of glass." Her fingertips found the bunched muscles in his shoulders and kneaded. And a kiss followed each delving pressure.

"Oh, Abby, you aren't going to be safe if you don't stop that," Nick murmured, bracing his weight on his hands.

Abby guided the back of his head against her neck, deliberately pressing her breasts into his shoulders until he groaned and twisted, pushing her onto her back. "Don't you understand what I'm asking you? Shouldn't we wait longer before we make love?" Bright color rose to his cheeks, and Abby couldn't hold back a grin.

"You're wonderful, Nick Dorset. I'm in perfect shape. The doctor says so. And if you keep this up, I'll think you don't want to."

His mouth on her breast made her back arch away from the bed. "I want to, ma'am. You don't know how much I want to. But I won't risk hurting you." His lips closed over first one nipple and then the other, and Abby's brain began to disconnect. She felt his teeth, his tongue, the rough texture of his chest hair, on every part of her body. The thigh that parted hers was rock hard, and the hands that caressed her were gentle.

The skin at his sides was smooth, and on his shoulder blades, where a thin film of sweat formed. His hair smelled clean and felt vibrant. "You're not going to hurt me. I'm ready for you," she whispered against his ear. "Now."

Nick supported his weight on his elbows, staring down into her face. He bowed his head to look at her breasts before he slid lower to kiss them, smooth them and pass his mouth over each rib until he kissed her belly repeatedly, making a line down, steadily down between her legs.

"No," Abby said, but faintly. He reached up to cover her breasts, rotated his palms slowly until she arched her pelvis against him. Her skin and flesh and blood were on fire. She heard a cry, her own, but distant and strange, before she thrust her hips helplessly up to meet the searing in her body and fell back, throbbing.

He lay unmoving for seconds, his cheek resting on her stomach, his hands clasping her hips. Then, slowly, he slid upward, retracing the kisses over her sensitive skin, until his mouth found her breasts again, and then her mouth.

"I love you, Nick," Abby managed at last.

Nick murmured something unintelligible. His breathing speeded, and he moved more urgently against her.

Closing her eyes tightly, Abby used all her strength to push him onto his back and slide her body on top of his. She reached to touch and stroke, missing no part of him until she caressed his most intimate places. "My turn," she said, and wondered at the sound of her own voice—the husky voice of a woman she didn't know.

"Oh, my sweet," Nick groaned when she sat astride his hips, "for a quiet lady, you're something."

Abby laughed softly as she joined them and moved them with an intense fervor she was powerless to stem. They turned onto their sides as one, rolling again. Abby wrapped her legs around Nick, looked up into his eyes and saw them glaze before all thought ceased.

When he slumped on top of her, she tasted damp salt on his skin, smelled the scent of their loving. "I love you, Nick," she heard herself say on a long breath. She sighed. "I keep saying that."

He shifted his weight and pulled her tightly into his arms. "You couldn't say it too often. And you couldn't love me as much as I love you. But I'll take as much as you've got. Did I hurt you? It was too fast, wasn't it?"

She laughed and cried, and clutched his flexing arms. "Yes, I can love you as much as you love me, and I'll give you everything I've got to give, and no, you didn't hurt me, and no, it wasn't too fast."

"Mmm." Nick peered into her eyes. "You'd better not be trying to fool me."

Abby stroked his tousled hair. "I wouldn't dare."

Abruptly Nick plumped up two pillows and sat against them, cross-legged. He maneuvered Abby's head onto his belly. "Let's get serious."

She kissed the taut skin beneath his navel. "I thought we were being very serious."

"You know what I mean. Justin's going to need a house with a yard. Plenty of room to run around in. We'd better start looking for a place."

"You want to discuss this *now?*" Abby peered disbelievingly up into his face. He gazed intently into the distance, and she groaned. "You do want to discuss it now. Okay. But Justin can't even turn over properly yet. All he needs is a crib and food."

"Kids grow up fast. We have to make plans."

"Of course," she agreed demurely. "But I'm going to have to get a job to help with a big expense like a house."

Nick frowned and looked away.

"What's the matter?" Abby sat up to face him. "Is something wrong, Nick?"

"I can't tell you what to do. Knowing you're going to be with me has to be enough."

"What aren't you saying?"

He kissed the corner of her mouth and stroked her cheek, pulling away to look acutely into her eyes. "Would it be so terrible to give Justin the time he needs with his mother—for a while, at least? I'm not suggesting you give up your career altogether, but a baby needs his own parents around as much as possible...I mean, his mother." He looked slightly confused.

"No," Abby said thoughtfully. "It wouldn't be at all terrible to stay with Justin. And if you feel awkward about behaving like one of his parents, don't. As far as I'm concerned, you are. You're taking us both on. But that doesn't mean I have to be a dead weight on you, financially."

"I can afford to keep a family, Abby. Later, if you want to go back to work—when our kids are older—fine."

"*Kids?*"

He smiled faintly and stroked her breast.

Abby felt an instant rekindling of desire. "I do want to have more children, Nick. How could I not with a man like you around to supervise?"

He rolled her tenderly onto her back and stretched beside her. "I want you to be happy, that's all. And I don't think you'd be happy if you left Justin too soon, okay?"

"Okay," she agreed slowly.

"So we'll take the work thing one day at a time, okay?"

"One day at a time. Nick—"

"Yeah?"

"My folks know about you."

"What do they think?"

"Well, my mother wondered how I'd had a chance to fall in love with a stranger."

He laughed against her breast, nuzzled the sensitive skin and wrapped a heavy thigh over both of hers. He looked pensive.

Abby pulled a pillow under her arm and propped up her head. "What are you thinking about, Nick?"

He outlined the contours of her body. "I was thinking we'd better get married fast—like immediately."

"Why the hurry?"

Nick brought his lips close to hers. "Because I want your folks to see us legally hitched before they figure out I'm no stranger."

# WEDDING BELL BLUES

## HEATHER GRAHAM POZZESSERE

Prologue

As long as she lived, Kaitlin would never forget the day Brendan asked her to marry him. A wedding, a beautiful wedding with a white gown and all the trimmings, had been a dream of hers all her life.

And through the past three years, the dream had always included Brendan.

He proposed with style. With the same style that had attracted her from the beginning, with the handsome appeal and charisma that had swiftly and surely convinced her that it was not puppy love, with the tenderness that had proved to her that there was much, much more between them than young passion and, as her mother warned, growing hormones.

No, she was in love with him.

And he was in love with her. The forever kind of love, the "'til death do us part'' kind of love. A lifetime of commitment, of vows, of promises, pure and bright and shining forever.

In years to come she would remember the night and the picture they made together. He had reached his full height of a solid six foot two, and his shoulders were powerful and squared, and still he seemed lean, both mature and youthful. And with the straying lock of ebony hair that fell over his eyes, he was handsome enough to attract the attention of women of all ages. She had known that she was shining that night, too. Shining with excitement.

She had always been delighted that he was hers. The quarterback of the high school football team, the captain of the debating team, somehow managing to convey a certain sexy wildness while maintaining an average very close to a perfect 4.0. And from the moment they had met, their eyes locking despite the length of the hallway between them, their relationship had seemed fated.

She'd known who he was, of course. Everyone at school did. And he had smiled. Slowly. With cocky assurance. And his gold-flecked emerald gaze had swept the length of her. That had been slowly, too.

And then he had turned away, with utter confidence. She would be there when he was ready for her, the gesture seemed to say.

Kaitlin had never had any intention of being anyone's easy conquest. And neither did she need to be. From her grandmother she had inherited her rich, beautiful strawberry blond hair. Hair that rippled and waved down the length of her back, soft and abundant. She had her grandmother's startling blue eyes, too, light, crystalline and clear. And her Irish complexion, soft and creamy, with rose-tinted cheeks. She was her mother's daughter, too, determined, bright, savvy…and nicely built.

So at the first dance of the year, she was a flirt. A terrible flirt. She laughed outrageously. She moved as if she was dancing on air. She teased the boys mercilessly but grandly, and…

And she kept her eyes on Brendan. But he didn't come near her. Not until the last dance was announced, and then she was suddenly in his arms, and he was staring at her.

"Are you happy, Kaitlin? That whole pack of lost puppies is over there tripping over their hanging tongues. You've set their self-confidence back a decade."

"Oh, have I?" she challenged him. But something in his eyes was very serious, even though he was still offering her his slightly mocking smile. "I was dancing, that's all. Enjoying the night."

"Teasing every guy here to distraction."

"Really? Well, if you don't mind, then, Brendan, let me go, and I won't be teasing anyone any longer."

He shook his head. "No more, Kaitlin. You're with me now because you want to be. Because you want me."

She had smiled disdainfully at his sheer effrontery. "I want you? Don't be so certain."

"But I am. You'll always go after what you want, Kaitlin. And right now, you want me."

"You're awfully egotistical, Brendan O'Herlihy—" she began. Then his lips were suddenly on hers, and he kissed her. The kind of kiss she'd never dared imagine. Open-mouthed, hot, demanding, coercive, a kiss that stole her breath away. She could barely hear the music; she could barely stand. She forgot what she had been saying.

Then the kiss ended, and when she looked into his eyes, she knew that her world had changed. He smiled again, gently. Assured, mature, certain.

"You're where you belong right now," he told her softly. "And it's where you're staying."

''But I—I might be teasing you,'' she stammered.

He shook his head. ''No. Because whatever you promise me, Kaitlin, you will give.''

She had meant to jerk away from his arms, but she never did. She met his eyes, saw the challenge there, and they danced until long after the music had stopped.

From that moment on, they were one.

Oh, they fought. She *was* something of a flirt, and he was possessive and had a rather infamous temper. And she was jealous. Jealous as she had never thought she could be in her life. But there was no one quite so fascinating. No one quite so startlingly handsome. No one with enough casual, masculine charm to sweep away an entire class. Girls liked Brendan. She knew that half her classmates—half of her good ''friends''—were just waiting for them to break up so they could have a chance at him.

But despite the wild fights and her continual determination to prove that she was her own woman, they never did split up. Not for a weekend. Not even for a day.

By her eighteenth birthday they had been together for three years. For the occasion, Brendan had rented a small suite at an old hotel in the country. He had ordered up dinner and even thought to see that there were flowers and candles on the table, and that everything was as elegant as possible.

She had worn a strapless sea-green satin dress, and they had shared a bottle of white wine across the candlelit table.

And then he had stood up and taken her into his arms. She had known, on that night, that they were going to make love.

Everyone who had dated as long and as steadily as they had had already done so. Her interest had certainly been piqued; she was both eager and scared. She'd heard stories from her friends about awkwardness and pain and frenzied groping—and the back seats of old cars.

But she should have known that it would be nothing like that with Brendan.

His kiss was something she already knew well. Deep and searing, hot and passionate, soul-stealing. And the exquisite, shivery feeling as his lips moved down the length of her throat was also something she knew.

But always before, there had been a certain restraint.

Not this night.

She was swept into his arms and carried through the living area of the suite to the bedroom, where he placed her on the queen-size bed. He lay down beside her and kissed her again, then showered her shoulders with searing tongue strokes that left her quivering in their wake.

At last he found the zipper of the sea-green dress and slid it down. And where the material of the dress parted, the lightest caress of his lips followed. She never quite realized how, but suddenly the dress was gone, and then he just stopped and stared at her, drawing his breath in very sharply before he touched her. Her lacy strapless bra was shell pink, as were her panties and her elegant little garter belt. He had seen her in less, actually, since he had seen her in the half dozen bikinis she had owned over the past few years. But it didn't seem to matter when he moved again and whispered that the garter belt was the sexiest thing he had seen in his entire life. Then he tossed aside her shoes, and she was amazed when he clutched her foot and teased her flesh through her sheer stocking, massaging, kissing her arch and then her ankle, the length of her calf, the back of her knee and along her thigh, before stripping the stocking away. And when he repeated the process with her other leg, she found herself shivering as if she was frozen, even while her skin was flaming from his touch.

She was hot. Hot as she had never been in all her life, barely able to keep still, to think, to comprehend. There would be nothing for her tonight except sensation...touch...the feel of his lips against her naked flesh.

Once her stockings were gone, her bra was next. He nuzzled her breasts tenderly and gently, and then he told her that he had been wrong before. The garter belt was something, but nothing in the world was as erotic as her breasts. He kissed each one in turn, starting slowly, then moving inward with erotic, soft flicks of his tongue until he surrounded the hardening rosy center and swept it into his mouth, creating a startling fire that left her moaning and thrashing restlessly beside him.

It burned deep in the center of her, hot and aching, there, at the juncture of her thighs.

Always he touched her, always he seared her. Kissed and whispered. The garter belt came next, and then the shell-colored lace panties. And his touch moved closer and closer to the fire, until he stroked the flame itself, igniting her, causing her to cry out in soft, incomprehensible whispers. He rose to remove his own clothing, and in the shadows he was magnificent, tall and broad-shouldered, lean and hard, and when he lay beside her, he was all hot, rippling muscle, smooth and sleek and beautiful. And he was more. He was the man she loved. Had loved for all these years. And she knew that she would love him forever.

His body moved over hers, and she gasped, startled at the feel of him.

She had thought she knew him so well....

But she hadn't quite known this part of him. Huge, throbbing, arrogant against the bare flesh of her thigh, threatening, promising, warm against the gates of her femininity.

But she did know his voice. Heated, intense, passionate. Encouraging...telling her that she should touch him, too.

She did so, nearly crying aloud at the vital heat of him. And then she was burying her face against his shoulder, amazed that when she had touched him, the fire within her had grown. She ached. She wanted him. She needed him.

But he waited. Waited for the words of need to come tearing from her throat. And when they did, he entered at last. Slowly, carefully, tenderly. When the first startled cry of pain came to her lips, he whispered and held still, then slowly moved again. Kissing her. Touching her. Until the delicious feelings returned again. Until the ache became a drumbeat, a pounding, a pulse. Something nearly desperate. So sweet and searing that it was agony, and so exquisite that it was ecstasy. She felt herself climbing, flying, reaching the clouds, where at last the sweetness exploded within her like the bursting of the sun in the sky. Hot, melting rays swept through her body, filling her with molten honey and sensations of love and warmth beyond anything she had ever imagined.

The heat, she thought, was him. Filling her. And it was wonderful, because she knew that she had not reached that searing splendor alone, that she had been everything he had wanted, that he had filled her, been a part of her, and would be, from now until forever.

Even afterward, it was beautiful. He pulled her close into his arms and held her tenderly, smoothing back her damp hair and whispering softly that he loved her.

The night was still young, and it became a time for explorations. They bathed together, and made love in the shower. She began by pressing sensual kisses against his chest, nipping at his shoulders and back, and stroking his hard, muscled buttocks as the shower cascaded over them. Even when they were ready to leave, they couldn't quite bear it. She wrapped her arms fiercely around his neck, and he backed her against the wall, lifting her until she locked her legs around him, and they made love right there, standing up. And it was as passionately fulfilling as before.

She would never be the same, she knew. Never.

He had told her many times through the years that he loved her. But now, somehow, that love seemed so complete. They had shared the secret of their intimacy. No one could know the depths of their love.

It was two weeks later that he asked her to marry him. And he did it with the same careful thought and love and tenderness.

They were out with her family, at the annual spring dinner in Petersham, and he had led her out to the porch, where they could be alone. He'd seated her on the wicker swing, and the rich beauty of the new season surrounded them. There were birds above them in the trees, and flowers everywhere. The breeze was soft and caressing, and sunlight poured down upon them.

To her amazement, he was suddenly on his knees. Brendan, so handsome in his suit, so masculine, and grinning just a little, was kneeling as he took her hands in his. She trembled, remembering what it was like to make love with him, and he spoke the words that were so simple, so traditional.

"Kaitlin, I love you. And I want you to be my wife. I want us to spend our lives together. Will you marry me?"

She stared at him, her eyes growing wider and wider, and then she screamed and threw her arms around him. She didn't care whether anyone came on them while they were kissing so passionately, out there on the porch. Not her little cousins, not her mother, not even her father.

But no one came out. And eventually they were sitting together on the swing, and he flicked open a jewel case.

It held a diamond ring.

It wasn't huge, but it was the most beautiful ring Kaitlin had ever seen. The stone was set in a simple gold scroll, and Brendan explained that the wedding ring would surround it, completing the design, two entwined roses.

He slipped the ring on her finger, and she leaned back, unable to stop admiring it, and rested her head on his shoulder.

Then they started to dream.

College was ahead of them, but Brendan wasn't worried about that. He had earned a scholarship to the school of marine biology in Miami, and, beyond that, he had a trust fund that his bootlegging grandfather had left him. And her parents would be willing to help, too; college had always been important to them. Of course, they would both work, too, preferably on campus. They would manage. They would manage very well.

She wasn't concerned about the future, although she knew her father would be. But her father liked Brendan, had always liked him. He liked the fact that Brendan had only touched liquor sparingly, and he liked the fact that Brendan had always seemed to listen and weigh and watch before coming to a decision. Her parents wouldn't mind. They would understand.

It was the immediate future that fascinated Kaitlin.

"Oh, Brendan! Can we have a big wedding? Everyone in both our families? Everything?"

He laughed. "I think you're more excited about the prospect of the wedding than you are about being married. But we'll have whatever you want. You've always known how to smile and tease and come after whatever you want, Kaitlin."

"All I want is you."

"And the biggest wedding in the world."

She shook her head and touched his cheek; her eyelashes were damp. "No! I can't think of anything that I'd rather do than wake up beside you every day of my life. But I'll never forget my Aunt Gwen's wedding. It was the most beautiful thing I'd ever seen. She had three flower girls and five bridesmaids, and there were flowers and candles everywhere, and they wrote their own vows, and she was so beautiful in that white wedding gown. Oh, Brendan, I want it all, the train halfway down the church, the music and the flowers—especially the flowers!"

He hugged her tight. "It's fine with me. Except that I think I'd better work this summer, then. I'm not sure your parents can pay for all that, even if you are an only daughter." He smiled, and she laughed and promised that she intended to work hard, too. After all, it was her dream.

But he was still Brendan. The Brendan she had fallen in love with, the one she had battled and adored for what already seemed like her entire life. He was her secret lover, her pride, her delight. And she knew the depth of his love for her.

"We'll have everything," he promised her. "Everything you want. The long white gown with a train so long the guests will have to be careful not to trip on it. And we'll have champagne, and candles, and most of all, we'll have flowers. So many flowers that we'll be smelling them for the first ten years of our marriage."

"And I'll be your wife, and I'll take your name, and we'll live happily ever after," she vowed in return.

Brendan spoke to her father, and they announced their engagement that very night.

They even managed to slip away alone together, for at least an hour, to a beautiful old inn on the Vermont side of the border. As they made love, they spoke of their love again. He promised to love her forever, and she vowed that she would always be there for him.

And he meant the promise that he made to her. He meant to give her everything. Just as she meant to keep her vow.

But fate did not intend for it to be.

In time, she would take his name.

But she was not going to walk down the aisle in a long white gown.

Nor were they going to live happily ever after.

Often, in the years ahead, Kaitlin would be glad of that time. She would look back on the girl she had been, on the broken promises and shattered dreams. And she would think, *At least I had that day.*

And the really funny, yet horribly painful, thing was that she still loved him.

The shining glimmer of love, of that dream, would never quite go out.

Chapter 1

*Twelve years later...*

The fact that Kaitlin first misunderstood her grandmother was entirely her own fault.

They had gone out to breakfast together, just as they did every Wednesday morning. But the Seashell Sunblock commercial presentation had to be given to the company VIPs that afternoon, and even though Kaitlin was prepared, she was restless. This was her own ad agency, and the account was a very important one. And the verdict had just come in on a particularly scandalous assault trial and she couldn't help but notice the headlines on the *Miami Herald*, so she was reading the story out of the corner of her eye when Gram first spoke.

"Kaitlin, I'm going to be mur—"

Mur—and something garbled. It didn't help any that after fifty years in this country Gram still spoke with a brogue so strong it could be sliced clean through with a knife.

Mur-something. Gram was going to be mur-somethinged. That was all Kaitlin heard. She looked up, but Gram was looking down. It had sounded very much as if she had said, "Kaitlin, I'm going to be murdered."

Murdered. Well, it was natural that Gram would be nervous. She was nearly seventy, and alone. She had refused to live with Kaitlin, who had offered her separate living quarters on her own property. Gram liked the condominium where she lived; the building was filled with other active retirees. She missed children, of course. Gram loved children, and she missed them when she was in Florida. But she went north every winter to spend the holidays with the family. She had ten great grandchildren, aged eight months to eighteen years, to greet her lovingly on each visit. Gram was precious to all of them. She was their link; she was, in essence, the Ireland of their ancestry. She told wonderful stories, and when Kaitlin had been a little girl, Gram had her really believing in leprechauns and convinced that if men practiced evil deeds, the banshees, the wailing death ghosts of Eire, might really come for them.

So, with her brogue, she was difficult to understand at best. But then, that big hairy German shepherd of hers had eaten her best set of teeth, and Gram hated the new ones, said they didn't fit right.

So she was afraid of being killed. There had been a rash of robberies—home invasions, they called them now—and it was natural that she should be frightened.

"Oh, Gram!" Kaitlin said. She took Gram's hands in her own. "Now, listen to me. You are not going to be murdered. This is a very scary world that we live in, but you're really not going to be murdered. Gram, if you want, you can come and stay with me, just for a while—"

"And I'll be damned if I do, that I will!" Gram said, her tone surprised—and her words startlingly clear. She was still such a beautiful woman, small, with brilliant blue eyes. **And** she kept her hair a very attractive silver-blue color. She still looked as sweet as a saint, and to hear such a statement come so explosively from her seemed quite an irony.

"But if you're afraid of being murdered—"

"I didna say 'murdered,' Kaitlin O'Herlihy. I didna. You didna listen to me."

Kaitlin folded her hands on the table. She tried not to glance at her watch; she would be at work in plenty of time, and this—whatever it was—seemed important to her grandmother. She lowered her head, smiling with a certain relief. "I'm sorry, Gram. What were you saying?"

"Kaitlin, I'm going to be married. Not murdered—what did you think, that I'd become a hysterical old recluse? Married, Kaitlin. Married."

"Married!"

Kaitlin couldn't have been more stunned if her grandmother had been absolutely certain that she was going to be murdered in the next five minutes.

Married…

Gram, married?

She'd been a widow for nearly forty years. She'd raised five children on her own in a new country, and she'd gone these many, many years without even dating.

And now she was going to be married.

Kaitlin's jaw wouldn't quite work. Then she managed to repeat the word. "Married?"

"Married, young lady. Aye, now you've heard me right," Gram said with a sigh. "And shut your mouth, love. People will start staring at us."

Kaitlin didn't know whether to smile or laugh or worry. Then she managed to say, "But, Gram, you haven't even been dating—"

"Oh, but I have. And I didna say a word to you or your mother or any of your cousins, because I didna intend to take the likes of the teasin' you'd all be givin' me. But I've been seeing Mr. Rosen every week at bingo for over a year now. And we've been meeting Sunday night for dinner, and going to the theatre and movies and—"

"Rosen? Gram, is he a Jewish gentleman?"

"Aye, that he is. And don't you be sayin' a word about it to me, Kaitlin O'Herlihy. At me age, it just don't seem to matter anymore. He's got a beautiful house by the water, and we're going to move into it. And we'll have Hanukkah candles and a Christmas tree, and don't ye dare be sayin' a word to me about it, eh, Kaitlin?"

She was going to laugh. She was going to burst into laughter. She could remember how terrified they had all been to go to Gram and tell her that Kaitlin's cousin Mary Elena was going to marry outside the church—and Lance Hendricks was merely a Lutheran.

"Kaitlin—" Gram warned.

She caught her grandmother's hands again. "Gram, I'm delighted."

And then the tough determination that had brought her through many years of hardship left Gram's eyes, and a charming, girlish uncertainty filled them. "Are you certain, Kaitlin? Will the family mind? I've not even told me sons and daughters yet."

"They'll be thrilled," Kaitlin promised her. And then she laughed again. "Gram, you little devil, you. All this activity, and we didn't know a thing. It's wonderful. Absolutely wonderful. When is the big occasion? And when do I get to meet Mr. Rosen?"

"This weekend, for dinner, Kaitlin. I thought that maybe you wouldn't mind having something small at your house."

Kaitlin grinned. "Not a bit. I'll be delighted. When is the wedding?"

"Two weeks from now. At the Lotus Gardens. Justice of the Peace Merkin has promised to wed us, and both Rabbi Nathan and Father Tangini have promised to bless the ceremony."

"How wonderful!"

"Aye, Kaitlin. And I'm countin' on you, girl, that I am. Will you stand by me?"

"Be your witness?"

"My maid of honor."

"Oh, Gram, of course! But what about your daughters, or your friends——"

"You're family, Kaitlin. Me daughters will understand. You're the one who's looked after me down here all these years, don't ye be denyin' it. I want you with me when I wed Mr. Rosen. Will you stand for me?"

"Of course! I'd be honored, Gram! I'll charge right into it. The Lotus Gardens! It will be beautiful. Have you chosen a dress yet?"

For the remainder of the meal they planned a night to shop for dresses, then a night to go by the florists, then a day to find the proper cake.

Kaitlin was thrilled, although for a moment it was there—a tiny little jab of pain in the center of her heart. It always came, despite the pleasure she often felt for others. She loved weddings, but things just... Sometimes they just still hurt.

Then the pain ebbed away. She'd never been bitter and she'd never been jealous. And she loved Gram almost as deeply as she loved her own mother. This was funny, sweet, charming—and wonderful. Nothing in the world seemed quite as wonderful as getting to help plan her grandmother's wedding.

Kaitlin forgot her commercial until she happened to glance at her watch. Then she was truly sorry that she was going to have to leave. "Gram, where can I drop you? I've got to get to work."

Gram didn't want to go anywhere; she wanted to stay in the mall and maybe buy "a wee bit of new under-type things." Kaitlin smiled, kissing her goodbye and watching her disappear into a throng of shoppers. She looked great, Kaitlin decided. Truly radiant. Just like a bride. A beautiful woman with those ageless eyes and her wonderful peaches-and-cream complexion. And after all these years...

Kaitlin seemed to float in to work on her grandmother's euphoria. Janis Epstein, her assistant, was waiting in her office, gathering together the storyboards for the presentation. "Hey, boss," Janis grinned. "I thought you'd be early today. Worried, chomping away at those nails of yours."

Kaitlin made a face and set her handbag beneath her desk. "Janis, guess what?"

"What?"

"My grandmother is getting married."

Janis's brows shot up with surprise, then she laughed. "Married! I didn't even know she'd been out on a date!"

"Neither did I," admitted Kaitlin. Janis handed her a cup of coffee, and she sat in her chair for a moment, telling Janis all about her grandmother's plans.

Janis clicked her tongue. "Can you imagine? All of us, supposedly in our primes—or semi-primes, at least!—out there looking for Mr. Right, and Lizzie Boyle sweeps him right out of a bingo game. Can you imagine?"

Kaitlin grinned and admitted that it was tough to picture.

Then Janis jumped up. "Hey, we've got about ten minutes before we need to show up in the boardroom."

"Um. And face Mr. Harley," Kaitlin admitted. "I'm rushing into the ladies. I just need two seconds."

The "ladies" was actually her private bath in the corner of her office. She went in quickly, drawing her brush from her handbag even as she did so. In the mirror above the handsome marble sink, she surveyed her reflection. Not bad, she reflected. Not when she had turned the corner this year and celebrated her thirtieth birthday just a month ago.

She smiled suddenly, wondering if she would grow old like Gram. Maybe she would, with luck. She still possessed a headful of wild strawberry blond hair, thick, wavy hair that curled around her shoulders and halfway down her back. Today it was all neatly tied into a French braid, to complement her deep maroon paisley skirt and loose blouse. It was an outfit that was all business but still very feminine. Her eyes, she thought, were her best feature, wide and light blue. She had Gram's skin, too. Maybe she *would* age well. So far, she assured herself, she hadn't done too badly for thirty. The company was hers. Eventually she wanted to make Janis a partner, just so that she could have more spare time. She had a good reputation in the business, and she worked very hard and loved it.

The only thing that she didn't have at thirty, the only thing... Was anything that resembled a personal life, she told herself dryly.

Well, she reminded herself, she hadn't wanted a personal life, had she?

She smoothed back the loose strands of hair over her forehead and applied a little lipstick, then decided that she was as presentable as she was going to be.

She turned out the light and headed back through her office. She was just about to leave the room when she heard her personal line buzz. She picked up the receiver to tell Samantha that she'd have to call whoever it was back, but before she could say anything, Samantha spoke quickly.

"It's your cousin Donna from Massachusetts. She says she just needs two seconds. Is that all right?"

"Yeah, fine, thanks, Sam." She pushed the extension button on the phone. Donna would understand her need for haste, and if she wanted to say something, it must be important.

"Donna, hi, me. I am in a hurry, but—"

"I know, I know. Seashell Sunblock, right?" Donna didn't wait for an answer; she plunged on. "Kaitlin, I'm getting married."

"Married?" Kaitlin gasped. Married, the same as Gram had told her. Donna had all her teeth—there was no mistaking the word for "murdered" this time.

Kaitlin shut her mouth. How many times had she already said that word—and as stupidly—today? She recovered much more quickly this time. "Oh, Donna, that's wonderful. Congratulations."

"Thanks."

"Bill?" Kaitlin asked hesitantly. The last time she had spoken with Donna, they had been going through a rocky patch, even though they were both great people. Kaitlin had known Bill Piccolo all her life and liked him very much.

Bill would have been in her own wedding. If there had been a real wedding.

The little jab of pain was sharper this time. She exhaled and willed it away.

"Yes, Bill, who else?" Donna said. Then she rushed on. "I just wanted to tell you now because I couldn't stand waiting. I'll let you go, and I'll talk to you tonight. Kaitlin, I want you to be my maid of honor. Will you think about it, please?"

"It's an honor. I don't need to think about it," Kaitlin assured her. "But when is it? We've got time, don't we? You're never going to believe this, but I'm standing up for someone else."

"Who?" Donna asked.

"Gram."

"Gram!" Donna shouted over the wires. "Gram?"

"Yes, Gram. Don't say anything, though. She just told me this morning, and I'm sure she wants to tell the aunts and uncles herself."

"Why, that little devil!"

"That's exactly what I said, and straight to her face!" Kaitlin agreed. "She's being married very quickly, though—she says she doesn't want to waste time at her age, or something like that. Anyway, she can tell you, which I'm sure she'll do."

"She'll get to her grandchildren after she makes it through all her children!" Donna laughed. "But no, we won't be married right away. We've got an awful lot of planning to do. Thanks for saying you'll be my maid of honor. Now hurry up, knock 'em dead, and I'll talk to you later. Oh, Kaitlin, I'm so excited!"

"Right, talk to you soon," Kaitlin promised, and hung up the phone.

But she didn't rush out of the room. Instead she stared at the receiver. First Gram and now Donna. It was wonderful. She loved both of them dearly. And they were both asking her to be a part of their joy.

She couldn't even blame it on the water. They didn't live in the same cities.

Seashell Sunblock, she reminded herself sternly. She marched out of her office and down the hall.

In the conference room, Mr. Garrett Harley, president and chairman of the board of Seashell Products, was already seated at the long mahogany table, with Tom Pinchon, his promotions man, and his sister, Netty Green, the VP.

"Good morning," Kaitlin greeted them all, sweeping into the

room with a broad smile. The storyboards were already set up in
the front of the room, and Janis had seen to coffee and ashtrays.
Garrett Harley, forty-five and broad as a barn, but smart as a whip
to have put Seashell Products where it was, grunted. Netty, older
and much, much thinner, murmured a thin-lipped reply, and Tom
nodded.

This was not a cheerful group, Kaitlin reminded herself. It
never had been. There wasn't going to be any light, comfortable
repartee in the room today, so she might as well plunge in. Janis
was standing in the back of the room, ready to give her silent
support. Kaitlin walked straight to the storyboard to make her
pitch.

"Mr. Harley, you told me that you want your new sunblock to
appeal to the young men and women flocking the beaches. Since
there's been so much publicity about the dangers of the sun, we
didn't want to concentrate on the product's tanning qualities, but
rather on its protective virtues."

"I told you to sell sex," Harley said. He looked at his sister
and said flatly, "Sex sells."

"Harley, I won't have anything lewd," Netty began irritably.

Kaitlin quickly interrupted her. "I think we have a commercial
that you'll both like very much. It's sexy, but not lewd, I promise." She flashed a smile to Netty, whose face didn't seem to
crack.

Harley, however, grinned broadly. "Let's see it."

Kaitlin showed them her first picture. "We've got a nice couple
on a beach. A really good-looking couple."

"Not kids," Netty protested.

"No, not kids," Kaitlin said. Then she grimaced inwardly at
the term she was about to use. "Yuppies. Late twenties, early
thirties. She's in a two-piece suit, as you see here—"

"Not one of those string things," Netty said.

"No, just a nice two-piece, a very decent bikini, I promise you.
I know just the suit I want—my artist has sketched it here, as you
can see." She pointed to the picture. "Now, Mr. Harley, this
couple may be a little bit older than what you first had in mind,
but they're very good-looking, and sexy. And old enough and
mature enough to be affluent, to vacation in the Caribbean and
Bermuda and Cozumel. So here they are, together on the beach.
And the narrator is saying, 'When you touch her this after-

noon…''' Kaitlin quickly moved on to the next picture, where the man was smoothing lotion over the woman's back. '''Touch her with Seashell Sunblock…''' Then she flipped another page, and the same couple was shown dancing beneath the moon, '''to be sure you can touch her tonight.'''

There was one last picture. Kaitlin flipped the page. The man was sweeping the woman into his arms and carrying her into an attractive hotel room. Sexy, but absolutely not explicit. Kaitlin had discarded idea after idea until she and Janis had come up with this one. And she was sure they had it just right.

But Harley was quiet for several long, long moments. Netty merely sat with her lips pursed, and it seemed that Tom didn't dare say a word until one of them spoke.

Then Harley slammed his hand against the table and pulled a plump cigar from his coat pocket. "I like it! By golly, I like it." He swung around to Netty. "Well, Netty?"

Kaitlin held her breath. Then Netty nodded slowly. "Except, of course, that I want to see these people when you've chosen the actor and actress. I don't want youngsters out there, truly, I don't."

"Netty, I promise, I'll make them both thirty," Kaitlin swore solemnly.

"And I want to see the bathing suit."

"I've got a picture in my office." She glanced at Janis, who didn't need to hear a word. She quickly left the conference room, and returned with the picture while they discussed media other than television and the way the campaign might be modified.

Netty seemed pleased, and Garrett Harley seemed pleased, so Tom seemed pleased, too. They shook hands all around.

Samantha brought in the contracts, which were promptly signed, and everyone shook hands again. And then finally—finally!—Harley and crew were gone.

"Blessed Mary!" Kaitlin exclaimed, falling back into the swivel chair at the head of the table, then hopping up to hug both Samantha and Janis. "We did it! No muss, no fuss. We've got it! The Seashell commercial! Sam, call Danny in here. We've got to celebrate. There's a bottle of champagne in my fridge—I bought it just in case. Get Danny, and we'll have a toast."

Sam, grinning, ran out. Danny was Kaitlin's artist, an amazing young man who could create beautiful illusions and more—he could understand everything going on in Kaitlin's mind and get it on paper.

Janis shook her head. "I don't believe we did it!" Then she wagged a finger at Kaitlin. "And you almost blew it. Boy, was Harley getting edgy when you didn't walk in here precisely on the hour. What happened? Nothing bad, I hope?"

"No. My cousin is getting married, too. Donna. In Massachusetts. And I'm going to be her maid of honor."

Janis arched a brow. "Your grandmother and your cousin, all in one day? Maybe it's in the water," she said, echoing Kaitlin's original thought. Then she sighed wistfully. "Wish I could drink some of that stuff."

"Don't you dare. I'm going to need you here. I'm going to have to go back and forth to Massachusetts a few times, I'm sure."

"Never fear, Janis is here," she teased. Then her eyes widened. "No, wait, go right ahead, fear away. Panic, in fact! You are going to see to this commercial shoot before you leave, right? Oh, please, say right!"

"We've got Harley in the bag, and I plan to shoot by the end of the week. I want to shoot right on the beach, and we'll use Addison's Resort. I've already made a few tentative arrangements. It's elegant and has beautiful rooms. I'll guarantee everything this afternoon. And I'll call the talent agency and reserve the models I want. I already asked for Mark Ford and Cissy Grissom. They should be perfect. This is going to be perfect. Perfect! I don't see a problem in the world."

And she believed it. When Danny came in, she hugged him fiercely, then managed a bit of a speech telling them all that they'd accomplished a tremendous coup, sweeping Seashell Products away from some really hefty competition.

That afternoon she was able to make all the arrangements, and that night, she took the whole crew to dinner, where she drank more champagne, forgetting until she got home that champagne gave her an awful headache.

In the morning, she awoke with too many memories.

So, Gram was getting married.

She, at least, was having the decency to go through a small and simple ceremony.

But Donna's wedding...

Donna's would be sumptuous. Kaitlin's beautiful, dark-haired cousin would make a stunning bride. She'd wear a long white gown, just as Kaitlin had always dreamed of doing.

Well, Kaitlin told herself, that dream was over now. She could never dress in white, that was certain. And she had no right to envy Donna; she had already been a bride. She'd never had the wedding of her dreams, but she *had* been a bride.

What were dreams, anyway?

Nothing but crystal illusions to be shattered. The wedding she and Brendan had promised one another had never come about. Brendan's cousin had been killed in an automobile accident, and the wedding had been called off.

That hadn't mattered then. To all of them, Sean had been all that mattered.

She would never forget going to see Brendan the day after Sean had died, and she would never forget the funeral. Brendan's cousin Sean would have been his best man; the two had been best friends forever. Brendan hadn't cried. He had just stood there in the pouring rain, in the gray of the day, staring at the coffin where Sean lay. She'd been there. At his side. She'd cried for Sean, and she'd cried again that night. Her father had held her and told her that that was the worst part of growing up, the death of love and friendship and innocence. The death of dreams. Meeting the reality of life.

For Brendan, it had been a death of innocence indeed. After that he hadn't wanted to see Kaitlin. He should have been clinging to her; she should have been comforting him. But no one could reach him.

And then she'd gone away to school, while Brendan had stayed at home. She'd never stopped loving him, but she hadn't been able to reach him. And when he had enrolled in January, he had been different. Brooding, quiet, angry. Always angry. But she hadn't stopped loving him....

He had hurt her, though, and she had wanted to hurt him in return. He'd said that he was ready to plan the wedding again, but even as she called the caterers and tried to make arrangements long distance, something was unraveling on her. They nearly lived together. They continued to make love, wildly, passionately. But she didn't seem able to touch him anymore.

And then one night he didn't show up when he was supposed

to. James Brager did, though. James was one of Brendan's best friends, and that night he was so sweet and so good to her that she found herself pouring out her heart to him. And then James kissed her. There was no passion in it, just friendship.

But Brendan, who had shown up at last, didn't see it that way.

She would never forget how his eyes had looked that night. Fierce. Burning. There had been something about his face that had reminded her of the day he had stood by the grave, at Sean's funeral. Another death of innocence, Kaitlin's father might have said. She could have given him an explanation, but Brendan didn't want it. Not after he'd walked in and found them together. His rage had been terrible, and the fight that followed even worse. The shouting, the things they said. Until he had tossed her on the bed and made love to her in a frenzy. She had fought at first, but then she had clung to him, praying that they could get back something of the love they'd known....

But they hadn't. He had left. And the next thing she knew, he had volunteered for the Navy.

And then she found out about the baby.

Kaitlin rose, ignoring her headache, suddenly more aware of the agony of memory than of any present pain. She staggered into the bathroom, took two aspirin and decided that she looked every bit of her thirty years. No, she looked more. Much, much more.

She called the office and said she would be late. Sam sounded unhappy—as if she wished she could have called in late, too.

Oh, well, there were some advantages to being the boss, Kaitlin thought.

She started perking coffee, planning the shoot in her head. Then the phone rang, and she answered it. It was another one of her cousins, this one local. Soon after Kaitlin had graduated, Barbara had come south and lived with her for several years before falling in love and eventually moving in with her beloved down the street. Joe was another transplant from Massachusetts, and he had gone to the university, then fallen in love with the sunlight and the South and stayed on. He was a musician with one bad marriage behind him, but Barbara stayed with him, believing in her heart that one day Joe would realize that she was a very different woman from his ex-wife, and marry her and raise a family with her.

They had been living together for six years. Kaitlin had to give

Barbara credit for tenacity. It had taken Joe two years to let her move in, another two for him to allow her to bring in any furniture. Now it seemed they were married, they were such a normal couple. They were happy, and Kaitlin knew that Joe really loved her cousin. He just had difficulty with the marriage idea.

"Hey, Barbara, how'd you know I'd be home?" Kaitlin asked.

"'Cause I called the office," Barbara said. There was an edge of excitement in her voice, but Kaitlin's head was pounding and she was busy plugging in the coffeepot, and she didn't hear it. "You delinquent," Barbara accused. "What did you do? Go out drinking champagne?"

"Precisely."

"You landed Garret Harley's account. Congratulations. And now, guess what?"

Kaitlin leaned against the kitchen counter. "I don't know, but don't tell me you're getting married."

There was silence on the other end.

"Barbara?"

Then she heard her cousin inhale and exhale. "But, Kaitlin," she said, and her voice sounded hurt, "I am getting married." Then all the tremendous excitement returned. "Kaitlin, believe it or not—finally!—he wants to get married. I thought you'd be ecstatic for me. I know you've been with me through thick and thin on this one. Kaitlin—"

"Wait, wait, wait!" Kaitlin said. "You're serious? Joe proposed?"

"Proposed, put a diamond on my finger and even got us a church date."

"Oh, Barbara! That's wonderful. I really am happy for you! It's just such a—a surprise."

Barbara giggled. "I guess it is. After the week you've already been having."

"You heard about Gram?"

"I have."

"She called you already?"

"No, Donna called me already. So I know about Gram. And Donna. And Donna knows about me. And I know that you're going to be her maid of honor, but I want you to be mine, too. You should be mine, actually. I mean, we live so close, it seems we spend half our lives together."

"I'd—I'd love to be your maid of honor, too. When is the wedding?"

The pang, the stupid little nasty pang, struck her again. Hard, this time. Like a knife right to the heart. She clenched her teeth and ignored it. No one deserved this kind of happiness more than Barbara. It was just that Joe and Brendan were friends, and thinking of one man made her think of the other, too.

The past seemed to be crashing down upon her.

Go away! she screamed in silence. Then the pain faded, and she was truly happy, happy for Barbara.

She listened to Barbara, trying to think. If Donna's wedding was in October and Barbara's was in November, it could work. She would just have to do a lot of running back and forth, but she loved them both. How could she turn down either one of them?

And then there was her grandmother...but that would be over very soon. While she was listening, she scratched a note on her wall calendar to buy something nice for dinner that weekend. If Gram loved this nice Mr. Rosen, than Kaitlin was going to do her best to make him happy, comfortable and well-fed.

"Well?" Barbara prompted.

"Everything sounds fine," Kaitlin told her. "Oh, Barbara! Finally! After all this time! And he really wants a big wedding, the whole works?"

"He said that he'd do it however I wanted to do it." She laughed suddenly. "Don't forget—my parents still think I'm living with you."

Kaitlin was certain that Barbara's parents didn't really think so—they just wanted to—but she couldn't see any reason to remind Barbara of that now, when she was about to become legally wed—and totally legitimate.

"There's more to tell you," Barbara said. Then she was suddenly in a rush. "But I'll have to call back. Just promise me that you'll do it. You won't back out if things get a little sticky?"

"Sticky? What should get sticky?" Kaitlin asked.

"I'll explain later. But if you can handle it for Donna, then you can handle it for me."

"Handle it? What—"

"Oh! Donna didn't tell you? We're sharing more than a maid of honor. I can't get into it now, though. Just promise me you'll do it. Be my maid of honor. Promise me! I just realized I'm late as heck for work, and I'm not my own boss. I'll get back to you as soon as I can."

"Fine," Kaitlin said. "I promise." Then she hung up and stared out the window. "Damn!" she whispered aloud. "It *must* be something in the water."

She did make it to work by late afternoon. As she strolled through the attractive outer office she paused by Sam's desk.

"Screen my relatives for me, will you, Sam?"

"Your family?" Sam said, amazed.

Kaitlin nodded dryly. "If they're calling to ask me to be in a wedding, tell them I've disappeared. Even if they're only calling to ask me *to* a wedding, you can still tell them I've disappeared." She walked into her office and managed to get some scheduling done. She reached the director she wanted for the Seashell commercial, and she got Sally from the agency to verify that she had the actor and actress Kaitlin wanted.

That night she tried to reach Barbara, but all she got was the answering machine. She left Joe her congratulations and Barbara a message to get back to her. Knowing that she would be at the beach shooting all the next day, she left the resort's phone number.

The day of the commercial dawned beautifully.

Kaitlin arrived at Addison's Resort, on the Key, to find that her director and her actors had already arrived. Netty was in the coffee shop, and Janis drove up just as she did, bringing the swimsuits, the accessories and, of course, the product, Seashell Sunblock.

Kaitlin met Janis in the suite she had rented for the shoot and smiled. "So far, so good," she told her, then ran through her checklist again. Danny was on his way to set up the scene. He should arrive by the time Mark and Cissy were dressed and ready to go.

"Let's leave the suite to Mark and Cissy. We'll start with the beach scene. We'll meet Lenny down by the pool and grab some coffee ourselves. How does that sound?"

"Great," Janis said. "Why do I feel so jittery? As if something's bound to go wrong?"

"Nothing is going to go wrong," Kaitlin assured her. She herself felt great. Things seemed to be moving perfectly.

Lenny was already downstairs at one of the huge umbrella tables by the pool overlooking the beautiful white sands of the private beach. He pointed out his cameramen by the water, busily checking light levels and their equipment.

"I just hope we finish today," Lenny told her. He was thirty-three, blond and balding, and possessed of a definitely artistic temperament, but he was quick to laugh at himself and able to work well with Kaitlin's ideas. She used him as often as she was able to get him.

"Why shouldn't we?" she asked him with a frown. The wind was picking up by the water. She was wearing sunglasses, a big, droopy straw hat and a candy-striped sleeveless dress cinched at the waist with a wide red belt. It had been a mistake. Even as she sat at the table, the wind whipped at her skirt.

"Mark is having some problems."

With his lover? Kaitlin wondered. Mark Ford was a gorgeous male. Tall, dark, extremely hunky. He was also gay, but he was usually dependable and wonderful to work with. Kaitlin had chosen him very carefully. She liked him a lot, knew he liked her, and couldn't believe that he would jeopardize such an important job.

"It's been touch and go with one of his favorite aunts," Lenny told her. "Cancer. He was just on the phone in the hallway."

"Oh," she said softly. "I'm sorry." She *was* sorry. And she hoped that God would forgive her if she prayed that Mark's aunt stayed alive until after the shoot.

She realized how horrible she was being and told herself that they would just have to reschedule. Even as she did so, the waiter came up, and handed her the phone. "Call for you, Ms. O'Herlihy."

Kaitlin thanked him and picked up the receiver. It was Barbara.

"Barbara!" She had wanted to talk to her cousin so badly, and she had thought that she'd have plenty of time, waiting around the set.

"I'll check on things. I see Cissy coming," Lenny whispered to her.

"Thanks!" she said and watched him walk toward the model. "Barbara, I may have to get back to you—" she began. Then she noticed that Cissy was pouting at something Lenny said. The model stamped a foot.

"Kaitlin? You okay? Got a second? I just wanted to get back to you about what I was saying the other night."

"Yes, yes, of course. This mystery thing," she murmured. What was going on? Cissy was shouting about something.

Cissy, unlike Mark, was not easy to work with. She was stunningly beautiful, and she knew it. She thought that she should have been discovered for big-time movies by now.

Barbara was saying something. Kaitlin, watching the exchange between Cissy and Lenny, wasn't really listening.

"We share the same best man, too."

"Really?" Kaitlin murmured politely.

"And I don't want you to be upset."

"No, no, of course not." Upset? She was about to get hysterical. Cissy had just hauled off and given Lenny a big slap, then spun around and walked away.

"Oh, hell and damnation!" Kaitlin muttered. "Barb, I'll have to call you back."

"Right! Just let me tell you who it is—"

Lenny, enraged, was back. "Cissy says she isn't coming back. Mark is gone—he headed for New York. Cissy said he had no right to go. That she doesn't give a damn about Mark or his aunt. She won't work again in this town, not for me. I swear it, Kaitlin—if you're going to work with her again, don't call me."

She vaguely heard Lenny, and she vaguely heard Barbara. Vaguely. Just vaguely. Because her jaw had dropped and her ears were buzzing, and it seemed that the world was spinning.

There was a man coming toward her. A tall, dark-haired man in bathing trunks. A tall, beautifully bronzed man with wonderfully rugged features and startling green eyes with golden-fire specks.

Brendan.

She knew he had a home here. She knew he kept boats here. She'd read bits and pieces about him in the papers over the years. And she'd even seen him, in the Keys. Not so long ago. Not long enough ago.

But they hadn't met face to face, not here, and she hadn't imagined that they ever would. There were three million people in Dade and Broward counties.

But in the midst of all this, Brendan was coming toward her.

"Barbara, I really have to hang up now," she said to the receiver.

"Wait!" Barbara shrieked. "I have to tell you. He **wants** to talk to you. He took a room at the hotel, and I'm sure he's going to look you up today."

"He? Barbara, what are you talking about?"

Closer. He was coming closer. And suddenly she didn't feel a day over eighteen. If she had been standing, she would have fallen.

**There** was hair on his chest. Rich, dark hair. Very masculine. **A gold** St. Christopher's medal dangled there, somehow adding to **the** appeal. He'd aged. Some. There was just a touch of silver at his temples.

"He?" she whispered sickly.

"Brendan, Kaitlin. Brendan is our best man. And he's going to be Bill's best man, too. Anyway, he wanted Bill and Donna to ask you first, but when Joe approached him, well, he said he had to talk to you himself. That you're a relative and he's just a good friend, and that he's willing as long as you don't feel there would be any problem. And, well, I wanted time to talk to you, but you know Brendan, he said he had to know for himself that it was okay—Kaitlin, are you there?"

She was there. But Netty was suddenly there, too, staring at Brendan and smiling. Actually smiling.

"Oh, Ms. O'Herlihy, he *is* perfect! Definitely perfect!"

"But that's not Mark Ford!" Janis whispered anxiously.

"Kaitlin, are you there?" Barbara demanded.

By then Brendan was there, right there in front of her. Smooth and muscled and sleek—and half naked. He seemed to dwarf everything else. And he was talking softly, his voice low and rich and resonant.

"Kaitlin, I'm sorry to interrupt you—excuse me, really—but I just wanted to see if we could meet later. Barbara promised that she would have explained things to you by now and—,"

"Perfect!" Netty cried again, clapping her hands together. And then she put her arms on his shoulders and turned him to face her.

She actually put her hands on him—on Brendan!—and dragged him around.

Kaitlin saw his muscles tighten, saw his jaw go tense. He might have grown lots more hair on his chest, but it didn't seem that his temper had changed a bit.

"Wait!" she shrieked, leaping to her feet. The phone fell to the tiled floor. She could vaguely hear Barbara's voice, and she wished that Barbara was there at that moment, because she wanted to throttle her cousin into silence.

"Mrs. Green, this isn't my model. There's been quite a mix-up, I'm afraid—"

"Nonsense!" Netty insisted. "He's perfect."

Brendan's temper seemed to have faded. He was confused, he was irritated, but he wasn't going to do anything incredibly rude. "Perfect?" he inquired politely. "Well, thank you. But I don't think that Ms. O'Herlihy would agree with you."

"Oh, Kaitlin, come on! Seashell Sunblock is my product, and I think he's perfect."

"But he's not a model!" Kaitlin insisted.

"No, he's not," Brendan agreed, and his voice was very firm. "Kaitlin, if you can manage a few minutes later, I'll be down by the water." He stared at Netty Green. "Excuse me, ma'am, it's been a pleasure."

"Oh, wait! Wait!" Netty cried. "If you're not the model, just who are you?"

He paused, his back stiffening. Then he turned slowly, and the way his eyes fell on Kaitlin, she suddenly felt as if no time at all had passed since their last meeting.

As if dreams had never shattered between them.

Then his gaze was suddenly very cold and distant, and the smile he offered Netty was wry and amused. "I'm Mr. O'Herlihy. Brendan O'Herlihy, Miss...?"

"Green," Netty said quickly. "Netty Green."

"Yes, well, nice to have met you, Miss Green." Then he turned again, and his muscles rippled in the sunlight as he started to walk away.

Janis, working on delayed reaction, gasped and leaped to her feet, staring after Brendan. It seemed as if her jaw was about to hit the floor. "That's him? Your ex?" she breathed incredulously.

Kaitlin fell into her chair. She couldn't answer.

She didn't need to. Brendan paused and turned slowly. "Yes," he said, his gaze sweeping over the table. "I'm him. Her ex."

His eyes landed on Kaitlin one last time and swept over her curiously; then he was walking away.

Yes, it was very definitely Brendan. But he wasn't walking away, not really.

On the contrary, she thought, trembling. He had just walked back into her life.

Chapter 2

"That man is perfect!" Netty Green repeated obstinately.

Kaitlin, staring after Brendan's retreating back, clenched her teeth tightly to keep from replying too quickly. She even managed to smile past the grid lock of her teeth. Then, after a few deep breaths, she managed to speak with an even tone and a surprising amount of polite control.

"Netty, I really am sorry, but I can't make a man be a model who does not choose to be a model. And despite our very best efforts, I am afraid that I'm going to have to reschedule."

Netty set her thin little lips and raised her chin. "Ms. O'Herlihy, I am not willing to reschedule. My time is valuable. I'm afraid I can give you only thirty minutes to solve this dilemma, and that is that."

She turned, her narrow back ramrod straight, and disappeared into the hotel.

Kaitlin allowed her hand to crash straight down on the table, groaning. "Where did I go wrong? It was college, I know it. I should have gone to medical school. Gram always wanted someone in the family to be a doctor."

"Kaitlin!" Janis said, her voice low but edged with a trace of excitement. "This is still salvageable."

"Don't mention salvage. It's part of what he does for a living."

"Your ex?"

"Don't call him that."

"Okay. Mr. O'Herlihy?"

Kaitlin nodded bleakly, her head still on the table.

"Well, that doesn't matter," Janis said. "Listen to me now! Pay attention. He came here to see you. He wants peace between you. He's offering an olive branch——"

"If he's offering it, it's a barbed olive branch, believe me,"

Kaitlin moaned, but she managed to sit up.

"Kaitlin, how bad can this be? You've been apart a long time now——"

"No, no, not so long." All right, it was a long time. Eight years since they were divorced. But she had seen him less than four years ago, when she'd asked him if they couldn't seek an annulment to appease both sets of very Catholic parents.

She hadn't gotten an annulment. What she *had* gotten had been enough to make her very, very careful now.

"Kaitlin, you've got to ask him to model for this commercial."

"No!"

"Kaitlin, what is your problem? He seems mature and pleasant, and he's one of the most handsome, masculine men I've ever seen. He *is* perfect! A wonderful model—"

"He doesn't want to be a model."

"Tell him that it's acting."

"Janis, I can't!" she insisted.

"You have to! We're going to lose this account if you don't."

"We don't have a female model anymore," Kaitlin reminded her.

"We'll get one. Just go get that man!"

"Janis, so we lose the account..."

"And then I don't get paid!" Janis wailed. "Kaitlin, this is important. We could keep Seashell Products for years and years. Please!"

"Janis—"

"He wants something from you, right? So go out there and get something from him!"

"I need a drink," Kaitlin muttered.

"It's first thing in the morning!"

"Irish whiskey, neat."

"Go get him, Kaitlin. Think of our reputation. Think of the business."

"I'm thinking about my sanity," Kaitlin said wearily. She sipped at her cold coffee. It was fine. Anything to wet her parched throat.

What had she done that was so evil that it seemed God was punishing her with a day like today?

If she found that Gram had included Brendan in her wedding, too, well, then, Kaitlin would probably just explode in shock and that would be that. All over.

"Kaitlin!" Janis wailed. "We're running out of time."

Kaitlin stood. Janis was right. Kaitlin needed to salvage something out of this situation. It was just that it was so dangerous to go near him. She should know. After what happened when she had seen him about the annulment...

Because things didn't change. Things never changed between them. Emotions always roiled just beneath the surface. Anger, pain, even laughter, and that deep-lying thing had made it possible for time to erase anything between them.

But she was going to have to see him anyway. There was no way out of it. She couldn't possibly tell her cousins she wouldn't be involved in their weddings if Brendan were involved, too. She just couldn't.

"Go get him, tiger!" Janis applauded.

"Janis!"

"Well...?"

Kaitlin inhaled and started walking down the beach. She passed Lenny's cameraman with all his equipment and smiled, as if nothing in the world was wrong. "Are we still on, Ms. O'Herlihy?" he called to her.

"I—maybe," she answered. She could see Brendan again. He was a little further down the beach, seated in the sand, his elbows on his knees, a blade of beach grass in his mouth as he stared out to sea. A trembling began deep within her abdomen. What had gone so wrong between them? Had it been because they looked at life with the eyes of youth, expectant, hopeful, believing in ideals?

And then life had been so cruel. Even so, when she had seen him several years ago they had still managed to laugh. Then the laughter had died away, and they had discovered that other things remained, the passion remained...

He turned, as if he had sensed her. She kept walking, despite the lump in her throat. Then the wind picked up, and suddenly her candy-striped skirt was swirling around her thighs.

She swore, pressing it down. He was wearing his sunglasses, but she saw the smile that curved his lips and she knew he was aware of her discomfort.

She held the skirt at her side and anchored her hat with her other hand before the wind could whip it away, too.

It got harder as she got closer, but she kept walking, and within moments, she was standing before him.

"Hi," he said, and patted the sand. "Take a seat."

She bit into her bottom lip, but sat beside him. For a moment she, too, stared out to sea.

"I take it that Barbara hadn't told you anything?" he finally asked, turning to her.

She could feel his green gaze despite his dark glasses. She didn't look at him. She wished that she hadn't sat quite so close. He had showered recently and he smelled nicely of soap mingled with his own scent, and with the salty smell of the sea.

He *was* perfect.

His bare shoulders were bronzed, strong. He had gotten more attractive with age, she thought. His chest was so broad, so nicely muscled.

And so damn bare.

Even if she hadn't know him before, she would have been tempted to touch. To explore that rich, dark flurry of hair that grew over the rippling muscles...

"Kaitlin?"

"Ah...yes, Barbara did talk to me. About five minutes ago. Right while you were walking up to the table," she managed to say.

"No warning? I'm sorry."

She shrugged. "Well, you know Barbara."

"And Joe," he agreed, and though he was looking out to sea once again, she could see his easy smile from the corner of her eye. "Can you believe that they're finally getting married?" He chuckled softly.

"Yes, I can," she said with a trace of indignation in her tone. She added, "I still believe in magic," then regretted the words. They gave away so much.

He glanced at her and shrugged. "Yes, well, maybe it is out there," he said softly. Then he went quickly to the point. "Do you mind?"

"That they're getting married? Of course not. I think it's wonderful."

"No," Brendan groaned. "I meant, do you mind that I'm going to be involved in these weddings, too? Because if it's going to bother you at all, I'll step aside."

She lowered her head, staring at the sand. "It's really none of my business. Bill has a right to his choice, and so does Joe. And if they both want you—''

''Kaitlin, I asked if *you* minded.''

''And I said—''

''Kaitlin?''

''Well, of course I mind!'' she exploded, and she was instantly on her feet, in all of five minutes he'd managed to completely destroy her well-earned, customary control. ''Of course I mind, but—''

''Kaitlin, I said that I—''

''No! No! You're going to be Bill's best man, and you're going to be Joe's best man. You just can't have my blessing, that's all. I don't think I can be cheerful and smile every time I see you.''

''Then—''

''But I *will* see you. And we *will* get through it.''

He was smiling, she realized. And he was barely listening to her.

''Your skirt, Kaitlin. It's better than Marilyn Monroe on that subway grating.''

She gasped and collected her flying skirt. Afterward she felt his hand on her wrist, pulling her down beside him. ''Funny, isn't it? I don't have a right in the world where you're concerned, Ms. O'Herlihy, but though I'm impressed as hell by that sexy red garter and those sleek stockings, I still can't handle the thought of another man enjoying the show.''

''Brendan—''

''I won't seduce you, Kaitlin.''

''Oh, God!'' she whispered, mortified, trying to jerk her wrist from his grasp.

''The last time I saw you, I really couldn't help it. You wanted something from me. You wanted to pretend that we had never been married. After you'd spent all these years using my name. And you still wanted the name! You wanted the annulment, too. And it seemed as if you were willing to pay anything to get what you wanted. I really couldn't help myself.''

''Brendan, let go of my wrist!'' she whispered, then swung on him when he didn't let go. ''Your ego is incredible. I couldn't have been seduced—especially by you—if I hadn't let it happen. So don't assume that you can crook a finger and have me come running.''

"I never assumed that, Kaitlin," he said coldly. "There were times when I could have begged and it wouldn't have brought you near me."

She gasped, and suddenly her lips were trembling. She was so filled with emotion that she was shaking all over. "You left, Brendan O'Herlihy! You left me right after our wedding—or what sufficed for a wedding! And then you left the country. Even before that you left me. You left me when Sean died. You were gone even when you were standing right beside me."

"For God's sake, Kaitlin—"

"It still hurts, doesn't it? It still hurts that Sean died. Well, what happened between us still hurts, too."

She shut up suddenly, aware that her eyes were watering, aware that she had said things she had never intended to say. It was just that, when he was with her, time and distance disappeared. It had been the same when she had gone to see him before. When they had begun to talk. But she had been casual then. She had tried to pretend that time had taken away all the pain, all the longing. She had been mature and distant as she explained what she wanted and why it would be best for them both.

He had listened. Then he had moved closer, and she had felt all the same things that seeing him now was making her feel again. The urge to stroke his cheek, to run her fingers over his back, over his bronzed flesh. They'd been sipping wine, and he'd been listening so seriously to everything she'd had to say....

She couldn't regret it. Not what had happened between them. But she had been furious about the morning after. About his blunt reminder that she'd been using his name all these years, and that they had been married, and that he would never say any different. And then he'd been quick to leave, inviting her to come back whenever she wanted to see him, just see him, without expecting anything else.

She hadn't gone back. She'd felt like a fool. And now...

"Does it still hurt?" he asked her softly.

"Yes," she replied honestly. "Not every day." She smiled. "In fact, I pride myself on the fact that endless days can go by during which I don't think about you once. But yes, it's there, in a corner of my heart."

"Is it?" he asked very quietly, but then she realized that he was looking beyond her shoulder and frowning. He smiled at her, arching a brow. "Your friend is hopping up and down and waving wildly. And tapping her wristwatch."

"Oh!" Kaitlin gasped, startled. She stared at the sand miserably. She couldn't ask him. He had told her once not to come back unless she came because she wanted him—and not something from him. But he'd made such a fool of her, hurt her so badly, that she'd never been able to go back. And now...

"She seems to want you," Brendan observed.

"Yes," Kaitlin said. She turned so she could see Janis hopping up and down, too. She waved reassuringly and stared at the sand again.

"If you need to get to work..." Brendan began.

"I don't. Not really. The shoot fell apart and Netty Green is pulling the spot."

"Why?" he demanded sharply.

She gazed at him. "She wants you."

"Who wants me? For what?" he asked, annoyed.

Kaitlin exhaled and scrambled to her feet. She stared at him without answering, holding her skirt at her thigh. "Brendan, I wouldn't hurt my cousins or ruin their weddings for anything. We can get along for the little time we need to be together, I'm sure of it."

He had a very skeptical look on his face as he got to his feet. "Sure," he said briefly. Then he caught her hand. She felt his fingers moving against her palm, and she wanted to scream. "Now, tell me, what's going on with your shoot?"

"It isn't your problem, Brendan."

"Tell me."

"No."

"Why not?"

"Because it isn't any of your business. Because..." She hesitated.

"Go on."

"Because you told me not to ask you for anything again."

He stiffened. "Oh. So you did walk down the beach to ask me for something."

"Yes. No! I walked down the beach because I had to talk to you. Because we had to straighten this out. And because——"

"Because what?" he snapped. She had forgotten that his hold

could be so steely, that his fingers could clamp around her wrist like a vice.

"You heard her!" Kaitlin snapped. "She wants you to be her model."

"I've never modeled in my life! I race boats and I dive for wrecks."

"I know, Brendan, but—"

"You mean that woman is going to pull the entire campaign if she doesn't get me in her commercial?" he asked incredulously.

"Yes. She—she thinks you're perfect," Kaitlin replied irritably.

He was grinning as he released her suddenly. "Well," he murmured, stroking his chin.

"I'm not asking you to do it, Brendan. I can't afford your price."

His grin faded. She could read nothing of his thoughts from his features, and his dark glasses shadowed his eyes. "I told you I wouldn't seduce you again, Kaitlin," he said harshly. "If that's what you're afraid of."

"I'm not afraid of you, Brendan. I told you, it was as much my fault as yours."

"How interesting. And magnanimous."

"It's nothing."

"We're going to be seeing each other a number of times," he reminded her.

"Yes, we've established that—"

"And I won't stop you if you try to seduce me," he said softly. Huskily. His words seemed to hang on the breeze. To linger. To reach out and touch her more surely than any caress.

"That should hardly worry either of us," she murmured coolly.

"We'll see. What happened to your model?" he asked suddenly, changing the subject.

"What?"

"Your model. Why does your lady need a male body to begin with?"

"Oh." He had changed from her personal life to her professional life too quickly. She shrugged. "An illness in the family. And it doesn't matter. I lost my female model, too. I—"

"All right," he said suddenly.

"All right what?" she asked nervously.

"All right, I'll do it."

"You'll do what?"

"I'll model for your commercial. You're supposed to be talking me into it, right? That's why your friend keeps hopping around and tapping her watch. I'll do it. On one condition."

"And what's that?" Kaitlin asked softly, suspiciously.

He was quiet for a minute, watching her. The sun beat down on them, and she found herself studying him, seeing the man she had known forever, but also seeing the stranger he had become. The little touches of silver at his temples added to his mystique. The dark glasses shadowed his eyes, kept him from revealing any truths. The set of his jaw was as square as ever; his shoulders were as taut and broad and square as they had always been.

One condition...

Maybe he would ask for one last night. One last chance to be together, to believe in magic. To forget time and eternity and the world, and bask in the moonlight and the night air. To feel the caress of the breeze, and of one another. To soar and savor flesh and blood and passion.

Her cheeks colored, and she lowered her lashes, fearful that her eyes would betray her thoughts. She knotted her fingers into fists and held them behind her. The desire to touch him was suddenly so strong she could hardly resist. To touch, to stroke. To follow the thin dark line where the mat of chest hair narrowed provocatively at his waistband. To step closer and press her lips against his, to feel the hunger of his kiss...

"One condition," he repeated.

"Yes?" Her lashes were falling, closing over her eyes. Let it be decadent, let it be crude! She could protest, of course, and be indignant, but then...

"You have to model, too."

Her eyes flew open. "What?"

"Well, if I'm going to spend the day being a piece of meat, you can join me. I'll model—if you will."

Her secret desires came spiraling through her with shocking clarity, and she stared at him incredulously. He didn't want to go to bed with her. He didn't want one last night together.

Not even an hour.

He just wanted to make sure she didn't get anything for free.

She shook her head, backing away, feeling like a fool—and wishing she could dunk him in the ocean.

"I can't. It's out of the question."

"Why not? Gained too much weight in the thighs?"

"No!"

"I'm not a model!"

"Well, then?"

"And neither am I. But I'm willing to give it a fling to save your business. Why aren't you?"

"My whole business will not fall apart if I do not keep this account!"

"Ah, but it will be injured," he said smugly.

"How can you be so sure?"

"Because of that person up there, hopping away like a pogo stick."

"Oh!" She spun to see that Janis was desperately trying to get her attention. And Netty Green was walking toward the table. It was now or never.

The Seashell Sunblock account *was* important. No, she wouldn't lose her business, but...

Other clients would know that Seashell had pulled out. They would wonder why, and few people would stop to realize that Netty Green was a pain in the...

"Hey, kid, this one is up to you," Brendan reminded her softly. She spun to face him. "All right, all right!"

"Don't jump down my throat. It's your business, not mine."

"That's right. You make a living out of being a pirate."

"A pirate?" His brows shot up. "Because I search for ships that sank hundreds of years ago?" He wasn't really expecting an answer. "There's more, too," he told her.

"What do you mean, there's more?" she asked suspiciously. A little dance of heat was already taking place all along her spine.

"Dinner."

"What dinner?"

"Any dinner. You and I alone. Just to discuss the basics—"

"What damn basics?"

His brows shot up in surprise, and he smiled then, very slowly. "The weddings, Kaitlin. Some of the things I know Donna and Bill and Barbara and Joe would like. What I think we should do for them."

"What you think...!"

"Kaitlin, damn it, I want your opinion, too. That's why I'd like to go to dinner. A *friendly* dinner. To discuss things. Look, these ladies are your cousins, and I said I would step aside—"

"No! I told you I don't want that."

He was silent for a moment. As she watched him, she wondered why he couldn't have lost every hair on his head.

No...he probably would have been attractive bald, too. He'd need to lose his whole damn head. Turn pink. Cease to smile, to speak...

And he wanted dinner.

"Kaitlin, I know you wish I'd disappear from these weddings—actually, I imagine you wish I'd disappear from the face of the earth. But you don't want to be responsible for my absence."

She smiled sweetly. "Brendan, you're wrong. I hope you live forever."

"Just nowhere near you, right?"

She shrugged, and he laughed. Then his smile faded, and he demanded abruptly, "Have we got a deal?"

"What?"

"A deal, Kaitlin. I model if you model, and then I get dinner. The weekend after next. I'm working this weekend, and this *is* supposed to be at my convenience."

"But if I model—",

"It's your business, remember?"

The weekend after next was Gram's wedding.

"Wednesday. I don't have a weekend night free."

"I'll get you at eight."

Still, she hesitated. Dinner. With Brendan. Alone. Well, he wasn't going to seduce her. Did she trust him?

Damn. Did she trust herself? Twice burned...

He pointed toward the hotel once again. "Your friend is getting very nervous."

"Yes!"

"You'll model and join me for dinner?"

"All right, all right. I'll model, and—and go to dinner. And I won't renege."

"Fine," he said flatly.

Janis was slamming her fingers against her watch. Netty would be walking away any second.

"Okay, Brendan, come on, then," Kaitlin muttered, turning.

"Please, let's just do this and get it over with."

"Gee, when you phrase things so charmingly, it really is hard to resist," he mocked.

What was the matter with her? He could still back out of the deal.

But he was behind her. "It won't be quite over with," he reminded her.

"Right. Dinner," she said.

He laughed huskily, but he was with her. And that was important. He was behind her all the way past the cameraman and the equipment and to the table, where Netty Green was beaming.

"Oh, I am so pleased, Mr. O'Herlihy. I do understand that this is not your vocation, and I thank you sincerely. I promise you that my product is a very good one."

"I know your product, Mrs. Green," Brendan began.

Terrified of what he might say, Kaitlin jumped in quickly. "Is Lenny close by, Janis?"

Janis nodded, her eyes darting from Kaitlin to Brendan, and started to speak. "Yes, he's in the suite, waiting. He said—,"

"Well, Mr. O'Herlihy, what do you think of Seashell Sun-block?" Netty demanded.

Kaitlin held her breath. Brendan was going to tell the truth— no matter what it was.

"It's a good product. It compares with the established brands, and the price is low enough for the young mother with a bunch of kids to stock up on it. I wouldn't have agreed to this—no matter what—if I had been asked to sell something I couldn't truly endorse."

Netty was beaming, absolutely beaming. Kaitlin didn't think she could take any more of it. "Did Cissy leave the suit, do you know?" she asked Janis.

Janis stared at her blankly for a moment. "Oh, yes, yes, she did. But I haven't called for another model, because I didn't know—"

"It doesn't matter. I'm going to do it," Kaitlin said.

"You're going to call?"

"No, I'm going to be the model."

Janis dropped her jaw, Netty cocked her head, and Kaitlin could feel the smile on Brendan's face.

"You're—you're going to be the model?" Janis said.

"Yes!" Kaitlin snapped. Then she spun around. "I'll go change. I'll be right down. I'll send Lenny to the beach, and you alert the cameraman." Janis had yet to close her mouth. She kept looking from Brendan to Kaitlin, who ignored her.

"Brendan, Lenny may want to put some pancake makeup on your face. I know that—"

"Fine."

He wasn't going to fight with her. He was still wearing the glasses, but his features were calm and composed, and he was being completely charming, the easiest man in the world with whom to get along.

She wanted to hit him.

Instead, she smiled. "Well, then, I'll go change."

She swung around and hurried up to the suite. Lenny was sitting on the sofa, watching a talk show. He looked up, surprised, as she breezed in. "Are we on or off?"

"On!" Kaitlin snapped, marching by him and heading for the bedroom. The two-piece bathing suit was on the bed, and there was an array of makeup spread out on the dresser.

"Glad to hear you so pleased and excited!" Lenny called to her.

She slammed the door. In seconds she had stripped, throwing her clothes wherever they landed, and donned the suit. She sat before the mirror, darkening her eyes carefully and doing her face. There was a knock on the door.

"Hey, Kaitlin! What's up?" It was Lenny.

"Come on in," she called to him.

He opened the door and stared at her, then began to smile. "So…"

"Don't 'so' me."

"I think you're perfect."

She groaned softly. "And don't use that word, please!"

"Okay, you'll stink, but what the hell."

"Lenny…"

"Seriously, I think you'll be great. I think it's a major loss that you never put yourself in front of the camera before."

"Lenny, how's the makeup?"

He came over and studied her closely. "Seems perfect—sorry, seems fine. Where's Mr. Perfect—whoops! Sorry, can't seem to shake that word."

"Manage it, huh?" Kaitlin murmured.

He grinned.

"Why doesn't anyone take my temper seriously?" she moaned.

"An Irish temper? I take it very seriously, Kaitlin, me love," he teased. "I'll go down and check out your man."

"He's not my man."

"He is today," Lenny advised her. He closed the door, and Kaitlin closed her eyes, then opened them and studied her face once again. Maybe she would be all right. The makeup made her eyes huge, and, if nothing else, her hair had color and luster. It was probably too long, but she wasn't going to go around chopping off her hair for a sixty-second commercial.

Sixty seconds…that would take them hours. Hours and hours of putting sunblock on Brendan or—worse—feeling him put it on her.

She groaned and leaned her head against her arms. Well, she was committed. She might as well face the music.

She stood and hurried out of the room to the elevator. Then she realized she had brought nothing with her, no shoes, no towel, no cover-up. And there was a slightly balding man in the elevator with her. Leering. She felt naked. She was half naked. Anyone in her right mind would have grabbed a cover-up.

She wasn't in her right mind.

When the elevator stopped, she nearly ran to the table. Janis was waiting for her; the others were already down on the beach.

"You look like dynamite!" Janis assured her. "But how—"

"Don't ask."

"You'll be just per—"

"Don't! Don't say it! Let's just go, okay?"

Janis studied her and nodded, grinning from ear to ear despite her best efforts. "All right, you look like pure garbage. Is that better?"

"No!"

"I wouldn't be so grouchy if I was the one putting lotion on him," Janis commented.

"You weren't married to him."

"No," Janis said with a sigh. "I wouldn't have let him go."

"I didn't—oh, never mind. Please, let's just get this over with!"

It wasn't going to be that easy; she had been sure of that, and she'd been right.

Lenny had worked on Brendan, who was wearing makeup on his nose and cheeks and shoulders. His sunglasses were gone, and his eyes were a startling deep green against his bronze flesh, his dark hair a perfect frame for his face. He watched Kaitlin approach, and his gaze swept slowly over her. He smiled, but she wasn't sure whether it was because she hadn't changed—or because she had. She was about to speak when Netty came rushing forward.

"I knew it, I knew it! It's exactly the look I want. Older, sophisticated—well, not too old, of course, but—oh, Kaitlin, I am so pleased and eager to see the final product!"

"We should get to it," Lenny advised. "Morning light, you know."

"Sure," Kaitlin murmured.

There was a huge towel stretched out on the beach in front of the cameras, and a large bottle of Seashell Sunblock was waiting on it. An ice chest sat on one corner of the blanket; sandals and a couple of paperbacks were strewn on another. It was an average day at the beach.

"Kaitlin, Brendan, remember, there's going to be a voice-over. Don't worry about sound. The surf and breeze will be added to the mix later. Action is all that we need. Is that all right, Brendan? Do you understand?"

"I think I've got the basics," Brendan said dryly.

"Great."

"Brendan, the voice-over is saying, 'When you touch her this afternoon, touch her with Seashell Sunblock'—then the scene will switch. Janis will read the line. And what I want is Kaitlin on her knees, and you right behind her. Make use of her hair. Sweep it aside to get the lotion on her nape and along her back and shoulders. Okay? Kaitlin, down on your knees."

She went down. This was her commercial. She had written it. She hadn't planned on being the one on her knees...with Brendan behind her.

Touching her.

"Okay, Janis, give Brendan the line. Slowly."

So Janis read.

And Brendan touched.

He swept her hair aside, and his fingers moved smoothly over her skin. Slick, fragrant with the lotion. Warm, soothing, rippling along her shoulders and spine, touching her flesh, massaging her, moving down her back. She couldn't breathe. She could only feel him. His touch, his body, behind her. Close. His every breath touching her flesh where it was slick and smooth and cool with the lotion....

"Brendan, that's wonderful. Kaitlin, what the hell is the matter with you?"

"What?"

"That would have been it! A one-shot wrap. Kaitlin, this is your lover, your best friend in the world, the man you travel the globe with. Smile! You like him, remember? Loosen up! Glance his way over your shoulder. You like it! Got it?"

She gritted her teeth. "Got it."

"Okay, Jerry," Lenny called to the cameraman, checking the angle himself. "Action, please."

Janis began to read.

And Kaitlin found herself being bathed in lotion once again. She felt his fingertips. Felt the trembling they created deep down inside her. She moistened her lips and closed her eyes. She felt the sun, and she felt his touch. Stroking, his head bent close to hers. And she heard his barely breathed whisper. "Like it, Kaitlin?"

She didn't snap; she didn't break. She turned and smiled, just as she had been told, her eyes alive, her gaze as wicked as his fingertips....

Lenny groaned. Kaitlin had been fine this time, but a kid running on the sand had caused the fly-up that the camera would surely catch. And then Netty suggested that when Brendan was done, he should give the lotion to Kaitlin, who could apply it to him as the shot faded away.

They went for seven takes in all.

On the last take, Kaitlin thought she would scream if she had to do it one more time. Had to feel his fingers moving against her flesh and muscle. Had to sense him behind her. Had to feel the strength and bulk of his body, smell his scent, feel the warmth of his breath caress her against the coolness of the lotion. Had to feel him stroking the length of her spine, stroking her shoulders, massaging her nape...

She was trembling when she turned. Smiled. Murmured a low, sultry thank you and took the lotion from his hands.

Then she touched him. All over his back. His broad, rippling, bronze and sexy back. She touched him from just above the buttocks, and swept upward, sheeting his back in lotion, and nearly touching him with the length of her body. Then he turned suddenly and her fingers were in the mat of hair on his chest and she was looking into his eyes. And her fingers were spreading the stuff outward, upward and downward, and she was still staring at him...

"Cut!" Lenny cried. And he jumped up and down. "That's a wrap. Perfect, damn, but that was perfect, Kaitlin, you can't imagine how perfect!"

His eyes were still on hers. It was over; people were moving. The cameraman was picking up his equipment, Lenny was hugging Janis, and Brendan was still staring at her with his magnetic green gaze. She couldn't seem to pull away from it. She was still trembling.

Then he smiled slowly. "Perfect," he said softly, turning as Netty came up to him.

Suddenly, on the beach, with the sun beating down on her, she was cold, shaking with it deep inside. Then Janis was behind her, whirling her around and whispering. "Dear Lord, I have never—never!—seen something so simple become so sensuous. I'm telling you, Kaitlin, this spot is mesmerizing. I could barely breathe right, just watching!"

"Janis! Please, stop!" Kaitlin said, her cheeks flaming. Just how sensuous had it appeared? And in front of all these people, too!

"But, Kaitlin, it *was* sexy. This product is going to walk off the shelves, I'm telling you. Just imagine—"

"Imagine what?" Kaitlin demanded.

"Why, we've just begun. Now he gets to carry you into the suite. Oh, it's wonderful that things didn't work out with Cissy and Mark! You two have such chemistry!"

Chemistry. Damn chemistry! Kaitlin thought. But Janis was right. It was there.

And they still had more to do.

It was his fault. The whole damn thing was his fault, and Brendan knew it. He had never meant to say yes to her. And then, if he *was* going to agree to make an idiot of himself on camera, what had ever possessed him to demand that she join him, just so he could spend hour upon hour of torture, touching, stroking, caressing everything that he had vowed to himself—and to her—he wasn't going to have?

What a fool he had been.

Seashell Sunblock. Great. Wonderful. What on earth had gotten hold of him? After all these years, he should never be in such a position now.

Holding her. Dancing with her. Looking into her eyes, feeling the sway of her body, in the sweet heat of the night....

It had been bad enough at the beach. Touching her. Rubbing his fingers over her back, her shoulders. Sweeping her hair aside, inhaling her sweet scent. Touching her in front of all those people. Just how sensual could it have been?

Too sensual. The people had faded away, and he'd had trouble hearing. She had looked great in the blue two-piece bikini, tan, lean, compact, beautifully built.

Why couldn't she have gained about fifty pounds, accrued a few rotten teeth—or lost a whole mouthful of them—and maybe gone bald?

Then he wondered whether even those things would have changed anything.

He had wanted her all his life. Why should anything have changed?

They were off the beach now, and things were even worse. It was dark, and they were out on the patio. The moon was out, and they might have been alone, staring into one another's eyes. His fingers were curled around hers, his hand at the small of her back. It shouldn't have felt so natural; it shouldn't have been so easy. And he shouldn't have been waiting for so much of his life.

He should have gotten married by now. He should have made damn sure he was at least seriously involved with someone so that she couldn't slip back into his life.

And she was in his life, all right. In his arms. In a strapless deep maroon cocktail dress with a skirt of some silky fabric that moved and swayed with every step. Her shoulder couldn't have been softer. They'd been bathed in sunblock all day long, and now her skin felt just like an angel's wings. And they were dancing close together. So close that he felt the tension rising in his body, so close that he felt every curve of her.

Curves he knew well. He could close his eyes, in fact, and summon up a memory of every curve and dip and nuance of her body. Colors and shapes and scents and essences, he could remember them all.

He had to quit remembering. It was embarrassing, because they weren't really alone.

There was a camera crew not ten feet away. And good old Lenny. And Janis, still rapt, still staring at him intently, still stuttering when she tried to talk to him. He liked her. She had an honesty that wouldn't allow her to pretend she'd never heard of him.

But exactly what had she heard? He didn't know.

And he couldn't begin to tell from looking into Kaitlin's eyes. Blue eyes. Wild, and anything but innocent. He would never forget the first time he'd seen her. She'd been flirting away, and the guys had all been panting after her like puppy dogs, just about tripping over their tongues. She had been defiant, challenging...and watching him in return. It had been fun at first, because he had known she was after him, making a bid for his attention.

And then she'd gotten it. He wasn't sure if it had been before or after he had taken her into his arms and danced with her—just like this—that he had realized he was interested, that he could never let her go.

He felt his jaw tightening. She was looking at him just as she had looked at him that night so long ago. With eyes that could melt steel. With a never-ending cascade of strawberry blond hair rippling down her back in lush waves of fire and gold.

He told himself that it was a commercial. A damn commercial and nothing else. There was no honesty in her eyes, none at all. It was over between them, all over, and it had been for a long time. She talked to him only when she wanted something from him.

Last time he'd made sure she hadn't gotten it. And this time...

Well, this time, they had to make peace. And they might have done it, if only he didn't have to touch her. If only he didn't feel just like a teenager—with *his* tongue on the floor this time.

No, it wasn't his tongue he was worried about.

He'd promised her he wouldn't seduce her, and she'd told him he didn't have the power. Not anymore. That he'd only been able to seduce her before because she had wanted him to.

Want me now, he thought. Want me.

Good, O'Herlily, good, he told himself sarcastically. Let's start this whole thing off panting. It should make everything move right along.

It was just that when he held her like this, it was hard not to believe there was still something between them, no matter how much time had passed.

The last time he had held her this way had been almost four years ago, down in the Keys. The moon had been full and beautiful, and she had been in his arms, looking at him, her eyes very blue and very wide. He had been determined then that she wouldn't get away that night, that he would listen to her, that they would talk...

Then he had touched her, and when the music ended, he had carried her away...and refreshed his memory about her curves.

The scene felt so much the same now. No words between them, just the patio, the moonlight and Kaitlin in his arms. The only woman who both infuriated him and made him feel whole. He could lift her into his arms and sweep her away and—

"Brendan! Wonderful!" Lenny called. The people in the background suddenly came crashing forward. "You two look wonderful. Janis is going to give you the line now. Just listen to it and keep up the good work. The camera is rolling."

Janis began to read huskily. "If you touch her this afternoon, touch her with Seashell Sunblock and be sure that you can touch her again tonight."

Kaitlin was still staring into his eyes. Her lips were soft, gleaming. She had never seemed more beautiful.

He wanted to shout, It was my fault, damn it! When Sean died, the things that happened were my fault. I didn't stop loving you.

*It just seemed like everything else was so trivial. He'd been my best friend all my life, and he'd had so many hopes and plans and dreams, and suddenly they were all dead. I didn't know how to explain how I felt, how to cope with it. So I blocked you out, and then I lost you. I didn't even realize it until I saw you with another man. I thought it was my pride, but I really just didn't have the guts to admit that it was my fault, and I wanted to hurt you.*

"Okay, cut! That's a wrap!" Lenny was clapping his hands together.

Kaitlin dropped her hands and stepped away from him, a foot away. None of it had meant anything to her. It was just a commercial. A game. A tease.

Suddenly Lenny was there between the two of them, excited. "Kaitlin, I can't tell you how great the two of you look together!" He swung around to pump Brendan's hand. "You're wonderful. A natural. You should go into this for a living—"

"Oh, I've got a job, thank you. I'm a pirate," Brendan said, flashing a smile to Kaitlin, who didn't smile in return.

Lenny flashed Kaitlin a quick glance, then smiled at Brendan again. "We're almost finished here. We just need to go up to the hallway toward the suite. Pretend you're carrying your beloved off to bed. Think you can handle that as smoothly?"

Brendan met Kaitlin's eyes. "I can't wait," he said dryly.

She smiled sweetly. He could almost hear her teeth grating.

"Oh, neither can I," she assured him.

"Okay!" Lenny called. "Let's wrap it up here and move upstairs, okay?"

Janis gathered up her papers, and the cameraman and his assistant began collecting their lights and equipment. Netty Green, who had been there all day, was still smiling. She placed a hand on Brendan's tuxedo-clad arm. "I must thank you again. You've been just what I wanted."

"Don't thank me, Mrs. Green," he said, his eyes still on Kaitlin. "Thank Kaitlin. She's always known how to get just what she wants."

"I just wish I knew how to repay you—" Netty began.

"Please, don't worry about it. Kaitlin pays very well. Very well, indeed."

Again he could almost hear the grating of her teeth. But she was still smiling. "He's a sucker for minimum wage, Netty. But it's nice to hear that you're so pleased." She turned to Brendan. "Thank you for working so hard. By the way, I think you need to fix your makeup. Your nose is shiny."

"My nose is shiny? Oh, no," he said with mock concern.

"It's the lights," she said sweetly. "They make us all perspire just a bit."

There went that tongue of hers as she moistened her lips again. She was shaken, as shaken as he was. If only there weren't so many people around.

"I think it's lovely that you two managed to part and remain such good friends!" Netty exclaimed, her thin fingers twining together, her eyes alight.

"Oh, yes, such friends," Kaitlin murmured. "Excuse me, Netty, will you? I'm going to run up and check a few things."

She was going to get away from him for a while, and they both knew it, Brendan thought. Maybe that was all right. He didn't seem to have a whole lot of control over his own reactions.

We never talked, he thought. And now, if I started talking, I wonder if she'd even remember what the problems were.

She was gone, and he gave himself a shake. "I guess it's going to take a few minutes for them to move all this stuff around, right?" he asked Netty.

She nodded, smiling and taking the arm he offered her.

"Can I buy you a drink, Mrs. Green?"

"Let me buy you one."

"No, thanks, I'm an old-fashioned guy at heart. What can I get you?"

She decided to have a glass of white wine. He sat with her at the bar and listened to her talk about her brother, and the growth of Seashell Products, and why it might seem that she was being petty, but all she really wanted was to protect her product. He half listened to her.

And he half ignored her, dreading, anticipating the moments to come.

He'd come here today to talk about arranging a special party for Barbara and Joe. Instead, he was in a tux, drinking Scotch in hopes that it would numb his fingers.

He hadn't seen her in almost four years, and it didn't matter, not one bit. It felt as if it had been yesterday. Maybe that was because he had seen too much of her when he *had* seen her.

He finished his drink. "I hear I need more makeup. I guess I'd better head up."

"Yes, yes, of course," Netty agreed.

They took the elevator up to the suite. Lenny was talking to the cameraman, but he turned when he heard Brendan approaching.

"Kaitlin will be right with us. Brendan," he said, smiling ruefully, "you need to powder your nose."

"So I hear," Brendan said wryly. He excused himself and went into the suite. The woman doing makeup was set up in one of the bedrooms, and he hesitated, knowing that Kaitlin was there, too.

Then the door opened and she came out. For a minute they were alone. Really alone.

Then her eyes narrowed, and her smile wasn't the least bit sweet. "Thanks a lot, O'Herlihy. You made me feel really cheap out there."

He swallowed the feelings that had been growing throughout the long day. "Sorry, O'Herlihy. But then again, if the shoe fits…"

"The shoe is just about to fly in your face, Brendan. I shouldn't pay you a thing! I should opt out of these weddings myself. And don't you dare call me O'Herlihy like that again. Don't—"

He stepped forward, clamping his hand over her mouth before she could go on. Her eyes rose to meet his in a cool blue fire of unreasonable fury.

"Kaitlin, may I remind you that you chose to keep the name. For your business, you said. And then you wanted an annulment from me—after all those years of keeping my name! So if I want to call you by it, I damn well will! And let me remind you of something else, too. You were willing to pay a hell of a lot to have your way the last time I saw you."

She tried to bite him, but he moved his hand quickly, then pulled her against him. "Damn you, Kaitlin!"

"Brendan, stop it! Let go of me! There are people right outside. We have to finish this shoot."

"Oh, great! You're about to bite me, but when I fight back,

you scream about propriety. You don't fight fair, lady, so don't expect fairness from me.''

''I didn't know that we were fighting,'' she snapped.

''I walked in, and you attacked.''

''You haven't been attacking all evening?''

All evening. She had been in his arms all evening. And she was in his arms now. He was growing tenser and hotter by the minute. It was worse than ever here. Worse, being alone.

He shook his head slowly, then he released her. ''Let's go. Let's finish your damn commercial.''

She went very still, then she swept by him. When he started to follow her, she swung around and hissed, ''Go powder your nose!''

He stopped, staring at her, as she continued. ''If I'm paying you so damn well, I want my money's worth.''

He arched a brow, smiling. ''Oh, honey, you already *have* gotten your money's worth,'' he assured her.

But he swung around and stepped into the bedroom to have his makeup retouched, slamming the door behind him. When he came out, he allowed the door to slam behind him again. Then he was sorry he had. The girl, Janis, was obviously waiting for him. She jumped sky high at the crack of the door.

''Mr. O'Herlihy, they're ready for you. If you're ready, that is.''

''Brendan. And I'm ready. Thanks.''

She smiled nervously, still staring at him as he opened the outer door of the suite for her. She flushed. ''How could she have divorced you?'' she whispered.

''I wondered about that myself,'' he said, and smiled. ''Come on, this is almost over.''

Almost, but not quite. Lenny explained the scene to him. It was late, the end of a perfect day of sun and fun. And the evening was going to be even better, because they'd been doused in sunblock all day. No painful burns. No skin that couldn't bear to be touched.

''You're carrying her off for a night of ecstasy now. That's all you have to remember. Got it?''

''Oh, yeah, I've got it,'' Brendan said dryly.

Kaitlin was standing there. He took a step forward and lifted her off her feet. She gasped when he held her like a sack of potatoes. "Okay, Lenny, where am I supposed to be when I start looking forward to all this ecstasy?"

"Right there. Just stare into her eyes and come toward me."

Brendan walked to the end of the hall with Kaitlin in his arms.

"Ecstasy, Kaitlin," he said sarcastically. "Remember, we're anticipating ecstasy."

"Yes, because the night really *is* almost over," she said.

"No talking, you two," Lenny called. "Just eyes, nothing but eyes. Okay, action. Roll 'em!"

Brendan started down the hallway. Eyes. Eyes. Oh, yeah. Hers were the most delicate blue he had ever seen in his life. Eyes...but he could feel her fingertips at his nape. The beautiful sweeping skirt left her knees bare, and her elegant stockings were rubbing against his hip. He could feel the soaring heat of her body and the beating of his heart.

"Cut! Gosh, guys, I'm sorry, but we'll have to do it one more time. I just realized that there's a cord in the shot. Hey, get that out of there, huh?" he shouted to the nearest technician.

Kaitlin closed her eyes. "Damn! I thought we were done!"

"Hey, I'm the one doing all the work," Brendan reminded her curtly. "And you're not exactly a featherweight."

She kicked him, but he only held her closer. "Watch it, Ms. O'Herlihy. I'll drop you flat next time."

She narrowed her eyes. "You wouldn't dare."

"I dare anything, and you know it," he reminded her. She must have believed him, because her arms tightened around his neck. He smiled.

"Ready?" Lenny asked.

Brendan looked into her eyes again. "Yes."

Action...and the cameras rolled. Brendan walked with her to the door, then thrust it open with his foot before walking inside with her and closing the door behind him.

"Perfect!" Lenny called. "Perfect!"

They were alone in the room. She was still in his arms. And her eyes were still on his.

Slowly, very, very slowly, he eased her to her feet. Her body rubbed along the length of his, and it was torture.

Then she was standing on her own, and he knew he had to go. "Dinner next Wednesday. I'll pick you up at eight. Be ready."

She nodded.

"I'll send the tux to your office," he said harshly.

She nodded again.

Almost blindly, he swung around. Then he felt her hand on his shoulder, and he turned back. "What?"

"If I'm so good at getting what I want," she said softly, wistfully, "why is it that nothing ever went right for us?"

He had no answer for her. He wasn't even sure she had really voiced the soft, painful question.

"You're not going to stand me up?"

"No."

He turned and opened the door, then hurried down the hall, heedless of Lenny calling to him. Heedless of everything.

The day was over. And he needed to get away.

On Friday morning Kaitlin came into the office and found Danny, Sam and Janis watching a preliminary version of the commercial in the conference room.

She stood in the back, watching the day unfold before her eyes, and wanted to scream. It was too painful to watch.

She wanted Brendan to be real so she could run to the screen and smack him right in the face. Ever since he had walked—no, swaggered, or at the very least sauntered—back into her life, thoughts of him had been plaguing her.

She had spent a night with Gram, looking for dresses, and Gram had found a beautiful creation in dove-gray silk and lace. But Kaitlin hadn't quite managed to be as enthusiastic as she felt she should have been.

Her mind had wandered.

And wandered.

And then there had been her dreams. Decadent dreams. Dreams so real she had woken up in a cold sweat.

She had always done things wholeheartedly. When she had been with Brendan, life had been a feast. And since they had parted...

She hadn't had a single real involvement, throwing herself into her work instead. She had dated, but she had never let anyone come close. Now she wished she had. She wished she'd had all kinds of experiences. Then she could have dealt much better with her feelings for Brendan.

Instead, all she did was dream of him.

Sometimes the dreams were wonderful. She could almost hear the laughter, the sighs.

Other times the dreams were painful. She would be walking in a mist, and then she'd find herself in the cemetery. Brendan would be standing there, and she'd call to him, but he wouldn't look up. And then, when he did look up, he'd look right through her, and no matter how loudly she called, he didn't seem to hear.

And sometimes she would relive the agony when she had lost the baby. Once again she was there all alone, hearing the doctor tell her there was no heartbeat. She wondered again how anything could hurt so much, and she called to him again. Again and again.

But he didn't come....

The lights went on, calling her back to reality. The sixty seconds were over. The voice-over had faded away. And everyone in the room was staring at her.

Danny was grinning from ear to ear. "Wow, boss! I have never seen anything so hot in all my born days!"

"My fingers are still sizzling!" Sam laughed.

"All right, all right!" Kaitlin groaned. "No more."

"I have sweat breaking out all over my body!" Danny said.

"Good! Because you're about to sweat your way to the unemployment office," she assured him.

She turned and left the room quickly, hurrying to her office and slamming the door. It was a great commercial. So why wasn't she in seventh heaven?

"Damn you, Brendan O'Herlihy!" she swore. Then she noticed that her private line was buzzing. She picked it up. "Yes, Sam?"

"Private call," Sam said quickly and hung up.

"Hello?" Kaitlin said. It was probably Gram or Barbara.

"Hello. Just checking on Wednesday."

It was Brendan. She held her breath, counted slowly, then spoke. "I never welsh on a payment."

"I'll remember that. See you then."

And he was gone.

It was the name O'Herlihy. Why had she kept it?

Brendan had been gone so long. They'd sent him to the Middle East. Even when she had realized that he wasn't coming back to be with her, she hadn't been able to file the divorce papers at first. She had spent long nights awake and miserable, realizing slowly that no matter how tender he had once been, he hadn't really wanted the cold, quick ceremony that had made them man and wife. It had just been for the baby. And now the baby was gone.

When he'd finally come home, he had been both distant and hungry, hungry as she'd never known him. The service had changed him; the things that he had seen had changed him. He had seemed to need her, but he hadn't talked, and he hadn't been able to listen, either. And then he'd gone again.

All she'd had left were school and her part-time job with an ad agency. And by the time she was twenty-one, she'd already acquired a very nice professional reputation as Kaitlin O'Herlihy.

She had kept the name for business purposes.

Or had she kept the name because she had really prayed all along that he wouldn't allow her to give it up, to give him up? Kaitlin sighed, hesitated a moment, then sprang to her feet. She'd created a great ad, and she'd endured hell to do it. She deserved a break.

She left the office, stopping just long enough to tell Janis that she was in charge.

She spent the afternoon in a desperate flurry of shopping, then remembered just in time that Gram was bringing Mr. Rosen to dinner, and Barbara and Joe would be joining them, too.

And she didn't have a thing in the house for dinner, including the steaks she had told Gram she would make.

She bought the steaks, Idaho potatoes and the ingredients for a Caesar salad, then hurried home. She straightened the house quickly, then started the salad and the potatoes, watching the clock all the while.

When the doorbell rang, she swallowed a mouthful of wine and hurried to answer it.

It was Barbara and Joe. Kaitlin stepped aside quickly, welcoming her cousin with a warm embrace and giving Joe a big hug, too. They both seemed to have a glow about them. Barbara was beautiful to begin with, with her coppery curls and green eyes. And Joe was tall and lean, sandy-haired and hazel-eyed and very handsome. But tonight they both looked dazzling.

"You guys look great," she told them laughingly.

Barbara wiggled her hand beneath Kaitlin's nose. "It isn't us—it's the diamond. Oh, Kaitlin, isn't it beautiful?"

It was a beautiful diamond. Pear shaped, throwing off a million different colors in the light.

"Gorgeous," she agreed. "But the glow is coming from the two of you. Joe, I bought some champagne, want to crack it open? Gram is never late, she should be along any second."

"I'd love to crack open the champagne," Joe assured her. He and Barbara followed Kaitlin into the kitchen. "Kaitlin," he murmured, hesitating, then plunging in, "did Brendan come to see you?"

She managed to keep her smile. "Yes, he did."

Joe exhaled with relief. "Then everything is all right with you?"

"Of course," she said. "Here's the champagne." She heard the bell ring again. "And there's Gram. I'll bet she's glowing, too. I'm going to feel like a fifth wheel tonight. I'll be the only one not glowing." She grinned and started for the door, then paused, realizing that Joe and Barbara were staring at one another with nervous expressions.

"What?" she demanded.

Barbara shook her head. The bell was ringing more insistently. "Barbara...?"

"I'll get the door," Barbara said.

"No, it's my house. I'll go," Kaitlin told her.

It was Gram. And she was with a tall, handsome older man with a full cap of white hair, dancing blue eyes to match Gram's, and a delightful smile. Kaitlin welcomed him warmly and urged them both in.

"Kaitlin, this is Al Rosen. Al, me granddaughter, Kaitlin O'Herlihy."

"Al!" Kaitlin took his hand, and she liked him immediately. He had a firm grip and that great smile. And he had given Gram a glow.

"Barbara and Joe are already here, in the kitchen. Joe is just opening the champagne."

"Just Barbara and Joe?" Gram asked. They were already through the entryway, with its high ceiling, by the kitchen door. Kaitlin stopped and looked at Gram inquisitively.

"Who else is coming?"

Joe was behind her, clearing his throat. "I was trying to tell you, Kaitlin. Your grandmother ran into Brendan this afternoon at our house.''

She turned and stared at him. He grimaced and whispered, ''Well, at least you're not going to be a fifth wheel.'' She didn't smile. ''Kaitlin, I didn't invite him.''

The doorbell was ringing again, and Al Rosen was looking at her with a question in his eyes. Should he get the door for her? No...Gram wouldn't have done this to her!

Kaitlin hurried to the door and threw it open.

Gram had.

Brendan was standing there, wearing a red polo shirt and form-hugging jeans. And those glasses with the dark lenses that hid all his thoughts.

''No!'' she whispered.

And then Barbara was beside her, laughing nervously. ''Guess who's coming to dinner? Brendan, hi, come on in.''

''Brendan!'' It was Gram, coming forward. ''Thank you for comin'. I'm so glad you made it.'' She turned to Kaitlin. ''He told me that he couldna come, and I twisted his arm, I did. I assured him that ye'd be pleased, Kaitlin.''

''Pleased as punch,'' Kaitlin managed to say.

Gram smiled delightedly. ''Come on, Al, let's see to that champagne!''

She and Al Rosen disappeared through the swinging door to the kitchen, with Barbara nearly running at their heels. And once again Kaitlin was alone with Brendan. ''I thought I was supposed to see you on Wednesday!'' she said.

He pulled off his glasses and leaned against the door frame. ''You are. I just came tonight because I couldn't seem to resist your grandmother.''

''The evening has just gone straight to hell!'' Kaitlin groaned. He grinned and sauntered past her. ''Oh, I don't think so. I never did have a problem with your cooking. Steak, Joe tells me. Sounds like a good meal.''

He started for the kitchen. At the swinging door he paused. ''Coming, Ms. O'Herlihy?''

She closed the front door and leaned against it. He waited, and she groaned aloud. ''Yes, I'm coming.''

''I knew you'd see it my way.''

She swept by him as regally as she could, pausing just before entering the kitchen. "Your way, Mr. O'Herlihy? This is *my* house and it's *my* party!" she informed him heatedly, then pushed through the door.

She managed to look at Joe casually and ask, "Is the champagne open?"

"It is. Ready for a glass?"

She glanced at Brendan. "I'm ready for a bottle," she said pleasantly, then accepted the glass that Joe had poured for her, draining it quickly.

She was in for another long night.

There was a certain amount of chaos in the kitchen as the champagne was passed around, and Brendan met Al, and Joe greeted Brendan, and Barbara kissed Brendan like a long-lost relative. Then the noise level began to die down, and Barbara told Kaitlin that the table looked beautiful and that she would set another place for Brendan. Kaitlin drank her second glass of champagne, then a third, then she managed to shoo her grandmother and Al Rosen out of the kitchen so she could check on the meal. Joe, nearly as comfortable in her house as he was in his own, offered to show everyone the living room.

Kaitlin turned, only to find that she was rid of everyone except for her unexpected guest. He was standing at the refrigerator, pulling out the salad. She wanted to tell him to get out, but she poured herself another glass of champagne instead, watching him.

"Isn't that stuff still deadly for you?" he asked politely.

"I'm older," she said with a shrug. He let it go at that. He set the salad on the counter, along with the fixings for the dressing and the anchovies to be added at the last minute.

She brushed past him, wishing there was a little more room in her kitchen. "Wouldn't you like to go out and sit with the other guests? The invited ones?"

He leaned against the counter, grinning. "I thought I'd try to be helpful."

"If you'd really wanted to be helpful," she reminded him heatedly, "you would have turned down the invitation."

"How could I turn down your grandmother?"

"Oh, it might have taken some strength, but I'm sure you could have managed it."

He stepped past her, making himself at home and reaching into the refrigerator again. He rummaged around for a beer, popping it open as she stared at him. "I can only take so much champagne, no matter how great the celebration." He smiled.

She turned to her steaks, which were still marinating. She took them out of the mixture, set them on the broiler pan and put them into the oven. When she turned again, Brendan was finishing the salad. She let him, sweeping out of the room with the rolls and butter. Brendan followed her with the salad, and she went to turn the steaks. By the time she had pulled them out, everything else was already on the table. He took the platter from her to carry it out.

"You wanted me to turn down steaks?" he asked softly. "I'll give you this—you always did broil a great steak."

"And I'll give you this," she replied sweetly. "You…" She hesitated, knowing that what she was about to say was true. "You were always good at helping out in the kitchen."

"Was that a compliment?" he asked her.

She shrugged, then smiled. "No, that was probably four glasses of champagne." She walked out, and he followed with the platter. She called to everyone else, and they came to the table.

Ten minutes later, Kaitlin was glad of the champagne. She was feeling mellow, something she hadn't thought possible. Not with Brendan at her table.

But she realized that he and Joe and Barbara were very comfortable together. As comfortable as she was with them herself. And she knew then that they had seen a lot of Brendan—and that they had just been careful not to mention it to her.

As for Gram, she had always doted on Brendan. And Al Rosen had seemed to like him right away, too. Brendan had a way with people. Gaelic charm with a soft New England accent, she decided. Al Rosen, it seemed, was a passionate boat enthusiast. And few people knew the Eastern seaboard better than Brendan.

Brendan told Al about his latest project, searching for a small Spanish man-of-war that had been blown off course and probably sunk near the Upper Keys in the late fifteen hundreds. When Al told him wistfully that it sounded like the dream of a lifetime and a great way to make a living, Brendan cast Kaitlin a quick glance.

"Some might see it as modern-day piracy," he murmured politely.

She smiled back. "Some might."

She really had bought good champagne. And the ice bucket was right next to her. It was easy to reach for more. And it was nice. She didn't feel in the least as if she had over imbibed. She felt comfortably drowsy. Content. Able to weather any storm.

Including her ex-husband.

"So tell us more about the wedding," Brendan said to Gram, deftly drawing the others into the conversation.

Gram flushed. "Well, Kaitlin and I bought my dress the other night."

"It's beautiful. Really beautiful," Kaitlin said, smiling at Al.

"And simple. Like our ceremony will be. Some of the family will be coming, and a few close friends," Gram said. She and Al smiled at one another, and Kaitlin felt her heart warming.

"Well," Joe teased, "it sounds like a wild fling."

"A marriage is always a wild fling," Al said, his eyes on Gram.

"But as for the wedding...."

"I had my big wedding," Gram said softly. "When I married Granda. We had nothing in Dublin, really nothing at'all. But me mum made me gown, and me sisters sewed the pearls onto the train. And Da's best friend was a butcher, so he gave us a grand reception out in the yard. It was a great wedding, though, a wonderful wedding. Like the kind Barb and Joe will have. And that's good, Al, eh? But not for us. It's the marriage that matters."

"Your wedding will be beautiful, Gram," Barbara assured her. Brendan reached across the table for the red wine and poured a small portion into his glass. "But I agree with Liz," he said softly. "It's not the wedding but the marriage that counts."

He was looking at Kaitlin, and she wanted to slap him. She had wanted a big wedding, sure. But she had loved him. Really loved him with her whole heart. When they had been married in the midst of all the chaos, she had wanted it to last forever.

He was the one who hadn't wanted her when it came down to it.

She turned away from him coldly. "Well, here's to Gram and Al! May you live long and happily. Al, we're pleased to have you with us!"

"Here, here!" Joe said.

They all raised their glasses, and Gram and Al were duly toasted. Then Joe told them how hard it had been to get the church date he had wanted, and Barbara watched him with a soft smile. Kaitlin was still amazed that Joe had made the arrangements with the church.

"We need to go out looking for dresses," Kaitlin reminded her.

"Yes! How about this week?"

"Sure."

"How's your Wednesday night?"

"It's fine——" she began, then she felt Brendan watching her. How could she have forgotten? "Wednesday is bad for me," she said sweetly. "Tuesday?"

"How about Thursday?"

"Fine. I need something to wear for Gram and Al's wedding, so we can look for that at the same time."

"Sounds great," Barbara said. "I'm going to have to look pretty hard. I need something that's already in."

"Why can't you just order what you want?" Joe asked her.

She glanced at Kaitlin, shaking her head impatiently. "It can take a full year for a dress to be ordered and come in. There's usually a minimum of three to four months. I don't want to worry. I know there's something really beautiful out there, and I can just have it altered. Right, Kaitlin?"

Kaitlin nodded. Barbara poured more wine. "Of course, you do have to be careful. They've been having the strangest problem in Massachusetts. Donna was telling me about it the other day. There's a group of wedding bandits stealing shipments of gowns. Can you imagine?"

"Stealing wedding gowns?" Brendan said. "What for?"

"They change the labels and sell them in the South and out in the West. Lots of women want to buy gowns more quickly than they can be specially made. It's quite a racket, I understand."

"Well, if we're buying a gown to be altered," Kaitlin said, "at least we shouldn't have to worry. We'll find the gown if it takes all week, buy it and get a seamstress working on it right away."

Barbara had finished her meal, so she pushed back her chair and picked up her plate. She dusted a kiss on Gram's hair. "Not all week," she said with a soft smile. "Don't forget, we have plans for Saturday."

"Saturday. So close," Gram breathed.

"You can't be nervous!" Kaitlin told her.

"Not too nervous, I hope!" Al Rosen said.

They all laughed, and Kaitlin stood with Barbara to start picking up the dishes. She was dismayed to realize that she was swaying a little. She steadied herself on the chair and was certain that no one had caught her unintended movement.

Except for Brendan. He was watching her. Disapprovingly, she was certain.

Well, what and when she chose to drink was none of his affair.

"I'll help clear," Gram said.

"You'll do no such thing," Kaitlin told her. "You sit with Al, and we'll have cake and coffee coming right out."

She turned and carefully carried her collection of plates into the kitchen. She turned, expecting to find Barb behind her.

Brendan was there instead. He set a stack of dishes on the counter. "Want me to take the cake out?"

"I can take it out."

"I'd love to do it for you."

"You think that I've been—"

"Drinking too much champagne, yes. But hey, it's your house, your party. I just thought you might want someone else to carry the cake."

She plugged in the coffeepot. "Carry the cake, then. Make yourself happy."

He went out with it. Then Barb appeared with the last of the dishes, her eyes sparkling. "Well?"

"Well what? Oh, Mr. Rosen! I think he's charming. And he loves Gram, which is all that really matters, isn't it?"

"I'm not talking about Al! He *is* great. We liked him from the moment we met him—Joe and I. But what else would you expect from Gram other than a super guy?"

"Right," Kaitlin agreed, pulling out her best cups and saucers and cake plates. Then she paused and looked at Barb. "So what were you talking about?"

"You and Brendan."

Kaitlin stared at the coffee cups. "Brendan and me? We're adults. We'll manage."

"You'll manage?" Barbara said. "That's all?"

Kaitlin swung around and looked at her cousin. "Of course. You want me to be a bridesmaid, and I will. Even if Brendan's going to be there, too. Joe and Brendan have apparently seen a lot more of one another over the years than I realized. Maybe I should have known, though. After all, Joe did find him for me when I wanted to talk to him several years ago."

There must have been a trace of bitterness in her voice, because Barbara sighed. "And he wouldn't agree to have the marriage annulled. I'm sorry, Kaitlin, we both thought that if you just talked to him…well, Joe managed to get one very easily. And I did want to be married in the church. Not that it really matters. Married is married, just like Al said. The wedding goes by so quickly! But then you have the memories all your life. Kaitlin, I've waited so long! I do want a big wedding. I want a million people, and I want to be beautiful!"

Kaitlin smiled, then hugged her. "Joe wants you to have it all. It took him a while to come around, I'll grant you. But he seems to want it all to be perfect now."

Barbara nodded happily. "Just like you originally planned, before you and Brendan had that awful fight over that guy you were seeing." She paused, then gasped in horror. "Oh! I'm sorry, Kaitlin, I—"

"I wasn't seeing another guy," Kaitlin said wearily. "I told you that—"

"I know, I know, I'm so sorry! But that's what Brendan thought, wasn't it?"

"I guess. Barbara, it doesn't matter. It's all in the past."

"Oh, Kaitlin! I'm just so grateful to you both! It's so important for me to have you, and so important to Joe to have Brendan, too. And you've both been wonderful, trying to make it all just right for us."

"No problem," Kaitlin said, then turned away. The coffee was ready.

"I'll take out the cups," Barbara said. As she headed for the door she called back, "Joe put the liqueurs and the whiskey out. Did you get whipped cream? It's a great night for Irish coffee!"

"It sure is," Kaitlin agreed. She opened the refrigerator and found whipped cream. When she closed the door and turned again, Brendan was in the kitchen. Watching her.

"Want some help?" he asked. His gaze was fathomless, wandering up and down the length of her, then meeting her eyes.

She smiled. Sweetly. Defiantly. "Yes, please. Grab the cream and sugar and the coffeepot."

He did, still watching her as she sailed past him with the whipped cream.

The cake was wonderful, and Irish coffee went with it just right. Kaitlin had two cups.

Gram talked about her reception, and Barbara and Joe sat with their fingers entwined atop the table, listening, silently planning their own wedding. Kaitlin was surprised—then guilt-stricken—to find that her parents were coming down for the wedding. They would be arriving at the airport Friday afternoon.

"I said you'd pick them up, Kaitlin. Your mother will verify times with you sometime this week," Gram said.

"Of course," Kaitlin murmured.

Brendan, and now her parents. What more could she ask for? Oh, she loved her parents dearly, but she wasn't sure she wanted to be with them and Brendan in the same room, and she was certain that Gram had already invited Brendan to the wedding.

It didn't really matter, she decided. The champagne was curling around the whiskey in the Irish coffee. Or maybe the whiskey was curling around the champagne. It was going to be all right. Even if Brendan was at her dining room table, still staring at her. She smiled at him. He really did have those wonderful Irish good looks, with his ebony hair and beautiful green eyes, just sparked by those touches of gold. She wondered if life might not have been incredibly easier if she hadn't fallen so hard for him so long ago. It still seemed impossible that he was sitting in her dining room. And that she could smile so easily as he sat there!

Kaitlin realized then that Barbara had picked up most of the dishes, and Joe was standing behind her, saying that they had to leave.

Gram and Mr. Rosen were standing, too, and Brendan with them. She stood, and she wasn't sure if she swayed, or if she just thought that she did. At least she was still speaking rationally and coherently; she was certain of that.

But when she touched her lips, she had to press hard to make sure they were still there.

She ignored the feeling to smile and kiss Gram and Barbara and Joe goodbye, then she shook Al Rosen's hand. Then they were gone, and when she turned, she realized that Brendan was still in the house.

She didn't say anything. She just leaned against the door, watching him.

"Want me to leave?" he asked.

She smiled. "I'm not sure."

"Um," he murmured. His lashes seemed inky black, shielding

his eyes. "Why don't you sit down in the living room? I'll pick up the rest of the dishes."

"There's a dishwasher."

"I know. I saw it. Do you want me to brew another pot of coffee?"

"I think I've had enough coffee."

"I think you've had enough *Irish* coffee. You might just need some of the strong black stuff."

His hand was on her arm, and he was leading her to the living room couch. She sat, and he slipped off her shoes. She felt his fingers against the arch of her foot, and she stared into his eyes.

She smiled. "Do you know, Brendan, you're still extraordinarily good-looking."

"Am I? Thank you." He shoved her back until she was leaning against the overstuffed arm of the chesterfield. Her eyes were very wide, her smile sweet, and her hair fell like Rapunzel's, in long, soft tresses and waves. His eyes caught hers. "And you're still extraordinarily beautiful, Kaitlin. But then, you know that, don't you?"

"I'm getting old, Brendan."

"All of thirty."

She shook her head. "It's young if you've done something with your life. I haven't really done anything with mine."

"You've done lots with your life. You've got a great business. You're bright, creative, talented. You've succeeded. That meant an awful lot to you between the ages of twenty and twenty-two."

She stared at him searchingly. "I didn't think you noticed anything I was feeling in those years," she said lightly.

He sighed. "Kaitlin... Never mind. I'm going to make coffee and finish your dishes."

"You don't have to. I can do them in the morning."

"Kaitlin, you're going to have a horrible headache in the morning. You're going to wish that someone would come along and shoot you."

She closed her eyes, vaguely aware that he was right. "It's all your fault."

"What's my fault?"

"The champagne. I inhaled it because you walked in."

She didn't see his crooked smile as he walked away. She winced slightly, aware that he had been right. She couldn't drink champagne. She'd never been able to. And she'd already suffered one wretched hangover this week. Now she was going to have another.

The room was heaving. Her eyes were closed, but the room was heaving. Like an ocean, undulating around her. She could feel her foot where he had touched her. Just her foot.

When they'd filmed the commercial, he'd touched a lot more than her foot. And she had felt that, too....

But tonight, despite her intoxicated state, she was feeling more. She was seeing more. She'd never heard his voice quite so clearly, felt it dance along her spine so seductively.

She liked it. She felt caressed by it, beguiled by it. She thought about the other day on the beach. She had wanted to touch his chest, to feel the thick, dark hair that grew there in such a fascinating pattern.

She wanted to curl against him. She wanted to taste his kiss. She wanted to do more than that.

Something moved over her cheek. He was sitting beside her, stroking her face lightly with his knuckles. She smiled. She had dreamed him, and he had appeared.

"Hi," she murmured.

"Hi. The coffee is done."

"Great." She couldn't stop smiling as she caught his hand and inspected it. She liked the broad back with its slight spattering of freckles. She liked his fingers, too. They were rugged hands, but handsome. Masculine hands. And when they touched her...

"I think I should just put you to bed," he said huskily.

She smiled. "Are you coming with me?"

He swore softly. "Damn it, Kaitlin, don't do this to me."

"That's right," she said huskily. "You said you weren't going to seduce me."

"Right."

"That's so honorable of you, Brendan."

He sighed. "Kaitlin, you may not believe this, but I was always trying to do the honorable thing. I've never known how to explain the way I felt after Sean died. I know that I was at fault, and I have no excuse. I can only apologize."

Tears were coming to her eyes. She didn't want to get weepy. She was feeling so content and peaceful, so delicious and peaceful....

And hungry.

She set his hand against her cheek and closed her eyes. "I loved Sean, too, you know," she said softly. "Not the way you did, of course. I understood. I really did." Her eyes flew open, and she smiled. "Brendan, did I tell you that you've aged well?"

"Just like fine wine," he returned with a grin.

She sat up, curled her arms around his neck and met his gaze. She studied his eyes. And then it seemed too hard to resist, and she pulled him close to her. She had wanted to do it all day when they were filming.

She kissed him.

At first he stiffened, his mouth closed. But when she teased his lips with the tip of her tongue, prodding slightly, he gave in to her. He opened his mouth and seemed to consume her. Hot, sweet, searing, his tongue plunged deeply into her mouth, where it met and dueled with her own. When he broke the kiss it was only to press his lips against her ear, laving it, then the pulse at the base of her throat, tasting and feeling and savoring. Then his mouth fused with hers once again.

This was the kiss they had known before, only deeper, hungrier. More demanding and more giving. Her body trembled and shook. She moved her fingers into his hair, to touch and explore. Then she allowed her nails to trail down his back, her fingers tugging at his shirt, freeing it from his waistband so she could touch his hot flesh. She moved her hands from his back around to his chest and allowed her fingers to tease the crisp black mat that had so fascinated her the other day.

His mouth lifted from hers. "Kaitlin, I'm warning you..."

She found his lips again and pulled him down. The little pearl buttons on her white silk blouse were giving, melting away. His hands were on her, hefting the weight of her breasts, teasing them through her bra. And then he was freeing her flesh from its restraint. His palms moved over her nipples, and then his dark head lowered against her, and he was tasting her, filling his mouth with the hardness of one nipple, with the soft flesh and supple firmness of her breast. And she was clinging to him, soft gasps escaping her as she held him close.

His head rose, hair tousled, his look sensual. He lifted her, cast aside the blouse and the bra and laid her back, his eyes studying and devouring her. She wanted him so badly. And she loved the way he looked at her. Just like he had before....

"What you're doing to me should be illegal," he whispered to her raggedly. "Punishable by death."

She smiled and tried to reach for him. Her fingers caressed his tousled hair; then her arms fell to her sides.

He rose and lifted her into his arms. He moved down the hallway to her bedroom, where he carried her into the darkness and laid her down, tearing at the covers as he did so.

"Brendan!" she whispered.

His hands were on the zipper of her skirt. She could feel his touch against her bare flesh, and it was delicious. In the shadows she could see his eyes, could see the passion and determination within them, and she smiled again. He was with her, holding her.

"We should have made it," she told him vaguely. "We came from the same background, the same religion, the same ideals, the same desires. And I loved you so much. What happened to us, Brendan?"

Her breath was soft against his cheek. Her body was supple and liquid and beautiful, offering all the torments of hell and all the raptures of heaven.

A harsh, ragged moan escaped him as his lips fell lightly on her forehead, then her lips. And she felt the soft hair on his chest and the warm ripple of muscle beneath her fingers.

Kaitlin felt his lips on her own, his hands on her nakedness.

He rose and looked at her, then swore at the tension that gripped his body.

She was so damn beautiful, curled on the bed.

He swallowed hard, then tucked in his shirttails and did up his buttons. Her lashes were thick and lustrous against her cheeks, her hair a wild tangle. There was a stray lock over her cheek, and he reached tenderly to move it. His hand hovered, then he stroked her cheek gently again.

"Yes, we should have made it, Kaitlin. We should have made it."

Then he bent and kissed her lips once again. A soft sigh escaped her, and she smiled as she slipped into sleep.

Then he smiled as he pulled the sheet over her. She was going to have one hell of a morning.

He knew her well. And she was definitely going to have one hell of a morning.

## Chapter 5

**K**aitlin's head was spinning, and her tongue felt like sandpaper.

For the first few minutes as she began to wake up, all she could do was feel the subtle tortures within her body.

And from there on it only got worse.

There was a sheet covering her to her neck, but she felt funny beneath it.

She was naked.

And she wasn't one of those people who naturally slip naked into bed.

A groan escaped her, and she tried to remember the evening.

Brendan.

It could all be explained with a single word. He had arrived, and she had drained a glass of champagne in a fraction of a second. And more had followed. Then there had been dinner and cake and coffee. Irish coffee.

She groaned aloud again. She should have been born a devout Muslim. Muslims didn't drink at all, did they? She would never have tasted champagne in the first place.

Never, never again.

She tried to sit up, her head pounding. She wanted someone to shoot her and put her out of her misery.

To shoot her...

Someone had said something about that last night. That she would wake up with a headache so bad that she would want to be shot.

Brendan...

Oh, no. There had been dinner, then conversation and Irish coffee. That was where she had stopped before. Because she didn't really want to go on.

She had stood at the door. She had kissed Gram and Barbara good night. She had hugged Joe. She had waved to her almost step-grandfather. Then she had closed the door, and...

Brendan.

He had still been inside. He had brought her to the couch. He had said something about the dishes and coffee, and she had closed her eyes, and he had come back.

A very, very loud groan broke from her lips.

She hadn't been able to keep herself from telling him how good he looked. How well he had weathered time. He'd promised not to seduce her, but he'd also warned her that he couldn't be responsible if she seduced him.

And, oh! The things she could remember! Curling her fingers into his hair, welcoming—inviting—his kiss. And feeling his touch on her.

She could even remember that he had carried her in here, already half naked, and removed her skirt.

What else had happened?

Her memory was blanking out on her. It was as if she had forgotten everything after reaching the darkness of the room.

Rather evident, isn't it, Kaitlin? she tormented herself in silence, her head crashing painfully to the pillow. Then she rose, wishing she could just stay in bed forever. If only her head would stop pounding so badly! No, no, maybe it was good that her head was pounding, because she really didn't want to think.

She had to take something for her head.

She realized that she was naked and wrapped the sheet around herself.

Her clothing was tossed over the big wicker chair in the corner of the room. Her shoes were beneath it.

She staggered into the kitchen and discovered that everything was as neat as a pin. The coffeepot was cleaned out, with coffee measured into it so all she had to do this morning was flick a switch. She didn't. Not yet. She didn't want to wake up.

She fumbled through the cabinets for a packet of bicarbonate, mixed it with water and swallowed the concoction in seconds. She set the glass on the counter, her thoughts suddenly all too clear.

What a fool I am, she thought derisively. I meet him every four years and hop into bed, then spend the rest of my life dreaming. How could I have done such a thing! I'm thirty years old. Mature. I should be able to handle this, to pretend it never happened.

But she couldn't. Because there would be dinner Wednesday. And Gram's wedding. And parties. And more weddings.

She could beg out of dinner. She could be deathly ill all week. She felt as if she was deathly ill already.

With another moan, she staggered to the bedroom and crawled into bed, praying for sleep to claim her again. It did, but it was anything but restful, because she began to dream.

It was years ago, almost four years ago. She was home, and one of her cousins mentioned that another cousin had gotten an annulment so she could be married again in the church. Kaitlin's mother had been there, and she had mentioned softly that if only Kaitlin and Brendan had gotten an annulment, they both could have looked forward to marrying again within the church.

Her father had suggested that her mother lead her own life, but Kaitlin had seen the hurt and the hope in her mother's eyes.

Then Joe, good old Joe, had known where to find Brendan. He had set up a meeting, and she had driven down to the Keys to see Brendan.

He'd been surprised to see her. Cold, aloof. Then he'd made an about face, asking her to stay for dinner. He'd cooked for her at his house on the water, and she'd had to admit that the surroundings were really elegant. And there had been candlelight, and wine....

She could remember everything in her dream. The room had been beautifully paneled in light wood. There had been a rose on the table, a snowy cloth and beautiful crystal. And Brendan. When she saw him, she started drinking the wine too quickly. The food was delicious, but she barely touched it. He was charming, his green eyes ablaze in the candlelight. He asked about her family, and she asked about his. They talked about his latest venture, and she told him she was thinking about breaking away from her firm to form her own company. She flirted—outrageously, probably. But it was so easy to do, so natural. And then she began to explain why she had come, and why an annulment would benefit both of them. He listened, and she didn't notice his eyes narrowing. Then he suggested a stroll along the deck, over the water.

In the dream the mist was all around him, but she could still feel the balmy salt air, smell the rich scent of the sea—and the man. She didn't know when she stopped talking, except that it must have been when he kissed her. When he moved his lips over her bare shoulders. And she knew that she wasn't talking when he lifted her into his arms. And she knew what was happening, but she had no desire to stop it. He was seducing her, and the torment was sweet. Suddenly they were inside, and there was moonlight streaming into the room. She held her breath against the feel of his lips moving slowly over the glow-bathed length of her, until the longing became so strong that she was unable to endure it. The desperate desire for fulfillment, for the raw tempest and passion, rose within her, and she touched him, whispering incoherent words against his flesh. It was so good to feel him inside her again that tears came to her eyes.

He touched her again during the night. And again.

But in the morning she woke up alone. He had left a note saying that she should come back when all she wanted was him. And she had known then that he had played her so damn well that she didn't dare go back, ever.

The mist faded. She could hear a clock ticking. She was awake, but the dream had been so real that patches of it remained.

No, the dream only seemed to have been so real because of everything that had happened last night.

At least her head wasn't pounding so badly. She cracked one eye open.

She was going to live.

Then she realized that she could smell coffee. And she sensed that she was not alone. She sensed it so strongly that she screamed when she rolled over and discovered that there was a figure in the doorway.

"For God's sake, Kaitlin, it's me."

"Brendan!"

The sheet had fallen. It was down to her waist, and she was gaping at him.

She grabbed madly for the sheet.

What for? He had apparently gotten her into her present state of undress. Or else she had done it herself because of him.

She swore and leaped out of bed, trying to cloak herself in the sheet. "Damn it, Brendan, of all the nerve! I should call the police. After everything you did—"

One ebony brow shot up. "Everything I did?" he interrupted politely.

"Oh!" She spun around and stamped into her bathroom, locking the door behind her. She should have gotten rid of him. She should have told him to leave the house.

All she wanted now was a shower. To soak herself. To drown. No, no, she had to get a grip on herself. He was in her house. Maybe he'd never left. No, she'd been awake, and he'd been gone. Besides, he was dressed in tennis shorts and a sweatshirt, and he had that just bathed and shaved look about him. He'd been gone, but he'd come back. Why?

She let the water pour over her, easing her tension. Then she panicked again.

He had promised her that he wouldn't seduce her.

And he hadn't, she reminded herself. She had to be honest with herself. With him. She had to be cold and firm and dignified. She had to admit that it had been her fault, but that it could never, never happen again.

She turned off the water with a jerk and left the shower, then rigorously toweled her hair dry. She met her reflection in the large mirror over the sink. Her eyes were huge.

And bloodshot.

She reached into the cabinet for her makeup and did a quick repair job. Her fingers were trembling, and she was certain that she was going to have mascara down her nose, but it wasn't so bad.

She tied her terry robe around herself and stepped into the bedroom.

He wasn't there, and her door was closed. She bit her lower lip, then dressed quickly in jeans and a soft knit shirt. She brushed her hair, convinced herself that she didn't look nearly as green as she felt and turned toward the door.

She had to stand there for several seconds before she could bring herself to twist the knob. She was going to be strong, mature, aloof. She was going to—oh, hell.

She managed to leave the room at last. Brendan was at the dining room table, sipping coffee and reading the morning paper. He looked exceptionally awake and aware. Clean and fresh and masculine.

And surely he was gazing at her in a condescending fashion.

She walked to the table and curled her fingers around the wooden frame of one of the chairs.

"Why did you come back?" she asked him sharply.

"Why are you so angry?" he questioned in return, leaning back in his chair, arms crossed over his chest.

"I'm not angry."

His eyes widened in disbelief, and he lifted her keys from the table. "The only way I could bolt your door was from the outside. But I thought you might like these back."

"Oh," she said numbly. "Well, thank you." *I think,* she added in silence.

"The coffee is hot."

She nodded. Coffee. Maybe after one cup she could get rid of him. She walked into the kitchen, poured herself a cup, added sugar and milk generously and drank it right there in the kitchen. She poured herself another cup and went more lightly on both the cream and the sugar, then squared her shoulders and swung around to return to the dining room to face him again.

Except that she didn't have to return to the dining room. He was leaning on the doorway, watching her, smiling.

"You're gulping that stuff down just like you were inhaling the champagne last night," he commented.

"Thank you for noticing," she said.

He was still smiling. "You really shouldn't be mad at me."

Mad? She was pale white and wanted to crawl under a rock. She lifted her chin. Mature, dignified. "I'm not angry with you, Brendan. Really. You did...you did promise me..."

"Yes?"

She wasn't white anymore. She was flaming red. If only she could speak! She was never going to manage mature and dignified if she couldn't talk.

"You did promise not to seduce me."

"Yes, I did."

"And I know..."

"Yes?" he asked.

"Well, I know that what happened was my fault. That I, uh..."

He leaned more comfortably against the door frame.

"You're not making this easy, you know."

"No, I wouldn't think of it. I'm enjoying it way too much."

"It can't happen again!" she cried desperately.

"What can't happen? I didn't do anything."

She set her coffee cup down and curled her fingers around the countertop behind her. "Brendan, I've admitted that. And I'm not angry, really I'm not."

"You shouldn't be. You should be grateful."

"Grateful!"

"I picked up the place. I locked you in all nice and sound."

"Yes, yes, you locked the door. Thank you. Great. It was before you locked the door that I'm talking about."

"Yes?"

Damn it. He was having a good time. At her expense.

"I was responsible. It was my fault. But it isn't going to happen again."

"Just exactly what is it that isn't going to happen again?"

"Brendan, please!"

He arched his brows. "Seriously. I'd like to know."

She swore softly, picked up her coffee and pushed past him to take a seat at the table. He followed and stood behind her, making her very uneasy.

"Let's see. My memory is probably better than yours."

"Brendan, stop."

"Not on your life. Let's see, I got you to the sofa, I got the dishes in the dishwasher, and I put the coffee on. And then I came out and sat next to you. And then..." His husky whisper teased her ear as he leaned behind her, putting his hands on the table. "And then, wow. Kaitlin, you have a kiss that singes the hair."

"Brendan..."

"And then, you know what?"

"I don't want to know what!"

"Then your hands were all over me. In my hair, on my shoulders, touching me...and I was trying so hard to be noble, but you've got a great smile. And great eyes. And really great—"

"Brendan!"

"And I just couldn't resist. So there we were on the couch, and the next thing I knew, half your clothing was off. And you were ripping at my shirt—"

"I was not!"

"You were, I swear it. And your fingers were all over my chest and across my shoulders, then down my back. It was the most incredible, exquisite torture!" He slid around beside her and set his hand over hers. She tried to pull away, but he took her fingers between his hands, his thumb rubbing over her palm. "Just thinking about it right now, this very second...there's a cold sweat breaking out on my skin, and a hot rush sweeping through me—",

"Stop it!"

But he ignored her, pressing on. "I got you into the bed. And I kept telling myself that I had promised—promised!—not to seduce you. But you're such a flirt. Hot and sexy—and sweet. So there you were in bed, half dressed. I couldn't leave you that way."

Her eyes were wide on his, her expression one of absolute horror. She wanted to pull her hand away, but she couldn't. She wanted to scream, to hide beneath the table, but she couldn't do that, either.

"I touched you, and oh, Kaitlin, you moved so nicely. Your skirt just slid free in my hand. And your stockings came off, and then I..."

His voice trailed away as he shuddered. She stared at him, open-mouthed and paralyzed.

Then he dropped her hand and grinned disarmingly. "Then I threw the sheet over you, locked up and left."

"What!" She gasped.

He stood, still grinning. "I really did have to try very hard to be noble. But that was it, Kaitlin. I undressed you, put you to bed and left. You haven't sold your soul—or anything else, for that matter. For the moment, at least."

She stared at him blankly for a second; then her temper soared, and she stood to face him, her fingers wound so tightly into her palms that her nails were clawing into her flesh.

"What?"

"Kaitlin, I said that you didn't—"

She approached him in a fury, her left fist flying. He caught her wrist, swearing at her strength as he struggled to capture her tightly against him.

"Kaitlin, I said—"

"You said! You let me sit there and talk and stumble and nearly die of humiliation and shame. And you knew all along—"

"Well, of course, I knew! I wasn't the inebriated one. And, as a matter of fact," he added, his green gaze dangerously alight, "I was rather insulted that you could even imagine that we had gone through with anything. I could never have forgotten a single one of our sexual encounters. No matter what I'd been drinking."

"Oh!" She gritted her teeth and tried to free her wrists. When she couldn't, she tried to kick him, but he stepped back quickly, maintaining his grip on her.

"Come on, Kaitlin."

"You just sat there and let me think——"

"Kaitlin, you were thinking about a lot that was true! You did try damn hard to resist me. And it was hard to resist you, too. But I did."

"Congratulations!" she snapped.

He laughed, brought her wrists together and pushed her into her chair.

"Want to know why I did?" he asked her.

"I'm just dying to hear!"

"Good, because you're going to. I don't want you to have any champagne excuses."

"Champagne——"

"You see, Kaitlin, I did play hardball against you once. When I realized that you had come to see me just because you wanted me to participate in a lie——"

"Brendan, it would have been for both of us!"

He let out an expletive that told her precisely what he thought of that, then continued heatedly. "Listen, we played this badly once. I seduced you because you wanted something. Then you tried to seduce me because I was the only one in the house——"

"What a horrible thing to say!" she interrupted furiously.

Suddenly he didn't seem angry anymore. He laughed, his hold on her hands loosening, and his eyes were bright. "Okay, does that mean you tried to seduce me because I was me?"

She groaned softly, trying to pull away from his touch. "Brendan, please!"

"All right, it doesn't matter for the moment. What I'm trying to explain is why I held back last night when you were doing your best to be a nearly irresistible temptation. When we make love, I want it to be for the right reasons. I don't want you even slightly inebriated. And I don't want you thinking that you can bargain anything from me."

"I never did!" she flared.

He shrugged. "All right. But you never came back."

"You made a fool out of me—and then left."

"We both did some pretty sad things to one another over the years. But, Kaitlin, I still want you. More than ever. But if I'm going to have you, I want you to want me with your eyes wide open."

"Brendan, I told you that it can't—"

"Can't ever happen again. But it can, Kaitlin." He stood, grinning. "And I'm willing to bet that it will."

Her eyes flashed sharply. "You're not allowed to seduce me, remember."

"I remember. But I'm willing to bet that you decide to seduce me again—stone cold sober."

"Not a chance," she said sweetly.

"We'll see," he told her. "It really was one hell of a night. I could have told you more, but..."

"You told me quite enough!"

He laughed and headed toward the door. "See you Wednesday night, Kaitlin. At eight."

"Maybe."

"Be ready," he warned. He allowed the door to slam shut behind him.

The sound caused her ragged nerves to snap, and she jumped, then smacked a hand on the table. "Damn him!" she swore aloud. But swearing gave her a headache all over again. She leaned her face flat on the table and savored the coolness of the wood.

Well, at least they hadn't made love.

Did that really make it any better? After everything she had done?

She lifted her head. Damn him. She wasn't sure whether she was relieved or insulted that he had managed to refuse her invitation.

She hadn't been able to refuse him....

But he thought that she would issue him another invitation. Well, that would be a cold day in hell, she swore to herself silently. Never. Never! Too many things lay between them, things that could not be forgotten.

Then she trembled suddenly, remembering his words. He had said that he wanted her, that he wanted her more now than he ever had.

She wanted him, too. She always had.

And she was afraid that she always would.

"Ah, Kaitlin, me girl, we canna always have what we want!" she told herself aloud, mimicking Gram. "What we want, love, isna always so good for us, eh?"

Brendan was definitely not good for her.

And still...

She groaned and rose. Brendan made good coffee, and there was almost a whole pot of it left in the kitchen. No sense in letting good coffee go to waste.

By Sunday she felt like living again. Barbara called and asked her to come over. She was about to say yes, then hesitated.

"Barbara, is Brendan going to be there?"

Barbara hesitated, and Kaitlin knew that he was. "He and Joe will be watching the football game. We can ignore them and look through the bridal magazines out by the pool."

She was about to say no, but then Barbara began to plead.

"Kaitlin, please! Help me get things going!"

"All right. But I can't stay late."

Later on, she prided herself on that Sunday. Everything went very much as she planned.

Joe and Brendan did stay in the den, watching the football game. And she and Barbara stretched out by the pool and leafed through magazines, then looked through the menu for the hall that they had booked.

At six, the men and women joined one another at the kitchen counter for hot dogs and chili and beer.

At least, the others had beer. Kaitlin had a ginger ale. And she noticed that Brendan's inky lashes covered his eyes when he watched her now and then with amusement, and that his mouth curved with humor. But he didn't say anything. And neither did she.

They were polite to one another. Painfully polite. And she was very careful to keep a wide distance between them.

She had walked over, and she was determined to walk home. When she started off, she turned and looked back, certain that Brendan would be following her.

He wasn't.

She started walking again, then started violently when a hand fell on her shoulder. She swung around. Brendan smiled.

"Sorry, I—"

"Brendan, I've got an early morning tomorrow."

"So have I, Kaitlin. I just wanted to let you know that I booked Donna's favorite country club for the Saturday after your grandmother's wedding."

"What?"

"I managed to get a booking for a mixed shower. The Saturday following your grandmother's wedding. Is that all right? Can you manage it?"

"I—yes, I think so."

"Good. We can go over details at dinner."

"Fine."

"I'll let Donna know. It's what she and Bill wanted, a party with all their friends. Male and female."

She had always known that if and when Donna planned a wedding, she would want something with everyone together, rather than a shower with just the women. Kaitlin should have thought of it herself. She really couldn't complain that Brendan had done so.

He was staring at her, waiting. "Was there something else?" she asked defensively.

He shook his head. "No, nothing. As long as we're in agreement."

"We are."

"Good." He turned and left her. She watched him, resenting the feeling of disappointment that rose within her. He could seem so close....

And then so damn distant. He could demand, then walk away so quickly.

She had an awful night. And she did have a very early morning. She had a number of print ads to place, and she had to deal with the various stations to get the Seashell Sunblock commercial on the air. Her morning was busy enough to allow her to forget for long moments her mortification of Friday night.

But around lunchtime Janis came in and hopped up on her desk, swinging her feet. "I took a few personal messages for you from Sam when you were on the phone with the networks."

"Great, thanks. Shoot."

"Your mother. She really wants you to call her."

Kaitlin winced. "I will."

"And Donna called from Massachusetts. She said that she knew you were really busy, so she went ahead and made travel arrangements for you. She knows that you hate to fly unless it's a life-and-death situation, so you're on the morning train next

Tuesday. A messenger will drop the ticket here. You've got a sleeper to New York, then—''

"Then I have to change trains. I know. Thanks, go on." She winced again. Donna was going to be a bride. She was supposed to be helping Donna. Donna shouldn't be having to make arrangements for her just to make sure she showed up.

"Barbara wanted you to remember that you're looking for gowns with her on Thursday night."

"Right."

"Your grandmother wanted you to remember that her wedding is this Saturday."

"I remember," Kaitlin said wryly.

"And..."

"And?"

"Your ex called."

"Brendan?"

"Do you have another ex?" Janis asked with a definite hint of mischief.

"No, I do not. What did he want?"

Janis sighed. "Whatever he wanted from me, I'd be sure to give him. Kaitlin, that is one gorgeous man. Arriving out of your past! It's so wonderful."

"It isn't wonderful at all."

Janis wasn't listening to her. She sighed again. "You know, when men appear from my past, I'm always left wondering what I was ever doing with them in the first place! They all have these huge pot bellies and have to comb their hair from one side of their heads to the other to cover up the bald spots. They never, never look like your ex-husband."

Kaitlin smiled with an effort. "He is a nice looking man," she said casually.

"Nice looking!"

"Janis..."

"All right, all right. It's just that I understand now why you don't date."

"I do date!"

"Once a year."

"That's ridiculous."

"Never mind. If you're accustomed to prime rib, it's hard as heck to settle for ground chuck."

"I'm not accustomed to anything."

"See there—you don't date!" Janis said triumphantly.

Kaitlin groaned. "I am not getting anywhere with this conversation. Janis, listen closely. What did Brendan want when he called?"

"Oh—just to remind you that you've having dinner on Wednesday night."

"Right."

"Dinner, Kaitlin. You're dating him again! It's so romantic!"

"It's not romantic! It's—it's dinner."

Janis nodded knowingly. "Prime rib," she agreed.

"Janis!"

Janis leaped off her desk. "I'm going. If you need me, just holler."

"I'll holler, all right," Kaitlin promised. Janis grinned and disappeared.

The remainder of the day passed in a rush of work. She was glad of it, glad of the layouts she had to approve, glad of all the arrangements and haggling and scheduling she had to deal with. It was nearly seven when she finished, and everyone in the office had gone home except for Janis, who had waited for her.

They decided to have pizza together before going home. When Kaitlin reached her house, she showered and fell into bed, then enjoyed a completely dreamless night.

Tuesday passed quickly, too. There was still so much she had to attend to. And she made a point of calling Donna and her mother, which took a chunk out of the day, as well.

Tuesday night she had dinner with Netty Green and Garrett Harley. It was a wretched occasion with Netty endlessly praising the commercial. Kaitlin knew she should have enjoyed it. If only Netty hadn't been quite so gung-ho on Brendan.

By Wednesday she was still knee deep in reworking some of her local print ads. At five she glanced at her watch and decided that she had time left. She called Danny in and started reworking the ad for a local clothing store. She soon lost all track of time.

Then there was a tap on her office door, and she looked up. Janis quickly swept in, leaning dramatically against the desk.

"What is it?" Kaitlin asked her.

Janis grimaced. "Kaitlin, it's late."

"Yes?"

"Dinner, Kaitlin! Prime rib, remember? Well, Prime Rib is here, and he doesn't seem at all pleased that you forgot all about him!"

"Oh!" Kaitlin murmured.

The door opened again, and Brendan was there, darkly handsome in a suit, his eyes flashing, his jaw set.

"Excuse me, Ms. O'Herlihy. We did have an agreement, didn't we?"

She was a mess. Her hair was disheveled, her linen suit wrinkled, and she was certain that she had inkstains on her hands. How could she have forgotten?

And what did she care?

"Well?"

Danny and Janis were both staring at her, seemingly enjoying her predicament. She tried to smile.

"I'm sorry, Brendan, I really did lose track of time."

He didn't say a word. She picked up her handbag and told Danny, "We'll finish in the morning, all right?"

"Sure," he said agreeably. He walked over and shook Brendan's hand. "Hi. I'm Dan Clover. It's nice to meet you, Mr. O'Herlihy."

Brendan nodded cordially. His mouth was still tight.

Kaitlin ignored his look and sailed out of the office. Brendan said good night to Danny and Janis, then followed her. Suddenly he paused, frowning.

"What's the matter?" Kaitlin asked him.

"Your friend is saying something to you," he told her.

Kaitlin walked back to the door.

"Prime Rib!" Janis whispered.

"Prime!" Danny laughed.

Kaitlin slammed the office door on both of them, irritated to discover that she was moving as quickly as she could.

Prime Rib had a temper.

They were out of the office and on the street before Kaitlin paused. Then she spun around with vehemence. "Don't come into my office like that again, Brendan O'Herlihy."

"Don't stand me up again."

"I wasn't standing you up. I was just—"

"You were just biding your time, right?"

"I was busy."

"Well, Ms. O'Herlihy, I have a schedule of my own, but I do keep appointments."

Appointments! Their dinner was an appointment?

She turned, heading down the street toward her car. He came up quickly behind her, catching her arm. "I'll drive."

She jerked free from his hold. "You'll drive? I need my car. We don't live in the same place, remember?"

He released her arm suddenly. She realized then that his hair was still damp from a recent shower, his cologne was light and enticing, and he looked wonderful in a navy suit with a peach shirt beneath, emphasizing the bronzed coloring of his rugged features. She was instantly sorry, although she wasn't at all sure why. It was his fault.

"I don't *think* we ever *did* live together," he said softly and turned, then started walking away.

Good. She needed him out of her life. And he'd had no right to swing his temper around in her office. She hadn't been trying to ignore him or back out of anything.

Yes, she was in the right.…

But she didn't want him to leave. She bit her lip, swallowed her pride and strode after him.

Damn him. His legs were long, and she had to run. Her temper started soaring again when she realized that she was running after him. She was thirty—and she was still running after Brendan O'Herlihy.

"Brendan!" Enough was enough. She stopped dead and called his name.

He stopped, too, and turned to her. So, it seemed, did half the people on the street.

"I'm sorry I was late. I really didn't do it on purpose. It's going to be difficult for me to take time off next week, and I got involved in things."

He stared at her for a long moment.

She ground her teeth together, about to turn and walk off.

Of course, his strides were longer. If he chose to catch up with her, he wouldn't have to run.

He always had the advantage, or so it seemed.

But she didn't have to turn away. He was striding toward her.

"Let's just take my car for now," he told her. "I'll bring you back for yours later, and follow you home."

She mused over his suggestion. "All right," she consented at last.

He took her arm, and they started down the street. She didn't know what kind of car they were heading for, but it didn't surprise her when they reached a sleek black Mercedes sedan with a tan interior. It was a small car, comfortable, subtly elegant inside.

"Piracy must pay very well," she murmured, sinking into her seat.

He met her gaze in the mirror. "Piracy has always been a high-paying profession," he replied casually.

She fell silent as he turned the key in the ignition and drove into the traffic. He didn't speak, either, as they drove. Eventually she realized that they were heading toward her house. "You're just taking me home? I should have brought my own car."

Not until they reached her place and he had turned off the car did he lean back and look at her. "I'm sorry," he said. "And I didn't think about your car. I just thought you might want to shower and change. We can get the car later, I promise."

She smiled. "It's all right. But you know, you still have one awful temper."

"Blame it on the Irish," he murmured.

"Well, we're in the same boat there, aren't we?" she teased.

But he was studying her seriously. "You said something like that the other night," he murmured.

"Like what?"

He wasn't looking at her anymore. He was staring at the deserted street. "That we had so much in common. Ancestry, religion, ideals...you...you see so many people combat different cultures and faiths, and they make it. We had everything going for us."

"Maybe there just wasn't enough love," she said softly.

He swung around on her, his eyes very green and intense. "I don't believe that, Kaitlin. I don't believe it for a minute."

She felt suddenly trapped, as if she needed air, needed to escape. "I don't know, Brendan," she said lightly. "All I knew then was that you withdrew from me."

"I never really left you."

"You might as well have," she said softly, and before he could respond, she had opened the car door and was heading toward the house. She was suddenly very afraid of the conversation going any deeper. She didn't want him to pursue it.

Tears were stinging her eyes, and she didn't know why. It hadn't been for lack of love! she thought. Not on her part!

He followed her more slowly. She couldn't quite seem to get her key to fit properly in the lock. It finally gave just as he came up behind her. She felt his hands on her waist, his breath against her ear.

"Want to start the evening over?" There was something wonderfully warm and yet decadently provocative about the way he said the words. About the moist heat of that whisper against her earlobe. She felt that touch, and she felt his hands, and deep inside, she trembled.

She turned quickly. "You're not supposed to seduce me, Brendan."

His eyebrows shot up. "Am I that good? It was really just an innocent question."

"No, you're not that good," she lied. "I just don't want you getting any ideas."

"Sweetheart, you were the one with the ideas, remember?"

She let out a soft oath and hurried into the house. He followed, flicking on the light. She left him in the living room and headed for her bedroom, then paused, calling back, "Yes!"

"Yes, what?"

"I want to start the evening over."

"Good, we're going to have to. I'll try to postpone our dinner reservations, since we're not going to make eight-thirty by any stretch of the imagination.''

She winced and called, ''That's no way to start the evening over.''

''Hey, it's the truth!''

''But there was a lot of sarcasm in your voice. Like it's all my fault.''

''Well...''

''As if you're not willing to forgive.''

She paused by her bedroom door. She couldn't see him, so she just waited. And then he said softly, ''All right, I forgive you for being late.''

She smiled. ''And I forgive you for walking into my office like an avenging angel.''

He didn't answer her. A second later she heard him on the phone with the restaurant where he had made their dinner reservations.

She hurried through her shower, then slipped into clean stockings and swore softly as she searched through her closet. She found an elegant black knit with subtle beadwork and a softly flaring skirt and slipped it on, then stepped into her high-heeled black pumps. She paused briefly before the mirror to do her makeup, then started to wind up her hair. After a moment, she let it fall. Brendan had always liked her hair loose.

''Stop it,'' she warned herself. ''You're acting as if we're dating again. Again? We never really dated. We fell in love, we fell into estrangement, we fell into anger, into almost parenthood, then into distance and divorce. We never really dated. Oh, and then we had dinner once. Dinner and sex!'' Her reflection stared at her mockingly.

''No champagne, I swear. I'll drink iced tea all night!'' she vowed to her reflection.

She dumped a few things from her big leather purse into a small beaded bag and glanced at her watch. Thirty minutes. He couldn't complain.

He didn't. He was sitting on the sofa, watching a newscast, waiting for her. When she appeared, he rose quickly.

''Was I too long?'' she asked him.

He smiled slowly. Rakishly. Just like he had smiled in high school. ''You're definitely worth waiting for,'' he told her. He came to stand before her and took her arm. His whisper touched her cheek, and for a moment she thought he was going to kiss her. "Very definitely," he said softly.

Then he turned away and opened the door for her. When they reached the car, he opened that door for her, too. Brendan had a knack for such things. She had to admit that he'd always been courteous without being patronizing. Now, leaning against the comfortable upholstery, she smiled.

"You're not a bad date," she told him. "Sorry—appointment."

He cast her a dry glance. "Is this an appointment?"

"You tell me."

"I have appointments with professors and congressmen and students and my divers. I think I want this to be a date."

"We never really dated, you know," she told him.

He flashed her another quick, amused glance. "Well, we did just about everything else, so we might as well get the dating in now, huh?"

She didn't answer him, but she could tell that he wasn't expecting an answer. And it was a nice silence that developed between them. A companionable silence. The car had a wonderful speaker system, and soft rock rolled out from it as gracefully as the car itself rolled down the road.

The restaurant was in an old hotel in Coral Gables. It was one that Kaitlin loved. When they were seated, the maître d' handed her a rose. A waiter took her shoes, and a soft satin pillow was placed beneath her feet.

Brendan arched a skeptical brow to her when he was given the wine list. "As long as it's not champagne...," he offered.

"I'll have tea," she said primly. "Iced tea."

But he pointed out that the restaurant had half bottles of a very nice white wine, and she decided that she could manage just a little wine with dinner. Then they ordered escargot and crab cocktails, and Kaitlin decided that she just might enjoy the night.

He told her about the place he had booked for Donna's party, then he drew out the menu and handed it to her. She looked at him and sighed. "Brendan, I really don't have any right. You've been planning this—"

"I've gotten a place for the party, Kaitlin, that's all. We're in this together."

She took the menu from him. "Only if I get to pay for half."

"Kaitlin, it's really no big thing."

"Yes, it is! It's their shower!"

He was silent for a moment. "When I left the beach the other day, your assistant insisted on paying me for modeling."

Kaitlin grinned, looking at her plate. "Brendan, we had to pay you. It would have been illegal not to."

"Okay. Did you pay yourself?"

"Actually, yes."

"Neither of us intended to do that commercial, right? So we'll use the money we made to pay for the party." He leaned back and waited for her answer.

Her smile broadened. "Perfect!" she told him softly. Then she bent and began to study the menu. "This sounds wonderful." She laughed. "Really wonderful! We couldn't begin to get such a nice selection for these prices down here. I'm glad Barbara wants a traditional girl thing."

"I don't think what Joe wants is really traditional," he told her.

She looked up. "Oh? What does Joe want?"

"A cruise. One of those one-day things."

"A cruise?" She frowned.

Brendan laughed. "He doesn't want a blonde to jump out of a cake. He just wants to gamble."

She grinned and turned her attention to the menu. She read off the appetizers, and they both decided on Donna's and Bill's favorites, then went on to the salad, the main course and dessert. She promised to make up the invitations and get them out by the next night if he could give her the guest list.

The crab cocktails disappeared, then the escargot. The chef suggested a fish delicately seasoned and cooked in a paper bag. Although Kaitlin had never really gotten used to the idea of eating a fish that still had its head intact, she felt daring and opted for it when Brendan enthusiastically endorsed it.

The fish was delicious, the wine perfect. She felt both relaxed and clearheaded. She and Brendan discussed going in together for their gifts to the various bridal couples. They toyed with several ideas, then decided that they still had time to choose.

Finally their waiter brought them espresso, and they lingered over the tiny cups.

Kaitlin idly stirred sugar into hers and found herself studying Brendan intently. He looked at her, and she quickly turned her attention to her cup. Then she looked at him again.

"Yes?" he prompted.

"I was just curious."

"About what?"

It sometimes seemed that he hadn't changed at all, that things hadn't changed. He'd barely walked back into her life, yet it almost seemed as if he'd never been out of it. But he had. There were eons between them, yet it seemed that he had never really been very far away.

"You have your house in the Keys," she said.

He shrugged. "Yes."

"But you must go home often enough. You're still such good friends with Bill that he wants you to be his best man."

"I keep a house in Massachusetts, too," he told her.

"In the Worcester area?"

He shook his head. "I have a place in the country. Out by Orange, almost on the New Hampshire border. I have about twenty acres there."

She was staring at him blankly.

"Is that all right with you?" he asked.

She gave herself a little shake. Of course. It was fine. It was just that no one had ever told her.

Well, she had said once that she didn't want to hear about Brendan O'Herlihy. And it seemed that all her family and friends had taken her words to heart.

"Of course it's all right. I guess I had just been wondering...what you'd been up to all these years."

"Piracy, remember?"

She nodded. "Yes, right." She was silent for a moment. "And I take it that you've seen a lot of Barbara and Joe over the years, too."

"Obviously. You know that."

"You come up from the Keys very often?"

He hesitated for a moment, then shrugged again. "Sure. I need to go by the research facilities at the university now and then. And I take students out for dives. I have a lot of colleagues who are professors. I keep an apartment on Brickell."

Brickell! It was right down the street from her office.

And Barbara had known all along, but never said a word to her.

"How long have you had the apartment?" she asked stiffly.

"About two years."

"And they all knew..." she muttered beneath her breath.

He made an impatient sound. "Kaitlin, you've known that Joe and I kept up. And that meant that Barbara and I did, too."

"I didn't know how much. I knew that Joe knew where you were, since he told me where to find you when—"

"When you came down to offer me your...bargain."

"I didn't come down to bargain."

"What *were* you doing, then?"

"I came in an effort to make things easier for both of us."

"Like hell!"

"I wasn't seeing anyone seriously at the time."

"Well," he mused, his green gaze bright as he leaned back in his chair, studying her broadly, "I'm glad to hear that."

"What—",

"I'm glad you weren't deeply involved with another man while you were bargaining with me."

"Brendan, how can you make it all sound so—so decadent!"

"Because it was," he said flatly.

"I lead the life of a cloistered nun—" she began furiously, then broke off, aware of just how much she was giving away about her own life.

"What?"

"Nothing! I wasn't bargaining with you!"

"Well, you did fall into bed with me rather easily. I'm glad that you weren't contemplating another marriage at the time."

She gasped, her temper rising. "Damn you, Brendan. Maybe I fell into bed easily with you, but you fell into bed with me easily, too!"

He didn't reply for an instant. Then he said, very softly, "But I wasn't asking you for an annulment." She suddenly sensed that he was looking behind her rather than at her.

She twisted around to see that their waiter, his face an impossible shade of crimson, discreetly attempting to give Brendan the check.

She felt the blood rush to her face as she recalled the last few lines of their conversation. She wanted to explode, to sink beneath the table....

Or tear out every ebony hair in Brendan's head. The silver ones, too.

She stood, grabbing her handbag. "Thank you for dinner," she said stiffly, then hurried blindly out of the restaurant.

She had barely made it through the front door, though, when he came striding up behind her, catching her arm and swinging her around.

"What do you think you're doing?" he demanded.

"Going home. I'll get a cab—"

"The hell you will."

"I'll do—"

"You came out with me tonight, Kaitlin. You'll damn well go home with me, too."

His hand was on her elbow. She gritted her teeth, looking down the street. There wasn't a cab in sight, and there wasn't likely to be. Not at this time of night, in such a quiet area.

He started walking toward his car, with her following slowly, digging her heels in stubbornly. He opened the door for her. "Will you get in, please? And quit being so mad at me because the waiter heard you talking about your sex life—or lack thereof."

Her eyes flew to his with renewed fury. "You son of a—"

"Kaitlin, it's late. Get in."

She did so only because she had no choice. He quickly walked around and slid into the driver's seat, then revved the engine. After he had pulled onto the street, he met her eyes.

"If you weren't seeing anyone, why did you want the annulment?"

She shook her head, unwilling to explain.

"Why?"

She lifted her hands vaguely. "My parents had mentioned a cousin who was married again. The right way. In—"

"The right way!" he exploded, his green eyes dark and shadowed and angry in the night. "What is the right way to be married, Kaitlin? Is it still only real to you if there are a million guests and you wear a dress worth a few thousand bucks? Is that it?"

She gasped, furious. "No, that is not it! The right way is the way that any individual deems to be important! For me that means in the church. For others it may be different. And it doesn't matter in the least what the hell anyone wears, or who attends. It's in the heart, Brendan, it's—oh, never mind!"

"You're damn right I'll never mind. However the hell it was done, Kaitlin, we were married. Man and wife. And we were expecting a child, and we lost that child. And I'll never pretend that it didn't happen. I'll never sign any piece of paper that says it didn't. So get that straight right now."

"I got it straight!"

He pulled over to the curb abruptly. She was suddenly afraid of his temper, wondering what he was doing. Then she realized that they were in front of her house. He got out of the car. She knew that he was going to come around and open her door, so she leaped out hastily, unwilling to have him come too close.

"Thank you for dinner!" she snapped.

"Oh, no, we're not done yet."

"Yes, we are. I wouldn't dream of asking you in. That might be construed as bargaining!"

"Kaitlin—"

"Go to hell, Brendan!"

She headed for the front door. She strode up the walkway in a searing temper, but as soon as she reached the door, she remembered that her car was still parked by the office.

She turned. Brendan was waiting for her to remember. He was leaning against the passenger door, looking superior.

She strode down the walk. "You knew all along that my car was still at the office," she snapped. "So why did you drive me here?"

"I didn't know all along. I remembered right after you went flouncing out of the car."

"I do not flounce, Brendan O'Herlihy. And I don't appreci-ate—"

"Kaitlin, let's go get your car."

"I can get a cab in the morning, thank you."

He shrugged. "Suit yourself. It will only take us ten minutes to go back. And taking a cab in the morning isn't going to change the fact that you will be seeing me again."

"Yes, but I'll have a few days' grace," she said sweetly.

"Not so many. Your grandmother invited me to her wedding, you know."

"Yes, I assumed that Gram would do something like that."

"I have to go."

"I imagine."

"And I really should be your escort."

Her mouth fell open. "What?"

"Do you have a date for her wedding?"

"I don't need a date!"

He smiled. "All right, then, an escort."

"If I wanted an escort, Brendan, I would get one."

His smile deepened. For a moment he looked at the ground, his dark lashes sweeping over his eyes. "You still sound like the very proud young woman I met all those years ago. Kaitlin, I know that you can get a date. You can get what you want from almost anyone just by opening those baby blues and batting an eyelash or two."

"Brendan—"

"Get in. I'll take you to get your car."

She hesitated. He stepped away and opened the door for her. She got in.

He was silent as he drove through the quiet night streets to reach her car. He parked behind it, got out and walked her over to it.

"I'll follow you home," he told her.

"It isn't necessary," she said stiffly.

"It is to me."

She got into her car and started it.

Yet as she drove home, she saw that he had followed her, and that he was following her all the way.

She parked in her driveway. When she got out, he was leaning against his car once again, watching as she headed up the walk, fitted her key into the lock and turned to wave.

"I'm home. Safely," she said.

He nodded. "Call me if you change your mind about Saturday. We could use the practice."

"For what?"

"Weddings," he called back. "We've got two to attend together."

"I won't change my mind," she said sweetly.

He chuckled softly. "Call me if you do. But not too late. I might pull a date out of a hat myself."

She didn't answer as she stepped into the house, then closed and locked the door.

She stripped off her clothing and donned a nightgown quickly. She was exhausted.

But she didn't sleep. She wondered what Brendan did with his time when he wasn't working. She had told him that she wasn't seriously involved.

She had told him that she lived like a nun!

She sighed and tossed around, and tried again to sleep. When she finally dozed, she was beset by dreams.

Of Brendan. And in her dreams, he was curled up beside her; they were naked, and he was holding her close.

In her dream they were married again. Sleeping together, entwined. His chin was resting on the top of her head, and she was comfortable and secure....

She woke with a start. It was still the middle of the night. She rose and hurried into the kitchen, where she made a cup of tea.

As she sat sipping it, she realized that she had never remarried because she had not met anyone who could make her feel the way that Brendan did.

But it was always so painful when they were together! Their tempers flared, and their words were bitter. But there was so much more, so much they never said. The words wouldn't come, so the bitterness remained.

She stayed awake for a while, then she made herself go back to bed.

The next day was insane from start to finish.

She had work to do, and more. After work she had to check dinner arrangements with Gram, then they had to check on the cake.

Next she had to meet with Barbara, and they went from shop to shop trying to find the perfect gown.

At the sixth place, they found it at last.

The gown was stunning. The satin bodice and low-cut back were enhanced by a soft mesh that covered Barbara's back and collarbone, ending in a slim row of pearls below her throat. A small teardrop pearl sat where the satin met the gauze at the cleft of her breasts.

The train was exquisite, long, beaded and sequined. And the gown fit Barbara perfectly.

"It's stunning!" Kaitlin told her. Watching Barbara, she felt tears well in her eyes. Her cousin was so beautiful. And she had waited so long to be a bride.

"Will Joe like it?" Barbara asked anxiously.

"He'll love it!" Kaitlin promised her. "Oh, Barbara! It's perfect!"

So Barbara left a down payment on the gown, and then they looked at dresses for the bridesmaids, deciding on black and white gowns. They were wonderful, too, with black velvet bodices and beautiful white skirts.

That done, they went and had dinner and a drink. Barbara had a champagne cocktail, and Kaitlin carefully chose a white wine spritzer. She was relieved that Barbara didn't mention Brendan.

By the time Kaitlin reached home, she was too tired to think, or even to dream.

The next afternoon her parents arrived. She picked them up at the airport, and as soon as she saw them, she was besieged with guilt.

They were wonderful. Her mother was a younger version of Gram, an older version of herself. She had flawless skin and beautiful blue eyes, and though she looked like a woman of fifty, she was a very, very lovely fifty. She was dressed smartly, and she walked with her arm linked through Kaitlin's father's.

Her dad was great, too. A very tall, gray-haired man with steely gray eyes and strong, handsome features.

They'd been married since they were twenty, and they had obviously never fallen out of love. Kaitlin was an only child simply because there hadn't been any others, even though her mother would have liked a houseful. She was the one object of their affection, and they were very loving, yet careful never to smother her.

They deserve so much more than I give them! Kaitlin thought. And having located them in the crowd, she suddenly tore through the mob to reach them.

"Mom! Dad!" She hugged them both enthusiastically, not at all sure why her eyes were suddenly so wet.

"Kaitlin!" Her mother hugged her, then she was in her father's arms. He held her very close, then he released her slowly.

"Sweetheart, it's so good to see you!"

She nodded. "Let's get out of here. It's a zoo!"

She linked arms with them both and led them to her car. She chatted all the while about the wedding plans, and her mother told her who was going to be able to make it down.

"Donna wanted to come, and so did Patrick." Patrick was Donna's older brother. "But Patrick's wife is having a baby, and she hasn't been very well, so she's been in and out of the hospital. Donna's been taking care of Brandy, and they didn't make up that saying about the terrible twos for nothing!"

Kaitlin felt a pang of guilt. She was supposed to be helping Donna, and she hadn't even known that Donna was taking care of her nephew. "Maybe I can help when I come up next week," she said.

"Don't miss your train, young lady," her father warned her.

She smiled. "I won't, Dad. I promise."

"It's too bad you don't like to fly," he said.

"I hate to fly—unless I absolutely have to," she admitted.

"Maybe it's good for you to take trains, anyway," her father said shrewdly. "You relax a bit, at least."

Her mother frowned slightly, warning her dad not to tread on her private concerns. "So tell me about Mr. Rosen!" she said.

Kaitlin smiled and did so. They reached her car and drove to her house, and the conversation didn't lull once. Once they arrived, Kaitlin heated some soup she had made, while her mother and father settled into the guest room. Her dad was the first one into the kitchen. He tasted the soup, winked and told her it was terrific.

"So how is everything with you?" he asked her.

"Great, Dad. The agency is really holding its own."

"I'm proud of you, you know."

She hugged him again just because she loved him so much. She knew it was hard for him that she lived fifteen hundred miles away from home.

"I've spent my whole life being proud of you, you know," she told him.

"Thanks," he said huskily. He leaned against the counter and asked about her work.

She told him that they'd just brought in a really big account.

She didn't tell him that she'd participated in her own commercial. With Brendan.

He listened, commenting on her minor problems. Then he asked her, "What about you?"

"About me?"

"Are you happy, Kaitlin?"

"Oh! Well, of course, I'm happy."

"Are you seeing anyone?"

She turned to the soup. "I've been really busy lately."

"You're not seeing anyone at all?"

It was her mother's dismayed voice that she heard, and she turned and smiled. "Mom, I do see people. Really."

"Will we meet anyone at Gram's wedding?" she asked anxiously.

Now it was her father's turn to frown at her mother, who ignored him.

"Well, not at Gram's wedding." They were both staring at her. "I've been so busy. I'm her maid of honor, you know, Mom." They were still staring at her. "I won't be there alone. I couldn't really bring anyone because...well, she asked Brendan. So I thought that I really should let him escort me."

Her father's jaw dropped; her mother beamed. "Brendan? I knew that he'd be Bill's best man, but he's here? Now? And we'll see him at Gram's wedding?"

Kaitlin wondered with a certain annoyance if her parents weren't more excited about seeing Brendan than they were about seeing their own daughter.

Then she felt guilty.

She turned to the soup again. Damn you, Brendan! she thought furiously. Then she realized in a small panic that she needed to call him and let him know that she needed a date after all.

Whatever had possessed her to say anything to her parents? It had been the way they looked at her, so anxiously....

She managed to steer the conversation away from him during dinner. And at least her parents made it an early night.

As soon as they were in bed, she closed herself into her own room. She called information, only to learn that Brendan's number was unlisted. Then she swallowed hard, bit the proverbial bullet and called Joe.

She ignored the curious tone of his voice, got Brendan's number and called him quickly, before she could chicken out.

He took forever to answer! She closed her eyes and wondered what he was doing. His apartment might well be an impressive bachelor pad, with a Jacuzzi on the balcony. And he might already be working on a date. She'd be dark. Very dark, and very sexy…

"Hello?"

She moistened her lips. She couldn't speak.

"Hello?" he repeated with annoyance. She knew Brendan; he wouldn't stay on the line long.

Her fingers wound around the phone cord. "Brendan, it's me. Kaitlin. O'Herlihy," she added inanely, and winced.

"O'Herlihy, eh?" he said, and she heard a trace of amusement in his tone. "And what can I do for you, Ms. O'Herlihy?"

"I need you. I mean, I don't need you. I want you—no, no, that's not what I mean."

"Just what *do* you mean?"

"I've changed my mind. About the wedding. Gram's. That is, if you haven't already gotten another date."

He was silent for so long that she began to wish she had never called. She was ready to slam the receiver down when she heard him speak again, his voice husky and deep.

"No, I haven't made any other arrangements. I'd be delighted to escort you, Ms. O'Herlihy. What time shall you require my services?"

## Chapter 7

It was really a beautiful wedding.

Gram and Al Rosen were married beneath a flowered trellis in a courtyard. It was a simple ceremony, but the two of them had written their own vows, which were very traditional. They promised to love, honor and cherish each other for all the time that God should grant them, until death should them part.

Standing by her grandmother's side, Kaitlin felt tears welling in her eyes. She thought honesty was the only thing that mattered between two people. Gram and Al were both so sure of what they were doing. And their love was evident to everyone present.

For a small wedding, it was a surprisingly large affair. Donna and her brother hadn't been able to make it, but their folks were there. All four of Gram's daughters—Maeve, Kaitlin's mother; Margaret, Donna's mother; Bede, Barbara's mother; and Siobhan, their youngest sister—were there. Gram's sons, Galen and Michael, were there, too, with their wives. And there were seven cousins, counting her and Barbara—Michael, Jeremy, Joshua, Liam and Catherine Mary. Al Rosen had a big family, too, and many of them were in attendance. And then there were Gram's and Mr. Rosen's friends, the oldest and spryest gentleman being an old friend of Al's father, a Timothy Tyron.

After the bride and groom had been on the dance floor for a few minutes, Al's best man, his son Jacob, brought Kaitlin out to the floor. Then everyone joined in, and Brendan cut in on Jacob to take Kaitlin into his arms.

"How are you holding up?" he asked her.

"Fine, thanks."

"Your parents look good."

She nodded.

"They like to believe in miracles."

"They're beaming at us."

He grinned. "It hurt like hell to call me, huh?"

"It wasn't easy," she admitted. And it hadn't gotten any easier.

Her parents had been glad to see Brendan, and she'd discovered that even her mother and father had seen him occasionally over the years without mentioning the fact to her. And he looked great. He had picked her up in a blue suit with very thin pinstripes and a handsome vest. The magnificent cut of the suit enhanced his hard physique, his muscled shoulders, his lean hips. And he smelled great, too. She hated it when he was this appealing. It was hard enough to be with him to begin with. They had grown so far apart, yet so many thing felt so familiar.

"It's a beautiful wedding," he murmured softly. "Your grand-mother is a very classy lady."

Kaitlin had to smile. "She is."

"She's in love with him. She's going through the paces, but you can tell that the music, the trappings, none of that really matters. He's the only thing that matters to her."

She looked at him. Was he implying again that all she had ever wanted were the trappings?

"Brendan, don't—"

"You know, I still remember meeting you. Seeing your eyes. The challenge, the determination. I don't think I'd ever seen any-thing as beautiful, as captivating, as your face."

His eyes were on her, and his body was close, brushing hers, hot against hers, as they moved. She wanted to tear herself away; she was breathless and afraid. There was too much history be-tween them. He had not only broken her heart, he had stamped on it. And then he had humiliated her. If only he wasn't looking at her so....

The song was over, but they were still standing there in each other's arms. Then the band began to play something else, and Brendan moved to the faster tempo. As Kaitlin followed his lead, she realized that a majority of her family was watching her. And she knew that they were all thinking she had been a fool, that it was her fault she was no longer married to Brendan O'Herlihy.

"Remember the good old days, Kaitlin?" he asked lightly.

"I remember that you left me," she told him defensively.

He shook his head. "I never left you."

"You ran off and joined the Navy. I call that leaving me."

"I thought you wanted to be with someone else."

Then her father was there, cutting in on Brendan, and she was swept away again. She tried to smile, tried to act delighted, tried to chat and laugh. But she knew she was failing dismally, and her father knew, too, but he didn't let on.

"Brendan looks good," he told her.

"Brendan always looks good," she said wearily. "And he's smart, and he's successful, and I was the biggest fool on earth to file those papers."

Her dad frowned. "Kaitlin, what—"

"I can tell. I can see it in everyone's eyes. I come out the heavy."

"Honey, there is no heavy in a situation like that."

"Dad, no one could understand. No one who didn't know him like I did. Sean died, and a piece of Brendan died, too. He was there after that, but he was never with me."

"Kaitlin, no one is blaming you."

"I wish he'd fall on his face."

Her dad laughed. "That's bitter. It doesn't sound like you."

"Well, I am bitter." She was silent for a minute. "I don't really want anything bad to happen to him. I just want all his hair to fall out and his weight to balloon. Maybe a blackened tooth or two would help."

Her father laughed and swung her around. "Sounds to me like you're still in love."

She shook her head vehemently. "No, Dad, never. It hurts too much."

He was serious. "Remember Sean, honey? I do. And that was something that he always saw. There has to be discord for us to know harmony. Pain so we can feel pleasure. Tragedy so there can be comedy."

"I remember Sean," she murmured. He had been right, of course. But he had never warned her that the pain could go on for years and years and years.

Then Al Rosen cut in, and her father had no choice but to release her.

Then she was needed by the maître d'. There were too many people for the present seating arrangements. Desperate, she rearranged everything, careful not to offend Mr. Rosen's family or her own.

By the time she finished, she felt exhausted, frazzled. And when she came out, she found out that she had forgotten about one very major guest—Al's rabbi. She hurried back and started over. Thank God for the band. They kept playing and playing.

Finally things were set and the guests could pick up their table numbers.

She danced with her uncles and with her cousins. And with her new step-grandfather. Even when the meal was served, she barely saw Brendan.

Then the band struck up again, and she had a moment to herself when she leaned against the wall and fanned herself, laughing as Gram tossed her bouquet—and Barbara caught it. Then Al Rosen slipped off Gram's garter and managed to toss it to Joe, who made quite a production of getting it onto Barbara's leg.

Then there was more dancing. From her vantage point Kaitlin could see that Timothy Tyron was keeping pace with all the activity. He was definitely in the swing of things. He didn't care whether the band was playing the hora or a waltz or an Irish jig, he was right in the middle of it.

After a while she was called into the bride's room, because the gifts were overflowing the tables that had been set up for them. While she was looking for a busboy to help her carry things to various cars, she suddenly heard a loud scream, then numerous shouts and absolute chaos.

She came running out and saw a large crowd around the dance floor.

"An ambulance!" someone shouted.

"It's been called!"

Then another voice, smooth and authoritative, warned everyone to get back. Kaitlin didn't know what was going on, but her heart was in her throat.

Gram!

Where was her grandmother? She wanted to worry about Al Rosen, but she couldn't change the fact that she had been blessed with a grandmother for thirty years, and Al was still a stranger.

"What's happened?" she shouted.

Then an arm slipped through hers. Her father was at her side, and she looked up at him with wide, terrified eyes. "Gram!"

He shook his head. She could hear the ambulance siren wailing. "Gram is fine," her father told her. "It's that nice old Timothy Tyron. I think he danced a bit too much."

"Oh!" she cried.

Then the ambulance was there, and the paramedics were coming through, carrying a stretcher.

Yet even as they did, Timothy Tyron was opening his eyes, his hand held by none other than Brendan O'Herlihy. Then the crowd closed in again, cheering and applauding as Timothy was helped onto the stretcher. He was still gripping Brendan's hand, and Al was walking at his other side. ''It was that last hora, I think,'' Timothy said.

''You'll be up and about soon,'' Al promised him.

Timothy grinned and closed his eyes while the paramedics managed to get an oxygen mask on him. Then Kaitlin stared after the stretcher and the departing backs of Al, Brendan and the attendants.

''What happened?'' she whispered.

Her cousin Michael was behind her. ''He fainted, I think. It's a good thing Brendan was around, or the old guy might have breathed his last.''

''Brendan!'' Kaitlin exclaimed.

''Somehow Timothy stopped breathing, but Brendan got him started again.''

''Oh,'' Kaitlin murmured, so glad that Timothy was going to be okay.

And she didn't know why she resented the fact that Brendan had been the big hero of the day.

Al came in, announcing that Timothy seemed to be doing well. There was more cheering, but the party was winding down.

Gram found Kaitlin and gave her a big kiss and a teary-eyed thank you. Then she kissed the rest of her family, and she and Al departed for their honeymoon.

There was more dancing, but soon the guests began to drift away.

Kaitlin felt that the responsibility of holding down the fort until the very end was hers, so she said goodbye to the last of the guests, then slipped off her shoes and collapsed into a chair at one of the tables. Her parents were beside her, and she knew that Brendan was behind her, waiting.

Politely, the perfect escort.

The hero of the whole affair.

Why was she so resentful? Or was it just that she was tired?

"I think that's the end of it," Brendan murmured. "I'll get the car and meet you out front."

She nodded without looking at him. Her mother thanked him. Kaitlin wasn't sure if she was glad her parents were there, or if she just wished that she could be alone with him to tell him... Tell him what?

She wanted to scream at him, to smash her fists against his chest. And she wasn't even sure why.

"Tired?" her mother asked her softly.

"Exhausted."

"And you've got two to go," Maeve reminded her.

"But it's fun, it's great—"

"And exhausting," her dad said, laughing.

"Everything was perfect except for poor Mr. Tyron," Kaitlin said.

"Let me warn you, Kaitlin," her dad said. "There's always some little trauma at a wedding."

"I'm not going to allow any more little traumas," she said firmly. And when her parents exchanged amused glances, she insisted, "I'm not!"

Neither of them corrected her. They had reached the door, and Brendan was there with the car. Kaitlin's dad opened the door for her and her mother, and Kaitlin slid into the seat next to Brendan. And then she didn't know what happened.

Suddenly Brendan was waking her up. She blinked furiously as she realized that she was sleeping with her head on his lap, and they were parked in front of her house.

"Kaitlin, your parents have already gone in."

"Oh. Oh!" Her fingers were curled around his thigh. She felt his warmth, the slight movement of a muscle.

She jerked upright.

"Let me help you—"

"No. No, please, I'm awake. I'm going in. I—thank you. I do appreciate you serving as my escort," she said coldly.

She started to slide out of the car, but he caught her arm and pulled her back. Despite the darkness, she could see the glitter in his eyes. "If you're so damn appreciative, why are you being so rude?"

"I'm not. I'm just tired."

"I'll walk you to the door."

"No! It's all right!"

But he was already out of the car and coming around to open her door. She jumped out quickly, not wanting to give him an excuse to touch her.

"What the hell is the matter with you?" he demanded.

"Nothing. I don't know." She backed away from him. "I just—I just think we need to put a little distance between us."

"Kaitlin, we've got years of distance."

"Right. Well, thank you, good night."

His jaw twisted. "You know, Kaitlin, once, just once, I'd love to hear from you when you didn't want something."

"You said to call you—"

"You called me because your family was here. Because you didn't feel like dredging up a date who meant nothing to you. A date who would expect to be entertained like any other guest."

"What difference does it make?" she demanded.

He came close, threading his fingers into her hair and pulling her against him before she could protest. "A lot, Kaitlin. It makes a lot of difference to me."

"We're not all perfect like you," she said.

"Like me? You think I'm perfect?"

"Always. The perfect damn hero."

"You're mad at me over Mr. Tyron!" he said incredulously.

"I'm not!" she gasped, horrified. "My God, I wouldn't want anything to happen to anyone—"

"But you wish someone else had seen to him, right?"

She was stubbornly silent.

"Kaitlin, it's part of what I do! I have to know emergency medical procedures. I have divers who get injured. Things go wrong."

"I'm not mad! I'm delighted that you could help. I'm just—"

"Just what?"

"Sick of you being so damn perfect," she muttered.

His hold tightened, and she thought he was going to kiss her. And though she was angry and confused, she wanted that kiss. She wanted the fierce heat of his lips. She wanted to taste the anger and the passion, and she wanted to let it rise and simmer and explode....

But he didn't kiss her. He released her. "Good night, Kaitlin. I guess I'll see you in Massachusetts."

"Right," she murmured. "In Massachusetts."

He opened her door and waited for her to go inside. She did, then closed the door and locked it.

Her mother and father had apparently gone to bed, because the house was dark.

She sank slowly into the couch. Her cheeks were damp, and she touched them, amazed to realize that she was crying.

And she didn't even know why.

She was afraid, she realized. Afraid of taking a chance, afraid of reaching out.

And yet she wanted Brendan. She wanted to talk to him, to make love with him. She wanted to lay her head against his shoulder and cry for the past.

And maybe find a future.

When Brendan dropped Kaitlin and her parents off, he didn't feel like returning to his apartment. It was a nice place, but it felt cramped to him. It felt like the city. It was late, but the Upper Keys weren't very far away; his house was only an hour and forty-five minutes from Kaitlin's place.

But when he reached his place in the Keys, he knew that that wasn't really where he wanted to be, either. He wanted the water, he realized.

He changed his suit for jeans and a T-shirt, then walked to the dock. His yacht, the *Lilliputian*, was gently rocking in her berth.

He hopped aboard. He knew he wasn't going anywhere; he just wanted to sit on the open deck and smell the sea breeze.

The yacht was a fine piece of craftsmanship. The woodwork was beautiful, the two staterooms were great, and even the smaller crew cabins were nice. She was equipped with all the latest in sonar devices for underwater discovery, and she could carry all the diving gear and paraphernalia he needed. When he had a big find he had to call out the heavy-duty salvage vessels, but the *Lilliputian* was the perfect vessel for discovery. There was nowhere he would rather be.

He went down the steps to the main cabin and headed to the galley for a beer, then went on deck, popped the top, sat down, leaned back and looked up at the stars. It was a beautiful night. It had been a great night for Lizzie Boyle's wedding.

"To you, Lizzie," he said softly, lifting his can. Few women were so wise, he thought. She was a very great lady.

And she was what Kaitlin would be, he thought, years and years from now.

He wished suddenly that she was here with him. It seemed that they were always fighting when they were together. They would just start to get close to the truth, then they would erupt in some argument, and the things that should have been said were left unvoiced.

**If only** she was here now...

**But she wasn't.**

He closed his eyes and felt the air move over him. It was soothing, but not soothing enough to wash away the past. He'd led such a great life in so many ways. Nice parents who supported him. Things always seemed to fall his way. He was naturally athletic, and good at academics, too. His grandparents had been Irish immigrants, just like Kaitlin's. They had believed deeply in the American dream and tried hard to give their children everything they'd never had. His grandfather had gone over history with him, then geography, and once Brendan found the oceans of the world, his dream had been born.

Best of all, he'd had Kaitlin. The most beautiful and exquisite creature he had ever seen, with her soft blue eyes and radiant hair, her pride, her laughter and her passion. No one could have asked for more, but he had more anyway. His cousin Sean.

Sean O'Herlihy had been an actor. From kindergarten on, it had seemed that Sean knew his dream. He could read circles around the rest of the family by second grade. He studied literature, and he studied plays. He loved the great Irish playwrights. He wanted one day to perform at the Abbey Theatre in Dublin, but he wanted to act on Broadway, too.

By their senior year, Sean was the hero of the high school. He played MacBeth, Romeo, anything of Shakespeare's. He produced and directed and starred in Behan's *Hostage*. He was offered several prestigious scholarships, a role on a soap opera and bit movie parts. He could mimic any accent, but his Irish was naturally the best.

For eighteen years, they had been more than cousins. They had been best friends.

Brendan would never forget the last time he'd seen Sean alive.

They'd gone to the park in Rutland, just to walk. School was over; it was almost time to say goodbye. Not forever—just to the old way of life. Within a month Brendan and Kaitlin would be married and headed south, and Sean would be off on his own, headed for school in New York. Sean was enthusiastic about the bachelor party he was planning. When Brendan assured him that he was really far past the need for a blonde to jump out of a cake, Sean laughed.

"Aye, sure and begorrah!" he said and leaped atop a rock. Then he rested his chin in his hands and sighed. "No girls out of cakes, Brendan. I couldn't find one to compare with Kaitlin, anyway. You're a lucky man, you know. She's the most beautiful girl I've ever seen, and bright and sweet to boot. And I can't wait for the wedding. It will be solemn and regal and wonderful, and then it will be time to party, party, party!"

Brendan laughed and sat across from him on another boulder. "Party time, all right. We're going to be married. It's what I want more than anything, and sometimes I still can't believe it's really going to happen."

"Believe it, my boy," Sean told him; then his handsome, freckled face went serious. "Brendan, it gives me goose bumps just thinking about it. I'm going to be your best man. I can't wait. I think I'm more excited than either of you. And I love her, Brendan, you know that. I feel like she's my relative already. You're lucky. You've got love. When you've got love, you've got everything."

"Yeah, I know."

And they had sat there on those boulders, then skipped rocks across the creek the way they had done when they were kids. They had talked about their plans, their dreams. And they had promised that they would always come home.

"I think home for you is going to be any patch of salt water," Sean told Brendan.

"And home for you is going to be any stage, with the footlights shining on you."

"'All the world's a stage!'" Sean quoted. "Sometimes comedy, and sometimes tragedy. But you've got to have the tragedy, you know. Otherwise there couldn't be heights of the ridiculous and the sublime, right?"

"Right."

They gripped hands suddenly. "We'll always be blood," Sean vowed, grinning. "Sharing dreams."

"Always blood," Brendan agreed. "Sharing dreams."

But there would be no more dreams for them to share. The next week his mother had come by the dive shop where he was working for the summer. There were tears in her eyes, and it was the middle of the day, and right away he knew that something was terribly wrong.

Sean was dead. He had been hit by a truck driver and killed instantly.

Brendan had never cried like that before in his life. And there was more. There was the funeral. Sean, always so full of life, lay there cold and silent and still, and he wasn't Sean anymore.

After that, nothing seemed right. If Sean was dead, then he shouldn't be alive. He shouldn't be able to feel the breeze, to see the sun, to smell the flowers.

Or Kaitlin's perfume. Or touch her, or feel the softness of her hair sweep around him. When the first stunned agony faded, he became numb, and no one could touch him. He didn't want to be touched. Nothing in his life had prepared him for losing Sean. He tried to understand that his aunt and his uncle and his other cousins were in the same pain, and he tried to understand that Kaitlin had loved Sean just as Sean had loved Kaitlin.

But he had known that he couldn't go through with the wedding. No one expected them to marry as planned, anyway. Not so soon. Sean's death was an incredible loss to both families, and everyone was going to have to struggle to go on.

But Brendan never quite got over it. When he talked to Kaitlin, he wanted to reach out to her. He wanted to drown in her whispers, in her tears, in her touch. He wanted to make love until he could feel nothing but the sweet ecstasy that would take him away, but he couldn't go near her.

Because he shouldn't be able to feel. Sean was dead. Sean would never feel again.

Brendan tried to bring himself back to her. But he still couldn't stand the idea of a wedding. Because Sean should have been at the wedding. Should have been standing beside them.

In the end Brendan had lost Kaitlin, too. She was still with him, but he had lost her. Two years passed, and they were still together. Studying, learning, leaving high school far behind them, becoming adults. And planning a wedding again. Or, at least, he kept quiet while Kaitlin planned it.

And then he found her laughing in the arms of a friend. His friend.

He had exploded and left. The next thing he knew, he had signed up for the Navy and was knee-deep in basic training.

And wishing he could go back. Once he was away from her, he knew how deeply he loved her.

The service didn't leave a guy much time for apologies. And he didn't know what to say, anyway. Then he had heard from her. A very stiff and stilted letter, telling him that she felt obliged to let him know that she was expecting a child. He needn't feel obligated to do anything about it.

He'd been able to come back then, feeling guilty, because he was thrilled. He had Kaitlin back. As his wife. And he was going to have a child, along with all the love he had discovered, nearly too late, that he needed so badly, the love that had sustained him. Quiet, undemanding, always there for him.

Then Kaitlin had lost the baby, but the news hadn't reached him until he was in the middle of the Persian Gulf.

He'd wanted to be with her. He'd wanted to be with her so badly that it ate at his insides, but by the time the news reached him, she was already out of the hospital and he had months at sea ahead of him.

By the time he returned home, Kaitlin was distant. Untouchable. And in his heart he knew long before he received the official papers that she had withdrawn herself from him.

He had been twenty-two at the time. With nothing left except his pride.

"The stuff that goeth before a fall," he reminded himself out loud. He finished his beer, staring at the stars. He thought of the years since then and the women who had passed through his life. The ones who had cared, the ones who had been casual.

He'd never been more than casual himself. He had never managed to fall out of love.

"And I still love you, Kaitlin," he whispered softly to the darkness.

But how the hell did you start over after a past like theirs?

He had missed Sean so badly. It seemed an ironic shame that it had taken him all these years to understand what his cousin had known all along. Life was a mixture of laughter and of tears. And you were just lucky if you could be loved through them both.

Once upon a time, he had had a love that strong.

And now he wanted it back.

He sat for a minute, then smiled slowly and closed his eyes against the night breeze.

Thank God for all these weddings. He was going to have a chance to try to have it all one more time.

He was older and wiser, and this time he knew that love was everything. When it was offered, you had to reach for it, and grab it, then hold it tight, through the laughter and the tears.

Yes, love was everything....

Kaitlin was everything.

And he would have the chance to spend a lot more time with her next week.

With that thought in mind, he rose, threw his beer can away and patted the *Lilliputian* good night for the evening.

He was whistling as he headed to the house.

## Chapter 8

Kaitlin arrived at the train station in a state of confusion.

Her parents had left just yesterday morning, she'd survived a meeting with Harley and Netty of Seashell Sunblock that afternoon, and then this morning she'd overslept, her taxi had gotten lost, and she had been afraid, what with the early morning traffic, that she was never going to reach her destination.

She did make it in time. Eight minutes before the train was due to leave.

She couldn't wait to get on board. Into a small sleeper, alone. She could read, or sleep, or relax. Actually, she could even work, but the idea of relaxing, of grouping her forces, seemed too sweet. She didn't need to work. Janis was on the job. Harley was as pleased with the finished commercial as his sister was, and the ad was already scheduled to air.

The doors to the train were open, and she trailed her wheeled baggage cart behind her as she hurried along. The conductor pointed out her car. When she reached it, the attendant helped her with her luggage, then took her ticket.

"O'Herlihy," he muttered. He was a young man with sandy hair and light freckles. He flipped his reservation chart over and muttered her name again.

"You're traveling alone?"

"Yes."

"Okay…let's see. What's your first initial?"

"K. For Kaitlin," she told him.

He shook his head again. "How unusual."

"What's the matter?"

"Oh, nothing. Really." He smiled cheerfully

"Is there some problem?"

"Problem? No! Well, let's see, we'll try cabin A," he told her. He moved along the narrow hallway and opened a door. The cabin was empty, and he smiled broadly. "A it is!"

"Was there something wrong with my reservation?" Kaitlin asked him.

"No. Come on in, and I'll show you the cabin. This sleeping car is one of our newest."

He said it with such pride that Kaitlin didn't dare comment on the very tiny size of the room.

"That's the top bunk up there, folded into the wall. And there's plenty of storage space above it. The seats are pulled down—I'll make up the bed for you tonight—and there's your sink." She could see the sink. It was only a foot away from the seat. Once the bunk was down, she realized, she'd have to kneel on the mattress in order to brush her teeth.

She pointed to a door. "Is that the bathroom?"

"Oh, no, that leads to another cabin. These are really wonderful cars. Each cabin can sleep two, so if a family is traveling together, the door between the two can be opened, and the kids can run back and forth."

They would have to be very tiny kids, Kaitlin decided, if they were going to run anywhere between these cabins. No bigger than dolls.

"The bathroom," he told her with pride, "is right here, behind the sink."

The bathroom...

There was a fiberglass toilet in a space that seemed to be two feet by two feet at the most. The shower head was in the wall. To use it, the toilet seat needed to be closed, and the water would just spray around the entire cubicle.

Well, she had wanted small and cozy. This was certainly that.

She smiled. "Thanks. I think I see where everything is, all right."

He grinned. "Great. If you need me, give a holler. I'm here to serve you."

She nodded and thanked him again. As he left, the train began to pull away from the station.

She heard thudding in the cabin connected to hers. Apparently her neighbor had arrived even later than she had.

She decided to settle in. She had hours and hours before they crossed the Georgia border.

She unpacked her toiletries, then took another look in the bathroom. It was so small that it made her shudder. She wondered what a larger person would do in such a space.

Well, it wasn't quite home, she thought a few minutes later, but everything was in its place and her suitcases were stowed away. She took off her shoes, curled up on the seat by the window and brought out a mystery novel by one of her favorite authors, a book she had been saving especially for this occasion.

She tried to read, but the first pages didn't seem to make sense. She read them over, then she realized that she was thinking about Brendan.

She leaned back and closed her eyes.

She would see Brendan again very soon, in two days. His secretary had called Janis to arrange a lunch meeting for them at the hall where they were having the party. They would go over the menu and check the seating arrangements. And they'd be together at the dinner, of course.

Then she wouldn't really need to see him again for a while. Barbara was having a standard shower, and Joe was having an all-male bachelor party. After this trip, weeks could go by before she had to see him again.

She didn't know whether she was relieved or anxious.

She set her book down, keeping her eyes closed. The motion of the train was gentle and soothing, and she drifted to sleep.

When she awoke she was amazed to discover that it was already dark outside. She glanced at her watch. It was almost six; she had slept for nearly eight hours. In a ridiculous position on the tiny seat. Her neck was cramped, and she was stiff and miserable. And hungry.

With a sigh she rose and stretched, then stumbled the fifteen inches to the tiny sink. She washed her face and combed out her hair, and decided that dinner seemed like a good idea. She had noticed that the dining car was forward when she boarded the train, so she walked that way, passing through another car of sleepers and one of seats.

There was a buffet line, and she joined it, then had to choose between chicken, fish and beef for the entrée. She decided on the breaded chicken and iced tea, then followed the attendant, who carried her tray along a line of tables.

She saw only the top of his head at first, yet even then, she felt little prickles along her skin. The attendant was still walking, but she was standing still in the aisle.

Then he raised his head. There was no mistaking him. Brendan was on the train. Sitting at a booth, sipping coffee and reading a newsmagazine. And now...

And now he was staring at her. He didn't smile, and he definitely looked surprised to see her.

Someone bumped into her from behind as the train jolted. She almost toppled over, but Brendan was instantly on his feet and down the aisle, catching her before she could fall.

"Let's sit down before this gets any worse, shall we?" he murmured, leading her to the booth where he had been sitting. Her food seemed to be long gone.

"What are you doing on this train?" she demanded, more sharply than she had intended. She winced inwardly. Why couldn't she be nice?

"Kaitlin, there are two trains a day out of Miami, one in the morning, one at night. This train was the only one I could take!"

"You should have taken an airplane!" she accused him.

"You could have flown," he reminded her.

"I hate to fly."

"You're terrified of flying."

"No, I'm not. I just hate to do it," she lied. "And I do fly."

"Yes, I've heard about the way you fly," he informed her, frowning. "Inebriated into insensibility. Barely conscious," he commented.

"That's why *you* should have flown!" she informed him.

He arched a brow. "I like trains, Kaitlin. I work on the train. I read on the train. I look at the countryside, and I even enjoy the seedy side of the landscape. And the last I heard, this is a free country, so why the hell can't I take a train if I so choose? Are you that afraid of me?"

"I'm not afraid of you!"

"Can't stay away from me, huh? Afraid you'll wind up sleeping with me because there won't be anywhere for you to run once you start things?"

"I am not going to sleep with you!" she exclaimed, far more loudly than she realized.

There was a crashing sound beside her. She looked over to realize that her attendant and the waiter who had bumped into her were both standing beside the table, one to bring a complimentary glass of wine, the other, who had found her at last, to deliver her dinner tray. Only he had dropped her tray, his face reddening, when he overheard their conversation.

She realized then that she must have spoken very loudly, because the diners around them were staring at her, too.

"Now look what you've done," Brendan told her.

She wanted to throttle him or, at the very least, dump the wine over his head. She gritted her teeth while the first waiter assured her that he'd be back with her dinner in just a minute. "I—I had lost you," he explained, picking up the remnants of the chicken from the aisle. She smiled sickly. Then the wine was set down, and both men hurried away.

Her fellow passengers, however, continued to stare for several seconds.

Brendan was smiling. "Want to leave?"

"With my tail between my legs? No, thanks," she assured him.

There was still one pinched-faced lady staring at her. Kaitlin couldn't help herself. She gripped Brendan's hand passionately and leaned toward him. "All right, I *will* sleep with you again."

"Right here?"

"Have we got the space?"

"I guess not."

"We'll just have to wait."

The woman rose, wide-eyed. Brendan gave her a wink, and she huffed. Then he laughed, and Kaitlin found that she was smiling. "She's probably thinking that the trains really are filled with derelicts these days," he assured her.

She flushed. Her tray of food arrived, and she toyed with it idly, feeling his gaze. "It was all your fault," she told him. "Mine?"

"For being on the train. I would never have stopped dead still if I hadn't seen you. And then the man wouldn't have rushed into me. And the other waiter wouldn't have lost me."

"I see. I'm guilty of existing."

She made a face and pushed her tray away. "You really should fly."

His lashes were heavy over his eyes as he leaned back, watching her. "So should you. It saves time." And then to her surprise, he rose. "I'll let you dine in peace, Ms. O'Herlihy." But he paused next to her and whispered softly, "Since you won't sleep with me here and now. Too bad. You had me all excited."

She spun around, but he was already starting down the aisle. She stared at her food for a minute, decided that she wasn't hungry after all, then stood and left the waiter a tip. She started down the hallway, passed through the other cars to hers, where she stared at the letters on the cabin doors. The attendant had been in to pull down the bunks, and the drapes were pulled over the windows in the doors.

She came to cabin AA and opened it. The door slammed into something, and she shoved at it, certain that her luggage must have gotten in the way.

"Hey!" came an aggrieved voice. The door swung open, and she almost fell in.

Brendan was there. He was shirtless, taking up all the space between the lowered bunk and the sink. He glowered at her.

"What are you doing?"

"This—this is my cabin."

"Sorry, it's mine."

She pointed to the letter on the door. "Brendan, I know it's my cabin."

"No, Kaitlin, it's mine." A woman was coming down the narrow hall. Kaitlin had to get out of her way, so she moved into the cabin, almost on top of him. He backed away from the door to give her room. Then he sighed with exasperation and drew her all the way in. He flicked a bolt on the door connecting his cabin to the one next door, opened it and thrust her through. She saw her belongings.

"You're cabin A—not AA," he told her, then turned, returning to the sink.

He hadn't closed the door. She followed him the three steps in. "Well, I'm sorry. Very sorry."

His head clunked into the medicine cabinet as he started to raise his face from the water. He hadn't quite been able to get his body bent into the space to begin with. He looked so angry that she thought he was going to start to growl.

He slammed his hands on the sink. "Sorry. How nice. You know, Kaitlin, I've never heard you say you were sorry about anything before."

"I haven't had anything to be sorry about!" she flared, swinging around and slamming the door between them. She took the two steps to her own sink, determined to brush her teeth, wash her face and curl up with her book again. She could—and would—forget that he was there next to her.

But the connecting door slammed open again, and he was standing there, legs spread, bare chested, his hair damp, his eyes glittering. "Because everything was always my fault, right, Kaitlin?"

She turned. He was walking toward her, and she was trapped in the tiny space between the bunk and the sink.

"Yes," she said simply.

"I never filed papers against you!" he rasped out furiously.

She gasped, then fell silent for a moment. He had never protested, never tried to contact her, never said a word.

Not until this moment had she realized that their divorce had meant anything to him at all.

"You—you left me!" she whispered.

"I joined the Navy," he said more quietly. "Because I thought you wanted more out of life than I could give you."

"I did want more. But I wanted it from you," she said.

He was standing at least a foot away. She could see the rise and fall of his chest, the damp sprinkles of water upon it, the rippling of the muscles there. He lifted his hands. "All that we had," he murmured. "All that we had, and we could never talk."

Tears were rising behind her eyelids, dampening her lashes. She gritted her teeth to keep the tears from falling.

He turned, starting to go to his own cabin. "Well, it's too late for this now, isn't it?" he murmured softly. "Good night, Kaitlin."

He disappeared through the door and closed it behind him. She stared at it for a moment, her hands on her hips. Then she strode toward it and flung it open. He had just stripped off his jeans and was standing by the bunk in his briefs. She paused for a moment, staring at him, then she inhaled sharply and stared into his eyes.

"You didn't even come home when I lost the baby!" she flared.

"I didn't know!" he snapped.

"You had to know. I wrote to you—"

"And I was already on a ship. Kaitlin, it was the Navy, not a joyride!" He was walking toward her. She had to retreat. She needed time to assimilate the things they were saying. She spun, but he caught her arm and turned her back. He ran his free hand through his hair. "Kaitlin, damn it, you know I would have come if I had known!"

She tried desperately to free herself. He released her, and she crashed into the door to the bath and fell on the commode, bringing him with her. Then the door slammed shut on them both. They might have been a pair of sardines caught in a too-small can.

Brendan swore, finding it impossible even to turn around. Kaitlin, caught beneath him, tried to catch hold of something and rise. Her fingers closed over the rubber shower arm, and suddenly water was spraying all over them.

"Damnation, Kaitlin—" He managed to shut off the water, then find the catch on the door. When he swung it open, he turned for her, pulling her over the step, soaked and sodden, in his arms.

They both started to laugh. Her skirt was plastered against her body, and her hair was slicked against her head. She was touching him, and she could feel the dampness of his briefs—the heat beneath them.

Then their laughter faded. Suddenly they were staring at one another. Emotions simmered, seeming to rise like steam between them.

Kaitlin started to tremble and tried to pull away, but Brendan's hands were tight on her arms, and he held her flush against him. She went still as, slowly, slowly, his head descended toward hers. His lips, hot and wet, moved over hers, and his tongue invaded her mouth, all of him warm and wet and assertive. The fingers of his right hand tangled into her damp hair as his left hand pressed into the small of her back, bringing her more tightly against him. As she freely tasted her mouth, the resistance within her faded. He stroked both hands down the length of her back, cupped her buttocks and brought her up high against the rising steel of his desire.

He kissed her until she knew that she had no strength within her, until she was weak from the wonder and intimacy of his body against hers. Her clothes and his briefs seemed to offer no real barrier between them. And he was still kissing her. Finding her lips, playing his tongue over her earlobe, her throat, her cheeks, her lips. Licking, taunting, probing the deep recesses of her mouth.

Then he pulled away, holding her cheeks, studying her eyes. She knew that her lips were wet and swollen, that her expression was dazed, and he smiled slowly, and with pain.

"I can't seduce you," he whispered.

"No," she agreed.

"And you're not going to sleep with me on the train."

"That's what I said I'd do," she murmured.

"But then again, you were going to have sex with me right on the dining room table."

"Between the rolls and the wine," she agreed, her whisper swallowed up by his soft kiss. Then the teasing quality left his voice, and he told her, "I can't just date you, Kaitlin. I thought that was what we needed, at first. But just like I can't change the pain of the past, I can't change the intimacy of it. I can't pretend that you were never mine, or that I don't want you now. I don't expect you to swear away your life to me. I don't want promises, or a commitment. But I do need honesty."

She didn't quite understand what he was saying to her. It could have been so easy. He had just kissed her, and their passion had risen and soared. They could have followed through to the natural conclusion without awkwardness, without a word being exchanged. And she knew that he still wanted her, desperately. She could feel the pulse and the heat of his wanting. Feel it make her want him in return...

She shook her head slightly and dampened her lips. "What do you want from me, Brendan? I can't make the years disappear, either. You say you don't want promises, but what promises could we give one another, anyway? I can't erase the pain either. And I..."

"And you what?" he demanded, his green gaze fierce as he stared at her.

"I can't just date you, either, I suppose. I don't know. I

don't..." She shook her head. "What do you want?" she whispered.

And he told her. He leaned down, his lips against her ear, his whisper soft and yet searing. And his thumb trailed down her spine, and he drew her close once again.

"I want you to want me," he told her. "No repercussions, no running away in the morning. I just want you to want me."

She met his eyes again and smiled very slowly. She reached up, wrapping her arms around him, pulling his lips to hers. And she kissed him with an ardor to match his, tasting his lips with her tongue, fusing them sweetly together in an ardent dance of desire. Then she spoke against his lips, her lashes heavy against her eyes. "I wanted you at my house that night. When you left."

"The night when you didn't even know that we hadn't made love when it was all over?" he whispered, and she flushed. He shook his head. "I promised you that you'd remember," he said softly. "Tell me you want me now."

His hands were on her blouse, undoing the small buttons. He didn't fumble, his fingers moving even as his eyes met hers.

She inhaled sharply as his knuckles grazed over the flesh of her breast.

"I want you now," she told him.

He stripped away her shirt and let it fall to the floor. He kissed her shoulder blades, lifting her lacy bra straps and pulling them sensually down her arms, then releasing the snaps in back. At last he lowered his head, taking her breast into his mouth, laving the nipple with his tongue, then suckling hard on the peak so that she arched against him in a sudden swift rush of sensation so sharp that she cried out softly. Suddenly he was kneeling before her, finding the zipper to her skirt, pulling it down slowly. She stepped from her clothes, and he teased the flesh at her waist, then swept away her pantyhose and bikinis in a quick motion before burying his face against the softness of her belly.

He caught her buttocks and brought her hard against him as he kissed her abdomen and upper thighs. She closed her eyes, throwing her head back in response. And she trembled, wondering what he would do next, the anticipation exciting her nearly as desperately as the touch that followed.

For when he touched her so intimately, the shock tore through her system, the sweetness pervaded her, and she could not think.

She could barely stand as she felt the delicious rush drenching her inside with hot, honeyed wonder. Then the world seemed to burst into brilliance and rush into black, and she could not stand. She was falling as the nectar and the ecstasy spilled from her.

She was in his arms as she fell, and he was catching her so that she landed on the lower bunk. He kissed her, and her fingers raked over his back, then slipped beneath the waistband of his briefs. Lovingly, slowly, she peeled them down, stroking the flesh of his hips, her fingers moving to the soft down at his navel, then closing around the hard, pulsing life of him. He groaned, shuddering, and wedged his way between her thighs, then caught her hands and curled her fingers within his own, and plunged deep within her.

She cried out softly, loving the feel of him within her. Then he began to move, and she felt as if the earth itself was shifting beneath her. He stroked the flesh within her, touched, caressed and teased, then plunged deeply again, cradling her against him, savoring the sensation of being locked so tightly together. Slowly, then swiftly, he moved, and she rocked with him, sweetly aware that she was straining against him, wanting more of him, closing around him. She could feel the sheen of perspiration that covered her body and his, and the ever spiraling hunger that drove them both. Then release burst upon her, and she trembled and shook with the strength of her response. She felt the force of his body shuddering against hers again and again, felt the heated rush of his seed filling her.

And still he lay taut against her, holding her close. Then he groaned softly against her throat, kissed her, nipped her flesh and kissed it again. And in the growing shadows he lifted his head, and she saw that he was smiling. Only then did she realize that they were really only half on the bunk, and that he was twisted in a truly unreasonable position. She pulled him over her, stretching out against the wall of the cabin. They barely fit onto the bunk together.

"You know, Ms. O'Herlihy," he whispered softly against her cheek, his fingers tenderly, idly stroking her flesh from her collarbone to her breast, "there have been numerous times—numerous times!—when we have been alone near sumptuous, comfortable beds. Beds with space, with softness, with support, with clean, fresh sheets and endless pillows. And you pick a two-by-four train car.''

''What?'' she demanded, struggling to sit up.

''I may never walk again,'' he told her solemnly.

''Oh!''

He laughed, pulling her close again. And his whisper filled her ear sweetly. ''It was worth it. Whatever the sacrifice, it was worth it.''

''Sacrifice!''

''My spine is a pretzel.''

''Well, I'll just go to my own cabin, then!'' she told him.

He shook his head. ''Not on your life, Kaitlin O'Herlihy,'' he told her, carefully balancing his weight, his green gaze somehow sharp and tender and wicked all at once. ''This is an odyssey, a challenge...an adventure.'' He lowered himself against her slowly, still smiling.

The train whistled shrilly in the darkness, but neither of them noticed as he began to kiss and arouse her again, feeling the rebirth of a hot and flickering fire within him.

She shimmied down his body, giving in to every decadent and wanton desire that had ever filled her fantasies, touching him, caressing him, tormenting his hips and chest with tiny flicks of her tongue, rubbing her body against his. The space at their disposal was quite limited, but this was an adventure....

She breathed in the masculine scent that had haunted her dreams for years. She tasted the salty remnants of their love against his flesh. She teased and taunted with her hair and lips, kissing and arousing him everywhere until at last she closed her fingers around his renewed desire. Unbearably aroused herself, she kissed, she caressed.

Until he swore and proved that he could fit fully atop her, despite the limitations of the bunk.

The whistle shrilled again, or it could have been her cry of desire, of ecstasy fulfilled.

The night went on and on, as she lay against him, his arms around her, and he whispered with a trace of amusement and a satisfied shudder, ''Beyond a doubt, Kaitlin, me love...this is the way to see America!''

# Chapter 9

As it happened, it was one of the best train rides Kaitlin had ever taken. In more ways than one.

She was glad she had slept all day, because she didn't sleep a wink during the night. And since they would have to change trains very early in New York, Brendan suggested with a sigh that they should rise at about five-thirty to shower and dress.

Then, listening to Brendan swear vociferously as he tried to fit in the shower and bathe at the same time, she laughed as she was sure she hadn't laughed in years. He heard her and came bolting out, soaked and sudsy and insisting she come in and help him. She swore that they wouldn't fit, but somehow they managed. And then he began to tickle her, until she was laughing and gasping at the same time, and they wound up making love one last time and having to shower all over again.

She slipped into her own cabin in time for the attendant to deliver her coffee and croissants, then she breakfasted while she applied her makeup. She had barely finished when the attendant came by again, warning her that they were about to reach New York.

Brendan came to get her luggage down, and they detrained together. The layover in New York was a little more than an hour, plenty of time to have a second cup of coffee and pick up a newspaper.

Kaitlin was surprised at just how warm and wonderful it felt to hurry for the next train together, to have him take her bags, hold her hand, be with her. She hadn't realized just how alone she had been.

This time they were on a commuter train, sitting in regular seats, with dozens of people around them. They didn't talk at all. He was reading a magazine, and she took out her mystery. Somehow, with Brendan beside her, she found herself absolutely delighted by the book, and she read on, turning the pages faster and faster until she realized that they had arrived in Boston.

They detrained again and walked to the street. And there a bit of the bubble burst, because they had to separate, having ordered rental cars from different companies.

"Do you really need a car?" Brendan asked her.

She nodded. "I'll be running around with Donna and you'll be running around with Bill. And I'm not staying with my parents, either. I decided on a motel in Auburn because I really didn't know what hours I would be keeping."

"I'm not staying with my parents, either."

"I suppose you're staying at your own place?"

He shook his head. "I told you—it's too far out." Then he smiled wickedly. "But, since the choices in Auburn are limited, I'm willing to bet we're staying at the same motel."

She smiled slowly. "I wonder if maybe I shouldn't go home after all."

"Oh?"

"My father could protect me."

He scowled. "Kaitlin, I didn't—"

"You didn't," she interrupted, then added quickly, "not from you. From myself."

"Tell you what. I'll cancel my car, we'll take yours into Worcester, and I'll get myself a car there."

She lowered her eyes quickly. Her heart was beating furiously, and she was ridiculously pleased because they were going to be spending a little more time together. They were going to be staying at the same motel. But they would be running around with Donna and Bill, and their time together would be limited.

He was already on the street, hailing a cab. He must have had the knack, because one came along instantly. They had the driver take them to the rental car company by the airport. Kaitlin stepped forward to pick up her car, and Brendan waited for her. When she had finished the paperwork, she met him with the keys in her hand. "Want to drive?"

"Sure." He took the keys from her, and she smiled.

"I hate the Boston traffic. I'm not here enough. I always make a wrong turn and end up going in circles."

"Well, I've got a confession to make," he told her. "I still go in circles now and then, too."

But he didn't make any mistakes. He knew the expressway and the way to the turnpike, and from there it was simple.

He drove to Worcester, to another rental agency, parked and got out. Then he leaned over and kissed her lightly on the lips. "I'll see you later?"

She nodded. He retrieved his luggage, then stepped back and waved. She twisted the key and drove away.

By six o'clock that night she had checked into the motel, driven out to a neighboring town to see her parents and come back to Auburn to meet Donna for dinner. They hugged fiercely, not just relatives but friends all their lives. Donna, with her dark auburn hair and light blue eyes, looked enough like Kaitlin to be her sister. They had shared everything throughout the years, their opinions on boys, on clothing and music, then, when they had matured, their ideas on morality and ethics. Kaitlin was happy for Donna, but what should have been an easy occasion was suddenly very hard for her.

Things had changed last night. Unbelievably. She didn't know what to think or feel, and she wanted to spill out the whole story to her cousin and ask for advice. She wanted to cry for help, but she was also desperate to keep her own counsel. She was more afraid than ever. Get out of my heart and out of my mind! she silently warned an absent Brendan as she listened to Donna's enthusiasm, looked at the picture of the dress she had ordered and praised the bridesmaids' dresses Donna liked.

They talked about the wedding, and Donna talked about Bill, and Kaitlin kept the subject away from herself for hours. They ate dinner, then went to the bridal shop at the mall, where Kaitlin was fitted for her gown. Then they took a ride to the reception hall and went by the church to listen to the organist and choose the music.

Finally they stopped for a drink at a club near Kaitlin's motel, and Donna asked her how the train ride had been.

"The train ride?" Kaitlin murmured, stalling.

"Sure, how was it? Boring?"

Boring. Kaitlin lowered her eyes and ran her fingers over the table. "Uh, no, it wasn't boring."

"Long?"

"It, uh, it didn't seem that long, either." She kept her lashes lowered. Laughter was welling up inside her. She wanted to tell Donna about the episode in the shower. Donna would laugh, too, just like when they were young.

But she couldn't say anything, no matter how close they were. The future was more frightening to her than it had ever been before.

Finally she raised her eyes and looked at Donna. "Brendan was on the same train."

"Oh! That's right, Bill told me he likes to take the train, that he needs the time."

"Yes, something like that."

"Well?" Donna's eyes were wide, and there was a whisper of excitement in her voice. "Well?"

"Well, what?" Kaitlin asked smoothly.

"Are you two getting along? Are the sparks flying?"

"We're both in your wedding party. And we want the wedding to be great. We're working well enough together."

"And that's all?" Donna asked.

"That's all," Kaitlin lied sweetly.

"But he made the train ride go more quickly, huh? You two talked. He was entertaining?"

"Oh, uh, very entertaining."

She realized Donna was grinning and looking past her. She whirled around to see that Bill and Brendan had come into the club and were standing behind her. Her cheeks reddened. Brendan was tossing his jacket over the chair beside her and taking a seat, his green eyes flashing with amusement.

"Kaitlin was darned entertaining, too, Donna," he told her. He said it with a very straight face.

Kaitlin cast him a quick glare, then rose to kiss and hug Bill. Then she sat, and the men ordered drinks.

The conversation flowed smoothly. At least, Kaitlin thought it did. She wasn't really a part of it; she just listened. And she felt Brendan so close beside her, and a chill streaked up and down her spine.

It might have been years ago. They'd all known each other so long. They'd taken day trips together as kids, long rides out to the cape, excursions into New Hampshire and Maine. Nights in New York City. It might have been forever ago.

But it wasn't. She didn't really know Brendan anymore. She had to keep telling herself that. He didn't want to date, but despite what had happened on the train, she was afraid to rush. They'd hurt one another too badly in the past.

Suddenly she rose, kissed them all—even Brendan—and excused herself, saying that she was exhausted. She promised Brendan she would meet him at noon at the restaurant where they'd be having the party, and she told Donna and Bill she'd see them the next night. Then she left.

At the door, she felt Brendan's gaze and turned. He was staring after her intently, but she couldn't begin to read his expression, or his mind.

She met him at noon, as promised. He was precise and cool as they went over the menu, checked on the entertainment and listened to the war stories the maître d' had to tell them. But when they were seated alone with sandwiches for lunch, he wasted no time.

"What was going on last night?" he asked her tensely. "Nothing."

He almost smiled. "It was definitely nothing," he agreed. "Why did you walk away?"

"I was tired."

"It was more than that."

"All right," she said softly. "You want to know what happened last night? I was afraid."

"Of me?"

She leaned forward, plunging in. "Yes, of you. Brendan, we were divorced almost eight years ago. We were married for less than two. And when I went to the Keys to see you that time, one night destroyed my equilibrium for another year. I don't want to fall for you again. We didn't just hurt each other before—it was torture."

He leaned back, staring at her. "So what do you want to do?" he asked softly.

"I—I don't know."

"Run away from it?"

She was silent, afraid that he would stand up and walk away, that they would never have a chance to really talk again.

What she wanted, she realized, was a declaration of undying love and devotion, a promise that they would make it. She wanted him to say that he had loved her forever, that there had never been anyone else.

But he couldn't tell her that, and she knew it. There was too much time, and too much distance, between them.

"I don't know what I want," she said very softly.

He rose, and she thought he was going to storm away. But he didn't. He touched her cheek lightly. "I *do* know what I want," he said quietly.

And then he walked away.

When she followed moments later, he was nowhere to be seen.

At the motel she sat by her phone, staring at it, thinking she should call him and suggest that they drive to the party together—they were coming from the same place. But she couldn't quite manage to dial. No, she couldn't even manage to pick up the receiver. Brendan should have called her.

But he wasn't going to. Not after the way they had left things at the restaurant.

She showered and dressed with plenty of time to spare. Then she sat by the telephone again. She had just about convinced herself to pick up the receiver when there was a knock at her door. She hurried over and threw it open.

Brendan was there. "I wondered if you were ready," he said. She nodded, not trusting herself to speak. He was striking in his dove-gray suit, white shirt and maroon vest. His hair was clean and damp, a shining ebony. He wore clothes well, she decided.

And when he didn't wear clothes...

Her mind was slipping. "I'm ready," she said, and she was breathless. "But it's too early to head out—"

"Let's take a ride," he told her.

She didn't know where they were going, but she nodded. He picked up her shawl and drew it around her shoulders, then caught her hand and walked her along the hall.

They still hadn't spoken when he seated her in his car, and she asked him softly, "Where are we going?"

His lips curved slowly into a smile as he stared ahead at the road. "I don't know," he admitted, and she smiled, too.

The car might have been a horse, allowed to take its own lead. They just started driving, and suddenly they were in the heart of Worcester, driving by the old neighborhood. They went by the triple decker where the O'Herlihys had first lived, then down to Burncoat Street, where her father had built their first house. They went by the high school and the pool and the park, and then they decided to see if the best little family-run Italian restaurant in town was still in business. It was.

"Too bad we're out of time," Brendan said morosely.

She laughed. "Brendan, we're throwing a dinner party. An expensive dinner party, at that. And you want to stop for pasta first?"

He nodded. "Yeah, but we haven't got the time."

He started driving again, and Kaitlin felt a faint and curious prickling along her spine. They were passing the cemetery where members of both their families had been buried. Including Sean.

"You think the gates might still be open?" she asked.

He glanced at her sharply. Dusk was falling. He glanced at the car clock. "There're about ten minutes left. Why?"

"Let's go in."

"Kaitlin—"

"Please, Brendan, I want to."

He shrugged, then swung the car around the corner and through the gates. He drove as far as he could, then pulled the car up to the side of the road.

The cemetery was very quiet. There didn't seem to be another soul there. To the left, the old slate tombstones that gave credence to the cemetery's age rose against the twilight. Here, in the newer section, there was a multitude of beautiful twentieth-century stones. Praying angels, saints, obelisks, all kinds of memorials to loved ones who had passed from the world.

Kaitlin didn't head for the bowing angel above the graves of her father's parents and grandparents. She walked straight to the large statue of a beautiful Saint Theresa standing guard over the earthly remains of Sean O'Herlihy.

In the dusk, Saint Theresa seemed almost to live and breathe. And there was a gentle, curious smile on her lips that reminded Kaitlin of Sean.

Brendan was standing behind her, and he didn't come any closer.

There were flowers on the grave.

"You've been here already," she said.

"I've been here," he told her. "But I didn't bring the flowers. Someone in the family always brings flowers at this time every year."

Kaitlin nodded, staring at the grave. Suddenly she wanted to cry as badly as she had all those years ago. What would have happened if Sean had lived? Would she and Brendan be celebrating more than a decade of marriage? Would there have been other children to replace the one they had lost? It was a mystery, buried deep within the earth with Sean O'Herlihy.

"We should go," Brendan said, and she nodded. He led her from the grave and helped her into the car. And when they had moved into the traffic he asked her, "Why did you want to stop?"

"I don't know."

"Kaitlin, he's been dead for twelve years."

She glanced at him sharply. "Has he ever really died for you, Brendan?"

He frowned, catching her eyes in the rear view mirror. "I'll never forget him, if that's what you're saying. He was my best friend. Any time you lose someone, a certain emptiness remains."

She didn't answer him, only looked out the window. Then she murmured softly, "He left us because he had no choice. But the emptiness was worse when you left me, too, because you didn't have to go."

He suddenly pulled the car onto the sidewalk.

"What are you talking about?" he demanded.

"Brendan, you're on the damn sidewalk!"

"I don't care! Answer me!"

"I was still there, Brendan. And you were still there. But you left **me**. You were gone. Sean didn't leave on purpose. You did. You **had** a choice."

"I didn't leave."

"You weren't there."

He leaned back against the seat and swore. "What the hell do you want from me, Kaitlin? I've said I was wrong. I've tried to explain. I know you understood. You were wonderful, you were quiet and supportive, and you just waited. And I hurt you. I'm sorry." He swung around to face her. "Maybe I was even wrong later, when I caught you with another guy—"

"It was nothing!" she choked out furiously.

"I just said I was wrong!" he told her harshly. "But once we were married, I wasn't the one to end it all with the clean stroke of a knife! What the hell was it? You didn't get the wedding you wanted, so you decided you had to try again? I'm surprised you didn't bargain for an annulment from the first. Then you could have had everything you wanted."

Eyes burning, she turned toward him, telling him exactly what she thought he was, her hand suddenly flying. She didn't slap his cheek only because he caught her wrist. And then she was in his arms again, his kiss searing her lips with a passion and fury and trembling vehemence more volatile than anything that had passed between them before. His lips and tongue tasted of his fury, his violence, of despair and of longing. The kiss spoke of time and of tears, and it seemed to shatter her heart.

He released her slowly, staring into her eyes. She felt a dampness on her cheeks, and she knew she was crying.

"Oh, Kaitlin," he whispered.

He kissed her very lightly then, and drew out his handkerchief, dabbing at her mouth. "I cut your lip," he said with regret. "I'm sorry, Kaitlin. Really."

She shook her head, taking the handkerchief as he revved the motor and eased the car into traffic. Darkness surrounded them, and the streetlights played across his features. Kaitlin wiped her cheeks and dabbed at her lips, and her heart suddenly ached as she watched him. She wondered if she had ever felt closer to him than she did at that moment, and she wondered how that could be.

Swallowing her pride and the pain that had built up over the years, she moved closer, laying her hand gently on his thigh. "I didn't really want a divorce, Brendan," she said in rush. "It was just that when I lost the baby, I was so hurt and so alone, and I wanted you so badly. And you didn't come——,"

"I couldn't come! I didn't even know at first!"

"I know that now," she said. "But then, even when you were with me, you were still living in your own world. Brendan, I wanted you to protest. I wanted you to fight me. I wanted you to mourn Sean and our baby. I just wanted you to realize that we were both still alive!"

He didn't say anything for a long moment. Then he held the steering wheel with his left hand, and his right hand curved over hers.

Then they were at the restaurant, and he was swinging into the parking lot. He found a spot for the car and turned off the engine, then turned to her. He took the handkerchief from her and dabbed at her lip. "Damn, it looks like I gave you a good one to the jaw."

She laughed. "It can't be that bad. Oh, well, we'll chalk it all up to that Irish temper of yours."

"My Irish temper!"

She smiled, and so did he, but then his smile faded. "I gave you the divorce because I thought that it was what you wanted," he said. "How could I protest when everything had gone so badly?"

She shook her head, afraid she would start crying all over again.

"All those years," he murmured. "Kaitlin, I—"

She never knew what he had intended to say, because there was a tap at his window. They both started and turned their heads. Kaitlin's cousin Patrick was standing there, smiling. "Hey, you guys coming in or what?"

He walked around to open Kaitlin's door. "Patrick!" she murmured with forced enthusiasm. Patrick was great—she loved him. But she wondered why he'd had to show up at that exact moment. Still, she got out and gave him a big hug.

Brendan was out of the car, too, and beside them both, greeting Patrick. Then the three of them walked into the restaurant together.

It was a wonderful party. More than wonderful. Donna and Bill looked so happy together. Brendan gave the groom a great speech, and Donna received all sorts of beautiful things. Both families were there; the meal was delicious, and the band Brendan had hired played a range of songs that appealed to every age group.

They didn't leave until nearly 2:00 a.m. Donna and Bill stayed to the last, thanking them both profusely.

"It wasn't anything," Brendan told Donna.

"Yes, it was," Donna insisted. "It was wonderful. I just wish you two didn't have to lay out quite so much—"

"Honestly, it was nothing. Kaitlin has a new business," Brendan told her solemnly.

"Brendan's in on it, too," Kaitlin said sweetly. She explained about the commercial, then wished she hadn't. Now everyone in the world was going to be looking for it. She'd never hear the end of it from her relatives.

Donna went on and on, but finally she and Bill left, and Kaitlin and Brendan walked to his rental car. She leaned her head back as soon as she touched the seat. She was exhausted, drained.

He drove to the motel in silence, then escorted her up to her room. When she stopped by the door, he paused, then kissed her lips gently. She waited, tired, but growing flushed with excitement. He was going to stay, she thought. He would come in with her, and they would make love.

But he only told her good night very softly, then turned and walked away.

Kaitlin carefully disrobed and hung up her dress, then slipped into a soft flannel gown. Then she lay down and tried to sleep, but suddenly she felt the dampness on her cheeks, silent tears again, tears for all they had shared, all they had lost.

The love had never died. They had just thrown it away.

Perhaps everything was out in the open between them now. But could anything they said make it right now? Or had too much time passed, too many years? Could they ever rectify the past? She lay awake for a long time, but exhaustion finally claimed her.

She was awakened very early by a pounding on her door. She hadn't even blinked enough to be coherent, but she bounded out of bed and threw open the door.

It was Brendan. An irritated Brendan. "Look at you, Kaitlin. Barely dressed, just throwing that door wide open. Hell, I could have been anyone. A burglar, a rapist!"

She stared at him blankly. "It's nice to see you, too, Brendan."

"Kaitlin, I'd just rather you didn't get yourself killed."

She nodded. "Sure." She shook her head. "Excuse me for a moment, will you?"

"Briefly," he warned ner.

She shut herself into the bathroom and doused her head in cold water, then scrubbed her teeth. She felt lucid again.

When she walked out of the bathroom, she didn't see him at first, and she thought he had left.

Then he called her name softly. "Kaitlin."

She whirled and stared at him, stunned for a moment; then her lips slowly curved into a smile.

He was stretched out on her bed, stark naked. It could have been a calendar pose if it hadn't looked so natural. He was glorious and tempting beyond all measure, leaning on one elbow, his head resting on his hand, watching her. One ebony lock fell with a slightly rakish air over his forehead, and his green eyes were gleaming, the gold specks seeming to catch the morning sun. He was all bronze muscle, the thick thatch of dark hair on his chest immensely inviting. And below that…his intent was certainly visible.

"Come here," he said, patting the bed.

"What the hell are you doing?" she whispered.

"You'll have a good time, I promise," he told her with absolute confidence.

She still hadn't moved, so he did. He rose and walked over to her, and deftly began to undo the tiny buttons on her flannel gown. She still didn't make a move, but she allowed him to strip her, paradoxically feeling both lethargy and excitement sweep through her as the gown fell to the floor. He moved behind her, and she felt his naked body brushing her back and buttocks. His hands curled around her breasts, and his lips brushed heat and fire against her ear as his tongue dampened her flesh in small circles. He swept her hair aside, and his kiss moved down the length of her spine. She turned in his arms, choking as the sensations of sweet fire claimed her. His tongue dipped into her navel and flicked along her belly. Unable to stand any longer, she knelt before him and caught his lips in a fierce and hungry kiss.

He meant to sweep her into his arms, to carry her over to the endless soft expanse of the bed. To make love to her there. But her lips were on his, her fingers moving over his back, stroking, while their tongues met and mated in an age-old rhythm. And she was there, beneath his hands. So he touched her. He teased her legs apart and feathered his fingers over the juncture of her thighs, then teased the bud of her desire and probed deeply into the heart of her sexuality. Her soft cries aroused him to a frenzy, and it seemed that her hands were beautifully, miraculously everywhere. On his shoulders, taunting his buttocks, curling around the very life and strength and force of him. Touching him, stroking him, until he thought he would die if he didn't take her soon.

He laid her on the thick carpet and wedged her legs apart, convinced—in his heart, in his mind, in his hunger—that she could never forget this morning. And then he had her with the force of his kiss and his tongue, parting her fiercely, tasting her endlessly. Ignoring her cries and her pleas, and taking an ever-increasing pleasure in the wild undulations of her body as he forced a searing burst of ecstasy upon her, tasting the response of her body to his hunger and demand.

He did not let her drift down, but wrapped her in his embrace and cried out hoarsely, plunging the need of his body into the promise of hers, shaking as she gloved him with warmth and fire and liquid heat. Tender, violent, he rode out his desire. Felt her move, her legs locking around his back, and breathed out words of passion, burying his face against her throat, then his lips against her breast. He felt her stiffen, heard her cry, and knew the sweet liquid flooding around him once again. And he sank into her, shuddering, climaxing, and praying that he could fill her with the love that had been lost to them both for so long.

He closed his eyes and held her.

Then, slowly, they both became aware of the hum of the air conditioner and movement in the hall outside the door. The world was awakening.

He turned to look at her. At the blue beauty of her eyes, at the sheen of perspiration covering her, the damp strawberry-blond locks tangling over her breasts and cheeks. He moved her hair, smiling. "What is it that you have against beds, Kaitlin?"

"Me!" she protested.

He stared at her, loving her, and kissed her lips again, very slowly. "I'd want you anywhere," he told her. "Anywhere at all."

Then, to Kaitlin's amazement, he rose and stretched a hand to her, still grinning. "Although it would be nice to try a bed next time." His smile eased, and his eyes searched hers. "If there is a next time," he said softly.

He turned and walked into her shower. Stunned, she listened as the water started. She walked to the bathroom door.

"What do you think you're doing, Brendan?" she asked, and tried the door. It was locked.

He was quick, though, emerging moments later, toweling himself strenuously. He paused to lightly kiss her lips, then dressed. "I'm going home, Kaitlin. I fly out in about two hours. I've got to get back to Boston."

She felt her temper soaring. "Nice of you to stop by," she told him.

He reached for the coverlet, wrapping it around her shoulders. She tried to wrench away from him, but she couldn't. He laughed easily, still holding her.

"Brendan—"

His finger fell across her lips. "I told you yesterday, Kaitlin. I know what I want. You don't. So think about it. Take your time. Neither of us can undo all the things we did before. We've thrown away years of our lives. Let's not do it again."

"Brendan, I—"

"I don't want you to say anything. Think about it. I'm going to go home and go to work. I'll see you at Donna and Bill's wedding. And when I see you again, I want an answer!"

Then he was gone, and she was left to stare after him, dressed only in the coverlet.

"An answer to what, Brendan?" she shouted.

She sank down on the bed, and she didn't know whether to laugh or cry.

"An answer to what, Brendan?" she repeated softly. "An answer to what?"

## Chapter 10

Nearly four weeks later, Kaitlin was again in Massachusetts.

She'd gone home, gone to work, had a very traditional all-girl shower for her cousin Barbara. And she and Barbara had ordered flowers, checked on the menu and listened to bands. They'd run around looking for favors for the reception table, and they'd made a very elegant little box where gifts of money could be safely left.

They'd survived a few rough spots, like the reception hall sending out a warning that it might file for bankruptcy before Barbara's wedding. Barbara had called, hysterical, and she and Kaitlin had hurried to the hall, only to be assured that things had already changed, that new money had been invested in the business, and everything would be perfect.

Kaitlin didn't see Brendan. Brendan told her that he and Bill and some others were going to be taking off for a special one-night cruise to Freeport and back. Later she heard that they had gone, but that the hotel had been overbooked, and they'd had to wait until nearly 2:00 a.m. to get rooms, and one room had been filled with bedbugs.

She hoped it had been Brendan's room. He deserved bedbugs.

But Joe laughed when she asked him about it, and told her that despite their problems, they'd all had the time of their lives.

And still she didn't hear from Brendan.

Before she knew it, it was time to leave for Donna's wedding.

There was plenty to do when she arrived in Auburn. She and Donna covered what seemed like half of Massachusetts in a matter of days. They drove to one small town for the special ribbons Donna wanted on the flowers, then to another to deliver the ribbons. They picked up the elegant party favors that Donna and Patrick and his wife had painstakingly been making for weeks, then they brought them to the hall. They went for the last fitting on the gowns and agreed to pick them up at ten o'clock on the day of the wedding.

"We'll bring them all to my mother's house and get dressed there," Donna said. "Bill and the guys can dress at his house."

Finally the day of the rehearsal dinner arrived.

Tremors had set into Kaitlin with the sure knowledge that she would see Brendan that night. She had chosen her dress with care for that very reason. It was sheer black satin and covered her from neck to knee, but it fit her so closely that it was one of the sexiest things she had ever seen.

She wondered if Brendan was staying at the motel, but she doubted it. She wasn't staying there herself this time. With the wedding so close, she was rooming with Donna at her mother's house.

At six-thirty they left for the rehearsal. The church was already filled with family and friends.

And then Kaitlin saw Brendan. He was across the aisle, talking to one of Bill's ushers, when he caught sight of her.

His eyes moved up and down her so pointedly that she flushed and turned away. Her little cousin, Brandy, was about to start attacking the candles, so she chased quickly after her. Then her mother found her and whispered, "What's taking so long?"

Startled, Kaitlin told her, "I don't know."

Then Barbara came by, almost in tears. "We've lost an usher."

"What do you mean, you've lost an usher?"

"Terry Simmons isn't here. He's forgotten the wedding! He's left the country—I'm sure of it!"

"Barbara, don't cry, don't panic. He's just late. He'll be here," Kaitlin assured her.

But as it turned out, they didn't have to find another body. Brendan managed to track Terry down at his office. He had merely written down the wrong time for the rehearsal. The priest paced, Barbara wept and Brandy tried to eat the candles while they all waited.

When Terry appeared he apologized profusely to Donna, and she kissed him and hugged him and told him she didn't give a damn, as long as he was finally there.

Kaitlin caught Brendan's eye and saw that he was smiling with amusement. She smiled, and the rehearsal was on.

Bill's mother had arranged for the dinner at a country club. Kaitlin and Brendan would be sitting with Donna and Bill, as well as another couple from the bridal party.

Brendan looked striking that night. No matter how elegant his clothes, the rugged planes of his face gave him an aura of masculinity that was sharp and appealing.

He didn't touch her after the rehearsal. He had led her along the aisle, and they had stood together beside Donna and Bill. But once they left the church, he didn't touch her.

Except with his eyes. And the look in them was decadent.

Dinner was delicious. The conversation flowed smoothly, and the champagne was great. Kaitlin knew she was drinking too much champagne again, but she couldn't help it. She was flushed, her palms damp. She wanted to be alone with Brendan. She wanted to watch him.

She wanted him to touch her....

And she still wasn't the least bit sure what question she was supposed to be answering.

Apparently she wasn't going to find out, either. When dinner was over, he helped her out of her chair. "Watch the champagne tomorrow night," he warned her. "I'll see you then."

Early the next morning she discovered that she wasn't going to have to wait until the wedding to see him after all.

Donna had asked him to follow them to pick up the dresses because the gowns were bulky, and they needed the extra space in his car to carry them. When they arrived at the bridal shop, Donna went over to the counter to speak with her consultant.

Brendan came over to Kaitlin. "Have you been thinking?" he asked tensely.

"You son of a bitch!" she hissed softly. "I've been doing nothing but thinking, and I don't even know what the hell it is I'm supposed to be thinking about!"

Before he could reply, Donna let out a cry of distress.

They stared at one another, then hurried to her. Tears were glimmering in her eyes. "She can't find them! Mrs. Taylor can't find my gowns!"

Mrs. Taylor came hurrying in from the pressing room where the ready-to-go gowns were usually kept. "Donna, don't worry now, they have to be here somewhere. Relax, I'll keep looking."

Donna threw herself into Brendan's arms, moaning that her whole wedding was being destroyed. Kaitlin glanced at him over her cousin's head, then turned, determined to search the place herself. She wandered into the rear of the store, then found that she was in a long hallway hung with endless rows of gowns. She followed it back, toward the alley behind the store.

Then she heard the whispering. ''Let's go. Now!''

She pushed through the last of the gowns. The back door was open, and a small panel truck was parked beside it. The sliding door of the truck was open, too.

There were no words written on the truck, Kaitlin realized. Nothing that advertised the bridal shop.

And the man loading it was doing so quickly. Very quickly. Looking over his shoulder now and then.

She gasped as she saw the last of the load being thrown on top. Five of them—the color of the dresses for Donna's bridal party—and a wedding gown.

Donna's wedding gown!

''Hey!'' she protested. She went tearing after the truck. One of the two men loading it was just pulling down the sliding door.

''Stop! You can't take those! Those are our gowns!'' she cried. Then she saw the two of them exchange glances. One was tall and dark, the other was small and fair.

''What are we gonna do, Spike?'' the short one asked the older, dark-haired man.

Spike swore.

Footsteps sounded in the hall, and Kaitlin spun, praying it was Brendan, and that he could make the men give the gowns back.

''Get her, Henry, that's what!'' Spike said quickly.

''What?'' she gasped. Then she realized the obvious. These men didn't work for the shop. They were stealing the wedding gowns!

And now they were planning on taking *her*, too.

''No!'' she gasped and turned to flee.

Fingers wound into her hair. She opened her mouth to scream, but a hand clamped down hard over her mouth. And then she was lifted up and sent flying head first into the pile of wedding gowns. Her head cracked against something, and the world grew dark for a moment. She was only dimly aware when the door was closed.

Spike and Henry were in the back with her, she realized a moment later. She tried to rise, tried to scream, tried to throw herself against the sliding door. Spike made a flying leap for her legs as the truck jerked into the traffic, and she went down again, half-smothered by the gowns.

"Get her hands!" Spike roared to Henry.

Pudgy little Henry did so, even though Kaitlin fought and tried to bite. With Spike sitting on her legs, nothing she could do was much good.

It was only when her hands and ankles were tied that she panicked. Absolutely panicked. She had heard something about a ring of people who stole bridal gowns in the north and sold them in the south. Donna had told Barbara about it.

And now she was in the middle of it. She was in a truck, going only God knew where, and she was tied hand and foot.

Chills seized her; she shivered violently. They could kill her. She opened her mouth, gasping for air, desperate to scream.

"Gag her," Spike ordered flatly.

And a grubby handkerchief was tied over her mouth, so tightly that she could scarcely stand the pain. She couldn't barely breathe, and the world was darkening again.

Brendan reached the back of the shop just in time to see the plain white truck disappearing. He hadn't seen Kaitlin; he hadn't heard her.

But when he looked down, he saw one of the little faux-pearl teardrops she had been wearing in her ears. He swore, catching sight of the license plate and watching the direction the truck had chosen, then went tearing through the shop.

"Call the cops," he told Donna quickly, scratching out the license number.

"Thieves have my dresses!" Donna cried.

"They have more than your dresses," Brendan warned her. "They have your maid of honor!"

He didn't wait for any of her questions but went running out the front door to his car. He revved it and went jerking into the street. He nearly hit a garbage can, then gritted his teeth hard, his heart thudding, when he had to slow to allow an old lady to pass.

Damn Kaitlin! She didn't think!

He was so mad at her he wanted to explode!

Then he realized that he wasn't mad, he was just scared as hell. He'd waited all this time to see her. All these weeks. He'd wanted to give her some space.

And now…

Who knew what the hell was happening!

He turned another corner, burning rubber. And there, heading onto the highway, was the truck.

He increased his speed and followed it.

They were heading to the countryside, he realized. Passing from town to town.

Where the hell were the police? he wondered. He had been driving forever. No, he admitted, glancing at his watch. Only about fifteen minutes.

Then the truck turned off the highway and, before long, headed up a dirt road. Brendan forced himself to slow down, then he followed, too.

And there, behind a high row of trees, was a long line of warehouses. The truck pulled up to the first.

Brendan parked under the trees and sat for a moment, gritting his teeth. He wished to hell he had some kind of weapon. A gun, preferably. The police were nowhere around. And Kaitlin was in there.

He got out of the car. Hell, he liked to think he'd done more than learn how to sail in the Navy.

He moved quietly toward the building and slipped around the side. And then he found a window.

They were arguing about her. They had her propped up in a chair, her hands and feet tied, the filthy gag still in her mouth. And Spike had a gun. He was waving it around, fighting with Henry and another man, Sam, the driver.

Sam didn't want to hurt her. "I ain't going to jail for murder one!"

"I ain't going to jail at all, but if we don't get rid of her, we're all going to rot. Hell, we truss her up, blow her away and sink her in concrete. No one will ever be the wiser," Spike said.

"You're disgusting!" Henry told him.

She wasn't going to cry, Kaitlin determined. She wasn't going to panic anymore. What good would it do? She couldn't even begin to move. She just had to pray that Henry and Sam would have the deciding influence. Oh, God! How had she gotten into this?

Tears stung her eyes despite herself.

Stubby little blond Henry was looking at her with sympathy. Spike started to say something about blowing her away, and Henry exploded.

"Not here, Spike, you hear me? Not here!" And he caught Spike's arm and dragged him down a corridor, with Sam close on their heels.

Kaitlin closed her eyes and tried to loosen the ties around her wrists. Absurdly, she thought that it wouldn't matter if she chafed her wrists. They were wearing gloves for the wedding.

They can bury me in gloves, too, she thought.

Oh, she was going to be sick....

Don't panic, don't panic....

Brendan, I love you. I'll never get to tell you, but I'd answer yes to anything. I don't care if we ever marry again. I don't give a damn about a wedding, I'd live with you. I'd follow you. I'd forgive you. I'd love you.

There was suddenly someone behind her, someone with a knife. A little switchblade type thing; she could hear it as it snapped open. A moan sounded in her throat.

"Shh! It's me!" warned a voice.

And then she sensed it. The clean scent of his cologne, and another scent that was all man, the man she loved. She wasn't going to be stabbed in the back. It was Brendan. Relief almost made her black out.

The rope was nearly shredded. It wasn't a switchblade, she realized, just a little pocket knife. He loosened her gag. "Oh, Brendan!" she murmured. Then, "Hurry. There's three of them. Spike, Henry and Sam. Spike's the mean guy with the gun. Henry's the short, paunchy one, the easiest to get past, I think. And—"

There were footsteps coming toward them. Brendan swore and slipped the gag over her mouth as Henry appeared in the room, Spike and Sam behind him.

Brendan left Kaitlin and swaggered into the center of the room. "She's a real pain in the butt, isn't she?" he demanded, before they could speak.

Spike had his gun pointed at Brendan's chest. "Who the hell are you?" he demanded.

"I'm here to make a deal," Brendan told him, hoping the other man wouldn't stop to wonder how he had known where "here" was.

"What?" Henry demanded.

"Yeah, I want some of these down San Antonio way. Fifty-fifty. I'm telling you, I can sell them right and left, no questions asked."

Spike swaggered up to him, wagging the gun beneath his nose. It was a .38, an old police issue, probably stolen, Brendan decided.

What difference did that make? he wondered. No matter where it had come from, it was a lethal weapon.

But Spike didn't seem to be comfortable with it. Yeah, he waved it around. But Brendan was almost certain that he'd never used it on a human being. Spike was more talk than action.

"I want the girl, too."

Spike shook his head. "You can't—"

"I'm glad you tied her up. She's Irish, you know. She's got one of those god-awful tempers. And she's trouble. Lots of it. But she kind of grows on you. Now, I'll give you big money for the dresses, but I want the girl thrown in, too."

Henry turned to Spike. "These are going to be as hot as tamales! Let's give him the damn things—and the girl, too."

Spike wasn't looking at Brendan, who realized that this was his chance. He slammed his arm down in a heavy chop on Spike's. The .38 went flying.

He punched Spike, who went down, but then Sam came after him, trying to butt him like a bull. He sidestepped Sam and chopped down on his neck and shoulders. Sam went down, too, but then Henry was running for the gun.

Brendan made a dive for him, caught his ankles and brought him down heavily. He made an oomph sound and went still, but Brendan knew that Spike was up and coming after him again. He had to reach the gun himself.

Then he didn't need to. Kaitlin was up, the ties discarded, her mouth free from the gag. She went racing past him, sweeping down on the gun just as Spike began to get near it.

She spun around, furious, aiming it at Spike's heart. "I don't know how to use one of these things, and I'm nervous as hell, but I think you just tug on the trigger here. You wanted to blow me away, so if you take one more step in my direction, I swear I'll blow *you* right to kingdom come!''

Spike must have believed her, because he went dead still. Brendan rose, walked over to her, reached for the .38 and smiled. ''That was pretty good. But I do know how to use that thing, so do you want to let me have it?''

She gave him a brilliant smile and handed him the gun.

And then she passed out cold, not falling hard, just wilting slowly to the ground.

Brendan heard the sirens at the same moment. At last, he thought gratefully.

All in all, Kaitlin decided later, it was a wonderful wedding. A beautiful wedding. The stuff that dreams were made of. Eventually.

First she'd had to bargain with the police, flirting outrageously with a young officer to get him to give her Donna's gowns when they should have been evidence. And, of course, Brendan had been furious with her for flirting.

Then they'd split up. She'd helped Donna dress, along with the other bridesmaids. Then the limo had come for them, and they'd sipped champagne on the way to the church.

Then came the next snag.

There was no groom. Donna's father found out that the driver had gone to the wrong town, so there was no way on earth the groom and his best man could show up at the church anywhere near on time.

But they did. Brendan and Bill arrived in an old pickup truck, smiling and proud of themselves. Cheers went up, and the wedding was on. And it was beautiful, just beautiful, with Brendan and Kaitlin waging a discreetly silent war over the placement of Donna's train.

Then her cousin was wed, and they were leaving the church amidst the glow of candles.

Someone had forgotten the champagne for the limo ride to the reception, but no one seemed to mind. The embarrassed driver offered them a six-pack of Canadian beer, and they all laughed and decided that they'd just have to smell like a brewery when they arrived at the hall.

The flower girl didn't quite make it across the floor when she was announced at the reception—her daddy was in the band, so she stopped and swayed to the music. But Kaitlin, smiling, knew that it was part of the beauty, part of the humanity and part of the wonder that Donna would get to remember all her life.

Suddenly she thought she was going to cry.

Gram had always had it right. It wasn't the wedding that mattered. It was the marriage. And any way it was done, it was the vows that mattered, not the tinsel. It was people, and it was love....

The first dance was announced. Donna danced with Bill, then with her father. And then Kaitlin was able to dance with Brendan.

But there were so many people there. They weren't able to talk.

Not for a long time.

Not until Donna had tossed the bouquet—aiming straight for Kaitlin. And she had caught it.

And Bill somehow managed to slam Brendan right in the forehead with Donna's garter. He had to catch it; the darned thing fell right in his hands.

And so Brendan was on his knees before Kaitlin again, as he had been so many years before, his fingers moving deliciously over her stockinged thigh. She knew that she was smiling, and that her eyes were glittering, and he probably didn't need an answer to anything anymore.

He must know that she loved him, that she always had.

Finally the garter was on her leg, and everyone was cheering and laughing.

"Think I can get it all in with this one shot?" he asked her, gazing into her eyes. He was striking in his black tux and tails, but it was his crooked smile that seized her heart. That and the huskiness in his voice.

"Get what in with one shot?"

"Well, you know, it just always seems that I'm on my knees for you. Asking you to marry me."

"What?" she whispered.

"I want you to marry me again, Kaitlin. I've never stopped loving you. I never will. And I believe with all my heart that we belong together. I want a family now, Kaitlin. I want to go sailing with you, and I want you to tell me all about your problems at work. And most of all, I want to sleep beside you, to hold you. I want to see the blue of your eyes every single morning. I want to cherish the time that we have left. I want to give you the wedding of your dreams this time. I promise that I'll never shut you out again. I'll probably still have a bad temper, but then, you do, too, so we should be able to deal with that, as long as we always talk. I never want to lose you again, so I know I'll always be there. I'll give you the biggest diamond you've ever seen—'',

"No!" she cried. She had forgotten where they were. She slid off the chair to her knees and caught his fingers, lacing them through her own. "No, I don't want a different diamond, I want the old one—'',

"You still have it?"

"Yes!"

"And the wedding ring?"

"That, too."

"I have mine, too. And I've asked your father for you all over again, I thought that our parents had a right to know, and—''

"I love you, Brendan," she interrupted, and kissed him. And then, when a loud roar went up, Kaitlin realized at last that they had one hell of an audience.

"Excuse us, will you?" Brendan said casually. He stood, pulling her up with him, and smiled, then swept her from the hall and ran through the corridors with her until he found an empty room.

And, once inside, he kissed her.

Open-mouthed, sweetly, hotly passionate. The kind of kiss that had made her melt at eighteen.

The kind of kiss that made her melt right now. And then, trembling, she was in his arms, trying to say all the things she had to tell him.

"I don't need a big wedding. I never did, really. I just didn't realize it. Oh, Brendan, I don't care, I don't—''

"I care," he insisted, his eyes gleaming. "This is the last time I want to marry you, Kaitlin. I want it to be perfect. I found out that since we were married by a justice of the peace the first time, we can get a dispensation to be married in the church."

"Brendan, I don't care—''

"Kaitlin, I do. And think how good we'll be at weddings by the time we get to our own! We still have to see Barbara and Joe legally wed, then we can get to our own."

"Oh, Brendan..."

"You haven't answered me yet, Kaitlin."

Very, very slowly, she smiled, her arms looped around his neck, her eyes radiant, dazzling. "Okay, a big wedding. On one condition."

"What's that?"

"You don't disappear for almost a month again. We, er..."

"We what?"

"We get to fool around in the meantime. Maybe we could even go ahead and start thinking family a wee bit before the ceremony, as Gram might say."

"With her teeth in," Brendan agreed.

Kaitlin laughed and, once again, he took her in his arms.

She was certain in that very moment that their vows were sealed. She didn't need the wedding. She never had. She needed Brendan. She loved Brendan.

And she had never really lost him....

But weddings were wonderful, she decided long moments later. At this one, she had found her way back home.

Epilogue

Okay, so it was worth it.

Yes, definitely worth it, Brendan decided.

This just might be the most beautiful wedding he had ever seen, and it was his own.

The church was dressed in flowers, red and white, and regal candles burned atop elegant long brass poles attached to every pew. Kaitlin's mother and his own were seated to the glorious notes of "Ave Maria," and then, as the organ continued to play, their wedding party began to appear.

First came her little cousin, Brandy, in the elegant cream and black dress Kaitlin had chosen, her red curls adorned with a tiara of flowers. Then her junior bridesmaid walked down the aisle with the ring bearer, handsome in his very traditional tux. The ushers escorted her bridesmaids and her two matrons of honor, Donna and Barbara.

And then came Kaitlin.

Escorted on her father's arm, she was achingly beautiful. She wore a traditional gown, but it was a soft dove gray, not white. Yet Brendan had never seen anything more elegant. Seed pearls had been sewn into a beautiful design, along with soft, glimmering sequins. A veil covered her face, and a sweeping train followed behind her. Her hair was free and flowing down her back, just shaded by the gauze of her veil. The gown's bodice was medieval, the sleeves long and tapering, and the veil was held in place by a narrow crown of seed pearls and flowers.

And yet, most beautiful of all were her eyes. Sapphire blue that day, glimmering through the gauze of her veil until she reached the altar. Then her father lifted her veil, and the two of them smiled at one another with pride and love and just a hint of tears.

Someone sniffed loudly. Either her mother or Brendan's, she was certain.

And then her father was handing her over to him, and the love in her eyes touched him. Somewhere deep inside his heart, he felt a quiver. And even before the service began, long before they exchanged their vows, he knew that this time it would last forever.

His voice was steady and firm as they exchanged their vows. Hers was crystal clear, but her finger trembled slightly when he slipped on her wedding ring.

It was the same ring he had given her twelve years before. She had kept it, just as he had kept the ring she had given him. Perhaps the diamond was small. It didn't matter to either of them. What did matter was that they both still had the rings. And they both knew that no other rings could possibly do.

They pledged their love. They knelt, they rose, Barbara adjusted Kaitlin's train.

There was another sniff from somewhere. Brendan smiled. Gram. Lizzie Boyle Rosen. She was right behind them, he knew, next to Brendan's mom, her arm linked through her beloved Al's. Bless you, Lizzie, Brendan thought. You were always rooting for me, weren't you?

He heard the words and the music. But most of all, he felt Kaitlin beside him. Felt her hand when they touched, felt the trembling inside her. Breathed in the sweetness of her perfume, and met the shining happiness in her eyes.

To love, honor and cherish....

He smiled, and as Father Mulraney said that he could kiss the bride, he swept her into his arms to a cacophony of applause.

She was his wife again. Kaitlin, with her laughter, her spirit, her beauty, her sky-blue eyes and waves of strawberry curls. With her temper, too, but with all her wisdom and, most importantly, all her love.

It had been beautiful. A perfect wedding, he thought as he tasted her kiss. The wedding she had always seen in her dreams.

It was perfect for him, too. The wedding he had envisioned when he had been so much younger. If only Sean had been there.

Even as that thought touched his heart, she broke from his embrace, and smiled at him radiantly, her fingers still locked in his own.

Once again he felt the trembling deep within his heart. Her emotions were so easily read within the blue beauty of her eyes. Her lips were curved into a smile of such sweet warmth that even now he felt a growing wonder that it could be for him. It almost seemed that there was a whisper breathed against his ear. Sean's whisper. "You're lucky, cousin. You've got love. When you've got love, you've got everything."

He had to kiss her again. He pulled her into his arms, and there was a burst of applause as their lips met and he kissed her for another eternity.

When he released her, there was laughter in her eyes, and just a hint of tears. Then he took her hand, the music started, and he led her down the aisle and out of the church.

Before the others could follow too closely behind him, he swept her into his arms, delicately planting a kiss on her forehead.

"I love you, Kaitlin O'Herlihy," he told her.

"Oh, Brendan! I love you, too, so much! You gave me everything! Everything I wanted!"

Barbara and Joe were behind them by then. Joe was claiming a kiss from the bride, while Barbara congratulated Brendan and hugged him warmly. And then Barbara and Donna were hugging Kaitlin, and Joe and Bill were there to pump Brendan's hand, while the others were pouring out of the church.

So many good friends and relatives to greet them.

Lizzie and Al. Brendan's mother, with tears in her eyes. His father, proud, pleased. His cousins, her cousins. His family, her family.

Their family, now. And all their friends.

Everyone told them what a perfect wedding it had been. And it had been perfect, he thought, closing his eyes for just a second as a smile teased his lips. It seemed that Sean had made this wedding. In wisdom, in spirit.

Before anyone could part them again, he found his bride's hand and pulled her into his arms. "No," he told her. "You gave me everything. I have your love, Kaitlin, and love is everything."

Just for good measure, he kissed her long and hard again, heedless of those around them.

They would just have to wait…because love was everything.

* * * *

# Looking For More Romance?

Visit Romance.net

## Check in daily for these and other exciting features:

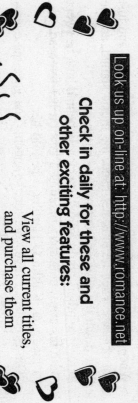

View all current titles, and purchase them on-line.

## Hot off the press

What do the stars have in store for you?

### Horoscope

Exclusive offers available only at Romance.net

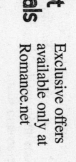

## Hot deals

Plus, don't miss our interactive quizzes, contests and bonus gifts.

PWEB-T

# HARLEQUIN®
*Makes any time special.*™

**HARLEQUIN®**
**AMERICAN ROMANCE®**

Upbeat, all-American romances about the pursuit of love, marriage and family.

**HARLEQUIN**
*Duets*™

Two brand-new, full-length romantic comedy novels for one low price.

**Harlequin® Historical**

Rich and vivid historical romances that capture the imagination with their dramatic scope, passion and adventure.

**HARLEQUIN®**
*Temptation*®

Sexy, sassy and seductive— Temptation is hot sizzling romance.

**HARLEQUIN®**
**SUPERROMANCE**

A bigger romance read with more plot, more story-line variety, more pages and a romance that's evocatively explored.

*Harlequin Romance*®

Love stories that capture the essence of traditional romance.

**HARLEQUIN®**
**INTRIGUE®**

Dynamic mysteries with a thrilling combination of breathtaking romance and heart-stopping suspense.

**HARLEQUIN PRESENTS®**

Meet sophisticated men of the world and captivating women in glamorous, international settings.

Look us up on-line at: http://www.romance.net

HGEN99-T

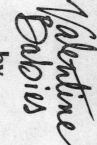